SHADOW-FORGE
REVELATIONS

ANDREW'S ADVENTURE SERIES

STEPHEN J. BAUER

To order additional copies of this book, contact:
Bookwhip
1-855-339-3589
https://www.bookwhip.com

Contents

DEDICATION

In remembrance of family, both living and deceased, whose support gave me new meaning for this revelation.

Author's Note

This novel is a sequel to the original science fiction fantasy adventure story, 'Quest of the Shadow-Forge', and it is the second in the 'Andrew's Adventures Series'. It continues to intertwine life experiences with theoretical concepts gleaned from the continuing companion book series, 'The Evolutioning of Creation'. While this second story is intended as a sequel to the first in this book series, it provides a fanciful vehicle for the presentation of the theoretical ideas developed in the companion book, 'The Evolutioning of Creation: Volume 2'. Although not solely dependent upon a reading of the previous novel, or an understanding of the continuing companion book series, such an exposure would enhance the reader's understanding of characters and references to the first book, providing a vision into the author's mindset upon the unfolding events contained within. It is my hope that these stories will continue to provide for the wondrous explorations that are the discoveries of our individual purposes for being, from both a scientific and metaphysic perspective. It is also my continued hope that this story will inspire others to pursue their dreams and review what life has to offer them if they only take the time to look within themselves for their own answers.

Prologue

**[The nature of evolution contributes to
the reality of our existence]**

Within our traditional sense of fourth dimensional spacetime, in which existence is currently defined, it appears everything evolves from one moment to the next: e.g., people, animals, plants, and even inorganic matter like our own planet Earth. Still the evolution of inorganic matter does not stop here. As we have continued to explore, we have also discovered the planetary bodies that makeup our Solar System, the innumerable solar systems and loose stars that makeup the mechanism of our Milky Way galaxy. And further, we have seen how the fantastical apparatus of such mature galaxies, and even nebulae, are the nurseries of the ever emerging life that makes up our Local Group galaxy cluster.

Nonetheless, the inner workings of our evolving cosmos are even more complicated and larger than the collection of matter that makes up our Local Group cluster; for our Local Group is just part of the Laniakea Supercluster: one of many superclusters which are seemingly grouped about a Great Attractor. While this becomes the extent of what we have discovered so far, we have imagined that all this is bounded within a forever evolving universe. And this, the theoretical concept of fourth dimensional spacetime that makes up our evolutionary existence, we endeavor to bind in the precision of our mathematical equations. It is our fervent hope that these equations will permit us to make sense of our ability to be a part of this ever mutable environment, which we know as the awesome evolutionary being that is our universe.

Satirically, it is a furthering innovation of the human perspective to be able to separate the concepts of Space and Time from its cohesive union defined by the term 'spacetime', in order to provide for a philosophical representation of their abstractions and how they might interact. Where Space can be viewed in a myriad of dimensional frames of reference to facilitate our many versions of mathematical proofs, by which we define its ability to be, we pretend to fashion a logical representation of our own existence as it is imbued within a dimensional framework of Time.

It is a theoretical vision of our existence in which we choose to parcel Time into divisions akin to a Past time, a Present time, and a Future time; all to agree with the internal operations of our thought processes. The Present time is best defined as the being of continuous evolutionary change, and is ofttimes referred to as the perceptible intermediary between Past time and Future time. Yet, for however we attempt to parcel the notion of Time, there is only ever the truism of a Present time. For while Present time always mediates from a dependency of consequence, the manifestations of a Past time and a Future time are purely illusionary inferences of our own cognitive properties. Subsequently, our allusions to a Past time and a Future time merely provide for a conscious articulation of this continuous change; i.e., a continuous change of surreptitious events from which one might understand the breadth of evolution and the extent to which our evolution may come to fruition. Consequently, evolution is the only physical reality of events acting outside the conscious mind that ultimately decides all fate within our universe.

Fate aside, there is nothing more important than the evolution of the psychic intangibles within the living landscape of our own mental being. For regardless of the impact that our physical reality imposes upon us outside of our conscious mind, it is the autonomous surreality of our own individual mental chemistry and free will that seeks to shape our own individual destiny. Where fate is the purveyor of tangible interactions, destiny is the surveyor of intangible interactions. Ergo, where interactions have consequences, if one seeks to influence their own destiny within the scope of their allotted fate, then they would need to understand the evolution of their own internal psyche; for one can only ever influence their own evolutionary existence upon the window of opportunity that each Present time moment presents. Ironically, for such analysis, evolution can only be collected, stored, measured and studied from within the interpretation of our own conscious mind. At best we might agree on a consensus of it. Ultimately therefore, our ultimate fate really depends on how all contained forces interact within the physical reality of these events occurring outside our conscious mind.

And if these concepts of Space, Time, Fate, and Destiny were not enough variables by which our maturity might be influenced, there are also the imaginable possibilities. Indeed, these fictional possibilities can influence the non-fictional probabilities by which one matures and evolves over time; i.e., 'knowledge is power'. Consider the notion of 'close encounters' as first suggested in 1972, in the book, 'The UFO Experience: A Scientific Inquiry'. These definitions of 'close encounters' had to do with the fictional possibility of a non-fictional probable event in which a person might interacted with an unidentified flying object. However, as the source for intelligent life beyond our own, on this planet, has been imagined from so many other origins, it currently presents an outdated notion of such interactions between humans and other intelligent life. Such is it that these definitions need to be updated to keep up with the times.

Reconsidering, then, the probability of a 'close encounter' as an event in which a person might interact with any intelligent life, other than our own, these 'close encounters' could then be categorized into eight groups: i.e., as 'close encounters' of the first, second, third, fourth, fifth, sixth, seventh, and eighth kind. Visual sightings which are seemingly attributed to other intelligent life events, and that show any considerable detail, can be considered a close encounter of the 'first kind'. Identifying or providing physical evidence of other intelligent life which could be scientifically evaluated can be considered a close encounter of the 'second kind'. Visual sightings of other intelligent life, where an encounter in which another intelligent life form is visually observed, can be considered a close encounter of the 'third kind'. A described physical encounter with another intelligent life form, with or without physical evidence, can be considered a close encounter of the 'fourth kind'. An event that involves direct communication between a person and another intelligent life form, in any capacity, can be considered a close encounter of the 'fifth kind'. An event that involves the death of either a person or another intelligent life form, due to a 'fourth kind' of close encounter, can be considered a close encounter of the 'sixth kind'. An event that involves the engendering of a new life from either a person or another intelligent life form, due to a 'fourth kind' of close encounter, can be considered to be a close encounter of the 'seventh kind'. And finally, a described psychic 'connection' with another intelligent life form, with or without physical evidence of communication, can be considered a close encounter of the 'eighth kind'.

[The nature of secrets contributes to the nature of our evolution]

Then there is our inner cosmos, which resonates as the gateway to our connections within the universe via an alternative dimensional interface. As we grow older, we begin to become increasingly more aware of how these 'connections' affect us. We build our connections with others, from outside of our own sentient condition: i.e., a condition from which we have only our bilateral mental capability of consciousness to keep us company. And yet, we also build connections with the universe, from inside our own presentient condition: i.e., a condition from which we have only our bilateral mental capacity of unconsciousness to help keep us sane. Over our allotted time to mature, we continually develop this awareness of how we interconnect within and without the world at large.

Still, rather than just residing within the echo of our own conscious ego or unconscious id, we are even given to try and orchestrate our conscious connections, in an attempt to fashion how we want to be perceived by others. However, we have little control, if any, over our ability to orchestrate our unconscious connections, which tends to fashion how we affect others. These connections are the nature of our secrets which evolve over time; where once the cherished secrets of our youth existed as the fantastical imaginations of our childhood indulgences, these selfsame secrets eventually evolve into the ponderous burdens of our more adult desires and our need to connect. Indeed, over time, our secrets transform from the naive expression of who we are, to become the imagined impression of who we want to be. Where our secrets were once enjoyed within the solus of our own daydreams, they eventually mature, and can become the scourge of our own incarcerated identities or the armor that maintains our very sanity.

The unshared, unspoken secrets inhabit the mind and inhibit the free-flowing and unencumbered thoughts that we transform into forms of communication. Not unlike the unspoken lie, the unspoken secret dwells in the consciousness as a gate; dispersing and redirecting cognitive thought and memories onto an alternate, or rehearsed, story line. It keeps one's true identity restricted, while splintering out alternate identities of dysfunctional facades that run counter to one's true self and feelings. Hiding the secret becomes part of the socialization of our thoughts with others and pollutes the foundation of our self-esteem; for our self-esteem is no longer based on who they really are, but rather on who they want to be, and on how they want to be viewed by others. Over time, one becomes socially impaired by their own perceived persona. Or worse, they are conflicted by their self-created identities. It is a dubious condition from which to influence one's destiny.

The shared secret, not unlike the shared lie, promotes more of a duality in what is deemed to be acceptable behavior and creates a questionable dependency with its audience. Similar to 'peer pressure', if the audience adopts a certain shared secret or behavior as unobjectionable, regardless of its moral or ethical implications, it then becomes the norm for the entire audience. Such secrets also account for the adapted dysfunctionality of much larger organizations, even if they were previously established on the foundation of more altruistic motives. It is the decisions we make that define the consequences of our actions. And such consequences are most egregious when in conflict with the candor of our ultimate destinies. Either way, unshared or shared, secrets inhabit and inhibit the individual development of one's true nature of self-actualization and, in turn, one's natural altruism. At best, such secrets beg the concern that one's destiny is not their own, but is rather that of a group consensus.

Then there are the unseen secrets, or subliminal lies. The unseen secrets are a consequence of the secrets predicated upon those who are not party to the introduction of the secrets. Unseen secrets are often camouflaged within the illusionary magic of misdirection. Such illusionary magic is the innocent lie that provides us with the mysterious color or flavor of imagination in an otherwise monochromic perspective of life. These unseen secrets, unshared or shared, are the lies that we predicate upon others. They become the lies that others then incorporate into their own psyche, without even knowing it, because the magician makes acclimating them more believable. These unseen secrets then become the foundation upon which those, who are party to the secret, impose a social dynamic on others that are not party to the deception. Forthright or not, those who are party to the unseen secret become bound by their shared deceitfulness. And fair or not, others not party to the truth of the deception, begin to adopt and react to their perceptions of the socially dysfunctionality dynamic predicated upon them.

Unseen secrets can be harmless lies that are crafted to promote a more positive outcome: e.g., the whimsy of hope for a better future or the unwitting chance for salvation. However unseen secrets can also be harmful lies that are crafted to promote a more negative outcome: e.g., the accidental condition of cause and effect, which can make the unthinkable come to fruition, duping others to act in opposition to their ideals and beliefs, spreading an untruth which needs to be defended, fostering or participating in a shared joke or drama at someone's expense.

Such chaos belies the hidden truth of such divergence from conformity in an otherwise monotonous perspective of life.

These unseen secrets can be the purveyor of a more chaotic and uncontrollable reality, the obsession of despair for an unattainable purpose, or the probable inclination toward a harmful temptation. Liken to a weed in a garden, the unseen secrets of self-righteousness or avarice can be planted in our subconscious, with or without consent. And without constant tending, the inception of these unseen secrets can take hold and alter one's true nature and identity beyond even their ability to control their own 'free will'. Thus the unseen secret is the wild card of destiny; a secret of which one knows neither of its ambition nor of its terminus. And any combination of these differing types of secrets can seek to embrace chaos or harmony.

It has been previously postulated that chaos is 'the state of the universe before there was any order', based on our accepted notions for order and disorder. However, likened to the ideation that the infinity of Space in Time provided the soup of formless matter for our more chaotic existence, such universal chaos is supposed to have been preceded by the void of Space in Time; the void from which there pre-existed a more ordered universe. This notion affords that a framework of evolution in a dimension of Time is essential for being, regardless of its purity in a dimension of Space. However the conceptual perspective of defined entropy in thermodynamics belies the inherent nature of a more spacial abyss.

Still, the inherent nature of universal symmetry promotes that chaos and harmony are the progeny upon which the universal balance is predicated. In which case, where symmetry is the progenitor of universal balance, harmony is the aspiration of the spacetime boundaries upon which the universe 'is', and chaos is the inspiration of random interactions, or the 'free will', within which the universe 'does'. In truth, the notion of 'being' as an event measured by change predefines a condition of 'does' from 'is', while allowing for the elective rationale of 'was' and 'will be' as a concept outside of such actual entification. It is these qualities of aspiration and inspiration that forever bind the destiny of these two unlikely siblings; which, in turn, drives the fate of our universal existence.

It is the 'yin and yang' of existence, or sometimes referred to as the metaphysical nature of two hearts beating as one. Therefore, universal balance is not the result of unlikely extremes in chaos and harmony, but rather the evolution of a universal being which purports change, or growth, from within its inception in symmetry towards a more asymmetric balance between the two. It is a journey in degrees of space and time maturing upon the matterless void from whence it was conceived and hypostatized within the cooperative dissolution of these extremes.

The secularists would have us embrace the oxymoronic concept of an 'ordered universe' as an expression of an evolution towards a more order state in the condition of mass rather than a process in disarray; i.e., the purpose of evolution is to change upon a previous condition, whether that change is an improvement or a detriment to the actual overall essence of being.

The religious would like us to believe in the oxymoronic concept of an 'ordered universe' as an expression of our significance within this universal order: i.e., the universe was preordained for our creation and the superlative evolutionary form in which it was conceived.

Concordianism is centered on the idea that both order and disorder exist and contribute to understanding of existence within the universal experience. Concordia is the Latin word for 'harmony', literally meaning 'with (one) heart', or hearts in agreement. Another way to perceive harmony is as it relates to a meaning in the consistency of uniformity, or the conformity of peace. Nevertheless, this is not to imply that harmony or peace can only be attained via conformity or agreement to one ideal.

Discordianism, on the other hand, is centered on the idea that both order and disorder are illusions imposed on the universe by the human psyche, and that neither of these illusions of apparent order and disorder are any more accurate or objectively true than the other. Discordia is the Latin derivative for "chaos," derivatively meaning 'without (one) heart' [of heart apart], or hearts in disagreement. Whereupon, the doctrine of 'concordia discors' is the idea that the numerous conflicts between the four elements in nature (air, earth, fire, water) paradoxically create an overall harmony within the world, or a semblance of order out of chaos, or order from chaos. It is a philosophy that the world is shaped by the enduring, perpetual strife among these four elements and it is ordered by their co-existence into a jarring unity. Similarly a philosophy implying it is alright to 'agree to disagree'. Or as the contemplation of a musical metaphor, it is held in the notion of a more 'discordant harmony'.

As a variant of this 'discordant harmony', cosmology comes from the Greek word 'kosmos' which means 'the world or universe as in 'an ordered harmony' or 'a harmonious system'. The term cosmology then comes to mean the theory of an 'ordered universe', or 'the universe as an ordered whole'. According to Greek thought, the cosmos came out of chaos, which they understood to be 'the formless void' as a state of utter confusion and disorder. This concept is often associated with cosmogony, a term defined as 'a theory, system, or account of the generation of the universe' and the celestial bodies found within it.

Interestingly, as an aside to such a discussion of cosmogony, a Greek philosopher came up with the ancient philosophical notion that the celestial bodies emit a form of music. This concept was known as the 'Musica Universalis'. Pythagoras has been credited with being the creator of this concept. 'Musica Universalis' (from Latin for 'universal music'), also called 'Music of the Spheres' or 'Harmony of the Spheres', is an ancient philosophical concept that regards proportions in the movements of celestial bodies as an incorporation of the metaphysical principle that mathematical relationships express qualities or "tones" of energy; i.e., such energy which can be manifest in numbers, visual angles, shapes and sound, which are all connected within these patterns of proportion. This is not unlike how we scientifically view our reality; where everything we see around us is vibrating at one frequency or another. Subsequently, Plato described astronomy and music as "twinned" studies of sensual recognition: "astronomy for the eyes, music for the ears, and both requiring knowledge of numerical proportions."

So it would appear that even the universe has its unseen secrets to which we are bound. The consequences of which are imposed upon us, even though we are not party to its secrets, and are camouflaged within the illusionary magic of energy and matter. And as yet another layer to this intriguing philosophy is the inferences of dark energy and dark matter.

For the main character in this story, Andrew, who is to be once again involved in a quest with far reaching consequences, it is an evolutionary step in his maturity. This time it is Andrew who must choose and outline the quest, and thereby forge his own destiny. Where once again the fate of the universe continues to be a question of balance, Andrew partners up with an old friend to divine the nature of a new threat. And while the stakes are similar, the adventure is different. Andrew becomes the involuntary pawn of universal chaos and perhaps the unwitting trigger for a more uncertain fate. And where fate is usually outside the realm of an individual's control, unlike our destinies, Andrew discovers that fate is still subject to the principals of cause and effect. And where cause and effect includes the even the destiny of a more overall universal 'being', presumably prescribed as the decreed cause of predetermined events that unavoidably plays out over time, fate is the sum of all destinies.

In truth, there are still some ultimate agencies by which the order of fate can be altered. One such agency of evolutionary change is secretly known among its members as the Guild of the Shadow-Forge. It is a calling that few can realize and even fewer take part in. These are the special few who have been recruited to fight the hidden battles within an unseen realm of universal forces that shape the fate of our very universal existence. It is a guild that does not discriminate between the forces of harmony or chaos, but rather it is one that embraces the notion of universal balance for the continuation of an evolutionary universal being. It is this guild which remains as the guiding force for change in the overall destinies that drive the eventual fate of our individual realities. However, ultimately it is the 'free will' of every life force within the universe that decides the consummate reality of our ubiuitous existence.

C H A P T E R

1

Family Secrets

[The unshared secret can become a self-imposed prison]

Andrew's story continues some five and a half years later after his first quest. His first quest was the baptism of his special connection with the universe, a tribulation wherein he first began to assimilate an understanding of this extraordinary association. It was an experience that would be forever seared into his being as a recruited member of that elite group known as the Shadow-Forge. But who is Andrew now?

Favoring his Earth born environment, he has lost his capacity for depending upon his Shadow-Forge skills. And by ignoring these abilities, Andrew is no longer able to get in touch with that part of him which was most important: his amazing ability to join with the universe. His special connection had previously given him a real purpose for living. But now, without this connection, his philosophical balance has begun to teeter on the edge of despair. He remains forever lost in a world of his own self-deprecating introspection. It is a perception of his life that he adopted only after having once existed as a Shadow-Forge, in another time and in another place, far away from where he now resides on Earth.

If only he could forget his former life as a Shadow-Forge on the planet Glorthocks; a life that allowed him to journey about and influence the inner workings of the universe. If he could forget, then, like everyone else, his now mediocre existence wouldn't be such an affliction to him. And with his ability to disremember his previous life, like the philosophical beliefs of reincarnation, he would have no other memory of a time when he wasn't human.

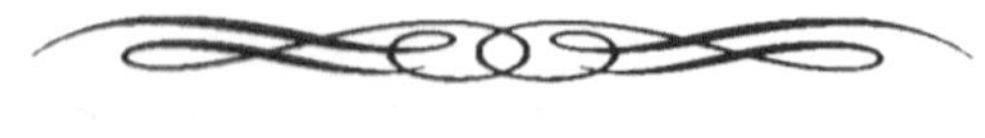

[Andrew's Narrative]

Here I stood with my left shoe in one hand and the remnants of a bush in the other. Looking quite the disheveled version of myself, my pants were torn at the cuff, my shirt was half shredded, and my face and hair were covered with fresh dirt. Taking stock of my situation, liken to a snapshot in time, I was still alive; and that was a good thing. About me was an impressive girl, who was seemingly there to ensure my safety, and a gnarly beast, who was seemingly there to ensure my demise.

From my battered appearance, one wouldn't have guessed that such an attractive girl would have been looking out for my well-being. To say we were companions would be a bit presumptuous, as I had not met her before today. And this, being our first chance meeting, was not the type of first impression I would have strived to make upon meeting with a pretty girl. But circumstances being what they were, I'll take it.

As for her, she had made a fantastic first impression upon me. I'm not sure what about her I found more appealing; the fact that she can handle herself in a fight or the fact that she could do so without getting all mussed up. In truth, she was my rescuer, and her timely intervention was none too soon for me. From what I had witnessed of her moves so far, I would swear she was like one of characters out of a martial arts movie. Observing her in a ninja like stance to the front of me, I couldn't believe my luck. Having been knocked down and dragged away by some weird creature, I thought I was a goner for sure. Had her arrival been any later, then she might have been meeting up with a corpse; or at least that is how it seemed from my perspective.

The weird beast on the other hand, which was the nature of the threat to my continued living, was a particularly eerie looking beast. The creature looked to be like some demon straight out of hell. It appeared to be some amalgam of a monkey, a coyote, and who knows what else. As it was, I may have never really known of its real intention for me had it not started speaking to the girl; which in itself was creeping me out to no end. Yet, even more bizarre than this beast speaking was the attitude of the girl responding back to it in kind. It was as if they already knew each other.

While it may have almost been Halloween, accordingly to the calendar, this was not the kind of scare or spooky encounter that I was used to dealing with this time of year. Considering the inexplicable nature of this whole experience, I was shaken to my very core. As I thought on it further, I wasn't sure whether a talking beast was a sign of the apocalypse, but this one appeared to be talking about just that. I am certain of one thing, though. While how I got into this situation is one story, I'm confident it will most certainly pale in comparison to what lie ahead for me. And although I'm not really sure where how this girl fits in with all this, I felt she was going to be a big part of how this all plays out. Where our story goes from here, I could not imagine. However, what I do know is that it must've all started just yesterday.

Thinking back to yesterday, it was the end of a very distraught week for me. In fact, yesterday was the anniversary of the destruction of my meeting place in the woods where it all started: five years ago today. To me this meeting place, behind our house, was like a shrine to my survival from my first audacious quest. And with its destruction went my hopes of every connecting up again with my friend, Harmony, who tutored me in the ways of the Shadow-Forge; or so I imagined it. Indeed with this remembrance, yesterday had unquestionably begun as the shit swirl topping on my scoop of unpleasant events yet to be suffered.

Still, as I am standing here today, having survived the attack of this beast, I actually felt revitalized. I guess an adrenaline rush will do that to a person. I must admit it was all a rather thrilling break from my current humdrum routine, these past five years or so. To me, this routine was more of a self-induced sentence that I imposed upon myself after the destruction of my shrine. I mean choices, good or bad, are not the fault of anyone except for the one who makes them. Though, in my case, I believe fate had a hand in altering my destiny. After all, when you are only given a choice between bad and worse, it is not really a choice at all.

As it happens, this sentence started out as a blessing that turned into a curse. The blessing of it was that I had this fantastic adventure that I could never forget. The curse of it was that my fantastical adventure now overshadowed my every thought and action, making the rest of my life pale by experience. Even yesterday, as school came into sight, I continued to mull over the idea of reincarnation and how I had survived the greatest adventure of my lifetime on another planet. And even after these five years, my thoughts are still peppered with visions of those exploit. It was like having watched a fantastic sci-fi movie, and recalling the moments that I liked best. In my soul, I knew it to be real; as real as our family fun trip to Disneyworld this summer. And yet, even the memory of my summer vacation trip was diminished by the recalled journey of being spirited away to an off-world adventure on some random alien planet. Perhaps, in my solace, I was unconsciously just trying to keep these older memories alive; so as to dull the pain of missing it: my lost past life.

As one distant memory begets another, yesterday I also remembered back on my first day of high school. I was like any other poorly socialized teenager. I was nervous, disoriented, and unprepared for the contest of egos that swelled the hallowed halls of Washington High. And the worse part of all was that I was really a 'somebody', but I couldn't tell anybody. Had I been recognized as a superstar, at least I might have been given some respect and would've been spared the indignities of anonymity. At best, if people knew of how I saved the universe, it would have greatly improved my acceptance and popularity. In point of fact, I was a hero. No better; I was a superhero!

The fact of the matter was that I couldn't confide in anyone about my experience, other than my parents; for they lived it through me. Even if I could divulge this secret to anyone else, who would ever actually believe me? As most of my peers from middle school considered my discussions kind of strange already, they would just think I was telling another one of my imaginative stories. And like the story of the boy who cried wolf, I'm guessing being considered the teller of strange tales would not be the kind of notoriety that would help endear me to my fellow students. After all, being accepted by your peers is what being a teenager is all about; or so my mother would tell me. Her consoling logic let me know that I was not alone in this feeling. I wondered if my comic superheroes ever had to deal with these identity issues.

It seemed that every day the process would be repeated. I would remember these exploits in my own thoughts. Then, for all my sequestered self-esteem, in the realization of being back on Earth, I was still only me. I mean, I still had the same socially unacceptable quirks that hampered my conversational skills. My memories of a more confident me remained inconsequential as to how I am able to relate to and with others. For, while my bizarre experiences had taught me to be somewhat more patient and less impulsive, it was still not enough to keep the behavioral symptoms of my ADHD at bay. Truly, I would have thought that my off world experiences might have sufficiently bolstered my ego for any eventuality. However, it would seem that my ability to control some of my symptomatic idiosyncrasies was not really enough to reinforce my confidence in this respect.

So the events of yesterday began for me, as I walked into the school building. With my random mental narrative to trouble me, I just wanted the school day to be over. And, as if I didn't have enough to distract myself, now four school bullies decided they wanted bother me. Yes, even now as I enter my last year of high school, there are still these idiots with nothing better to do than to taunt others. After enjoying a couple months of avoiding just this kind of unwanted attention, this group decided once again to challenge my demeanor. At first, they just followed behind. Seemingly savoring the moment when they would strike, I suppose. I just ignored them.

Now, having explored the nature of bullies over the years, I came up with a supposition, of sorts, to explain their behavior. Bullies, I decided, were kind of a species unto themselves, who practiced in tormenting individuals when the grown-ups weren't looking. And, actually, these four seemed to have digressed, rather than matured, over time. Or at least that's how I thought of them. I mean, what is their problem anyway? What gratification do they get out of bothering people? And yet, it did motivate me to exercise my body upon the chance encounter of such a confrontation. And while I'll admit I am not physically the strongest of my class, I had been bullied by worse creatures. If they only knew about my life on Glorthocks, they might not be so eager to bother me.

As it is now, my human body is a bit of a letdown from the one I had on that planet Glorthocks. Back on Glorthocks, I was a nimble ninja. I stood toe-to-toe with the king of the planet DeMutron. Well kind of; as he was more of an insect than a humaniod, he really didn't have any toes. I even faced his DeMutronion minions in combat. And as if that weren't enough, I also had the courage to dive headlong into and through a red sun in a crystal-like starship. And by the grace of the universe, I had survived the terror rendering forces of the black hole's event horizon. Call me stupid, but I was no longer one to back away quietly. After all, it was difficult to support such mental bluster if I couldn't back it up. And under the influence of such mental bluster, I felt they were no longer an intimidation to me so much as they were just really annoying. For me, it was kind of a mix between my temper control problem and lack of patience.

My temper control problem, as my mother mom explained to me, was because of the unique symptoms of my behavioral condition. In other words, I was likely to have a shorter fuse than most of my peers. Conversely, my dad's advice in this matter was to just get control of my emotions. I shouldn't let other's teasing me get under my skin. Dad felt that if bullies see that their harassment does not rattle me, then they'll look for easier prey elsewhere.

As it was, it didn't take long before this group of four, tailing me down the hallway, became more of a verbal annoyance. They started at a low volume, "Andrew. Andrew. Andrew. Andrew. Andrew. Andrew." Continuing, they chanted my name in unison as if they were acting out some weird ceremonial ritual.

Somehow dad's advice just didn't seem fair to the next victim. Somehow, I just couldn't allow this to happen to someone else. Consequently, I became engaged in a campaign of standing my ground while not actually provoking the situation. It was a delicate balance, I'll grant you that, but this usually worked. This being the opposite of the advice my dad had given me. Rather, dad had drummed into me that if I sensed a real threat, then I needed to do whatever it took to escape the situation, and then report it. Knowing school policy, he did not want me to get suspended or expelled. I guess he felt I had enough to deal with. He would exemplify his lecture with some stories in which he decided to take matters in his own hands, when he was in school, and it didn't turn out so well for him in the end. There is just so much more emotional baggage to deal with in high school other than just book learning. The sarcastic sentiment that comes to mind in these situations is, 'Welcome to Washington High'!

Then, for good measure, a few others seemed to join in. As the group continued to march behind me, the volume increased with the addition of new voices, "Andrew. Andrew. Andrew. Andrew. Andrew. Andrew."

Having acquired a bit of an audience, this was beginning to get a little embarrassing. I started to hear other random phrases in the back, "What's going on? Hey, what is it all about?"

I imagined the others, who joined in, just thought it was all in fun, but they contributed to the taunting just the same. That's mob mentality at its finest. Finally, I just turned to face them down; hoping, of course, that they would all back down, but they didn't. In fact they didn't seem to me to be quite their selves. While not advancing toward me as I stood my ground, they did nothing else but continue to chant my name, "Andrew. Andrew. Andrew. Andrew. Andrew. Andrew."

While the others in the crowd had stopped chanting, it was no less disconcerting having them waiting around to see what would happen. I looked around to see if there were any grown-ups who might want to intervene on my behalf. Of course there were no grown-ups in sight, or these four instigators wouldn't be acting like troglodytes. As I waited for some unexpected physical or verbal abuse to be flung in my direction, I couldn't help noticing a strange shadowy presence about these four ring leaders. While I wanted to dismiss it as bad hallway lighting, resulting from the dreary and overcast morning, I couldn't help notice that they weren't actually looking at me. I looked behind me to see if there was someone else behind me, but there was no obvious threat. As I searched my options for fight or flight, they did not approach me. Rather, they kept their distance and just continued to chant my name, "Andrew. Andrew. Andrew. Andrew. Andrew. Andrew."

Now having just argued with my father this morning about the untidy condition of my room, yet again, was still feeling the sting of that moment. And I wasn't in the mood for such taunting. Having chosen my words already, I unloaded loud enough for others nearby to hear, "Oh, go and find someone else to bother!"

Not awe inspiring phraseology, I'll grant you, but I was not really shooting for an academy award performance. To my surprise, this not only seemed to snap them out of their weird chanting, it also attracted the attention of the PE teacher, who was now at least in ear shot of my outburst. Where was he when the crowd was chanting my name, I thought to myself? Maybe some Good Samaritan got his attention for me.

While the crowd quickly dispersed, the original four perpetrators looked at each other in confusion; seemingly as if awakening from some hypnotic condition. And in their confusion, I just turned around and left, continuing onto my class. As a consequence of their disorientation, these four did not escape retribution for their actions. Instead, they were cornered for more serious consultation from the PE teacher. Thinking back on the incident, as it did seem to me that the four were in some kind of trance, perhaps they weren't completely at fault. But more than likely it was some cruel joke they cooked up to get under my skin. Being the strange kid at school had its drawbacks. Although when they stopped, it did appear that they seemed dazed; as if they just woke up from a daydream. Still, it was not my first encounter with them, or others like them. So I felt they had it coming.

During class, I continued to be distracted by my thoughts of this tedious encounter with the four. What did I do to warrant them singling me out? I couldn't remember doing anything new that might have encouraged them to target me specifically. I soon became lost in thought, trying to figure out what had set them off. However, being lost in one's own thoughts during class had its own distinct disadvantages. It is quite disarming when one is suddenly brought back to reality by a teacher's question.

Fortunately for me, Mrs. Lancaster was not one to take advantage of a potentially embarrassing situation, and quickly moved on to another student. Having been brought back to the real world, I began to realize that I had missed part of the classroom lecture. It also reinforced to me how those four must have felt when they finally snapped out of it.

Not a wonderful morning, to be sure, but there was always the lunchtime break to look forward to. During lunchtime, I met up in the cafeteria with the usual group with which I was more comfortable.

"Hey Andrew, the PE teacher is looking for you," said Tug. "He just wanted me to let you know that he wanted to talk to you."

"What's going on?" asked Sharon.

"Oh, nothing much," I replied, "just four troglodytes with nothing better to do."

"Who were they?" asked Tug, wanting to know more.

"You know, Rich Lang and the football jocks that hang around with him," I informed them.

"What did they want with you?" Sharon questioned me with concern.

Sharon and I were kind of going together, but nothing serious. We didn't even spend time together outside of school, but I had no trouble talking with her at all.

"What do they ever really want? Probably just wanted to get a rise out of me," I told her. "In fact, all they did, really, was to just chant my name, over and over again. They were being really annoying. To look at them, one would almost believe they were on drugs or something."

"Weird; like something out of a 'B' movie," acknowledged Tug.

"Yeah; in fact, it appeared to me, that they didn't seem to even know what they were doing," I noted to them. "I mean their eyes seem to stare beyond me instead of at me. It was a little creepy."

"Well it is almost Halloween," Tug acknowledged. "Perhaps, it was just your active imagination working overtime. Besides, they're jerks and that is all there is to it."

"Not everyone is a jerk, Tug," Sharon chided him. "But I will agree with you that those four are jerks. I wouldn't be surprised if they cooked up the whole thing, just because it is almost Halloween," Sharon said, making light of the whole situation.

"Are you going to report them?" asked Tug.

"Don't really have to," I replied. The PE teacher already cornered them about it, as I was leaving. That's probably what he wants to talk with me about."

"Well, whatever happens to them, they have it coming," offered Sharon. "Last week they got my best friend in trouble during class. They're always doing something to bother people, and then feigning the blame off on someone else."

The rest of lunchtime we traded stories about such bullying encounters. As my mind was still on other things, I found the rest of the day at school to be uneventful. Although I did end up spending some time with the PE teacher discussing the incident in the hall, but we both agreed not to make a big deal about it. After all, nobody was hurt. And having had similar consultations with teachers about such encounters, this seemed to be their barometer for such interactions. As long as nobody got physically hurt, they didn't want to pursue it.

After the school day ended, I opted to take the school bus home. Even as the sun had come out to brighten the day, I comforted myself in supportive conversation with the few friends I had on the bus. As the school bus dropped me off, I still wasn't in a mood to face family just yet. Instead, I decided to take a walk in the woods and lose myself in the comfort of happier thoughts. It always seemed relaxing to walk among the very trees where I met Harmony just five years earlier. As I noted earlier, it was like five years ago from this very day that the landscape of our meeting place was changed forever. I'll never forget it; just as I will never forget the day of her bizarre arrival on Earth, in a sphere of water drawn from the pond. These two incidents seemed to mark the beginning and end of my extraordinary time with her.

It all appeared to happen overnight, or so it seemed to me. The reality of my experience, and of all the physical evidence about her appearance, had been mysteriously erased from the landscape. No one I talked with knew why. In truth, everyone I talked with didn't even know there was a pond in the woods. It had just somehow seemed to have evaporated or drain away. In its place there now lies a lush meadow; a grassy tract of land which was adorned with all variety of meadow prairie-like plants. Ongoing visitations gave me time to learn much of the new terrain. I sat down among the undergrowth of what was once the large pond. There I had become eccentrically familiar with the variety of plant life that grew in its place: meadowsweet, meadow rue, meadow foam, meadow saffron, meadow sage, meadow beauty, and even the meadow spike-moss and meadow mushrooms. I believe meadow rue was my favorite. Meadow rue was like a miniature patch of clouds hovering close to the ground, especially when mixed within the meadow spike-moss. It rather reminded me of the mist that brought me to this spot on that first fateful summer day, some five and a half years earlier.

While musing about my fading memories of that time, it seemed the wind, upon the outlying trees, was echoing a song of past incarnations in remembrance of that time. Sing sweet comfort to me, I thought to myself, and ease my sadness on this beautiful afternoon. As I lay on my stomach close to the ground, I gazed over the miniature vista of this meadowland.

Just then, from out of the corner of my eye, I noticed a glimmer of light floating among the bushes, at the edge of the tree line. Perhaps it could have just been the reflective surface of some brightly colored leaf, I first thought to myself. Then upon second glance, I tried to focus upon the glimmer. Moving my head from side to side, the bit of light seemed to evade my direct view. I finally dismissed the whole thing as an illusionary trick of the eye. And now, having broken away from musing by this momentary distraction, I got up and continued toward home. In a week or so, even these leaves will lose all their luster; for summer was over and autumn was fast approaching.

It seemed Harmony was forefront in my thoughts today, as was the adventure initiated by her. And yet, after all this time, these memories had intertwined themselves within my new normalcy. Although it happened so long ago now, it still felt like just yesterday. My every other thought was littered with images and events from my grand quest, which I had revisited over and over again. Sometimes the immixture of my past and present memories was like trying to do homework while watching a movie at the same time: nothing gets resolved. In a strange way, I desperately needed the comforting reassurance that these past memories were real and not just an induced hallucination. It was as if part of me was just a mystery.

While I strolled through the woods, of which I had become so familiar, I reminisced about those simpler times. Even as the excitement of that quest had worn thin over time, in comparison to my everyday life as it is now, I still remember it like it was yesterday. That fantastical journey was seared into my mind's eye and seemed to influence anything I did. And it all started with Harmony. Harmony was …, well what one might call a celestial entity, looking every bit the part of her character. She left me with the impression that her appearance was my doing, and her only goal was to recruit me to save the universe. But before sending me out to save the universe, I had an awesome time training with her in the woods behind our house. Like 'The Wizard of Oz', she showed me what was behind the curtain of our four dimensional universe. Each day with her presented a new and more wonderful anticipation to be experienced. Those were the great memories.

But then there were the not so great memories, as she had convinced me to go it alone on a quest whose journey brought me across time and space. Let's just say that when I returned, I was no longer the naive little boy I was when we first met. She opened my eyes to a whole new way of understanding life and the universe. And perhaps I should thank her for that experience. But all in all, almost every day away from Earth seemed like a struggle to survive. In the end, I was just happy to even be alive.

In fact, I'm ecstatic to be back home again, on familiar ground, with both my parents. Heck, I was even glad to be back in school again. Anything was better than having my essence separated from my body and turned inside out, only to be propelled through varying dimensional frames of reference across spacetime. I mean, who knew it was even possible to travel outside of our fourth dimensional existence. Then, not to mention having my quintessential self transfigured, recreated, and then shredded into oblivion from within a galactic black hole. Oh, and least I forget, having been reassembled with spare parts from who knows where and then being returned to my comatose body, which had been languishing about in the woods.

So yes, I survived. And perhaps that should have been enough of an adventure for me, or anyone. Still, somehow, I missed it all. For in the wake of my survival, I felt I had attained a sense of immortality, as I had survived what no other human has ever experienced or could even imagine. I had traveled beyond the stars, through the limits of our dimensional spacetime, and touched upon the aethereal plane of existence itself; or that is how my dad had explained it to me. So if boredom is the measure of one's ability to not be excited, then I am doomed to be forever bored. I mean, how could I possibly top this extraterrestrial experience?

Still, I guess it's just like my dad told me: You cannot live a full life without moving forward with the current of Time. Going against the current of Time will only make you grow older before your time. That is to say, you would still grow older, but without embracing any of the new experiences with which to fill your life. You know, the kind of new experiences that help to keep one young. A bit cryptic, but I think I got it: You can't live for the future if you're always dwelling in the past. Anyway, I felt my life was overflowing with experiences already; having already lived two lives.

After all, holding onto these memories was like a reassuring confirmation that it all really happened. I wanted ..., no, I needed some validation of my past experience to support the absence of my previous alien life and the alien memories I still retained. And I needed these memories to reassure me of my own sanity. Consequently it was important to me, that who I told of this secret would believe in what I said. I knew I could always count on my parents. And yet, I also hoped for some further corroboration. Something like the reappearance of Harmony. Just something, anything, that would allow me in my normal life to acknowledge the truth of my more alien experience. I closed my eyes and soaked up the atmosphere.

As I stood there with my eyes closed, I even had the strangest feeling that I was being watched over by her even now. It was like a weird sensation or sixth sense which made the hairs on the back of my neck tingle. But moreover, I was distraught with the feeling that I would never again embrace the scent of peppermint and roses that used to linger after Harmony left. Frustrated, I thought to myself that maybe no one was meant to live more than one lifetime. After all, you can't miss a past life that you never had.

Before it got too depressing, I decided to return home. Entering through the back gate off the woods, I passed by our redbud tree where the fairy statue was set beneath it. It was a benign reminder of my time with Fairy, and reminiscent of my mother's description for the redbud tree. She called it our fairy tree. Mom said it made her gardening chores easier if she could imagine that she was creating a beautiful home for the fairy folk. She even planted some mint scented plants and some rose scented geraniums for me. A sweet gesture to be sure, but perhaps not true to what I remembered. Perhaps she had just read one too many fairy tales.

Still, after my last adventure, who was I to argue as to what was real and what was a fairy tale. It wasn't that I didn't believe in the possibility of fairies, mind you, but just not around here. The only fairies I ever met up with were part of the hazy recollections of my experience after diving headlong into a black hole. And how real those were, I could not even tell, for my mental state was not at its best. I mean, I just don't know if I could trust my scrambled memories of that event anymore. Perhaps I had imagined the whole thing about the small bright lights being fairies from out of that dark limitless void. Having been a disembodied essence of life itself, my only connection with my environment would have been one felt via a weirder, supernatural sixth sense.

Anyway, my mom would go on about how a redbud tree holds the magic of fairy dreams. Something to do with it blooming redbuds before it becomes a normal tree with green leaves. So it can be implied that the magic is really in the redbud flower. The story goes that if you eat the redbud flower, you will either have good dreams or see fairies in your dreams. Although sometimes I think she made the whole thing up just so I would eat her exotic redbud salads. Not quite the magical reputation of the Alder, or the Elder trees that the Eastern Redbud tree is sometimes compared with, the Elder tree boasts being the home of fairies.

But there was also another story that merited less favor in my mother's eyes. Being in a negative mood myself just now, I also remembered that she was upset about it being nicknamed the Judas tree. She doesn't hold with those negative tales as reasons for the blood red blooms. Still, mom did say that dad did cut himself planting the tree, so blood there was. She related how it is was such a chore to transport the big tree and plant it by hand that dad's back was out of whack for weeks. And all because he wanted the biggest redbud tree he could find, so he wouldn't have to wait for it to grow. And they say I am impatient.

Reaching the house, I found the back patio door locked. I assumed my mother was off somewhere, so I went around to the front and let myself in. It was not an uncommon occurrence, but I wouldn't say I was a latch-key kid. Still, I had to remember to grab my house key every morning. It reminded me of my morning routine with dad's cumbersome litany of daily reminders for me: did I remember the house key, did I remember to pack my homework from last night, did I remember which band instrument I needed for the day, did I remember to pack the correct music, etc. Although I resented his constant checking up on me, I would occasionally seem to forget an item or two in the morning. I had decided that the brain was just not ready to function on the particular morning of school days. Such inability to function in the morning would often make for some awkward drives to school, when I did ride with dad. I believe it to be one of the best reasons that I couldn't wait to finish Driver's Ed. The opportunity to be more mobile and independent would not come too soon for me.

From conversations I had with other students, this seemed to be a common phenomenon for most of my classmates as well. Though, I could never convince my parents that this morning phenomenon was an indisputable fact of life. Needless to say, my father and I were at odds on most such considerations. To me, all of his well-meaning reminders seemed be geared around him making his life easier and mine more difficult. Yet, it was the price I had to pay if I wanted a ride to school in the morning, after missing the school bus.

After my obligatory call to dad every afternoon, to let him know that I was home, I then spent time getting my homework done. I knew that it would almost always be dad's first question to me upon his return from work. And although my parents had taken the time to provide me with a workspace in my bedroom, my favorite spot to do my homework was at my dad's desk up in the library. It just seemed to be the place from which ideas flowed.

I reminisced how dad would always spend his weekend mornings writing down his thoughts, or mine, depending on which book he decided to work on that day. He spent a lot of time over the last few years documenting the tales of my great adventure and how I saved the twin planets of Glorthocks and DeMutron. When we would talk of it, I could feel the excitement and pride my father had for me, his reluctant hero; even more so than when I got my grade point average up beyond 3.0 or my periodic participations at school concerts or even my performances in high school drama plays.

I also remembered how, as we worked together on the book, dad believed it was very important to always relate the facts accurately. It was as if he believed it would help him to better understand what happened to me. And while I enjoyed my dad taking an active interest in my experiences, in the end it seemed to be all about 'his' book rather than 'our' book. He even used the information he gleaned from my adventure, to help him refine his concept of the universal order in his companion book, *'The Evolutioning of Creation: Volume Two'*. It was as if he placed more significance on recording the event than on sympathizing with me about how I just survived a near death experience. Or maybe, I really did die. It is difficult to understand what death really is. His approach was not so much that he was unsympathetic, but rather that he took an analytical approach to my whole adventure. While dad would sit, listen, and then provide some sage advice, it was more mom who tried to understand how I felt or how it all affected me as a person.

These feelings aside, it just seemed to me that dad's desk was a better place to do my homework as it was more open to the house and to the outside at the same time. From the desk's corner position in the loft area, I could survey the expanse of the library and the family room below, while being able to monitor the entrance to the front door, basement, and kitchen. Behind me natural sunlight streamed in through a row of large windows facing the back yard to the south, which backed up to the woods. It was strategically the best way to keep track of most everything inside the house and outside the house. Perhaps that's why dad chose this particular location in the house. Contrarily, my desk was placed up against the wall of my bedroom. And, behind me, only diffused light made it through the shade of the north side windows, as I preferred the shades to be drawn down. Although my windows could be opened to the front of the house, they were still at the opposite end of the room, leaving little opportunity to connect with the outside world. It was probably their intention to cut back on any outside distractions, but I might have as well have been back in the Feldspar Caves of Glorthocks.

As I went about the business of resolving mathematical word problems, I had that weird feeling that I was being watched. Looking out the library windows behind me, I again noticed a faint glimmer of light flitting about the redbud tree in the backyard. I looked away and then back, only to see it now in the forefront of the woods. As before, the glimmer of light seemed to evade my every ability to focus directly upon it. Rather it seemed to float off to the side of my view, just within the shallow of the forest shrubbery. Again, I passed it off as a trick of the eye; kind of like the 'floaters' in one's eyes, I thought.

'Floaters' were a term I became familiar with during some cautionary lecture from the eye doctor about taking proper care of my eyesight. Maybe my eyes were starting to go bad, I briefly thought to myself. It certainly made more sense than not being able to focus upon a moving object. And yet, the glimmer of flitting light brought to mind a memory of those lights that appeared to me in the midst of my darkest hour from within the galactic black hole. Of this event, my memory is still quite blurred. As to my imprinted recollections during this time, it was as if I were in some semiconscious state between being awake and dreaming. And as remembrances go, these events would be forever hidden; only to be unlocked and played out within my dreams.

My father and I spent some time trying to sort out what actually happened to me while I was in the black hole. But he took great care not to press me on the details of this particular event. Although I could tell that he was genuinely interested, and even excited, about the events of my experience within the black hole, he would always tread very gently about this portion of my fragmented memory. As far as he could surmise of the event, dad related to me that my experience, beyond the black hole's horizon, was actually part of an alternate dimensional state. It was a dimensional state outside the defined boundaries of normal Time and Space. Rather, it was what dad termed approaching his concept of 'No Time and All Space'. It wasn't a concept that I understood very well, but he postulated that my experience was a verification of his theories for the universe.

Still, however fragmented, that memory of my experience in the black hole was also of my companion, Fairy. I never found out what her real name was, or if she even had one, but then there wasn't a lot of time for introductions. From the time we met until the time we crashed through the red sun and into the event horizon of the black hole, we jumped from the frying pan and into the fire. I wondered where she was now, and what she might be doing. I know that I would've never survived it all without her.

As I mused over whether I'd ever see Fairy or Harmony again, I refocused my efforts toward finishing off my homework. After all, once homework is done, I can play Wii or watch TV; either of which to me is much more interesting than my homework. Probably not the best motivation, but that is where my mind was at.

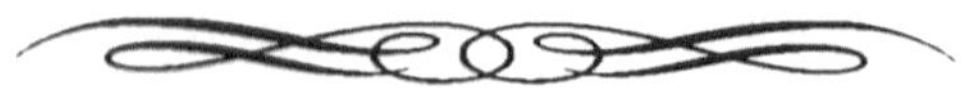

[Scene Change - Narrator's Perspective]

[The unseen secret of the meadowland]

As Andrew continued to focus more on his homework, a wisp of autumn air could be seen kicking up a gentle whirlwind within his back yard. The vortex of the whirlwind pulled up a swirl of fallen leaves into a mini tornado. And within this mini tornado, a single redbud seed could be seen ascending ever higher into the sky, as if it was being lifted by some unseen force. As happenstance would have it, a closer view revealed that the singular redbud seed was followed by that same gimmer of light that evaded Andrews's direct detection earlier. The seed flew as if it was being piloted, and was now soaring across the tops of the trees towards the meadowlands. In the distance, the sun was slowly setting and there was a splash of red cascading across the clouds of the neighborhood sky.

In the course of finishing up his homework, Andrew's mother came home. And as daylight faded into dusk, they engaged in the normal activity of catching up on each other's individual time away. Soon dad would be home and the family would be together again, before the day ended. Having previously dismissed the distraction of the glinting light, Andrew has no idea that there is more to this little glimmer than even he might have imagined. So it came to be, upon the very site of Andrew's original first encounter with Harmony, the normalcy of Andrew's life was about to be turned upside down again; just as it had done before, five and half years earlier. So it is that the focus of our story moves away from the family for now.

Deep within the supplanted meadowlands, dusk began to approach where the large pond had once been. Deer could be seen meandering about as they passed through the area; some pausing to forage upon the floor of the meadowlands, while others fed upon the scattered berry bushes. High above the tree line, there was to be one of those rare events when both the sun and the full moon were to trade places in the sky. As the sun was seen to kiss the horizon, that single redbud tree seed could be seen dropping from out of a red tinted sunset. And as the full moon rose, the redbud seed had just now found its way to the center of the lush meadow. Once the setting of the sun was no longer visible, the full Moon could still be seen rising in the distance.

Serendipitously, this twilight phenomenon was coincidentally followed by another rare event. As the sky above grew darker against a moonlit landscape, the bright dancing lights of an aurora borealis began to come into view. It was indeed unusual that the northern lights could be seen this far south. Becoming ever more visible, it was even more unique for the aurora to be demonstrated with such intensity. Such was the intensity that it filtered into the meadowlands, reflecting with an eerie glow of pale green and purple colors as it rippled across the sky.

Even stranger still, the aurora broke out into a dazzling display of bright green rays in the visage of a phoenix. Unexpectedly, from the heart of the phoenix, there came an abrupt flash of unnatural green and yellow electrostatic discharge emanating down into the familiar meadowlands like a slow motion flash of lightning. A ghostly blast of air silently pushed out in every direction, having projected from the grounding of the mysteriously colored lightning bolt.

It was here, just above that singular redbud tree seed now lying in the meadowlands, which the mysterious lightning bolt terminated. The strange lightning did not dissipate abruptly, but rather it splayed out; inducing an eerie, fog-like ground covering in a large circumference around the seed. At the center of the unique circle, the meadowland opened up just enough to accept the redbud seed. After that mysterious lightning strike, there was no enduring evidence of this unnatural lighting from the sky, save the scorched earth about the planted seed and the eerie fog-like blanket of green light.

Furtively, as fate would have it, the strange lightning was witnessed by no one. There was not even a single thunder clap, from the displaced air around the area of the strike, for anyone to have heard. Instead, all that remained of that strange event was the eerie blanket of seemingly bioluminescent fog that appeared to retain the strange energy of the northern lights just above the ground surrounding the seed.

Upon accepting this new gift within the meadowland, the apparently magical seed immediately took root in the still fertile soil and began to be nurtured under the eerily glowing fog that blanketed the area. The unnatural display of dancing lights above the site continued to accentuate shadowy differences in the surrounding landscape. While other trees, shrubs, and plants just outside of the meadowlands were falling dormant to the condition of an autumn season, this newly planted redbud seed was just now coming alive.

An emerging redbud tree would soon be seen springing forth within the magic of this unusual oasis; for indeed this meadowland was rich in the life force of Mother Earth, or Gaia as related in Greek mythology. Even Andrew, upon his many visitations to this location over the months, had not noticed the strangeness of these meadowlands. He had not noticed how this singular meadow had continued to thrive while the rest of the surrounding woods had already begun to wane within the embrace of the fall season; acquiescing toward its well-deserved winter slumber.

And now, under the brightness of this moonlit night, the newly rooted redbud plant slowly expanded in two directions. Below the earth, its root system snaked through the underground medium seeking out water and nutrients from the soil. Above the earth, the emerging redbud plant began to grow, upon the support of its newly entrenched root system, to meet the warmer nurturing atmosphere of the eerie blanket of fog above.

Slowly the woodland understory was breached to allow the emerging deciduous sprout to drink in the reflected sunlight that was bouncing off the full moon. And as the young tree sapling reached out for more energy, it began to bud the first basal sprout into a slender twig; which, in turn, was provided with short, dark brown knotty spurs upon its length. The polycormic pattern of the twig could then be seen filling out into spreading branches which zigzagged into a form that rose higher, rounding out the tree's profile. In addition to all during this remarkable growth, the ghostly green glow that still danced in the sky above, now appeared to emanate, liken to St. Elmo's fire, from the tree itself.

If not for seclusion of its location, the phenomenal speed at which this redbud tree was growing, and the oddity of its blooming in the fall season, would not have gone unnoticed. Growing at an unimaginable rate, the intertwining branches were actively being supported by multiple trunks that cropped up from its suckers. Soon the shape of the redbud spread out as wide as it was tall. Within just a few hours, the redbud tree, as seen silhouetted against the full moon, had impressively achieved its full growth size of 30 feet tall and 25 feet wide.

Slowly, perhaps even in parallel with this growth spurt, the small, sweet pea–shaped, lavender pink and rosy purple flowers began to sprout on the newly formed branches, and even along its main trunks. As the redbud's pinkish-red flowers blossomed and matured, they were accompanied by their emerging heart shaped leaves. Oddly enough, just as the heart shaped leaves appeared, the red blooms began to be supplanted and discarded. Normally a much slower process, the abundance of discarded redbud flowers could now be seen gently raining down upon the ground below, like a gentle crimson colored snow storm. The unneeded red flower blooms were then all but lost beneath the strange blanket of fog, which continued to flourish, but had now changed color to a more purple hue.

Within the center of this activity, and among the network of intertwining branches, the familiar foliage of the emerging flattened leguminous bean-like dry seedpods had begun to replace the redbud's flowers. Amidst the every maturing foliage, an unusually large redbud seed pod began to arise and evolve. As the larger seed did so, the eerie glow began to be concentrated onto this single, special seed pod. As the glow became brighter, this special seed pod continued to expand and grow until it grew up to 6 feet in length and 3 feet wide about its center.

The now completed redbud tree, with its new gift artfully nestled within its network of branches, swayed in the breeze; swinging the pod like a small cradle in the wind. As the dazzling display of northern lights began fading from the sky, so too the eerie glow about the seed pod began to be diminished as well. There, the seed pod will remain unseen and undiscovered, for now, concealed behind a fresh blanket of lush green heart shaped leaves.

The moonlight could be seen illuminating the many colored autumn leaves within the shallow of the changing woods that surrounded the meadowland. It seemed a fitting backdrop for the miraculous scene that had just taken place, as it resembled the look of light shining through a stained glass window. As the last hint of direct moonlight from along the tops of the trees began to wane, the broad green leaves slowly changed to an appropriate bright yellow; which was more in keeping with the expected seasonal fashion.

In fact the entire meadowland had now changed overnight in kind to match the season. And now, after every trace of the eerie greenish and purple glow faded from sight, the secreted seed pod also faded in color to match the bark of the tree; camouflaging its true form and purpose. Such is the unseen secret; a secret of which one knows neither of its true purpose nor of its ultimate destiny.

CHAPTER

2

Life Intervenes

[The key to surviving life is to understand how to survive strife.]

With his mother now home, Andrew is seen playing on the family room, big screen TV. Just outside the family room window, dusk has been giving way to twilight. His mother can be seen in her routine of preparing dinner for the family, when Andrew's selfish mood is broken upon the entrance of his father.

[Andrew's Narrative]

Yesterday evening dad came home in a very different mood. It was as if he had just given up on life. I had seen him stressed out before, even grief stricken upon the death of his younger sister or, more recently, in the months after the passing of his eldest brother. But this seemed to be something quite different altogether. It was a soulful depression, not unlike what I had been experiencing over the last six months. Coincidentally, it was the same six months after which dad was dealing with his eldest brother's death, while doing his best to grapple with the recent changes in management at work. Suspiciously, it would seem, my mood was reflective of dad's inability to lift my spirits during this troubled time in his life. It is ironic how such a loss can imposed so much weight upon one's contemplation.

Although I had related today's weird incident at school with mom, I could see no reason to worry dad about it. He seemed to have enough on his plate right now. I surreptitiously listened in as dad despondently explained to mom how he had found himself backed into a corner at work, with no real decent alternatives. From what I gathered, his earlier contact with the company Ombudsman ended up just making matters worse. Subsequently, after years of diligently working towards a promotion, the recent management changes put him the awkward position of failing to meet their favor and prospect.

Now what I knew of dad was that he was very proud of his work ethic. He had always been confident in his ability to provide whatever it took to accomplish his tasks, regardless of any favorable management support. It was more of a personal ordinance which he imposed upon himself. Consequently, what dad was not use to was failing in any form, regardless of the conditions. So it was quite a shock when management told that he was not meeting their expectations. I wanted to sympathize with my dad's dilemma, but he never really wanted to look vulnerable in front of me. So now, in the midst of his current fear of failure, he appeared to believe that he lacked the capability to succeed.

I could see that the work stress was such that dad wanted to outright quit. However, his family obligations required that he continue to endure in the unforgiving and bias environment of his workplace. This he did, so that he would be eligible under the current rules of unemployment compensation, to stay the family while looking for another job. He very seldom lashed out at anyone, if at all. I could just tell that it was tearing him up inside.

"Remember how I told you that on my first interview with this new manager?" I heard dad quizzing mom. "She all but told me that I shouldn't be in the leadership position that my previous manager had just recently promoted me into. I mean, it was the first time we had even met and she didn't even know me yet. How am I expected to work with a manager who has all but decided the fate of my career? I have no idea from where this distain is coming. Either she, or her manager, wants me out. I am not sure why, but they want me out. Perhaps it's my age. How can two managers be so different?"

"You need to relax," mom started in. "I know it's not fair, but we can work through this."

"Work through this?" dad remarked. "Do you know what she did today? She scheduled a status meeting with me, but then she didn't want to discuss the status of the project at all. Instead she just started in telling me that someone told her I was arrogant and condescending. And then that was it. I accepted her critique and tried to learn more about this alleged incident so I could make reparations. She just dismissed me; reaffirming her position that I need to curb my behavior. She wouldn't even tell me who reported it or what it was that I said. I tend to believe she just trumped up the whole thing, but I can't prove it."

"OK, so quit," mom recommended. "We can afford to live on our savings while you look for another job."

"Oh, they'd like that. Then they wouldn't have to pay me unemployment," dad complained. "No, you're right. I'll just have to work through this no matter what it takes. And I can't expect any help from the Ombudsman or HR. From the way she is trying to my job difficult, it just appears that the Ombudsman has been feeding my complaints about her behavior right back to her. It's just not fair."

Seemingly, dad was internalizing the pain in upon himself. It was at this moment that I realized perhaps my problems were not as bad as I had made them out to be. Introspective of his predicament, he had a maxim to which he would often referred, 'Just as it appears you have control of your own destiny, life intervenes'.

Interestingly, this maxim of 'Life Intervenes' is actually an addendum to the adage of 'Murphy's Law', which dad also invoked with some frequency and consistency. 'Murphy's Law' is typically understood as stipulating, 'Anything that can go wrong will go wrong'. It appropriately speaks to the resultants of fate, in which he relegates his lack of control to that which is happening around him. Subsequently, this new adage of 'Life intervenes', ends up as the clash between fate and destiny. It tends to speak more to the rhythmic flow of destiny. In which case, 'Life Intervenes' is understood as stipulating, 'Just as soon as things are going good, life takes a turn for the worst'.

It was as if life, or living, had its own biometric rhythm of highs and lows. Liken to working the stock market, you had to know when to buy in. It may be why some of us can never get ahead. And if the difference is large enough, then one might just crash and burn; leaving one without the strength to get up again. I 'googled' it on the internet and found that the philosophy behind 'Life Intervenes' is more commonly referred to as Forsyth's Second Corollary to Murphy's Law; which states, 'Just when you see the light at the end of the tunnel, the roof caves in'. And clearly it did seem that way for dad.

I imagine it all becomes very confusing and messed up when our destiny shifts under us. It is rather like an existential earthquake, of sorts. I can see how one can easily get lost in a recusal of their own self-worth, exposing the notion of 'Where did I go wrong'? And when there is no thoughtfully logical answer to this preponderance of introspection, the confusion can become worse. This 'loss of control' over one's own ability to influence their own destiny is a difficult concept to ponder, and an even more difficult burden to accept. It erodes one's very confidence. Until finally, this feeling of soulful confusion transmogrifies itself into one of depression. It is a depression wherein as one tries, in vain, to fight off the negative thoughts of self-pity; a feeling of self-pity that begs the invocation of the sentiment of 'Why me'.

Oh, how I have gone down that road before in another life, in my previous quest, only to realize that my only guide in such despair were the written thoughts of my father which he captured in his work, *The*

Evolutioning of Creation'. Those, and then what I could interpret from my training with my celestial mentor, Harmony, They were my only guide posts for any hope and salvation. Though, trying to make sense of either dad's logic or Harmony's riddles is like trying to make sense of the 'Wonderland' from which 'Alice' was a part. It was a wonder that I even made it back alive at all. Truthfully, the adventure proved to be both my high and low moments in life. Perhaps dad just needed to regain his 'high' momentum back again.

It was just then, from my vantage point, that I noticed a hint of green light dancing across the back yard lawn. I rushed over to the parents and alerted them to this unusual spectacle.

"Dad, Mom, you have to see this," I said briefly as I pointed to the sunroom windows.

"What's going on?" dad asked.

"There is a strange light in the backyard," I answered with excitement.

"Yes, I see it," mom acknowledged as she followed dad into the sunroom.

Watching from the sunroom for just a moment, the weird green color seemed to cover the entire valley. We left the confines of the sunroom and walked out onto the deck. The sky was lite up from just above the tree line and over the woods that bordered our back yard. It was a spectacularly dazzling display of the aurora borealis that captivated us, and everyone else in the neighborhood, it would seem; as I saw them slowly filter out of their homes.

As I leaned over the railing of our deck, seemingly trying to get a better view, dad laid his hand upon my shoulder. "Better drink this in son," he said. "I don't think we'll see anything like this again in our lifetime; at least, not from this lower latitude. The northern lights almost never reach down this far."

As mom move in closer, dad wrapped his free arm around her. Yes, I thought to myself, this is a well needed respite from the cloud off despair that seemed to engulf our family, at present. As we watched, the aurora broke out into an astounding display of bright green rays in the visage of a phoenix. Then, for just a moment, there appeared to be a pulsating heart within the manifested image of the phoenix. It was all rather awe inspiring.

The bizarre nature of this happenstance only increased its enticement upon my thoughts. Looking about, I noticed the neighbors engaging in similar activities. Everyone seemed entranced by the colorful spectacle that was being exhibited high in the night sky. If only such moments could last forever, I thought to myself.

As the night's spectacle wore on, it seemed that dad had resigned himself to lay in the yard swing looking up into the sky. Mom had already gone back in by this time, while I sat on the deck steps. When I could see that lights had faded enough, I challenged dad to a game of chess. I was hoping to keep him distracted from indwelling upon his depression. Though playing the game of chess was not necessarily my real intent, playing chess was a good way to open up channels of random conversation with dad.

Dad agreed and brought out the good board from the closet, where he kept it stored with the rest of the board games. Having grabbed a bottle of coke from the fridge, dad sat down at the kitchen table across from me and opened the box.

"Not so fast you two," mom yelled over to us. "I didn't cook all this food just to fill the fridge."

While we ate, I thought to myself that my first question should redirect dad's attention and engage his passion for the thoughtful resolution of existence. By the time we got back to the game, I was ready.

"Dad, what do you think happens when you die?" I asked, as we completed setting up the board. It was perhaps not the best choice of subjects, considering his demeanor, but he joined in just the same.

"Are you looking for a faith based answer or a science based answer?" he asked, fishing for a more lucid question. "I ask that because there can be no real science based answer without objective empirical data," he stated. "And all we really have now is the subjective first hand data from those who have returned from a near death experience, like you, without any empirical data to support their testimony. And, like you, there is no way for anyone to examine the evidence of what happened to them, or to reproduce how it transpired."

"You say that mine was a near death experience, but it didn't feel like that to me," I responded with some regret. "I never really felt I was dead, or even near death as I could recall, because the death of my alien body wasn't really my actual body; if that makes any sense to you. And as you yourself said on previous discussions, it was more like I was living in an alternate dimension, rather than really being dead," I said to remind him.

I started the game, but couldn't help thinking back to the moment when I awoke from my trance, upon my return to my body on Earth. "I mean, my body was still working. It was just my brain that was on vacation; so to speak."

"I see what you mean," dad paused to take in what I was saying.

Jokingly, I thought, he didn't even take advantage of the opening I gave him about my brain being on vacation, which he might have said was more often than not.

"Then what it really comes down to is how one defines death," he reframed the conversation. "Is one's death just the end of their corporal existence, as we understand it in this fourth dimensional version of our own reality within this universe? Or is one's death something more egregious, like the loss of one's identity? Rather like losing our own sentience of self, beyond our corporal existence; one's soul, if you will."

"When you put it that way, then I guess I'm looking for a faith based answer," I responded in kind. "I was considering what it would be like if my astral incarnation was unable to return back within my host body. Do you think I would continue to exist, like in a perpetual state of astral projection? I could deal with that. Perhaps something like consciousness without my physical body to host my thoughts," I probed, drawing upon the established foundation of our earlier discussions on the subject. "Or do you think it would be, as you have suggested, more like the loss of one's conscious control and self-awareness altogether?"

"From what I have gathered from a cursory study of the differing religious philosophies, over the years, the general belief of death is the process by which one's soul is set free from its more physical form. Beyond this initial belief, the theosophical speculation is that everything in the universe is alive, and that nothing truly dies. Most theosophists maintain that there is a deeper spiritual reality beyond the natural order of our more physical universe. And to contact or experience this more metaphysical plane of existence, one must establish a deep state of meditation, or some other way of transcending normal consciousness," dad explained. "And I guess a near death experience would constitute as another way of transcending normal consciousness."

"And this 'more metaphysical plane of existence' is where we go after death?" I prodded for more of dad's insight.

"Well, of that I cannot be sure. You were quite alive when traveling about the universe without your body. So based on your adventure, we know such an astral plane of existence does indeed exist for you. But as to whether such an astral persistence requires an elemental connection with your physical host appears to be the mysterious piece of this puzzle," he conjectured. "Still it begs the question, do our physical bodies subsist to support our astral selves or is it our astral selves that are supporting our physical bodies?"

"Kind of like the 'chicken or the egg' analogy if you ask me," I remarked. "However, I do remember Harmony saying that she could not help me on my journey because she needed to protect my body," I contributed with some air of understanding. "How did she put it?" I recalled aloud– *"No harm may befall your mortal body. Your body will be under my protection at all times. This I tell you, so that you will not be afraid to try. But even my protection has it limits. I cannot aid you in your great journey lest the liability of this protection and your quest be jeopardized. Although I can monitor your immortal spirit, I can only interfere to return you from whence you came."*

"And because of that piece of the puzzle," dad speculated, "I expect that the living body is an important connection to be maintained, else one would lose control of their own self-awareness in reality and then they would be truly dead."

"I ofttimes have imagined the after-life to be a comingling with this metaphysical plane of existence, but without the anchor of our more physical form. More aptly put, it would be analogous to the mindless dream that never ends," dad said thoughtfully.

He then deliberated over the chess game as it was his turn. After dad completed his turn, he continued, "For the most part, dreams are the mind's way of working through one's feelings. You know; in the attempt to heal the mental stresses or scars that haunts one's psyche."

"The transitioning of our psyche, or soul, after death is not an easy concept to postulate or theorize upon," he began changing his train of thought. "In fact, mythology is filled with many examples of the human struggle to understand an afterlife. Many are influenced upon their imaginative musings on a more anthropomorphic representation of the id, ego, and superego as the vestige of one's soul. So they believe the soul you have nurtured in life, is the soul you take with you upon your death. Where upon the condition or character of your soul would then be your heaven or your hell."

While not everything dad said was a kernel of wisdom, this statement was pretty close. Still, I could not discern whether he paused to prompt me to take my next move on the chess board or whether he was waiting for some response from me, but clearly the next move was mine. As I worked out my next move, I began to work out what we were discussing.

"So then," I continued our discussion, "while my boundless soul becomes my new formless being of existence in this mystical dreamland, I would still have no actual control over my own consciousness because I would be in a perpetual state of sub-conscious dreaming," I asserted with some certainty as to my reflections.

From what I remember of what mom and dad told me, dreams were essentially just the ramblings of one's subconscious trying to make sense of emotions via their collected conscious memories.

"And since dreams are the mind's way of working out one's emotional state, or sub-conscious feelings, and trying to provide us with emotional balance for the issues that bug us, then how can I ever exercise any control over my life force after death?" I questioned.

Wow, I don't even know how I came up with that thought. My dad's face lit up and I could see he was engaged in our conversation, but perhaps more so in my contribution to the discussion.

He engaged me with some of his more cherished introspections, "Yes, you have it; the concepts of control or 'free will' are aspects of a more real existence. Conversely it follows that the loss of control, or the loss of 'free will', are aspects of a more abstract non-existence. This abstract of non-existence can be understood as the existence of nothing, where nothing exists. So all that is left is just the ego-driven dream of our previous memories in a more ideated existence. It is that existence, which being the stream of our emotional subconsciousness, that continues to reorganize our psyche as it tries to make sense of it all."

While I couldn't completely process what dad had just related to me, I felt more engaged and emboldened to dig further into this understanding that we were creating. Rather than answer, I was lost in the thought of working through how to build upon our collective discussion. It evoked memories of conversations that I had with Harmony; 'the dreams yet to be dreamt.' How did Harmony put it?

For life is the illusion, the dreams to be dreamt
Dreams are the hope of Time in Space spent
Time is the being, the now here of no where
Space is the tenability of Time in despair

Finally I blurted out, "And then perhaps death, not life, becomes just our dreams yet to be dreamt."

"Yes, I like that. A very insightful and deep thought," dad relayed back to me with some pride in my answer.

But then my fourth dimensional logic started to kick in again, and I asked, "But if dreams are only our way of working through our emotional states, based on captured memories, wouldn't our ability to dream require a physical brain from which to draw upon?"

"An intriguing question," dad started, but then paused again. "Perhaps you could take your next move, while I think on it," he prompted me.

As I took my next move, dad started in again, "I got stuck on that very thought for the longest time. It made me wonder if a state of death was somehow dependent on maintaining a connection with our living host. Then I reflected upon what the stories of ghosts, hauntings, poltergeists, or possessions may provide as a plausible avenue for this hypothesis. I later worked on the exploring of a connection between death and the concept of extrasensory perception. I even tried to imagine a combination of the two; both concepts melded together in which to provide for a way of continuing to exist in some alternative hyper-dimensional frame of reference."

"Existence in some alternative hyper-dimensional frame of reference," I thought aloud.

"Yes. You know; somewhat like your connection with the universe," he introduced his supposition. "As such, one might still be able maintain their individuality and their ability to influence their own destiny by interacting within the living universe more directly. In the end, I found that trying to fathom such a realm of an afterlife was more akin to understanding non-existence than I had first realized. It ends up being a black hole of circular reasoning that pulls one invariably out of their own reality."

"Makes for great movies, though," I interjected, partially because I could not completely follow dad's logic and partially because it was his turn. "And now you're the one holding the game up," I prompted my father.

While I started this discussion to pull my father out his funk, I found I was dismayed at our inability to come up with an answer upon which I could build my own sense of understanding for what comes after death.

"I would like to think that I could control or continue to create my own dream world in my own afterlife; kind of like in that movie, *Inception*,'" I postulated aloud.

Dad joined in, "Yeah, that would be nice. You know the first film that I saw like that was 'Dreamscape'. But even before it became a movie, it was also the intent of my meditation to not only be able to tell whether

I was dreaming, but to be able to control my thoughts and actions within the dream."

His declaration intrigued me. "So you would try to control your dream by first recognizing that you were dreaming," I acknowledged.

"However, as you have so poignantly put it, I also concluded that such abilities would still require the subconscious portion of my psyche, or a brain, to manipulate the dream. So this ability would therefore be dependent on a connection with a brain, or some form of living that I couldn't imagine would be available after death," he surmised.

"Then that's it," I stated with disappointment; "death is just the like 'holding patterns' of what we have previously dreamt? So once the brain is gone, so is the ability to make new dreams," I declared.

I turn my attention back to our chess game. It appeared dad waited until I completed my move. Then he approached me anew with his new theory.

"Oh, don't be so negative. I didn't mean to propose that there is no controllable afterlife," he revealed to me. "What I said was that I couldn't imagine one would be available after the death of one's brain. But as I think of it, after your amazing experience, a whole new avenue of possibilities opens up. It challenges me to reshape my basis and bias for existence and nonexistence as part of the universal balance."

"How so?" I asked, intrigue by the prospect of a possible answer.

'Well, it is your ability to receive impressions through living connections in the universe that demonstrates to me that there is perhaps another form of living communication, or existence, beyond our separate and unique psyches," he said, seemingly working to put it altogether. "I'm beginning to think of these psychic abilities as our unconscious capability to tap into these more universal connections. It is as if the concept of a soul makes more sense in this more holistic view. I mean, think on it. You were able to travel the universe and then back to home using only these connections."

As dad continued, I could tell that his depressing mood was becoming lost in his zest for understanding.

"This brings about a whole new philosophy for how our individual psychic energies, our souls if you will, may interact within this being of a living universe. Think of it as a fifth force," he tried to explain it to me; "one outside of the four fundamentals forces that drive our fourth dimensional existence. There might be another form of being that continues our existence in another dimensional frame of reference. Perhaps it would be one not even bounded by just our variable degrees of Space and Time, but rather more of a cooperative comingling of Space and Time like in the form of a tesseract."

"A tesseract?" I inquired of dad for more understanding. "You mean like in the book, *A Wrinkle in Time*?"

"Exactly so; a tesseract that provides for a fifth dimensional perspective in spacetime: a medium wherein Space and Time might be interchangeable frames of reference. Such a perspective would allow us to view the universe as a morphing evolutionary being in both Past time and Future time, rather than just as an evolutionary progression of cause and effect in the Present."

"But the tesseract of that story, is just that," I argued back. "It is a fantasy of fiction."

"In the most rigid sense, that is true," dad continued to justify his reference. "The tesseract is indeed just a geometric, four-dimensional analog of a cube. However, if you start by thinking of it like the non-fictional geometric consternation of spacetime, then the tesseract can also be considered as a four-dimensional hypercube for the representation of Space and Time. If interpreted relativistically, it would interfuse the traditional three spatial dimensions with the one temporal dimension of our fourth dimensional frame of reference," dad stated, seemingly working his theory out in real time.

"Now, accordingly to Klein's definition of four-dimensional geometry as a study of the invariant properties of a spacetime, the tesseract, under transformations within itself, is reflective of a fifth dimension geometry that can be utilized to study the invariant properties of such a spacetime event, as we move within it," he related aloud.

While it was amazing to see dad working out his theories in real time, I could not follow his logic.

"Now you've lost me completely," I admitted. "Can you provide me with a more abbreviated version?"

"OK," dad thought for a moment and then provided some background for what he was relating. "Much of the early work on fifth dimensional space was in an attempt to develop a theory that would unify the four fundamental forces in nature: i.e., strong and weak nuclear forces, gravity and electromagnetism. Although their approaches were not without flaws, the concept provided a basis for further research into multiple dimensional studies and, in time, the basis for hyperspace. Whereupon the fifth dimension could be similarly viewed as ripples in hyperspace or a folding of space, reflective of 'faster than light' travel," he presented, using ambiguous hand motions.

"In fact, many physicists believe that light is an effect of the cause created by these five-dimensional spacetime ripples," he remarked, seemingly needing to validate his thought process.

"It is an abstraction that seeks to quantify the theory of everything in the nature of existence from non-existence. In this theoretical expectation, Present time is the basis for existence itself, pervading as the substrate of all relativistic time, and imbuing spacetime with degrees of relativistic possibilities; or differing spacetime streams. While this would allow for immediate connections anywhere in spacetime, the method of traversing such a fifth dimension hyperspace still eludes the probability of achieving a 'faster than light' travel capability. I myself have spent much of my time on working through this enigmatic mechanism," he concluded.

An awkward silence briefly ensued as dad perceived a vacant look on my face.

"You never really read any of my books unless you had to, did you?" he asked rhetorically, nodding his head as if to indicate a 'no' response on my part. Not really waiting for any corroborating response from me, he continued, "You know, despite how I compiled the information, my book is more than just a reference; it is more of a theoretical primer for the creation of an evolutionary universe."

I continued to sit in silent anticipation for some clarity in what dad was explaining to me.

"OK, more simply put then," he continued, "I needed to come up with a concept of providing a frame of reference for where non-existence could interact and influence existence. As I was already working out my own understanding for the notions of dark energy and dark matter, I had a vehicle from which I could lay the foundation for such a living omnisentient being. I understood that it was essential for these notions of dark energy and matter to be just as real as gravity. And, for these notions to be real, they would need to require a measurement outside the normal range of quantum mechanics. I eventually came up with the concept of 'negative mass density' as a corollary to the accepted understanding of 'positive mass density'."

"Dad, stop – you're losing me here. In fact, you lost me at tesseract," I admitted.

From time to time dad would drift back in his mode of spouting 'too much information'.

"It's wasn't that I didn't read your books, or even how I read your books, so much as it was that I was unable to understand the plethora of information being related within its contents, without constantly conferring with you or the dictionary as to its context," I confessed. "Reading them just makes me feel stupid."

Thus a more pregnant pause superseded his lecture, as he backed off from trying to rationalize his explanation with scientific theory. I could see that dad was excited to explain these new and revolutionary theories with anyone who might listen to him, rather than by anyone who judge him or his ideas. But the problem with that logic was that you had to have had some background to understand his ideas.

And I still wanted to get back to our original discussion, of which I was apart, "Anyway, what does all of what you are explaining have to do with death, or the afterlife?"

"OK, OK," dad said, as he began to regroup his thoughts. He then initiated a new strategy, "By your own recollections, as you related it to me, your meditative state turned your fourth dimensional perspective inside-out. You entered into a state that was beyond our fourth dimensional norm of reference, and you were able to maintain a 360 degree sense of what was going on around you."

"Yes, I remember that," I agreed.

"And then, at some point in your journey, you lost awareness of yourself as you let go of any control over our ability to be. It was as if you gave yourself over to some psychic connection that you could sense within the universal being; as if you were on autopilot. After that, as you explained it to me, this connection, which allowed the essence of 'who you are' to journey through Space and Time, was more or less like an old-fashion telephone 'party-line'; involving your essence in a shared pool of thoughts. Perhaps one might even think of it as a co-mingling of souls. And yet it was a co-mingling that allowed for separate realities."

"Right," I recalled. "It was like I was peering on others within their own world."

Dad continued, "It was like Harmony warned you, if she sensed that you were losing your sense of self: you know, getting lost in the rift of spacetime, or in this pool of souls, then she would have had to bring you back. Therefore, I believe you were traveling about via these universal connections in this rift of Space in Time; kind of like within a super hyperspace highway. What did she refer to this rift as? Oh yes, the dreamscape of your subconscious is how she put it." Then dad seemed to quote from memory, *"You will be traveling via the dreamscape of your subconscious, as it is the only way to travel the rift of Space."*

"Don't you see?" he asked, looking to see whether there was some indication that I understood his thought process. "Your traveling through the cosmos was more than just what we understand as astral projection. Your journey across the cosmos was more like a form of transference for your energy, your very essence. It was a transference of your working thoughts and identity within another dimensional plane of existence."

Dad paused again to take account of my countenance. Then continuing he suggested, "Perhaps it is like the 'thought transference' of your psyche along a set of universal neurons within this universal being. After which, you were actually transmogrified upon your arrival on the alien planet. It is just as you said; you lived a whole other life, in a whole other physical form, and in a whole other area of the universe."

"So you are asking me to think of the universe as if it is a living brain?" I questioned of my father's premise.

"Yes, of course, a shared brain; a shared-brain outside of a fourth dimensional frame of reference," dad proclaimed as if he was identifying some new eureka moment. "If we consider that 'thought transference' is a real possibility within this fifth dimensional expression, as demonstrated by your real experience, then it would follow that 'thought' is a unique and separate form of energy that is not bound by the laws of physics; as are the other forms of quantum energy."

"In fact, based on your account, it would follow that such 'thought transference' is then faster than the speed of light," dad declared with a sense of certainty. "While incredulous, this makes perfect sense when you infer that the speed of energy is dependent on the density of mass from within which the energy persists. Whereas the speed of energy persists within 'negative mass density', the speed of thought transference could be all but instantaneous."

"And this explains the nature of the afterlife... how?" I continued to pursue an answer.

"Sorry, I get a little carried away sometimes," dad said, apologizing for his diversion. "But I do want to remember this for later."

I waited as dad scribbled random notes on some paper.

"Anyway, back to your question," he continued. "In physics, there is a concept known as the 'Law of Conservation of Energy', also known as the 'First Law of Thermodynamics', which should be inherent in any system involving Space and Time. This law expresses the theory that that matter and energy cannot be created or destroyed, but rather it transforms from one form to another. Therefore if we believe that that 'thought transference' is a real form of energy, then it would follow that it could transform into other forms of energy, even beyond our physical fourth dimensional existence. And as I think of it, dark energy could also be conveyed into our existence instantaneously. Or, better yet, dark energy could be the medium by which asymmetrical energy is transformed for our very existence."

Suddenly dad seemed to be lost in the throes of his own thoughts. I was actually interested in what he had to say on the subject of my question, so I need to get the train of his thoughts back on the rails.

"So when we die, we automatically go to the dark side," I jokingly related by using a 'Star Wars' reference on dad's introduction to the concepts of dark energy.

"Now that's funny," dad chuckled at the reference and my understanding of his information. "But while an interesting aside, what I was trying to say is that I believe the nature of death is a transformation of the individual psyche, or unique soul, in which one is forever co-mingled within this shared perspective of universal thought transference."

Dad's game seemed to be going downhill with the increasing distraction from our more focused exchange. Not that I really intended to take advantage of his 'Achilles heel', but a win is a win.

Moving my queen into position, I alerted him to my progress, "Looks like I have your king in 'checkmate'."

"Well done," he praised me. "So let's try something a little more challenging," he concluded. "I believe the key to resolving this conundrum is in the introduction of this concept for a measure in 'negative mass density'," he stated with some resolve.

"Not right now. Besides, that's more your thing dad," I said, distancing myself from getting involved in one of dad's 'think-fests'. He wasn't really aware of his behavior when he would become entangled within in his own thoughts. It was like the right side of his brain would go into overdrive, while the left side of his brain was allowed to focus on working through his problem. He would really be 'off-line', or maybe better said as 'off-world', for a while. In fact, any communication with the outside world would only be processed on an 'as-needed' basis. He wouldn't even know I was there.

"Well, alright then," he acknowledged, "let mom know that I will be working at my desk."

"Sure thing, dad," I echoed back.

It would seem that dad never really learned to play well with others, in this respect. Maybe that's where I get it from. As I knew he would be off in his own little time warp, without any sense of the activities about him, I retired to my room. I donned a set of headphones and immersed myself within my favorite tunes. I was now isolated from the world within my own private 'think-tank'. It was a great way to just be myself, in my own little dimension of spacetime.

As chance would have it, the song 'Space Oddity' was being played. While I listened, I continued to mull over our conversation about how each individual soul might be lost to a shared pool of souls after death. What would it be like to be within a mixture of shared essence for all time? Would there be a time after death when our individual sentience to be absorbed into the one cooperative and unifying whole soul, as part of the universe? As I found out in my previous journey to Glorthocks, the relativity of Time and Space is quite subjective. Where time appears to be irrelevant outside our traditional fourth dimensional existence, it might even take forever for our individual souls to co-mingle with the others in the pool. After all, as an analogy, not all gases or liquids comingle at the same rate.

If I remember my physics correctly, the second law of thermodynamics implies that there is a tendency for entropy to increase, or a tendency of mixtures toward achieving negative order and positive equilibrium. Yet, there are still those immixtures of oil and water; a classic example for the tendency of increased entropy to cause the coalescing of oil to achieve equilibrium. In which case, it would still be possible to maintain some sense of identity in a mixture of shared essence. Still, since oil does mix with oil, the sense of uniqueness might eventually be lost to dissolution within the coalescing of shared essence. Actually, this might explain the separateness of heaven and hell in the afterlife. What a thought; I might be neighbors with some soul suffering in their own self-imposed hell.

Still, where souls do exist, so too may the ability to be able to maintain the uniqueness of one's own separate identity. However, would one really want to be separate if it meant being apart from the being of the living universe; apart from this pool of souls, I wondered, do souls experience loneliness? On the other hand, what if to know and be everything, one needed to be part of that everything? These are the kinds of hypothetical conundrums that leave one lost in a catharsis of their own making. Can one forego their eventual dissolution of uniqueness without losing the inheritance of this collective omniscience? The questions just came popping into my mind.

Whoa, I am becoming my father, I thought to myself. It was like I was building upon dad's previous introspections. It seemed to me that, what dad was really trying to explain was his belief in the universe's ability 'to be', or the established 'being' that was the universe. Therefore, the nature of its influence upon our fourth dimensional frame is just part of the whole that is existence. How did dad put it? I sought to recall it accurately, As God 'is', so exists the universe.

I also remembered that Harmony put it a little more simply. When Harmony spoke of the universe, she described it as just 'being'. Which then brings to mind the equally enigmatic bible quote, 'I am that I am', as a reference to 'being', or 'to be'; similarly like saying 'I exist because I can be'.

Or how did that 'Moody Blues' song put it, 'I think I am, therefore I must be'. So if I imagined the mechanism of this universal 'being' as the life force medium for this pool of souls, and this mechanism for this 'being' is thinking, then the universe could also be perceived as one gigantic brain. In which case, rather liken to the collective connection of individual neurons that allow us to think, the universal process for thinking would be conveyed as the connections among our collective souls. And if that is so, then the universal brain would not be just one dictate, but rather it would be the congress of all 'being' that provides for its collective omniscience in Present time; and thereof its balance of being.

Of course, it had to be what dad was trying to relate to me. Thinking back, I remember that I attained such an omniscient view of the universe in my previous journey through spacetime, on my first quest. I recalled that it was the most awesome and spiritually fulfilling sensation I ever felt. However, I also lost that momentous perspective almost as suddenly as I gained it. How odd is that, I thought to myself; to know everything, but only for an instant, and then not to be able to retain it. Perhaps knowing everything is too much for one living entity to contain.

Thinking on that moment, I thought that I must have touch upon the aethereal plane of existence where Time and Space are held in contention. Or perhaps it was where existence diverges from non-existence. I just can't recall any real details. Then a possible rationale came to me; it would appear that dissolution of one's individuality into this pool of souls is necessary to be forever part of this collective omniscience.

Still, if Harmony could interface between existence and non-existence, then there must still be such choices available in the afterlife as well. To be sure, Harmony spoke of life force connections that allowed her to find me, but I really never knew what she was talking about. Furthermore, she had explained to me how these connections helped her to monitor the universal balance, but I was never able to makes sense of it. How did she put it? *The universe is not a decidedly fragile balance of being, but it does require some frames of reference to maintain its balance*.

"That's it," I thought aloud, "These connections must be supporting, or perhaps communicating, some sort of collective sentience to maintain the balance of the universe, or at least the balance within this universe."

Suddenly realizing that I was talking to no one, and temporarily embarrassed by my exuberant outburst, I looked out my bedroom door to see if mom was within earshot. OK, no one was in sight. Returning to my own eureka moment, it seems that not only had I helped my father out of his 'blue funk', but I now had renewed my own purpose as well. Perhaps our mutual endeavors could foster a common purpose after all. And perhaps, I thought, I should not have dismissed dad so abruptly when he reached out to me.

As I went looking for dad, I ran into my mom. "Have you seen dad?" I enquired of her.

"You just missed him," mom replied. "You know, it was the strangest thing. Your father came in all excited about some idea that he was working on. As he tried to explain it to me, I made him a sandwich. At some point in our conversation, I got the idea that we had you to thank for your dad's renewed ambition."

"Well, it was beginning to be a bit gloomy around here," I observed.

"Hey, you haven't been Mr. Sunshine yourself lately," she reminded me.

"Yeah, I know. Perhaps I just needed to have a project to work on as well," I said without thinking it through my own selfishness.

"Oh, and what might that be?" mom enquired of me.

"Something dad and I were discussing about my experience with Harmony and such," I offered, knowing that mom would not try to help if it involved science.

"That's great," she replied emphatically. "So you and your father helped each other. It seems everything has a way of working itself out after all. And I know it has been tough for you. PTSD is nothing to be made light of, you know. I just wish we knew someone who could work with you to talk you through this," she stated empathetically.

"Yeah, I know. But remember the last time we tried that, things just got worse," I reminded her.

"Yes, it's difficult to discuss your problems when we have secrets to keep. But there was no other way without having you, or all of us, either committed or worse. We all agreed as a family that we needed to treat your experience as a great fictional adventure, and nothing more."

"Besides mom, I'm just fine," I stated; "really."

"Yes, you're fine for a boy with PTSD, maybe," she said with some resolve, "but you are not just fine."

"Oh, Mom," I stated, glaring at her.

"OK then, how about an after dinner jelly sandwich?" she offered.

With everything going on, mom was like the glue that kept the family together. At first I was the focus of her concern, for obvious reasons. Then more recently, with dad's situation taking a turn at work, she has had to prop us both up. I'm sure mom had her moments where she needed support, but it seemed that she would just soldier on with helping us.

"A sandwich would be fine," I replied to keep things moving along. "So..., you were saying about dad," I said, prodding her. As I still wanted to talk again with dad, it wasn't so easy to get distracted when there was extraordinary research urging to be explored.

Mom and I shared a mutual smile as she continued, "Oh yes; well your father got another coke from the 'frig'. And just as your father was about to retire to his study room, the phone rang. It was a phone call for your father. So I called him back to answer the phone. As he took the phone call, he sounded more serious and professional. Then, as the call continued, he became more cordial, and then even excited."

Whether mom knew it or not, she was not one to get right to the point. I'm guessing that it was just the way her brain worked, allowing her to recall and relate what had transpired. I just bided my time.

"The man on the other end of the phone must have been very convincing, because your dad made his decision on the spot to accept an invitation for a late night job interview. When he got off the phone, he told me that there was a job fair in town and he was going to reconsider his options. You know, I never thought to ask him who the gentleman on the phone was, or where the event was. It was just good to see your dad so engaged again, rather than just moping about," she stated contentedly.

"So he went to a job fair that someone is running at this time of the day," I indicated skeptically; "a job fair where they made a point to provide him with a special invitation at the last minute."

I don't know why mom had not found this suspicious, but it appeared to me to be a little incredulous.

"Well, it wouldn't do to have the job fair during working hours, now would it? Who would be able to attend?" mom rationalized the mystery with some logic, while ignoring the motive for a special invitation.

'Uh, maybe those who do not have a job," I chimed in. "They can attend a job fair at any time of the day, because they are not working. But you're not getting the point."

"And what point might that be?" mom asked, handing me a jelly sandwich.

"Well, doesn't it seem a bit strange that they knew how and where to call dad," I continued. "I'll bet he hasn't even put a job profile online or even attempted to fill out so much as a job application."

"That's quite an assumption you're herding there," mom replied. "Besides, I'm sure he must have. After all, it only makes logical sense that they got his information from somewhere. And that somewhere must've been online. You're just as suspicious of others as your father."

"That's not completely true," I fired back. "I am only suspicious when there is reason for it, whereas dad is suspicious all the time." Taking a bite of my sandwich, I impatiently came back to my needs. "So then you have no idea when dad will be back?" I asked.

"No," mom responded with very little concern. "All I remember is that he went to his study to grab some papers, and out the door he went with his briefcase in hand. I guess we'll find out soon enough, I suppose."

Thinking that I may have now caused my mom to worry, I shifted the discussion, "So I'm guessing this sandwich is to be my dessert?"

"We'll talk about eating more when your father gets home," she decreed. "Have you finished your homework yet?"

"Really, now?" I asked. "I have all weekend to do my homework," I pleaded with her.

"Well then, you can either help me with the dishes or you could read a book," she knowingly gave me an option to read a book.

As I left, I fired a parting 'salvo' to lighten the mood, "At least things are beginning to look up again around here." She smiled back in response.

Homework indeed; I don't think so. There is a mystery here to be solved. I stared out the library window into the night sky. Perhaps it might have been one of those 'head-hunters' clueing in dad on a job opportunity. He would occasionally tell mom about 'head-hunters' bothering him at work, even after he took down his old job profile. Somehow, I just couldn't believe that. It had to be something else, I thought; but what? I half-heartedly picked up a book to read, biding my time until dad came home.

[Andrew's Perspective continued]

[The key to surviving strife is to understand your approach toward living it.]

After what seemed like hours later, dad finally returned home. I could hear his and mom's voices, but I couldn't quite make out what they were saying. As my curiosity got the better of me, I moved out to the loft to get within hearing distance.

"It seems like a wonderful opportunity. Oh, it's almost too good to be true," I heard my mother say, with some happiness and relief. I know she couldn't bear to have dad sulk around in a blue funk for the next year or so. I just had to find out what was going on.

"Yes, I know, but it's the 'too good to be true' part that has me worried," dad responded.

That would be dad's philosophy behind 'Life Intervenes' drifting into his thought process. I believe he imagines fate to be some real presence that will always bring him down just when he is started to make some headway. Indeed, fate was not to be trusted.

"And yet, can I afford to pass this up? You know, with the situation at work being what it is. So what have I got to lose?" dad declared.

Those words never boded well for anyone I knew. It was like choosing between bad and worse.

"I mean, with the change in management at work, they've all but torpedoed my career in my current position. It seems as if they are just waiting to catch me on some little 'slip up' to put me on probation," he projected his suspicions. "At least with this new offer, I have a chance to forge a new career path," dad continued to convince himself.

"And they really liked your resume?" mom pursued the answer with a sense of hope.

"Enough so that they want me to fly our early tomorrow for a second interview with their management team," dad said, a little nervous at the thought of being unprepared. "They even set up my flight arrangements."

"Already; so soon?" mom responded. "How did they manage that?"

I know my mom never did like having to deal with last minute plans.

"It wasn't as if I was the only one there," he answered defensively. "They were handing out airline vouchers to other viable candidates as well. Besides, it's not like we were doing anything this weekend anyway," dad countered.

Mom didn't like when dad would impulsive make important decisions without first taking with her.

"And you know what the kicker is? It appears the guy I was interviewing with, had already even read my books as well," dad followed up, perhaps trying to avoid the possibility of conflict in their discussion.

"What, wait; they've read your books," mom inquired further?

"Yeah, I know what you mean," dad said, thinking they were on the same track. "What are the odds of that? No one reads my books."

"That's not what I meant," mom explained. "When you left for the job fair, I thought you said you were interviewing with another aerospace company. Just what is this job about?"

"Well, it is definitely about aerospace, with an emphasis on 'space'. The way they explained it, it's rather like a consulting position with their main branch," dad starting in with some excitement. "It is a research center where they are studying the negative and positive possibilities of practical space travel, and the effects on the integrity of both the means of travel and the travelers."

"It all sounds very exciting," mom started out, "but what has that to do with your books? Aren't you a bit in over your head?"

"It did seem to me to be a quite daunting offer as well," he responded some apprehension, "and yet he seemed insistent that I was a perfect candidate. They ended up convincing me. They said the research presented in my books was very promising, and they wanted me on their team as soon as possible. Heck, this means I wouldn't have to work at this research as just a hobby anymore. Perhaps I could work with the team on nailing down a way to provide proof of my 'negative mass density' concept for 'dark matter'."

"But you don't even have an advanced degree in physics. Won't you feel a bit out of place," asked mom?

"Perhaps this is a way to get some recognition. But more importantly, it is a chance to follow up on my theories with people who believe in me," dad responded, forever the hopeful optimist.

"It's not like I'm young anymore. How much time do I have to convince the scientific community by just 'self-publishing' my books? And you know the math behind my theory is one of my big failing points. It could take me years to come up with a working equation to prove the existence of 'negative mass density'; much less trying to persuade others, on my own, as for its relevance to 'dark matter'. I mean, this may be the opportunity that could bring mankind closer to reimagining the universal expansion theory, or even the event of its creation," dad presented his argument, seeking to gain mom's approval.

"Well, maybe mankind was not meant to understand creation," mom intervened with some existential argument. "Maybe, the mystery of cosmogony was not meant to be discovered."

"I'd rather think of it as not wanting to be discovered," dad provided as a comeback, so as not to be out maneuvered by mom. "But I would be just as happy with just fostering a new field of scientific study."

"OK, but didn't you say it was just a consulting position?" mom continued to query dad on the practical aspects of furthering his career. "Is this like you're working as a contractor, again?"

"No, it is a full time consulting position," he came back, "with a title, benefits, and everything." Then dad paused a moment, and sheepishly revealed, "However, they did say that it would involve a relocation. To start with, they said they would like for me to train at their satellite station for three months; to get a feel for the effects of space travel. And then I would be transferred to their onsite location."

"And what about the family?" mom interjected. "I've seen you like this before; you get obsessed and end up having less time for us. Is that what you really want?"

"Three months is not that long," dad responded in a consoling tone of voice. "It's a short time investment; and the pay has to be much more than what I am making now. Think of it; you won't have to work anymore to make ends meet. You can concentrate on what you really want to do; outside of employment, I mean."

"This all seems to be moving rather fast," mom cautioned. "Doesn't any of this strike you as strange? I mean, what company brings airline vouchers to a job fair anyway?"

"One with money to spend," dad replied flippantly.

I'd heard just enough to realize that things were about to change in a big way, and I wanted to be part of this decision. As the discussion started to get more emotional, I volunteered myself as the distraction.

"What's going on?" I interrupted.

"Well, it appears your dad has a job offer," answered mom, "however, it is not anywhere around here." It appears mom had little compunction about expressing her displeasure in front of me.

"Wait, What, Whoa!" I exclaimed with dismay. I guess I was about to make things worse. "I don't want to have to finish out my high school years in a new school. It would be like starting out as a freshman all over again. And what about my friends, they are my only outlet to the real world?" I poured on the arguments like a lawyer in a murder trial. "I am just not prepared to move again." And by friends, I meant I was just nurturing a great relationship with a girl I met at school, and this would be a definite deal-breaker for sure.

"Slow down," dad intervened, "there is no reason to get all work up. We aren't moving anywhere just yet. I still have to go for a second interview. And neither your mother nor I would expect you to move prior to finishing high school."

"That's right," mom agreed. "We can make this work."

"Sure, you could finish up your senior year here. In the meanwhile, I'll go on ahead and work with this company by myself. Then when you finish your senior year, we could talk about moving the whole family to closer to the new work location," dad said, not realizing that in his effort to calm me down, he interjected a new source of contention.

Feeling a little taken aback by my aggressive tone, he wandered over to the refrigerator and took out a coke. Knowing dad did not like confrontations, he was probably hoping that mom would continue to smooth things over with me.

"But I was planning to go to college here as well," I pleaded to my mom.

I desperately needed an argument that would allow me to stay in the area. It was comfortable here and things were starting to look up for me. Hell, I even had a girl that was interested in being with me.

"We can talk about college when you finish high school," mom joined in. "It takes money to go to college, and your father is working hard to make that happen; just maybe not here."

"I can get money for college. I can join the military like dad and grandpa," I blurted out, "and use the GI Bill."

Mom looked me in the eye and said to me, "Listen, this is not going to be easy for any of us, especially with your dad not being around. I need to know that you are part of this family. We are all trying to do what is best for the family."

I could see mom was having issues of her own. "And while this may not seem fair to you now, you have a lot of life to live. Just realize that we need to plan for a future that will serve everyone in this family, and I need to know that you are 'on board' with that."

Great, mom was pulling out the guilt card now. Yes, my arguments were selfish, but then when will I be a teenager again. I wanted to enjoy my time as a teenager, and I wanted it to be here and now. I began to review my life here. Like a character on TV whose life is ending, my life here was passing before my eyes. I reviewed the time spent with my friends in the drama club, time spent with my girlfriend, summers between school years, and of course there was Harmony.

"And what if Harmony should come back," I implored.

"Andrew," Dad broke in, "now you know that Harmony would be able to find you anywhere. She is not bounded to this home address or any specific location. She focuses in on you. Still, it has been years. It may be that she will never come back. What's the saying, lightning never strikes twice in the same place?"

"It's just a saying, dad," I couldn't let dad dissuade me from my best argument, "lightning strikes the highest buildings all the time." I know my dad could not refute the logic of my informational insight.

"Yes, OK, but that's not the point", dad paused for a moment to regroup. "But then again, this is not about Harmony at all, is it," dad asked rhetorically? "This is about a feeling of security for you. You surrounded yourself with people and places that you know and love. I know this is a big move for you, but it's not the end of the world. Just think about it. That's all I am asking for right now. We can't grow as a family under these conditions."

I was sure he was referring to his conditions at work.

"I need to be able to feel that I can support our life style and provide you with the best opportunities for your future," he tried to get me to understand that it as for me.

"Oh, don't get all psychoanalytical on me," I professed, rebuffing dad's good intentions. "I'm not living in the future. My life is here and now.

If you're always focused on my future, then you're missing what matters to me now."

Mom could see that dad and I were headed for train wreck and chimed in again with the obvious, "Come on now; let's not say anything we will regret. It's late and tomorrow is another day. Nothing is going to happen tonight anyway. Why don't we all sleep on it, and we'll talk more tomorrow. Maybe we can work something else out."

I was quick to agree, as it was best to keep on the good side of at least one of my parents. Cutting off all support from both parents was not a good strategy. Besides, with mom seemingly already on my side, this could work in my favor.

Having separated us, mom gave me some encouragement in private, "When I hear you defending your position so elegantly, I sometimes believe you are destined to be a politician. You are growing up so fast. Now off to bed to sleep, perchance to dream," she said smiling, slipping in a reference to Shakespeare.

As I left for bed, I could still hear mom and dad talking about parenting strategies. "You can't just talk away his feelings," I could hear mom tell dad.

"It's just when he get likes that, there is no real talking to him anyway," dad tried to explain. "He weighs his own emotions against all logical reasoning. It is like trying to talk down a raw nerve. Why does he get so worked up without thinking it through?" dad asked with frustration.

"It's not always about emotional control," mom explained to dad. "He sees your attempts to calm him down as dismissive; like you're not listening to him."

"I just think if he would amp it down a bit, we could have a civil discussion," dad continued to lament. "He thinks I'm always just talking down to him; lecturing him. I just don't like having to leave it like this."

"Well, it won't do any good to try and talk to him now," mom continued to arbitrate our discourse. "You just go and concentrate on your job interview. While you're gone, I'll talk with him."

My mind was filled with dozens of thoughts on the changes and misgivings of moving away from the only security I had known for my entire life. And each one of these thoughts seemed to branch out in a dozen more probabilities towards possible despair and tragedy. I could only dramatize upon the negative aspects of such a move, and the fear filled me with even more feelings of doubt and apprehension. Not quite the bedtime activity I wanted to take with me to bed. I'll probably have an endless flurry of nightmares, all focusing on my worst fears. I felt my life was about to change in the worst way possible, and prayed for some salvation. It seemed that just as my life was coming together, it was all about to come apart again. I was just now realizing what dad meant by 'Life Intervenes'.

I looked out my window and just by chance I saw a shooting star. While the coincidence was peculiar, I'd stopped believing in wishing upon a shooting star after many years of disappointments. There was nothing magical about a shooting star other than the probability of seeing one just as I looked out the window. And yet, maybe just once, fate would intercede on my behalf. Like a gambler trying to win his money back, I hoped against hope and wished for just one more adventure; for just one more time to ride the cosmos. Still, as dad always counseled me, no good every came from leaving one's destiny in the hands of fate. Indeed, fate was not to be trusted.

Close Encounters of the First Kind—Second Sight

[Serendipity and zemblanity are close bedfellows]

The following morning, Andrew was fighting to wake up from a restless night's sleep. Whether it was the engaging conversation about the after-life he had with dad, the previous evening, or the argument he had with dad, just before he went to bed, he seemed imprisoned within his own dreamscape, tormented by his own demons of doubts and indecision. Having found himself sorting through a nightmare, from which there seemed to be no end, he managed to become aware of the fact that he was dreaming.

Normally this was a good thing, as he could hope to control his surroundings and manipulate the events that plague his subconscious. However, this time it just seemed to induce him with a feeling of control where there was none to be had. Having convinced himself that he was the master of his dream, he now fought a battle of guerilla warfare against his own demons. He continued to playout the cat and mouse game, until he finally awoke from his nightmare.

He spent some time looking about the familiar stuff in his room; almost as if to convince himself that the nightmare was really over. He then noticed from the time that he had slept in, which means he would be late for school. He threw on some clothes and dashed to the bathroom to wash his face. Suddenly, there in the mirror, he was grabbed by a set of hairy arms. The shock of the unexpected attack woke him out of his layered slumber. He thought he was in control but it was a dream within a dream, and it had caught him off guard.

[Interlude - Narrator's Perspective]

Andrew was not the only one who would experience a tormented awakening this morning. Reminiscent of our deepest nightmares, a zemblanitous awakening was happening in the woods just behind the sanctuary of his home. A lone coyote, who had successfully avoided human encounters, woke up hungry and ready for another day's hunt. Without warning, he began to convulse and instinctively sought the shelter of the thicker underbrush. Upon further examination, he could be seen to losing his battle to a metamorphic transformation that had taken over his body. Slowly the figure of a creature emerged from the underbrush that was neither coyote nor forest creature. It had a muscular, hairy body that measured about three and a half feet high in stature. And although it somewhat resembled a monkey, it had the snout and fur of the coyote. It sniffed the air, and then took to making its way through the woods.

As fate would have it, it was not the only transformation to take place that morning in these same woods. Beyond the boundaries of Andrew's home, and upon a more familiar landmark deep in the woods, a serendipitous awakening was also taking place in the newly matured redbud tree. The large seed pod, which had been nestled among the tree's branches, is being gently extended to the foot of the tree. As it touches the ground, it opens to reveal the form of a young female who had been prodigiously wrapped in the foliage of the fairy tree. Her long brown hair was feathered at the ends, somewhat resembling the mature end of carex frosted curls. It lay thick upon her head and flowed down about her shoulders.

She slowly awakened to greet the new day with a prolonged stretch. As she sits upright, her hands separate the loose hair from in front of her face, allowing her to take in her surroundings. She watches for a moment, as the birds and animals of the forest forage in the meadow for their morning meal. She then stands up and smooths out the foliage of the makeshift garments that covered her body, knocking off the plantlike umbilical link that held her to the seed pod. Slowly she oriented herself within her surroundings, eventually focusing her attention in one specific direction. Without so much as making preparations or looking back, she started out walking towards her chosen bearing. Her demeanor implied that she had a definite purpose for her awakening.

[Andrew's Perspective]

I had awakened in a somewhat shaken and uneasy state. The layered dreams left me too groggy to just get up and out of bed. Rather, I laid there trying to phantom why, after all these years, I was having nightmares again. As a matter of reference, it had been awhile since I could remember waking up from a nightmare. And this abstinence of control was not really like me. I tried to phantom whether there was any meaning to my nightmare. Finally I just passed it off as a result of my fight with dad last night.

As I had grown older, it seems that I had slipped into a biorhythm which allowed me to sleep in on the weekends. So it was unusual for me to be up this early on a Saturday. Yet, here I was in that very situation, unable to take advantage of the weekend morning to sleep a little longer. I lay in my bed, considering my choices. It was too early to start up the computer and chat with friends. Tackling homework or even being involved in any work for me at this hour was out of the question.

My mind wandered as I perused the carefully crafted solar system that dad and I had assembled on the ceiling of my bedroom. Looking up at it, I amused myself thinking that it wasn't at all how I remembered traveling across the cosmos. However, unless I had the talent to actually come up with the drawings myself, the makeshift ceiling mural would merely trigger a memory of my initial journey, while never really being anywhere close to a representation of my experience as a bubble. Oh well, 'we can only work with what we have', dad would often say. But then that was dad; always tinkering with something in the basement. And I; well I was more of a thinker than a tinker, as it were. After all these years, I was still trying to figure it all out.

My dad and I had other differences that tended to pit us at odds from time to time. It seemed dad was more of a doer than I was; mostly on the weekends. And while I was also more outgoing and more socially inclined than either of my parents, I still had trouble being able to share my deepest thoughts with others; such as they were. Perhaps if the people I really connected with weren't twenty or thirty years older than I, then I would have been more like my parents who actually had siblings to grow up with. I would have grown up sharing my thoughts with my brothers and sisters. I wouldn't be seeing everything from the perspective of my own introspections. It was an odd combination indeed, to be more socially inclined but less able to vocalize my deepest thoughts with my peers. Sometimes, it was like my peers were speaking another language. And then it occurred to me, as thoughts often do, that I began to understand the irony of the term morning, as I mourned my lost sleep thinking about my own despair.

They say the truth will set you free, but in my case it only seemed to bring me more grief. I am the purveyor of an unwanted secret. It is not unwanted because it is a secret harboring some hidden shame or dark emotional conflict. Rather it is a secret involving the most noble of motives and the most altruistic of deeds. Still, like many altruistic deeds, its nature must remain hidden for the protection of all. Perhaps it didn't start out that way, but it did end up that way. It is a secret that, which by its very nature, must be forever locked away, lest its revealing bring about both hope and despair simultaneously. For, no matter how much people aspire to be perfect in every way, their ability to grasp the unknown is met with a variety of emotional baggage and preconceived ideation. In point of fact, people do not want to be reminded of their own vulnerabilities, or even their own shortcomings. Think of it this way: how does one deal with the concept that their very existence is but a limited part of their more universal being and that the purpose for all of existence itself is to indirectly influence the universal balance?

What is universal balance I often wonder? From what I read online, universal balance is the scale between harmony and chaos that drives the nature of being in the universe. Would people really want to know that, with their every unwitting action, they could possibly tip this scale of universal balance in the direction of either harmony of chaos? And that tipping it in a direction towards chaos could cause further strife to befall themselves and others, or, even worse, could even contribute to bringing about the end of their own universe? I don't think so. People want to be free to live life as selfishly or selflessly as they choose, without any regret.

Yes, 'free will'; that's what it's all about. No one wants to know that their lives, and the fate of others, are not completely under their own individual control, or that, by their very decisions and actions, they may cause an unfathomable ripple of consequences. Human minds are not built to be anything other than blissfully ignorant of their true participation in the evolutionary continuation of the universal 'being': i.e., the ability of the universe to be. And, for any sane person, such knowledge would come with cross purposes; a purpose that opens the mind to a greater understanding of existence, but a purpose that also opens the heart to greater burdens.

Why am I entertaining such thoughts, one may well wonder. One may think, why should I constantly dwell on such ominous possibilities? Surely there are lighter thoughts that a person of my age could entertain, and should entertain. Let children be children, may mother would say. There is time enough for growing up. However, having the remembrance of a past life does get in the way of growing up ignorant of our own transitive mortality. And what about the wondrous prospects of being part of a greater purpose, or the developing knowledge of knowing and potentially influencing the very nature of our lives and the lives around us? And now that expectation of a greater purpose, seemed all but jaded somehow.

However, I wasn't always so negative; for I knew of greater wonder and grander purpose, enough even for one lifetime. Still, as I found out early on, there are some truths that are just too fantastical to be believed, and just too far reaching in their consequences to be revealed. And, as such, the revealing of these truths will always be branded as insightly dangerous and delusional, or, even worse, as psychotic by the majority of the populace in which we must co-exist. As my father would counsel me, where a truth has no relevant basis for understanding, it can only be revealed via experience.

And so my family and I had unwittily become drafted members of our own private and secretive union, simply by virtue of our joint experience. Not so much by choice, but rather more inadvertently through my impulsive participation in matters of universal order, no less. Hey, what can I say; when I take a leap of curiosity, I go big. And as for those who would choose to believe, or even could believe, in these truths upon such revelation, their support would most assuredly bring about the worse of unwanted attention.

Indeed, as we found out, our lives would no longer be our own to live as we would choose. My father was always of the opinion that, although individuals can be intelligent and open minded, collectively, people can become unreasonable and close minded. It is mostly because the thoughts of these same intelligent individuals could be either limited by or driven by the consensus of peer acceptance. Collectively larger groups of like-minded individuals are more easily swayed by the loudest, or most charismatic, or even the most believable of speakers, while dissenters are intentionally driven to doubt or drowned out. It is not so much the truth of the matter being revealed, as it is the situation in which it is revealed. If a lie is told often enough, people may believe there is some basis for its propagation.

Such is it that the resulting lie or propaganda becomes more believable than the actual sincerity of its nature. Some believe that truth will eventually win out, but then these are the same people that believe that good will always win over evil. And what of the unseen secret, you might wonder? Such is the unseen secret that if enough people tell you that you're wrong, or delusional, then you're apt to begin to believe it yourself. Well, for most people anyway.

Fear and stupidity, my father would say, can come from any walk of life. Since intelligent people believe they are too smart to be stupid, it is precisely their belief in their own competence which leads them to underestimate the flaw in their own thinking. It's kind of like proof reading your own written work; i.e., since one knows what they wanted to say when they wrote it, one reads it with the same assumptions they made when writing it down. So, while the only correct version is really in the mind of the author, the thought may not be coherently communicated to others. I guess that would account, in part, for my dealings with the opposite gender as well, but that is an issue for another time. Anyway, the point being, there was no way to tell what people might think, or do for that matter, even if they could actually believe in our secret.

And although my mother believed that my father was basically distrustful of most everyone, she was not one to seek unwanted attention in any form; e.g., my mom was the kind of person that felt she was in someone else's way in a line at the grocery counter, or even in a line of cars at a stop sign. She did not see herself a one of many in a larger queue, but rather as the one who was in the way of many. She could not accept the mechanics of everyday living without infusing it with some emotional distress. Indeed, her thinking was not in harmony with the order of the universe. But then she was never a scientifically minded individual. Rather, she felt that there had to be more than just cause and effect driving how everything works. Of the two, dad, was the more pragmatic. I mean talk about opposites attracting; dad did not deal in trying to understand what drives the human psyche, but rather in what drove our universal continuance.

For dad, there were just too many variables to emotional interactions. Emotions did not follow any consistent logic, laws or theorems. Rather, such interactions mostly got in the way of logic. I could see how dad came to his conclusion about the nature of swaying the populace through emotional, or faith based rationale, rather than through logical reasoning. And, as to further support my father's insecurities on the subject of group intelligence, the short time I spent under psychological care was not a good family experience. While it was meant to help me with my emotional baggage, of which I had acquired much, it became the object of my conflict; a conflict that became increasingly worse after I confided in the doctor about our secret, and after which we all came under the judicious scrutiny that threatened to have the family institutionalized. This led me to believe that some truths are best kept secret.

I, on the other hand, have had previous experience with other more typical secrets that I still wanted to be kept private. Therefore keeping a secret was not foreign to me. Foremost of these secrets was the fact that I had been diagnosed with ADHD. It's not like it was a real disease, or something contagious. Rather, it was just that the mere mention of it was like imposing some kind of brand or stigma upon the nature of my character. While it was difficult enough just being a teenager, as to which my parents would attest, absolutely no one my age wants to be different, or in any odd way. However, while I'll admit social situations were a bit of a struggle for me, oftentimes I would be able connect one-on-one with someone; usually someone with a little more maturity. But this could also be attributed to having been brought up like an only child. Still, I could not, for the life of me, interact with large socially diverse groups or even join in well-meaning team experiences. I mean, I just couldn't understand why teenagers just didn't act more like adults, or at least with my perspective of how adults interacted. I couldn't comprehend that they were unable to see the simple mechanics of everyday living.

While my mother struggled to help me get involved into more social situations, my propensity to diverge from the norm seemed to be part of my having this ADHD. She related to me that having ADHD wasn't the end of the world, because in retrospect she believes dad has had ADHD all his life. And still, dad manages to maintain a job that provides us with a comfortable living. The trick, mom would say, is to curb my impulses and to be aware of strategies that allow me to be more accepted in the areas of social interactions. Of course, my dad's approach was quite different. To say my dad had a strategy to deal with ADHD would be kind. He seemed to just simply limit his social interactions with others and avoid emotional confrontations altogether. His advice would be to adopt a routine of organization and social temperance.

In fact, my dad viewed small talk as the bane of social interaction; mostly because his mind is always elsewhere. And if one fails at small talk, they're often labeled as shy, introverted, apathetic or even as self-centered and egotistical; and, well, shall I go on. People just tended to label their interactions with others, putting them in separate little boxes in the mind. How does the saying go? "Better to remain silent and be thought a fool, than to speak and remove all doubt." In this case, it was better to remain silent and be labeled as shy, quiet, introverted, or apathetic, than to be outspoken and labeled as self-centered, boisterous, not empathic, or even egotistical. Labels are like bad reputations, in that they take a lot of work to change once they've been applied. And knowing this makes first impressions very stressful; a situation sometimes best avoided, if at all possible.

Still, if you think about it, everyone has a secret, or so it seemed to be of my peers. It seems like everyone at school was trying to hide some secret or other: e.g., an embarrassing life experience or family relative, an abusive or overprotective parent, an ailing family member, an individual identity problem, or even just an annoying sibling. So keeping a secret was not that unusual. Perhaps every family unit tends to form their own separate, secretive unions. Therefore, in this respect at least, maybe I wasn't really all that different from everyone else after all.

Maybe; but then as I thought for just a moment, I decided who am I kidding. Other secrets were like the story plots of dramas about communal people interactions, similar to the movie dramas about 'real-life' or dysfunctional family experiences. And while their secrets may be more shocking if revealed, they are at least more down to Earth and believable. I, on the other hand, had lived the very real life of an otherworld alien; which was not so down to Earth. And perhaps there was even some part of me that was still alien; or at least that is how I felt sometimes. How am I even supposed to deal with this? However, to be more fair, my problems seemed to stem more from my holding onto the secret rather than from the secret itself. So in that respect, we may all be more alike, even if I could not always see it that way.

And yet, to make matters worse, I was actually the focus and the cause of our secretive family union. While others would not see themselves as the guilty party, I could only see myself that way. Yes, it was my otherworld experience that my parents and I were all keeping repressed for fear of being ridiculed or institutionalized, or, even worst, being pursued by fanatics. And then there were always the bad memories that haunted my waking thoughts and sometimes even my dreams as well. Memories of some horrors that I wished I could forget. Like a war veteran, my psychological baggage was deep. One should never have to experience the pain of being dematerialized, or even worse, the absent of self inside of a black hole. You can't push that much experience on a twelve year old and not expect that it won't have some adverse impact.

But it wasn't all bad, as I recalled. In fact, some of my fondest memories were of the wonderfully incredible experiences of that fantastical adventure with characters like Pooncha, Avian, Guide, and Fairy. Even our recent vacation to Disney World this summer took a back seat to the distraction of my ongoing thoughts; thoughts that ever dwelled in my mind from that momentous event of my cosmic journey. But it was more than just an event, wasn't it? I mean, after all, I spent a full lifetime on Glorthocks; or at least that part of my life where I was not human anyway. And I survived it all. But what of Pooncha, Avian, and Guide; did they make it out alright? I regretted that I never did give Guide a proper name. I mean, his name was merely his profession. Still, oddly enough, it was these wonderful memories of my grand quest that left me even more depressed than those I would rather shut out. Not at first, of course, but over time. Having something that amazing and wondrous taken away, it was like working through a drug withdrawal. I couldn't win for losing.

During my recovery, if I could call it that, my mind was assaulted by hundreds of ideas and images of which had now become integrated as part of my shared psyche. I say shared psyche because of my shared life experiences from this and my previous other alien life. It was an absolute adrenaline rush of foreign and downright weird experiences that cannot be applied to my life here on Earth. My mind spent weeks, maybe even months, trying to reassemble and process mental connections, while trying to makes sense of it all. Where this process of reworking mental connections from one's daily experiences is normally relegated to dreaming, or REM sleep, my brain had been working overtime even during my waking hours. I was barraged with a variety of extraordinary information at a fantastic rate; all of which needed to be sorted, managed, and stored. I guess all this activity is the mind's way of keeping us sane.

I spent the first six months back feeling like I had just gotten off an extreme roller coaster ride. While it was thrilling, I was elated to have survived such an adventure. And still, I was thrilled to have been part of such an adventure that others would never know. But most importantly, I was happy to be back home. Still, survival alone is not always a resolution to life's problems. As I became to understand, keeping this secret was not the worst of it. Rather, in the wake of all these extreme feelings, my life seemed to be lacking. Like a superstar who peaked too soon, I lamented the doldrums of my everyday life. Is this what the rest of my life holds for me, I continued to nag myself? Even more to the point, what was there for me to look forward to after all this sensational adventure? Nothing will ever equal this experience. These are the questions I had asked myself hundreds of times since my return to normalcy. Normalcy, I thought to myself; what could I even consider normal anymore? Can I ever be normal again? How can a normal life provide me with anywhere near the adrenaline rush and accolades of self-esteem that was part of my awesome adventure? Longing for that, which I did not want to have to survive again, I found myself to be a real emotional mess.

I needed to get out of bed. Being in bed just enabled me to rehash my own random thoughts. I needed some other distractions. Perhaps it wasn't the best way to deal with my stream of consciousness, but it was either distraction or focus, and focus was never my best attribute; especially in the morning. I dressed for a lazy day about the house, and left my room to greet the day on my own terms. Being a weekend morning, I pretty much had the house to myself; especially today, because my mom drove dad to the airport.

As I didn't feeling like just hanging around the house, I grabbed a quick bowl of cereal and decided to take a walk. When life seemed a bit overwhelming, I would often wander off to the site of my encounter with Harmony. I found that these walks would provide me with both new and old distractions, as I would navigate the woods like an early pioneer explorer. Entertaining the distractions of my trip to the meadowlands, I sought to sort through the events of this past week. Instead, I actually felt a little uneasy and vexed; small wonder as not much was going the way that I would've scripted my life. It was similar to the feeling

I had yesterday, while trying to do homework, but it felt a little more threatening. It was like I was being watched. However, when I looked around this time, there was no dancing light in the distance.

Ignoring my inner animal instincts, I shrugged it off as the imaginations of a paranoid mindset. Yet as I continued to walk, I could hear a distant rustling of the underbrush, and the faint sound of an animal breathing heavily. The last time I had such an encounter was on vacation, where I found I had walked up on a bear grazing at the woods edge. Not an encounter that I would like to repeat twice. Still there were no bears here in the suburbs. Should I continue forward or back away, I thought to myself. I sorted through my memories to try and identify the sound. It was rather like the shallow breathing of my cousin's dog. Certainly it was not as big as a bear. While most animals would avoid human contact, a dog might tend to seek out people. Still strange or feral dogs are unpredictable. They might lick you or they might bite you. The distraction was more than enough to dispel my troubled thoughts of yesterday. Indeed, I thought, this path through the woods has held more than its share of zemblanitous surprises in my short lifetime.

Then all at once, there it was in front of me! But what was it was, I could not say. I was both surprised by the weird look of the beast and startled by its sudden appearance. At first glance it seemed to be more of a mix between a dog and a monkey. As I studied it more, trying to ascertain its next move, it appeared to me to have the head and snout of a dog, but the limbs of a monkey; perhaps more like the abnormal visage of a deformed baboon. In the next instant it bounded toward me, hitting me in the chest and pushing me off balance at the same time. Having caught me 'off guard', it grabbed me by both ankles and started dragging me off down the trail. Damn, it was my nightmare come to life. Maybe I'm still asleep, I thought, but no such luck. It was real and it hurt.

Just taking it all in, ahead I could see it was pulling me towards a large hole in the ground. 'I should be doing something', I thought in panic, 'rather than just allowing myself to be carried away like this'. 'Do something', I could hear my thoughts yelling at me. I started grabbing at the underbrush in vain, hoping to gain some semblance of control. As the beast tried to pull me down into the large hole, it turned out that my body was too large for the opening it made. And yet, even when the opportunity to fight back presented itself, all I could think about was wishing the pain would stop. It felt like the beast was going to pull my legs off, or tear me off at the ankles. Indeed, for a beast half my size, it was unexpectedly strong.

When I felt I could no longer deal with the pain, I hollered a mix of shocking obscenities at it. While it seemed to help me deal with the pain, at that time, it wasn't really helping me to free myself. I dug at the ground, hoping to pull free, and throwing whatever I dug up, down the hole at the beast. Then, changing my strategy, I began to alternately kick my legs in rapid succession; which seemed to help a bit.

Then, quite unexpectedly and to my amazement, I could see a girl behind me on the trail. Knowing my plight had not gone unnoticed by the female passerby, I yelled, "Get some help."

And while I would've expected her to run away in terror, she instead came running towards me with determination. I watched as she snapped off a dead branch from a low hanging tree, without so much as breaking her stride. She then continued to charge into the fray by soaring over the length of my body, with tree branch in hand. She seemed to fly into the air, in slow motion, as she came down with a savage stab into and through the dirt. The maneuver freed me from my attacker. All I could think of was to crawl back out and away from the large hole, before the beast could reassert his grip on me. Knowing that the beast would not be far behind, I found myself scampering further away, as best I could, along the ground. As the pain began to subsided, the girl retreated to my position, still holding onto her makeshift spear.

She reached out in my direction as if to help me up. "Are you alright?" she asked with some concern.

Dazed from the encounter and surprised at being rescued in this fashion, and by a girl no less, I was speechless to respond at first. And having felt a little emasculated, I ignored her outstretched hand.

"Are you hurt?" she asked me again.

"Yes…, I mean no; not very much," I said, trying to put on a more macho front. I the grabbed her outstretched arm and pulled myself up. As she helped me to my feet, I could see that I was bleeding through a tear in one of my pant legs. "Aw damn, this can't be good," I said.

"Well snap out of it," she commanded, pointing just beyond me and to my right. "It's not over yet, Elvis."

I turned to see the creature, coming up behind me. The creature, which had previously been pulling me down into the ground, was now up and out of the ground. Snarling like a rabid dog, it lunged again to attack me. Almost instinctively, I fell back and kicked up hard below its rib cage with my uninjured leg, just above the solar plexus of the beast. The beast went flying over me and right toward my female rescuer. She smashed the creature across the right side of its snout with the same stick she had used earlier to free me. The beast yelped as the blow to its snout forced it into a side roll and flip. The beast fell on its back behind some brush just off to the side of the trail and quickly disappeared from sight.

While still on my back, I yelled to this girl in disbelief, "What the hell is that thing?" Not that I expected her to really know, but it was nice to have someone with whom to communicate my anxiety.

"You don't know the half of it," she stated with earnest over her right shoulder, keeping her back turned to me. "So, are you going to help," she asked rhetorically, "or are you just going to lay there?"

"Oh, yeah," I meekly responded as I got back up to my feet again.

As I looked around for something to arm myself with, the beast came flying out of the brush; attacking us yet again. With its teeth bared and its claws reaching out, it appeared to be charging in for a kill. And this time its target appeared to be the girl. Without hesitation, and with unerring accuracy, she shoved the spear-like branch into its gapping maw and launched the beast over her head and mine. I saw it pass over me with the stick still in its mouth.

"OK, it's your turn now," she alerted me to the danger. "And don't let it get behind you."

"What, are we a tag team here?" I shouted, as I backed up to her.

"Would you really rather I handle this all by myself?" she asked sarcastically.

"Uh, no; I mean, that is no what I meant," I blurted out with some confusion.

As I watched her scanning the landscape for a replacement weapon, I turned my attention back towards the creature that she had catapulted over my head. The beast was still recovering from her unexpected defense. Defiantly snapping at the branch, the beast broke it off in its jaws. It then coughed up the smaller remainder of the crude weapon, and resumed its threatening stance. The beast really looked pissed off.

"This can't be good," I said aloud. I then watched, as the beast seemed hesitant to continue his attack. Circling us in apprehension, it appeared to be sizing up our defensive strategy.

"Hey, Elvis," the girl shouted. Having gained my attention, she tossed me a stick in the shape of a club. "I'm guessing you know what to do with that."

The beast appeared 'no worse the wear' for the injuries the girl had inflicted upon him. As I braced for the eventual onslaught of another attack, the beast mysteriously began to slowly back off into the underbrush. I looked to my rescuer, motioning to her with a facial expression that would suggest that I was looking to her for what to do next. She motioned back with an expression suggesting she was just as confused as I was. At that moment, we were both alerted to a rustling sound coming from the underbrush.

Again the beast lunged, this time between us. Catching us both off guard, the creature split us up and knocked us both to the ground. The girl rebounded like a seasoned veteran. With a tuck and shoulder roll, she was back up on her feet, with the club I had dropped now in her hand. She repositioned herself between me and the creature before it could maneuver back for another attack. From behind her, I gathered myself up, grabbed what ended up being a bush, and made ready for another advance.

And then, to my astonishment, the beast turned to the girl, speaking in a quite eerily human voice, "This is not your fight, girl!"

To which she retorted, "You take a lot upon yourself. Who are you to decide the fate of this human?"

"Wait… What?" I said aloud. I suddenly realized I was the only one who didn't know what was going on, or was even surprised about the beast speaking. And what did she mean by calling me human? "Who is not human here," I asked in befuddlement. Completely ignoring me, they continued their discourse.

"Him…, he is but a pawn," the beast growled out with contempt. "I am here to herald the fate of all humanity. He is but the first to be counted."

"It's a bit early in the fight to declare victory, I think," she continued, poised with the stick club in her outstretched hand. "So why is this 'pawn' so important to you? Or…, is he really more than a pawn?"

The question seemed to rile the beast, as he slowly backed off again. "He is but a minor consequence in the foreshadowing of events to occur. You need not concern yourself with his life."

"Well, if his life has such a minor role in events yet to come, then you have little reason to pursue him. That is, of course, unless you are attempting to win by deception," she probed the monster's reasoning.

"All life is but nugatory to the course of fate now unfolding. You need not be concerned with his one's destiny," was his cryptic response. "For his fate has already been written. And he cannot escape his fate."

"Not true spawn of discord. The illusion of fate is dependent on one's ability to influence their own destiny. You would know that if you had any influence over your own," she yelled, rebuking his logic."

"Me thinks you fool yourself, elf spawn. Fate is the sum of all destinies, and certainly greater than any influence his might play in this universe." Then the beast seemed to reserve his thoughts, "Do you wish to save his soul? Me thinks you have little to offer. I just assume leave him to your bumbling about," he said, intending to insult her.

"I do not have time to bandy about with your deceitful reasoning. Be off with you, or I will finish what you have started here today. Leave; lest I bring upon a host of familiars to come to our aid," she threatened.

"Like you did on Glorthocks?" he mocked her. "That did not go so well for you, me thinks. Many died in your favor. Fairies…," he said with disgust, "you are all the same. You seek to thwart us with your empty threats, and interfere where you are not regarded."

"You pretentious demagogue, I don't need anyone else to thwart your kind," she returned with vigor. "I only meant to match your pathetic threat of events yet to occur. Shall we be the first martyrs for this cause?"

Admittedly I may have been a little lost in trying to follow their conversion, but I was not excited with the possibility of becoming a martyr.

"You waste my time, fairy," the beast imparted to her. "I have much to do. The time of Ragnarok is almost upon us."

"Who are you beast?" she demanded to know of the creature's identity. "Introduce yourself, lest we know the gravity of your words."

"Knowing my name will not help any of you now," he stated with resolve. The beast looked in my direction and then back to the girl, saying "You'll not always be about to help this human. Me thinks we'll meet again at another time." And then the beast backed away and ran down through his crude tunnel.

As I watched, the large hole seemed to magically close up behind the beast. With the danger seemingly abated I noticed I was missing a shoe. Scanning the area, I found it a few feet from where I had been knocked down. Then I looked to my rescuer with a lot of confusion.

"A bush?" she asked. "You were going to use a bush to fight off that monster?"

With my left shoe in one hand and the remnants of a bush in the other, I took stock of my situation. As I was still alive, I considered that to be a good thing.

Finally I responded to her sarcasm, saying, "It's a sharp bush. I mean it has a lot of sharp points." I then discarded the bush out of hand.

"Well, at least you held your own, Elvis," she complimented me. "I guess you haven't forgotten all your fighting skills."

Fighting skills, I questioned of myself. I was just trying to survive. Then her words finally hit home.

"Wait, Elvis? Glorthocks?!" I inquired with single word questioning.

As I uttered these words, they seemed to trigger long forgotten memories from my previous quest. Seeking to understand and make sense of what just happened, my mind keyed in on the few clues that were provided to me. Then, as if the adrenaline in my system was repurposed from my muscles to my brain, a flood of memories came back to me like a tidal wave. I was almost at a loss for words, having conflicting emotions upon the possible realization of my rescuer's identity. What was it that the beast called her, I thought to myself? "Fairy?!" I guessed aloud and with excitement.

The girl gave a slight bow with an accompanying hand gesture, acknowledging my guess with a simple affirmative nod. While it was difficult to believe, it was not as bewildering as a talking 'whatever that thing was'. Putting things in perspective, it made much more sense than any other rationale that I might have come up with.

"Is it really you?" I continued to ask. "You're Fairy?"

Again she acknowledged simply with only a nod. Instead she appeared to let me work it out for myself. "It's all real then," I stammered aloud!

The triggering of past memories being networked within my mind began to be reanimated in a succession of senses surrounding our previous encounters. I merely met her briefly within the crystal source seed at the end of our preceding quest. I imagined her with wings and guessed her to be a fairy princess. So I only ever knew her as Fairy.

"But how; how is it that you are here?" I asked in bewilderment.

My mind was racing now, and I had trouble containing myself upon the realization of her being here right in front of me. It was Fairy, I told myself; perhaps not just exactly as I remembered her from within the crystal, but it was her just the same. Then I thought if she was here, maybe Harmony was here as well.

Before Fairy could answer, I asked, "Is Harmony here as well?" "No… no Harmony; just me," she responded.

"Oh," I uttered in acknowledgement, hoping on the assumed anticipation for a more complete reunion. As I could feel the adrenaline wearing off, I felt a little weak in the knees. I sat down on the ground to get a good look at my wound.

"You sound disappointed," she remarked. "Perhaps I should've left you to handle the beast by yourself."

She then tossed her crude weapon aside and knelt beside me to gingerly attend the wound under my torn pant leg.

"No, it's not that. I didn't mean to sound so ungrateful," I said, apologizing. "It's just that I had been waiting a long time for her return; or for any real evidence of my…, eh, our adventure together."

"Waiting?" she asked, looking up to see my expression. "Waiting for what?"

"Oh, I don't know," I searched for the words to convey my feelings. "It's just that everything just ended, and then my life just became ordinary again."

"As I remember it, you were almost erased from existence," she reminded me. "I would think you would have enjoyed your little respite. Don't tell me you have been wasting your life here reliving the past."

It's like she didn't even understand. But then how could she; she probably never stopped operating as a full time Shadow-Forge. In fact, for her, there may have not been any time off. Hell, as for her sense of time, it probably wasn't even the same as mine, relativistically speaking. After all, she was from, I don't know, another dimensional frame of spacetime reference altogether. For all I know, her last encounter with me was her yesterday. As for her appearance today, our previous relationship was a tangled mess of memories. I remained momentarily speechless, trying to sort it all out. But it was all coming back to me now.

Sliding my torn pant leg up and lifting towards her, she declared, "This looks like a bite mark. This is definitely going to need more attention than a quick wash."

I hobbled a bit, shifting my weight to one leg. It seemed to me that Fairy had spent no such time for introspection. Perhaps it was not even in her nature to dwell on the past. She appeared to be only ever interested in the present, and anticipating the future. Yes, we were definitely polar opposites.

Then sliding my pant leg back down again, she continued, "We need to get that leg of yours some better treatment. Can you walk?"

Having momentarily been lost in thought, her question jogged my concerns back to reality. "Yes, of course, my house is just over there," I said, pointing in the direction of my house.

As I started to walk, putting weight on my injured leg, I reflexively winced, "Shit! Damn that hurts."

"Here let me give you a hand," Fairy said, as she moved in to assist me along.

The macho side of me immediately went on the defense at her recognition of my vulnerability.

"I can take care of myself," I assert, manly warding her off. "Maybe if I just had a walking stick, or something to lean onto," I insisted.

With that she went over and picked up the larger remnant of the branch she had previously shoved into the beast's maw. Although it was now about the right size to use as a crutch, I would have none of it.

"Maybe not that one," I said.

"Why, it's looks like it would work out just fine?" she asked without thinking on it much.

"But it has drool on it," was my initial response.

"Oh, don't be such a big baby, Elvis," she jeered.

Realizing how it may have made me sound like a bit of a wimp, I reflexively rebuked her statement about my acting like a big baby, "and I asked you not to call me Elvis. My name is Andrew."

"Oh yes, I forgot," she responded with a smile. "First things first, let's get you cleaned up," she said as she pulled my arm over her shoulder, and began walking.

However, unbeknownst to me she was leading me in the opposite direction of my house. "I like the name Andrew better anyway," she remarked as we walked together.

"And all I really know you as is 'Fairy'," I said, accepting of her apologetic response. "Do you have a name?

"I have been called by many names," she started to explain. "I have been to many worlds, and they all have their own notion of what I represented to them. That being said, to the kin of my realm I am known as ILMR. But I am more fond of your label for me Fairy."

"But I can't call you Fairy here. Nobody here is named 'Fairy'. It might sound strange," I said. Pausing for a moment, I tried to imitate the sound of her name. "IL-MER," I said, trying to pronounce her name.

"That's close," she said smiling, "but the way you say it sounds strange to me. Try rolling your tongue in towards the back of your mouth. I-L-M-R," she instructed.

"IL-MAR," I said, hearing no discernable difference. "No, that won't do," I said, impatient with my inability to make the sound correctly the first time. "I know, what about a mix of the two; something between ILMR and Fairy? IL-Fairy-MAR, IL-F-Mairy, or Elf Mairy," I related, trying out differing combinations. No Elf Mairy is almost as strange as just calling you Fairy. How about just 'Mairy', replacing the 'F' with an 'M'? Yes, that's a common enough sounding name. All my aunts have the middle name Mary."

"Hmm, Mairy has a gracious sound about it," Fairy mused about her new moniker. "Yes, I like it."

"OK, then Mairy it is," I responded in consensus.

[Scene Change – Andrew's Perspective continued]

[The big reveal about the Shadow-Forge origin.]

As we continued to walk, there was a nagging amount of discomfort coming from about my wound. Periodically, the conversation sank into with awkward silences as I tried to hold back any reaction to the ache in my leg. I tended to ask questions that would require Fairy to talk more. Half-listening in the silence of my pain, I was furtively curious about the sudden visitation of Fairy and that beast. Why did she show up now after all these years? Did she know I was going to be attacked? If so, how did she know?

I prompted her to take command of the conversation by asking short questions. "So my guess is that beasty thing was no accident then," I surmised. I paused and waited, but from Fairy there came no response.

"I'm guessing it was out to get me. I wonder how it even knew I was here," I continued to prompt her. Still, there was no response from Fairy.

It was as if she was preoccupied or ignoring me. Hearing myself express these feelings, I had the same questions of Fairy.

"For that matter, where did you come from and how did you even know where I was?" I asked pointedly.

"Well, you don't become a Shadow-Forge on your own, as you know," was her flippant reply. "And by virtue of being a Shadow-Forge, we have each realized our special connection with the universe. It is that connection which led me to you."

"OK, I get that, but why you?" I inquired.

"Why me, why anyone," she replied. "As it is, there never seems to be enough of us to keep up the good fight to preserve the balance of the universe. Needless to say, we need to look after our own. In fact if it wasn't for my connection with you, I would have still been stuck in that crystal on Glorthocks."

"OK, let me ask the question in another way. Why, after all these years, have you decided to show up here and now?" I rephrased my inquiry.

Then, before she could answer, I threw in another question, "Wait, are you saying that it was you who initiated the connection with me from Glorthocks?"

"Yes, that was me," she said with unabashed candor.

Having had the sudden realization that Harmony did seek me out because of my connection to the events on Glorthocks, but it was just not the connection that I had assumed. I had believed it to be the multitude of voices calling out to anyone in their anguish. Perhaps if I was older, I might have realized that it would have been improbable for me to dream upon the thoughts of these many warring aliens, battling for dominance of their merging environments on some distant planet. Instead, it was but one special link.

"So it was you who was the one filling my mind with the imaginings of battle on an alien planet," I deduced.

"Yes, but it was no imagined battle that I conveyed to you," she exposed.

"Yeah, I found that out when I arrived," I acknowledged.

"You have to realize that I had no other option, but to find another," she stated apologetically. "I would have been frozen in that crystal prison for all time. I couldn't even kill myself to escape my fate."

"Another what?" I asked.

"Another who was able to see the universe for what it is," she cryptically answered.

"And what is it?" I pursued.

"It is the being of all things; interconnected upon every life force," she answered with a touch of reverence.

"OK," I accepted her response without probing it further. Rather I was still concerned with her arrival. "Well then if we had such a great connection, and you were so grateful for my assistance, why had you not contacted me before this," I asked, thinking of the time I spent distressing over my life of mediocrity.

"It's not always a simple choice of deciding where to go," Fairy stated abruptly. "It is not always about what I wanted to do, but with what needed to be done. Our quest together was not the only problematic event that needed attention. You should be mature enough to know that by now," she said defensively. "Besides, you needed time to grow up," she put it to me.

"Grow up!" I exclaimed, but then backed down from my outburst. "Well, perhaps that was true. But I have been more grown up for a while now."

"We all like to think that, but growing is ongoing," she stated from experience.

"Well, it would've been a lot easier growing up if I never went on that quest at all," I declared. "All the time I was there, I just remember wanting to return to my life as a child. I wanted to be safe and irresponsible again. I just wasn't ready to make all those decisions and take on the responsibility of other's welfare."

"And yet you did. What you did out there was a marvelous sacrifice. To think of you giving your life like that; well, it made me rethink my own priorities," she confessed. "That showed real courage on your part."

"Thank you," I responded. "I appreciate the compliment, but I never really saw it that way. Most of the time I was just reacting impulsively, without any idea of what I was doing. Anyway, it would've been nice to have a friend my age here to talk with about it," I lamented.

"I know," was Fairy's simple reply, trying to be empathetic I suppose.

"You know?" I asked, thinking that was an odd response. "Do you even understand what it is to be lonely? And I don't mean alone. I mean not being able to confide in any one person completely."

"Where I come from, one is never alone," she answered. "However, I do understand the term. As for your being alone, it always seemed to me to be something of your own choosing."

"What?" I asked.

"I have visited you from time to time; just not in a form that you would recognize," she stated with a playful candor.

I stopped to look her in the eyes. "You been around and have not contacted me? You can't just drop a bomb like that without some sort of explanation. How have you been around?" I requested more detail.

"Oh, my kind can exist for a short time in any of the other worlds," Fairy explained. "Only as a Shadow-Forge can we exist inside another world for any length of time. But then once transformed as a Shadow-Forge, are we committed for the duration; just as we both were on Glorthocks."

"We?" I questioned. "Of which 'we' are we talking about here?" I asked.

"We, as in you and me, and my kin," Fairy acknowledged matter-of-factly. "But only you and I, out of all my kin, have the ability to become Shadow-Forge. In fact, you are the only other Shadow-Forge of my kind that I have ever really been in contact with."

This gets better all the time. I haven't had a real conversation with Fairy since we first met in the crystal.

"Yes, I was a Shadow-Forge on Glorthocks," I agreed, "but I have not existed for any length of time in any other spacetime location, other than this one. And I certainly haven't been visiting any other worlds, other than my own."

"And yet, as a Shadow-Forge, even you should share in this ability with us to exist for a short time in any of the other worlds," she explained.

"Me?" I asked unbelievingly, as I never imagined having such an ability.

"Yes," she continued, "you are one of us now. It was the only way I could have saved you. It was the only way for us to make you whole again. Remember," she said, placing her hand over my heart, "you have a piece of me within you for all time. You are part of me."

What she said and did, when she placed her hand over my heart, touch me in a most peculiar way. I suddenly felt a deep connection with her.

"Yes," I uttered softly, thinking back on the encounter, "somehow I do remember."

It was odd that I was able to feel it all just then. As I turned to look into the eyes of her visage, I became light-headed. Not knowing whether it was from my wound or our connection, my sight began to blank out. I could no longer see Fairy, or even the forest where I knew we should be. And in this moment, I had the vision of her as she was in the crystal and then again as I was made whole by her beyond the event horizon of that black hole. It was unsettling. In the blackness, I began to relive that terrible moment from within the black hole. It was as if I was actually there again. I suddenly lost my balance in a short fainting spell and became limp in her arms.

"Whoa," Fairy exclaimed, "that's seems to be enough for now."

I had no idea to what she was referring, but she seemed to be implying something other than walking. "Your wound is worse than I first realized," she said, assisting me to the ground. "Let's take a rest."

As I felt myself regaining my composure, I turned down her offer to rest, "No, I'm fine now. Let's just continue walking."

"I think not," Fairy insisted, as she helped me down. "It seems like your body is not handling this wound very well. Perhaps the gash is infected and poisoning your system."

I felt light headed and couldn't focus in on the importance of what Fairy was explaining to me. In my disorientation, I believed it to be something quite different than Fairy described. It was as if she reached in my mind and highlighted the event of my reanimation within my own consciousness.

"How did you do that?" I had to ask. "It was like I was really back there; I mean not here. Like a daydream, but only more vivid."

"I only meant to convey to you of whom and what you are," Fairy revealed. "Normally a life force condition fragments such recollections to allow for the continued control of body and mind. Nonetheless, the full experience is always lingering in their memory for such a full retrieval."

"After all this time, that is the first time I fully remembered that experience," I declared with amazement. "You can show me my own memories!"

"I am only able to help you to relive the emotional interaction. Rather like when you are dreaming," she replied. "The feeling I elicited in you, triggered your own lost memory."

Still a little disoriented, I lost my original train of thought. Reliving that extreme experience was almost more than I could handle. That is probably why dad always tread lightly on it while we working on his book. In truth, my survival mechanism seemed to kick in and dictate my next question.

"Say, who is after me anyway? Is it some mad doctor who is experimenting on animals to make them talk?" I asked.

While I believed that I asked a question, the question seemed strange even to me. I don't remember if Fairy responded. I looked away and said aloud, "No, that wouldn't be it. It must be something else."

The memory also brought to mind other associations and the possibility of another quest.

"Will Harmony be coming here as well?" I ask, without remembering having asked it before.

"No, no Harmony; just me," she answered with amusement at my disjointed stream of thought. "Although she is genuinely fond of that reference for her, that you came up with."

I felt unusually tired and wanted to sleep, but Fairy would have none of it. It was as if she was driven to get me some treatment for my wound.

"Alright, I think we've had enough rest now. Come on; let's get you back on feet again," Fairy urged. "Try and stay awake with me. We were talking about Harmony."

"Oh yes," I replied. "Why is it that Harmony will not be coming?" I asked.

"Actually, she has no reason to be coming here. In fact, no one sent me," she confessed. "So who sent the beast?" I asked.

"Oh, as for the beast," she continued, "I believe it was just a matter of time before it was able to locate you."

"What; so there is no quest for me here," I said pausing for a moment to try and think this through? "But you are here. And so why are you here, if we are not involved in another quest together?" I asked.

"For your safety," she replied matter of factly. "I am here to keep you safe, and none too soon I might add."

"How did you even know I would be in trouble?" I inquired.

"The same way I knew how to find you," she replied tersely, "we are connected. I could feel it."

I didn't know whether it was my foggy state of mind or just the way she was explaining things to me, but I was not getting the answers I needed to piece the puzzle together. So in my impatience, I began jumping to my own conclusions. I thought to myself: I haven't been daydreaming or night dreaming about any other quests since I got back. Maybe this is not about me at all.

Then my frazzle mind came up with another insight. "Hey, wait a minute here. No, no, no … You're the Shadow-Forge here. So this is not my quest, it is your quest," I stated.

"Slow down Elvis, I mean Andrew," she said, correcting herself. "There is no quest," she said; "or at least not one that I was aware of before I came here. Let's talk no more about Harmony."

As I stared her down in my confusion, we had stopped walking; or as least it appeared that way. Perhaps she was trying to come up with a new way to explain it to me. Then she started again.

"OK, not everything is a quest," she related. "Think of it this way: what is happening here is happening to you, and not me. It is clearly not enough for the Guardians to get involved, and certainly enough to sanction a quest for. So it is just me. And I would think you could show a little more appreciation to me for committing myself as a Shadow-Forge just to save you," she declared.

While I thought on what she had said, she abruptly changed subject. "You need to focus more. If you are just going to die on me, I might as well just kill myself now and return to my own world."

"No, don't leave. I'm sorry, I'm awake now," I apologized, as if regaining my composure from a deep sleep. Not only was I able to think clearly, but I no longer felt the previous intensity of pain from my leg.

As she relented, we begin walking again. I began to regain some clarity, as if our little respite had revitalized me a bit. I didn't quite know what to think, but I did not want to her to think I didn't appreciate her sacrifice.

"So why me?" I asked. "Why am I suddenly on the most wanted list for these wackos?"

"Why you, why anyone; life intervenes," was her only answer.

"Life intervenes," I echoed her candor. "What does that ever even mean? You're the Shadow-Forge here, you must know something."

"We are both Shadow-Forge here," Fairy deflected. "Just because you may not have taken on another form, here on your home planet, you are still one of us."

"Right, one of the chosen few; one of the guild of 'good guys'," I responded somewhat sarcastically, reflecting on my current wounded condition. I swore aloud at experiencing another sudden sharp pain. "Ouch, damn it."

Thinking more on her retort about our affinity as Shadow-Forge, I tended toward dwelling on how we were different.

"I don't have half the talent you have. Why, if it wasn't for your fighting skills, that beast would've figured out a way to get me down that tunnel of his," I lamented.

"It would appear that I was only chosen to intercede on your behalf because of my subconscious connection with you," I bemoaned. "It's like they had no other choice but to choose me to help on your quest. After you got in trouble, I was your only back up; lucky you."

"It was very fortunate indeed for me that you could come to my aid. Do not belittle your abilities," she scolded me.

My self-pity was getting me off track from what I really wanted to know. As I tried to focus more, Fairy revealed something I had not considered before.

"Actually, I was never chosen for the quest on Glorthocks," Fairy sheepishly admitted. "You were the first and only choice of the Guardians. You see, it is not about being a warrior. You have other abilities, as well as other sensibilities. My being there when you arrived was of my own doing. I intervened where I thought I was needed. I wanted to save lives. But as a consequence of my actions, there was much suffering and death. In fact, sometimes I think you should have left me in the crystal; as punishment for my interference."

Upon hearing her change in mood, my mind began to focus on helping her. I felt bad about badgering her for information. In my impatience, I had gone too far.

"OK, so you messed up. I always mess up," I stated, seeking to correct my tenor with her. "So maybe it wasn't your quest. And maybe this isn't your quest either. But it needs to be someone's quest. I mean, think about it. If that creature is really forecasting the end of the world, then it needs to be someone's quest. So why not make it our quest?" I declared of our alliance.

"Well, I am committed here as a Shadow-Forge anyway," she admitted. "And the only way to leave here is by my dying. So why not die for a real cause, I always say."

"Sure, OK," I replied, "but I wouldn't really call it dying. In your present form, you'll just return to your host body." She seemed a bit dramatic and 'gung ho' to say the least.

"Hey, perhaps you could teach me to fight, or something, while you are here," I requested. "I mean, what you did back there with that beast was really something. I could sure use a few pointers. By the way, do you really say 'why not die for a cause' all the time?"

She just smiled back. I guess I had gotten past her sullen mood.

As my mind became clearer, I realized that we were not heading toward my house. "Hey, where are we going anyway?" I asked casually.

"We need to take care of that wound of yours," she answered. "I can't bring you home like this, so I am taking you to see my kin."

"What!" I said, taken by surprise. "Are you saying that there are more fairies here?" I asked. "I thought you said that you were the only one who could transform into a Shadow-Forge."

"Well, they are not really here yet, and they can't stay long," Fairy answered. "And no, they are not going to transcend as Shadow-Forge. I am the only one of my kin that can exist inside another spacetime for any length of time. Just like you, I have the gift of realizing my connection with the universe."

"So what are you saying, then?" I asked, trying to put it altogether. "If they are not here yet, and you are insinuating that the will be, then I gather they can just 'pop in and out' whenever they want."

"Yes, but our time and power is limited when 'popping' in and out," she answered with some amusement.

I wondered how many times she had done this 'popping' about, or even how many times she had taken on the form of a Shadow-Forge. I felt like a novice and wondered why I had not been chosen by the Guardians more often; just to hone my abilities, so to speak. Then, I began to remember back to our first encounter. While I was chosen for the quest, she had already been on Glorthocks. If she was not chosen, then becoming a Shadow-Forge was not tied to being part of a quest. Having finally made sense of some of the puzzle pieces, I announced my conclusion like a detective in the movies.

"Hey, I get it now," I announced. "You 'jumped the gun' again; just like you did on Glorthocks. And now you are stranded here alone again, just like when you were on Glorthocks."

"Well, not quite the same. I could end my Shadow-Forge life here," she stated matter of factly.

"True enough; you do have more options here," I agreed.

"What does it mean to 'jump the gun'?" Fairy inquired.

"Sorry," I apologized, forgetting that idioms are not universally understood. "It means you acted without thinking, or you started too soon; like before you were asked to get involved."

"Yes, I tend to sense the future of events," she stated with pride. "The Guardians tend to react to events as they are unfolding; shaping them, rather than truly avoiding them. I, on the other hand, believe that fate is not predestined. While the Guardians tend to take a 'wait-and-see' attitude as to whether the universe will heal itself, I feel the need to prevent it from ever happening in the first place. Only once the balance has been tipped, do they ever react. I, myself, cannot wait for such destruction to be inflicted. I cannot wait to see who will die and who will live. So, like life, I intervene."

I turned to look ahead. I began to recognize that we were following my same path to the meadowlands. "I know this path; this is the way to the meadowlands at the center of the woods."

As we rounded the tall brush, I was amazed to see a full grown tree upon the center of the meadow. "Truly unbelievable; how is this possible? That wasn't here last week," I said. Fairy only smiled. Thinking on it just a little bit more, I concluded, "I always believed there was something strange and magical about this place."

As we approached the tree, I discovered that I forgot about the pain of my wound. Fairy did say she could induce feelings. My guess was that she had gotten me to focus on other feelings, rather more than on my pain. I was awash with a sense of contentment. Fairy was much better than taking an aspirin pain reliever.

As the sunlight waned, the broad, rounded yellow leaves showed brightly among the array of autumn colored foliage. "It's as if it had been here all along," I thought aloud.

It all seemed as natural as the large pond that previously resided here. Fairy only smiled back at my childish wonderment.

"This place is truly magical," I convinced myself aloud. "Like some long lucid dream; everything keeps changing around and yet it always appears as if it is in its own natural setting." Again, Fairy said nothing.

It seemed to me that Harmony's arrival at this location had enlivened a magical portal. Yet, magic or not, I felt comfort in the realization that it was all real. The years of depression and doubt were swept by the wayside. I felt renewed, as if my life now had meaning and purpose once again.

"Alright, have a seat, and let's get that wound of yours cleaned up," Fairy offered.

Helping me down to a comfortable seating location on the ground, she did not tend to my cuts directly. Rather she walked away towards the tree. She then placed her hands on the tree, closed her eyes, and leaned into it as if she were attempting to move the tree. As she did so, the tree began to be reanimated to a more spring-like seasonal state right before my eyes. It was a surreal vision that I had only previously witnessed in movies. It was as if she could will a change in the seasons. I watched as her touch was able to bring the tree back to a more green leafy state.

It was difficult to accept the truth of it; like being in a daydream or watching some high-end computer generated graphics effect. I wondered if this was another of her special powers. Could she do this with all vegetation, I wondered? Perhaps it is an ability that I may have as well.

As the 'special effects' change completed, I began to focus more on her appearance. She was much different from when last I imagined of her in the crystal. It was not as if she had aged much at all. If fact, we were probably the same age now. She seemed real enough; I mean normal enough. So much so that she could easily pass for any other girl in my high school. The transformation for her was good, I'll give her that. She had magenta colored hair, similar in color to the redbud flower. Her eyes were a bright azure blue, like the color of the crystal source seed on Glorthocks. She was barefooted, and both her finger and toe nails were shown off in a bright, blue-green color with a leafy veined texture. Her skin was soft as a redbud flower petal, and her clothes seemed almost organic in both their color and the way they adorned her form. In fact, I wonder if they were even clothes at all. Somewhat like Harmony before her, her form was surreptitiously covered; but by what, I could not say. Her body proportions were both athletic and demure. And her visage was somehow reminiscent of my dreams of girls that I had never met.

While I watched, the tree miraculously started to bloom. The redbud tree began to flower again amidst a mix of green and gold leaves. As quickly as the magenta colored flowers sprouted, the petals began to fall. I lay back and relaxed below a seemingly dreamlike shower of redbud petals. Looking up, I could see little flashes of light flitting about the lower branches of the tree. Upon the branches themselves, I noticed these flashes of light appearing in place of each falling redbud flower. In a short time, there were a multitude of these flashing lights flying about. Between the rain of flowering redbud petals and the abundance of little flashes flitting about me, I quite forgot where I was. It was as if I had been transported to a more enchanted world, quite unlike anything on Earth.

As Fairy opened her eyes and looked over to me, I asked, "Not lightning bugs?"

"No, not lightning bugs," she repeated with a smile. "But we have been known to dance with them from time to time when they come out. I've even done it a time or two myself. It's quite exhilarating."

In short order, these fairies began to descend upon my wound. My leg tingled as they went about their business. It was difficult to make them out in any real detail, either due to their glow or the swiftness of their movements. As I tried to study them, I noticed that they were not all the same. There were a variety of telltale variations in the diversity of the wings they featured. Some were graced with what looked like larger butterfly wings, while others displayed smaller dragonfly wings or even smaller bee-like wings.

"Why are they so small?" I asked.

"It is as Harmony wills it to be," Fairy enigmatically answered. "All emerging life forces must go through a process of attaining a form, or host, based on their entry point into their emerging environment. Having appeared upon the redbud blossom, as they did, they are rather a mix of the smaller forest life forms that were present in this environment when they arrived."

"Oh, you mean they are bugs," I impulsively replied. Then thinking better of what I said, I attempted to make it sound less offensive.

"Well, at least they don't look like bugs. I mean, they have wings and all. In fact, they look more like normal…, uh well…, you know. They look like the way a normal fairy would look like; that is, if fairies actually existed. I mean, more human-like rather than bug-like," I finally remarked, blushing with embarrassment in thinking I may have offended Fairy. Fairy only smiled upon my sense of innocence.

I watched as the colors of their light seamlessly shifted among the hues of the rainbow with their altering movements: blue for stillness, white for slower changes, and yellow to red for quicker movements. "So I guess this is how fairies came to be," I said trying to recover from my earlier clumsy use of words, "and why they can never be found; because they don't live here to begin with."

It was fascinating to watch them flit about. In doing so, I had not even noticed what they were actually doing. Somehow it appears they were able to heal my wound as easily as they mended my pants.

"Yes, this is how these fairies are transformed into being here, on this planet," she stated, following along with my sense of imagery. "But we can actually appear anywhere in what you refer to as spacetime for a short time. And with each appearance, we can only don a new guise from the life forces about us. Verily, we always seem to be smaller in stature for these short duration visits."

"Except you," I stated the obvious, "you're quite big; I mean to say that you are more normal size." I again changed my wording upon remembered how self-conscious some women are about their weight.

"Yes, the Shadow-Forge transformation takes much more energy to infuse its life force, and requires a form that best suits its needs. Remember what you looked like on Glorthocks? The one you call Harmony is much better at this than her counterpart. It is only by her grace that we may serve the universal being," she said with real feeling.

Then looking with pride on the accomplishments of these small fairies, she announced, "There, good as new."

I looked under my pant leg, and found that my wound was no longer visible; having not even a scar upon its mending. Having done what had been requested of them, the little fairies began to disperse.

Being much more alert and clear headed now, I held up my hand to wave goodbye to them. As I did, one came to rest on my finger. In a soft voice, I enunciated my gratitude, "Great job; please extend my thanks to everyone."

I could swear I could see a little face with a smile upon it. The fairy figure presented a low bow to me, and then flew to Fairy's ear for just a moment before flying away with the others.

"What did the fairy say to you?" I enquired of Fairy with curiosity.

"It was a message for you. Loosely translated, she wanted me to convey to you that it was their pleasure to serve one who serves the universal being," Fairy said with her own smile.

With that, I watched as the last of the fairies flitted away into the dusk of the day. One by one, their lights faded away into the autumn forest.

"Where are they going?" I asked.

"To have a little fun before the magic wears off," was Fairy's reply. "And now you need to get home before you are missed," she said with a hint of caution in her voice.

"OK; but before I go anywhere, I need to know what that beast was and why it wanted to kill me," I pursued answers from our earlier conversation. Considering my need for answers, sat down next to me.

"I don't really know that it wanted to kill you," she replied. "But they are not the gentlest of beings, to be sure."

"That's an understatement. Wait, they," I expressed with some surprise. "There are more of those?"

"Yes, or there can be. I'm afraid everything has a balance," she continued. "For every servant of the universal being, there is one who would tip the balance toward harmony or chaos," she started to explain.

She looked to me for some hint of acknowledgement. Then pausing for a moment to collect her thoughts, she continued, "Where there is a harmony, there is also discord. The Shadow-Forge consists of forces for both harmony and chaos."

"You mean it was a Shadow-Forge as well?" I asked, overwhelmed by the possibility. "So the Shadow-Forge are something like the light-side and dark-side of the life force," I interrupted with some concepts from the 'Star Wars' movie series I had watched. "Kind of like good and evil."

"Perhaps; but good and evil are relatively moral notions of right and wrong," she tried to translate her understanding of the universal balance to me. "Good and evil are not necessarily relevant to the universal balance of being."

"I must admit, it is not always easy to say what is good and what is evil," I agreed with her. "Take for example the collateral damage of the warring creatures on Glorthocks. Is it any less good to defeat those who believe in their own cause?"

"In truth, you and I together dealt the forces of discord a mighty blow upon our last quest," Fairy declared.

"What do you mean?" I asked. "Are you referring to that old man who was with us at the end?"

"Not just him alone," she poised for a longer explanation. "All those wanting more than one life can offer. Everyone on that planet, from which the crystal was launched, was influenced by the forces of chaos, to tip the balance. They were all part of a discord in the universal balance that you and I were able to put right."

"Perhaps, but at what cost," I asserted, remembering the multitude of dead aliens in the floating cemetery between Glorthocks and DeMutron.

"What was happening on Glorthocks was not right, I'll grant you that. But it would have happened whether we intervened or not. Besides, I was not trying to save just one civilization," she said, trying to justify her actions. "There was the whole of the universe to consider. If not for what we did on Glorthocks, many other worlds would have most certainly shared the same fate. And many other life forces would have been lost," she tried to impress upon me. "There was no other way."

"And what of all those millions of life forces on that planet near the event horizon?" I lamented. "When we sent the source seed crashing through their red sun, they never had a chance."

"You know the science of spacetime. There was no way they were going to stave off the rending forces of that black hole forever. It was just a matter of time. The only thing we ended, for all those millions, was their pain of re-living their same time cycle over and over again; persisting in the same feeling of despair in 'hope against hope' for any change. And without hope of any change, they were doomed to re-live the agony of their same mistakes over and over again. In their current condition, they were forever predestined to re-live the inescapable torment of their wanting for an existence they could never truly retain," she related to me, trying to ease my guilt.

"Was it really pre-destined?" I asked. "Was there really no other way? I wonder."

"In truth, they were supported only by their ability to transgress against the tidal forces of the event horizon. Their continued existence was distorting any real sense of being. For all intents and purpose, they were only supporting a soulless existence from which there was no true 'being'. At least now they have been allowed to move on, to become part of that 'being' which is the universe."

I thought of how my dad lamented over the decision to take his eldest brother off life support, and the guilt he felt deciding whether it was the right thing to do. How does one ever know when it is the right time for a soul to pass on? Indeed, fate was not to be trusted.

In that quiet pause, she reached over and took my hands in hers. She then looked into my eyes and said, "It's not so much about living in spacetime, as it is about continuing 'to be' within the universe. Whether inside or outside of spacetime, all life forces continue 'to be' in one form or another," she tried to explain.

I gently let go of her hands and hugged her, thinking of how maybe there was an afterlife after all. I realized she had to deal with this guilt as much as I had; maybe more. Then releasing her, we both stood up near the tree. As she rested against it, I leaned in next to her, gripping the branch above. As I thought about her explanation, she allowed me to linger without interruption.

Searching my thoughts, I remembered some of the mythological tales surrounding entities representing good and evil. I related them to Fairy, saying, "Did you know that ancient civilizations used to come up with all manner of god-like beings to explain the forces of nature, or the bizarre phenomenon outside of known physical behavior?"

"In fact, I believe Harmonia and Discordia were two such characters who were rationalized to influence the balance of human life. Discordia was the goddess of disorder and a being with life form, while Harmonia was the goddess of order and a being without life form. Maybe the ancients had it right all along," I thought aloud.

"Order and disorder are relative notions of life forces; both are required for a life form to persist. Verily, we are all part of the one universal being," she acknowledged as if to agree with me.

"So then, there is only one universal being?" I asked, trying to make sense of it all. "Why just one?"

"It is more than the philosophical vision of the universe reduced for our understanding. Think of it like this: where 'zero' and 'one' are defined as the only absolute units of being. Zero is nothing, in contradiction of one being something," was her cryptic response.

"I must confess my confusion," I remarked of her simplistic comparison. "It's difficult to makes sense of it all, when it seems like you are all talking in riddles."

"I understood that on Earth mathematics was the universal language to explain the universe, so it is how I sought to explain it to you. However think of it like mathematics with form; where zero is the vessel that contains the oneness of being," she stated, employing a modicum of patience in simplifying the concept for me.

"OK, zero is a vessel but it is nothing," I echoed back what I heard. "So how does nothing contain something?"

"One, in and of itself, is but the potential unit of existence; like Space without Time. Zero, in and of itself, is but the potential unit of non-existence; like Time without Space. Subsequently, 'one' is defined by its ability to be part of zero (or zero divided by one), because any value by which zero is multiplied is always non-existent; hence zero is the vessel," she explained.

After a momentary pause, she continued, "Conversely, zero cannot be defined by its ability to be part of one (or one divided by zero), because there is no value by which zero is multiplied that will ever be existent; hence one is the unit. So, together, just as zero can be divided by one, Space can be part of Time, and just as 'one' cannot be divided by zero, Space cannot be apart, or separate, of Time."

I had to really think about it, but there was no real denying her logic. "That actually makes sense," I acknowledged. "I never real thought about it that way. But of our differing realities, how do you explain that?" I asked, seeking to understand her world, if only a little better.

"Containments within this vessel are subject to dimensional disparities," she continued to relay her understanding of the universe. "The interaction of Space with Time is not constant, but is it is consistent. As such, dimensional interactions are complex and provide for a multitude of varying realities within the one universe being."

"Actually, from what I read, scientists theorize about the existence of a multiverse, in which the whole of existence can be manifested in the form of many universes," I provided as an alternate perspective.

"I have assimilated much of your cultural ideology, but this theoretical concept presents, how would you say it, a hodgepodge of irreconcilable suppositions," she pressed the point. "These diverse theories tending to allow for many universes, do so because of such self-imposed suppositions about the dimensional disparities, without the distinction of the one universal being. In truth, these disparities are not boundaries upon which the universe is subdivided. Rather the one universe is a varying immixture of layered realities in differing dimensional frames of reference."

"OK, I'll grant you that, but I am not seeing there is much difference in the two approaches," I presented her with my inability to comprehend.

"The difference is that, even upon the related persistence of your visible universe, your science can not see beyond the limits of what it can measure. There is so much more to 'being' than any one life force can experience. Each disparity is dependent on another because we all share in the universal experience through our connections with every other life force. This is the 'being' that is our universe. You've been there, you know this," she compelled me to understand.

"I do remember some of what you are saying during my journey. But that ability to 'know all' through these connections kind of faded away by the time I reached my destination," I explained to her.

"It is because you had a destination that impaired your ability to maintain these connections," she insisted.

I took advantage of the pause, as I was getting lost in what she was trying to relate to me. This discussion was more my dad's speed than mine. Yet, having been there and back, I never really understood what it truly meant to me or how it happened to me. To me the whole journey was all magic. Maybe it was all about my immature viewpoint, but I felt it was something not to be questioned lest the magic would disappear forever.

Still, there was that one point in my journey through the cosmos when I sensed everything around and within me all at once. And in that moment, I somehow understood it all. It was an instant of complete bliss that overflows one's soul with a feeling of complete comprehension. Then, being like the moment it was, the feeling of bliss and understanding all faded in the next instant. Liken to a lucid dream, it was an experience not obtained via my normal five senses.

Then Fairy moved from the tree and brought me back down to Earth. "OK, maybe we should be starting toward your home now," she decided. "And maybe we should be discussing the here and now," she professed. "Ultimately, that is where our problem is now, or so said the beast."

"Yes, we were talking about the forces of chaos in the ranks of the Shadow-Forge, here on Earth," I said, trying to make sense of this very real threat. "So now I am here, and here is where these creatures have come to haunt me, and my family, and maybe of all life on this planet. And as I remember of the events that surrounded my last quest," I inserted, "we are pretty much on our own when dealing with these creatures. So if there are to be more of these creatures, I need to know a little more about what we are dealing with," I asked her in earnest.

"The creatures do not really have a name, as they are whatever or whoever they can be," she began to explain, as we left the meadowlands. "Just as I have been forged within the life force of this planet, so have they been brought among us in their form."

"Why do they look like animals, and yet talk and act like humans?" I continued to interrupt, hoping to spare myself another long-winded explanation; "you don't."

"Discordia, as you put it, does not concern itself with the well-being of its manifestations. Unlike Harmony, Discordia personifies a selfish existence whose only purpose is to expand the disorder of the universal being. She takes little care in resolving her will upon these creatures. In fact, I believe she would rather they had very little free will of their own," Fairy concluded.

As we walked away from the newly transformed meadow, I thought a moment about what Fairy said about the manifestation of weird and half-human creatures appearing on Earth. The concept seemed to resonate within my memories, among the stories of legends that I have read about in mythology. Then it hit me.

"Yes, that's it! They've been here before, haven't they?" I asked. Like a detective on a case, I began putting together clues towards a logical hypothesis; or, at least, logical to me.

"Of course, Discordia's reach is far and wide. She intends to impress her resolve upon all living things. And she has been particularly vested in the variety and discordance of this planet's environment," she said.

"I thought so; so again, mythology is the key," I continued. "Because people are so ready to dismiss these creatures of legend, they never considered that there might be some truth to it."

I wasn't always right about things outside of school problems, or for which I had not been trained to think about. And the only puzzles I tended to work out were ones that my parents would present to me as gifts. However, it all started to fit together and make sense to me. I hadn't felt this good about myself since my last quest.

"The mythological beasts of past legends were like the Minotaur, Medusa, Echidna, Lamia, Chimera, Cyclops, Charybdis, and; well I can't remember them all. They were all part animal and could have been Discordia's creations. So then, these mythological creatures of legend might have all been real."

"Perhaps," Fairy acknowledged of my insight. "Would these remembered life forms have been the kind that would have been in league with forces of chaos?"

"To be sure," I confirmed of her suspicions. "They pretty much went about wrecking, killing, and consuming everything in their path; kind of like the embodiment of black holes."

"Conversely then," I speculated without any real rationale to support my inferences, "that would make the heroes and heroines of mythology as having all been Shadow-Forge members as well. And they would be the creations of Harmony."

Harmony implied as much, but I never got a straight answer out of her either.

"She referred to having approached other children on Earth, but lamented about not always being able to enlist them to go to other planets, as she did with me. So conceivably, it would be just as probable that she would have chosen other Shadow-Forge members from other worlds to visit upon Earth."

"Were that so, then truly I am not the first," Fairy acknowledged of my speculation. "However, I caution you," she warned of my conclusions. "You may be 'jumping the gun' with these suspicions of yours. Your heroines and heroes of legend may not have really been Shadow-Forge members at all. The only difference between being a real hero and others like us, appearing on this planet, is the compassion of their heart and the desire of their will to put others welfare above their own. The only special power they may have wielded is their ability to embrace a destiny greater than their own. In a way, they are fulfilling the role of their connection within the universal 'being', without realizing they even have a connection."

As I was only half-listening, Fairy's cautionary advice fell on 'deaf-ears'. I was outputting information from my own rationalizing, while randomly ignoring any input other than the information from my memory.

"This connection is kind of like the 'force' from Star Wars," I interjected; "where there is a light side and a dark side to this connection." Making this association was so cool, I never acknowledged my rudeness. "OK, so if there is a Legion of Chaos, with members of the Dark Guild, then there must be a Legion of Order, with members of a Light Guild as well. But then who might be these other members of the Light Guild?"

"Are you enjoying yourself?" Fairy asked, not playing along with my narrative. "You say you are serious, and then you start talking this nonsense."

"Yes, yes, I know," I pressed in anticipation of the answer, "but who might be some of the others that were here on Earth as Shadow-Forge members of the Light Guild? Let's see, maybe like Hercules, Perseus, Achilles, or Diana the Huntress are some of the legend names on this planet that spring to mind. Hercules and Perseus for sure fought off some of these weird man-beasts. And then perhaps even Samson, Jesus, and Joan of Arc could have been; for they are the names of some of our religious heroes and heroines. Still, Samson, Joan of Arc, and Jesus were all particularly tragic figures, as they were betrayed by the very people they defended," I thought aloud.

Upon my last comment, Fairy remarked, "One always remembers the sting of betrayal." I must have hit home because Fairy gave it real emphasis, pausing as though she could feel the pain of her prior experience on Glorthocks. If it was, then I'm sure it had something to do with that old man.

"Discordia's reach is deep, but the balanced must be retained, lest the life of the universe cease to be," she stated with purpose. Again I heard and spoke only to myself. It was as if we were talking past each other now; having two completely different streams of thought.

"However, I do believe that these heroes and heroines felt not unlike myself; alone, unappreciated, wanting to be more, or wanting to do more, or even wanting to be part of something more," I affirmed of their feelings on my behalf. "So why might these two diverse members of the Shadow-Forge have come to influence Earth's history? And what did their influence on Earth's history have to do with preserving the balance of the universe?"

"The universal balance can be influenced by something as fragile as a seed of thought," Fairy began to explained, trying to bring things into perspective. "So it was for you on our first quest, where you were convinced to free the source seed. The life forces of order and chaos are both rooted within the universal being itself. And these life forces can be used to influence or sway the universal balance in either direction, regardless of their origins."

Her directed analysis fed right into my narrative, so we ended up back on track with our trains of thought.

"But the source seed was more than an idea," I tried to persuade myself. "The source seed was real, as was its influence on the red sun and the black hole. We helped to keep the universe in balance by keeping chaos from manipulating matter without regard to the consequences of cause and effect. Had we not intervened, the creation of a runaway black hole might have altered the evolution of the universe itself."

"It appears you have given this a fair amount of thought," Fairy acknowledged. "As it happens, I believe perhaps both are true. The mechanism of the universe and the connections within the universal being are not uniquely separate. Each supports the other to maintain the existences of our many realities, and each can influence the consequences of cause and effect on the other. An ideation is more than the supplicant of an ideology, or the action taken," she stated with conviction.

"Know this then Andrew; there is no ledger of Shadow-Forge participants or their accomplishments, or even from where they may have come," Fairy explained. "Only Harmony may really know more, for she is the sentinel and recruiter of these quests."

"As to your affirmation of those feeling alone, unappreciated, wanting to be more," she started in, "it is a strange compulsion of some life forces to want beyond their own limitations, much like chaos. Perhaps there is a little chaos in all of us. Perhaps to be human, is to want for more."

"So said 'Oliver Twist'," I joked, without regard to my audience. "But I think I can explain how it feels: to succeed against all odds, to accomplish something great, and to have barely survived. That is what it feels like to be really human. However when this feeling falls away, it all tends to leave behind a longing that needs to be filled; a longing to be more and to do more. For if we have this power, should we not then use it," I asked aloud, as much for myself as to my companion Fairy.

Fairy must have sensed that I was not done, for she did not respond. Rather, Fairy listened as I ranted on about my philosophical revelations.

"This is the insanity that drives our addictions to overcome strife when there is no real hope of survival. It is only in our failures, or in our thoughts of failing, that we are likely to be dissuaded from doing more," I concluded.

Upon my pause, Fairy offered up her opinion, saying, "Actually, I see this insanity as probably just the seed of thought from which your addictions would continue to grow ever stronger. It appears to be a spiral of deceit that feeds the very demon you wish to control."

"There is more truth in what you say than you know," I acknowledged of her contribution. "Though there is actually more to these addictions than just the selfish feeling of fulfillment. It is also about the feeling of purpose, as well," I contemplated further. "I mean, why are some people so readily willing to be shepherded; to be given that which they cannot earn through their own strife? People continually reach out for some way around the strife, whether it be a religious or secular savior. Their want to believe in something greater then themselves appears to be fueled by an inherent need to be saved or chosen for something more. Whether it be a belief in faith, magic, or advanced alien civilizations, humankind hopes for some intervention to transform them to someplace better, or into something better."

Continuing in my monologue, I thought of how it affected me personally. "And yet I have to ask myself, is it better to be the savior or the saved? We all have our psychological baggage. It is part of the curse bestowed upon us as 'sentient' beings," I stated as if to preach about my own circumstances. "If there was a Garden of Eden, then it must have been one of insentient bliss; for to know, is to want for more. I mean, would it be so bad if humankind were the advanced alien civilization, the harbingers of magic, and the bringers of faith for which sentient beings reach out? And if we all believed this, then perhaps we would not be the victims of our own addictions."

As I paused in thought, Fairy again joined in the conversation, saying, "I do see what you mean. It would seem that it is not enough for humans to be part and parcel of the universal being, which is 'all life'. Instead, these sentient beings of Earth desire more than to just emulate 'all life'. Rather it would seem that it is their desire to influence or control 'all life', so as to further their own continuance beyond their own sense of mortality," she hypothesized.

In this she had strong opinions, remarking, "Indeed, Discordia already has a greater hold on this Earth than even I realized. The influence of chaos is similar to how one might relate the insanity of existence; where existence seeks to control non-existence," she expressed. "And similarly, it is the irony of existence that it would seek to validate its identity by denying its own genesis from non-existence; for without non-existence, existence cannot be."

"Now that is deep," I replied. "You sound just like my dad."

"Deep? Non-existence is without measure, for it is rather only the infinite medium of spacetime," she attempted to correct me. "It is the infinite abyss from which Time and Space are brought into convergence."

"No, that's not what I meant. I meant 'deep' as in very thoughtful," I explained to her. "It's a compliment."

"Oh, then I will take it as such," she responded, and then resumed her role as defender. "As to your point about being the target of this creature, did anything else strange or untold recently happen to you?"

"You mean aside from being attacked by a vicious half dog, half monkey phantasm, and then being rescued by my Shadow-Forge companion from previous quest," I asked sarcastically?

"Yes, aside from that," she replied quite amused. "I meant even before today's events."

"Well, there was an incident at school yesterday with some troglodytes," I recalled. "They were behaving stranger than normal. They followed behind me and just kept chanting my name."

"What is a 'troglodyte'," she inquired again, not being familiar with my use of the English language?

"Oh, nothing to worry about," I informed her. "It is just a name I use when describing the behavior of some of my more callous classmates who were on my back that day," I explained, without thinking.

I looked over at Fairy's quizzical expression and explained further, "No, not literally on my back. I mean getting on my nerves, but not literally touching my nerves."

I stopped and thought better of my descriptive use of metaphors, restating, "They were bothering me. Anyway, they seemed to be unaware of their behavior. Another thing I noticed was that there was like this shadow hovering over them."

"Seems to me like they we're being driven by the forces of chaos, who were actively looking for you. I'm guessing from our earlier encounter, that they had no trouble finding you after that encounter," she surmised from the information I presented her. "So the creature we fought in the woods was probably there as a direct result of your being identified by those troglodytes. So why are they looking for you, is the question we need to answer next," Fairy said thoughtfully.

"Can't you just contact Harmony, and ask her," I enquired.

"It's not that easy," she responded.

"Of course not," I stated sarcastically. "I forgot we are on our own again."

"The manifestation of Harmony is a response to an imbalance in the universe, as I explained to you before," Fairy began to expound. "It is only a one-way connection from the universal being to us. There is no contacting Harmony. So yes, we are on our own until Harmony is required."

"Required," I said with some pessimism. "I required her to appear many times, but to no avail. What is she, some celestial computer program or something; doesn't she ever check up on us," I ranted on. Then I paused for a moment to manage my frustration.

"Feeling better?" Fairy asked, breaking my solemn mood.

"Yes," I affirmed. We walked for a bit in silence and then I changed the subject saying, "By the way, your little friends do good work."

She nodded in acknowledgement as I continued to lead her through the woods to my house. It was only as I got closer to home that I thought about how Fairy was now going to exist in this form on Earth.

"Hey, now that you're here, I think you should come and stay with us," I offered. "You know, rather than wandering about alone in the woods. After all, you could use a little cleaning up yourself as well."

"And how are you going to explain me to your family?" she inquired.

"Actually," I thought for a moment. "Nope, that won't work. OK, I believe the truth is the only thing I can think of that will work in this situation," I surmised. "Anything else will have mom calling the police or worse: social services."

"Do you believe they can handle the truth?" she asked.

"Dad's not the problem," I started to explain. "He may be a little skeptical at first, but he's been waiting for confirmation of intelligent extraterrestrial life probably all his life."

I paused, thinking of how mom would handle it. "It's mom that will take some convincing. Oh, she wants to believe, but I always suspected that she will have her doubts when it comes to things she does not readily understand. It's as if she feigns belief of my stories, for my sake, because she believes I'm teetering on the edge of sanity as it is."

"She worries about you," Fairy abridged, in an understanding tone.

"Yes, perhaps too much," I continued. "Not that I can't tell her anything and everything. She's always there for me. It's just that her sincerity only belies her concern for me. Sometimes it is just too much."

"And then she's just not really into science at all. She is more of a 'people person' is probably the best way to put it. So it is rather against her nature to understand why things are. She'd rather just explore how things are. It would be easier for her to believe that I dreamt the whole thing up, like that story of 'Alice in Wonderland'."

"I'm not familiar with that story," Fairy informed me.

"Yeah, I figured that," I acknowledged. "Remind me to tell you about it sometime. Anyway my mom may not take to you right away, so don't be put off by her. She'll is really a very good person at heart."

"If she is anything like you, then we should get along just fine," Fairy stated, being quite sure of herself.

"Well, she is older," I explained. "And a little set in her way of seeing the world. But she is my mother."

"Her name is 'My Mother'?" Fairy asked.

"No, I mean 'she is' my mother," I repeated, hoping that if I intonated the same sentence differently that she would understand. "The expression of 'my mother' is the same as when I talk about 'my mom.'

As I saw the quizzical look upon her face, she reached out and touched my cheek. I felt surprised by her sense of familiarity. Then I seemed to be remembering more than just what she related to me about her origin. "Oh that's right, you were never born. You and your kind are incarnate beings; unrealized life forces of the universe. How is it that I just remembered that?" I questioned aloud.

"In seeking to understand the nature of your relationship with your mother, I introduced to you as sense of my relationship with my own kind," Fairy revealed to me.

Then recalling what she had done to me before, I realized what she did. "You placed your memory in my mind" I replied with incredulity. "That's a handy talent you have there."

"Not a memory," she insisted once again, "just a feeling. Your thought processes made the connections from which you could recall and make sense of that feeling."

"Weird; you're just full of surprises," I acknowledged. Anyway, how can I put this? Having a mother is like when we were on the planet Glorthocks, and each creature was brought into being from another of its kind. They were all physically connected at one time, but then became physically separated. Similarly, I was born of my father and my mother. That is to say, my mother bore me into being. So I was once a part of her, but now I am my very own person. Anyway, her name, or what she is called is 'Sandi'."

"I see," Fairy revealed of her comprehension. However, my guess is that she learned more from her ability to get into my head. "It is a strange thought that corporeal being is reproduced physically. Still, in truth, it could be said that I am an extension of a greater energy force."

"You mean to say that you never took on a physical form before you became a Shadow-Forge?" I asked in astonishment.

This was truly like the stuff of science fiction. No wonder her and her kind has little trouble popping in and out of other worlds. She must be equivalent to that of an interdimensional entity with the capability of traveling through dimensional rifts that few other entities can enter.

"Although we are a sort of pan-dimensional life forces, our ability to exist independent within any other reality is one of impermanence. However in our own reality, we exist together as the embodiment of the living force that embraces the entirety of the universe. In truth, each of us is brought into realization as our own life force distinction upon the being of our interdependence from within the living force. I never really questioned the why or how of it," Fairy stated, musing upon the thought for just a moment.

"Dad is really going to love you," I stated with certainty. "You are like the incarnation of his total thought process. You're like every sci-fi fantasy rolled up into one."

"I am sure I will get along well with your mother, as well," Fairy recounted of our current goal. "Your feelings for her are quite genuine and very strong. I'm sure she will come to realize that I am only here to help. In this sense, I believe us to be kindred spirits."

"Yes, I'm sure she'll take to having you around without any problem," I acknowledged. "Once she gets past all the science about you came to be here."

Being with Fairy after all these years was comfortable. It wasn't like the clumsy introductions of first meeting a girl. I remembered how I could always talk to girls before I began liking them too much. And then when I found one I really liked, I couldn't stop talking. It was like I was possessed by some dark magic that only allowed me to speak in kind of a nervous chatter. In my mind, my pestering rationale was that if I allowed a pause in the conversation, then I would have to deal with that awkward silence. Talk about a 'time warp'; nothing slows down time so much as awkward silence.

Although my dad's advice was for me to slow down and allow the girl to talk as well, it just never seemed to come natural to me. I mean, what if she didn't want to talk? And what does dad know about dating anyway? Heck, he never even dated until he was like 27 or 28 years old; or so he told me. He just simply avoided the whole complication of dealing with girls as a teenager. Mom said that it was probably a side effect of his own ADHD. My mom's advice wasn't much better. She would tell me that if a girl was really interested in me, as a person, then it wouldn't matter who I was or how I came across. Geez, parents can be so naïve.

As we continued toward the house, I began to wonder how dad was doing. I was beginning to feel quite guilty about how I blew up at him when he told us about his new job. Each of us has our own problems, and I didn't help to make him feel any better. I wish I could've gotten up sooner to see him off.

CHAPTER

4

The Allusion of Destiny

**[Sometimes one becomes part of a secret
without even knowing it.]**

While Andrew spent his Saturday morning with Fairy, Steve arrived at the San Francisco International Airport, CA, for his second interview. However his second interview would be more like his first day on the job, because he was asked to prepare a presentation of his research on dark energy. Something he neglected to tell his wife, Sandi, as there was no need for both of them to be feeling anxious.

As he traveled to the baggage claim area, he continued mull over the highlights of his presentation. He was preoccupied by the obligation to do right by his research and to subsequently make a good impression for himself. He felt that his work was well thought out and it just needed a chance to be properly represented.

It was his hope that his ideas would be appreciated for what they were, independent of his ability to support them. He was always fascinated by the ability of the written word in books or the written notes in musical scores to transcend spacetime. Indeed, while books or musical compositions, and even their individual pages, would deteriorate over time, the ideas captured and the story they formed would live on. And for him, each book and composition of which he was familiar triggered many memories. As each memory retained a portion of his identity, each portion then helped to shape his own destiny, and thus helped shape the fate of the universe; as it was now and forever a part of an evolving universe.

[Scene Change - Father's Perspective]

I made my way through the bustling crowd of airport travelers and arrived to pick up my travel bags. While I paused at the baggage claim area to read signs, I was momentarily interrupted by a family group trying to decide from which baggage turnstile their luggage would be appearing. I glanced out through a window to the outside to embrace a sense of the warmer atmosphere, thinking of how my family would enjoy living in this new climate.

As prearranged by the job fair interviewer, I had been given a phone number, along with the tickets, to call upon my arrival. I was to let the company contact know when I got in San Francisco and they would give me further instructions on where to go. I assumed the company had made reservations for me somewhere, but first I would need to procure some transportation. It did not seem to me to be an altogether unusual arrangement, as I was acquainted with companies that left foreign personnel to fend for themselves upon their arrival for work.

Yet, amid the hustling of new arrivals, like myself, making their way for a car rental, my attention was averted by a person who was holding up a sign with my name on it. As I looked up from the name card to the face of the card holder, she smiled back at him in recognition. She appeared to be a well-dressed woman of Polynesian descent; an assessment I made based on her facial features alone. I walked up to her and introduced myself.

"I'm Stephen Bauer," I informed her. "Your sign has my name on it."

"Yes, of course sir; I'm Kiana. I recognized you immediately from your photo on the outside of your book. I will be your escort for this leg of your trip. We actually have you scheduled on another flight out, and it is due to board in about 23 minutes," she announced to me as she confirmed the time on her watch.

Odd, I thought, there was that reference to my book again, and I thought this was to be my destination. She did not attempt to help me with my travel bags, but instead held the sign in one hand and started for a waiting airport electric cart.

"I thought San Francisco was to be the end of this trip. I was on my way to pick up a rental car before calling your company," I said, but she gave no response. "Do I at least have time to go to the restroom?" I ask, putting down his bags in front of the electric cart.

"Only if you hurry," Kiana said smiling, as she pointed in the direction of the restrooms.

"I've be doing nothing but hurrying today," I acknowledged with a reflective smile.

I thought back to this morning activities when I said goodbye to Sandi and seemingly rushed to the airport to make my flight. After returning from the short restroom break, I confessed, "I was in such a rush this morning that I left my son sleeping; only saying good bye to my wife. I just didn't have the heart to wake him up."

As she again did not respond, I just left it alone. I was never very good at small talk. "Where are we off to?" I inquired.

"Just a short hop to an island off the mainland; but you wouldn't want me to spoil the surprise now, would you?" Kiana asked with a playful air of familiarity.

"Depends on the surprise I guess. I like nice surprises," I said with apprehension, deciding to play along.

I was not particularly very trusting of people in general. Still, we were in an airport with dozens of witnesses. As I noticed my bags had already been put into the cart, I decided to go with the new arrangements.

"Well, this is a nice surprise, I can assure you," Kiana stated. "And I encourage you to relax, for now, and enjoy our hospitality. You'll even have time to call your family once we are in the air," Kiana clarified.

I followed after her into the electric cart. "Kind of 'cloak-and-dagger'; isn't it?" I asked as an aside, thinking it all to be a bit strange. "I thought I was supposed to call for directions."

"Not at all; the company thought it would be better to roll out the welcome mat, so to speak," replied Kiana. "The phone number you were directed to call is (808) 961-2180, correct?"

"Yes, exactly so," I acknowledged, confident that she couldn't have known that number unless she was a viable representative of the company. "So then, who are you exactly?" I asked.

"Oh yes, of course," Kiana says, while reaching inside of her suite pocket to pull out some identification.

Her identification badge banner read 'National Security Agency', and below the banner was her name, Kiana Nakoa. I thought to myself that I wouldn't know an official identification card even if my life depended on it. I was actually a member of the 'Army Security Agency' when I was in the military, but we never really had any elaborate identification.

"Is that a Hawaiian name?" I asked about the origin of her name. Just then the cart then came to a stop in front of gate A10.

"Yes, and we better get a move on if we're going to make our connecting flight," Kiana insisted. Seeing my hesitation to immediately follow along with her, she pointedly asked me, "You accepted this position for a reason. Do you really want to back out now before even giving it a chance?"

I admitted to myself that she made a good point, and I got out of the cart.

"Well no; but I had thought my entrance orientation and presentation was going to take place here in California," I provided as rationale for my apprehension. "It just would have been nice to know that it was going to be in Hawaii."

"Well, sorry for the 'cloak and dagger' routine, but our company values their privacy. Besides, not everyone we gave airline vouchers to, will be going to Hawaii. It was just more expedient to have them available that way to be handed out at the job fair," Kiana admitted.

As we arrived at the airline ticket counter and I was given my boarding pass for my flight to Hawaii. Well, things are looking up, I thought to myself; my tickets were for first class seating. And one can't beat Hawaii for a place to work. Curiously enough, even though Kiana was getting on the same flight, she was seated in the back of the first class section, away from me. As we walked through the jet way, neither of us spoke.

Then, as we entered the jet, Kiana smiled and said, "See you on the other side."

I nodded uncomfortably, as I was unaccustomed to such last minute change in plans. I found my seat, and settled in. It was a window seat. It all seemed a rather strange situation. It was nice to have been set up with the first class accommodations, and a window seat to boot, but it would have been better to have known the complete travel itinerary up front. I pulled out my cell phone to make a call to Sandi. A passing stewardess cautioned me that the plane was about to taxi out, and I would have to wait until the plane was airborne. I bided my time by gazing out of the window as we took off. Once airborne, I called home.

Sandi: "Hello."

Steve: "Hello, sweetie; it's me."

Sandi: Sandi recognized my voice and started the conversation, "I was thinking it was time you were arriving in San Francisco. How was the flight?"

Steve: "Actually, the flight is not over yet. It appears the want me to give my presentation in Hawaii. So I am on my way to…," Steve pauses to read his boarding ticket, "it looks like the next stop is at the Hilo International Airport."

Sandi: "Wow, if we have to move, I can't think of a better location. Where in Hawaii? I can look it up."

Steve: "I don't really know yet. But this could be a good thing; you know, more prestigious scientists."

Sandi: "I can hear it in your voice already. You need to calm down. Remember this is what you always wanted; to be heard." Sandi paused for a moment, but I did not respond. "Just be yourself, and remember to slow down when you are talking."

Steve: "You're right; I just don't want to make a bad first impression."

Sandi: "You won't. Just take it one step at a time." Sandi changed the subject, "How's the flight."

Steve: "Well, they booked me in first class. It's pretty roomy up here; I've never been in first class before. And it looks like they may be providing movies."

Sandi: "Movies, huh, that should keep your mind off your worries."

Steve: "What did you say?" I asked, as my cell phone connection seemed to fade. "I can only hear every other word. I guess there are no cell towers in the Pacific," Steve said trying to make a joke of it.

Sandi: It seemed Sandi had the same problem on her end, as well, and she verbally ended the call, "OK, call me when you get there then. Love you."

Steve: "Love you too."

I closed my flip phone and settled in for the long travel to Hawaii. As I relaxed, I began to think of the vacation we took to Hawaii back in 1999. I figured it would be about a 5 hour flight. I smiled at the thought of the problems we had keeping track of all that extra luggage and carrying that baby car seat around for Andrew. It seemed comical now. How old was he back then, I tried to recall; probably just about 2 or 3?

I remembered our hike up to the top of Diamond Head. Andrew fell asleep in my arms and woke up just as we were nearing the top. Once he woke up he wanted to get down and walk up the last set of stairs to the top by himself. I was more than willing to let him do so, after carrying him uphill for the last mile and a half. Then to our surprise, the other hikers were amazed to see this toddler working his way up the last 99 steps. They all cheered him on as he kept moving right along to the top. Yeah, everyone enjoyed that.

As I reminisced about our vacation, all those years back, I began to relax more and even caught a nap. My only interruptions were the complimentary offer of beverages and a meal. I chose a movie title from the sci-fi genre to fill in some of the time, and paged through their magazines. Five hours later, we were landing in Hilo. As we were de-boarding the jet, I once again met up with Kiana.

"Did you have a nice flight?" Kiana said, trying to make light of the extended trip.

"Wonderful," Steve commented. "Will there be any more surprises?"

"Actually coming to Hawaii was not the only surprise," Kiana stated with an air of mystery. "The real surprise is that you will be making your company presentation from a conference room in Mauna Kea."

"Is that near the Mauna Kea Observatories?" I asked with excitement. "I always wanted to visit a working observatory, but such opportunities were always part of a larger tour and we just never made time for it in our vacation plans."

"We thought you would appreciate the setting. Actually, the conference site is on the campus of the Mauna Kea Science Reserve," Kiana explained.

"Do you think they'll be able to provide me with a private tour of the observatory?" I continued to inquire.

"Of course," Kiana responded. "It just so happens they have a lot of free time this week. We'd be happy to set it up for you."

"Thank You," I replied appreciatively.

Kiana had my baggage transferred to a limousine and hustled me off to my final destination. She made small talk about the Big Island's weather and how its terrain hosted 10 of the 14 climate zones, which I had similarly heard upon my previous vacation to Hawaii, and then some interesting facts about the Mauna Kea Observatories.

"Hawaii is touted as Earth's overlooking summit to the rest of the Universe," she started in to say. "The top of Mauna Kea is host to the world's largest astronomical observatory, with telescopes operated by astronomers from eleven countries," she recited as if she were a seasoned tour guide. "The combined light-gathering power of these telescopes is fifteen times greater than that of the Palomar telescope in California and sixty times greater than that of the Hubble Space Telescope."

Indeed, Kiana sounded like an advertising pamphlet for the University of Hawaii. If nothing else, I would enjoy the getting to view these facilities first hand. And what I backdrop for my presentation; it was all quite inspiring.

We arrived at the conference site, where I was ushered into a room which gave me a sense of what my audience size would be. I positioned myself near the white board and situated my materials for my presentation. One by one, five people entered the room and introduced themselves. Tom was the first to enter the room. Introducing himself to me, his title revealing his association with the company as the CEO, he carried himself in a quite professional manner. The others seemed to take their cue from him, all being quite polite. Their titles let me know that they all had advanced degrees in physics or astronomy.

Kiana hooked up her laptop to the large monitor in the room, while one of the five dialed in on a conference call. I gave her the thumb drive upon which I had crafted my presentation. On a second adjacent monitor in the room appeared to be another set of people sitting round a large oval table from a remote site.

"OK Tom, you're all connected," Kiana announced.

"Thank you Kiana," Tom cordially acknowledged of her assistance. Then he turned his attention to me. "Stephen, may I call Steve?"

"Yes, that would be fine," I agreed as I wasn't one to stand on formality.

"I want to set you at ease," Tom began to explain. "This is not really an interview, and there is no one here that is going to judge you or even 'fact-check' you on your information. I took the liberty of providing sections of your book as handouts, so we all have had a chance to familiarize ourselves with some of your work. Kiana will be assisting you with the slide presentation, so you can just let her know when to begin."

Tom continued to set the stage for the discussion and even had everyone participating remotely introduce themselves. I felt a little intimidated introducing myself, as I was lacking in the higher degrees which seemed to be representative of a majority of the crowd. It seemed the only one, other than me, who might not have an advanced degree in physics, was Kiana.

I motioned to Kiana to start the presentation. With a slide showing my rendition of a simplistic perspective of my unified theory, in a philosophical sense, I started to talk.

"Since everyone is somewhat familiar with at least an exposure of the information I am about to present, I'd like to skip right to the specific reason for your company's interest in my work. Simplistically, my view of physical matter is defined from the equation for a set of mass where density equals mass/volume. Such that as the volume decreases for a set value of the mass, so the density for that mass increases. Whereupon the smaller the volume, the greater the density is for that set of mass."

"Similar of this example, a set of separate masses in close proximity can be considered as the volume of accumulated matter. And as this volume decreases, this collective matter, or collective mass set, become smaller in size; increasing its density and its resultant gravitational force beyond what is normally attainable by any of its individual masses. In a sense, the laws of physics for the included smaller mass set is somewhat altered by the collective matter environment. And this is because the environment of the collective matter group has altered the medium in which they are existent. In this way, the size of the collective matter begins to embrace the physics of both the macro and micro universe."

"So what are the forces to be considered in this relationship of this collective environment?" I asked as a transitioning into my next slide. "Considering there are four fundamental forces at work in the universe: the strong force, the weak force, the electromagnetic force, and the gravitational force; these fundamental forces work over different ranges and have different strengths depending on their interaction within either the macro or micro universe. At a micro-level, gravity is the weakest but it has an infinite range. The electromagnetic force also has infinite range but it is many times stronger than gravity at this micro-level. The weak and strong forces are effective only over a very short range and dominate only at this micro-level of subatomic particles. Despite its name, the weak force is much stronger than gravity at this micro-level. However it is indeed the weakest of the other three forces. Normally, when it comes to the minuscule scale of particles, the effects of gravity are so weak as to be negligible. The strong force, as its name suggests, is the strongest of all four fundamental interactions at this micro-level environment. It has so been defined because the strong force holds the nucleus of atomic and subatomic particles together against all other forces in the universe."

I motion again to Kiana, and she changed to the next slide showing a rendition of a black hole in space.

"Now, I would like to make use of the dynamics of a black hole in this discussion of the four fundamental forces at a macro level. Comparatively, the density of atomic particles can be suggested to be part of a larger scale collective; for example, their effective gravitational force dominates their collective matter. This brings the interaction of these fundamental forces at a micro-level into conflict with the Standard Model of particle physics, which also includes their subatomic carrier particles; which, in turn, also alters the dynamic of how these forces interact with each other and how they act upon all of the other atomic particles within the collective. Normally the strong force, which holds the nucleus together against the enormous forces of proton repulsion, would be dominant within the micro-level universe. However, within a mix of these particles, wherein one or more particle densities are greater than many solar masses, the strong force of the nuclear model fails and the surrounding matter is stripped away into a soup of positrons and negatrons."

"This, in turn, would then allow for furthering a reduction in the volume of matter, inducing it with an increased gravitational acceleration within its greater density. At which point, unless one believes all these subatomic particles can truly be reduced in a form of matter equal to the size of an electron, then this would be an improbable state for the accumulated matter within a black hole as well. Following this rationale, it should also be evident that the dynamics of positive density matter could not play any larger role within the forces of a black hole beyond its ability to be densely packed," I said, setting up for my proposal.

I motioned again to Kiana, and she changes to the next slide showing a more detailed cross section of the black hole. "Rather, the gravitational force of the black hole is better understood as the marriage of positive density matter and negative density matter. In effect, for the density of positive density matter to increase, the volume of the matter must decrease while maintaining its overall mass. While this works great within mathematical equations, it does not represent a valid form for positive density matter. Arguably, it would be more logical that the dynamics of the black hole is either representative of a point at which the volume of matter contained can no longer decrease or there are other forces in play. These other 'forces in play' being that the volume of accumulated matter is more representative of interaction with negative density matter. Therefore, we have a choice:

> If the former is true, then there is a maximum achievable density, based in the size of it subatomic particles, which is controlling the volume by which matter can be compacted. This is similar in notion to the maximum achievable velocity for positive density matter (i.e., the speed of light). In which case, the addition of greater mass, as imagined of black hole consumption, or

black hole merger, could only add to the volume of the positive density matter beyond this maximum achievable density. As the maximum achievable density is restricted by the existence of positive density matter, the black hole cannot increase in volume consistent with its inability to exceed its maximum gravitational velocity. This is consistent with the boundary defined by the Schwarzschild radius as the event horizon, where the maximum density is contained by the speed of light.

> ➢ If the latter is true, then there is no volume by which matter is controlled and the maximum achievable density is essentially limitless. And while this concept mimics the theoretical belief that all positive density matter inside a black hole collapses into a singularity: i.e., an infinitely small and infinitely dense point well inside the boundary defined by the Schwarzschild radius, I would like to propose a singularly new hypothesis. One in which, within a volume of negative density matter, the positive density matter need not be reduced to a singularity to attain the needed greater gravitational acceleration required to support a black hole. It is therefore, rather the ability of negative density matter to be divorced from positive density matter; allowing for a deepening well of difference that continues to drive an ever increasing gravitational acceleration."

"So while there is a general understanding of the traditional black hole theory, based on the standard model and facilitated via positive density matter, I would like to explore the notion of principles involving negative density matter's interaction within the heart of a black hole. And actually, I would like to propose that the dimensional transformation from within a zero state medium of dark energy is the basis for both positive and negative density matter; where dark energy is representative of a displacement in the original medium of a pre-Big Bang universe." I felt I was on a roll now, and I just needed to drive my point home.

"While the Big Bang creation event, via an unfolding of its condition from singularity, is generally accepted to have introduced the intrusion of our existence, there is a flip side. Where our existence is defined as a reality of positive density matter within a traditional fourth dimensional frame of reference, as the makeup of our spacetime continuum, consider that a pre-Big Bang universe had zero positive density matter. Consequently, the manifestation of an evolutionary unfolding of a unidimensional frame of reference, in the spacetime continuum, is really the intrusion of positive density matter that is the presentment of a creation for our positive matter based universe. This intrusion, then, displaces the previous pre-Big Bang condition of a zero state medium," I explained.

"Such is it that this displacement effect is expressed as if the mass has intruded upon its relative consistent, or inertial, condition of non-mass within the spacetime continuum. In this way, this displacement effect simultaneously provided for introduction of negative density matter, or dark matter, in complement to the intrusion of positive density matter. Thereby the net gain to the modified zero state medium would still be maintained as a zero sum gain. The resultant effected motivation for the disturbed medium would be a need to bring the universe back into a more ordered condition, consistent with its pre-Big Bang persistence. This, it could do so by the expanding of the positive density matter from within our fourth dimensional spacetime construct. This expansion of the positive density matter would then allow for a reduction in the condition of difference that defines both positive and negative density matter. As positive density matter expands, it becomes less dense. Whereupon the negative density matter affects also becomes less pronounced," I proposed. "Another way to put it is that positive and negative density matter offset each other to allow for a modified dilation in relativistic time within space."

I motion yet again to Kiana, and she again changes to the next slide showing a black hole enveloped within a plasmonic ring structure, with the imagined black hole event horizon between the ring and the black hole's center. "Based on the dispersion of particles that would normally define the mass providing for the force of gravitational acceleration, we can see here that the center of gravity does not need to exist due to an impossibly shrunken volume of condensed positive density matter. Rather, the baryonic matter can remain expanded while allowing for a dark matter focus to define an imagined gravitational center. In this way, the relativistic difference is based not solely on positive density matter, but instead on the difference between the extremes of positive and negative density matter. As positive density matter increases, so too does negative density matter increase, providing for the exponential increase in gravitational acceleration that gives rise to an increased time dilation."

Suddenly Tom interrupts, "Thank you Steve. I believe you will be a valuable asset to our research." Tom then speaks to the audience, "Gentlemen, is he all that I said he would be. This new perspective should allow us to take our research to the next level and get back on schedule with this project development."

This surprised me as I had not even gotten to speak to the more meaningful details of my proposal. It was indeed as Tom had said, no one was judging or fact-checking me. In fact, no one was even curious enough to ask questions during my talk. Or so I thought. Perhaps they were instructed by Tom not to ask questions. Still, except for the last part on the introduction to negative density matter, the presentation was probably more remedial than they any of them expected to sit through. So perhaps there were no questions to be asked during this remedial overview. Yet, it did seem to me to sill hold their attention.

There was a din of mixed conversations, both in the room and on the monitor from the remote location. I couldn't help wondering why Tom cut my presentation short. Hopefully this would not hurt my chances of being accepted.

Then one of the five spoke up, "Yes, we agree that if this is the direction in which you are taking this project, Steve will be a valuable addition to the team."

This seemed to be an odd way to phrase their recommendation of my being hired. But perhaps not everyone was 'on board' for the Tom's direction for this project. This could make my job a little more difficult. If there was not a complete consensus on the changes that I would be bringing to the project, then I would have to mitigate their resistance to change and arbitrate upon the possible infighting between members of the team. All this I would have to accomplish, without the benefit of an advanced education degree to bolster their respect for my vision. This is not going to be an easy transition for me.

Tom then spoke to me directly, "Steve, I would like for you to join us at our onsite location. I believe you'll be quite excited when you understand the immensity of the project with which you are about to become involved. Kiana will set you up tomorrow for a pre-orientation with HR, and they will work out the details of your compensation. I'll see you both again in three months' time."

"Sounds wonderful," I said with an air of ease, as my stress just dissipated, "and I thank you for this opportunity." Well that went easier than I thought; what next? Tom and the others left the room in an unceremonious manner; no doubt, having several side conversations about me.

As I left the room with Kiana on our way back to the limousine, I asked, "Where is the onsite location?"

Kiana looked expressionless as she responded, "It's all classified for now, but you'll know soon enough." She handed me a card, "For the time being, you will have access to our driver, Calvin. He will be able to take you where-ever you would like to go. I have some arrangements to make." She motioned to Calvin to lower the car window and then let him know at what hotel I would be staying.

"Thank you," I said, thinking of how I was being given the royal treatment. I was feeling a bit out of my element, and I wondered if I had 'bitten off more than I could chew' by pursuing this job opportunity.

"If there is nothing else, then tomorrow you can contact Calvin to drive you out to meet me at this campus entrance, and we'll get you started," she instructed me.

"Yes, great," I responded, "and thank you again." I got into the limousine without her, somewhat preoccupied by the secrecy of it all.

"Where to," Calvin inquired?

"Oh, the hotel please; I'd like to get settled in before dinner," I answered.

When I finally got settled in my room, I called Sandi to let her know the good news.

Steve: Picking up on the conversation in mid stride, "You would not believe the 5 star treatment that I am being given. I am not sure how to act. Should I present myself with an air of confidence and self-assuredness or should I be more quietly amenable and humble?"

Sandi: "Oh, listen to you," was her level headed response. "Things must've gone well."

Steve: "Yes, but actually in some ways it was difficult to tell. There was no real discussion with me. Everyone just seemed to go along with whatever I said. I couldn't tell whether they agreed or disagreed with the thesis of my presentation."

Sandi: "Just remember, they pursued you; or at least their management did. They want what you have to offer. You'll find out where or how you fit in soon enough."

Steve: "Oh and I still haven't a clue where I'll be working, or where we'll be living. They are so secretive. I didn't have this much of a problem back when I worked for the Army Security Agency. Still it is not enough to put me off from accepting their offer, whatever it may be. So what do you think? Are you ready for an adventure?"

Sandi: "Life with you is always an adventure. Still, Hawaii is quite a distance from our relatives and friends," she stated with some misgivings.

Steve: "We don't have to make it as a lifetime commitment. We'll try it out for five years or so, and see if it is a good fit. From what I have negotiated up until now, I should have enough money for you to make trips back and forth to see the family."

Sandi: "Well, I married you for better or worse. And right now, between the stress of your current work place situation and the looming prospect of your being unemployed, it is putting a strain on our relationship. So if that is the worst of it, then perhaps going forward would be the best of it. I would rather have you sane than sorry. We'll make it work."

Steve: "Work; I almost forgot, I still have to give my notice. And what about Andrew?" I inquired, worrying about how this would impact his life.

Sandi: "You worry too much. Our parents never worried about us as much as you worry about our son. We'll make it work. Just go and pursue your dreams."

Steve: "Sweetie, I don't know how I would ever get along without you." As the conversation continued for a while, I began to build up my fortitude for the upcoming events. The rest of my evening was uneventful. I had dinner by myself in the hotel restaurant and then spent the rest of the evening preparing myself for tomorrow's campus tour. Usually Sandi did the planning for vacation, but here I was checking out the tour itinerary for tomorrow.

[Scene Change – Andrew's Perspective]

[Andrew shares a new secret with his mother]

Having talked a bit, on the trek to my house, it seemed we reached home sooner than I expected; or at least sooner than I was ready for. All the way back home, I had thought little of the introduction of Fairy to mom. Rather I spent my time relating my life story to Fairy. But now, having arrived home, reality set in. As the backyard came into view, I hadn't decided on a strategy for breaking the news to mom.

"Well, here we are," I announced to Fairy. Not really sure how this introduction was going to go down, I employed bravado over humility. "I'll handle this," was my suggestion. "Let me break it to her slow and easy."

"How is breaking something going to help with this situation?" Fairy asked. "Is it meant as a distraction?"

"I'm not really breaking anything. It is just an expression," I explained. "Just let me do the talking."

Walking in unannounced, I followed a maze of half empty boxes that filled the room. Looks like mom was all out in full work mode, preparing for our eventually move. But when mom and dad find out about Mairy, that should all change. It was a good plan, I thought to myself.

I called out in confusion for her, "Mom, where are you? And what's going on?"

As I turned the corner to the kitchen, I found her head deep in a tall empty box.

Rising up out of the tall box my mother answered back, "Ah, the prodigal son returns. And I thought you were purposely avoiding your chores," she said jokingly, while grabbing other items with which to fill the box she was working on. "Now that you're back, you can help by bringing me the extra pots and pans. You know the one's we don't use regularly."

Finding my mother in a good mood, I motioned for Mairy to come over. I immediately introduced Mairy to her, "Mom, this is Mairy."

Mom looked up to see the girl I was talking about, and started over to greet her. Brushing any dust from her hands on her jeans, she walked over and extending her hand in greeting.

"Well hello, Mairy. I'm Sandi. You'll have to excuse the way the house looks, I wasn't expecting company," she started in by apologizing. "Besides, it's not every day that Andrew brings friends back home unannounced."

Mairy politely responded, "Yes, well, we rather bumped into each other just today."

"Oh, are you one of his friends from school?" mom asked, trying to make conversation.

While my intentions were good, my impatience got the better of me, yet again. I was never very good at wading through small talk when I had something to say. My anxiousness began to preoccupy my thoughts; neither allowing me to listen objectively nor to delay the introduction of my news, pending the niceties of polite and restrained conversation.

So I jumped right into the conversation, saying, "Mom, we didn't just bump into each other today. Mairy actually saved my life. She arrived just in the nick of time to save me from an animal attack."

"Saved your life," mom exclaimed with suspicious surprise. I couldn't blame her as there was no evidence of either one of us having been in a fight. "Well that was fortunate. What kind of animal was it?"

"I got to say that it was weirdest looking monkey creature I ever did see," I answered tersely, without really wishing to follow up on the circumstances. "And I know it may not look it now, but we had a tough time fighting off the beast."

"A monkey?" mom questioned. "How unusual."

"Well, something like a monkey," I acknowledged, "but I couldn't be for sure. And I might as well just tell it to you straight out. Mairy is really 'Fairy', from my first quest as a Shadow-Forge on Glorthocks. You know; the girl I told you about when I got back. In fact, she was the first Shadow-Forge to show up on that planet. She came with her fairy friends, but they had to go back. So now only Fairy is here."

My mother's attitude then changed, as she seemed to be taken aback and a bit put off, implying, "Yes, I know. I read your father's book." Feeling she had been caught quite off-guard, she stumbled to process the information I blurted out. Feeling a little duped, she was quick to dismiss the account as not real.

"Sounds like a little play acting fun, but I really have a lot to do this morning. And once you're done play acting, I could really use some help. You know that we have a lot to prepare for, now that your dad has found a new job," mom pointed out to me.

Then she turned to Mairy and then to me, stating, "Perhaps whatever you two are doing, you could put off until tomorrow."

"OK, sorry for blurting it out like this, but this is not play acting. It really happened," I plead with mom to make things right. "Perhaps if you could just stop for a moment and listen, I can start over again."

Mom sat down at the dining room table, submitting to my request. "Alright, go ahead," she conceded.

"Well, it wasn't play acting. And we can't put it off until tomorrow, because it just happened today; as I have already told you," I loudly stammered at trying to communicate with my mother. "The truth of the matter is, Mairy has nowhere else to go because she doesn't even living here on Earth. She is an alien from another world altogether that I only previously met on Glorthocks," I explained, continuing my broken train of thought.

"So now she is an alien from another world?" mom said with incredulity.

I continued to support my claim, clarifying, "Perhaps not so much from another world. She is more from another dimension of reality. She is, in point of fact, not even from within our current spacetime."

I could see that mom found this revelation a bit unbelievable, to say nothing of the monkey creature attack I spouted to her earlier.

"What's this really all about?" she asked in a more interrogating manner.

Mom was obviously familiar with the story I shared with her and dad over and over again, when I first got back. And while she believed the story I told them, it was always kind of like a fantasy to her. Somewhat like a sci-fi movie she watched a long time ago, it was never real to her.

As mom was not embracing my explanation, I looked to Mairy for some help. Mairy rolled her eyes and looked disapprovingly at me. She could see that it was a lot for my mother to take in all at once.

As if to scold me, Mairy pulled me aside, and then proceeded to complain in a hushed voice, "This is your idea of handling it slow and easy?"

As an excuse or explanation of my outburst, I could only shrug in silence at Mairy's displeasure.

"I'm sorry Mairy," mom said, seemingly apologizing for my behavior. "I'm sure this seems all very peculiar to you, but my son's timing is not very good. Could I just have a moment alone with him," mom asked her, ever so politely?

Mom and I walked to the kitchen, where she felt she would be out of earshot.

"Andrew, we talked about this. I'm not sure what happened today, but I can see it has affected you deeply. I know things have been rough for you; nonetheless we were supposed to keep this secret within our family. I can understand that you do not want to leave your home. But you can't fake an episode in order to forestall the inevitable. And bringing your friend into this is just not helping anyone."

"No, mom, she is the real deal," I professed to her.

"No, she's not," mom interrupted. "I understand that moving is something you don't want to deal with right now, but I have to. And really, a monkey creature and an alien; did you really believe that I would not see through this fabrication? Think about it. Do you want to end up on a psychiatrist's couch again?"

"Mom, I know what you're thinking. You're thinking I'm just reacting to our moving away," I said, trying to reason with her. I needed to get mom to understand that I was not bonkers. "Perhaps, I am not the best at communicating. And I'm still a little excited because what happened was just insane; but it is also true. I am not crazy and I am not making this up. Mom, just talk to her and you'll see what I mean."

"Talk to her," mom said with disbelief. "Who is she anyway? Does she even know what this is that you are playing at?" Mom hung her head down low and then looked up at me, saying, "You know how I worry about you. This is just cruel. And for you to involve someone else in this charade is just embarrassing me."

Obviously mom had not moved far enough away to have this conversation with me, because the next thing I saw was Mairy coming in.

"Sandi, I know this is all too much for you to take in at once, but you need to have a more open mind," Mairy suggested, trying to mediate our disagreement.

"Listen little girl," mom stated in a condescending manner. "I'm not sure what Andrew may have told you, and I know you think you are helping him. But this is not the way."

"I see," said Mairy, quite contrarily. "I didn't intend for any of this to upset you. I'll take my leave of you. Andrew, will you walk me home," Mairy asked of me quite unexpectedly? I couldn't believe she was just giving up.

Mairy grabbed my hand and then reached out her hand to mom as mom had done when we first arrived, "Again, I'm sorry if we caused you any distress."

"Thank you," mom replied sincerely. "And I didn't mean to bite your head off," she apologized, reaching out to shake Mairy's hand goodbye.

As mom took Mairy's hand in hers, she seemed overwhelmed and confused. Her eyes looked up and around, as if she were focused on something other than us. Suddenly tears began to stream down her face, as she seemingly stared beyond us. I let go of Mairy's hand to help mom. As I grabbed mom by the shoulders, she seemed to be strangely unaware of my presence. It was as if she was dreaming, or maybe even hallucinating, and couldn't see me. I shook her by the shoulders, and hers eyes slowly focused on me.

"Mom, what's wrong?" I called to her. "Please snap out of it."

I looked back to Mairy and accused her of being the cause of mom's behavior, saying, "What did you do?"

A bit disoriented, mom apologized for her actions, "Excuse me, I have to sit down." Mom moved to sit at the kitchen table, amid the clutter of empty boxes about the room. I helped her to a chair and sat beside her.

Mom then looked deep into my eyes, saying, "I never realized what you went through; all this time, and not knowing of your anguish."

"Nothing was ever all that bad," I said, trying to empathize with her. I had no idea what mom was going on about, but I could see she was on the verge of crying again. "I'm really alright. There is nothing for you to cry about."

Mom stated in a worrisome voice, "Knowing what you went through, I don't know if I can let you go through this again." Mom seemed to be babbling and I didn't know why.

"Mom, it's alright now," I repeated, trying to console her, but I wasn't quite sure to what she was referring.

I was beside myself, trying to figure out where this was all coming from. Perhaps I should just let it play out, I told myself. I had never seen my mother at such a loss for words, or in such an emotional state, since I came back to her from my last quest. I gathered there was more going on then I first realized. I thought back to the sequence of events that led up to her emotional outpouring of sentiment, and it all came back to Mairy.

"What did you do?" I demanded of Mairy.

"I just helped your mother to recognize the sincerity of your explanation," was Mairy's response. "You might say that I opened your mother's mind to the truth of your feelings."

I stopped to make sense of Mairy's response. It must've been the same thing she did to me in the meadowlands. I didn't know whether to be angry with her or not. No son wants to make their mother cry. From what my mother was saying, I deduced that Mairy must've acted as a conduit between my mother and me. Indeed there was more to being a Shadow-Forge than I had ever realized.

Then, purposely looking up to Mairy, mom continued, "I know who you are."

Mairy moved in closer. Feeling a bit helpless, I just got up and gave Mairy my seat next to mom. Mairy sat down and took her hand.

As mom began to collect herself, her protection mode kicked in. "So what is this all about? Will Andrew be going away again?" she enquired of Mairy.

"Sandi, please calm down. Andrew is not going anywhere. And he is in no immediate danger at this time," Mairy replied.

It was as if mom's emotional insight about me was on overload. Truly if she was able to sense my emotions, it may be more than she could accept.

"No, he is danger," mom insisted. "You have to help him to get home."

"But mom, I am home; I am right here beside you," I remarked.

As Mairy looked deep into mom's eyes, I couldn't see whether her connection was having the desired effect. I blamed it all on Mairy, saying, "You showed her too much. It is too much for her to believe."

"It is just as Andrew said; you are not of this world," mom declared, realizing the truth of Andrew's words.

Mairy continued speaking, "It's true that I am not of this world, but I am not a real threat either. However, I am no more alien here, on your world, than your son was, when he first arrived on Glorthocks. I have been assimilated into the environment of your reality upon my transformation. I have done so that I can be a part of your reality and to interact with all of you."

"So that's what happened to me on Glorthocks," I thought aloud. "No wonder I could understand and talk with everyone."

I looked up to see Mairy glaring back at me. And I understood her glare to mean that I had interrupted the mood and conversation that Mairy was having with mom.

"Oh, sorry; please continue," I said embarrassedly.

Mairy turned her attention back to my mother. Pausing to consider her next words carefully, Mairy explained her rationale for coming to Earth, "As for what this is all about; it is about Andrew's safety. I had a sense that Andrew was in danger, and I acted upon it. So here I am."

"And it was a good thing for me, too," I interrupted again, hoping to support her account, "or I would have been ripped to shreds by that monkey creature."

Mairy rolled her eyes again and once again looked disapprovingly back at me.

"Or maybe not," I said sheepishly, trying to take back what I just said. "Besides, I'm just fine now."

She then turned again back to mom, trying to regain any ground she may have lost from my unscripted outburst.

In a consoling voice, Mairy explained to mom, "It was not really quite as dangerous as all that."

Mairy's intent was clearly to not alarm my mom any more than I already had.

"I believe the creature may have only been trying to scare him," she explained.

"Well, it certainly did do that," I added in a lower voice, thinking back to my initial encounter with the beast.

Mom, recovering from the shock of the emotional deluge imparted to her, had calmed down considerably. Taking stock of all that she heard, including the blunt statements provided by me, she took Mairy hands into her own, saying, "Thank you. Really, thank you for being here to help Andrew."

Then changing her tone a bit, she stated, "But this is all a bit surreal for me. I mean, I do believe what you both are saying, to be sure. I can't deny what you have shown me. But the genuineness of these events is all a bit overwhelming. I'm just glad that you are both safe from whatever it was that threatened you. But it is difficult to imagine that any of this has really happened; and yet, I do believe that it all did happen."

"I understand," Mairy continued to console her. "Let's take it a little slower. What would you like to know?"

Clever girl, I thought to myself, she had given control of the conversation back to mom. But rather than responding to Mairy's request, mom continued to praise Mairy's actions.

"You're quite the guardian angel," mom complimented her. "And to just leap into our world, without any thought to leaving your own home," she said, continuing to show her appreciation, while trying to process it all. "You're very courageous."

"That's what she does, mom; she's a Shadow-Forge," I added, as if my statement alone was enough of an explanation for her motives. "She pops in and out of other worlds all the time. Remember, I also made a similar journey upon my first quest?" I concluded, attempting to support my assumption.

"Yes, I think she got that from when you told her the first time," Mairy seemed to convey to me with a bit of sarcasm.

It appeared that Mairy had adopted some of the idiosyncrasies of communicating on this planet, during her short time with me. Or maybe I was just feeling the sting of truth in her words.

Mom looked to me saying, "Well, so are you, it seems. You were also a Shadow-Forge on another world. I don't really think I ever appreciated what that meant until now. I am very proud of you. You know that don't you," mom asked me rhetorically?

"You must have saved many lives with your sacrifice. And to think of how I almost lost you forever," mom choked on the words, and then cleared her mood again. And I, in turn, was choked up by what she said.

"All the same, I happy you haven't taken it upon yourself to just go 'popping in and out' of other worlds. It shows very good restraint on your part." I could see she was almost smiling, like she made a joke. Then, perhaps thinking twice about her assumption, she asked me, "You haven't been 'popping in and out' of other worlds, have you?"

"No mom," I answered with an air of embarrassment. Not that I hadn't tried, of course. I was just never able to achieve the accomplishment of astral projection on my own.

"That's good," she said, probably satisfied in believing that she still had some control over what I did.

Mom then looked up again to Mairy and asked with some concern, asking, "Well then, how long will you be staying here to help keep my Andrew safe?"

I was also interested in Mairy's response to mom's question, asking for a bit more clarification on top of her query, "Yes, is this a quick stop over between rescue missions, or is there more to come?"

"From what the creature told us, I believe there is more to come," was Mairy's answer, rather ignoring mom's question to answer mine. "But I cannot be sure of what might be coming; at least, not just yet."

Picking up on the implications of Mairy's answer, mom gave a bewildered looked. It was much like mine when I first heard the creature speak. Mom had to ask, "Are you saying that this animal could speak?"

"Well, as it happens, it is not quite an animal," I offered of my earlier speculation. "It was more like a 'dark' version of a Shadow-Forge."

It was just one surprise after another for mom, as she looked to us, asking, "There are more of you here?"

"Yes," I admitted, cringing at being the bearer of more bad news.

"I'm afraid so," Mairy replied, "and they must be planning something big to be so blatantly attacking your son, without fear of discovery. They usually managed their attacks in a much more subtle manner."

"Will Andrew be safe here with us?" mom expressed to Mairy, with some concern. "Perhaps we should take Andrew away from here."

Well, that was counter to what I had planned from this discussion. "Hey, I'm right here," I interrupted. "And I'm not completely helpless, I might add."

To think that two women were discussing how best to keep me safe, without any reference to their own vulnerabilities was quite an emasculating experience.

"We should all be safe for now," Mairy stated. "Whatever they are planning, it doesn't appear to involve anyone's immediate death, or the beast would not have broken off its attack as it did."

"If it is as you say, perhaps they may have anticipated my coming here to thwart their attack," mom suggested. "It may even be that they orchestrated the attack just to pull you into our world."

"So they wanted her here," I surmised of mom's supposition.

"Or, maybe, they wanted both of us here," Mairy remarked.

"Great; maybe it is some sort of retribution for our actions on Glorthocks," I suggested of their motives.

"These Shadow-Forge guild members of chaos are not driven by such trivial motives as retribution or revenge," Mairy stated with distinction. "There is little loyalty to be spared among their kind. They are always about the next battle to move their cause forward. For them, it is a constant state of war. It is a war that has been going on since the beginning of time; even before there was ever a form of organic life."

"Their cause; what is their cause?" mom asked.

"They are the nemesis of our efforts to keep the universe in balance. They seek to undo the evolutioning of all creation by providing for the continued disorder of the universe," Mairy replied.

"Continued disorder?" mom asked with confusion, "I always thought of the universe as being well ordered; something more or less like along the lines of an intelligent design."

"While disorder is what may have brought about and helped to maintain our current reality," Mairy began to explain, "the actuality of such disorder on the fabric of spacetime is that it pervades as a continual cycle of consumption which seeks to supplant its evolutionary existence within the universal being."

A little lost in her logical rationale, I questioned her motives, "Maintaining our reality is a good thing, isn't it?" I had to ask myself if I was on the right side of this clash between these opposing members of the Shadow-Forge. I posed the query, "I mean, without this continuum of spacetime, there is no existence for anyone, right?"

"The universal being is with and without an existence. Just as we can become Shadow-Forge, the realities of the universe are maintained upon its presence in a variety of dimensions in Space and Time. The aspect of a universal being beyond our own realities begets a far greater prescience than we can ever fathom," Mairy tried to explain.

"The existence of the universe is more based on a more transcendent nature of being, which has no real bounding limitations. It is more about this spiritual nature of the universal, being beyond existence, which animates the living force. It imbues all of existence with purpose and connections. It is this aspect that is the motivation for all of creation and its resultant evolution, parsing out the life forces from within its universal being. Too much disorder perpetuates an ambiguity in these life forces for a more non-evolving existence."

"Wait; if favoring disorder promotes a non-evolving existence, at least it is an existence. So does that mean we are not supporting the perpetuating of our own existence?" I asked with some confused sense of outrage. "I think that makes us more the bad guys, rather than the good guys."

"You're reasoning is flawed. You are deducing a difference based on the verb rather than on the subject.

We are supporting the perpetuity of an ever evolving existence. The disorder of being is the continual cycling of Time that bounds Space in an existence which has a specific beginning and an end," Mairy continue to explain; "whereas the order of being is the continual recycling of Space unbounded by Time in an existence which has a no beginning or end. For Time is not just a measure of existence; it is also a distinction of reality without form. And this 'reality without form' promotes the ever present evolutioning of purpose over substance."

"You'll forgive me, but my form is all have just now," I declared. "Good or bad, it is just who I am."

"It is your form that binds you to this reality in spacetime," Mairy replied, "and as such, your form is predestined to end with the passing of Time. However, the evolutioning of purpose perpetuates the evolution of our life force within the being that is our universe. Without this evolution of the life force, the chaos of a non-evolving existence promotes the 'non-being' of all life force, via its termination in Space rather than a continuation in Time."

She debated the issue like a seasoned philosopher, which was beyond my ability to grasp. "As per your previous preference to form over purpose, it should be noted that while all forms are in constant change, such physical existence promotes consumption and support for greater disorder and chaos. Whereupon all form is consumed over time, purpose imbibes no such dissolution."

A thoughtful silence filled the room. It was one of those moments when the individual mind races without the awareness of others. It is the moment in which the mind works to maintain a semblance of sanity within the individual realities that we have created for ourselves. I couldn't help wishing dad were here to make sense of it all, but I could not continue to refute Mairy's logic. As my mind sorted through this information blitzkrieg, it produced a new relationship from which I had not previously approached the issue at hand.

"Ends with Time," I repeated out loud to myself. "Or perhaps it might also be thought of as the end of all Time, or better yet as the 'end of times'. Yes!" I blurted out, bringing everyone back to our shared reality.

"It was as if the creature was providing us a warning about the 'end of times'. Or maybe more to a religious point, perhaps it was about the 'end of days'," I reasoned. "That being the case, then I am thinking that there might be some reference to legend or religious folklore about the nature of the creature and what the creature said. How did he put it?" I tried to recall aloud.

"Yes, I believe he framed what he said as *the fate of all humans*," I espoused upon my perspective for our discussion. Sometimes the unlikely side effect of my condition with ADHD can bring about some new insight and comparable alternatives to a problem. "It stated, I am here to herald the fate of all humans".

"So how does the 'end of days' relate to the 'fate of all humans'?" Mairy echoed in a quizzical tone.

"What my son is referring to is a reference to the religious or cultish prognostication about the 'end of days', or 'end time'," mom began to explain. "For those of Christian belief, the 'end time' is captured in the 'Book of Revelations' as our 'Judgement Day', and it is facilitated through the opening of a book with seven seals. For Protestants, it is known as the Rapture and the Tribulation. Still, for both Christians and Protestants, 'Judgement Day' signals the end of Armageddon and the second coming of the son of God."

"But it is not always about God," I broke in to clarify. "In Buddhism, the ultimate destruction of the world is expected to come through seven suns. In Judaism, it is the coming of a savior and the resurrection of the righteous to bring about their version of utopia. For Islam and Hinduism, the day of judgement is preceded by the appearance of their savior atop a white stallion. In this incarnation, the savior brings about an end to the demise of civilization, along with the suffering and death that it promotes; rather like the four horsemen of the apocalypse."

"I am unfamiliar with this concept of religious beliefs," Mairy regretted.

It was ironic to see Mairy in this position, as she seemed to have all the answers. Then thinking that I may have overshadowed my mom's contribution, I quickly back peddled to show more appreciation.

"Wow, I didn't know you checked out other religions like that," I echoed of my surprise to mom. "However, what I was referring to was the nature of the beast. I believe it is the 'Book of Revelations' that makes reference to a beast, as well, heralding the 'end of times'," I added.

"Yes, in 'Revelations', there is reference to a beast, and the beast will bear mark of the 666," mom stated. "In fact, I remember your father's interpretation for this mark of '666' as part of our own human chemistry; where '666' stands for the carbon atom, one of five elements within our human DNA," I contributed.

"Or more to the point, it is part of the makeup of all carbon based life forms," I added. "Carbon is a key component of all known life on Earth: 6 protons bonded to 6 neutrons, surrounded by 6 electrons."

Mairy just listened as we batted about random secular perspectives related to cultural religious beliefs.

"I too remember some of what I have read on this topic," mom proposed, eager to join into the resolution of this mystery. "There are other references to a real beast that would bring about a renewed and fertile world. It is a reference in Old Norse mythology that predates Christianity's view of '666'. In Old Norse mythology, there are references to a wolf, or hound, known as Fenrir, or Garmr. This wolf was a messenger of the gods which comes prior to the time of 'Ragnarok'," mom restated from her recollection.

"That's it!" I exclaimed. "The beast made reference to the time of Ragnarok. He said *'the time of Ragnarok is almost upon us'.*"

"Alright then, maybe we can find something online that would help us to identify the type of creature you encountered," mom concluded. "Now where did I leave my laptop?"

"I'll get it," I said, offering to get her laptop, "I know where it is." We were definitely on a roll. Not bad for simple humans, I thought to myself.

We all stared at the laptop screen while mom searched the internet for possible matches. One by one, we studied the images of beasts affiliated with 'end time' prognostications. Like witnesses searching the police photos for possible offenders, we spent several minutes going through the catalogue of possible suspects being displayed before us. Then all at once, I identified a candidate from the listed images presented in front of us. "That's it," I announced with a high degree of certainty.

Focusing in deeper on the selected image, mom read the information reference. "This is the Tokoloshe," mom recited. "The Xhosa people of South Africa tell a story of the Tokoloshe wherein it murdered many people. Originally the Tokoloshe was considered a harmless fairy that was fond of children; probably more or less like the tooth fairy. It appears to be derived from the beliefs of the Nguni people. However, when the Christian missionaries arrived in Africa they demonized the Tokoloshe, referring to it as a dangerous monkey-like animal. It then to be called as the Tikoloshe, which was later referred to as the Tokoloshe."

Mom then sat back in her chair, lamenting, "There doesn't appear to be any reference to it as a harbinger for the 'end time', like in the legend of Old Norse mythology."

"Don't be so quick to attribute the appearance of this new creature to the ancient myths of your diverse cultures," Mairy cautioned. "This was a Shadow-Forge, and a Shadow-Forge can take any shape, or any combination of shapes, from its environment when it emerges."

"I get it," I immediately conceded to her point. "While mythology and legend flourished about in ancient cultures, they are only a record of the past. Each re-emergence of a Shadow-Forge brings about a new manifestation; a new shape for the Shadow-Forge to use. And these past remembered events cannot possibly predict the future manifestations of these new creatures."

"OK, then what about the creature's warning," mom inserted with a sense of urgency. "Perhaps maybe there is a clue in what the creature said."

"Of that, I am also concerned," Mairy agreed. "And I fear it is not something we will be able to determine from your records of past events."

"You'd be surprised what out records of past events holds. What does it say about the time of Ragnarok?" I asked mom impatiently. I felt we were on the trail of uncovering the true purpose of its portend.

"Here it is," mom identified of the entry. "In Norse mythology, the apocalyptic battle that the gods will fight against the giants before the world perishes in flame and is created anew. Also known as the Twilight of the Gods: wherein the destruction of the gods, and of humankind, will occur in a final battle between the Aesir and the Vanir. On the day of Ragnarok, Fenrir will break his chains and join the giants in their battle against the gods, wherein he would be responsible for the destruction of the world," she recited.

Mom paused to learn more about this reference to Fenrir, "Let's see; yes - Fenrir is the terrible monster in the shape of a wolf."

There was a quiet pause, as everyone stopped to digest what mom just read. "Can we expect more attacks from this creature?" mom questioned of Mairy.

"Without knowing what their plan is, it is difficult to predict," Mairy replied with uncertainty. "Eventually, I believe; but of the actual timing I cannot say with any degree of certainty. There is a method to their actions, of that I am sure. I am just not sure of what universal events they are intending to alter this time."

I began to think more seriously about our immediate situation. "Is dad coming home soon?" I asked.

It was not so much that dad seemed to foster a feeling of security for me, but rather that dad seemed to somehow be in touch with this concept of universal balance. Dad was always more pragmatic. He could bring in a more scientific perspective to an otherwise sci-fi like scenario.

"He did call while you were out," mom answered, "and he has been offered the job. So perhaps the timing couldn't be any better for us move out of this area. I mean, why tempt fate? If this can happen again, then it would behoove us not to be here when the opportunity presents itself. Are we all in agreement?"

"I have nothing that endears me to this one location in your world," offered Mairy.

But I was not so quick to answer. I thought of the friendships I had made over my high school years. While I certainly would not miss the troglodytes that would spring up from time to time, there were the more endearing aspects of high school friendships as well. I especially thought of my new found girlfriend of these last 7 months. I actually had great hopes of working on our relationship. The relationship actually started with our getting together in junior year, just before last summer. And then, we renewed our relationship upon our return in the fall season for our senior year, we had even made some plans about where we would go to college. And, well, everything revolved around my being here; not someplace else.

"Andrew," mom prodded, "what's going on?"

"How will we stop the coming apocalypse if we are not here to stop the beast?" I questioned.

"The beast came for you," Mairy remarked. "I don't believe it will be creating the apocalypse from here."

"Perhaps, but we might learn more from it, if we could encounter it again," I countered. "And this time we'll be ready for it."

"I don't share in your passion to invite trouble. Capturing the creature may bring more of them to his rescue," mom warned. "I can't believe that is the only reason you want to stay."

"Well, it's a lot to give up and start over again, you know," I said, expressing doubt in my decision. "I feel like I belong here; like I have lived here all my life."

"Your lifetime here in Iowa is not much longer than your previous lifetime in Illinois, before we moved," mom consoled me. "I understand you may not remember much of our previous stay in Illinois, and you have become much more your own person here, but you've only been here since the second grade."

"Sure, I remember some of when I was much younger and living there," I said, thinking aloud, "but if it weren't for the picture and videos you and dad took, I don't think I would remember any of it. My memories are mostly about here. I grew up in our backyard and in this neighborhood. My greatest adventure ever was in the woods behind this house." I could have gone on and on with excuses. I had a sense that I should preserve my way of life here, no matter what.

"I don't know if this helps," Mairy joined in, "but you have already moved away from here once before. You had a whole other lifetime in another more alien world, away from everyone. What of your friends there? You would have lived there with your new friends for a full lifetime, if not for your sacrifice. Who is to say which lifetime is more real?"

"That was different," I expounded upon my rationale. "I was young, and without any real friends before I left. And I didn't really grasp that the quest was going to take as much time as it did. And even with everything that was going on there, I always held on to the fact that I would be going home, here. And while I did make friends there that I will miss, I still felt out of place, because it was not here. I wanted to get back to the more familiar and safe environment in which I actually grew up and mattered to someone."

As I paused in indecision, Mairy approached me with a different perspective, "And now it is no longer a safe environment for you here, or your family. Somehow they found out about you and this place here on Earth. You've seen what the Shadow-Forge members of Discordia can do. Do you really want to submit your family to that kind of danger? At least if we keep on the move, you have a chance to work things out. And maybe once the danger is gone, you can all return back to this place and make it your home again."

Mom came over and gave me a hug. "Where ever we are together, that will always be home," mom added. "It's time I got rid of some of this clutter anyway. We've collected way too much stuff over the years."

"In a more universal sense, all of Earth is your home; this solar system, as well as this galaxy, is your home," Mairy added.

Perhaps mom was right, I thought to myself. Perhaps it was more of me missing the family, while I was off Earth, rather than this house and the stuff within it. Besides, I'd never forgive myself if something happened to anyone I cared about. I looked to Mairy and then to mom, "So what about Mairy" I open-endedly asked?

"She comes with us, of course," mom declared without reservation. "She's you're guardian angel. She came here only for your protection. So I don't see why that ends here and now."

"That's not what I meant," I said with a sense of the future. "What about Mairy after the danger is over?"

"I believe that is up to Mairy. While I would consider her a member of our family always, there will always come a time when the children move out on their own." Mom looked to Mairy and asked, "Was there somewhere that you need to go or elsewhere that you needed to be after all this?"

"Being a Shadow-Forge is a lifetime commitment," was Mairy short answer. "Once I crossed over to your Space and Time, my lifetime began anew. That being said, short or long duration, this is but only one lifetime. I'm not sure how events will play out on this plane of existence in the future."

"However, for right now, we need to find out why the members of chaos felt it necessary to attack another Shadow-Forge member here. It must have something to do with the chain of events in this current spacetime stream," she surmised.

Mom looked a little bewildered with her response and turned to me, saying, "You're right, she needs to talk with your father."

"When's he coming home?" I asked again.

"He's due to arrive tomorrow afternoon," mom replied. "Until then, you must both be hungry. Why don't you two both relax while I cook up some pancakes."

"I believe I am quite hungry," Mairy replied.

"While you're in this form, it is all about consuming to stay alive," I said, reminding her of her earlier comparison of us.

I just plopped myself down in an empty space on the couch. My whole world had changed in a single 24 hour period. All of my plans, in which I was emotionally vested, were now turned upside down. It all seemed quite surreal and struck a somewhat familiar chord; as if this was all just part of another quest gone wrong. I knew this was the right thing to do, of course, but it was the first time I had made a conscious decision to support such a drastic change for my own future destiny, since I got back.

Maybe that is what being an adult was all about. Or maybe I actually grew up too soon on Glorthocks, and needed this hiatus to recover from my lost childhood. Normally as a child, I would have just felt that I was being dragged along without any real voice in how my life played out around me. This was a big move for me, to put aside my selfish wants and needs to support my family's survival. More importantly, I felt the weight of a more familiar depression shedding; freeing me of my emotional baggage. It was as if my self-imposed depression was the cocoon that enveloped me and kept me safe in the comfort of my own lost childhood.

For now, my feelings of belonging to a special group, a special cause, came flooding back. I was indeed a member in the Guild of the Shadow-Forge, enlisted to restore order where chaos threatened the universal balance. The stakes, however, would be a bit higher this time, as it seemed more personal this time. Indeed this new adventure was about to fashion my destiny yet again.

I looked to Mairy and smiled. I thought of how it would be nice to have someone around to keep me sane; someone other than my parents to talk with about our family secret. And she was now to be one more secret that we would all share.

As mom cleared a space on the table for us to eat, Mairy smiled over at me. I could not say what she might be thinking, but it all appeared to please her. I watched as she went over to mom, asking, "Can I help?"

Mom did not hesitate in her response to an offer of help, "Now that's not something I hear very often. How about I show you how to make pancakes?"

I watched as mom and Mairy faded off into the kitchen together. The future didn't seem so bleak to me now. Although, we hadn't talked in length about it yet, there was still our situation of moving away prior to the end of the school year. It was still not clear whether I would be staying until the end, or not, but I was inclined to believe mom would not be voting in my favor.

To be sure, we were not the first family ever to be in this situation. That is, the situation of moving away, and not the situation where we were being attacked by a Shadow-Forge member of chaos. Still, this time I had all the support I needed. I was on my home turf with my parents to rely on as a resource, and Mairy to take some of the pressure off of me. She was there to either back me up or lead me forward.

So this wasn't a sanctioned quest from Harmony; or not just yet anyway. But somehow I had the feeling that very soon it would be. One thing I did know is that if we don't act now, then we will be that much further behind when Harmony does finally show up. As Harmony once said, "where we are unable to meet the expectations of our liable keep, our mutual destinies and that of our life force connections will forever remain unresolved." I'm not sure why that quote came to me just now, but it seemed appropriate to our circumstances. It seemed that destiny had a sense of purpose and clarity all of its own.

CHAPTER

5

The Illusion of Fate

[The unseen secret influences destiny, whose
true nature is concealed in the future.]

As Andrew's family ends their day in welcome slumber, a stranger day begins in an unknown laboratory, in an equally unfamiliar location; or at least, a location unfamiliar to them. It would seem that Andrew's foreboding sense of doom was not unwarranted, yet not for the reasons he was now struggling to endure.

Events were even now unfolding that would adversely involve him in yet another unexpected adventure, and the consequences were no less threatening than in his previous quest. Still, while Andrew may have secretly wished to be once again immersed into a thrilling emprise, he also secretly doubted his abilities to survive another such risky exploit. But what he could not know is that this time such danger could involve his entire family, with a possibility of anyone of them who might not survive.

[Scene Change – Narrator's Perspective]

A group of observers in red lab coats can be seen intently monitoring experimental data on several large screen monitors arranged along a wall, on one side of a well-lit room. The room was longer than it was wide, about 100 feet by 60 feet. These large monitors were set up side by side at one end of the room. To the right of this array of large screen monitors are six modular containers, each about the size of a single passenger electric car, bolted to the floor. The six units were in varying operating positions: e.g., some open and some closed.

When closed, the modular units remained horizontal. They resembled the look of a thinly shaped computer mouse on steroids, as the containers were taller in the middle than on the front and back ends. The top and bottom of these modular containers were split horizontally along the side upon a gentle slope that rose from the front to the back, so that the bottom portion was higher at the back end. The back end of the top portion was conspicuously wider than the back end of the bottom portion, where the horizontal seam between top and bottom met. However at the front end, both the top and bottom portions were almost indistinguishable matched along this same horizontal seam.

On the outside of these modular containers, the surface was clean and reflective like a polished car. The top portion of the outside surface was graduated from translucent to completely transparent, while the bottom portion remained quite opaque. About the bottom portion of the modular container, embedded within the skin of their reflective surface, there were several smaller computer screens and gages. These smaller screens and gages were well attended by other technicians, in blue lab jackets, who conversed with the observers in the red lab coats.

Viewing a few of the open containers, there appeared to be two additional operating positions: one where the closed unit was raised up to a 45% angle and another, where the bottom remained at a 45% angle and the top was opened in a position parallel to the floor. Watching the operation of the module container in motion, as it opened, it appeared that the top portion was designed to rise up and over the outside back of the bottom portion when it reached its 45% angle. Inside the bottom portion, there was a bedlike platform that seemed suspended along the extent of its length, as nowhere could the bedlike platform be seen as touching the inside walls. The mechanism of the bedlike platform appeared to be such that it could be slid up along the inside of the bottom portion, while it also slid out along the inside of the top portion. In this position, the platform seemed to be completely extended at about a 75% angle, while the bottom portion remained at a 45% angle.

While the head of the platform could be extended out along the inside of the top portion, and away from the inside of the bottom portion, the foot of the platform remained seemingly hinged at the bottom.

Inside one of the open containers, the bedlike platform could clearly be seen to be padded, providing for a surface on which one might rest comfortably. Below the bedlike platform, the inside of the bottom portion can be seen to be hollowed out, similar to a large canoe or bathtub; save for several wire harnesses that were arranged along the inside lip of the bottom portion. Additionally, there was a wire harness extending from the upper portion at the point where the head of the platform met it squarely when it was extended to its 75% angle. Oddly, when seen from a distance, the top and bottom portions of the container somewhat resembled the large open beak of a pelican.

As the room is visually panned from left to right, a blue jacketed technician is seen working at the back end of one of the closed modular containers. An observer in a red lab coat is seen monitoring signals on the large screen across the room and reports back in the direction of the engineering technician, "No, we've lost the signal again; damn it!"

As the panning reaches 180% from the technician, another observer is seen leaving the room through a sliding door, centered on the wall that is left of the large screen monitors. The sliding door is on the side of the room that is opposite of these arranged units. The door automatically opens and closes upon an adjacent corridor running both left and right. On either side of the door, windows in the wall provide for a view of the outside corridor, and also of the observer who just left the room. The observer outside the room can be seen walking away along the outside of the right bank of windows. As the panning continues, other observers can be seen working with other engineering technicians, before the focus finally returns back to the first engineering technician.

The first engineering technician provides a somewhat delayed response, "Yeah, I think I found the fault. It's this pod harness setup again." The engineering technician, looking visibly annoyed, begins to complain, "I've requested a replacement for this pod harness over a week ago now. This one is too 'glitchy' to be relied upon. No matter what I do with it, it just promotes too much signal loss at this connection joint."

"You know replacement parts are difficult to get here," replied the observer. "You'll just have to make do with the spare parts that we have. How difficult can it be to fix a connection fault anyway? We should have more than enough spare connectors from which to choose. They brought in a new order just last month."

"Well, these are the new ones, and I'm guessing these are representative of our low bid offering," the technician acknowledge. "It's not like residential wiring you know. There is an amount of precision involved in getting these connectors built correctly. If we had some decent fiber optic network interface connectors,

there would be a whole lot less maintenance needed in trying to keep these pods working," the tech rebuts the observer, referring to the modular unit as a 'pod'.

"Besides, we can't always depend on cannibalizing other units when we get a bad batch, just to keep these command pods working. At some point in time, they are going to need all of them to work," he concluded.

The engineering tech is seen fumbling with a metal connector tool, which then slips from his grip. As if in a dream, the tool appears to be falling slower than normal to the floor. The technician easily manages to scoop up the falling tool before it hits the floor and comments on the rate of the falling object, "I don't think I'll never get used to this low gravity."

"Yeah, at least you won't ever have to worry about injuring yourself in a trip, slip, or short fall," acknowledged the observer with some amusement. He was quick to chime in with a comparatively positive spin on the low gravity environment. While this experience would have indeed been strange behavior for any falling object on Earth, these two seemed more than comfortable with this weird effect as being just a momentary distraction.

"Why can't they just make the system work with the other four pods for now? At least they've been tested out to be working at 100%." says the tech, motioning to the other pods. "Every time one of these harnesses goes bad, they shut down a whole test cycle. And, for that matter, why did they make it so that these two special units need to have a unique network hook up from the others anyway. It just makes it more difficult to keep up with the maintenance on all these parts."

"These pods were not designed to make your life easier, I'm sure," the observer is quick to point out. "But if you really want to know the reason behind it, you would need to ask the only one who really understands the whole design: the chief research engineer. Oh, wait, you can't; because it is above your pay grade."

"Are you referring to John?" the tech refers to the chief by name. "I thought he went back to corporate weeks ago to plead for a schedule extension."

"Nope, he's still here until the completed system tests out successfully. And to have the complete system to test out successfully, it means that these six CONS unit harness hook ups to the IGIE require a minimum of six working pod connections to provide a comparative determination for the superpositioning of viewed spacetime events. Noting, of course, that these two particular pods, one of which you are now working on, are the special prototypes that are meant to direct and enhance the resolution limits of the dimensional stabilization for these spacetime events. That makes them essential for the completed system test set up. So they'll need all six pods working at 100%." [Note to reader: The acronym, CONS, refers to the Cognitive Operator Neuro-positioning System and IGIE refers to the Interferometric Gravitational Influx Emanator.]

"Well, that was quite a mouthful. Did you just make all that up?" the tech asked sarcastically, and with some confusion. "Tell you what; How about you spell it out for me, without all the science babble?"

"You could just pay more attention in the meetings when we are briefed, and save me the trouble of having to explain everything to you all the time," responds the observer.

"Right, well I don't think they pay me enough to pay attention. I believe that is more in keeping with your pay grade," he fired back. "Besides, they never bother to dumb it down for us in those briefings. You need an advance graduate degree just to get pass the acronyms they use."

"OK fine; remember when they briefed us on IGIE and explained how it houses the computer array on the superconducting gravimeter for the acquisition of gravity variations?" asked the observer, who paused for a moment to see if he could discern some semblance of the engineering tech's acknowledgement. As he saw no such acknowledgement, he then continued with a more detailed explanation, "No; OK then, IGIE is the computer system that processes the combined integration of gravitational and electrical brain wave forms as generated from these CONS units."

"Oh, yeah, IGIE," replied the tech sarcastically. "They say is it more complex than the NASA system for mapping planetary travel; definitely not my area of expertise. Hey, but here's a bit of trivia for you: Do you know what the term 'igie' translates into?" he asked rhetorically. He paused for effect and then continued, "Igie is an African term meaning the 'one that is on high'."

Abandoning his attempt to explain, upon the tech's more distracted response, the observer acknowledged his interpretation of the tech's implied meaning. "Sounds appropriate, you can't get much higher than this. This is the most advanced observatory of its kind yet to view the stars. And its orbit is 'higher' than any other satellite's geostationary position. It should provide us with an unrivaled perspective of gravitational anomalies in deep space. That is what we are here for, after all."

"Yes, but there is also another rare African interpretation for this term," the tech continued with his distraction, "as the 'one who is delivered breech'."

"So what are you saying?" the observer plays along. "Are you then predicting that the computer imaging will be coming out backwards?"

"Well actually, as the African superstition goes," he goes on to explain, "such a baby was considered the incarnation of evil spirits. And as such, the elders of the tribe would deem that the baby was too dangerous to keep around and have it put to death."

"Brutal," observed the observer. "But I'm sure the only evil spirits plaguing this project are the budget managers," joked the observer.

"The Romans, on the other hand, were a bit more magnanimous with their beliefs," continued the tech.

"Oh, there is more to this then, is there," acknowledged the disgruntled observer.

"Yes, indeed," he responded. "The Romans believed a breech birthed baby was destined to be somehow crippled in an accident or to be gifted with either second sight or magical healing powers."

"Well, I don't know if we could afford to deal with an accident," the observer joked again. "Hell, we are way over budget now as it is." The observer paused to look over the collection of pods, and then more conservatively stated, "Let's hope it is the 'second sight' choice. After all, that is the whole purpose of this endeavor now, isn't it? This baby is supposed to provide us with a 3D rendering and greater resolution than any other radioscopes on Earth."

Intrigued by what he heard, a second observer crosses the room and joins in on the conversation.

"Second sight indeed; knowing that they are trying to generate deep space images through the filtered brain waves of these pod operators is almost psychic," chimed in a second observer. "With a little more effort, perhaps we could just remotely project the totality of our five senses into deep space. So instead of just translating images, we could immerse ourselves in a more holographic, fourth dimensional experience."

"I would rather it was the 'magical healing powers' choice myself," insisted the tech, "then I wouldn't have to keep working these minor faults all the time. Speaking of which, how are we supposed to meet schedule if they have us doing double duty as structural engineers in this station, as well?"

"Well, better inside this station than out," replied the second observer, who continued to interject himself into the conversation. "Magical healing powers are definitely what you would need if you had to work outside this station all the time."

"Yes, there would be no facility at all if it wasn't for the work of our advanced maintenance robotrons," stated the first observer.

"You know, at one time, they had toyed with the idea of having just those robotrons to work on this entire moon station," the second observer shared with them, "rather than all these extra people. Think of it; we could've been back on Earth managing this whole operation remotely."

"Oh, and add a satellite connection into the mix; that's all we would need," remarked the tech. "Who do you think they would need to keep that monster connection working? I'd rather have my feet on the ground, such as it is. Anyway, those 'advanced' robotrons are overrated," responded the tech. "With everything else we do around here, we spend half of our time fixing up those tin cans as well. If it's not 'hot carrier degradation' with their hardware or 'multiple-bit upset' with their software, then it is something else. And that's not to mention the various software patch upgrades needed to repurpose them or orchestrate their more complex movements."

"Yes, but without them, it would have to be you working out there," responded the first observer, "…and I, personally, would not relish the idea of being exposed to that much radiation, even in a radiation suit. Do you realize the surface of the Moon itself is a rich source of reflected radiation? There must be a 12 foot foundation of shielding below this station alone, separating us from the surface of the Moon."

"Yep, composed of layers of lead, aluminum, magnesium and lithium hydride, and all under a six foot thick foundation of DUCRETE; not to mention that it is all capped off with a rich topping of varying composites in polyetherimide, pyroxene, regolith-epoxy mixtures for an extra layer of safety," said the second observer, looking out the lab room's window and across through the corridor windows to the outside moonscape.

"DUCRETE?" questioned the first observer. "Is that some special form of concrete?"

"That's the best part of it all," the second observer began to explained. "The 'DU' in DUCRETE stands for depleted uranium. DUCRETE is product name for the use of uranium oxide in nonmetallic matrices;

as in concrete. This entire facility is built within layers of spent nuclear fuel, making it the largest radioactive waste site in the solar system. In fact, much of the revenue to build this facility was funded on this service that we provide for Earth: that being the disposal of nuclear waste. We pretty much have a monopoly on the disposal and storage of spent nuclear fuel."

"I thought the idea was to keep us shielded from radiation," remarked the engineering technician.

"Oh, it all safe; in fact, it is better than safe," answered the second observer. "The use of DU in these materials acts like a neutron-moderating or neutron-absorbing binder. So in their dense, compact mixture, these materials provide for both an efficient gamma absorber and a neutron-slowing substrate which makes them ideal for radiation shielding. What more could you ask for?"

"I don't know how much I trust all that shielding, even if we are on the dark side of the moon half of the time," cautioned the engineering tech. "Why do you think they provide us with this lead-lined footwear?" he asks rhetorically, "Which, by the way, does nothing for my knees or these 'jewels' when I am working this low to the floor," he said jokingly, while grabbing his private parts.

"The lead in your shoes is not to shield you from radiation, so much," remarked the first observer. "It is to keep you from floating about with each step in this low gravity environment."

"Dark side of the Moon, indeed," interjected the second observer; "Did you know that it really only means the far side of the Moon from the Earth? It is the hemisphere of the Moon that always faces away from Earth's prying surveillance. In fact, the far side was referred to as the dark side originally in the sense of it being unknown, rather than for its lack of light."

"Yeah, and it's only dark half the time, with respect to the sun's position," added the first observer. "About every 13.5 Earth days, this dark side is still lit up, without so much as cloud to interrupt its brightness; giving us two weeks of pure daylight followed by two Earth weeks of night."

"Not to mention a dusk and a dawn that are 6.8 Earth days apart," observed the technician. "You might say our 1 full day is like 27 days on Earth, with the possibility of a direct hit from the solar winds every 20 days."

"Oh, come on, you two, you're on the Moon," continued the second observer. "Don't fret the small stuff. They've even integrated lead into the glass, so we could have an excellent unfettered view of space. What better observation point in the universe could you have?"

"It's like standing next to a microwave oven, if you ask me," cautioned the engineering tech. "I'd feel safer if they provided us with lead-lined underwear."

"Wouldn't that be comfy," interjected the first observer satirically.

"Suit yourself, but you're missing a wonderful panorama," responded the second observer, walking over to the laboratory door. He paused in the open doorway to admire the vista of stars, "It's is almost as if you could reach out and pluck them from space."

The plastic-like covering of the wall in the corridor was inlayed with an array of windows to the outside, just opposite of the room. Outside the windows, there was a clear view of the night sky and the constellation of stars; the position of which could reveal the position of the Moon relative to the Earth, even if Earth couldn't be seen. Along the grounds of the moon station, could be seen the sparse lighting of robotrons moving about. The reader's perspective pans out of the lab, following the second observer as he is seen walking out from the laboratory and down the wide corridor.

As this introduction of the covert operation comes to a closure, the reader's perspective pans out for a view of the moon station from outside of the facility, as if from a helicopter. From the outside, looking back toward the facility on the Moon, a geodesic structure is observed to be nestled into the basin of one of the Moon's craters. Lateral sections of building can be seen snaking their way into and under a large partially glass lined, geodesic dome structure. Like the area in which the pods resided, some buildings can be seen to extend beyond the partial cover of the dome, wherein lies the research facility for their deep space interferometer telescope. Where only the pod laboratory for the research facility and the building housing it had been extended beyond the cover of the dome on this side, the rest of the structure resembled the back shell of a tortoise.

The expanse of the dome itself appeared to be about a mile in diameter, making it the largest manmade geodesic structure. The engineering of its gigantic size, a little more than 7.5 times larger than any manmade geodesic on Earth, can be attributed to the Moon's lower gravity. It had large supportive pillars, arranged in a ring within the center of the geodesic structure, reaching up to the dome's roof. Where the pillars met the dome ceiling, the glass was replaced with metal plates. Only that portion of the dome about and above this point had no glass. Rather liken to an old fashion propeller beanie cap, there was an array of communication antennas and other hardware extending from the more solid center of the dome's roof.

As the perspective pans out even farther, the widening overview shows similar conjoining structures added onto the entrance to the research facility, from the inside. However, no portions of these adjoining buildings, on the inside, were exposed to the outside beyond the safety of the dome. The perspective continues to pan up to a view of the Earth positioned high in the sky over a backdrop of low lying hills of the crater's rim. The landscape of the low lying hills, void of any organic life, presented a stark contrast to the blue and green color of Earth in the horizon.

Opposite the pod laboratory and research center, relative to this dome structure, could be seen some type of aerospace bay platform for transport. The expectation of this transport facility could be assumed to handle travel between this moon station and the Earth. Robotrons could be seen milling about the outside among a diverse set of aerospace crafts. From the size and look of the smaller crafts docked about the open bay area, it was not easy to discern whether the intention of these smaller crafts might be to facilitate a more limited shuttle travel about the Moon's surface, or whether they might be used to ferry back and forth to a larger space craft, already off the surface of the Moon. In any event, it could be seen that the scope of this moon station was both bold and ambitious. This panning overview continues along the outside of the building until it focuses upon a row of windows; and then to one where people can be seen.

[Scene Change – Narrator's Perspective continued]

[The shared secret, often the basis of intercompany intrigue, is based on allegiance.]

The scene shifts to an inside view of the window which had just been focused upon, via of the panning perspective overview. The scene setting inside is recognizable as a conference room, housing a large table and a number chairs about it. The people inside would appear to be representatives of the various laboratories used to orchestrate this grand and prodigious project, for which the moon station was built. In this conference room is Thomas Vanagandr, the founder and presiding CEO of the facility. It is upon his invitation that these representatives were scheduled to convene a meeting on the status of the project.

Tom sits at one end of the large oval table, with his back to the door, opposite a set of 'floor to ceiling' windows that grace the anterior of the room. It is an awe-inspiring view of the moon station's view on an evolving universe. The current perspective was now a scene of twilight against the harsh moon landscape.

Tom is surrounded by associate managers who occupy the seats on his left and right of an office size table. However, no one is seated at the opposite end of the large table to discourage from their view to the outside. Everyone presiding at the meeting is a manager responsible for some of the various disciplines required to keep the moon station working.

While most members of the company, residing on the moon station, are attending in person, other associates are participating remotely. On the web conference line, two associates can be overheard having a side conversation prior to the meeting's commencement.

Associate 1: "I've heard they're bringing in some science fiction author to consult on the project."

Associate 2: "I can't understand why we would need him," another expresses his doubt. "Besides, the science is well understood for this application and we are doing well on the trials thus far. What knowledge could he possibly be able to bring to the table anyway?"

Associate 1: "Well, it's not the first time NASA has used a non-scientist to consult for the space program. You remember that guy, Glen Brinely; or was it Brinner?" he stumbles on the wording, trying to remember the man's name. "He is a sci-fi novelist, and he is currently consulting with NASA."

Associate 2: "Yes, I know who you're talking about, but he was already a scientist with multiple degrees before he started authoring science fiction novels. At least there is some basis for his consultation."

Associate 1: "OK, but what about that other sci-fi writer, 'Somebody' Sayer, I heard NASA called on him and he is no scientist."

Associate 2: "I had heard that it was the other way around. It was rather he that consulted with NASA for one of his books or movies. A lot of science fiction writers team up with NASA personnel to make their works appear more believable. Besides, it's good publicity for NASA, and the NASA consultant makes some money in the deal for his time and expertise."

Tom then calls the meeting to order, "Gentlemen, I know it has been awhile since we called everyone together, but we've all been quite busy as you can imagine. I understand the progress on the IGIE program is going well. And while I realize the project has an ambitious schedule, I would like point out that our credibility and accomplishments are limited only by our ability to keep the project's testing on schedule."

Associate 2: "Pardon me for saying, but the schedule requires support. You would think we could afford more experienced personnel and better equipment to get this project moving along at a better pace."

Dr. John Leighy speaks up defensively, "It's not necessarily a question of experienced personnel or financing. As you well know we have taken great strides to maintain a low profile and keep the military in the dark on this program. It is this secrecy, and of course our location for this research facility, that limits our ability to manage personnel and inventory. The technical problems will be corrected in time. However, our ability to find subjects who have the talents required to interface within our moon station is another consequence altogether. In point of order, I would like to add that the acquisition of more qualified pod operators is of paramount importance to the success of the IGIE project. Having less than six pod operators is tantamount to a complete failure for this program."

Tom mediates to diffuse John's attempt to hijack the organized deliberation of this meeting, "Yes, yes; thank you John. As noted in John's test results, we have successfully integrated the gravitational wave variations among the human brain wave patterns to transpose and generate images from deep space targets. This is a fantastic accomplishment, and one in which we would like to thank John and his dedicated team of professionals. And as we know, this is only possible because of technical completion and ongoing maintenance of the CONS units, which are able to integrate this data for IGIE's consumption."

"Working back from the IGIE system, the generation of images is only possible due to the coordination of our individual pod operator's unique abilities. Their ability to filter on these acquired gravitational wave patterns have been instrumental in the successfully piloting of the four, out of the six, operating pods," he noted.

"However, as John mentioned, we are still short two operators for each of the six working pods needed to coordinate the collective focusing of wave intermediation required to provide for a completed cooperative brain hive."

Tom recognizes Dr. Phil Berry to his right, "Phil, has presented a short presentation of the projects status thus far. Phil, if you would be so kind."

As a projector screen is lowered in front on the windows, Phil stands up to speak. "Can everyone on the remote connection see the title page?" he asks politely. A mix of voices agrees to seeing the slides.

"Alright; even though we have successfully been able to integrate captured gravitational wave segments within the pod sleeper's brain waves for these pictures, there are some inconsistencies in these sample images that the CONS has been able to process through IGIE thus far. These are the actual generated images for the Lagoon Nebula, as provided via IGIE," Phil indicates as he points to the screen.

"Compare them with the images captured via the Hubble telescope, for the same given spatial target area," he requests of the group. "You'll note the Hubble's resolution is still better. These IGIE processed images are not providing the enhanced digital resolutions we were expecting," he explains.

As he proceeds to a visual of the two images being displayed side by side on the projector screen, he continues speaking, "As you can see, there are still some visual blurs in the images being built by the pod operator telemetry simulator (or POTS) software program."

The room fills with silence as the participants dwell over the images. "However we believe that the IGIE design is still very viable, and just needs the networking of last two pods for a more complete and detailed resolution. Consequently, we still need to find at least two more of these pod sleepers to complete the expected compliment of six operators: one each for the six pod configurations," John concludes.

Associate 1: "Surely this process of trying to find viable candidates is wasting valuable resources. Wouldn't our time be better spent just integrating and training some of our own science personnel to pilot these pods? I mean, have you even tried?"

Associate 3: "You can't provide proper wave intermediation by introducing incompatible brain chemistry into the cooperative brain hive. So it's not a question of training. It's more like finding a donor for a medical transplant. We were lucky to have identified these current subjects as compatible."

Associate 1: "Compatible? I wouldn't necessarily use the term compatible. Their compatibility is specifically built into the system, around these candidate pod operators. Each CONS unit is tailored to the individual used to pilot it. Why couldn't we just do the same with some more scientifically minded individuals?"

Tom intervenes, "Actually, having more scientifically minded individuals is part of the problem. We are dealing with brain waves here, and not someone's understanding of astronomy or cosmology."

Phil continues, "Just so; a scientifically minded individual, as you put it, has a more strictly structured neural network; one which doesn't allow for the free flowing creativity needed to integrate with the carefully introduced gravitational waves. I know, because I've tried it on myself. We scientists tend to have preconceived notions of what we are expecting to see. In fact, most people have preconceived interpretations of how a vague shape or shadow should be organized. And this preconception is built differently into a person's psyche."

Phil explains in more detail, "It's like that psychological phenomenon, pareidolia (par-i-DOH-lee-a), which causes some people to see faces in vague or random images. It's a form of apophenia (a-pa-FEE-nee-a); which is a more general term for the human tendency to seek patterns in random information and data. Everyone experiences it from time to time. It is, rather, an evolutionary predisposition for survival. That is to say, it is an ability which allows one to avoid predators, or at least predators with eyes. It is this instinctive tendency that influences one's perspective, and provides for a less accurate rendering of the generated imaging. It is, in fact, this unconscious interpretation that interferes with a more structured mind's ability to provide for an accurate rendering of these images."

Dr. Margaret Beecher then joins into the discussion, "Additionally, the input to the CONS units for this brain wave integration is through dreaming: the subconscious feedback mechanism of images, ideas, emotions, and sensations that usually occur involuntarily in the mind of the subject during certain stages of REM sleep. Notably, dreaming is not just a random collection of sensations and emotions experienced in a state resembling mental confusion. Rather, dreams have an internal structure which reflects the individual's ongoing cognitive processes. Like waking cognition, the dreamer's experiences depend on a large-scale neural network, subtending distinct neuropsychological domains such as attention, memory, language, and mental imagery. Comparatively, lucid dreaming requires an increased awareness, similar to waking cognition. And it is this lucid dreaming that is required to provide for a viable basis for this integration."

Associate 2: "You say lucid dreaming similar to being awake?"

"Yes, in a fashion," Dr. Beecher continued. "Lucid dreaming is a form of dreaming in which the dreamer is, to some extent, conscious of their dreaming. And while not everyone is capable of understanding this conscious connection, those that do are actually able to participate in the dreaming process. And since an ordinary dreamer is not actively using any one part of their brain during the normal dream process, a lucid dreamer, especially one who can participate, actively uses conscious controls in their prefrontal cortex while the rest of their brain remains in a dream-like state."

"It is this mental ability that allows for the integration of the pod operators' brainwaves with the received gravitational waves. Essentially, we need individuals who can, to some extent, participate within their own dreams," Dr. Beecher states, driving her point home. "You can't train someone to be a lucid dreamer participant. As it is, some people can't even remember if they had ever been dreaming at all. These few pod operators have been selected for their lucid dreaming ability and their capability to influence their own neurological output, as determined during our individual sleep studies on them."

Associate 3: Expressing a demeanor of 'I told you so', he interrupts to add, "Just as I said: You can't provide proper wave intermediation by introducing incompatible brain chemistry."

Associate 1: "Well, if individuals cannot be trained to be pod operators and you have to build the unit around them, then how can we ever expect to predict a definite schedule for the project's completion?"

Associate 3: "I believe Dr. Beecher can continue to speak to this. After all, if it wasn't for her team's pioneering research in neuroimaging, in which these candidate pod operators were identified, we wouldn't be as far along as we are now. Isn't that right Dr. Beecher?"

Dr. Margaret Beecher responds to the open-ended inclusion of her expertise as a neuroscientist, "It is important to continue with the subjects from whom we have learned so much already. We have been able to map activity in their higher order brain regions that accurately predicts the content of the participants' dream state imaging. From this map, we were able to decode brain activity associated with the earliest stages of visual processing to provide a model that reconstruct these images. Matching their brain wave patterns during this reconstruction process allowed us to understand that their dreaming and visual perception share similar neural representations in the higher order visual areas of their brains. With this research, we are confident that we can onboard any new subjects in a much shorter time frame."

Associate 3: Hoping not to lose his audience, he intervenes: "Yes, yes; anyway, I have seen these neural imaging reconstructions. And they are remarkably similar to the computer animation of a movie, when strung together. These reconstructed images have the same visual key identifiers from our everyday experiences: light, dark, ground, sky, walls, floor, trees, grass, people, and even emotional interactions."

Tom mediates from the distraction, "I think you've made your point. So we will continue to have our teams on Earth aid us in identify new personnel that would be good candidates for operating our last two pods."

Associate 2: "I understand our teams on Earth have exhausted their search of potential subjects within the current professional pool of research laboratories working on neuroscience imaging. It's been almost a year since the last compatible subject was identified. Verdandi, wasn't it? Shouldn't we work on a solution for refining IGIE to work with four pods instead of six? Or perhaps using Verdandi in one of the command modules? I understand she has shown remarkable promise."

Dr. John Leighy speaks up more offensively, "Theoretically, it is not possible to work with just four units, no matter how you combine them together. It is more than just making it work with the current pod operators through just one command module. IGIE's algorithms are built upon a network defining the dimensional boundaries of any deep space location in our universe. And I don't have to tell you that the universe is constantly evolving."

"Think of it like this: where we have defined our space within the universe in four dimensions, we have traditionally defined it from a static perspective with respect to the evolving universe. So, from within this static spacial reconstruction, we can only ever identify ourselves within a four dimensional perspective of spacetime," he expounds upon the system interface. "Where there are three dimensions of Space and one dimension of Time to account for only three spacial directions, we are only able to generate its perspective from our singular directional bias. In a sense, it is a 2d picture which is manipulated to be a 3D image."

Associate 2: "It works fine for the Hubble. So how else do we want to be able to view it?"

"We need a more variable direction for Time if we intent to provide for a more 3D rendering from these received gravitational waves," Dr. Leighy answered. "As our fourth dimensional perspective only attributes one dimension for Time, it is merely meant to differentiate changes within our perspective of logical Space in three dimensions: height, width, and depth. That is to say, that our treating of Time in a singular dimension is primarily a concept of its ability to support a view of cause and effect from only one direction. This concept of one dimensional Time direction is often explained as the arrow of Time. We want to be able to analyze succeeding wave forms, layering them like a 3D printer to produce a 3D view of the target. In a sense we would be building a 4D holographic perspective of the deep space target from the real time processing of gravitational waves."

Associate 2: "And my thinking is that, with reconverted algorithms, four dimensions could be configured around four pods."

Dr. John Leighy responds to his simplistic solution, "Except that defining our existence in within this four dimensional perspective would only provide us with a three dimensional location from within a static spacial reconstruction. And since the universe is constantly evolving, we cannot expect to identify ourselves within such a simplistic, four dimensional perspective of spacetime. Time is not only moving in accordance with these cause and effect changes for a single target, but there is still a predominance of inflationary momentum, as well. Together with the concept of relativity due to gravitational forces, we needed to account for the temporal displacement of matter over variations in time, as well as for variations in space."

"In our case, from within a dynamic temporal reconstruction, we cannot track these spacial transitions within just a four dimensional perspective of spacetime, as defined in three spacial dimensions. Rather we must consider the fourth dimension is also a collaboration of these three dimensional frames of reference for time variations, as well as for space, we end up with six separate points to plot a location in spacetime. Essentially we need to identify the target location as it is perceived in the volume of a cube," he concluded.

Associate 3: "Six points; where there points are representative of time in three directions, as well as space."

Dr. Leighy continued, "Exactly! Subsequently, this measure allows us to use these three temporal directions in a manner with which to track and capture a more bidirectional perspective of a spacial reconstruction," he completes his foundational explanation, and stops to have a drink of water.

As he knows they are following his logic, he continues to lecture, "Thus, this modeling of spacetime norms within six dimensions, upon a fourth dimensional frame of reference, facilitates a 4D holographic perspective of the location in three dimensions of Space and three dimensions of Time. This is especially true of ingratiating gravitational variances within an expanding universe. So, in attempting to identify a non-static location in spacetime, not only must we identify Space in three dimensions, but we need also to define Time in three directions. The theoretical normalization of this technique would be similar to the concept of identifying a target area's position and tracking its motion within a cubical area of spacetime, whereupon its temporal momentum in each of the three spacial dimensions: height, width, and depth."

Associate 1: "That is a very elegant theory. How did you come up with it? I mean, I hope it wasn't from the movie, 'Stargate'," he stated in an attempt to be funny or demean its credibility.

So as not to get lost in the details of how they came up with the theory, Tom mediates once again, "The long and short of it, is that our instruments would have to be relatively co-located within the location being studied for us to use only four pods. Not to mention that the entire application of the theory on which IGIE is already based, is consistent with using these six dimensional parameters; and thus six pods are needed."

Associate 2: "So then we are committed to finding more of these compatible pod operators."

"Yes," Tom acknowledged, "and to this end, we have widened our search method to include institutes that specialize in Clinical Neuropsychology and lower level sleep studies. Admittedly a precursor to neuro imaging, but we might increase our chances of identifying a suitable candidate for our purposes."

Associate 1: "And how are the 'pod people' dealing with their life out here in outer space? I've heard rumors of psychological stress interfering with the computer system's ability to gather and process gravitational waves within the cooperative brain hive."

Tom calls on Dr. Beecher, "Margaret, perhaps you could address this concern?"

Dr. Margaret Beecher again joins in the discussion, responding, "Yes, there have been some anomalies that might be attributed to the well-being of our pod operators. But involving such biologics into the system is not like switching on a machine. Each individual has their own emotional baggage and needs for social interaction. We can try to orchestrate and limit their social interaction by hosting the group in separate buildings on the complex, away from the influence of non-research personnel, but it has its disadvantages. In each building, the staff needs to be counseled to cater to their needs, while the resident working population is counseled to make social interaction with them as comfortable as possible, and not to engage them in any manner that would cause them undo anxiety."

"Additionally, we also maintain weekly monitoring sessions with each of them separately, and as well as working with them daily in a controlled group," she concluded.

Associate 1: "That is all fine and well, Margaret. But what is the analysis for this summary of anomalies?" Associate 2: "Yes, how does 'how they feel' interfere with what we are seeing in the generated images?"

John speaks up, "I don't really see it as an issue with the CONS to IGIE technical interface. The associative brain waves are being mapped out by the integrator to allow only those neural circuits, with a specific focus on the neural substrates of the mental processes for cognition, to interface with the CONS. Simply stated; we do not need to target their entire brain. Additionally, there is an element of redundancy used by IGIE to compare and norm the data from all four operators."

Having brought up an interesting point, Margaret explains further, "What John is implying is that the portion of the brain that is being manipulated for interpretation, translation, and neural imaging of these gravitational waves is not really effected by the other less controllable portions of the brain. In fact, the advances we have made in non-invasive functional neuroimaging and associated data analysis methods have also made it possible to manage and mask the highly naturalistic stimuli and tasks associated with social interactions. In simpler terms, we can distinguish between the cognitive processes for the dynamic brain activations of spatial reasoning from that of the more creative or social cognitive processes."

Then Margaret suggested the alternative considerations for their ongoing monitoring. "However, what John might not be taking into account is that the holistic property of the brain's activity influences the ability of its parts to work with one another."

Associate 1: "So in affect, you're talking about right brain versus left brain activity; right?"

"Somewhat, but not quite," Margaret clarifies. "Creativity does not involve a single region of the brain nor even a single side of the brain. Rather, the entire creative process, from instantiation to illumination to verification, consists of many interacting cognitive processes, both conscious and unconscious, as well as the inclusion of emotions. Depending on the stage of the creative process, and what you're actually attempting to create, different brain regions are recruited to handle the various tasks. Many of these brain regions must work together to get the job done, from both the left and right side of the brain. Therefore, cognition results from the dynamic interactions of distributed brain areas operating in large-scale networks. So depending on the task, different brain networks would need to be engaged."

Associate 3: "So then how are you able to resolve the conflict of overlapping disciplines in the mind?"

"To some extent, we engage their creativity in a set predictable pattern by controlling their dreams," Margaret discloses to her audience.

Associate 2: "Controlling their dreams?"

"To be sure," Margaret answered. "We have provided for scripted dream scenarios, which are uniquely tailored to each subject. In this way, we can engage and distract their more creative or social cognitive processes. Basically, we divert those regions of the higher brain functions, in a predictable manner, so as to prevent them from interfering with their overall assigned tasks of interpreting and translating our input feed of capture gravitational variances for integration and neural imaging."

Phil interjects himself into the conversation to explain further, hoping to per-address any unnecessary side discussions, "And as each scripted dream is uniquely tailored in some form, the uniqueness of each brain requires that each pod unit must be customized and synchronized to their individual pod operator. This is also based on how we have been able to map activity in the higher order brain regions to accurately predict the content of the participants' lucid dream state involvement. Then a difference algorithm, used to differentiate and target the proper area of the brain, becomes a major portion of the customizable software needed to control what is fed through from the CONS units to IGIE."

Tom sees that the two associates are losing patience with the extended explanations being presented. Tom intercedes on the team's behalf, "Phil, Margaret, what I think the project team wants to know is that we, or you, understand the source of the anomalies and can account for it in your software, or even in your psychological group therapy, so that it does not continue to be a persistent pest of a problem."

"Uh, yes, well my team is continuing to analyze the results," Phil states almost apologetically. "They believe the current issue might be a partition problem in the logic difference for these algorithms. And although it is not yet nailed down, we are confident it will be resolved before the six pods are on line and networked."

"Fine, will take an action to revisit this issue at the next meeting," Tom announces, putting to bed any further discussion of this topic at this time. "Now does anyone have anything else to discuss?"

Associate 1: "I understand that you will be bringing in a non-scientist to consult on the project. What's that all about?"

Tom explains, "Yes, indeed; the Human Exploration and Operations Committee of the NASA Advisory Council would like for us to explore the concept of extending our program in the direction of dark energy research. And in short, we believe that there is more to this layman's research than mere science fiction."

Associate 2: "So what you are implying, then, is that we don't have his kind of expertise up here already. Please tell me that we have more qualified people to support this effort than just this writer."

Tom continues, "Yes, of course; we've established a team on Earth for this effort, and we are planning to employ them in seven weeks' time. The team on Earth is headed up by Dr. Valeria Pettorice, a physicist and cosmologist at the University of Geneva in Switzerland."

Associate 1: "What can we expect in the way of collaboration from this team?"

"They will augment the current research for detection of deep space gravitational density and motion," Tom stated diplomatically. "IGIE's prime operation will continue to be the creation of a precise 4D model map of astronomical objects throughout the Milky Way, using their gravitational density, direction and motions. The 'dark matter' team will be involved on a shared, trial period in which the IGIE images will be compared with GAIA images to validate its viability for dark matter detection, before focusing it on deep space target areas."

"Then, in a few months' time, the Dark Energy Space Telescope (Destiny), planned by NASA and DOE, will be deployed," he continued. "They are designed to perform precision measurements of the universe to provide an understanding of dark energy. The deep space observatory is expected to derive the expansion of the universe by measuring up to 3,000 distant supernovae each year of its three-year mission lifetime. Further, it will additionally study the structure of matter in the universe by measuring millions of galaxies in a weak gravitational lensing survey. Dr. Valeria Pettorice will be instrumental in helping us to coordinate the results of their research on Earth with ours up here."

Associate 2: "And what of our team up here?"

"Our team up here will be using this data to do a similar comparison with IGIE to validate its viability for modeling the nature of dark matter and exploring the behavior of dark energy as the mechanism driving the inflationary acceleration of the universe," Tom explained, without going into any detail as to who might be working on the team, or how the writer would be assisting the team.

Associate 1: "Fine, Fine…As long as it doesn't interfere with IGIE's primary operation. We don't want anything to deter any more from our planned schedule. And we certainly do not want to announce our mission capability until we are confident of our own results. While our investors are pleased with our results so far, they do not want this project open to undue scrutiny."

Associate 3: "Speaking of which, how are you managing the non-research overhead? Are we still under budget for this year?"

"Marco, maybe you could speak to this concern," Tom said, giving the floor to Marco Georgen. As Marco stood up to address the group, the screen was raised to brighten the mood in the room a bit.

"As you know, the staffing of non-research disciplines accounts for 55% of the facilities overhead, with another 20% spent on services to maintain quality of life. There is a continuing need for health and psychiatric personnel to monitor and participate in the governing and distribution of services for the non-research community. For the most part, it is in keeping with the predicted societal degeneration curve for two generations. However, the incidents of petty and misdemeanor crimes are starting to increase with the advent of a maturing second generation. If it continues, we may not be able to hold to the ten year non-disclosure clause to which we had everyone agree," Marco cautioned.

Associate 3: "Yes, these experiments in utopianism don't usually last beyond two or three generations. For any repeat offenders, I would suggest deporting the perpetrating member's family, or some portion of their family, back to Earth. After all, within the company contract, it is a privilege to work on the moon and not a right. We can better deal with the dysfunctional families back here, down on Earth, where it does not interfere with our project execution." He then adds, an aside, "Is the birth rate within acceptable limits?"

"Yes, so far. But due to the additional staffing we had to accept within the last two years, we had to start transferring some of the staff's families back to Earth," Marco reported. "And the current communities of the Kalama Atoll and its sister islands may not be enough to control this growth overflow within this ten year span."

Associate 3: "Well, you just leave that to us down here. However, if you can give us some project results sooner, then we can make our big announcement sooner, which may then alleviate the whole problem. The earlier we can start debriefing these families, the better we will be in the long run. In the meantime, just keep them busy and happy."

As Tom continues the administrative process of drawing the meeting to its conclusion, he is comfortable with the knowledge that the company is unaware of any military oversight on the project. Funding has been tight, and he had been forced to subsidize their venture with a little extra capital from the air force. A condition that he believes not anyone really needs to know this outside his small circle of trusted employees. Additionally, he is confident of his assurance that his alternative plans for the IGIE program have been well camouflaged; for it was he who initiated the contact with NASA to bring about an interest in dark energy research.

As for his hidden purpose to alter IGIE's primary operation, with the acquisition of the writer, Stephen Bauer, he had not given himself away. Rather, the inclusion of Stephen onto his team was not just a convenience; it was a necessity for the success of his more clandestine plan of operation. And of his knowledge in the credibility of Stephen's research, both fiction and non-fiction, he was not yet prepared to divulge; lest he reveal too much about the nature of his own credibility. Interestingly enough, their 'Stargate' theory was formalized on the basis of Stephen work in 'The Evolutioning of Creation: Volume 2'.

CHAPTER

6

The Synchronicity of Spacetime

**[Synchronicity between dreams and reality
are the gateways to understanding.]**

The following day Steve arrives home with a mix of emotions, not knowing whether the pursuit of his life's ambition isn't a bit selfish motive for 'pulling up roots'. They would all have to start over again, but it's better than having it all end in eventually ruin. Still, is it really fair to everyone else? Sure he will be making more money, and that is good for the family, but is that enough of a reason to displace them from the familiarity their family and friends.

Although such a displacement wasn't as difficult for Steve, who was used to distancing himself from society, Sandi seemed to always be homesick for security of her entrenched roots. Perhaps if he made a point of spending more time with family, the passing of time might fill her with more recent memories. Perhaps then chasing his dream would not be the regret of his more elder years, but could he say the same for her. Still, soon he would see Sandi, and that should bring everything back into focus.

[Narrator's Perspective]

Anxious to have her family all together again, Sandi patiently waits at the airport for Steve to arrive at their agreed meeting point. Upon seeing each other, both of them focus on reaching each other through the throngs of commuters that are seemingly wandering about. After a soulful hug and kiss, Steve notices the absence of Andrew, "Is he still upset with the move?"

"No, actually he's quite on board with the idea now," answered Sandi in an upbeat tone.

"Well that's good news," said Steve. "I felt guilty enough uprooting the family, without having to worry about being the cause of my son's depression." As they travel to the baggage claim area, Steve embraced the familiar sense of family and thinks of how it feels to be home again. "How did you change his mind?"

"Well, I can't take all the credit for that," she answered. "Things have changed for us since yesterday."

"Yes, they have," he agreed, thinking he knew what she was talking about. "They made me an offer that I couldn't refuse, or rather that I wouldn't want to refuse." Steve spotted his luggage and grabbed it off of the conveyor belt. As they walked towards the airport garage, he continued, "They offered to pay me a salary of $220,000. Can you believe it?"

"That's amazing," she replied. "That's more that than 3 times what you are making now."

"That's not all," he continued. "They have even offered to pay off our mortgage and to finance our entire move to their overseas location."

"Overseas; so then to where are we moving?" Sandi guessed with excitement. "To Hawaii?!"

"I can't say for sure," Steve responded, with some apprehension in his voice. "They're playing it 'close to the vest', so to speak. Initially they are moving us to an island in the Pacific, known as the Johnston Atoll."

"Initially?" she inquired. "Where is this job located?"

"They haven't told me more than that," he replied. "I had to agree to keep the project secret, before they would even 'officially' hire me on."

"Secret, huh? Well, where ever it is, it can't be all bad if we are together," she responded with optimism.

"Well, don't get your hopes up too much. I googled the location and it looks to be a collective of islands, the largest one being about 1 square mile, or about 12 blocks square; rather a small community," Steve said apologetically. "And pretty much away from everything."

"A place that size wouldn't even last through a hurricane. I wonder how it's lasted this long," Sandi responded with confusion. "It's almost as bad as having cabin fever, but without the cabin. Not only is there is nowhere to go, but it's nowhere to bring up a child," Sandi said as she sat down on an available empty bench.

It was difficult for her to work through her emotions while knowingly she was keeping a secret. She hadn't yet told Steve about the attack on Andrew, and that she was already thinking about moving away to a better location. But to such a small island; it just seemed all too harsh. It was as if her dreams of moving to safer environment had just been scrambled up in the bittersweet symmetry of life.

"It used to be an old navy air base, so I'm sure they have structures that can withstand a hurricane," Steve said, supporting the notion of it be safe. "It would only be for a short time. Think of it as an adventure."

"I'll go crazy there, I just know it. And it's certainly no place to bring up a child," Sandi complained to Steve. "There is no amount of money that could make such a small rustic island habitat attractive to me."

"Again, it's only a short stint," Steve reminded her. "They say it is just a 3 month period on the island; kind of like an orientation. It's not where the job is, so it can't be where we are going to stay."

"Then why would they be moving all of our belongings there?" she asked in an agitated tone. "Why don't they just wait to have it move to your new job location? And what about Andrew finishing high school and getting his degree? I can't imagine they have a real school environment there."

"I don't have all the answers," Steve responded calmly. "But the move will be completely paid for, and they assure me that they will be accountable for everything." Steve could see this wasn't going well, so he offered an alternative. "Listen, how about I make other arrangements? I'll go on ahead by myself for the next three months, and call you when I reach the final job location. Then you can stay back with Andrew until he can finish out his senior of high school back at home and get his degree."

Sandi thought for a moment. She worried that staying back at home would invite more attacks. After all, it would only be three months; about the duration of a summer vacation. "No, we are a family," she started out. "We need to support you in this."

"Really?" he asked with surprise. "I appreciate the offer, but I don't want to put a strain on our relationship. It's just not worth it to me."

"Really," was her simple reply. "It's like you said, it'll be our adventure."

"I was hoping you would see it that way, especially because I had to sign up for a ten year contract of exclusivity with the company. I agreed to work in this capacity only with them," he disclosed. "And they agreed that I would have job security for the same ten years, barring any breach of contract."

"You what?" she retorted. "You might as well be an indentured servant. We'll be stuck out who knows where until 2024."

"True, but I would be an indentured servant earning $220,000 a year. Think of what we can do with that kind of money. We could fully pay for Andrew's college and still have a hefty nest egg for our retirement," Steve tried to present the situation in the best light possible. "And I will get to do what I love, while still providing for the family I love. Besides, with this kind of money, you can make trips back to the mainland as often as you like."

"I can't help thinking that there is something they're not telling you," she thought aloud.

"I guess that would be the secret part to which I agreed to in the contract," he said with candor. "Whatever it is, it can't be worse than my current position. And if we ever decide to retire earlier, we'll have that much more money. As for the 'exclusivity' part of the contract, who else would ever want to hire me to consult on dark matter research? It's not a common profession, especially for someone without a graduate degree."

As Sandi drove them home, Steve related to her the events of his trip and the discussions around his job. During their discussion, Sandi kept the conversation flowing, but held back any information of Andrew's encounter and the appearance of Mairy. However, as they pulled up in the driveway, she couldn't contain the secret any longer, revealing, "We also have something to celebrate; or perhaps I should say someone."

His assumption was that she planned some surprise for his homecoming, "Oh, and what might that be?"

"Well, Andrew has a very special friend that he wants you to meet," she replied.

"Oh, OK, but it was a long flight. Perhaps he could just make it a short introduction?" he hinted.

"Well actually no, because she is more of a guest," was Sandi's answer, "and she is staying with us."

"What; Andrew brings his girlfriend from school home to stay with us, and you agreed to this. Wait, is she pregnant?" Steve teased.

"Oh, please; it is nothing like that at all," was Sandi's mischievous answer. "And she is not Andrew's girlfriend, so don't embarrass him about it. He's in a much better mood now, so don't ruin it."

Steve could discern that Sandi was being a bit playful, if not forth coming, so he was willing to play along. "Well then, who is she?" Steve continued to pry. "Is she part of some exchange student program?"

"Please, just let the introduction play out," Sandi insisted of him.

"OK, I guess I can deal with a guest for a little while." As Steve opened the door, he saw Andrew and some girl he had never met. Andrew spoke first.

"Hey, dad," Andrew greeted his father, "How's it going?"

"It's going great, and it's good to be back," he replied, giving him a quick hug. Looking beyond the hug, Steve caught a glimpse of Mairy. "So this is the friend of yours that your mom has been telling me about?"

"Yes, this is Mairy," Andrew answered.

"Well it's a pleasure to meet you young lady," Steve responded, shaking her hand. "You can call me Steve." Steve looked backed to Sandi for her approval, as well as for some help as how to what to do next.

"Thank you; and you can call me Mairy," she replied, repeating back what she thought to be an appropriate introduction. "Andrew has told me a little about you already."

"Dad, Mairy is a Shadow-Forge member of the Light Guild," Andrew added, trying to slip the 'Light Guild' reference in as part of the introduction.

Steve didn't know what to think. His first thought was that Andrew might be 'setting him up' for some elaborate joke. But since he was happy to see that Andrew was in a better mood, he decided to play along.

"A Shadow-Forge member; really?" Steve said with mixture of fake surprise and whimsy. "And are you also a member of this Light Guild then?" he asked of Andrew.

"Yes, I guess I am," Andrew answered with a hint of pride. "When I travel off world, that is."

"So when did you both become members of this important guild," Steve asked?

His first impression was that Andrew opened up to her about himself. And while it was an experience which the family had been keeping secret for some time, he could see that Andrew was in a much better state of mind.

"OK, Andrew; could you get your father's luggage from the car?" Sandi requested of Andrew.

She was not happy about the way the conversation was going. Sandi could see that Steve was just playing along with what he believed to be some sort of role play. But then she knew that was Steve's way; he would keep things non-confrontational until he could get a handle on what was going on.

Sandi then pulled Steve by the arm, saying, "We need to talk."

"What; I was being nice," Steve responded to Sandi.

As Steve walked off with Sandi, Andrew spoke with Mairy, asking, "Why didn't you just grab our hands again, as you did with mom?"

"You said that your dad's believing wouldn't be a problem," Mairy answered rather matter-of-factly.

Having pulled Steve off to the side, Sandi began to convince him of the seriousness of the situation.

"At first I was just as skeptical, and I thought the same as you did. But look at me; she is the real deal. She is really one of these Shadow-Forge characters. I mean, she merely touched me and I could see the truth of who she really was. I don't know how she did it, or how to explain it, but that girl in there is not human."

Steve had been with Sandi long enough to know when she wasn't kidding around. "You're serious, aren't you," he asked of her politely, trying to get his bearings on the situation?

"Yes, of course; when have you ever known me to deceive you in fun," Sandi confronted him?

Steve realized that this wasn't the moment to scan his memories for an answer to her question. It was probably best to let this question go by the wayside. "I hadn't realized," Steve replied apologetically. "Thank you; how do you think we should proceed with this then?"

"Just don't be so suspicious all the time," she advised. "I should have known better than to let Andrew surprise you like that," she acknowledged. "You don't take surprise well. But now that you know, perhaps you could display a modicum of respect and control over your mistrust."

"Sure, I can do that," Steve replied, not really knowing where to begin.

"She actually saved your son's life yesterday," she informed him.

"Saved him?!" Steve said, as he was taken aback. "Saved him how? What actually happened?"

"One thing at a time," Sandi cautioned him.

Sandi felt better now, having at least provided Steve with a context from which to engage them in a more meaningful conversation. And having been convinced of the reality of the situation, Steve became much more interested and somewhat enthusiastic. The more he believed, the more intense the discussion became. Over the next half hour, they discussed the events of yesterday and how Mairy came to save Andrew and be with them.

After being satisfied that they survived their encounter without injury, or at least without permanent injury, he immediately asked about her transformation to Earth. In point of fact, Steve had many questions about her which prompted a prolong discussion about her transition into their dimension, and what it was really like in her reality. In truth, Mairy fielded a variety a questions from every family member sitting round the kitchen table. Each response was scrutinized by Steve and logically weighed for consistency.

Eventually, the conversation began to involve a blur of distinction between the concept of a universal being and the religious reference of 'God'. Subsequently, with all this talk about the universe and God,

Sandi couldn't help asking her own important question, "With all the death and insanity that exist on our world, why can't the Shadow-Forge do more than just care for the health of the universe? If you are really doing his bidding, then why does he allow for such chaos to trample upon our lives? Some see this life as a gift from God, but for others this is not paradise. I mean, don't get me wrong, I feel blessed most of the time. But no one would wish to have any part of the mindless death and destruction that abides in this world. A paradise would not require the taking of one life to keep another alive. And it certainly would not embrace the selfish desires of some people to weigh their survival and comfort above all others. There should be no disease or mental state of abrogation to allow for this."

Steve reached across the table and held Sandi's hand. "Sweetheart, living and dying is not what the universe is all about, it is what evolution is all about. And as for the control of it all, it may not even be what the concept of 'God' is all about. The grand nature of existence has been set in motion. As I understand it, these celestially orchestrated beings can no more alter our destinies, or theirs, than they can stop the Earth from evolving, or the universe from expanding. And yet, as we are led to believe, without them, our very existence may falter at any moment. It is a strange relationship, to be sure, that they are connected in a way that continues to only promote the health of our universe, but I see it as a good thing. In my opinion, it is kind of like the way white blood cells protect us in our own bodies."

Mairy interjected herself into the discussion, explaining, "Actually we are all connected. But the choice to embrace chaos or harmony is not an obvious one, but it is a choice. But to use your analogy, we are not all white blood cells. The universe is but a vessel for all our states of being. Just as we are the embodiments of our own 'being' within the living universe, so the living universe is but the embodiment of its own 'being'. And this 'being' has many degrees of reality. Within your degree of reality, the containment of your 'being' is expressed from within the limitations of your physical host. Similarly, the containment of the universal 'being' is expressed, for us, from within the limitations of its existence. Do you follow me so far?"

While they all nodded in agreement, there was no assurance that any of them, save Steve, could really grasp some the complexities of what Mairy was trying to relate to them. Like a college professor, Mairy continued to slowly introduce them to these new concepts.

"At another degree of reality, the containment of your 'being' is expressed from within the limitations of your essence. You can think of your essence as the convergence of your life force, which flows within and throughout all of existence," she enlightened them. "So where the limitations of your more physical manifestations are maintained via your body and skin, the limitations of your essence are maintained within the aural veil of your convergence. This aural veil is fundamental to the health and harmony of your essence, as well as to you more physical form. The health and harmony of your essence is central the balance of your life force and the field of your connections within the universal being. At least this is how it was passed down to me, and my kind."

While they tried to take it all in, it turns out Mairy was leading up to Sandi's earlier question, observing, "However in my many reincarnations, I have learned a great many things. As it was revealed to me on Glorthocks, this reality is but a transformation to the next. Whereupon this paradise, you speak of, is not a place. Rather it is more of an understanding of purpose and our overall connections to the life force. It seems to be a cruel trick of fate that we must live one life in a more physically limited reality before passing into the next. It is as if we are meant to develop and prepare ourselves for what is to come. And even we, who exist outside of your reality and embrace multiple incarnations, do not understand it all."

Pausing a moment, Mairy set up with a purposeful conclusion for her revelations, remarking, "Though, inexplicably, there are but only few of these many life forms who are able to embrace the balance of their own life force, and are able access their field of connections within the being of the universe. These few have can become to be known as the Shadow-Forge. As a Shadow-Forge works from within the expression of their aural veil, the health and harmony of their essence is essential. Any disharmony within their essence can promote the cause of disease, chaos, or even insanity within their life force."

"As such, disharmony can manifest itself within the physical host body, in which their aura is contained, as well. If one's essence is out of balance, it is a reflection of the chaos within one's force. Similarly, if the balance of the universe is out of sorts, good or bad, then the whole of one's reality reflects the nature of that imbalance. For it is one's reality that drives the identism of their next reality, and our even their transformation into it," she concluded, expounding upon her beliefs.

"Well, it is just cruel," Sandi continued to dwell on the injustice of life's unfairness in her present reality. "It's like dangling water out of the reach to a populace insane with thirst. The universe may as well be promoting the gladiator games of old Roman times. And to think madness may even continue into the afterlife is quit maddening."

"Of the afterlife, I cannot say. But for this life, chaos will always continue to pervade as the cycle of consumption which seeks to supplant existence within the universe," Mairy acknowledged.

Just then, Andrew suddenly realized that he had drifted into experiencing a déjà vu event. He was familiar with these experiences which have come upon him from time to time, over the years.

Steve tried to re-summarize, "So you are saying that all of us are maintained by way of our life force, our own inner aural veil. And it is the balance of our life force, or qi, which keeps us healthy and centered." Steve went on to correlate the similarities of this explanation to existing Chinese philosophy, "What you are saying is amazing. It is so like the duality of yin and yang as an indivisible whole; where the imbalance begins to affect one's health, sleep, emotions, focus and relationships."

As the family discussion progressed, Andrew became aware of Mairy's presence as a repeat of another time before, in this same location. As the placement of people in the room became just as familiar and he found he could predict their actions, even as they unfolded before him.

Then Mairy looked straight to Andrew. "And this is the most important principal of being a Shadow-Forge," Mairy said in a tone of caution. "Where one's balanced cannot be maintained, one's aural veil can give way, allowing one's essence to be turned inside out. Once this happens, then one's aural veil, or field of life force containment, is lost. And without containment, one's essence renews its balance by embracing its purpose within the aural veil containment of the universal being. And as the balance of the universe being is paramount to all existence, there is no known returning from this loss of individual aura containment."

As this hit home with Andrew, he couldn't help wondering how he had survived the rages of the black hole. So he explored further, questioning Mairy, and prognostically knowing what he was to say even as he said it, "With what you just said, how was it that I then survive the disintegration of the black hole?"

It was strange to for Andrew to hear himself say the words during this déjà vu experience. It was as if whatever he said was just what he was supposed to have said; like he had no control over the experience. It was as if he was removed from his own experience; being able to participate while also knowing what he would be saying as he said it. In fact, for the next 3 to 4 minutes, he knew what everyone in the room was going to say and do, as well as the change displayed in the flickering of house lighting and the familiar smell of Mairy's aroma as she leaned over the table. It all seemed to be the reawakening of a lost memory.

"You proved yourself to be a true Shadow-Forge upon that day," Mairy started. "Fortunately our auras do not operate within the same degree of reality as our corporeal host bodies. Rather our auras exist within a more metaphysical frame of dimensional reference inside the astral plane. So while your transition into the black hole scrambled your essence, your aural veil remained intact."

"Verily, with our help, we were able to make you whole again. Yet the process was not without problems. Your spirit could not be reanimated without an inspiration of purpose. Having made you whole again, it was still not enough to entify your spirit," Mairy recalled.

"Not enough to 'entify' my spirit... what do you mean by entify?" Andrew asked.

"It means that we were not able to properly reconnect you within your own reality, or to your own host form for that matter," Mairy tried to relate a meaning to the term. As Andrew gave a puzzled look, Mairy tried to gather the words that would explain the situation.

"Oh, how would you say it? We were not able to bring you back into existence because your life force had no real purpose anymore. So I comingle some of my essence within your own. In this way, I was able to conjoin our mutual life forces to provide for the spark in which to reanimate your scrambled essence within larger aural veil of our group aura. Harmony did the rest," she summarized. "Harmony was able to rejoin you back within your own individual containment as a life force."

Steve then broke in, trying to highlight what Mairy had explained to us, "If I understand you correctly then, you were able to bring Andrew back into existence by re-enlivening his purpose; kind of like using a defibrillator to bring one's heart back into rhythm. And by re-enlivening his purpose, he was eventually able to reform his own aura, with Harmony's help, and regain the true balance within his own essence."

"Fascinating; so this aural veil is just one more layer of containment for a Shadow-Forge to be able to exist outside of our own bodies," was his presumption.

Steve was in his element, translating the secrets of an unknown universe to us, as being relayed to us by Mairy. It was probably the best family discussion they have ever had.

As Andrew continued to examine the details of his déjà vu experience as they unfolded, the experienced faded. Kind of like when he tried to focus upon the flitting lights in the woods. Such déjà vu events always left him second guessing the nature of their timing. Did this all really happen before; or is there something special about the experience that needed to be understood? Or was it that he had he lived this life before, but could only remember this particular moment in time?

Like a bridge in time, perhaps he was he being presented with a decision point from which his life might go in differing directions? What choice might he had taken previously? Would this decision have any special import on his destiny or fate? Could this be an inspirational pause speaking to him from his universal connection? Still, he thought to himself, maybe it was enough that he gave the information, which was presented in their discussion, just a little more focus.

Indeed, the discussion challenged the concepts of what they all thought they knew about ideas that they had been taught since they entered the age of reason. The conversation enlivened and renewed an otherwise dysfunctional family, unifying them with a grand purpose to be part of something greater than themselves.

It may have not been how they originally thought their lives would have evolved over time, nor would it be the retirement the parents expected, but it would be something they could all experience individually and together. And living, for all its strife as the engine that drives the evolution of the universe itself, was thereby proposing an even grander purpose for the collective in the being of their existence; each evolving soul being true unto its own purpose.

For Sandi, this was validation of her belief in her son, as well as a renewed faith in Mairy, who kept Andrew safe and brought him back to her. For Steve, who was always a believer, he felt re-invigorated about his prospects and the promise of the part he was about to play in this grand purpose. For Mairy, haunted by the mistakes of her past, it seemed to be her chance at redemption. And as for Andrew, who always felt cheated by Fate, everything seemed to come together. It was as if his wish on that shooting star had been granted, for better or worse. In fact, it was upon this day, this very evening, in which they created a bond that would support each of them in their time of need; a bond that would support each of them in the quest they had yet to realize.

And while the Shadow-Forge may not have been great caretakers of the poor, weak, or helpless, they are be able to keep the universal being in balance so that everyone could live yet another day. And, if Fate would allow it, this would be the day upon which their mutual destinies would come together to meet the greatest challenge the evolving universal being would ever encounter: The involvement of chaos to reorder the universe in their image.

[Narrator's Perspective continued]

[The causality of fate is reflective of a fifth dimension.]

Andrew slept deeply that night, remembering his dream clearly upon waking up. Or was it really a dream? He remembered that he fell into an odd sort of sleep. While his encounter with the beast the day before was still fresh on his mind, his unexpected déjà vu experience that evening made for an uncomfortable atmosphere from which he maintained a wary sense of foreboding. His mind raced with the few clues it had, trying to piece together a resolution to the enigma of their encounter with the beast, and its mission.

Was the beast's mission been crafted as merely a ploy to bring Mairy into our reality, Andrew speculated; and if so, then why now and why here? Or was its mission to involve both of them in a new quest. And if this were a new quest, then why wasn't it presented to them through Harmony?

Then again there was the ominous pre-warning which couldn't have been clearer: 'I am here to herald the fate of all humans'. It seemed quite bizarre to him that his reality would once again clash with such a real threat, here in his own backyard. Still, would just the fate of all the humans on Earth be enough to tip the universal balance?

Still, it would certainly be the end for him; for not being of Shadow-Forge form himself, he would surely die in his physical form. And there would be no coming back from it this time. However mindful he was of the danger that they were in, and however determined he was to work out the nature of this unknown quest that lay before them, he finally succumbed to the mental fatigue created in the solace of his own thoughts.

Strangely enough, it would be Andrew's singular determination for the survival of his family that would allow him to reconnect with a previously forgotten mental state of meditation. It was a subconscious state which he had long abandoned upon many years of disappointments. While Andrew would regularly dream, he had seemingly lost or ignored his ability to recognize his participation in the dream.

It was this situation of renewed danger in which he found himself, and his family, that had finally unlocked the subliminal repression of his abilities as a Shadow-Forge. Whether it was the memory of his journey through space and time, or his near death experience within the black hole, his mental acuity was now on autopilot. He fell deeply into a meditative state of REM sleep that immersed him into a zero gravity state of connection outside of his consciousness.

Before him, Andrew could see a sea of stars twinkling in the night sky. As he gazed downward, he found himself standing in the backyard of the house. It was a familiar for him to be looking up to the stars, as he has often done since his return to home after his previous quest. However, this time he was mindfully unaware of how he got there. He left the backyard and attempted to retrace a path back into the house. He continued up the stairs towards his bedroom to see if being in the room would jog his memory. Maybe he had been sleepwalking, he thought to himself.

As he persisted up the stairs, the route seemed unusually steep and long. Oddly enough, the further he made his way up, the more his vision became blurry. As he continued to ascend, he slowly began to lose sight of his immediate environment and tried to make out some detail of familiar impressions that would reaffirm to him where he was. Not seeing clearly as to where he was going, he finally reached the top, only to find himself in the basement of his former high school. He chose the nearest exit door, which only lead him into an open area where the high school swimming pool was located. The pool emitted an eerie brightness, refracting the design of the water's motion upon the ceiling and walls of the room. As he made his way to the pool, he could see trails of light swimming about beneath the surface of the water. Trying in vain to get a grasp on what was happening to him, Andrew continued to move forward towards the water.

In his astonishment, he began to witness the snakelike streams of light extending up from out of the pool and into the air above and then around him. As he reached out to touch the lighted surface, he found himself immersed within a sphere of water above the pool. Hoping to reorient himself, he looked up to the ceiling, only to see stars once again through the translucent surface of the water.

Refocusing downward, he was amazed to find that he was now hovering over a large pond. Looking below, beyond the bubble of his containment, he realized that it was a more familiar setting than he had first realized. It was the large pond from where he first met Harmony. All of the sudden, his supportive bubble-like capsule began to fail and burst in mid-air, as if it was all being maintained in a zero gravity environment. Below him, the ground was breaking up and swallowing the pond water into a swirling abyss.

While his bubble-like containment kept him afloat, he watched as the newly implanted redbud tree was revealed. Inexplicitly the bubble started to descend until it burst upon the branches of the redbud tree. All at once, the redbud tree began to be suck down into the vibrating earth. Without the safety of his containment, he found himself plummeting towards the ever enlarging sinkhole. Andrew's instinctive sense of survival appeared to stop him short of being swallowed up along with everything else. He hovered just above the ongoing destruction below, trying to remember his training and his ability to fly. Focusing upon center of his life force, as he had been taught, he escaped the predicament of his situation by ascending above it all. The higher he soared, the faster he traveled.

Now, rising up into the sky, his remembrance of Harmony drew him to search for her. If she would not come to him, then he would seek her out. Seeking the security of Harmony, Andrew's search took him up beyond the atmosphere of Earth. Yet as he looked back again, he found himself overlooking a spherical structure amongst a barren wasteland; neither of which he had ever seen before. His continued his search deep into space, amidst a visage of galaxies and nebulae.

As he floated through deep space, it all seemed quite second nature to him. He envisioned the distant stars embedded in false colored gaseous images. However such false color imaging was only similar to what he had previously seen in books with pictures of the universe, as taken by the Hubble telescope. It was a clue to his lucid dream state that he precipitously discounted. As the false colored images faded, he embraced a familiar but distant memory of having been, were he now was, before; a kind of astral déjà vu.

Indeed, he recalled, this is what he sensed before when he connected within the great omnipresence that is the universe. Indeed, he thought to himself, this is the prescient point at which he found he could comprehend creation as the dimensional potentials of non-existence held forth to be animate in the expatiation of a presence for existence. It all seemed to make perfect sense to him again. All was right and true within the nature of his own being. He had thought the memory of this moment in time to have been lost to him forever and yet here is was again. It was all upon this moment in Time and Space that he seemed to understand the grandeur of it all; for it was everything all at once. It felt like he was touching upon the aethereal plane of existence, once again, within that moment. This is where Harmony must be, he surmised. Still, it was only for a moment, and then the moment passed. And yet somehow, this next moment was different.

He felt as if he was suddenly embraced by some larger force beyond his control. As he attempted to identify and learn more about this force, Mairy came into view. As he reached out to Mairy, he suddenly touched upon the identity of the force that had seemingly entangled him. Upon this touching, there was a crack of light that appeared out of nowhere in front of him. As the crack began to grow, it persisted against a darker background. Andrew watched as Mairy was pulled backwards into the rift and away from him. He frantically chased after Mairy into the rift, where he was filled with a sense of ongoing electrical shock.

Then abruptly, he felt an even stranger gripping sensation rippling through him and throughout the aether of spacetime about him. His omniscient perspective of the stars and distant nebulae became distorted in the ever increasing illumination that overcame his purview. And of his familiar sense of enlightenment, all that he felt, all that he knew, and all that he was, was disappearing.

The light poured in upon Andrew like a deluge; from every direction and he was without sensation of any kind. It seemed to him to be like the opposite of omnipresence; where he was no longer in touch with any part of the universal being. In point of fact, it was as if he seemed to exist outside of any Space and Time. He was not so much lonely as he was alone; separate of any known reality and excluded within an eternal void. And yet the void was not an abyss of darkness, but rather one of light where there was no imagining of what could not be perceived. There were no shadows of ambiguity because there was nothing to be perceived.

Nothing felt real to him forever more; he was in the 'nowhere' that was 'now here'. He could only subsist within the solace of his own reflection upon what he used to be; or of what he used to be a part, but was no longer. And that reflection was not enough to maintain the sanity of his realm. In this blinding light, his memories were illuminated upon the hallucinogenic canvas of his psyche. He felt he was in contact with his old friend, Harmony. He believed he could hear her thoughts being communicated to him, *"Consider who you are and where you are going. Let your hopes and dreams guide you through your darkest fears. You are more than physical form. Find the center of your life force. Only there can you realize the purpose and vehicle of your journey."*

Then, without warning, there was a second sensation of electricity sent rippling throughout his being. And all at once, Andrew felt reconnected; once again plugged into the universe. And yet, this connection was somehow strangely foreign to him. For some odd reason, he no longer felt that he had the same feeling and understanding about his spacetime as before the unusual event. Rather he felt he was at the center of a new existence, or perhaps more like at the moment of a new creation. He did not perceive any of the familiar sensations of form and volume that were once part of his known universe. Where was his sense of an evolved universe, he thought? What happened to the 'being' that was his universe? As the bright light now dimmed, he was unable to perceive of any forming miasmas of swirling gases; there were no evolving star systems, nor even any systems of interacting black holes. It was as if the universal being had been wipe cleaned and was beginning anew. This new environment was so unnatural that it became the nightmare from which he awoke from his deep slumber.

As Andrew lay in bed and dwelled on his dream, he felt secure in the realization that it had actually never happened. Somehow this surreality which had been embraced by him, as part of his conscious memories, was perhaps another vision of some distant event. He could even remember the details, much like what his dad had related to him of his astral projection experience while he was in the military service. But these were not of any places that he had ever visited or of which he was ever really even a part.

Maybe Andrew had tripped upon a way for the brain to tap into a fifth dimension, of which his father once related to him. Perhaps there was a way to traverse all of our possible fates, and come up with memories that could guide us during our lifetime, and then, somehow, convey a premonition of future events. After all, that's what dreams do, as mother had previously told him. Dreams work through emotional states and reorganize the information to allow one to continue to survive. Being able to connect with the future possibilities via such a fifth dimensional threshold would certainly make sense of his déjà vu experiences. It would be rather like unlocking a mystic portal within the landscape of his own dream to travel into his own mind's eye; the eye of a more psychic storm.

He recalled the particularity of his first experience, when he was invited to join his friends in forming a rock and roll band. As the band practice progressed in the strange surroundings of a 'friend of his friend's basement, he brusquely became aware of having been there before, though he never had been. His surroundings became weirdly familiar, and he found he could predict all of their actions as they unfolded. For the next 3 to 4 minutes, he knew what everyone in the room was going to say and do, as well as himself. He expected the change in natural lighting from the window against the basement furniture, as if the sun went behind a wisp of a cloud for only a moment. Once again, he recognized the familiar smell of chlorine from an almost empty bottle of bleach that the dog had just tipped it over. As he continued to press for more prognostic details, the experienced ended. After that experience, he never returned to that basement and he never became a member of that band. To this day, he is not sure how much his déjà vu experience played into whether that choice was a conscious decision on his part.

Indeed, his déjà vu experiences tended to fill him with a strong sensation of simultaneous prognostication and predestination. Yet, the interpretation of this sensation was certainly elusive. Could the event, currently being experienced, have already been experienced perhaps in some past lifetime? Or could it have just been the actual experiencing of a future possibility that had perhaps been previously stored in his memory via one of his dreams. For in one's dreams, the mind is set free to expand upon the probabilities of cause and effect. That might explain the unique perspective of reliving an event that had not previously happened, but has been stored in one's memory.

Still, anyone who has experienced déjà vu can relate how each sense is in sync with the event as it unfolds; The sight, the sound, the smell, even touch and taste. One can almost predict how it will play out as it is occurring. And then, just as suddenly as the experience happens, it ends and everything is back to normal again.

However, Andrew thought to himself, these déjà vu experiences might be more than mere happenstance. Perhaps, rather, they could be guideposts of opportunities: Serendipitous or Zemblanitous opportunities to influence one's destiny. Whereupon these more haunting experiences are more reflective of reliving a moment in time, they may be decision points that need to be reflected upon; so as to keep ourselves on the right path. But if the intent is to keep one on the right path, how is one to really know which is the right path? For if one is really just about to relive an upcoming future possibility, as being reflective of a repeated past lifetime event, isn't it like a resetting of that past lifetime event except for this decision point.

Consequently, if we are reliving a reincarnation of a past decision point, then how is one to know which path they chose previously? It's like having one's memory reset, except for this decision point. So, even as we are presented with this guidepost of opportunity again, are we then not doomed to repeat the same mistakes? Perhaps it is all just a cruel jest of Fate that would allow us to believe that we even have free will.

CHAPTER

7

The Chain of Events Unfold

[Be Careful what you wish for]

Steve slept uneasily, kind of 'on watch', due to the unsettling nature of their discussion. This beast sounded like it was a nasty character, who might come back to raise more havoc. As the rest of the family slept more deeply through the evening, he was inclined to sleep more lightly; periodically aware of the odd strange noise. Partly it was difficult to sleep because his mind was racing with the information Mairy had presented to them. He had often obsessed upon the cosmological makeup of the universe. And now, here, he was privy to more secrets than he ever thought possible. Partly he thought of how he might keep everyone safe, while still having to leave in the morning to start his new job. Such choices need to be weighed and measured. Such decisions were not meant to be made in haste. Perhaps, he thought, it would be best to take some time off before beginning his new job.

Mairy, on the other hand, was not used to sleeping much at all. It was never really ingrained as part of her nature. Her periodic transformations into Shadow-Forge form were not enough to instill her with the circadian rhythm of other organic life. She was not one to wait for life to happen around here. Rather she would seek out and explore her environment; mapping out its dangers and pitfalls. She was a survivor. While the rest of the family drifted off into slumber, she returned to the scene of their encounter with the beast, to investigate for clues as to its existence and purpose.

A strange storm rolled in overnight, bringing with it the revelry of thunder and lightning that are characteristic of autumn storms. The night sky light up in the distance, only allowing the echo of thunder to reach their location. It would not rain here tonight, but the storm would provide cover for other atrocities. There would be no 'cat and mouse' hunting this evening, as the beast had other targets in mind for this evening. Mairy stealthfully retraced her steps, searching for clues along the lightning lit path. As fate would have it, their paths would only cross indirectly at the site of her emergence into this world. Upon her arrival at the site, she witnessed the scourge of the beast's wrath. In the sporadic lighting of the impending storm, she beheld the vandalism of her birthplace. The magic of the meadowlands was lost forever to its carnage.

[Andrew's Perspective]

I came down to the smell of breakfast, only to find that I was the last one to wake up. I was still haunted by the nightmare from which I had no control. I guess I had much to consider upon the chain of events that were now unfolding before us. And the 'jury was still out' on whether dad would be comfortable with us staying here while he would be miles away from us. Perhaps now, that Mairy is here to watch over mom and I, it would not be necessary to leave; or at least, not right away.

"There he is," his mom joked, greeting him with a smile. "I thought you were going to sleep the day away."

"I feel like I've been gone for the whole day," I replied.

"Whatever do you mean," mom asked with curiosity?

"Did you have a rough night's sleep," dad asked with equal curiosity?

"I did have a wicked dream," I started, "and it was really vivid. It was much like the one I had when working with Harmony before my journey to Glorthocks; as if some alternate reality was being revealed to me."

"Yes, finally," Mairy joined in with excitement. "You say this happened before; before you went to Glorthocks? Tell me about that earlier dream."

"OK; from what I can remember, even before I even left from Earth and went to Glorthocks, I dreamt about the shooting star that came streaking in between the two bonded planets of Glorthocks and DeMutron. While in that same dream, I even remember watching the crystal as it seemingly enlarged a portal into and through the black hole. Then again, later, while I was on the Glorthocks, I dreamt about finding you in the crystal in advance of it even encountering the black hole."

"This is a very rare gift, indeed," Mairy stated with excitement. "While I can only sense a feeling of future events, it appears you actually have visions of them. So what did you see in your dream last night?"

"Well, 'the long and short of it' was that I ended up at the site of the meadowlands, but not as it is now. It still had a large pond, like it was before and during the appearance of Harmony. I was floating over the pond in a water bubble, as I had seen upon her arrivals. Suddenly the water drained away to reveal the redbud tree, where you brought me yesterday. Upon my touching the redbud tree, my bubble burst and the ground began breaking up beneath me. I watched as the redbud tree began to sink into the vibrating earth," I recalled of my dream.

"I was only able to escape being pulled into the sinkhole as well, because was able to rise above it; as Harmony had taught me. Having been reunited with this feeling of flying, I launched myself into space to find Harmony. Instead, I found you," I related.

"But only for a moment, because a crack then opened up in the emptiness of space, and you were sucked out from my reality. In my panic to save you, I had a revelation. I remember thinking that the whole of an empty space, outside of my existence, didn't seem to make any sense. It was like the universe was leaking out into some kind of alternative abyss. But the abyss was not dark. Instead, it was filled with blinding light from every direction. Then, all at once, everything seemed to revert back to normal. Yet, it was somehow all different; like I was a different universe altogether," I explained of my reasoning.

"Perhaps the crack opening up in the emptiness of space could have been something like a temporary rift in spacetime," dad spoke up to hypothesize. "In which case, the abyss beyond the opening could very well have been a perspective of dark energy."

I watched as mom looked disapprovingly at dad, similar to how Mairy had done with me when I interrupted her connecting with mom.

"It is part of a theory on which I have been working," dad stated, seemingly to imply as an apology for his interruption. "Within a black hole, the perspective should be of light coming in, but never getting out. The black hole's center should be one of complementary negative mass density, wherein nothingness would be amplified to its extreme," dad explained. "So, from the perspective of someone inside, all light would be rushing towards them."

"Yes, that's what it seemed like in my dream," I admitted. "Or, at least, your explanation sounds right to me.

"This is quite interesting," Mairy surmised. "I believe we are all meant to take a part in your father's research. Somehow between your vision and your father's interpretation, there is a connection."

"Vision?" mom remarked with doubt. "Isn't that that quite a leap from dream to reality," mom stated, trying to deal with the new information as best as she could. "We can't live our lives through our dreams. What even makes you believe that he even has this ability for visions? We don't even know if any of this is real."

"Actually, I do. I didn't want to say anything until we were altogether, but I got up early this morning and took a walk back the meadowlands," Mairy conveyed to us. "It's all destroyed. It was as if the great redbud tree had sunken into the ground, and everything else looks as if it was pulled under with it. How could he have known about all that?"

"How could that much destruction have even happen overnight, would be a better question," dad remarked; "and without me hearing it."

"I'm not sure. But I'm afraid if it could happen there, then it could happen here," mom portended.

"You make a good point," dad agreed. "I propose we should be ready to leave as soon as possible."

"What, now?" I exclaimed. "Aren't you both just being a little overdramatic here?"

"Andrew, think about it. I'm sure we have to the beast to thank for this. It has to be the work of the chaos," Mairy explained to me. "Discordia is cutting us off from being able to contact my kind. We are truly on our own now."

"Great, now the universe is against my staying here," I bemoaned.

"Not the universe, just Discordia," Mairy inferred.

"These events are just too dangerous to ignore," mom chimed in.

"Agreed," dad acknowledged. "We can always make arrangements to have our stuff moved later."

"Are you sure your company is willing to make that commitment now," mom asked?

"They'll have to if they still want me. Besides, they offered to buy the house and finance our entire move," dad reminded mom. "So that is what we are going to do. Let's pack just what we need for an extended two week vacation, and be ready to leave by this afternoon. In the meantime, I'll give them a call and get things rolling."

I sat down in disappointment, as I saw his parents kick into 'high gear' panic mode. For all my planning about staying behind for just a little while longer, it appears that fate had just open the 'flood gates' of anxiety from which there was no return. I knew fate was not to be trusted. Even as I knew it was the right thing to do, I still felt the loss of my connection with this place and the memories it held for me.

"You kids finish having some breakfast, while we make some phone calls," was mom's immediate task for us. "Then you can start packing for a two week vacation."

Although her command was really only meant me, because Mairy had nothing to pack, it really wasn't going to be just a vacation because we wouldn't be coming back. I looked to Mairy, who had just arrived via that singular redbud tree.

"There was nothing left there of the redbud tree?" I asked her empathetically.

She just shook her head in a negative manner, as she continued to eat.

⁂

[Scene Change – Mother's Perspective]

[Maturing can take on many forms.]

As I made final preparations for our travels, I watch as Andrew seemed to embrace the solace of the moment. How does one just leave behind their childhood, their ultimate identity, I thought to myself? As an adult, it is usually a choice to break free of one's childhood. But when one is not ready to move on, it can leave a scar that is not easily healed. Sure they did this once before with Andrew, but he was younger and less attached to his surroundings. And indeed it can be said that he had left home before without us, but it was only in his belief that he would be coming back. However, this time it would be for good, rather like when we first moved here. I could only imagine that all his memories were conspiring to pull him back to a simpler time: a time before he knew nothing about an existence of life beyond Earth. To him, his home, this neighborhood, and even the friends he made were a big part of his maturing identity.

Yet, in truth, everyone was growing up all around him, and soon he would be the one left behind. It's just the nature of things; with growing up comes separation. Sometimes, no matter how hard one tries to nurture a relationship, friendships just grow apart.

I remember Steve explaining how his life was turned upside down when he was drafted into military service. He had to make the decision to either run away from his obligations or to accept his fate. And all along he knew that he would not be able to share these new experiences with anyone he had previously known or befriended. Hoping that, upon his final return home to stay, he could expect that everything and everyone would be the same. He assumed the investment of his former relationships would survive.

I thought of how he embraced that decision, knowing that he was never one to avoid a challenge. Perhaps that's from where Andrew gets his tenacity. But life goes on, and he soon realized that his old familiar neighborhood had changed and his friends had moved on to other interests. And while he was gone, he had made new friends; friends which had shared his experiences and thus invested in him. Still, for Andrew, it would be like ripping off a band-aid; painful at first.

Having collected what we needed for this impromptu vacation, I had everyone arrange their stuff on the driveway while we waited for Steve's return. I then spent time reviewing the ordinance of items gathered to see it there was anything missing or not thought of. I looked to Andrew to engage him in verifying what he had packed, but it just didn't seem to be his major concern at the moment. A mother can tell when their child is in pain, or at least a mother should be able to tell.

I passed my list off to Mairy, asking, "Could you check out these last few items on the list?"

She had no problem granting my request. I then walked over to Andrew and gave him a hug.

"Time to go," I said simply.

"I know," he acknowledged. "I spent my entire life in that house; well almost."

"Think of it like another adventure," I reiterated the mantra of the family. "You've been to another planet. Surely a move to another location just across the globe won't inconvenience you too much. Besides you have responsibilities now; you need to look after your new friend, Mairy."

"I'm not sure who is looking after whom," he acknowledged, "but I get your point."

With that, Steve pulled up in his car and secured it in the garage, and then joined us on the driveway.

"Everything go as planned?" I asked.

"Without a hitch; I gave notice at my old job and left my personal stuff in the car. Our new employer was able to provide for the emergency papers to get Mairy on the plane with us to Hawaii. From there, we will be picking up private transport, so papers won't be a problem. Everyone ready?" he asked, as he does prior to each family trip. "The limousine should be here soon."

But this time he was not joking about traveling in the family car, it was to be a real limousine. "Here it is now," I observed, as the limousine pulled up. The driver spared little time with introductions and helped load our luggage into his trunk. With that, we all took one last look at the home we would all be leaving for good and then all piled in our seats.

"OK, last chance before we leave. Anyone forgetting anything?" I heard Steve asking the kids.

"Well, if they are forgetting anything, then they're not apt to be remembering it now; will they?" she joked.

"Good point," he acknowledged. "OK, what we don't have, we'll pick up when we get there."

As we left for the airport, I too began to realize the finality of it all. I figured my emotions would catch up to me at some point, but I needed to show support for this move. And besides, the alternative of waiting for some disaster to be imposed upon us was not worth the stress.

I embraced the notion of this ride to the airport as the beginning of a vacation, and thought of how the family would enjoy living a warmer climate. After being dropped off in front of the airport departure entrance, we made our way through the bustling crowd of travelers and checked in our travel bags. We then picked up our one-way tickets at the kiosk, and walked to the airport security checkpoint. Mairy was wide-eyed and alert, like some bodyguard surveilling ever action about us. Andrew seemed to be in a better mood, and I could see that he was talking her ear off.

Steve was just as nervous as ever. He never did enjoy unplanned traveling. I likened it to the way he would always drive the shortest route; never veering from his destination. It was just his nature. I myself enjoyed the journey, and I would normally spend a lot of time planning our route and differing diversions to be experienced on the way.

"How long are they giving us in Hawaii?" I asked.

"Great news," Steve replied with excitement! "Since they weren't really ready to orient all of us onsite, we'll have a full three weeks to spend in sunny Hawaii altogether. They even insisted that I take the time off as well. Our reservations have been made, and someone will be meeting us at the airport in Hawaii."

I thought of how we took a trip to Hawaii back in 1999, but Andrew was quite young then. I remember that, at the time, we had a difficult travel; what with trying to handle all the extra baby luggage and a baby to boot. I was actually looking forward revisiting Hawaii without the responsibility and worry of carrying a toddler around.

After checking in our bags, we proceeded to wait to be boarded. Steve gave some money to Andrew, and the kids bought some snacks. As we purchased our tickets at the last minute, Steve and I sat in the row behind but separate from the kids. I reviewed our itinerary: we had a two hour layover in San Francisco, prior to picking up our last flight to Hawaii, so we enjoyed a 'sit down' lunch at the airport. There was little or no talking about the events of the last two days. Rather we immersed ourselves in other conversations about what we would be doing on our vacation.

The plane trip was long, and uneventful, except for Mairy who has never traveled in this manner. It was delightful to see everything new through

Mairy's eyes. Even as I imagined she had been to many other worlds before, she seemed genuinely taken by everything she encountered. By the time we finally landed at Honolulu, we were more of a family unit; just one of the many tourists who came to enjoy a pleasant vacation. We gathered up our luggage at the baggage handler and maneuvered over towards the rental car stations.

Amid the hustle of new arrivals, like ourselves, I was surprised to see that we were greeted by a woman who was holding up a sign with Steve's name on it. Steve recognized her and he greeted her in a familiar manner. She was well-dressed and quite pretty. I began to wonder how well Steve actually knew of her.

"Good to see you again," Steve started. He then turned to me, saying, "This is my wife, Sandi, and the children, Andrew and Mairy."

"Hello, my name is Kiana. It's wonderful to meet all of you," Kiana replied. I just smiled back in silence.

Steve joked with her, "You're not here to make any last minute changes to our itinerary again are you?"

"Not this time," she replied with a smile. "I am here to personally look after your needs for the next three weeks or so, until they are ready to adopt your family into our little company island community."

She appeared to me to be a bit thin and a little on the muscular side. I thought to myself that she had probably never had a child. She even seemed a little pretentious in her manner, as she introduced herself to me and the children.

"Sandi, is it?" Kiana asked. "I work with the Kalama Atoll Science Foundation, where you will all eventually be staying," she started in to say. "I'd like to say how happy we are that your whole family will be working with us.

"But only for the first three months," I interrupted her. "Can you tell us where we'll actually be living after that?" I felt a little embarrassed about my abruptness, but it had been on my mind for some time.

"All that will be revealed at the proper time," she replied. "It rather depends on where the company needs Stephen to be, to complete his research. We have research teams in many parts of the world." She seemed to sidestep the question like a well-seasoned diplomat.

"But right now, I'm sure you would rather like to know where you'll be spending the next three weeks here on Oahu. If you will all come with me, I will escort you to our company limousine." Kiana lead the kids toward the airport entrance.

Steve motioned my attention to the limousine driver, who was coming to gather up our luggage. Making exaggerated facial expressions, he declared, "Wow, that's service for you." He seemed to be trying really hard to cater to me, which was always a tip off that he felt uncomfortable.

"Yes, that is nice," I rolled my eyes and acknowledged his optimism, "but are we really going to have to depend on the company limousine to drive us everywhere for the next three weeks?" I didn't know if I wanted to spend the next three weeks with Kiana hanging about.

"Oh, I'm sure we can arrange to have our own rental car once we get to the hotel," he said, downplaying the inconvenience of not getting a rental at the airport. "Besides, how often do we get to enjoy such first class treatment?"

As we turned our attention back to our host, she commented, "Oh, you'll have no need to arrange for a rental. We took the liberty of providing a company car at the bed and breakfast where you will be staying."

"You've thought of everything, haven't you?" I said with a smile. I thought how infectious Steve's attitude of non-trust was playing on me as I found myself being suspicious of her constant attention to our needs.

As Steve and the children showered our host with a barrage of questions, I went on-line to become more familiar with our next destination, the Johnston Atoll: *[The Johnston Atoll, also known as Kalama Atoll to Native Hawaiians, is an unincorporated territory of the United States currently administered by the United States Air Force (USAF) of the United States Department of Defense. The islands are visited annually by the U.S. Fish and Wildlife Service. Public entry is only by special-use permit from the United States Air Force. For nearly seventy years, the atoll was under the control of the American military. In that time it was used as a bird sanctuary, as a naval refueling depot, as an airbase, for nuclear and biological weapons testing and for space recovery, as a secret missile base, and as a chemical weapons storage and disposal site. These activities left the area environmentally contaminated, so remediation and monitoring continue.]* It was not a very hospitable description, to be sure.

Steve brought me back into the conversation by pointing to a picture in a brochure, he commented, "Look sweetie, the bed and breakfast even provides for its own outdoor pool."

"I know where I'm spending most of my time," Andrew said, acknowledging the use of the outdoor pool. "Is there a hot tub as well?"

"Yes, it appears there is," Steve replied.

As I was given the brochure to familiarize myself with its amenities, I notice the name of the location was the Manoa Valley Inn. I read further: *[The Manoa Valley Inn was a three-story gabled cottage near the campus of the University of Hawaii at Manoa, which hosted eight guest rooms furnished with fine antiques. Among its architectural features are multiple extended gables with decorative buttresses, a porte-cochere in the same style on the valley side of the house, and a broad, sheltered lanai with a view over the city on the sea side of the house.]* "It does seem to be very nice location," I acknowledged. "It looks expensive."

"Not to worry, Sandi," Kiana responded with reassurance. "This is all part of your moving allowance. You need only relax and have fun for the next three weeks."

"I can't wait to get there," Andrew said, inserted himself into the conversation.

Even Mairy appeared to be enjoying herself more. The trip to the Manoa Valley Inn was delightfully scenic. This is just what the family needed to regroup and recoup, I thought to myself. As we pulled up to the front entrance, I retraced the trip in my mind. The house was actually just another property within a larger neighborhood, away from the touristy locations of the ocean front hotels. While it was less remote than our honeymoon bed and breakfast in Arkansas, the house lot seemed very spacious and well-maintained.

Kiana turned her attention to the limousine driver, asking, "Calvin, can you take their luggage into the lobby?" She then turned her attention to us, saying, "Well, I leave you to it for now. The Inn's host is aware of all your arrangements, and is at your disposal should you need them. I will be in contact with you later on the move to your next location. Please enjoy yourselves for now." As she turned to leave, she paused and returned. Then she extended us an invitation, saying, "Oh, and if it wouldn't be too much trouble, Tom would like to invite you to dinner tonight at 'Morton's Steak House'."

"That sounds wonderful," Steve volunteered an answer. "What do you say, sweetie; ready to eat?"

"I know I'm hungry," Andrew announced. Mairy did not voice an opinion, but then see was always hungry.

"Yes, we would be delighted to accept his invitation," I replied politely. But inside I was stressing out.

"Fine," Kiana acknowledged. "It's a bit tricky to navigate downtown during the evening, so I'll send Calvin to pick you up at eight o'clock. The dress code is casual, but you might be more comfortable in dress clothes. See you then." With that, Kiana turned and left with Calvin driving.

We turned our attention to the front desk and I asked, "So where is our room?"

"You'll be staying in the 'Guild Master Suite', and your children can either stay in the sitting room area of your suite or we can provide them with individual rooms," stated the host of the bed and breakfast.

Looking to Mairy, I hadn't yet worked out how she might feel about her privacy. Perhaps we could have two rooms, one for the guys and one for the gals. "What about your other guests?" I inquired.

"Oh, that is not a concern as you are the only ones who have reserved a stay here for the next three weeks," he answered. "And I've have been told to accommodate your every need. So what shall it be?" he asked.

"Alright then, we'll go with the three separate rooms," I declared as our decision.

"Good choice mom," Andrew piped in. Mairy just smiled.

"All the rooms are on the second floor, and all your luggage will be delivered to the 'Guild Master Suite'," he instructed us. "Let me know which other rooms you would like and we will set up the accommodations accordingly."

"Is this company great, or what?" Steve rhetorically asked.

We made our way to the second floor, as the children preceded us to choose a room for themselves. The suite opened up on an elaborate sitting room which adjoined a beautifully decorated bedroom, and was reminiscent of the late 1800's. The room was a spacious and had an antique king size bed. There was also an equally spacious bathroom, with a full bath and shower room, laden with colorful tiles. Andrew came bolting back in, announcing, "I found my room."

Mairy spoke, "I believe Andrew and I can both sleep comfortably in the room he has chosen. It is the most easily defensible of the remaining rooms."

Guess her mission was more important than her privacy, I thought to myself. Not that I worried about Mairy anyway, as she seemed well able to handle herself in most any situation. "Of course," I agreed without hesitation, "and which room would that be?"

"It's the one called the 'Dole Junior Suite'," Andrew answered for them. "And it has two bedrooms."

"A very sensible choice," Steve acknowledged.

I too was somewhat relieved to hear it had two bedrooms. For the next hour or so, the family spent their time unpacking and exploring their new surroundings. There was a heated salt water pool with a waterfall, which was surrounded by lush vegetation; perfect for Steve. It seemed to me that the inn had a certain island flair and country feel, with hidden nooks spread about the property. But I must admit; the best part about it was that we wouldn't be sharing it with anyone, save the kids of course. So I could truly relax here.

As it neared the eight o'clock hour, we all got ready for our dinner with Steve's boss. Calvin showed up at the appointed time and we reached the restaurant in short order.

"For a steak house, this place sure is fancy," Steve commented.

"Seems a bit touristy to me," I commented, "but in an elegant way."

"I can smell the meat already," Andrew offered. Mairy just nodded and moved along with the crowd.

Steve talked with the seating hostess, who directed us to the table where Tom and Kiana were already seated. Noticing our approach, Tom stood up to greet us, "There you are, and right on time."

"Yes, your driver is quite efficient," Steve replied. "I would like you to meet my wife, Sandi, and our children, Andrew and Mairy." Steve and I individually shook hands with Tom and Kiana.

"It was very nice of you to invite us," I added. "One would think you would have better things to do, than to worry about a new employee."

"Well, I like to know all my employees on a more personal basis," said Tom. "It minimizes the guess work about any undue influences to their productivity. Besides, I have to eat anyway and I like the conversation," he added. Tom then made a point of shaking hands with Andrew and Mairy as well. "And you must be the Andrew I've read so much about in your dad's book," he greeted, shaking my son's hand. "And you are, of course, Mairy," he greeted, taking her hand in his. "It appears your father neglected to include you in his fantasy adventure stories."

"It was more of a father-son project," Mairy was quick to answer. "I have little interest in science."

"I'm afraid she takes after me in that respect," I offered in support of her response.

While the waiter seated us at the table and took our orders, I could hear Tom tell the waiter, "No, we both will just have the appetizer; thank you." Tom then continued to chair our conversation. "Are the accommodations to your liking?"

"Yes, of course," Steve answered. "I hope our rush to get on board has not inconvenience your company."

"Not at all, although I was surprised to hear about the urgency of your request to relocate," Tom acknowledged. "However, it is nothing our company can't deal with. Nothing unsettling I hope. It's not like you're running from the law or anything like that," he seemed to enquire jokingly.

"No, not at all," Steve said, as we laughed off his attempt to be funny.

"It was just that we wanted to get the children resettled as soon as possible," I added; "school and all." "Of course," Tom replied, seemingly accepting my reasoning.

"We don't really support a traditional school environment," Kiana spoke up. "It's more like home school and providing accessibility to online classes in support of completing a GED. However, perhaps you would rather remain on the island, while Steve continues to work with us on-site."

"I'd rather not," I countered. "You see we are a close knit family, and we feel a family environment is essential to raising our children."

"I feel the same way," Tom agreed. "I believe Steve will need the support of his family to provide the kind of productivity we are expecting from him."

"No pressure there," Steve interjected comically."

It was at that time, the waiter arrived with our appetizers. While it seemed surprisingly quick service, perhaps Tom was just a good customer of theirs. Anyway, we all just dug into our pre-meal treats.

"All kidding aside," Tom continued, "we have many families in similar situations, as Kiana can explain."

"Indeed; because of our unique working conditions, we sponsor a private association of home school facilities that allow our employees access to training from pre-school to college level courses," Kiana stated, as if she had rehearsed it. "Additionally, we provide for on the job assistance programs that allow the students to engage what they have learned in a more practical setting."

"That's wonderful," I responded with disbelief. "How does your company manage the overhead of such involvement?"

"Well, it has more to do with maintaining the secrecy of our project," Tom explained.

"Yes, that and we have been granted a government subsidy to study how a closed cultural society can exist separate of Earthlike resources. It is kind of a study in human behavior for recolonization on another planet."

"Quite cutting edge research, to be sure," Tom interrupted. "But tell me more about yourselves. Is this something that your family can get on board with?"

"Oh, to be sure," Steve answered for all of us. "We are all in this together."

"For myself, I am looking forward to engaging in conversation with like-minded individuals," Mairy offered. "I believe I would feel out of place in the traditional setting of a regular high school culture."

"And I could do with a fresh start myself," Andrew joined in. "I can't seem to break free of other's opinions. They seem to want to keep people pigeon hold with set labels. It's a cast system that seems set in stone."

"Well, that's great to hear," said Tom directly to Andrew. "I'm sure you have much more to offer than people give you credit for. I am hoping that you can reach your true potential by joining our team."

"And what is it that your team is doing," Mairy boldly questioned Tom?

"We are helping your father realize his dream," Tom explained. "And in doing so, we hope to realize our dreams as well. But I don't want to get ahead of myself. The company has a strict orientation process."

It sounded strange to hear how Tom interacted with us. It almost seemed as if we were joining a cult like Scientology or the Branch Davidians. While the warning signs were there, I was also aware of our need to complete our quest. If we ever wanted to lead a normal life again, we would all need to have to make some hard choices. Mairy doesn't show up from another off world altogether for no reason.

"Well, that's what we are here for; to follow our dreams," I agreed, holding my suspicions in check.

"Good, then we will see you in three weeks' time," Tom said, ending the conversation. "Now if you'll pardon me, I'll leave you all to enjoy your meal and the rest of your vacation." With that, Tom and Kiana got up to leave. We should up as well, out of courtesy.

"It was nice meeting with all of you. Will have Calvin come back to pick you up before you finish your meals," Kiana said, following behind Tom.

Once there were out of earshot, I spoke up, "Did that seem strange to anyone else?"

"Yes, I thought this was supposed to be a dinner engagement," Steve acknowledge, "and it appears to have been more of a ...," Steve paused for lack of completing his thought.

I picked up on his stream of thought, saying, "Yes, more of a follow up interview. What was that all about?"

"Not sure," Steve replied, "Maybe something came up at the last minute for him."

"Maybe somebody could clue me in," Andrew inquired of everyone assumptions. "What was so strange? I heard them only order the appetizers for themselves, and they ate what they ordered. Maybe they have another appointment. I, for one, am happy they are gone," admitted Andrew. "There were putting a damper on this vacation, for me."

Only Mairy seem to reserve her judgement for now. She seemed to just be taking it all in.

"Agreed, we need to start enjoying our vacation as of right now," Steve added.

And that's what we did; we enjoyed the rest of the meal and the rest of our vacation as a family unit. It was time well spent. Both Steve and Andrew were in much better spirits than they had been in a long time. And I now had a female to converse with, albeit she was unfamiliar with the male of our species. I had been too long without a companion that could understand my point of view and be sympathetic with my needs as a woman. She was indeed a delightful distraction from the world of men. Also, owing to her unfamiliarity with our culture, I had a wonderful time shopping around with her.

I felt that is was just the distraction that we all needed, especially at this time. I felt we needed to come together as a family unit, if we were to accomplish the task that this quest may impose on us. I, for one, was not going allow any harm to come to anyone in my family unit. And while I may not be a Shadow-Forge, we all have our own individual talents from which to contribute towards the family's welfare.

8

The Sum of All Destinies

[Hidden secrets have a way of being surreptitiously revealed]

Sometimes even the fate of the universe can be altered by influencing the destiny of just a few key players. Though, how to the influence such 'cause and effect' so that it can be manipulated in one's favor is forever a gamble. What might be strategically auspicious in one evolutionary incarnation, in truth may foster an unknowable future path towards one's own disaster. When the stakes are this extraordinary, life is an unbounded chess game, where the rules are not set. Unless one has complete knowledge of both fate and individual destinies of the affected players, there is no way to know if you're playing a winning strategy. One can only choose from the opportunities presented them to gauge the level of strife that defines how they will interact and survive. In the end, even the most elegant systems devised to describe the mechanics of these causal interactions, which are used to formulate the physics of such universal feedback, are subject to a degree of randomness; a degree of randomness that is exacerbated by the addition of emotions.

[Scene Change – Narrator's Perspective]

At the end of three weeks' time, Kiana showed up at their front door just as expected. The family gathered their belongings together and met the limousine outside.

"Are you all up for a new adventure?" Kiana prodded.

"Yes, but we are going to need more than just our vacation luggage to get through the next few months," Steve responded.

Steve never liked temporarily living out of a suitcase. It always felt to him as though he didn't belong, and it was all so unorganized. He was quite the homebody, seeking the solace of a rooted base from which he could seemingly control or predict his routine reality and assure the safety of his family and property. Liken to having home field advantage, he believed the randomness of unknown variables to be limited.

"Not a problem," Kiana replied. "As per your request, your belongings have been moved to storage on the atoll; which, of course, is to be your new home for the next 3 months."

"From what I read online, that island is quite bleak and deserted," Sandi said with some reservation. "There appears to be no real community. What can we expect in the way of living conditions and support?"

Sandi was more of a nest builder, and she did not look forward to being an empty nester. She liked to have a home that reflected her identity and the support of her family and community. She definitely needed an outlet for her emotional connection with her environment.

"So are we going to be roughing it for the next 3 months?" Steve asked, hoping to accent Sandi's concern.

"The appearance of the island, as it has been presented on the internet, has changed quite a bit," Kiana replied with a bit of intrigue. "Those internet images have not been update, by design, since our company bought the island back in 2011."

"Interesting, why buy an island?" Andrew asked. "It must have been mondo expensive."

The thought of owning an island roused Andrew's attention and interest. His life was still an open book with all the possibilities of being whoever he thought he could be and living wherever his heart desired. Such was his imagination of a future he had yet to experience. His only expectation of identity and security was the family where most all his needs were met without prejudice; where he was able to be himself.

"It was actually quite cheap for the amount of amenities it provided in its heyday," Kiana, said, trying to ease their misgivings. "And it provides for the isolation that our company requires to complete its mission."

Mairy thought about the phrase she used, 'to complete its mission'. It sounded suspiciously more military than their promoted appearance as a private company would had implied. Mairy was a bit guarded in her expectations. Outside of her dimensional frame of reference, there was no real place she felt at home. She tended to bring her home field advantage with her. It was her sharpness of her skills and the proficiency of her reflexive training and life experience that kept her confident in her surroundings. She depended and trusted only upon herself to survive from day to day.

"And what about the advertised levels of radiation?" Mairy asked bluntly. Mairy thought it strange that Kiana had ignored to mention the obvious health hazards that Sandi had to her from the internet.

"It has been way overblown, also by design, to keep the curiosity seekers at bay," Kiana answered. "Now, if you'll all relax a bit and wait until we board the plane, I can brief you further on the site as we go."

Upon their arrival at the Honolulu International Airport, the driver continued around back to the airport at Hickam Field. Andrew and Mairy watched out the window. While not as accommodating as a commercial airport, it did have a lot less security oversight to deal with. Kiana had Calvin managed our entry and the 'check in' of the family luggage without the encumbrance of long lines and overt security concerns. The family then followed Kiana to the location of a waiting Bell Boeing V-22 Osprey helicopter. The helicopter sported the logo of the company name, for which Steve was now working, TESSERACT.

"That is so cool," Andrew commented, recognizing the aircraft immediately. "I've seen those before. That's the Osprey, isn't it? It can flip its wings to provide for a vertical liftoff. That's so awesome!"

But Andrew's question went unanswered as Steve asked a question of his own, "I meant to ask earlier. What is the significance of the company name?"

"It's an acronym. It expands to read as the 'Theoretical Eidetic Space Surveillance, Environmental Research, and Aerospace Conceptual Transport'," Kiana explained. "The company tried to capture its mission statement of diverse operations, within the aerospace industry, in its logo. We're the only company using the term as an acronym instead of an actually part of the company name. It helps to mitigate any copyright issues."

As Mairy watched their luggage being loaded in the back of the plane, they all boarded the Osprey for their 750 nautical mile trip to the Johnston Atoll. Other than the pilot and crew, they appeared to be the only passengers on the plane. Andrew, taking advantage of the fact that there was no preassigned seating, walked with Mairy to the front of the plane to choose their own seats. Steve and Sandi followed behind.

Kiana continued on to the pilot's cabin. Upon her return, Kiana announced, "We should be there in a little over an hour. Being a commercial version of its military cousin, the lavatory accommodations are towards the front and to the left, behind the cockpit. You'll find the seats are similarly fitted for passenger transport. Please make yourselves comfortable," recommended Kiana.

The captain came on the loudspeaker, making his introductions, "My name is Captain Jack Spiro, and I understand there has been a request for a vertical lift off. This maneuver can be a little unsettling, so please remain seated with your seatbelts fasten until the seatbelts lights go off."

Andrew was beside himself, anxiously waiting as if he were in an amusement ride. It appears his comments had not gone unheard by Kiana. As the aircraft lifted vertically off the ground, they were all memorized; that is everyone but Kiana and the crew. The family had been flying before, but they had never flown in a helicopter. As this was the next best thing to a helicopter, the experience was quite thrilling.

As the plane leveled out, Sandi pursued her questioning. "So you said you would tell us a little more about where we are going," Sandi prompted Kiana for more information.

"Oh, yes," Kiana acknowledged. "When President Barack Obama signed the NASA 2010 Authorization Act into law, it fostered a growing commercial space transportation industry that allowed NASA to focus on the orbital space station and the science of interplanetary travel. Our parent company was quick to take advantage of this opportunity and bought up the Johnston Atoll to house its operations. Since then, the company has expanded and improved upon its renovation of a complex construction, above and below ground, to house its more commercial space transportation interests. This allows for the above ground buildings to house a very diverse community of people, who continually occupy the atoll and surrounding islands."

"There is nothing about this or your ownership in Wikipedia," Sandi pursued, questioning of her accuracy.

"You'll find that the internet has been scripted for our purposes, as all involved value their privacy," Kiana said. "As such, we are also afforded a small military contingent that allows us to operate a 'no fly zone' for any aircraft other than our own."

"That would account for the lack of updated photographs on the internet," Steve commented to Sandi.

"I'm sure you'll all be pleasantly surprised at the scenic accommodations. In fact, prior to our buying the island, one of the possible sale objectives for this location was as a vacation destination," Kiana explained.

"One would think the concern for radiation contamination would have been a negative selling point," Sandi inserted, as a concern for the health of her and her family. Sandi was quick to follow up, "It says here, *Five weapons were also dropped from aircraft for airbursts in the vicinity of Johnston Island. The high altitude tests were designed to discover the effect on communications or stopping incoming ballistic missiles. The effect of these high level explosions lit the sky from Australia to Hawaii, causing an enormous electromagnetic pulse which put out street lights in Honolulu, 1300 kilometers away'.*"

"I can understand your apprehension," responded Kiana. "However I can assure you that I would not be working there if I was not personally assured of it being a safe environment."

Sandi continued, "It also says that, *'The Johnston Atoll was used to store chemical weapons from Okinawa after 1970 and drums of Agent Orange defoliant from the Vietnam War in 1972. The Johnston Atoll Chemical Agents Disposal System (JACADS) facility was completed in July 1990. JACADS is used for the incineration of US chemical weapons removed from Germany at the end of the Cold War'.*"

"Yes, all that toxic waste was dealt with during the cleanup and renovation of this site some years ago. We currently house over 5,000 family members and maintenance crew members at this facility. I personally overlooked the off-site disposal of all nuclear waste," Kiana declared.

"So you've been with the company for a long time then?" Steve asked, attempting to change the tone of their conversation.

"Almost since the beginning," Kiana replied. "And in all that time, our population on the island has not reported a case of cancer related diagnosis due to radiation exposure."

"That's very impressive," Steve acknowledged of Kiana's declaration. "Don't you think so, sweetie?"

"Yes, quite impressive," Sandi reluctantly agreed, as her concerns were satisfied with what appeared to be a 'canned' statement which she could not refute. She looked to see the kids enjoying the trip, and settled in.

The flight over the Pacific during the daylight hours was a sight to behold. One could see endlessly in all directions, without a single landmark to gauge one's journey. Even the horizon provided no reference from which to calculate distance. One could only count the minutes until there would once again be some land.

Andrew couldn't help but think what is must have been like for those intrepid explorers who navigated the oceans to reach these seemingly lost islands. If they were off by even a little bit on their calculations, they may never see land. Even a plane might run out of fuel and be swallowed up by these harsh waters.

For Steve, this Pacific run from Hawaii to the Johnston Atoll provided a backdrop for his thoughts on how he imagined the Pacific was formed. While others were comfortable with the traditional theory that the Pacific Rim was merely the result of plate tectonics movements, he had long ideated its development as the cataclysmic clash of planetary bodies.

He was not alone in this thinking, as other scientists have mused on theories about a giant impact model for the formation of the Moon. Steve's working hypothesis was that the Earth and Mars once shared a similar revolutionary orbital movement about the Sun. Whereupon the orbital motion of Mars eventually came into conflict with the orbital motion of the Earth, their proximity resulted in a titanic collision. In this way, Mars rammed the Earth with a glancing blow. Liken to two billiard balls hitting, Mars was nudged from its 'goldilocks' position in our solar system.

The consequence being that the Earth forever stole from Mars its predominant reign for evolutionary procreation. Steve remembered how he accounted for the evidence of this imagined impact in his first book, 'The Evolutioning of Creation – Volume 1'. Of this imagined impact, he original conjectured it being the result of a mammoth asteroid, about the size of the Moon. Only later, after additional research, had he concluded the alternative Mars collision hypothesis.

In his book, Steve noted the evidence for such an impact. There was the Pacific's outline of a titanic crater traced about the resultant Central Pacific Basin. The enormous circumference of this basin encompassed the deep concave shape of its forced inward depression by literally scraping away the Earth's mantle. It was an area that was significantly larger than Earth's entire landmass. Consequentially, the signature upheaval along the Pacific Rim had forever changed the physiography of the Earth: From the Pacific-Antarctic Ridge in the south, up the Eastern Pacific Rise and along the coast of North America on the east, to the Aleutian Trench in the north, then down to the Kamchatka, Kuril, Japan, Bonin, and Mariana Trenches on the west. Also known as the 'Ring of Fire' because of the volcanic activity, prevailing in the pregravated remnants of the Earth's depleted mantle. The ongoing earthquake activity of this molten valley continues to sculpt this edifice even now. The gigantic entry wound, only healing over with the scars of lava outflows, as debris comingled with the settling ash to produce the tectonic plates.

It is how he ideated the combination of relevant forces came to initiate life's evolution. He thought of how the upward thrust of land, outlining this area of impact, is a testament to the power and extent of such an impact. The environment of the Pacific area reflecting the effect of this evidence: e.g., the pulverized, sand-like makeup of the Pacific shores versus the rocky, gravel-like makeup of the Atlantic shores. There was even the characterization of the Atlantic and the Pacific specific physiography to consider. While the Pacific Ocean floor reflects a bowl shape, on one side of the globe, there is a gigantic crack in the Atlantic Ocean floor, known as the Mid-Atlantic Ridge, on the other side of the globe. In its simplest analogy it demonstrates the forensics of a punch to a partially dried mud ball: i.e., where the one side is seen as a crater-like bowl depression and the other side shows a gigantic expanding crack. The formation of such an extensive crack in the Atlantic, from the North Pole to the South Pole, would seem to support the notion of an extrusive force from underneath; perhaps even slightly shifting the Earth's core to account for its more lopsided rotation.

Considering the energy of its punch force, an extrusion up from the inner density of the Earth's central molten mass, it is easy to imagine how it could split the land mass in half on the other side, forming the Atlantic Basin. It can be seen in the evidence surmised of the land masses; wherein North and South America had been torn apart from the land masses of Europe and Africa, leaving only fossil records and the outline of their continental shelves as reminders of their campaginations. Even more definitive of this force, he speculated upon the amount of pressure required to compress carbon into diamond, as in its relative position for Africa with respect to the predicted area of the impact. Yet in all this fury, from such an overwhelming catastrophe, even the destructive edifice of this efficacy could not deter the survival of planet Earth. Rather this impact was probably the progenitor of its evolutionary progression towards life.

"We should just about be in view of the islands now," Kiana announced, breaking his thoughtful musings.

During Steve's musings, Andrew had restlessly moved about the plane. While Andrew and Steve remained fascinated by the view outside, over the duration of the trip, Sandi and Mairy spent time getting to know each other better. It wasn't long before they came upon the visage of the islands, which would be there home for the next few months. Other than its small size, building arrangements could be viewed as a 'cut out' of a suburban development. Of particular interest, however, was the one largest building at the end of the massive airport landing area. Even as the main island was some 2 miles long, the runway seemed to extend way beyond the main island, and onto to the adjoining islands.

"How long is that runway?" Steve asked Kiana.

"It's a little over 3 miles long, extending all the way to Hikina Island," Kiana answered him. "It is actually quite a feat of engineering, anchoring itself along the shallow reef bottom."

"That's the size of a runway for space shuttle," Andrew broke in. "Why so long?"

"You are quite astute," Kiana complimented him. "It has to do with the fact that it doubles as a highway, bridging across three of the four islands," Kiana answered, covertly keeping it true nature a secret, for now.

"They have made a lot of improvements since these images on the internet," Sandi joined in. "It must be a very lucrative operation you are running here."

"Yes, we are very proud of the impact we've made here on this planet," Kiana replied.

"That's an unusual choice of words," Mairy noted out loud; "…on this planet."

"Perhaps, but the company sees themselves as more than a global network," Kiana responded to her confusion. "They are proud of their contribution to save the planet; thus the larger scope of reference."

"How very magnanimous of them," Mairy responded, still suspicious of the events that led them here.

"Well, there is that," replied Kiana. "However, now that you are all here, there is a much larger truth to this statement, as well. And you are all invited to join us to be part of this larger scope of reference, under the employment of TESSERACT."

Andrew felt a little uneasy about how her statement, which sounded like the introduction to *Jurassic Park*'.

"Now if you will all be sure that your seat belts are fastened securely; we are preparing for landing," announced the captain over the intercom.

Thus remained the unanswered question of what might be the larger scope to which she made reference.

The Osprey landed on the runway, near an adjoining airport building where they deboarded from the aircraft. The airport building was small by comparison to the runway; just about the size of a hotel lobby. They literally walked into and out of the airport building in less than a minute, as Kiana motioned to the administration desk of their advancement towards the front doors. There, they were met by a waiting shuttle, which eventually drove them to their home away from home; or at least for the next 3 months.

As the Polynesian chauffeur held open the doors for them, he greeted, "Welcome to the Kalama Atoll."

The family continued to survey their new community, marveling at the exoticness of their location. Arriving at the arranged residence, Kiana explained, "This used to be the base commander residence, back when this was a military base in the mid-1900s." As they got off the shuttle, she added, "It is usually used by the company brass when they have occasion to travel here. But right now, it is unoccupied."

"It is just like a continuing vacation," Sandi expressed, commenting her approval of the accommodations.

Andrew was not one to wait on ceremony, and began looking around the outside of the residence. Mairy followed behind, wanting to get the lay of the land, so to speak.

"Hey mom, it has its own private beach and everything," yelled Andrew from a distance.

"Actually, the beach is just for show," Kiana told Steve and Sandi. "These are ocean waters and there are sharks and other dangerous aquatic life that frequent the area. However, if the children want to swim, the island has a great recreational center near the condominiums we passed, down the road a bit from here. There's a pamphlet in the house that provides the layout of the whole island."

"This is all very wonderful, but where do I work?" asked Steve, expecting to get started as soon as possible.

"Eager to start, I see," Kiana replied, rather avoiding the question. The shuttle driver handed her some paper, which she promptly handed over to Steve and Sandi. "First things first," she continued. "Here is a map of the area. Family orientation is tomorrow at 9:00 am in the auditorium of the recreation building."

"Oh, orientation for the whole family," Steve acknowledged with some confusion.

"Yes; also took the liberty of having your clothes cleaned up, and we will be sending them to you, with the rest of your luggage, in the morning at 8:00 am. Everything else you might need is in the residence. Now I'll excuse me, while you all get settled. We hope you enjoy your stay here," she concluded.

As they all made our goodbyes, Sandi couldn't help being suspicious about why they kept their luggage.

The family spent the rest of the day getting settled, and then exploring the surrounding location on foot. It was easy to see that the company had invested a lot of capital in renovating this island. However, the island, for the most part, was small and utilitarian. From what they saw on the way in, the airport runway was the largest structure on the island, followed by the condominium complex. The runway also divided some of the larger single family homes, which they were in, from the more urban area of the island.

Their walk allowed them to meet some of the locals and get familiar with the neighborhood restaurant. Everyone seemed to be quite friendly. And while it all had kind of a Polynesian flare about it, the locals appeared to be a mix of several diverse cultures. It seemed quite overwhelming for a singular company property. It was more like a company retreat of sorts. As such, if this was representative of their training center, it gave them a true sense of the immense breadth of the company's operations.

[Time Change - Mother's Perspective]

[Indoctrination is often the method of giving a scripted purpose to others.]

The next morning, Steve woke up early as usual; a predictable practice which started the clockwork of the family unit to get into gear. I was the first to leave the comfort of my bed to wake the others, apprehensive of being late for our scheduled orientation. Steve went to the front door with the expectation of finding our luggage. He was not disappointed. He found our clothing to be well packed in separate boxes, and I accounted for the items inventory. Nothing was missing. Even the few souvenirs we bought on our vacation were seemingly undisturbed. I woke up the others before starting my own daily routine.

I looked over the kitchen counter, out the row of large windows that frame the backyard, to see the sun rise over the breakwaters of our shoreline view. I had to admit, of all the times we requested an ocean view, this was the first time we actually had one. The others filed in, one by one, as the family unit came together.

"Wow, now is that a sight to wake up to, or what," was Steve's observation of the view upon meeting me in the kitchen. "I especially like the way the sun shines through your hair. This is what I always wanted for us."

Andrew was not far behind Steve, commenting, "You look great mom. Do we all have to dress up?" As of yet, Andrew was still in his pajamas.

"No," I acknowledged. "But it would be nice to make a great first impression," I added, while drinking a bit of fresh brewed coffee.

"What's for breakfast?" Andrew asked.

"It appears there is cereal in the cabinets and milk in the frig," Steve answered. "Have at it."

"I'll check on Mairy," I offered.

I found Mairy up and getting ready to meet the new day. "Did you have a nice rest?" I asked.

"Strangely yes," was her response. "I found the sound of the ocean waves to be quite soothing. And you?"

"Well enough," I replied. "I couldn't help thinking about having to be ready this early in the morning. I rather liked being on vacation time."

Our breakfast was sufficient, but light; as it wouldn't due to be inattentive at an orientation. Just prior to the appointed time, we crossed the runway and made our way to the auditorium in the recreation center. As we entered, we could see that we would be part of a group of about 40 or more people. Seating appeared to be informally situated at round tables, arranged much like it would be for a wedding party.

"This reminds me of that time-share presentation we went to in Florida," Steve mentioned to me.

It was too long after we arrived that the orientation started. "Welcome all; we hope you are enjoying your stay on the island. Despite the accommodations, this is not meant to be a vacation," the presenter stated quite bluntly.

"That really puts things in perspective," I quietly joked to Steve. He acknowledged with one of his smiley facial expressions.

"You have all been hired on to participate in our research development program to study the effects of living and working in a more foreign environment; that foreign environment being, for now, the simulated effects of surviving on another planet. Each of you has been screened for your interests, education, and expertise. And every adult has signed an agreement to either a six or ten year non-disclosure, non-contact commitment to this project. And, of course, the non-contact commitment refers to the world outside of this company and not to your family," the company coordinator quipped.

"We appreciate your courage and your sacrifice. Ten years takes quite a bite out of anyone's life, but you have all agreed to your specific compensation packages," he expressed with resolve. "Notwithstanding, your presence here acknowledges that you and your families, are all employees. As such, we expect that you will all represent yourselves as such and treat each member of the team with the respect and dignity that each of you deserve, while you are in our employ. Together, your commitment to this project and your participation in our research will be appreciated by future generations to come. As part and parcel of this commitment and compensation, there are those of you whose primary expertise will be required on-site, but have families who have agreed to support your employment from this of-site island location, or from some other off island location. While this agreement was based on the needs of the on-site environment, and not its exact location, this agreement remains a negotiable option. However it is still dependent upon the on-site space availability, as well as adherence to company policy and procedures."

The speaker persisted, "Let me be clear. While your family members have the choice of whether they want to remain here on the island or continue with you to our on-site location, the principle employees have agreed to the same six or ten year pledge on behalf of their dependents. Those who stay on the island will become part of our working, self-sufficient community. They would be expected to support themselves and their obligation to this program. And while it is a rather planned community, no one is obligated to work or even stay on the island. However, you'll find that not working becomes very boring, very fast."

Another company representative joins the speaker, explaining, "Off-site jobs are listed in handouts pursuant to your selected participation. Furthermore, as a caveat of this ten year pledge, any transgressions committed by any family member may result in contract termination and debriefing of the family unit to their place of origin. Also, as an addendum to this remedial consequence, the company is not here to police the activity of any of our employees. First and foremost, this is company, and we defer all legalities and legal enforcements to off island jurisdictions. Containment and removal from the island is managed via the small military contingent that serves the needs of this company."

The speaker then continued, "For those of you who have agreed to continue with the primary employees to our on-site location, the company needs you all to be able to transition to our new space like environment as soon as possible. Therefore for the next 3 months, those participating in the 'on-site experiment' will be provided training to operate in a more space-like environment."

The secondary representative speaks again, "On-site jobs for non-primary employees will also be listed in a separate handout, to be provided to you during your separate orientations. Now, before we separate you for orientation by working location, are there any questions?" asked the company coordinator.

"Can you tell us now where the on-site location is?" asked an on-site participant.

"Not at this time," she replied. "Until we have a firm commitment from the family to participate with the primary employee, either here or on-site, we choose not to reveal any proprietary information. Based on your contract, and for plausible deniability, the on-site location will only be revealed to those on-site participants in a separate orientation. However, for those of you who remain here with off-site personal, we do not object to your receiving this information second hand via any on-site participant. So I'm guessing you'll all know by the end of the day, with the exception of those who do not wish to stay."

There was a brief bit of laughter emanating from the group.

"Will we be able to freely communicate between sites?" asked another member of the group.

"Freely is a relative term. Due to security protocol, all communication between sites is subject to being monitored; and no classified data is allowed to be discussed on an open line. However, normal discussions of a non-classified nature will be allowed via email," answered the company coordinator.

"Will there be a 'skype' or 'on-line chat' type of communication between sites?" asked another participant.

"I believe I understand where this is going," cited the coordinator. "As we are simulating an off planet like environmental study, there will be no real-time communication," replied the coordinator. "And as before, all communication between sites is subject to being monitored. Therefore, you might want to save any more racy discussions with your site specific counterparts for when you are face to face."

Another round of laughter sprang from the group.

"As I plan to support my husband from this off-site location, I would like to know when we will be able to meet face to face?" shouted out a woman from the group.

"Leaves from the on-site location are allowed to be scheduled as the situation permits," she responded. "Remember, the intent is to simulate the actual conditions between off planet and on planet relationships. Everyone has their part to play. Still, such leaves can be regulated for up to two months to be taken as much as once a year. If this becomes untenable, remember there is the negotiable option to participate on-site. Anyone else?" the coordinator asked of the audience.

"What are the schooling opportunities available for our children?" asked another female participant.

"I believe that your inquiry could be best responded to in your separate orientations," answered the coordinator. "If there are no other more general questions, then please organize yourselves into two groups by location of participation, and our group moderators will be with you shortly. Thank you."

I had been patiently waiting to talk with Steve about what I heard from this general orientation. I turned to Steve, accusingly asking him, "There was a choice for six or ten years?"

Steve responded defensively, but calmly, "They didn't give me that choice. Would you like me to ask about it?"

"No, I just want to know that you are not keeping secrets from me," I replied with a change of attitude.

"Well, it might be worth looking into it for yours and the kid's sakes," Steve continued. "But really I was looking for a more permanent position anyway."

"Of course," I agreed with Steve; "but what about that non-contact clause? Do we really want to divorce ourselves from the outside world for the next ten years? Also, what about vacations; are they all to be on this island?"

"Almost sounds like a cultist-like culture; doesn't it," Steve discussed aloud. "Why didn't you direct your questions to the company speaker?"

"It's really not as bad as all that," Kiana stated, slightly startling us with her abrupt arrival.

"Oh, hello again," I acknowledged of her sudden appearance. It was a somewhat jarring surprise, as I wondered how long she had been within earshot of our conversation. I even felt a little embarrassed about my negative comments toward the company.

"The non-contact clause does not mean that you cannot travel off the island, she continued, as if she was always part of the conversation. "It just means that you are bound by contract not to discuss your work outside of the company confines. Of course, it also means that you agree to let the company conduct a background check of anyone you have contact with outside of the company."

"Oh, thank you," I replied, still feeling a little uncomfortable.

"I didn't expect to see you today," Steve joined in. "Is there something you need from us?"

"As it turns out, there is," Kiana replied. "We would like to extend a welcome to your whole family to attend the on-site orientation. And if Sandi decides it is not for her, then we can have them switched back to the off-site orientation later."

"That's very nice of you," I replied, feeling somewhat maneuvered.

"Not at all," Kiana tactfully replied. "We're hoping that you would all be able to join us on-site. It is quite the life changing experience."

"My, you have a high opinion of your company," said Mairy, inserting herself in the conversation. "What could be so life changing about working for another company in a foreign environment?"

"My dear, Mairy is it, you have no idea how foreign our on-site environment is," Kiana answered in kind.

"Well if it is anything like this place, I'm in," Andrew chimed in. Mairy just rolled her eyes at Andrew's impulsive eagerness to try something new.

"Alright then," Kiana acknowledged of the family's decision.

She then introduced herself to the larger crowd and took charge of the on-site orientation.

"For those of you taking the on-site orientation, if you will all follow me down the hall to the next auditorium. We like to get you situated as soon as possible," she announced.

While the off-site group stayed behind with the original coordinator, the rest of us followed Kiana to a conference room where they had a large flat screen monitor on the far wall.

"Please take your seats so we can get started," Kiana requested of the group.

There was the usual churn of bodies as people jockeyed for position in front of the monitor. We worked our way up to the third row from the front, as Steve had problems with long distance viewing. Once everyone was seated, the lights dimmed and the monitor was turned on. Kiana sat down in the front row as well, deferring to the introduction on the screen.

The presentation started with a man standing over what appeared to be a mock up model of the on-site location on a table in front of him. It seemed like something out of a sci-fi movie, as the complex looked to be quite an ambitious undertaking.

The presentation started: "You have all been handpicked by your handlers and have agreed to participate in our research study of surviving on another planet. As you may have already figured out for yourselves, we can't take really take you all to another planet. However, we can do the next best thing. Here, before me, is a model of the base station to which you will all be residing for the next six to ten years. The base is completely self-contained and self-sufficient with the exception of periodic supply transports. The reason behind this isolation and secrecy is that this on-site base station is located on the Moon."

There was a noticeable gasp in the room, as everyone was taken by surprise.

"Yes, you heard me correctly; the Moon. While some of you are old enough to remember the TV series 'Space 1999', we have improved upon their concept of living off world. However, the nature of technology and assignments on this moon station will be vastly different. The reason for this site is two-fold: 1. It provides a readymade environment for our study of isolated cultures and society normalization; 2. The base station also houses a deep space observatory like no other on Earth. While not everyone will be permitted into the research labs where this observatory is situated, the base station provides a habitable environment much like that of a cruise ship. And to brief you, in more detail, I would like to introduce our ship's purser, Nathaniel."

The presentation shifts to Nathaniel, with what appears to be the backdrop of a large mall: "While you will all have your own individual jobs to support this off world research, the nature of your employment will be vastly different from that on Earth. Although it remains a company own environment, a lot of what you see requires the participation of everyone on board. We all have a responsibility to care and nurture the one another, so that each of you are treated with the dignity and respect that each of you deserves."

There it was I thought to myself; that company line up front and center.

The presentation continued: "This is the mezzanine floor of our habitat. As you can see, it hosts the main cafeteria and it is lined with a variety of services about this main floor. It is the lowest point at which to view the atrium up to the lateral sections of the building that snaked their way into and under a large glass lined, geodesic dome structure that support the spherical structure of the station's interior."

"This architectural marvel is the crowning jewel of our Moon station. The expanse of the dome itself is about a mile in diameter, making it the largest manmade geodesic structure. The remarkable size and accomplishment of this architectural feat, a little more than 7.5 times larger than any manmade geodesic on Earth, can be attributed to the Moon's lower gravity. The foundation for the internal structure of this geodesic shape is supported via four foot diameter pillars. These pillars, which are designed to ring about the center of the geodesic structure, are grounded deep below the Moon's surface. The pillars extend from the lowest point of the spherical structure all the way up to the dome roof."

"The recreation area resides on the fifth floor, where we host a variety of distracting experiences to keep the body and mind in tiptop shape."

Visuals of movies, bars, clubs, and dancing are shown for socialization, as well as an arcade area and individual computer cubicles are shown on the large screen.

"Because of the Moon's lower gravity, you will be required to spend 2 hours each day accessing some form of physical training. Physical training is scheduled so as to accommodate the entire population of the moon station, so please adhere to the timing of your individual durations. Further training for surviving in low gravity will be provided to you over the next 3 months."

A variety of activities are demonstrated on screen, from the walking lane about the fifth floor atrium to the aerobics classes and fitness centers in the various rooms.

"During this time, your health will be regularly monitored for disease borne illnesses. As the body, itself, hosts many bacterium and dormant viruses, which are utilized to regulate your chemical makeup, there is always the possibility of unintended triggers for more harmful contagions. Your ability to continue with the on-site population is dependent on your capability to stay healthy. However should you encounter any medical issues on-site, our first recourse is to treat you in our 'state of the art' medical facilities residing on the upper floors. The medical facility is just under the communication offices at the top of the dome."

"And to keep from becoming claustrophobic, the exterior of the living floors are lined with lead laden, polarized safety glass, which allows for your viewing pleasure without the worry of harmful solar radiation."

The presentation perspective then pans out beyond the glass surface to the landscape of the low lying hills, void of any organic life. The perspective continues to pan up high over the top of the Moon to show a view of the Earth positioned high in the sky over a backdrop of low lying hills. From my perspective, the foreground presented a stark contrast to the blue color of Earth in the horizon. All in all, it did not appear to me to be very inviting, to say the least.

The presentation ends like a travel brochure, with Nathaniel saying: "Hope to see you all up here soon."

The lights go up in the room again.

Kiana stand up to address the group. "Amazing isn't it? And I dare say, a bit overwhelming at first. But I would like to assure each and every one of you, that your safety is of our utmost concern. Over the next three months, we intend to not only get you ready for this adventure, but we hope to convince you that you need not be apprehensive about your well-being or security. If you really think about it, the existence of this moon station is a testament to our ability to safely shuttle passengers to and from Earth."

She then asked, "Are there are question?"

Andrew was not bashful at all. Completely ignoring the consequence any safety concerns, he shouted out his question, "Is there a swimming pool?"

"Indeed there is," Kiana answered. "It is located on the main floor, under the facilities observatory. And might I add, swimming in low gravity is an especial unique experience."

"What are the food choices," asked another in the audience.

"Well, as we are simulating real off planet conditions, there are a variety of healthy food products, specially created and processed for our off world consumption. The food has specific requirements for efficient transport and storage, as well as for properly supplementing the balanced nutrition of individuals working in space," Kiana answered in a rehearsed manner.

"But how does it taste?" the same participant pursued.

"It's not the first time this concept has been considered. Thankfully, the current members of the station have, perhaps out of the own preference, provided for a variety of familiar flavors," she answered. "I am personally fond of the processed flavoring of their rocky road ice cream."

"Actually, I would like to know if the choices include non-animal byproducts," asked another participant.

"Of course," Kiana recognized of the individual's concern, "if something of a more vegetarian diet is to your liking, we can easily accommodate that as well." "Our food specialists have been challenged with a number of dietary requests, since we started transporting people up to the base station. They've had many years to develop a diverse group of food choices."

Kiana made a point of walking about, rather than talking only from an up-front position.

"Currently they are experimenting with a system which allows us to grow some plants in the moon station, capable of producing salad-type crops to provide the population with a palatable, nutritious, and safe source of fresh food supplements. The challenge here, of course, is that the conditions for growth are all artificial. We can only allow the use of moon soil, which has only organic matter from previous growth cycles. There are no insects to help such growth along, and there is no direct sunlight for 14 days at a time. Perhaps, if you have a green thumb, you could select it as a choice from the on-site job listings."

With that, Kiana, now walking by us, handed me an extra pamphlet with on-site job listings.

"You never know what you might be good at," she directed her comment to the audience at large, while looking directly at us. She then directed a helper to pass out the rest of the pamphlets.

"From the presentation, I noticed they have bars and clubs," asked gentleman from the audience. "As a family man, I was wondering about the effects of such socializing on the population."

"In what way; could you be more specific?" Kiana asked, not quite getting the gist of his concern.

"Will there be a problem with drinking, smoking, and possibly drugs?" he asked more pointedly.

"It will be no problem at all, because it is not allowed," Kiana replied back. "If you turn your attention to your pamphlets, there is to be no alcohol or cigarettes allowed anywhere on the islands, or on-site. As for drugs, they can only be administered by the medical team. What was being shown on the video was a juice bar. I'm afraid if you want more, you will have to wait until your scheduled vacation leave time when you are on Earth and off island."

"Are there any other questions?" Kiana asked again.

I looked to Steve, and then asked my question, "When does the training start?"

"Training starts tomorrow, promptly at 8:00 am," Kiana answered, recognizing her question as a choice to participate on-site.

"So you decide to join me on the Moon?" Steve asked with a smile.

"I wouldn't have it any other way," I answered back. "Who knows what distractions you might encounter up there?"

"Yes!" Andrew intervened. "I can't wait. I wonder what it will be like to swim about in low gravity."

"Just remember," Mairy added in her two cents, "we don't know enough about this quest to let our guard down. And we'll need a cover story to get into that research center. Also, we can't rely on only your dad to be able to provide us with information all the time."

"OK, but let's talk about this when there are not so many ears about," I urged.

"What does the number of ears have to do with what we talk about?" Mairy asked with curiosity.

"It's another expression," Andrew alerted Mairy. "We should be alone when we talk about the quest."

From the front of the room, Kiana then announced, "If there are no more question, then you are all free to leave for today. Be sure to be back here tomorrow at 8:00 am. Thank you all for volunteering for our next great adventure."

The crowd was noticeable elated with excitement at the prospect of going to the Moon. Rather than leaving immediately, a few discussion groups collected to compare notes. We were not really minglers.

As it was about lunchtime, I suggested, "OK, let's get something 'to go' from the restaurant, and we can talk more at the house."

Suddenly Kiana was behind us again. She was actually quite good at surprising us.

"I'm glad you decided to join us on-site. I'm sure you'll find the adventure to be well worth the sacrifice," Kiana stated with all sincerity."

"I'm sure I'll have plenty to do just keeping up with this family," I commented, "but I'm sure you are right."

"See you all tomorrow then," Kiana said, leaving them once again.

"There's something about her that bothers me," I said allowed. "It is just a feeling that I can't shake."

"Perhaps, it is because she is too friendly," Andrew quipped. "You sound a bit more like dad, lately, because he doesn't trust anyone. And he always worries about people's motives when they are too friendly."

"Oh, we can't have that now, can we?" I joked back, loud enough to be heard by Steve. Steve smiled back. With that, we all went to the restaurant and then crossed back over the runway to the captain's quarters.

Gathering the utensils for our dining activity, we settled ourselves down for leisurely meal out on the back patio, overlooking the ocean. "I finally get a vacation on an island, with a view that overlooks the ocean, and I can't go in the water for fear of sharks," Steve mused over their situation.

"Maybe it's somehow prophetic of our situation here," Andrew joked back.

"You may be more right than you know," added Mairy.

"You might as well enjoy it while it last," I interject a more somber tone. "There will be no oceanfront view on the Moon."

"Depends on how you view the universe," Steve countered. "From my point of view, space is a sea of stars." Then he spouted off a remembered quote, *'We are tied to the ocean. And when we go back to the sea, whether it is to sail or to watch - we are going back from whence we came'.*"

"Where have I heard that before," I asked, recalling the phrase but not knowing where?

"John F Kennedy," was Steve's reply.

"From the perspective of our all having originated among the elements of our creation, the stars provide for a metaphorical backdrop from which to describe the ocean of creation," Mairy said thoughtfully.

"Somehow, I don't think that is what he meant when he said it," I argued the point.

"You're right of course, but Mairy's interpretation works for me just the same," Steve answered. "How about this one: *All I ask is a tall ship and a star to steer her by',*" Andrew contributed.

"I like that one as well," Steve replied.

"That one is from Star Trek," Andrew stated.

Following their lead, I recited a favorite quote of my own, *"Heaven on Earth is a choice you must make, not a place you must find."*

"How about you Mairy, do you have a favorite saying," Andrew asked, prompting Mairy to join in?

"Behest of my heart and my soul will follow," Mairy responded.

"That's a wonderful thought," I commented. "I'd never heard you speak of a soul before. Is that something shared by your kind?"

"It is the way of the Shadow-Forge," Mairy answered back. "We serve at the behest of all life forces, with only our soul as our buoy of being."

"I've believed I've heard that before," Andrew said, now searching his mind for some connection to her words.

"Yes, you have," Steve thought to help Andrew. "It is something I borrowed from your rememberings of your time with Harmony. I used it a couple of times in my first book."

"Oh yeah," Andrew recalled, "Harmony referred to my virtues as my 'buoys of being'. So that's the way of the Shadow-Forge," Andrew remarked to Mairy. "I like that reference even more now." Then he repeated Mairy's quote out loud, "Behest of my heart and my soul will follow."

"Well, as long as we're all together, maybe our time away from Earth will go quickly," I said, resigning myself to what must be done.

"I've never known ten years to go fast," I responded to Steve's statement.

"Mom, in all honesty, if this is our quest, as we suppose it is, then we'll be lucky to last the year up there," Andrew stated quite 'matter-of-factly'. "Once the quest is resolved, we don't have to stay up there."

"What do you mean," asked Steve?

"What he means is that if this is another attempt to bring chaos into the universe, and tip the balance of power, then there is no telling what their schedule might be. And while this is but another lifetime for me, I can't imagine that it will take the full ten years for chaos to execute its plan," said Mairy, in support of Andrew's prediction."

"OK, I see what you mean now," Steve replied a little downhearted. "But to me it is still my full time job."

I could see that Steve had not thought this through any more than I had.

"I know this job means a lot to you, but there is no guarantee that any of this may be permanent," I tried to put my feelings into words. "I mean, there is no real way of knowing what might happen if we succeed or fail. Still we can't avoid it."

"She's right dad," Andrew agreed. "What has happened so far with the attack back at home, by that creature and its impending warning of doomsday, do you really think of this merely about your job?"

"Merely a job," Steve repeated in consternation? "It's my life's work. I mean, working jobs is what helps us keep afloat around here. Goodness knows, I'm never going to be a celebrated author."

"Yeah, I'm sorry; I get that," Andrew apologized for belittle his father's contribution. "But there is the larger picture to consider here."

"Actually now that you bring up your books, I'm still leery about how this sudden recognition of your books and your theories landed you this job in the first place. Doesn't it all seem to be, well, too much of a coincidence?" I asked, hoping the reality of my suspicions would not be too much of a letdown for him.

"Yes, I can't argue against the logic of what you are all saying. But perhaps, at least, I can enjoy it while it lasts," Steve professed with some despondency. "It's like you said, we can't avoid it. So I say, why not enjoy it while the opportunity presents itself."

"It wasn't quite my expectation to an employee of this company, but it'll do," I replied, hesitant to dwell on his phrasing as it might lead to an argument.

"Come on!" Steve said with bravado. "This will be our only chance to experience what it would be like to journey in outer space. I mean, we are going to the Moon!"

"Yes, the Moon," I acknowledged with reservation. "I know this is your dream. But before I met you, I only dreamt of traveling overseas to Hawaii, or even Europe; you know, somewhere on Earth. But the Moon; while it is all very exciting, it is filled with so many unknowns."

Mairy reached out and held my hand, saying, "While I originally came to help Andrew, I cannot deny my sense of obligation for all of you. Where fate is the sum of all destinies, we will get through this together."

I smiled back, knowing that I could not abandon those I loved for any reason. "Yes, together," I said, placing my other hand on top of hers.

Then brushing his hands on his shorts, Andrew joined in. Placing his hand on mine, he echoed in agreement, "Together."

Steve, having created an awkward pause by his absence, prompted Andrew to glare over in his direction.

"Oh, yes, together," Steve said with awkwardness, as he responded by reaching out and placing his hand on top of the pile. "Fate is the sum of all destinies," Steve added, repeating the mantra.

"So what's our plan?" Andrew queried of the group.

Mairy spoke first, "We'll need a cover story that will put us in with the research team, so we can get some 'first hand' information of what we're dealing with. Have you got that list of on-site jobs?" she asked me.

"I do have it," I admitted.

When I went to retrieve the pamphlet from my purse, I found that I had two of them. It seemed that no matter what was being collected during vacations, it all got passed to me. It was like Steve and Andrew needed to have their hands free all the time. I often wondered if it was something that had to do with their ADHD. I handed them out and we all looked through both lists, searching for something appropriate.

"Here's one that might work," Steve announced. "It has to do with computer simulation programming."

Andrew looked to Steve, saying, "Be serious dad, these are not school courses; they're jobs. We could never pass for programmers, even if you did coach us."

"I wonder what this one is all about," Mairy spoke up. "It says 'Sleep Study Pod Operator Internship'."

"Oh, look; they all have definitions on the next few pages," I said of my discovery. I was happy to be of any help, even if it was just to point out the obvious.

I observed Steve, looking to the pamphlet that Mairy and I had, and then to his own again. As he gave a puzzled looked, he made the observation, "That job position is not on this pamphlet. What does it say?"

I read out the definition for all to hear, "Sleep Study Pod Operator – Individuals who can assist in the calibration and operation of sleep pods used to study the effects of long-term neurological impact on the brain senses and functionality in space.

Basic Eligibility Criteria: Siblings between the ages of 16-26. Healthy volunteers who had been trained to become lucid dreamers and can signal lucidity through a pattern of horizontal eye movements, or have previously monitored brain activity demonstrating signs of dream hallucinations.

Inclusion Criteria: Basic learning skills consistent with working at a high school education level and ability to self-evaluate and document responses to a variety of inputs.

Exclusion Criteria: 1) pregnancy, 2) presence of a potentially dangerous metallic device, implanted or otherwise, 3) age less than 16 or greater than

40, 4) presence of a medical, neurological, or psychiatric condition that makes MR scanning dangerous or confounds experimental hypotheses (e.g., cardiac disease, seizure disorder, traumatic brain injury, or mental illness), 5) claustrophobia," I finally completed.

"We can do that," Mairy said again, looking to Andrew. "It is what being a Shadow-Forge is all about: controlling the mind and spirit."

"Maybe for you," Andrew recalled with doubt. "But I have yet to master any of these aspects for being a Shadow-Forge by myself. I'm afraid that without Harmony, I'm useless."

"But Harmony is with us always. And remember, I have given you part of me; which is also a part of my shared connection with Harmony," Mairy said, encouraging him on. "I'll coach you ever day until we leave. And by the time we reach the Moon, you will be ready."

"I'd feel much better knowing what a pod operator does," Andrew replied back. "I've barely finished high school. I don't even have a high school degree."

"Yes, I thought about that," I consoled him. "But you should be able to finish your last few months out here, and then take the tests to get your GED."

"That's still doesn't tell me if I can handle this job," Andrew replied back.

"So much doubt," Steve spoke up. "Where is the Andrew that I know; the one who traveled the stars and back again? We all have faith in you. We are all in this together."

Andrew gave no response.

Steve continued to work with him, "I'll tell you what, I'll find out what I can about the job. And you can just consider it being like on the job training. You've always been able to catch on to things quickly."

"OK, I'll give it a try," Andrew finally relented.

"That's my boy," Steve couldn't help replying back.

"Now where should we say that you both got your experience?" I said aloud, as I searched through the internet for a possible background story. "Ah, here's one: Request for volunteers at the 'Mind Research Network for Neurodiagnostic Discovery' in Albuquerque, NM."

"Anything closer," Steve asked. "We want to make it sound believable."

"Here's another one, but the program is a little more non-descript. It's at 'The Department of Neurology at the University of Illinois, College of Medicine at Chicago'," I suggested.

"Yes, that's good. And the more non-descript, the better," Steve agreed. "You can say you were part of their summer volunteer or internship program. Companies never real delve into corroborating such details. They are more interested in documentation like educational degrees and such."

"OK, easy peasy, I can pass as volunteer," agreed Andrew; "nothing technical about being a volunteer."

"And by the time you reach the Moon, Mairy will have you ready to play the part," I repeated.

"Thank goodness for all that time you spent in drama class in high school," Steve joked of the situation.

"Yes, I will be giving the greatest performance of my life," Andrew retorted; "Being something I'm not."

"OK, then it is off to the Moon," Steve announced.

"This is going to be one kick-ass vacation!" Andrew declared, using a tough guy movie reference.

I sat there thinking about what the next three months would reveal; for we were not just here to start our lives anew, but we were starting our lives as part of a covert team of Shadow-Forge quest operatives. Talk about stress. Indeed, this may all be temporary, depending on how the quest plays out.

I recalled how Andrew had told me of his adventures, and I had listened from the safety of my own displacement from his situation; like watching a fantasy adventure movie. But now I am participant. And despite my outward demeanor, I was not sure I was up to the task. Still, I knew that I could not just stand by while my family puts themselves in a dangerous situation. My only consolation was that, by being with them, perhaps I could somehow help keep them safer.

[Time Change – Mother's Perspective continued]

[Even the best-laid plans of mice and men often go awry.]

What I couldn't know then was that the company would accelerate their time table and take Steve after only two weeks of off-site training; leaving us behind to work out things for ourselves. The day of Steve's departure was truly memorable. In fact, it was the day revealed what was special about the humongous building at the end of the runway. It was the colossal hangar that housed both a 747 and a space shuttle. We all watched with exhilaration, the takeoff off of the piggyback shuttle.

After Steve had gone, it was all I could do to keep the kid's on task. While patience and restraint were never virtues that Andrew was able to master, his cautious nature usually kept him in check. Still, upon the influence of Mairy, the two filled their free time with unauthorized explorations of the islands facilities. Yet, within a week after Steve was gone they had already he worked out a plan on their own for how to travel together to the Moon. The fact that they would be leaving me alone didn't seem to bother either of them.

Of course, this would then leave me to cover for them, while continuing with my training, handling all of the required documentation, and coordinating the long term logistics of storage for our belongings. This is not how I planned to spend my time getting ready to go to the Moon. But, for this quest, I understood that everyone had their part to play; although mine seemed to be less glamourous than the others. Still, I had to admit, it wasn't so bad having a little down time of my own, without the kids, before leaving Earth.

Fortunately, I was able to persuade them to delay their departure until after their completion of scheduled orientation for shuttle boarding and deboarding, which included a live tour of the shuttle that would be carrying us all to the Moon. This would mean they would be around for another month, at least. My hope was to eventually convince the kid's to just follow the company program and adhere to the scheduled.

As it was, I was not sure what the two hoped to accomplish by leaving two months early anyway. Rather, it was Mairy who confided in us about her increasing sense of forewarning which she did not want to ignore. So for the next month, Andrew and Mairy helped me out with the chores and continued their training. All the while, they persisted in their exploration of the islands and the planning of their escape to the Moon.

All seemed, more or less, normal until the night of the hurricane. The company had planned for such eventualities, and safety was a constant theme in their training. The sustained wind gusts had already picked up to about 40 mph, before the sirens signaled for everyone to be evacuated to the shelters. We grabbed our flashlights and gathered up a few belongings to entertain ourselves for the duration of the storm. It had already begun to rain before we left the house. As we headed for the island's storm shelters, Mairy immediately became wary of our surroundings.

"Something is not right," Mairy announced. "Please go on ahead and I'll catch up with you later," she said, as she passed me everything but her flashlight.

"What do you mean you'll catch up with us later," Andrew exclaimed boisterously. "I know you. If something is not right, then that means something is very wrong." He then turned to me with the same request, "Mom, we'll catch up with you as soon as we check this out." He then, likewise, passed me everything but his flashlight.

"OK, don't be long. The weather is getting worse by the minute," I cautioned them.

I felt a bit of pride in my son's willingness to back up Mairy. I guess I raised him right. As the rain went horizontal, I watched as they quickly disappeared from view, round toward the back of the house. I could only worry as I proceeded across the runway to the shelter, laden with the plastic bags they gave me.

I met up with Kiana at the shelter entrance as she was ushering people in.

"Where are your kids," Kiana asked with some concern.

"The kids went back for something," I informed her. "I'm sure they'll be along shortly."

"OK then, I'll watch out for them," Kiana assured me. "Find a place in the shelter where you can save them some seats."

"Thank you," I acknowledged of her kindness.

But as I continued into the shelter, I looked back to see Kiana leaving towards the outside. As I had always been suspicious of her intent, I dropped everything but my flashlight and followed after her. In the dark of the night and with the pouring rain pelting me on my face, I was barely able to keep track of her. Finally, having lost sight of her, I was unable to even discern where Kiana might have gone. I thought to myself that it would've been better if the runway lights were a little brighter.

So I decided instead to go to the house and see what was taking the kids so long. I went around the back of the house because that is the last place I saw them go. As I rounded the corner, a big blast of wind and rain buffeted me back. The storm was indeed getting worse. As I made my way pass the bushes, I could see the glare of a flashlight on the ground. A little farther on I could Andrew lying on the ground. I rushed to his side.

"Andrew, what happened?!" I exclaimed.

He only motioned with his hand, but it was enough for me to satisfy myself that he was alright.

Then in a panic, I realized that I couldn't see Mairy. Hearing the clamor of a struggle off in the distance towards the pier, I shined my flashlight over in that direction. There, in the beam of my flashlight, it looked to me to be a large hairy beast of a figure on top of Mairy. The beast appeared to be forcing Mairy's head under water at the shoreline.

Without thinking, I left Andrew and ran to where they were fighting. Without slowing down, I rammed my body's weight against the beastly figure that was holding Mairy down. I heard the animal give a quick yelp, much like the sound of a dog in pain, before it fell off into the water on the other side of the pier. I immediately pulled Mairy up out of the water. As she coughed up water, she pointed back over to the pier. From out of the dark, I could make out the figure of the hairy beast. It appears it had recovered and was lunging over towards us.

Miraculously, as the animal bounded towards us, it appeared to have been forced away from us in midair, and at a right angle to our position in the water. It was Kiana. Upon a strike of lightning in the darkness of the storm, I could see Kiana recoiling from a kick and following after the beast with fervent resolve.

As I shined the light in their direction, I saw Kiana being wrestled down by the beast. I shined the light towards the ground to see it there was something to hit it with; some sort of stick or club. When I looked up again, I saw Kiana kicked him off. The creature went flying a few feet away, and was quick to get back up into a defensive stance on all four legs. As the beast made its way towards Kiana, I threw my flashlight and hit it square in the head. It instantly changed its attention toward me, but only for a moment; for now Mairy was up in the fight as well.

From the light of the fallen flashlight, I could only make out that Mairy had leaped up onto its back. As Mairy tried to put a strangle hold on the creature, it reared up and rolled over. The creature then appeared to grab Mairy with its front paws, tossing her aside like a ragdoll. As it turned attention from Mairy, I assumed it was leaving to attack Kiana again. Hearing multiple shots ring out, I turned toward the sound. In the flash of the gun's muzzle, I could make out the silhouette of Kiana as she was shooting the beast.

I ran over to where I saw Mairy being thrown, and realized that Andrew had caught up to me, with his flashlight in hand. Shining his light, we soon found Mairy, still lying on the ground. As we helped Mairy up, she had regained her senses enough to surveil the area for anymore danger. From behind us, Kiana appeared.

"Is everyone alright," Kiana asked.

"Yes, we're all fine," I answered for all of us.

"Way to go mom," I heard Andrew praise me for coming to their rescue.

"Yes, that was quite a lucky throw," Mairy agreed.

Then the three of us all hugged; in part to support ourselves from falling.

I then turned to see Kiana face and arms were scratched and bleeding a bit; not unlike Mairy's own cuts.

"I don't remember seeing an animal that large in the residence area," Kiana stated. "I'll check later to see if it came from one of the other islands along the runway. Right now we have to get out of this storm."

Holding Mairy up, we all started back to the shelters. After a while, Andrew took over with helping Mairy. I felt bad about doubting Kiana's intentions and lingered back to talk with her.

"I want to thank you for following after my kids the way you did," I said appreciably to Kiana.

I felt compelled to resolve my emotional suspiciousness of Kiana's attention toward us. Clearly she was looking out for us.

"Things may have turned out quite differently if you hadn't been here in time," I related to her.

She wrapped her left arm around my shoulder in acknowledgement, and we headed towards the storm shelter. As we settled into the shelter, I tended to the cuts and bruises that were now more visible in the light of the well-lit bunker. Kiana continued with her duties in the storm shelter, leaving us to talk among ourselves. Others came up from behind Kiana, offer up dry blankets for her and then to us to get warm.

As we were left alone, Andrew confided in me, "Mom, it was the Tokoloshe."

"What! How is that possible?" I asked. "It was on the mainland, and we are way out here." I had to believe that he was mistaken and countered his disclosure, "It must just have been a large dog, as Kiana said."

"No, it was him again alright," Mairy piped in. "And most definitely in a much larger version of itself. So it must have killed itself to have been re-hosted here," she concluded. "But to be re-hosted so quickly after its first manifestation seems very strange to me. I'll have to think on that. One thing for sure, it was after me. And if it had not been for you, I may have had to be re-hosted myself. For that, I thank you."

"And if it hadn't been for Kiana, we might all have been much worse off," I admitted.

"Well, thank you for coming back for us," Mairy said appreciatively to Sandi.

"It's what mothers do for their children," I acknowledged of her thoughtfulness. "I guess you were right about getting off this island earlier. I should've listened to you."

I no longer pushed for them to stay until the scheduled launch time and agreed to allow them to sneak out at their earliest opportunity. Weird to admit; but to keep them safe, I needed to get them off this planet.

9

Space Stowaways

**[The purpose of a quest is often revealed
in the discoveries of its journey.]**

As the shuttle was no longer just built for astronauts, the craft had to provide for the safety of civilian transport as well. To this end, the shuttle was intended to be launched from the edge of space, instead of from the ground. The trick was to get it to that point.

Perched atop the back of a massive 747, the shuttle could be transported up beyond the greater forces of Earth's gravitational pull. The extensively modified jet airliner was stripped down to reduce weight, employing just the essentials needed to carry its own fuel, two attached solid booster rockets, and the shuttle gently to 9 miles up and out into the Earth's upper atmosphere. The solid boosters would execute a two stage burn, pushing the jet and its piggyback payload up to a further 28 miles above the Earth. Such was the strategy needed for the shuttle to reach an altitude of 28 miles before launching from the edge of space. In this way, the shuttle would not need to carry the extra fuel, required of a ground based launch, to break free of the Earth's gravity. Rather the load of this extra fuel would be carried by the altered 747.

At the end of the jet liner's solid boosters' burn, the shuttle would disconnect from atop of the jet liner, whereupon the jet airliner would slowly drop and glide back into the Earth's lower atmosphere. Once the jet liner was out of the way, the shuttle's re-useable external twin tank, mounted underneath the shuttle, would then take over to launch the space shuttle from the edge of space, and into the upper boundary of the Earth's stratosphere. The overall shuttle design was meant to provide for a reduced fuel load and weight, while still allowing it to achieve an orbital velocity at the required 70 miles up into outer space.

[Andrew's Perspective]

At the time of our departure, the shuttle module was still set up just as it was during the orientation tour, presented just days earlier. Since the cargo hold of the space shuttle also doubled as an escape pod, it was conveniently equipped with seats and all the supplies one would need to survive a disaster in space. Although it made the shuttle design slightly heavier than its predecessors, it was a necessary improvement that allowed the crew to mitigate the risks of past shuttle disasters.

By this time, Mairy had rationalized that whatever Discordia and her legions of chaos were planning must have something to do with this dad's research and this moon station. And after the sneak attack from that beast during the hurricane, all involved decided we needed to get up there as soon as possible. But first we had to get aboard the shuttle without being seen.

Mairy and I sneaked into the airport hangar and stalked about the space shuttle, which was not yet mounted atop the massive 747 jet liner. As I followed behind her, she stealthfully maneuvered about the jet liner, trying to avoid inadvertent contact with the loading crew. Our timing had to be precise if we were to board the space shuttle undetected. While waiting for an opportunity to board the shuttle, it felt more like waiting to leap off the high dive. As nervous as I was, I would just have to trust that everything would turn out alright. I could only imagine that Mairy's experience would make it so.

Recalling the tour guide's presentation, I remembered being impressed with the innovated use of their reusable rocket technology. For rather than just launching the shuttle into space from Earth, their reusable rockets were employed as inflight boosters to assist the massive jet airliner, and its piggybacked payload, to escape Earth's gravity. So the reusable boosters were not to be discarded. Rather they would be brought back as part of the jet itself. Their strategy was two-fold; while the gradual ascent not only reduced the g-force stresses of a ground launch on the shuttle, and its associate parts, it also reduced the fuel required to be stored on the shuttle itself.

In this way, the shuttle boosters only needed enough fuel to propel it up into a higher altitude orbital velocity, just beyond the Earth's greater gravitational pull: about 50 miles up. From there, the shuttle slowly builds up enough speed to skirt the 'Kármán Line', located around 62 miles above the surface of the Earth. The 'Kármán Line' serves as the approximate border between space and the Earth' gravitational pull. Like a stone skipping on the water, the shuttle is open to take advantage of this 'free space', accelerating it to its final traveling speed of a little over 32,000 mph. At this rate, it would still take another two days to reach the Earth's Moon. But right now, we just needed to make it over about 75 feet into the space shuttle.

"This may not be the best idea that we've ever come up with," I declared with some nervousness.

"Do I detect a tone of apprehension in your voice?" Mairy joked. "Besides, what are you so worried about? They said this was just to be a cargo run. So there won't be any other passengers on board."

"It's not that," I answered back. "I am not used to traveling off world in this manner."

"Well, that makes two of us," Mairy insisted.

"I wouldn't mind using a 'Star Trek' transporter, once the shuttle was already in space. At least then, there is no time to regret your decision," I thought aloud.

"A 'Star Trek' what?" Mairy asked with confusion.

"Never mind; it's not a real thing anyway," I responded. I paused to think more on the subject while I kept watch. "Actually, don't you have some extra superpower that would allow us to be beamed up to the Moon, or is this the only way to get us there?"

"What is with you and powers?" Mairy asked with incredulity. "Everyone has powers of some sort or other. In fact, just being alive is a power, in and of itself."

"OK. I just thought I would ask," I replied defensively.

"Besides, we can only transition from one world to the next as a Shadow-Forge," Mairy related to me. "However, since I'm already in Shadow-Forge form, I can't really do that again; now can I," Mairy asked sarcastically. "And you're not quite ready to take that leap just yet, so we'll just have to do it this way."

"But I'm not like you. You are the one who just jumps into danger without a second thought," I said, trying to reason with her. "I often have a lot of second thoughts. I even have third and fourth thoughts."

"It's when you take the time to think about it, that you allow you demons to interfere in your thoughts," she replied.

"Demons," I repeated with some confusion? "Do you mean like 'indecision' and 'fear'? That's what we call our survival instincts kicking in, with a boost of adrenaline. They are not demons."

"If I have to battle them, then I do not see the difference," she stated firmly.

Finally an opening presented itself. "It looks like they have completed preparations for the cargo module," Mairy suggested to me as we watched the workers move onto another area of the space shuttle. "OK, they're out of sight; let's move."

If nothing else, she was bold and daring. Two attributes of hers that I had to admit helped save my butt more than once. We made our way across the hangar and up into the space shuttle cargo hold. As we boarded, we continued to assess our options, wandering about the cargo module.

"We'll have to hide somewhere until they are ready for takeoff. Once they're in flight, I doubt anyone will have any need to come back here," I guessed. "I'll see what I can find for us to hide in."

I wandered about the cargo hold, as if I was playing 'hide-and-seek', looking for just the perfect place to hide before 'takeoff'.

"Looks like they have their own 'port-o-potty' out here," I remarked opening a door to what appeared to be a mobile toilet.

"What's a 'port-o-potty'?" inquired Mairy.

"It's kind of a plastic restroom," I explained. "But this one is made of metal."

"Makes sense that they would need one back here if this was meant as a survival module," Mairy replied.

I looked to Mairy and stated, "Hey, perhaps we can hide in here until they're ready for takeoff."

"Do you really think it would be safe to hide in a 'port-o-potty' of the cargo hold during takeoff?" inquired Mairy sarcastically?

"Well, not when you say it that way," I responded. But then I thought better of my original plan, saying, "Come to think of it, maybe someone will need to use the restroom before takeoff," I thought aloud.

Mairy just rolled her eyes again. As she never did it with the intent of being mean, it was becoming to be one of her more endearing qualities.

"Nah, I'm sure they all took care of their business before boarding. Besides, they must have their own facilities outside the cargo module," I presented the assumption. "I really doubt anyone will have any need to come back here until we've reached the moon station," I stated of my chosen location for us to hide.

"And I guess it's not really the most secure location to be in if we hit any kind of turbulence," I corrected myself, from a more practical perspective.

"Hey, have we considered whether it is safe to ride in the cargo hold at all?" I asked in earnest.

"I mean, we are traveling into space, and life support may not be required back here if it is just for cargo," I surmised, as my survival instincts kicked in.

Being a little preoccupied, Mairy was not really listening to my nervous ramblings. "Sorry," Mairy questioned, "did you say something?"

"Not really; no; I was just thinking out loud," I replied, almost apologetically.

I was quick to get back on subject, recalling, "Wait; now I remember. According to the presentation, it's safe to ride back here because this is also an escape module. And as such, it must be maintained as if it were part of the cockpit to allow for the quick transfer of the crew." I continued to support my summarization of the tour guide's briefing, "So the cargo hold needs to be properly pressurized at all times to allow for full life support during the entire flight."

"That's good to know," Mairy acknowledged. "So I guess we won't be needing these space suits then," she remarked, as she looked over her find.

"I'll bet they are for space walks," I concluded.

"Or maybe the space shuttle lands outside the moon station and they have to wear them to go inside," Mairy provided an alternative rationale.

Rethinking about my apprehension, I stated, "So, if you are in Shadow-Forge form and something goes wrong, then you would just reappear back in your own realm. However, if I die," I paused to think of the consequences.

"If you die, then I have to come back and deal with this quest alone," Mairy responded, jokingly completing my sentence. "Anyway, I am not hiding in a restroom stall during takeoff." As she continued to search among the containers, she announced, "Now this looks more promising."

I came over to look. It appeared that the container Mairy had discovered was a kind of closet, full of new clothes. Yet another sign that this cargo hold could be used as an escape module.

"What do they have in here?" I asked aloud. "It would appear they have extra clothes, as well as space suits, complete with helmets. Better safe than sorry," I supposed.

"I believe the space suits might be a bit much for our purposes," Mairy responded with a smile as they rummaged through the clothing. "Now this looks to be my size." Without hesitation or embarrassment, Mairy stripped down to her undies and put on the full body, uniform-like, zip suit.

It was a little awkward for me, but I couldn't help staring. Although she was wearing no less than any other girl in a bikini on the beach, to me it was still like underwear. I also couldn't help noticing there was nothing about her that shouted out 'alien' to me, other than the color and texture of her nails. In fact, she had quite an attractive body for an alien.

Then as she looked over to me, I turned my gaze, with some embarrassment. Fumbling back through the clothing in the closet, I pretended to be looking for something in my size.

"Well, are you going to change, already?" she asked. "We don't want to be conspicuous when we get there. We need to blend in."

Not truly understanding her immediate concern, I responded, "If they find us back here, I don't think blending in will help us any."

"I didn't mean we needed to blend in here, on the space shuttle," she said smiling. "I meant that we need to blend in when we reach our destination."

"Oh, yes," I replied pulling out a garment at random. "That would make more sense."

"That one looks a little big for you," she commented. She then walked over and reached in for another selection. "Here, try this one on."

And so I did. Following her lead, I stripped down to my undies and slipped on the full body suit. It wasn't the kind of clothing I would normally wear. It reminded me of a child's snowsuit. But Mairy was right that we needed to blend in with everyone else. They even had a pair of shoes in my size. "These shoes are a bit heavy," I stated, noticing their weight.

[Narrator's Perspective]

There was a sudden jounce as the reusable space shuttle, Argo, was being transferred to its perch on the top of the modified jet, Daedalus.

Andrew and Mairy moved to the safety of built in seats, positioned along the back wall of the cargo hold, and drew their seat harnesses into place. Had there been windows in the cargo hold, Andrew and Mairy would have seen the shuttle was pulled up and over the nose of the jet onto a fixed scaffold. Once in place, the Argo was secured to the top of Daedalus. The Argo was now ready to piggyback into flight atop Daedalus.

The Daedalus taxied onto the runway that ran the entire length of the island. The massive airliner could be seen to dwarf the surrounding airport buildings, except for the one from which it came. As the jet taxied to the end of the island runway, it was positioned for takeoff. After just a few minutes, the Daedalus roared to life. The jet gradually picked up speed, as it sped along the ground toward the end of the runway and the open ocean. Once Daedalus reached the end of the runway, the jet did not waste time gaining altitude, and they were off into the night sky.

As it flew up to its absolute ceiling in the night sky, the 747's booster rockets ignited allowing the jetliner to reach the appropriate altitude for their maneuver. The stowaways were taken off guard by the extreme jolt of the igniting booster rockets. Hanging onto his seat harnesses, Andrew looked to see Mairy complacently sitting with her eyes closed. It was as if she was without worry, or was just resigned to her fate.

Once the booster rockets were turned off, there would be a short 5 minute window provided to protect the safety of both the shuttle and the airliner. Liken to riding on a rollercoaster, Andrew awaited the pause in anticipation of the next surprise. As the shuttle separated, the airliner continued flying out from under it, as it lowered to the safety of the jetliner's absolute ceiling once again.

Once separated, the space shuttle was now free to ignite its own internal booster rockets; allowing it to continue its ascent to a higher orbital altitude. Having no warning of the sudden acceleration from within the cargo hold, the stowaways were once again taken off balance.

Later, as the shuttle attained a more consistent speed, Andrew felt the weightlessness of his body lift from his seat. Wanting to share this moment, he looked to Mairy who was just opening her eyes. The moment there eyes met, they both smiled and released their seat harnesses. They floated out of their constraints, hand in hand. And with a slight push, they both traveled to opposite ends of the cargo module.

[Andrew's Perspective]

Bouncing about the cargo hold of the space shuttle in zero gravity, I felt a bit like Peter Pan once again. It brought back memories of my training with Harmony on Earth and my time on Glorthocks near its planet's convergence with DeMutron.

"It seems we've have done this before," Mairy quipped to lighten the mood; "you and I floating together in space." She was probably thinking about our time in the crystal, before we entered the black hole.

"Yes, but this time I don't have to worry about dying in the process," I stated, reflecting on my own recollection of that time together. "I'm still not sure how we managed to survive within the Source Seed. Without our Shadow-Forge bodies, we should have just reverted back to our original host bodies."

"Yes, I remember. It was as if we were held within our own transcendence between altering realities; much like when we travel via in Harmony's grace in bubble form," she offered up her opinion. "Perhaps there is more than one way for us to host our astral spirits."

Feeling a bit unsure of my present vulnerability, I expressed my feelings, "At least if something goes wrong here, you just transition back into your own existence."

"You've made that point more than once. Besides, maybe I am not ready to go back just yet," Mairy stated. "Still, if you were worried about dying, then you should have waited until you could transform yourself."

"Transform?" I inquired incredulously. "I'm not like you. I can't just pop in and out of spacetime at the 'drop of a hat'. I need Harmony to become a Shadow-Forge."

"No, not really; she just meant to show you the way," Mairy replied. "You should be able to transform on your own now."

"Besides, since our shared experience within the black hole," Mairy continued to explain, "you now share a connection with Harmony through me. In order to maintain your being and return you to your own existence, we had to give you something more. I had to give you part of me; a part of my shared connection with Harmony. So Harmony is always with you."

"Well, I haven't been able to," I retorted. "I tried many times without success."

"Perhaps you have properly linked up with the right connection," Mairy revealed.

"Connection?" I asked. "I need to be connected to something?"

"Without a connection, your only destination is your own host," she explained.

"You mean I could have transformed at any time during these last few years?" Andrew asked.

"Probably not without some proper practice," Mairy answered.

"Well, how was I to know that I even still had this ability?" I replied, contradicting myself. "Besides, what if I end up in a black hole again?"

"Well, there you have it," she said simply. "You're conflicted by your own fear of that experience. I guess, having the ability to transcend, and being capable of transcending are competing concepts in your mind."

"OK," I accepted her explanation without further scrutiny. "But what about what the other fairies can do? Do I also really have the ability to make short hops to other realms?"

"Yes, but remember the fairies came with a specific purpose as well," continued Mairy. "Remember, your focus and purpose are also important parts of any transformation. These concepts help you to make the proper connection."

There was a short pause before Mairy playfully asked, "So where would you go? What would you do?"

"It would have been nice to revisit Glorthocks from time to time," I answered a bit meekishly, thinking of how it would be nice to see how Pooncha and Avian were doing. "Have you ever gone back?"

"No," Mairy replied, "it does not hold good memories for me. Besides, I have no real life connections from that quest other than after I met up with you."

"Well, there's a certain little imp I would like to look in on," I muttered to myself, thinking about Pooncha.

For the next two days, as the shuttle sped to the Moon, we continued to survive in the cargo hold. Having found a reserve stash of food and beverages in another of the containers on board, we fended for ourselves much like we would have at home. Most of the time, we just played about the cargo hold like two kids with 'cabin fever'. We even fell asleep once or twice, floating about in the weightless embrace of our temporary residence, until we eventually reached their journey's end on the dark side of the moon.

As our weightlessness diminished, we were pulled slightly towards the side of the cargo hold, as if by the moon's gravity. We could even feel the shuttle changing direction. This was to be the part where the shuttle crew executed the maneuver to make their approach towards their path to the Moon. We quickly became serious and made our way back to our seats, as the shuttle realigned itself for landing.

[Scene Change – Andrew's Perspective continued]

[Participating in this quest was a bit like spy training.]

Finally, I felt the shuttle slow to a stop and I could hear that we were docking. As we unstrapped ourselves from our seats and moved out of sight of the cargo hatch, waiting for our chance to discretely disembark. It wasn't long before workers arrived to remove the cargo. As we hide among the cargo, Mairy picked up her civilian clothes. She then turned to me and whispered, "Do not forget to pick up your old clothes."

I nodded in compliance and grabbed mine as well. I could see that Mairy was right on top of things. She did not want us to leave any trace of our 'stowing away' on the shuttle for others to discover. She then saw our chance to blend in by helping the workers to unload the cargo. Hiding her clothing under the cargo she was carrying was a stroke of genius on her part. Following her lead, I mimicked her actions. I was surprised at the size of the carton I picked up, as it was deceiving lighter than expected.

Once outside the shuttle, we followed along and placed the cargo at the back of the pile. Slipped our civilian clothing under our arms, we made our way through the confusion of workers doing their jobs. With Mairy leading the way, we left down a long hallway that led away from the landing bay area. As we walked, I noticed the multilingual markings along the walls. When we came across one that said 'trash', we dumped our civilian clothing.

As we reached the end of the corridor, we faced our first 'fork in the road'. "Well, where do we go now?" I asked, looking around discretely. I felt a bit like the cowardly lion on the movie, *'The Wizard of Oz'*.

"What did your dad say?" Mairy asked. "There is supposed to be some research lab at the far end of the facility from the landing bay; headed up by some woman name Dr. Margaret Beecher."

Mairy then noticed my posture, and admonished me, "And stop skulking about. You look like your about to steal something. Remember, we are just new members to this facility. Try acting a little more natural."

"Oh yeah," I replied. She was right of course. I was probably drawing more attention to us by skulking about.

"They must have them coming in all the time," she said, supporting her statement.

"What; new arrivals?" I asked reflexively. "I suppose so."

"Pretend you're just on another quest, and blend in," she explained, as she stepped boldly in the crossway.

Befuddled by her brashness, I gave her a confused response, "So just pretend we are not here illegally?" I asked sarcastically. I mean, it wasn't like I had all that much practice; having only been on one quest.

"Now you have it. Demonstrate the same composure that you employed on Glorthocks to get around," she advised. "And don't be afraid to mingle a little."

"I really didn't mingle in well on Glorthocks," I added. "I was actually spotted as an outlander within minutes of arriving in their nearest settlement."

"Well, then, focus on me," she insisted, trying to distract me from our breaking and entering on the moon station. "Pretend we are just out for a pleasant walk together."

"A pleasant walk?" I asked incredulously. "My idea of a pleasant time is not breaking and entry into a secure facility in the middle of space. What if we get caught?"

"I like you," Mairy responded before giving me a quick peck on the cheek. "You're funny."

Well, that was unexpected; but it did the trick. While I was trying to interpret the intent behind her casual kiss, I paid less attention to worrying about our current state of affairs. By then we had walked along through several corridors of rooms, or offices. Pretending to be lost, when randomly questioned by the inhabitants of the moon station, we eventually made our way the heart of the facility. Curiously, each member of the facility, that we encountered, seemed to be less concerned about our business and more concerned about their own business. They were, instead, rather inclined to be helpful.

This spy stuff was a 'piece of cake', I thought to myself. Freeing up my mind from worry, also allowed me to think about other concerns; like where I came from and where I was going. I imagined the layout of the moon station to be a cross between a hotel, or office building, and a mall. Trying to orient myself in these strange surroundings, I instinctively began to map out the moon station in my mind, until we finally made it to what I presumed to be the center of moon station.

The center was a much larger area of the complex that opened up into a ten story rotunda of balconies and walkways. Frankly, it looked a lot like the 'Minnesota Mall of America', but it had more of an industrial airport ambiance about it. I then recalled the visual that they displayed to us on the first day of orientation. Coming out onto what appeared to be a third floor walkway of this rotunda, I stopped to take it all in.

This center area lent itself to an atrium-like atmosphere, and was more brightly lit than the corridors we had been traveling through. Looking up to the ring of windows, just below the non-transparent dome of the rotunda, I noticed that the lighting was more artificial than natural. It was brighter inside the complex than it was outside the windows. Must be dusk, I thought to myself. Having not yet acclimated myself to the Moon's condition, it wasn't at all strange to think of the Moon having a dusk and a dawn.

"This is some place," I said in amazement. "Who would've guessed they'd have a mall on the Moon."

It actually eased my tension over our clandestine activity, and encouraged me to just do what comes natural. Actually I always loved hanging around and exploring within the variety of mall stores. The mall gave me a feeling of security and independence at the same time. But my unsolicited comments went unacknowledged, as Mairy seemed to be preoccupied with scanning the lower floors.

Spying a cafeteria on the lower floor, Mairy said to me, "I'm hungry; let's get something to eat."

Mairy seemed more susceptible and reactive to the involuntary sensations prompting her new body: If she was tired, she would sleep; if she was hungry, she would eat; and if there was danger, she would spring into action. It was as if she reacted without any real emotional influence. I, on the other hand, had enough emotional worry for the both of us. And as such involuntary emotions were second nature to me, I had time to multitask about the nonessential concerns of our being there: like worrying what were we going to do if security got wise that we were up here on the moon station without permission.

Still, it was amazing the way she just took command of her surroundings. She was certainly in her element.

She was like a female version of 'James Bond'; having an air of confidence in her every action. We got on the elevator, which was an all glass enclosures like those I've ridden in at the mall. I continued to be awed by my surroundings as we descended the five floors down to where we saw the cafeteria.

As fate would have it, we got in line behind a group of people who were discussing their participation on some project in the area of the research lab. To my chagrin, Mairy picked up on their discussion and did not hesitate to join in.

"Excuse me," Mairy began asking the woman in front of her. "We couldn't help overhearing your conversation. Did you say you were working in the research lab?"

"Why yes, but where do you work?" she asked with some suspicion. It appeared Mairy had not considered there might be a security partitioning of differing tasks on the moon station.

Not being put off in the least, Mairy continued, "Oh, we haven't really started yet. We just arrived on the shuttle today, and we are supposed to report for training with Dr. Margaret Beecher in the research lab."

"Oh, you must be the two new pod sleepers we have been waiting for," her male cohort said looking at me.

"Ah, yes," I acknowledged uneasily, just 'kind of' going along with the storyline that Mairy was fabricating. "But we're still a little disoriented. You know, being up here for the first time and all."

I began to think that there was more to Mairy than I first thought. It was almost as if she had planned this all out in advance. But how could she have, I questioned of my assumption? It had to be just a serendipitous coincidence.

"Wasn't there anyone to meet you at the landing bay?" the woman asked, continuing to ply us with questions.

"No, I don't think they knew we were coming," I answered without thinking.

Just then Mairy bumped into me, jogging me to think about what I had just said. It was clear to me she was better at this than I was. Perhaps worried about what I might say next, Mairy interjected herself back into the conversation.

"What he means is that we were actually not scheduled until the next launch. But when an opportunity presented itself for us to come on this earlier flight, we took it. We were so excited to get started that we couldn't pass it up. It was all rather last minute."

"That was lucky," her male cohort responded of our story. "I understand the flights are sometime scheduled months apart."

"Only problem is, that when we got here, we couldn't even find our luggage," Mairy pressed on with her story. "And it had all our paperwork in it."

"And we are quite lost without our paperwork," I said, seemingly finishing her thought.

"Typical mix up in communications," another male member of the group joined in to the discussion.

"I had my domain name changed on my email, and it took weeks for them to acknowledge that I was working up here at all," he offered. "By the way, my name is Milo," he stated, introducing himself to Mairy.

Perhaps I was being a little overprotective, but it I interjected myself between Mairy and Milo.

"Good to know you Milo. My name is Andrew and this is Mairy," I introduced for both of us.

"Hi, I'm Timothy," the first male cohort said, extending his greeting. "It will be good to have some fresh ideas and faces around here. Conversations have been getting a little stale as of late."

"And I'm Lindsey," the woman said, introducing herself. "We've been working with Dr. Beecher right along," she stated, feeling safe enough to talk more freely. "Aren't you two are a bit young to be in this field of study? Where did they recruit you two from?"

"Actually we came in as part of the team with Stephen Bauer," I said, providing a little name dropping to corroborate our being there.

"Oh yes, we know of him. He came up about a month ago," Milo answered.

"Yes; he's that new consultant working with Dr. Leighy, isn't he?" Tim commented, looking to his female counterpart for some confirmation.

"Yes, I believe Stephen works with John," Lindsey answered using their first names, and then continued to drill us with more questions. "Where have you been training?"

As she still seemed a bit suspicious of our responses, I tried to maintain a poker face and make up something on the fly.

"Oh, training," I said aloud, trying to think of something fast. "I don't know if you would call it training. We were working as part of an internship program with some Sleep Disorder Center when we were recruited."

"I believe our recruitment had something to do with our performance during our psychological evaluations," I said, looking to Mairy for some help.

"Yes, it was all quite exciting. They would use us to calibrate the instruments on their machines for their sleep study program," Mairy promoted. "They would hook us up to all these monitors and then put us to sleep. Next thing you know, they offered us this job to help calibrate their equipment up here."

"Yes, as internships go, it was pretty easy," I stated with a feigned smile.

"Is that what they told you," Milo said, with what seemed like some reservations about the truthfulness of our imaginary employers. As the other two members of his group stared disapprovingly at him, he continued.

"They'll have a lot more for you do up here than just sleep."

"Well, I'm sure Dr. Leighy will be looking forward to filling in the last two pod operator placements," Tim added, accepting our explanation and continuing towards his food selections.

"They have been searching for months to fill those positions," he said, as he filled his food tray.

Then looking to see we hadn't grab a food tray, he suggested, "Are you eating light for dinner?"

"Actually, I am pretty hungry," Mairy admitted.

"Then you'll be needing one of these," Milo said, offering Mairy a food tray.

"Oh yeah, I wasn't thinking," I responded, accepting the food tray from Milo for both of us.

"Yes, the flight here can be a little disorienting," Lindsey stated, offering up an excuse for us. "We'll get you two settled straight away after dinner."

"Thank you; we would appreciate that very much," Mairy replied cordially.

Looking around, I could still not get over the grandeur of it all.

"How did they get all this up here," I finally had to ask?

"Beats me," Milo answered. "I just think it's awesome to be part of it all."

"You'll learn some more about the place during your orientation," Tim offered. "They actually started all this back when they were first building the International Space Station. As I understand it, they decided to keep it a secret because the company couldn't get NASA or the government to fund it without having to comply with a lot of bureaucratic red tape."

"Then who is funding it," I asked?

"The government, of course, but they just don't know it," Milo piped in.

"It's TESSERACT," Tim told me. Then he argued back at Milo, "And you don't know any different. Does everything have to be a conspiracy with you?"

"That's because everything is part of some conspiracy," Milo stated 'matter-of-factly'. "Besides a secret plan, by definition is a conspiracy.

And it doesn't get any more secret than this. Hell, I'll bet no one even remembers how many of us are up here."

"Well, I guess that would explain the unconventional location for the base we launched from on Earth," I said, trying to join in.

"Bingo!" Milo agreed. "It's only us, and the people on the island."

"But this place is massive. It must be some 100 times larger than the International Space Station. I wonder how it all remains a secret," I stated rhetorically, following up on our conversation. "It's not without cooperation, to be sure," Tim revealed. "You do launch anything into space, much less people, without NASA not knowing it. I'm sure they have some kind of agreement in place."

"I wouldn't have thought that anyone could have been able move this much stuff from Earth without attracting more attention," I professed. "It's like a five star resort up here."

"They didn't need to bring all of it from Earth, because most of this stuff is manufactured up here," Tim acknowledged. "They moved in the labor force and robots first. Then they started their own mining and manufacturing operations on the lower maintenance levels. Even the air and water are manufactured or recycled up here."

"We're completely self-sufficient. But whatever you do, don't ask how they manage the human waste," Milo quipped. "Some things are better left to the imagination, if you know what I mean."

I acknowledged Milo with a facial expression, but I was more interested in what Timothy just said. "Lower maintenance levels; do you mean there is a basement in this facility as well?" I couldn't have imagined there was more to this station than what I had already seen.

"And then some," Tim added. "The moon station is anchored in a crater five times the size of that Meteor Crater in Winslow, Arizona."

"The main body of this moon station is actually spherical in structure," Lindsey stated, feeling a little more comfortable with us.

"Yeah, like the Star Wars Death Star," Milo said, continuing with his comedic tenor.

Mairy looked to me with some confusion, so I responded directly to her, "It's a movie reference I'll explain it to you later." Then I turned my attention back to the group, asking, "Then half of this moon station is underground, below the Moon's surface?"

"I guess you could put it that way. But it is built onto the natural shape of the Moon's surface within the crater," Tim explained. "Think of it as if you built a building on top of the Winslow Crater, where only half of it was visible from ground level; kind of like sticking an egg into already formed egg carton."

"It is the failsafe of its design and architecture," Lindsey declared. "Should anything happen to damage the above surface portion of this station, the population could retreat to the safety of the underground levels. The underground level could then be sealed off until a proper rescue could be mounted."

"Indeed, it is like a whole separate self-contained city down there," Milo said, adding to the discussion. "Except that they handle most of the self-support systems, minus the shared medical facility."

"The whole set up is rather uniquely interdependent. The lower half of this moon station is even managed by a separate private firm, contracted to make sure everything works and continues running smoothly. The population of the lower half makes up most of the labor force for the entire moon station," Tim explained.

"However this division in the labor force also makes for a more natural separation between the population below, and us here above, because of the work we do," Lindsey said, enlightening us further.

"What she is saying is that you might want to stay out of the lower maintenance sections," Milo admitted in a more pessimistic tone, "because the culture tends to be more like the low income areas of large cities on Earth; if you know what I mean."

"Oh Milo, that's not what I am saying at all," Lindsey scolded him for his off-handed remark. "Rather, it's more like a dystopian society of 'blue collar' workers on the underground levels, who imagine us to be harboring a more utopian society of 'white collar' workers on the above ground levels."

"Dystopian you say?" I questioned, half not familiar with her comfortable use of the term, "how so?"

"Well, while they have everything they need, they are seemingly dissatisfied with what they imagine they don't have; thus, they always want for more," Lindsey expounded. "I believe it is the psychological need of the unchallenged mind. I can only imagine their daily purpose is so routine and repetitive that they do not realize that their labor is all so essential to the well-being and safety of this facility."

"It's 'cabin fever' mixed in with a little 'separation anxiety', plan and simply," Milo made light of her description. "They have too much time on their hands to worry about nothing, if you ask me. None of us have any real contact with what is going on down on Earth. And there is nothing we could do about it, even if we cared to. Hell, we are not really citizen of Earth anymore."

All the while, Mairy listened until they started talking about their interaction with the people down below.

"How so?" she asked, seemingly repeating my method of questioning.

"What I mean is that we don't really reside, or even exist, outside of this company," Milo expounded. "We don't vote, or really have much of a say in how things work up here. It is as if we are living under third world rules: kind of like the medieval system of feudalism, specifically as it relates to manorialism."

"Well, what we do have is our work. It keep us occupied with new and exciting challenges. It pretty much takes up all our time, and seems to make the time go by a little faster," Tim admitted with a sense of pride in his work. "However, the labor force work day down below is a bit routine, and boredom is the constant bane to an otherwise fulfilling existence. Without constant distraction, time drags on. I can see why they would want for more Earth-like activities; like going outside."

"Just like I said, it's 'cabin fever'," Milo repeated of his earlier suggestion; "although none of us can really go outside anyway. So, as you can probably imagine, they are a little rough around the edges down there."

"Well, it is hardly a paradise down there," Lindsey said with some disdain. "They have no natural lighting, their work and living conditions are cramp, and the food is…, well kind of like it is up here, a bit synthetic."

"A bit synthetic," Milo intervened rhetorically; "You almost have to be a vegetarian to like this daily diet. What I wouldn't give for a fat and juicy cheeseburger."

As Mairy hadn't yet had a cheeseburger, she could not appreciate his sentiment. She was more concerned with the population dynamics. "So how often do you interact with them?"

"Not often; there are scheduled times for them to use the upper facilities, which is usually during our sleep time. The management discourages fraternization between us due to the secretiveness of our research," Lindsey explained. "And all access to our specific work areas is locked down via security protocol. It is all rather an estrange co-existence."

"Besides, down there, being geek is weak. Up here, being geek is chic," Milo stated. "Respect for us is difficult to come by down there, even though it is our work that pays for most of this."

Milo then looked to my plate and asked, "Andrew, are you going to eat that?"

"Behave yourself," Lindsey stated in a motherly demeanor to Milo, and then looked to me. "Talk about being a little rough around the edges."

"Hey, so I got a big appetite," Milo rationalized.

"It's not so much his appetite as it is this damnable low gravity," Timothy claimed. "It's like no matter how much of this synthetic food you eat, it takes forever to digest. You'll see; up here, one never seems full."

I looked around to see that everyone was done eating. Even Mairy had cleaned her plate. My plate had some mix of greens on it.

"No - that's fine, I was never much for eating vegetables anyway," I said, passing my plate over to him, "if that is even what they are."

"Not much to look at, are they," Milo affirmed. "But at least the vegetables aren't synthetic."

"Really," I acknowledged.

"Yes; seems part of the research that they are doing up here provides for growing vegetation," Timothy elucidated. "It has something to do with scrubbing the carbon dioxide from the air and giving it an earth-like odor."

As this aspect of a divided society had little to do with our quest, I was more interested in steering the conversation toward something more uplifting. "So, what do you all do for fun up here?"

"There are actually a variety of physical recreation activities that are mandatory for everyone. They keep us from wasting away in this low gravity environment," Lindsey answered. "We can show them to you now."

With that, everyone got up, leaving their dishes on the table. Looking around, I noticed that although the food service was cafeteria style, they did seem to have their own cleanup crew. Perhaps it spoke more to their habits than their culture, but it was similar to what they do on Earth.

As we walked to the elevator, Timothy continued the conversation, saying, "With all our advances in science, there is no real way to induce gravity where there is none. So keeping fit is almost a daily routine around here."

"All work and no play makes Jack an overweight, out of shape boy, up here," Milo quipped.

"Vacations on Earth will seem more like a chore and less like a relaxing stay if you don't keep up with exercising," Lindsey predicted. "It puts the pep in your step."

"Now that you mention it, why am I not bouncing about like videos I've seen of astronauts on the Moon," I asked.

"It's the footwear; you don't even notice the extra weight," Tim answered. "They did a good job coming up with this footwear. It keeps us grounded without being overbearingly annoying."

"It also forces you to exercise without you even knowing it," Lindsey added.

I guess that would account for the weight of the footwear I found in the shuttle cargo bay, which I noticed while we were still on Earth. I hadn't really thought about it until now.

We all got on the elevator, as Lindsey hit the button for the fifth floor. This is where we came in, I thought to myself. I watched as the elevator provided an ever changing perspective of the main atrium below.

"The lower floors provide for a variety of cleaning, clothing, and eateries," Lindsey explained to Mairy. She then commented, "As you'll be needing some more colorful clothing, I can show you around. It will be nice to have another female in the group."

"Yes, because two of you weren't enough," Milo quipped.

Mairy only smiled. I assumed, without asking, that meant there was already another female in their group. With that, the elevator doors open to let us out on the fifth floor.

"Now up here, there is an unending selection of streaming movies, video and virtual reality gaming, and a random selection of clubs. My passion is virtual reality," Milo revealed. "You can't beat it for a full body escape from this rock in space."

Mairy pulled me over to the side, saying, "It sounds like a way off if we need to get back to Earth."

"What?" I asked with momentary confusion. "Oh, Milo's reference to escape; it's another expression. He means it makes him feel like he has escaped. It is a visual distraction; like watching a movie."

Mairy acknowledged my explanation and we continued along with the crowd. I looked through the store fronts to see what each had to offer. The movie theater seemed to provide for individual, as well as group viewing.

"My dad must love it up here. He has quite an extensive library of 'DVDs' and 'blue ray' disks. It's pretty much all in storage now," I recalled allowed.

"Disks are dead; the cloud is where it's happening," Milo responded of my comment.

"Is there a facility that provides internet or any communication with Earth," Mairy asked.

Just like a spy to want and identify the required resources of her trade, I thought to myself.

"I would've thought they would have covered that in the briefing on Earth. All communication with Earth is 'one way' only; we can receive information but we can't transmit," Lindsey clarified for her. "Or as least not in real time anyway."

Worrying that we might be losing our cover story, I had to think fast. "Yes, we knew that. We just thought that in special circumstances, or emergency situations, there would be some easing of restrictions."

Looking back over to Mairy, she continued, "Or, somewhere where we could go to let our family know that we arrived safely."

I picked up on her intention and supported her reasoning, "Surely, they must have some way to directly communicate shipments and business meetings."

"I'm sure they do, but it appears to be above our paygrade," Milo reacted with more pessimism.

"And what about all these people? There must be some way to allow them to communicate with their family and loved ones down on Earth," Mairy continued to prod for more information.

"It's what we all agreed to when we signed up," Timothy declared, confused at her line of questioning.

"Yep; we're off the grid up here: no cell phones, no Wi-Fi, no chat via internet; just the local network and hardline communications. It's like we have time traveled back into the 20th century," Milo chimed in.

Looking again to Mairy, Lindsey became sympathetic with her concern and stated, "Oh, don't pay attention to them. They are just being dramatic. You can still provide emails to the central communication service via your computer. The emails are reviewed and passed down to Earth on a quarterly basis."

"Think of this moon station like the way they maintained Area 51," Timothy said of our situation, and then began to illuminate us about his analogy. "Back in the mid 1900's, they had a secret facility where they managed advanced research. But only a few brainiacs knew the interplay of the whole project. Everyone else was sworn to secrecy, and they were divided into differing labor forces so that they had no idea what was going on. The segregated working conditions, and their own separate tasks, were being managed at Area 51, while a separate city was built near the facility to manage their daily living needs."

"But the problem is a little different up here," Milo expounded. "How do you keep it secret that there is a research facility on the dark side of the Moon? It's easy: you just don't allow them to communicate with the outside world. This is why everyone had to agree to a multi-year non-disclosure contract. It is also why all of our emails are screened by security. Only when their contracts are up, are they debriefed and returned to Earth. And they must continue to keep the secret is they want to continue getting their pension."

"And, like leaving Area 51, they are provided with a background story for their employment and there is a human resource facility on Earth to which they can coordinate their re-immersion back into society on Earth. Any mention of a moon station, or investigation thereof, is denied in full by their HR," Tim added.

"But it won't stay a secret forever. After a time, an announcement about this facility and the work being done here will be coordinated to the public when the company believes it is safe to do so," Lindsey stated.

It seemed evident to me that they had all discussed this among themselves many times before.

"So what happens if someone gets sick or injured," I asked with some concern.

"Oh, they have an excellent medical facility on the top floor," Lindsey informed us.

"However, for the more serious cases, they send them back to Earth," Timothy added.

"And those that get sent back are never seen or heard from again," Milo said with a sinister tone.

"And the reason they are not seen or heard from again is because they are on Earth and we're still up here," Timothy rationalized.

"Enough of that," Lindsey drew upon her motherly tone again. "Honestly, those two are incorrigible. You mustn't let them worry you so much. Time will go by fast enough for you; you'll see. There is a lot to keep one occupied outside of work."

She then quipped to Mairy with a smile, "Follow me."

She appeared oddly excited, as we walked the fifth floor until suddenly her anticipation was rewarded. She motioned to Mairy, "Look, there's Todd. There, on the weight bench in the corner. He's with security up here."

"Is he your boyfriend," Mairy asked.

"Better than that; Ulrick and I have been married for over a year now," Lindsey stated with girlish pride.

Milo pulled me aside, saying, "He's a typical jock. He spends most of his time in the workout rooms trying to maintain his physique."

I looked to see a man in his mid-20's working out. He did appear to be the more athletic type; probably majored in football while in college.

The fifth floor seemed to be dedicated to, among other things, physical and mental fitness. There were people running out on a partitioned walkway that overlooked the atrium. There were bridges at the far ends of the walkway, as well as a set up for rock climbing walls and zip lines. I could also see an array of arcade like play station machines alongside the movie theater complex we just passed. Indeed, it did look as if there were enough distractions to keep one placated for a long while.

"It's a little busy now, but it slows down at night, or what we call night," Timothy informed me. Sleep is still an essential demand of our biological rhythms. However, you want to try and be awake during the daylight hours, to pick up on your body's natural ability to produce vitamin D. They come around every 14 days or so. There are even four swimming pools down on the 2nd level, near the windows. Want to see them?"

"Maybe a little later; I feel a bit tired right now. Where are we going to sleep?" I asked, just as Mairy and her new partner caught up to us.

"Oh right, you been up for a while, haven't you? There are a few empty rooms near us," Timothy offered.

"Our rooms are just outside of this main complex, on the 3rd level; closer to the research center. Follow me," Lindsey directed us. As the others bid us goodnight, Lindsey walked us to their living quarters.

She walked us back towards the elevator, but then continued walking down the hallway. At the end of the hallway was a glass enclosed tunnel.

Looking out the windows, I noticed another similar glass enclosed tunnels down the way. The enclosed tunnels seemed to bridge the main complex with smaller building units.

Beyond the tunnels, I could see the landscape of the Moon in the waning sunlight. It was the first time that I was able to get a full view of this bizarre moonscape. As there were no clouds, I could also see the stars out in the distance. It was a surreal vista of a vivid starscape while it was still light enough to make out features on the Moon. There was no vision of Earth, as we were on the far side of the Moon.

As we reached the end of the bridge, we turned right and then left to an area that resembled a hotel hallway of conference rooms. As we walked to the end of the hall, we took a more normal elevator down to the third floor. Their living quarters were just off from the elevator, and down the adjoining hall.

"These two on the end are currently not being used," Lindsey instructed. "They can arrange a more permanent rooming for you two tomorrow. Morning briefings begin at 8 am in that room at the end of this hall, and you know where the cafeteria is already."

Mairy and I checked out both of the rooms together; first one and then the other. The lights came on automatically as we entered and then again as we approached each individual area of the rooms. Not sure why we were so curious to see each of the rooms, but at least it allowed us to pick ours rooms. The rooms were nothing special, but they were very clean. I'd have given it 4 stars.

Mairy seemed extra cautious about the accommodations. I guess knowing that we were deceiving others, made us more aware that others could be deceiving us. Being mistrustful of others and our surroundings spoiled our ability to just enjoy the moment. But the moment was already tainted with our own fatigue.

"You two seemed to be getting along pretty well," I said to Mairy of her relationship with Lindsey.

"Oh, Lindsey? Yes, it did seem like she wanted to be my best friend or something. I don't know if I really trust people who are too friendly too fast," Mairy admitted, "but it would be rude to ignore her. However, it best to keep our options open until we know who we can trust."

"I don't know that I really trust Milo," I admitted with some jealousy. "He seems a bit too attentive to you."

Mairy seemed to pick up on my feelings quick enough, but then that is one of her special powers.

"I'll keep that in mind," she remarked with a smile. Then she leaned over and kissed me on the cheek, saying coyly, "Besides, I'm only here for you."

That was unexpected. I accepted her kiss while expressing a little embarrassment in the color of my cheeks.

"I guess that makes sense," I said, acknowledging her explanation. "I mean about keeping our options open. Anyway, we have more important problems to worry about. Like how are we going to keep up these acting roles until we can coordinate with dad? Are you still sure this is where we need to be?"

"If you mean on the Moon, then yes," Mairy quipped. "After all, it was in your dream that we would be in space together. From what you told us, your mother and I could only narrow it down to this. Can you remember anything else?"

"No, just what we talked about earlier. I remember urgently needing to talk with dad about the vision of stars and fog all around us. And, oh yeah, then there was the floating about above a spherical structure amidst a barren wasteland that I had never before seen; or at least, not until today."

Still there was more that I was not divulging; at least not right now. For I felt I was in actually contact with my old acquaintance, Harmony, rather than just my memory of her. I believed I could even hear her thoughts being communicated to me, *'Consider who you are and where you are going. Let your hopes and dreams guide you through your darkest fears. You are more than physical form. Find the center of your life force. Only there can you realize the purpose and vehicle of your journey'*.

"Well, there you have it," Mairy deducted of my recollection. "You dreamt of this place even before you knew it was where we were going. It can only be the foretelling of our quest."

"Does it ever bother you," I asked; "all this fumbling about in the dark, and not knowing what comes next?"

"What is the point of living, if everything is handed to you?" was Mairy's rhetorical question. "I don't want to know the future. Predestination is for the meek of mind. The greater the challenge, the richer one's destiny is what I like to think."

There was a short pause as I processed Mairy's kernel of wisdom. "Maybe you'll dream more tonight. Anyway, it's been a long day and we could both use some sleep."

"Sleep," I echoed back to her. "That is the last thing on my mind. My thoughts are racing about in every direction. I'll probably be up all night," I told her, despite my fatigue.

Or so I thought; I left her in the room and went to the adjacent room next door. Even though there was definitely a lot to think about before tomorrow, this was the first time all day that I could actually relax. I didn't need to be anyone else but myself. In being myself, I wondered about mom and dad. I wondered how they were doing apart from each other. Then I questioned about Mairy and me. Although the kiss was nice, I thought to myself, it may have been he impulsive reaction to resolving my feeling of jealousy.

Then, I wondered what the quest had to do with us being on the Moon. And I speculated upon whether we had missed something about our interpretation of my dream. I recounted how I had more to go on with Harmony's riddles than I do now. At least Harmony's riddles gave me a sense that solving them would help me understand what needed to be done to complete the quest. What is this new quest all about, I had to continually ask of myself?

As doubt filled my mind, I pondered if this was how it will always to be with the Shadow-Forge; just impulsively reacting to feelings and visions, without ever really knowing what you're doing until you stumble upon something. Anyway, I guess it fits in with my condition of ADHD.

As I took off my weighted shoes, I felt a little lighter. And as I walked slowly to the bathroom it was as if I couldn't feel the full weight of my body. I took off the full body suit, so I could take a dump. Having relieved myself, I returned to dive onto the bed. Comparable to a similar experience on Earth, it was almost like I was gliding down to the bed. I could easily get use to this.

As I lay on the bed, the lights started to slowly dim until there were off completely. As I lay in bed, unable to sleep, I stared into the darkness. I was tired, to be sure, but wary at the same time. My senses were hyperactive, as my mind ran on autopilot trying to ensure my safety in these new surroundings. In the silence of my own stillness, I could hear my heartbeat. Without the familiar distractions of light and noise, the room felt almost claustrophobic. It was strange to me. Although I knew the room was large, the absence of familiar sensory visualization manifested itself to impose limitations on my surroundings.

As I lay there, my mind created an illusion in which I entertained the notion of an unlimited dreamlike expanse. As I began to go over in my mind about the adventure Mairy and I shared over the last two days as stowaways, I recalled the David Bowie song, 'Space Oddity'. As it played in my head, this was the cradle from which I could comfortably fall asleep.

In my sleep, I re-dreamt my earlier dream from just before we left on Earth. It started out like when I travelled through the universe on my first quest. And yet, it was not quite like before, where I sensed I was embodied within my own presence of being in bubble-form. It was rather more like I felt intangible. Perhaps more like a sense of astral projection. Indeed, he recalled, this is what he sensed before when he connected within the great omnipresence that is the universe. It all seemed to make perfect sense to him again. All was right and true within the nature of his own being.

He had thought the memory of this moment in time to have been lost to him forever and yet here is was again. It was all upon this moment in Time and Space that he seemed to understand the grandeur of it all; for it was everything all at once. It felt like he was touching upon the aethereal plane of existence, once again, within that moment. Again, it was only for a moment, and then the moment passed. Still, I could sense everything around me. It was as if I was part of the omnipresence, embraced by the universe. And I was somehow aware that I was not alone.

Then, as in my earlier dream, I felt as if he was suddenly embraced by some larger force beyond my control. As I attempted to identify and learn more about this force, Mairy came into view. As I reached out to Mairy, I suddenly touched upon the identity of the force that had seemingly entangled him. Upon this touching, there was a crack of light that appeared out of nowhere in front of me. And as the crack began to grow, it persisted against a darker background. I watched as Mairy was pulled backwards into the rift and away from him. I frantically chased after her into the rift, where I felt a rippling sensation throughout my being for a moment, like the tingling of an electric shock; followed by a sudden loss of all sensation.

Then abruptly, I felt an even stranger gripping sensation rippling through me and throughout the aether of spacetime about me. My omniscient perspective of the stars and distant nebulae became distorted in the ever increasing illumination that overcame my purview. The light poured in upon me like a deluge, from every direction, as I was without sensation of any kind. It seemed to me to be like the opposite of omnipresence; where I was no longer in touch with any part of the universal being. And of my familiar sense of enlightenment, all that I felt, all that I knew, and all that I was, was disappearing. It was as if I existed without any boundaries or containment; having a sense of being everywhere but without my previous connection.

After that, I was devoid of any presence or connection to the universe; but only for a brief time. And when the sensation of my 'being' was reanimated, I felt part of that omnipresence again. However, this time my sense of omnipresence was without that previous feeling of my connection to the universal being. Again, I no longer felt that I had the same feeling and understanding about this spacetime as before the unusual event. Rather I felt he was at the center of a new existence, or perhaps more like at the moment of a new creation. I did not perceive any of the familiar sensations for fullness of density or form that were once part of my known universe. What happened to my connections to 'being' that was part of my universe?

As the bright light now dimmed, I was unable to perceive of any forming miasmas of swirling gases; there were no evolving star systems, nor even any systems of interacting black holes. It was, again, as if the universal being had been wipe cleaned and was beginning anew. Indeed, it felt like a less busy and more comfortable presence of being: restful and without any distractions. It was almost as if I was the only entity in the germinal stages of universal creation; a whole universe unto myself, upon the very convergence of Space and Time. And although this new environment seemed so very unnatural to me, it became the pleasurable delusion from which I awoke well rested and serenely calm.

CHAPTER

10

Quest Preparation

**[The vehicle of the journey may involve
more than just transportation.]**

Earlier that morning, Andrew woke rested and calm. It was as if he had never left the sanctuary of his room back at home. But as soon as reality kicked in, he reoriented himself with his current situation. As he raised his arms, he noticed the wall lit up with the current time; it was 7 am. He felt relaxed knowing that he was not late in getting up. He recalled that Lindsey said there was to be a meeting at 8 pm. He reasoned that should be time enough for a quick shower. Leaping out of bed in the low gravity environment was a rude reminder that he was on the moon. Quickly regaining his balance, he headed for the bathroom.

In the bathroom, he found the toilet to be about as accommodating as the one in the airliner. Next to it was a sink that allowed for very little water flow; perhaps just enough to brush his teeth. After which, he discovered the shower stall. It was more of a small chamber with individual seating, but it was warm and inviting. In the shower chamber, there appeared to be no real water, and no way to dispense it. Rather there was a unit on the wall that dispensed oversized, premoistened washcloths and a variety of liquid soaps and shampoos. Having completed his somewhat waterless shower, he found the drying towels to be large, warm, and absorbent. All in all, he felt refreshed and clean, and he didn't even have to get wet.

320

Grabbing a robe from outside the shower, he walked over to a closet. There, in the closet, he found a clean change of clothes, but with very little diversity. The clothes appeared to be more of a uniform and probably non-gender specific. They were arranged in 3 sizes, which he assumed to be an estimated guess on their part based on his approximate size and weight. He then donned his pair of weighted shoes, and felt ready for a full day of intrigue. It was now about 7:45 am, and time for him to jump back into the thick of it.

[Andrew's Perspective]

As I went to knock on the door to Mairy's room, it opened before I could hit it. Up to her old tricks again, she must have sensed me coming. Not surprisingly, she was as ready as I was. With my knocking fist still in the air, I opened my hand and placed my palm against the door; as if to hold the door open for her. Passing me, she moved out into the hallway smiling, having witnessed the whole event.

"Did you sleep well last night?" I asked her.

"Not much," was her reply; "how about you?"

"Like a baby," I commented without thinking. Then remembering Mairy's problem with expressions and idioms, I added, "I mean to say that I slept without a care in the world."

As we walked down the hall towards the meeting room, I could see the others coming out of their rooms as well. And there, in front of us, I saw a new addition to the group. It was another female. She was a little younger than the three we met yesterday, but still older than us. Lindsey was quick to take the lead.

"Good morning," Lindsey greeted us. "I would like to introduce you to the other member of our team, Vera. She was the youngest member of our group until you two showed up."

"Good Morning, I'm Andrew and this is Mairy," I greeted Vera, considering that good manners expected me to introduce us both to Vera. Over her shoulder, I could see Milo arriving into the hallway.

"Good Morning fellow travelers," was Vera's rather strange greeting in response. "I heard we had some new additions. Have they had a chance to meet our handler?" she asked aloud to the group at large.

"No, they just arrived yesterday," Milo said, offering up an answer.

"I can see you're in good spirits this morning," Lindsey sarcastically responded to Vera's query. "And Dr. Beecher is our manager; not our handler," Lindsey corrected her. "We're not zoo animals, you know."

"Well, that's a matter of opinion; now isn't it?" Vera asked with a hint of sarcasm. "Anyway, let's not keep our 'manager' waiting then."

We followed after Vera and Milo as they walked down the hall towards the meeting room. As we all filed into the meeting room, we could see that Tim was already there. Upon entering, Lindsey paused to introduce Dr. Beecher to us, "Dr. Beecher, we have some new arrivals to the group. They arrived last night."

Turning her attention to us, Dr. Beecher turned away from her tablet and greeted us, "Good morning, my name is Dr. Margaret Beecher. And who might you two be?"

"Good morning, my name is Andrew and this is Mairy," I replied, politely repeating my earlier introduction.

"OK, Andrew and Mairy," Dr. Beecher began. "As I was only made aware of your arrival just this morning, I have yet to be informed of your reason for being here in my department."

"Oh, we volunteered to be part of your sleep study program," was my unprepared reaction.

"He means, we signed on as your new Sleep Study Pod Operators," Mairy was quick to correct me.

"Indeed," was Dr. Beecher's one word recognition of our responses.

She reminded me of one of those middle age school teachers from my high school on Earth. I could tell from her no nonsense attitude, that our answers would not be enough to placate her.

"Well, that is not the way we do things around here. We have a well-established procedure for high security work, and you two do not even have the proper clearance to work here yet. This is Muriel," she introduced of the woman standing just behind her. "She is with our Human Resources team. And, as there seems to have been a mistake made in protocol, somewhere along the line, hopefully she will be able to sort things out. And if everything works out, then I'll see you both later. If not, then goodbye for now."

"If you'll both just follow me," Muriel directed, motioning in the direction she wanted us to walk with her.

As we followed behind her, I looked back to see Dr. Beecher closing the door to the meeting room. Not really grasping the reality of the situation, and having never had dealings with the police, it felt like we were being called into the principal's office. As we lagged behind Muriel, I looked to Mairy for some guidance.

Whispering, I asked Mairy, "What do we do now?"

"You're asking me?" she whispered back in confusion. "This is your culture, not mine."

"Actually, we're on the Moon; so technically it is neither of our cultures," I argued the point. "Besides, you thought coming up here was a good idea yesterday. How did you think it would go?"

"Would you rather I disable her, and we make a break for it?" Mairy asked.

"Disable her; No!" I replied in a hush voice, nodding my head in a negative manner. Knowing what Mairy could do, I could foresee this alternative going badly if I were to unleash her.

"OK then; how about you just tell her to contact your father, and let him deal with all this cultural stuff?" Mairy remarked of her plan 'on-the-fly'.

"That's your big plan?" I asked with some frustration. "Let the grown-ups handle it?"

"Calm down. What can they do to us anyway?" she replied back snippily. "In their eyes, we're just kids. And I have seen how adults interact with kids. Children are given far too little responsibility in your culture."

"Of course; I don't know why I wasted all my time worrying about whether we would be found out, when all we really needed to do was to just turn ourselves in as stowaways and let the grown-ups handle it," I spouted off sarcastically.

"So if you agree with this plan, then why do you sound so upset?" Mairy asked with some confusion.

"Because it's not a plan at all," I declared. "And I was just being sarcastic."

"Oh, then it is I who should be upset," Mairy concluded; "because you are insulting my plan."

I raised my eyebrows in recognition of her reaction to my impulsive behavior, saying, "Perhaps."

"Oh, do look so apologetic," she remarked. "I was making a joke. Of course it is not a plan. You need to be able to improvise and adapt to changing situations on the battlefield. Be more flexible."

"This is hardly a battlefield," I remarked.

Muriel then turned her attention to us, as she led us into the elevator. We went up a few more floors, and then she escorted us out, down the hall, and into a waiting room.

"Now if you two will wait right here, I'll go and see if we can find your registration," she explained.

Registration, I questioned of myself? Believing this is going to be a problem, I wanted to head if off before this got anymore out of hand. And actually, as I thought about it, Mairy's guidance wasn't all that bad.

"Wait a moment," I requested, stopping her before she could reach her office. "Actually, our father was supposed to have registered us with your office some weeks ago. And since we never got any follow up instructions, we didn't know about the security clearance problem. So if there is any problem with our registration or security clearance, then you'll need to contact him."

"Alright, who is your father, then?" Muriel asked in an administrative tone.

"Stephen Bauer," I answered. "He came up some weeks ago."

"Thank you. This shouldn't be too long," Muriel stated with certainty. "Please have a seat."

She then continued on through to what appeared to be her office, adjacent to the waiting room. As we watched Muriel leave, I looked to Mairy and admitted, "OK, it was a good plan." Mairy just smiled back.

After a short time of looking about the room, I felt uncomfortably impatient. I remarked, "At least they could've provided some magazines or something." Mairy just gave a puzzled look in response to my off-handed comment, as I continued to bide my time.

[Narrator's Perspective]

While the two stowaways were left in the waiting room to await their verdict, Muriel settled down in her office in front of a computer. After spending some time working the keyboard, she was unable to come up with any pre-registration for the two from their father. So she then use the intercom to notify her manager. Her manager, being similarly in the dark about these two new arrivals, then called his superior.

Eventually, Tom was apprised of the situation, and contacted Muriel directly. Muriel then relayed to him the account of how the two new arrivals showed up last night without pre-registration or escort. Strangely enough, she found that Tom wasn't alarmed about the lapse in security. Rather Tom seemed curiously excited about their arrival. Having met Stephen's family in Hawaii, he was furtively fascinated by Andrew's part in Stephen's science fiction story. Secretly it was always his intention, all along, to involve both Andrew and Mairy, in this program.

When Tom learned that the two were already on board, ahead of schedule, he couldn't believe his luck. Having delayed Muriel with a reasonable excuse, he immediately logged into the company's administrative database and quickly set up a backdated communication assigning the two as pod operators in the sleeper program for the IGIE project. He also made it look like the two were invited to join the team yesterday, by backdating an assigned entry escort.

Having provided for the registration himself, Tom responded back to Muriel, "Oh yes, here it is. Yes, these two were assigned to work with Dr. Beecher."

Cleverly he covered up for their unannounced entry into the facility with the empty threat of a reprimand on the absence of protocol executed upon their arrival, "However, I am not seeing a follow up to the order for an entry escort."

He continued providing for a backstory at a frantic pace. He identified a scapegoat from the duty roster and backdated an assignment for Sheryl to be their entry escort. As Sheryl had been in the process of being moved, as part of a reassignment, she was the perfect choice. It was easy for him to manage this subterfuge while maintaining intercom contact with Muriel.

"No, here it is. Looks like Sheryl wasn't available to check her email, but we can sort that out later. So yes, this appears to have all been cleared through upon their father's request."

"That account agrees with their story," Muriel acknowledged. "So there is no need to involve security then?"

"No, not at all," Tom reassured her. "Are the two new arrivals aware of why you have detained them?"

"No, I felt is best to not alarm them until I was able to sort things out," Muriel conceded.

"Perfect, then set them up in an orientation for this morning," Tom commanded.

"But we haven't processed them in with security as pod operators yet," Muriel reminded him.

"You can set that up later, following their orientation," Tom instructed. "In fact, make it a priority. I'll contact them right away to let them know what is going on. We can have them pinned and inducted before lunchtime, and no one will be the wiser."

"Yes sir," Muriel submitted. "And about their father, should I inform him of their safe arrival?"

"No," Tom replied, pausing for a moment. "I'll be meeting with Stephen later today. However you should inform Kiana and their mother on Earth of their safe arrival up here. I'm sure she would be worrying about their safety as well."

Everything was falling into place. It was even better than Tom had planned. Certainly, Stephen and Sandi would be beholden to him for managing this incident discretely and assuring their safety.

Surreptitiously, Tom understood their fates were being orchestrated in his favor by a higher power. He felt emboldened to proceed with the plan for which he been enlisted by Discordia as a Shadow-Forge member. It all needed to be advanced as normally as possible, lest he reveal his intentions too early. He could not chance even the slightest distress in the universal connections, until he was ready to execute, as it might cause an upset in the balance of the universe too soon; triggering the involvement of Harmony.

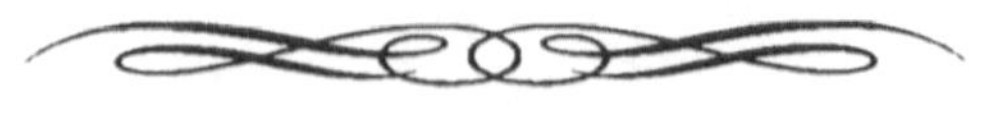

[Andrew's Perspective]

I began pacing about the waiting room, like a caged animal, as there was not much else to do. "It's taking too long. What do you think she's doing in there?" I inquired of Mairy. "She probably called for security."

"You worry too much," she replied, as she calmly waited for Muriel to arrive back.

"Well, it keeps me safe," I stated emphatically. Geez, I thought to myself, I was beginning to sound like my father. Just then Muriel walked back in.

"Alright, everything checks out," Muriel started in saying. "I have scheduled both of you for a 10 o'clock appointment with security to get your employee pins, right after orientation; which starts any moment now. Please follow me and I'll escort you to the orientation meeting room."

I looked to Mairy with relief. No retribution, I thought to myself. They bought our story 'hook, line, and sinker'. "Were you able to get ahold of our father," I asked politely.

"He's aware that you're both here, but we do have our security protocols to follow. So please keep up," Muriel stated as she continued to escort us into a large conference room. In the room, a group of people had already gathered.

"Help yourselves to some pastries," she said as we entered. Catching the attention of the HR representative at the front, she gave a nod to him as if to signal that it was alright to start.

The HR representative, at the front, then immediately announced, "If you could all please finish up with the 'meet and greet' portion of our pre-meeting, I would like to get started in 5 minutes. You can bring your food and drink to your tables. Thank you."

"I'll be back to pick up at 10," Muriel instructed us.

"Thank you. We'll be here," I stated of the obvious. We watch as Muriel left out the same door we entered.

"I don't know enough not to trust her," Mairy commented. "But something doesn't feel right about all this."

"What's to trust?" I stated flippantly; "Although it does seem a little strange that they just went along with our story. I was still waiting for some sort of reprimand. Maybe dad was available to clear things up after all."

We grab some donuts and drinks, and found our way to some empty spots at one of the tables. The presenter droned on for almost an hour before our first break. The orientation consisted of a short history on the establishment of the moon station, the company purpose, and the safety rules about staying inside and wearing weighted, semi-magnet shoes to counteract the low gravity.

It all seemed quite boring to me, which made it difficult for me to follow and remember everything that was said. So, even though I was well rested, I had a difficult time paying attention to everything that was being said. Perhaps it was more my ADHD filter, or maybe the monotonic temperament of his presentation. I mean, all in all, it was kind of like wading through a normal day at school.

Still, I did learn that the Moon's gravity was about 1/6th of Earth's gravity. And, while the lower gravity would allow a person to survive a fall from a height six times greater than on Earth, it appeared one could still actually get hurt here; even in low gravity.

When we finally reached our first break time, we made our way to the back of the room to get some more donuts, and talk.

"So did you dream again last night?" Mairy inquired.

"Oh yeah," I said, happy to be distracted. "And it was definitely weird. That much I can say about it. But I can't actually remember it in any great detail. For the most part, it was somewhat of a repeat of the dream I had on Earth before we left. From what I can still remember, it started out like when I travelled through the universe to arrive at Glorthocks. You know, in bubble-form. But then it changed, and I was no longer in bubble form. Still, I sensed I was embodied within my own presence of being. I felt rather more intangible this time, and yet I could still sense everything around me. It was as if I was actually part of the omnipresence that pervaded within the universe, rather than the embodiment of my own reality."

I took a quick drink, and continued with my recollection. "Then, in my ability to sense my surroundings, I was somehow aware that I was not alone. I suddenly felt a rippling sensation throughout my being for a moment, like the tingling of an electric shock, followed by an abrupt loss of all sensation in my 'being'. After which I was devoid of any presence or connection to the universe, but only for a brief time.

Though, when the sensation of my 'being' was reanimated, I was without my previous feeling of connection to the universal being. Somehow that was the strangest part of it all. It was like my sense of omnipresence independent of the universal 'being'. It was more like I was my own reality, separate of the universe; or maybe even my own universe."

"Without our connection to the universal being, there is no Harmony," Mairy commented; "for she is our connection."

Not sure how that all follows, but I went along with it. "Could my dream be a vision predicting that the Dark Guild is going to kill Harmony?" I speculated.

"There is little danger in that," Mairy assured me. "Harmony cannot be vanquished, as we understand the concept; at least not in this universe, for she is not real in the same sense as a hosted life force, like us."

"Not real?" I said disbelievingly. "How is that possible? I was with her; she talked to me and I touched her. She has to be real."

"Does she?" Mairy posed to me. "What is real? If you're talking about what you can sense of your ongoing experience around you, then what you feel, what you smell, and what you can taste or see, is simply a mental interpretation of that ongoing experience developed from your own memories. Think about it, it is your collective memories which dictate how you interact with your surroundings."

That's not something I thought about before. The fact that the way I react and interact with everything is just a trigger of previously arranged memories. When you think about it, it is almost reflective of who I am, or who I have inadvertently trained myself to be. Every choice, every decision programmed my identity.

"Did she really talk to you, or for that matter did you really ever touch her?" she asked, challenging me to rethink what I thought about my memories of Harmony.

As I thought about it for a while, I finally surrendered to the realization of what Mairy was implying. I could hear her communicate with me, but I don't remember her lips moving. As for touching, I remember the somewhat colder air of her exterior, and the smell of peppermint and roses, but there was nothing solid about her. Rather, Harmony seemed to seamlessly interact with her surroundings.

"No, I guess not," I conceded. "In our interaction together, she was always somewhat like the physical presence of an apparition. Perhaps more like in the nature of what I imagine of a visible ghost. Could it have all really been just a dream, or some impression she introduced into my mind?"

"No, the event was real enough," Mairy said, sounding as if she was backtracking from her earlier revelation. "All I meant was is that Harmony is not real in the sense that we are. She is not bounded by the dimensional limitations of Space and Time, as are we. She does not have a separate 'being' of her own, because she is part of the universal being. Or rather she is more like a projection of that 'being' which facilitates balance within our universe. Simply put, she is a response to a need for universal balance. Her very presence is just the embodiment of a metaphysical 'being'; like a force of nature, operating from within universal existence."

"OK, I think I get it," I stated, as I began to formulate an hypothesis of my understanding. "If Harmony is the order of balance with the universal 'being', then she is the 'yin' to Discordia's 'yang'."

"The what?" Mairy asked with confusion.

"Like what dad told us," I recalled. "Yin and Yang are references to the manifestation of duality as an indivisible whole. According to the Chinese philosophy of the universe, there are two forces in contention that allow the universe to exist: 'yin' and 'yang'. Their interaction is thought to maintain the harmony of the universe and to influence the destinies of all creatures and everything within it."

"Yin is rather like the more passive female principle in nature considered as the negative force, whose fusion in physical matter brings the phenomenal world into being. And yang is like the active male principle in nature considered as the positive force whose fusion in physical matter brings the phenomenal world into being. Although I would identify with Harmony as more closely associated with the principle of 'yin', I would find it difficult to imagine her as anything other than of feminine gender," I educed.

"Actually, Harmony has no real identity to a nature of gender," Mairy countered. "She came to you as you imagined her to be. For me, Harmony was a masculine figure. He taught me how to get in touch with my inner connections to the universe and travel about the cosmos, as Harmony taught you."

Just then the presenter interrupted our discussion, announcing, "If you will all get back to your seats, we can continue again."

As we sat through the rest of orientation, I tried to understand the enigma that was Harmony. Probably not the best course of action, as I was supposed to pay attention to the orientation, but it was difficult to not let this puzzle be a distraction. Between the orientation and my distracted thoughts, the second half hour went by quickly. At which time, Muriel returned and escorted us to the security office for badging, or should I say 'pinning'.

As an innovation to the clumsy badging of other companies, we were all provided with pins that, when scanned, provided all of one's vital statistics; or at least a profile, as they had it listed on our record for us in the internet cloud. Once we completed our morning orientation and 'pinning', Muriel directed us to the cafeteria to meet up with the other team members. As we entered the cafeteria, the events of the last 24 hours seem to come full circle. We met up with the other members of our team for lunch, but this time with a little more familiarity.

Now noticing that the other members of our group had pins, I commented, "So I guess now that we have our security pins, we are fully vested members of the team; just like all of you."

"None too soon either. In today's briefing, they talked about running IGIE at full tilt," Milo informed us; "which means greater involvement with our team."

"Oh and how exactly does that involve us?" Mairy asked.

"My, they do have some catching up to do," Vera interrupted. "How are they going to cram years of study in these kids? I just don't understand management. It'll take forever to get this program off the ground."

"You remember Vera from this morning in the hallway," Lindsey made a point of calling attention to her. "Her real name is Verdandi, but everyone calls her Vera."

"And as you can see she suffers from a lack of self-esteem," Milo stated sarcastically.

"Milo, please," Lindsey implored of Milo's teasing.

Mairy looked to me to be a little confused. Probably trying to understand how such a confident personality could she suffer from a lack of self-esteem.

"It's sarcasm," I said in a hushed voice. "It means that she thinks highly of herself."

"Then why didn't he just say that," asked Mairy, whispering back.

"It's funnier when you transpose the notion of opposites or exaggerations to express one's view. He was trying to be funny," I explained, not really paying attention to who might be listening.

Vera, having overheard our whispering, leans over to Lindsey, saying with quirky amusement, "Is she for real?"

Knowing that Mairy was sure to have heard Vera's snippy remark, I attempted to contrive a backstory for Mairy. "Actually Mairy is homeschooled and hasn't been exposed much to the notion of sarcasm or the use of idioms. Mom always thought of it as rude behavior."

"I think it's sweet," Lindsey responded to Mairy's innocence.

"You would," Vera acknowledge of Lindsey's response.

I could see that Mairy was getting a little perturbed about Vera's 'mean girl' attitude. Normally she would not be taking that kind of crap from anyone, but she was aware that we needed to keep a low profile.

"So how does it involve us?" I asked Milo, to reiterate Mairy's question and distract from Vera's comments.

But before Milo could answer, Tim interrupted by saying, "Well, we've been running with four pods for months now, while the engineers have been trying to fine tune the master CONS units."

"More like over a year," Milo said facetiously. "Before they brought in these two control pods, we were just continuing our ongoing research with Dr. Beecher: working to perfect the neurological imaging of dreams. So at least this will be a bit of a change."

"Oh, they watch you dreaming?" Mairy enquired further.

"Just like streaming video," Milo quipped.

"You see; this is what I mean. How are these two going to be of any help to us on the project? They don't even know what we are doing here," Vera insisted.

Tim responded for the group, "They just got here. You weren't exactly knowledgeable about the mission when you first got here either."

"And they don't even have any practice time on these pods," Vera countered. "Before management was just pandering to us by having us play these simple mind games in the CONS units to keep us busy, and now they are assigning these newbies to the control pods," Vera persisted.

"That's enough; you're not helping the project by creating this atmosphere of antagonism," Lindsey declared, scolding Vera.

With that, Vera just left the table. Lindsey reached out to Mairy saying in a more apologetic tone, "You'll have to forgive her. She's been working very hard to be the best at what we do. She's really quite driven."

"What did she mean when she said we were assigned to the control pods?" I asked.

"That's what we found out at this morning's meeting," Milo informed us. "You're the two new 'guinea pigs'. That's probably what's got Vera riled up with you two."

"When they first got the control pods up and running, we had all been kind of curious about what makes them different from what we were already doing. Vera, being the star pupil around here, had previously been used to calibrate them. So naturally, she was expecting to be one of the first candidates to operate the control pods when they were mission ready" Tim explained.

"Then about halfway through this morning's conference, it was announced that you two would be soloing the two new control pods. As you can see, the rejection is still fresh on her mind," Milo recounted.

"So as you can see, it's not you," Lindsey expressed apologetically. "She's been expressing that hostile tone since the meeting. I was hoping to calm her down before you two came back. But she continues to bear her disappointment quite openly."

"Well, we don't want to be the cause of any friction around here," I assured them. "Perhaps we could convince Dr. Beecher to use her to replace one of us. I don't see why one of us couldn't be assigned to a regular pod. Would that make her feel better about the decision? It may be a while before we can really contribute to the team's research, as it is."

"It doesn't work like that," Tim began to explain. "Initially they were using her to calibrate both control pods. But really, she could've only been assigned to one of them anyway because each pod is a programmed interface to an individual sleeper's brain waves. So now that they actually assign operators, it's not likely that they will be switching up ownership anytime soon."

"They say we are behind schedule. And since it takes time to adjust the equipment to recognize and interpret the brain wave patterns of any one individual, they would rather not have to reinitialize the drone pods," Milo adds to Tim's information. "Subsequently, everyone stays with their assigned drone pods, even Vera, and you two get the new ones."

"Well, you already said that Vera has also checked out in the control pods," I continued to press the point. "So I wouldn't mind being assigned to one of the drone pods. In this way, they would only need to readjust two of them."

"It'll only make things worse if they give in to Vera now," Lindsey stated. "Once she's in, she'll dig in like a tick. You'll never get her out whole again."

"Anyway, we have about a half hour before we're due back. Was there anything you wanted to do," Tim suggested.

"I think I would rather just freshen up a bit," Mairy admitted. "Are you coming Andrew?"

"Oh yes; I don't think we want to cart around this orientation material all day," I agreed. "We can just drop all of it off in your room for now."

"OK, we'll catch up with you at your rooms in a little bit," Lindsey stated in implied agreement.

Once we separated from the group, I started complaining, "What is going on? This is not what I understood the job description to be. I thought we would just be part of the maintenance crew or something. This fabricated cover story was supposed to keep us out of trouble, not get us enlisted into their operating their control pods. What are we supposed to be controlling anyway?"

"Not to mention, pitting us as adversaries to their best pod operator," Mairy added. "Besides, what choice do we have? We'll just have to pretend to be who they think we are until we can get more information."

"I mean, I don't even know what a pod operator does. And what about this dream imaging? Now I have to worry about what I'm dreaming?" I said in a panic. "Hey, do you even dream?"

"I do now; but I prefer the freedom of my astral experience," Mairy replied.

"OK, I think," I replied with confusion and astonishment.

"Again, you worry too much. Think about it; since our fake experience involved us being hooked up to equipment and going to sleep, what could they be possibly be expecting of us anyway?" Mairy proposed. "So how difficult could it be to just play along until we find your dad?"

"True; and dad or mom had probably talked with Kiana about it back before we left Earth. I mean, that is what we agreed on for our cover story," I rationalized away my misgivings.

The more I thought about it, the less confident I became. Then, as I thought more of our quest, I couldn't help wondering what the endgame was. "And I still don't see what any of this has to do with my dream."

"Now you're just trying to come up with an excuse to avoid working on the team," Mairy ventured. "Think of it this way; your dream was about being in space. And this is closer to space than you were on Earth."

"OK, point taken," I acknowledged. "But I still believe that we were out of our depth. We've only gotten this far on your courage and bravado," I admitted. "A little more information might help."

As we reached our rooms, we agree not to discuss our mission anymore in areas where we might be overheard. As Mairy used the bathroom, I dropped off our orientation material. It wasn't long before the others returned for us, knocking on our doors.

"Mairy, are you ready?" Lindsey asked loudly.

"Yes, I'll be right there," Mairy answered loudly.

We promptly came out of the room together, and noticed that Vera had now rejoined the group.

As Mairy walked off with Lindsey, Vera said to no one in particular, "I see Lindsey has a little sister now."

I waited until Vera walked by and caught the ear of Timothy, "What did she mean by that crack?"

Milo overheard my question and gave his own take on the situation, "She just wants things her own way, and you two are in the way; if you know what I mean."

"Vera wasn't really close to anyone, but she would spend time with Lindsey," Timothy informed me. "I guess you can't blame her for being a little jealous of the way Lindsey has taken to Mairy."

"At least she's aware that we're all watching out for you two," Milo hinted.

"Watching out for us," I asked with interest. "Why; is she dangerous?"

"Only where it comes to competing for job appraisals," Timothy alluded. "She's not one to share credit." Tim and Milo shared a laugh.

I followed them beyond the conference rooms where the group had their morning meeting yesterday. As we made our way to the research portion of the facility, I kept track of the route. The final entry required us to use our employee pins for entry. I was afraid of that. They would mean that they were most likely tracking everyone's individual entry and exit time. Still, I can't imagine that they would check such a record on a daily basis. Once inside, we met up with Dr. Beecher, who was just inside the security entrance. Dr. Beecher singled Mairy and I out from the group, while the rest of the team left us to do whatever they do.

"Good morning and welcome to our research center," Dr. Beecher re-introduced herself to us. "I believe I didn't properly introduce myself yesterday; security protocol and all. I am Dr. Margaret Beecher, the primary neuroscientist assigned to this project. I am also your primary manager and group coordinator. You already met the rest of the team yesterday. So if you'll follow me, I liked to explain what our team is doing here."

With the commencement of that introduction, she led us farther down the hall, saying, "Just to start with, I have only been working here, off and on, for the past four years myself."

"Four years is a long time. How long has this moon station been operational?" Mairy asked.

"The time goes by quickly when you like what you're doing," Dr. Beecher said in an upbeat tone. She then stopped in the hallway and continued to address Mairy's question.

"As I understand it, they built most of this station on the Moon during the latter half of the 1990's; just about the same time as they were working on the International Space Station. It started out to be a follow up mission to explore striking anomalies in the Lobachevsky Crater, as imaged by Apollo 16 and by the U.S. Navy's recent Clementine moon mapping mission of 1994. In fact, they scouted this station's present location using the data provided from the Clementine moon mapping mission. However, the station wasn't really operational until 2004."

Wow, I should have been taking notes I thought to myself. She really knows her stuff. I continued to probe further, asking, "So they've managed to keep the existence of this moon station hidden for all that time. How were they not found out long ago by the government or NASA?"

"Well, there have not really been any manned missions to the Moon since the early 1970's," Dr. Beecher explained. "And this station is not in the regular path of any lunar orbiters. However, I think that is more by design than luck."

Now, with my curiosity peaked, I continued my interrogation, "What about the GRAIL mission? You know; that lunar orbiter with the live camera taking video of the dark side of the Moon? Isn't there a danger of exposure from that ongoing study?"

"My, you are well read," she praised me.

"Not really; I just had a lot of time to 'read up' on the NASA space stuff, after I knew we were coming to the Moon," I said, playing it down.

"OK, so then you are probably also aware that there is also a planned mission by China to land a rover on the dark side of the Moon. Anyway, none of this is our concern. Management has security well in hand." Dr. Beecher said matter-of-factly.

Then she directed us to look out the window to the outside. "Now this is something truly special, and it does concern us. Over there you can see the top end of DeepSIT, the Deep Space Interferometer Telescope. It is the front end to the IGIE system."

"IGIE," I asked with curiosity?

"Yes, IGIE is an acronym for our Interferometric Gravitational Influx Emanator. It is based on the science behind the detection of gravitational waves, as captured by newly installed instrument GRAVITY at ESO's Very Large Telescope in Chile, in combination with the precision imaging of the Laser Interferometer Gravitational-Wave Observatory," Dr. Beecher said without taking a breath.

As I listened, I couldn't help hoping that we weren't going to be quizzed on any of this.

"This is all very interesting, but what does any of this have to do with our work assignments," Mairy insisted, hoping to skip past the background information? "We are not scientists. As I understand it we are just assigned to operate your control pods."

"True; in fact, none of the members of this team are scientists," Dr. Beecher agreed. "IGIE is the computer system that processes the data, provided from our team, to generate images. You see, the pod operators play a significant role in this research. Throughout the process of DeepSIT's detection and capture of gravitational variations in deep space, these gravitational waves are integrated within the electrical impulses of brain waves; to be precise, your brain waves. The associative brain wave patterns are then manipulated by an integrator algorithm, which allows for imaging of these gravitational waves. Our team was enlisted for the single purpose of acting as the intermediary for the imaging of these deep space gravitational wave variations."

We followed silently behind Dr. Beecher as she continued down the hall. Somehow she reaches the room where the rest of the group is working. Or perhaps considering their current positions, it might be more aptly conveyed as resting. For each of group members were hooked up to a machine, and each of the group members were silently reading a book. Off to the right of the group, I saw two empty machines.

"I take it that those other two machines are the ones you want to hook us up to," I presupposed.

"Don't be so modest. I read your applications. You both have previously been working in neuroscience centers to help them calibrate similar test units," Dr. Beecher said encouragingly. "Your applications say you're both highly proficient lucid dreamers."

"Yes, we are and we have; but more in a passive partnership capacity," I said, trying to downplay our fake resumes.

"The technologists really did all the work," Mairy added. She was quick to keep up the façade of our made up abilities.

"Yes, none of this works without the proper technology," Dr. Beecher admitted. "But what you two are able to do is very special; one in a ten million to be more precise. If only I could participate as a pod operator. I do envy you. What you two will be experiencing has been described by the others as truly breathtaking and magnificent," Dr. Beecher said, building us up to perform well. "You and the rest of the team will be exploring deepest space from the comfort of your own CONS units. And you will all be able to see with your own mind's eye what we can only watch on the computer monitor."

"CONS unit?" I asked.

"Oh yes, I have been throwing around some acronyms. I apologize for that," Dr. Beecher acknowledged. "I haven't had to work with new hires in a long time. The acronym, CONS, refers to the Cognitive Operator Neuro-positioning System and acronym, IGIE, refers to the

Interferometric Gravitational Influx Emanator. Oh, but I already told you that one."

"Yes, this all sounds very exciting," I said, as I motioned to Mairy for a washroom break. "I can't wait to get started," I told her, but I really had no idea what she was talking about.

"Is there a washroom close by?" Mairy asked.

"Yes, perhaps it is a good time for a quick break," Dr. Beecher relented. "The restroom is down the hall and around the corner to the right. I'll meet you both back here in the lab."

As we walked away from the research lab, I began to panic, "Is this the best that we could come up with? What was I thinking?"

"Well, it doesn't require a degree," Mairy rationalized. "Besides, what is the worse that could happen? Maybe they'll find out that the machines don't work well with us. After all, that wouldn't be our fault."

"I guess you're right," I had to agree. Mairy's conclusion made sense. I should be more like her, I thought, and just go with the flow. She follows her impulses and then adapts to new situations as they came up.

Upon arriving back at the research labs, the room was empty except for a lab assistant and Dr. Beecher.

"Where did everyone go?" I asked.

"I sent them to the recreation area," Dr. Beecher informed us. "We need to get both of you oriented in your own CONS units. This is Randy; he'll walk you through the basics on your machines. It will take all his focus and your cooperation to get your pod stations up and running." And with that, Dr. Beecher left the room.

"Mairy, Andrew; are you ready to get started?" Randy posed the question to us.

"That's what we are here for," Mairy answered.

"Great! First you both need to back up into your individual CONS units, and then lean back up onto the body platform. Be careful of the flooring, it is a little like walking on a very thick foam carpet," Randy instructed us.

"Should we keep our shoes on?" I asked, thinking I did not want to damage the foam.

"Yes please," he replied.

We followed along with his every instruction, smiling at each other and quipping throughout the procedure. Randy didn't seem to mind our nervous chatter. He had us don a cap with wires attached, as well as gloves, slippers, and a body vest. Then he gave each of us a book, similar to dad's copy of an atlas to the universe. From the cover, it appeared to be the same book that I had seen the others reading from. As we read through silently, as we were instructed, he continued his routine of remotely monitoring and adjusting our pod monitor controls. I can only imagine they were setting up the machine to work with our unique neural networks, as Timothy explained to us earlier.

As I read through the book, I could feel an occasional electrical vibration emanating from within the various articles of clothing which I was given to wear. While surprising, the shocks were no more powerful than from sparks of static electricity which I encountered on touching metal in the winter. Then without warning, I felt off-balance, as if the ground under me was shifting. My vision went dark. While a little unsettling, it reminded me of the times I would rise up fast from a squatting position and the blood would rush from my head.

"Is this going to happen very often," I asked, a little perturb at the odd feeling I was experiencing?

"What do you mean?" Randy inquired of my terse statement.

"I felt a little off; you know, dizzy," I answered in a more conciliatory tone.

"Do you feel nauseated?" Randy asked.

"No, just dizzy," I replied.

"Alright, then that's nothing to worry about. Certain frequency to the brain can elicit dizziness. As long as there is no motion sickness associated with it, then you'll be alright," he explained.

"OK then," I responded to his veiled reassurance. "This machine is not going to brainwash me into liking brussels sprouts or something, is it?"

"Actually, quite the opposite," he answered in an amused tone. "We are brainwashing the machine to interpret your neural activity."

"Oh, that's alright then," I responded reflexively, not really understanding what he was insinuating.

"Yes, that should do it," he said looking at his console. "Now you can both give me back your books."

As we handed back the books to him, I asked, "What's next?"

"We're going to see if we can induce your deep memories to come forward," Randy answered. "I'll be readjusting the position of your pod units and closing the lid. While this is not a full sensory immersion, it will be enough for our purposes. Now, just relax and try to recall the images that you have just being viewing during your reading exercise."

"I'm sorry," she spoke up, "I didn't pay much attention to the pictures in the book," Mairy admitted.

"That's not a problem; just try to recall what you imagined when you were reading the book," Randy instructed Mairy.

As I followed the technician instructions, I closed my eyes and tried recalling the images from the book. My reflexes automatically reacted to the pod being set in motion. As the pod bed was quite comfortable, I eventually settled in. I began to daydream about the events leading up to our current situation. As Randy closed the lid, my daydreams slowly drifted towards brief glimpses of long forgotten memories. Soon, I began to image some my earliest of childhood memories in some detail.

My mind eventually fixated upon one in particular. There was the time when I was about seven when I insisted on helping unload groceries from the car. I grabbed the handle of a milk gallon and proceeded up our front sidewalk toward the house. Before I could reach the door, I lost my grip on the handle and the glass milk gallon fell crashing to the sidewalk. My mother's reaction was overwhelmingly negative, "Andrew! You need to wake up and focus on what you're doing."

I remembered the intense guilt I felt for disappointing her with such a simple task. I remembered wanting to get back in her good graces. I knew I could do better. Perhaps it was the seed of motivation that had driven me to work on my mental focus. Strangely, I hadn't thought about that incident since that time. After that acknowledgement, my dream just seemed to drift away into darkness.

[Andrew's Perspective continued]

[Even impulse requires some control to be successful.]

"OK, Andrew, you need to wake up now," I could hear my mother saying. But as I woke up, I found it wasn't my mother at all. Rather it was Dr. Beecher who was talking to me.

"Wake up?" I asked with confusion, for my consciousness environment was totally displaced via my subconscious dream. "How long have I been out?" I inquired, remembering I was on the moon station.

"Oh, about an hour and 20 minutes or so," replied Randy, the lab technician. "We administered a slow acting gaseous mixture to help induce sleep, which was just enough to put you under. Then we let your natural chemistry take its course, so we could monitor your lucid dreaming."

"I dreamt the strangest thing. It was like the first time I saw my own face," I heard Mairy comment.

But only I knew the true meaning of her remark. She would have only seen a real face sometime after she had transformed into her Shadow-Forge form for the first time. I wondered whether she was very young when she was approached by Harmony or it represented the first time she was subject to a subconscious recall, after having taken on the form of a human.

"Yes, all in all, it was a successful test," Randy was quick to discuss the run with the assembled group.

I noticed there were more technicians in the room now. Then a male voice spoke from just outside of my view. I recognized it as the same man we had dinner with in Hawaii.

"So there is no mistake, then?" I heard him ask. There appeared to be an indistinct response to his query. The strange voice continued, "Do you have the final readout? I would like to bring this up with the committee before the end of the day."

"Yes, and I must admit, we are all quite amazed. These two had no problem interfacing with the CONS units whatsoever, on their first run," I could hear Randy discussing the results of the testing with someone outside of my view.

"I was hoping that at least one of the candidates would be viable, but it turns out that they are both quite unique. It is the best initial response time I've seen since I started working with your team over the last few years," Randy promoted. "We were able to map activity in the higher order brain regions that accurately predicts the content of their dream state imaging in record time. And with no side-effects, I would like to add. From this map, we will be able to decode their brain activities associated with the earliest stages of their visual processing."

No side effects; that was a bit of a 'white lie' I thought. But everyone wants to impress their boss.

Then Dr. Beecher seemingly cut short Randy's oral report, saying to the stranger, "So, Tom, it appears we have finally found the alpha pod operators for which we have been looking for so long."

"Yes, Margaret, it would seem so," Tom acknowledged. "This should allow you to accelerate the program much quicker than we previously anticipated. We should be back on schedule in no time at all."

"This is most fortuitous," Margaret recognized. "It appears the team on Earth came through after all."

"Yes, our team on Earth," Tom repeated, as if to accredit her assumption to be the truth of the situation.

Tom then turned her attention to us. "Your minds are quite resilient for your age. You both are very special, and your timing couldn't have been better."

"Well, we are just excited with being part of the team," Mairy replied to Tom, not quite knowing for what they were taking credit. "We hope you'll keep us apprised of our success in furthering your research," she added. "Just let us know if there is anything else we can do to help with the effort."

I couldn't be for sure, but it almost seemed as if Mairy was laying it on a bit thick. It was as if she was attempting to get into his good graces by virtue of deception.

"It's good to know that we can count on you, but I think that will be enough for today," Margaret responded. "I'll escort you to the meet up with the rest of the team."

Having met Tom, and believing this would be a good time to request favors, I asked, "Actually, we haven't seen my father since we got up here. Perhaps you could help us with that?"

"Yes, of course," Tom agreed. "I'm sure your father is just as eager to meet up with both of you."

"Who is your father?" Margaret asked.

"Stephen Bauer," Mairy said with some insolence, "but we already gave that information to your HR representative, earlier. Didn't you talk with her after she cleared us?"

"Sometimes the left hand doesn't know what the right hand is doing," Tom said, intervening on our behalf.

I could just imagine Mairy's confusion upon hearing that expression.

"Margaret, have Muriel check Stephen's schedule, and then set something up for these two. Perhaps dinner tonight?" Tom asked, looking in my direction.

"That would be great," I acknowledged.

"Wonderful," Tom replied. "If there is nothing else, I have a moon station to run. And please feel free to let Margaret know if there is anything else you need. That is what she is here for, among other things."

"Yes, of course," I affirmed. "And thank you again."

With that, Margaret called Muriel as we waited. While still talking with Muriel, she turned her attention back to us, asking, "You can all meet for dinner around six o'clock, if you're not doing anything else?"

"No, I can't imagine what else we might be doing," I replied. "Six o'clock would be alright. Thank you."

Dr. Beecher then escorted us to where we could join up with the rest of our group at the recreation center. As she led us there, she continued her discussion with us to promote the team's mission: to link up with the DeepSIT and provide detailed data from which to expand their knowledge about the universe. It was more information than a couple of teenagers, like ourselves, were willing to listen to outside of a classroom. However, we continue to nod our heads and smile as we walked with her. We eventually met up with Tim and Milo, as we were passing by the virtual reality room.

"Milo, you really need to challenge yourself on a more athletic level. We don't want that body of yours to be wasting away now, do we?" Dr. Beecher asked rhetorically.

"It would be an interesting experiment to see how much calcium depletion of the skeletal structure could still support his body weight," Tim said to me about Milo.

Lindsey then came out from the exercise room to meet up with us. I looked through the glass of the exercise room to see that Vera remained behind.

"So, how did it go?" she asked Mairy.

Margaret intervened, before Mairy could answer, saying, "Actually, they were both completely compatible with their CONS units. So we'll all be able to advance to the next level of the program. This, of course, will require an acceleration in the schedule to show some real results. So I will see you all tomorrow, bright and early." And with that being said, Dr. Beecher walked away.

"Finally; this is where things get real interesting," Tim exclaimed to me.

"You mean, this is where things get real weird," Milo hinted of their new expectations on the group. "I can't wait to get to the next level. Hopefully, this time we can meet the challenge this time around."

"We've had a couple of false starts, but it seems that is all behind us now," Tim offered to explain their enthusiasm.

"Are you ready for some exercise?" Lindsey said to Mairy, changing the subject.

"Yes, I think I would like to try that wall climbing exercise," Mairy said, pointing off into the distance.

"It's great for balance. It also features endless wall sections that allow for longer sessions," Lindsey agreed with her choice. And with that, Lindsey was off with her new best friend, leaving Vera in the exercise room.

I could see this partnership between Lindsey and Mairy wasn't sitting well with Vera. So, in trying to ease tensions in the group, I clumsily invited Vera to accompany us to the wall. But she would not have anything to do with us.

"Unlike these marshmallows, I've been working out for over an hour," Vera stated, taunting us. "I think I'll call it quits for today." With that she turned away from us in the opposite direction of the rock wall.

"She says it like it is, doesn't she?" Milo quipped.

Having previously left the confines of his video game, Milo decided to join in. Tim and I followed on behind the girls. Looking back over my shoulder, I watch as Vera continued away from us. Even though she came off rude, I couldn't help feeling a bit sorry for her.

After we reached the climbing wall, and were instructed on how to operate the equipment safely, I suggested a competition.

"OK, how about we do a 'men versus women' contest? Are you game?" I asked, hoping the competition would make it more fun. Although, after having heard myself say it, it did sound a little lame. I then thought the notion would be quickly dismissed.

However, Mairy being ever supportive of me, replied, "Alright then; I am game as long as you don't mind being embarrassed."

"Come on Milo, you can use the exercise," Tim urged on Milo. "I'll be your spotter."

"OK then, game on!" Milo agreed.

"I'll have to warn you guys, Mairy is very competitive. So you'll need to step up your game, if we are going to bet her," I said, hoping to enhance their own competitive spirit.

Although the term 'competitive' did not actually cover Mairy's real expertise; Mairy was warrior born and my body guard to boot. She may not be any good at any of the virtual reality games, but she was great with more pragmatic reality games.

Anyway, we might as well have a little fun while we can. As there was no telling what this quest will be requiring of us later on, bonding with others could work to our advantage. My mom always said playtime was where we learned lessons in preparation for real life; right down to the decisions we make and the spirit we employ.

We broke up into teams of spotters and climbers. Each of climbers started up the wall at the same time, upon an agreed signal. As this was a race, we all avoided the difficult side of the wall to see who could reach the top first. Lindsey won out against Milo, but then she lost out to Tim. Then, as predicted, Mairy had no trouble beating out Tim. So finally, I was paired up with Mairy at the end of the contest.

"If there is one thing I have learned from my time together with dad is that training may win battles, but strategy wins the war," I said, 'kind of' trash talking it up to Mairy.

"Oh, you think you can climb up this wall faster than me?" she responded in kind.

"I more than think I can make it to the top before you," I hinted of my strategy, not using the word 'climb'.

"I'll make it sporting for you," Mairy challenged me. "I'll go up on the more difficult side."

I could see she wanted to challenge herself, as well as she wanted to challenge me.

"OK, you're on," I agreed, feeling better about my chances.

As Tim was my spotter, I pulled him over to the side and cautioned him to be ready when we neared the top of the wall. I needed him to hang on tight to my safety rope for the maneuver I had planned.

Then Mairy and I both started up the wall with determination to do our best. Mairy was not holding back at all, and I quickly began to lag behind her.

Shouting down to me jokingly, Mairy taunted me, "It doesn't seem that your strategy is working very well."

"That's because I haven't employed it yet," I responded.

"OK, let me know when you're ready to employ that strategy of yours," Mairy teased me.

As Mairy continued to expand the distance between us, I waited until she was almost at the top before employing my strategy.

"Look out below," I shouted down, and kicked off my weighted shoes.

I then grabbed and pulled myself up along the fake rocks, successively hurling myself up in an ever faster ascent. As I gained on her, I gave myself a final explosive push with both my legs. I overshot the bar at the top to ensure my victory, expecting Tim to keep me from flying out of control.

Then I felt the expected tug of the safety rope that would bring me back down to the top of the rock wall. Yet, as I looked down, the tug was not Tim's doing. Rather it was Mairy who grab my safety rope, after she reached the top bar. It appeared that she was always looking after me; even it was not to her advantage.

"That was impulsive," Mairy chided me. "You know if you fall too far, you can still hurt yourself; low gravity or not. Looks like your strategy might've got you injured."

"Not with you around. You see, you were part of my strategy as well," I attempted to compromise. "Shall we call it a draw then?" I conceded, knowing that what I had done could be considered as cheating.

"OK, we'll call it a draw if you can admit who the better climber is," Mairy relented, as she pulled herself up on top of the wall.

"Agreed, you are the better climber. But then you have to admit who the smarter climber is," I said.

"Smarter or more impulsive?" she replied, considering her options as she moved closer to me. "It would seem that even impulse requires some control to be successful." Then pulling me out of sight of the others, she embraced and kissed me on the mouth. "Now that's how you manage impulse with control."

I was a bit stunned by her boldness, but I could not ignore her advances. As I kissed her back, she responded in kind. Then playfully she separated and moved away, in sight of the others down below.

As I couldn't believe that I was really her type, I was just happy being around her. I began to wonder if her advances were a result of her real feelings for me. I mean maybe it was just about her getting used to the hormones that were associated with her new body. Maybe this wasn't about me at all. I'm not sure what it is like where she came from, but the human body presents a whole new twist on maturing. Maybe, like eating pancakes, she was just reacting to her instincts. And she did like eating pancakes a lot.

"Well, don't just stand there," Mairy called to me. "Now let's see how you climb down without shoes."

She made her way over the edge and began repelling down the wall. She had a point though; without weighted shoes, repelling down the wall would not only be a bit uncomfortable but much slower as well. It was definitely not a consequence that I thought through. Still, in all, it was worth it.

Things were beginning to look up. As quests go, maybe being partnered up on this moon station with Mairy would not be without benefits. Anyway, it would certainly be better than our last quest together.

Navigating Clues of the Quest

[If the total positive density mass in the universe is calculated to only influence about 5% of the universe's total energy, then gravitation represents a narrow view of the universe.]

While the children played, Stephen was in his element. It could be said that he was exercising his mind, while the children exercised their bodies. As he focused on his dark energy hypothesis, he was lost in a time warp of his own making. Cosmological measurements indicate that dark energy contributes to about 6.15/9 (or ~2/3 or ~68%) of the total energy in the observable universe, he calculated. Of the ~1/3 remaining energy, dark matter is calculated to be 2.41/9 (or ~27% of the total energy); leaving baryonic matter to be 0.44/9 (or ~5% of the total energy). And while he estimated that there may be between 5 and 6 times more dark matter than baryonic matter, it would appear that this baryonic matter is still an essential ingredient for driving the creation and evolution of our reality in the universe. For without the introduction of baryonic matter, the universe would have very little incentive to evolve or create.

Mapping the perceivable universe via gravitational wave forms provides yet another tool with which to influence our perspective of space in time. Tom and Stephen have been working together for the first few weeks, following his arrival on the moon station, to enhance the CONS capability. The intent was that it should also interface with dark energy wave forms. Tom was been instrumental in bringing Stephen on board with the program and providing him with his every need. All their work is about to come to fruition as Stephen is set to give his first serious presentation of his theories and their impact on the program's advancement thus far. Arriving fashionably late, Tom walks in on Stephen's presentation, which is already in progress. As before, some of the associates are remoting in.

[Scene Change - Father's Perspective]

Associate 2: "So then, the concept here is to bridge in a connection for dark matter detection based on our current gravitational wave research?"

"Yes, the current model of the gravitational wave propagation is based on the well proven algorithm using Einstein's gravitational constant to calculate gravitational acceleration," I said, careful not to offend his traditional understanding of the universe.

"Even if we expanded on the notion of a synergetic gravitational influence for combined groupings of dispersed baryonic mass, it still doesn't account for the positive mass density required to hold rotating galaxies together. Rather, dark matter is expected to account for more than four fifths of the gravitational mass effect detected within the universe. Therefore, if we are to agree that dark matter accounts for this residual effect of gravitational acceleration required to keep these galaxies from falling apart, due to their evolutionary expansion, then we need to account for a theory that allows for this extra mass, which is not readily detectable, to exist," I presupposed for the sake of the discussion.

Associate 3: "And this is where you would like to propose your theory that there is a dimensional transformation from within a zero state medium of dark energy as the basis for both positive and negative density matter?"

"Yes," I replied, hoping to suspend their disbelief long enough to make my point. "What I am purporting is that dark energy would be the original medium of a pre-Big Bang universe. In this way dark energy may be viewed as reacting in a more flexible or fluid-like manner, exerting negative pressure from within the post-Big Bang universe to counteract the effects of gravity and gradually accelerate the expansion of the Universe."

Associate 1: "And it is then your theoretical proposal that what we have ideated as 'dark matter' is really this concept of yours for negative density matter. Alright, I believe I have it now. So what else do you have that we haven't already read from your prior brief?"

Seeing that others were attempting to steer the presentation, Tom interceded, "Gentlemen, if you'll allow Stephen to continue, and hold your question until later, I believe this will go a lot smoother." Tom then motioned to me requesting, "Please continue."

Feeling a little reassured upon receiving Tom's support, I continued, "The connection between the effects of these gravitational anomalies and dark matter are most easily approach in our general understanding of the traditional black hole theory. Based on the standard model of a black hole, where its gravitational acceleration is facilitated via positive density matter, the most traditional understanding for a black hole is suggestive of a compaction of matter to the point where little or no space can exist within the density of its combined mass components. Or more to the point, it is representative of a mass in stasis due to the absence of space among its component parts. This not only appears to refute the basic principles of quantum particle physics, but it also sets up an impossible spacetime condition by which the reaction of matter to energy transformation is maintained in perpetuity of it increasing contraction. In other words, it assumes a theoretical premise for the eventual condition of critical energy without physical mass."

I couldn't tell whether their silence was a courtesy due to their admonishment by Tom, or whether I was actually reaching them. Still, I continued without reservation, expounding upon my concept, "Considering the notion of a cosmic singularity that is predicated to have fueled creation, the simplistic model for the moment of creation implies an origin from where all the universe's mass and energy are compacted to a point of zero volume and infinite spacetime. As we refer to this point as the cosmic singularity, this model then entertains the notion of an expanding existence from this singular point of infinite spacetime; or rather the distribution of all Space for all Time. And yet, where does this initial condition of singularity reside? It is like Space in limbo, where Time has yet to effectuate its being. My answer to this is that it resides in a universal medium of no Space and no Time; a nonconvergence of Space and Time, if you will. In this way, our infinite view of spacetime within a singularity can be alternatively viewed as a dimensional framework for nonconvergent spacetime; whereupon its eventual convergence provides for the 'unfolding' of 'All Space and All Time'. Such is it that it engenders a being from within the degrees of Space and Time between 'All Space and All Time' and 'No Space and No Time'."

Having hopefully laid the groundwork for degrees of spacetime, I paused to drink some water. "So let's think about the nature of relativity for such degrees of Space and Time. As we currently understand the notion of the black hole, the relativity of its existence is reduced to calculations that reveal its nature in degrees of relativistically less Time in a more compact Space for greater gravitational acceleration. If we are to imply that a black hole represents the end of mass creation in the density toward greater dynamic energy, then can we can also infer that the beginning of mass creation would embody the nature of relativity in degrees of more Time in a less compact Space for greater gravitational deceleration. Consequently it would then represent the impetus of mass creation in the density of lesser dynamic energy, or greater potential energy. If this is our true dimensional framework for existence, then existence is bounded from 'All Time and No Space' to 'All Space and No Time'."

I now felt emboldened by my logical deductions, and pressed my point forward. "Coming full circle, back to our discussion of gravitational acceleration, we can then understand that the relativity of Time decreases as Space compaction increases with increased gravitational acceleration; where we understand that this spacial compaction as the shrinking volume of contained positive mass for increasing positive mass density. Alternatively, we can then understand that the relativity of Time increases as Space compaction decreases, resulting in decreased gravitational acceleration, or increased gravitational deceleration; where we understand that this temporal increase as the expanding volume of contained negative mass for increasing negative mass density."

"While this may seem rudimentary at best, it belies the disparate nature of opposing forces due to the dimensional transformation from within a zero state medium of dark energy as the basis for both positive and negative density matter. From a dark matter perspective, negative density is increased to counter any increase in positive density. From a dark energy perspective, negative energy increases as positive energy decreases. Consequently, dark energy increases as density, positive or negative, decreases."

Still, the fundamental principal of a zero state medium cannot be ignored. That principal being that spacetime is predefined as infinite with respect to zero state medium. It is rather the intrusion of these convergences for degrees in spacetime, or wrinkles in spacetime if you will, are precipitated in the creation of these cosmonic boundaries. Therefore, in the equability of a zero state medium, dark energy increases with increased gravitational deceleration to fill the infinity of an order toward 'No Time and No Space'," I stated as a fact. "But then this relationship only explains the current expanding distribution of our universal spacetime."

"So, in a reflection of fundamental forces that maintain these cosmogonic boundaries, negative mass density compliments positive mass density to provide for a synergetic increase in gravitational acceleration via its ability to absorb and accumulate the energy of disintegrated positive mass. As you can see, this theory of cooperative forces does not require the simplistic notion of a gravitational singularity based solely on baryonic density," I stated, concluding the basis for my foundation for dark matter and energy.

Associate 2: "We started out talking about dark matter and we end up with this discussion about negative density matter. Are you proposing that these two concepts are one and the same?"

"Yes, I am," I disclosed.

Associate 1: "Great, two equally improbable and unprovable theories! We are replacing an unknown force caused by an unknown element to speculate upon an unknown probability for the repulsive gravity activity of an expanding universe. . And how are we supposed to detect degrees of no mass?"

Associate 3: "Well, as I follow this proposed theory, it is not the concept of a repulsive gravity. Rather it is a concept of negative pressure pulling upon the introduction of positive matter density into our universe. So it would follow that such increased negative mass density should also be detectable by readjusting our instruments to measure for this negative pressure effect in terms of gravitational deceleration."

Associate 1: "Yes, the concept of 'pulling' tends to agree with the unequal distribution of force that would occur if the universe is being stretched. That is to say, it would agree with the observations that the universe appears to be expanding at an ever increasing rate, so that the velocities at which distant galaxies are receding from the observer are continuously increasing over time."

Pausing for a moment to rationalize this theoretical premise, 'Associate 1' came up with the question.

Associate 1: "So then you think it is possible to detect changes in gravitational deceleration, where there is no real mass?"

Associate 2: "Maybe not directly on the changes in gravitational deceleration, but perhaps more indirectly on the changes in the gravitational wave forms generated from the changes in gravitational deceleration. I mean, that is what IGIE was designed for anyway."

Associate 3: "So rather than just randomly capturing gravitational wave forms, we try to identify whether these waves forms are the result of increasing or decreasing gravitational acceleration."

Tom interjected himself, taking credit for hiring me, "Exactly my thinking when I first read Stephen's published works. However, I did not want to influence your decisions to come on board with this project."

Associate 1: "Well we would have to partition the new program interface, such that it would not interfere with our current progress on getting IGIE up and running. Our stockholders are expecting results."

Associate 2: "That should not be a problem. But how are we going to fund this new direction in research?"

"You can leave the budgeting to me," Tom declared. He then got my attention and suggested, "Steve, I believe this would be a great time to stop. We have some issues to work out, and you could present the rest of your theoretical premise at a later time."

"I understand," I agreed. "That would be fine."

Associate 3: "Thank you for an excellent presentation. You've given us a lot to think about."

"You're welcome. And, may I say that it's good to be appreciated," I accepted, responding to his praise.

As the audience chimed in with their kudos, I continued to respond in kind. Then as the audience began to disperse, I went to packed up my presentation materials. Tom then approached me as he started exiting from the conference room. I took this opportunity to thank Tom.

"I want to thank you for your mediation. It was quite timely and well-coordinated," I acknowledged of Tom's expertise.

"No problem; that's what I'm here for. I've been meaning to talk with you. Do you mind if we talk as we walk?" he insisted.

"Not at all; you're conversation is always welcomed," I invited him to continue.

"I understand your children are aboard the station with us. And they are already contributing greatly, as are you. You must be pretty proud of them," Tom lauded of our involvement.

I was taken quite by surprise as I was not informed of their arrival. However, I took the news in a low key demeanor and agreed to his high praise.

"Yes, they did very well as interns, and I thought they should at least be interviewed for the Sleep Study Pod Operator position," I commented as if it were all true.

"And right you were," Tom said, getting the response he was trying to elicit. "They are going to help us get this project right back on schedule. This, of course, means our team will need to accelerate its schedule in kind. I have high hopes for your assistance in our research."

"Thank You," I said simply.

"I understand HR has contacted you to meet and dine with your family at 6 pm tonight. I would consider it a great privilege to meet with the family team that is helping us to move this project forward. It isn't often that one finds so much talent within one family," Tom requested, inviting himself.

"Well, it's not the whole family, as my wife is still on Earth," I said, stumbling in my logic. Small talk was definitely not my forte. "But yes, of course your company would be welcome."

"Good; and about your wife, we will need to expedite her travel plans. We can't have the glue that keeps the family together being left behind," Tom responded, becoming uncomfortably more gracious.

"Besides, it wouldn't be good for the project to have the children worrying so much about their mother, or distracting you from your fine work," he mitigated as a need for her being there. "She can keep them occupied and out of trouble. It's amazing what teenagers get into when they are left alone. I'll have an order made out to have her brought up here on the next shuttle."

"Well, thank you again. It means a lot to me to have everyone here to support me in my work," I accepted; though I felt like I had no real choice in the matter as it was.

"Just what I wanted to hear. See you at 6 o'clock then," Tom repeated, cementing his invitation.

I felt somehow that things were going too well. Tom had not said anything about the fact that the children were not really supposed to arrive here until weeks later. I often cautioned my son about zemblanitous situations which can occur without warning. On top of that, I began to worry that the inclusion of Shadow-Forge participants into our experiments would alter the outcome. For as the Heisenberg Uncertainty Principle implied, the taking of measurements on certain systems cannot be made without affecting the systems; that is, without changing something in a system. I knew that by inclusion of Andrew and Mairy in this project, I would be introducing astral observers into the mix and risking the success of the research. I had not considered the variability of an observer with the system that I was to observe.

[Scene Change - Narrator's Perspective]

What Stephen could not know, at this time, was that was that Tom was counting on just this type of interaction. And unbeknownst to him, Tom was already meeting with his team, as he was traveling to meet the kids for dinner. In the few short weeks that Steve had worked with them, prior to Andrew and Mairy coming up, Steve had given them the breakthrough they were needed. Having this needed information, they managed to build and dry run two new prototypes with which to interface with the control pods. As of today, skipping their regular dinner in the cafeteria, Tom's team will be spending their time installing these two new prototypes on the back of the master control pod CONS units. Per the HR arrangements, he would be meeting with Stephen, Andrew, and Mairy to cement his deception, and allay their suspicions.

The original purpose for IGIE was to detect and image waveforms of gravitational 'acceleration' in deep space. DeepSIT would gather and integrate these gravitational waveforms within the 'alpha' wave patterns of the pod operator's brain, via the CONS units. The technique had worked for nine months now, but it only provided for the enhanced neuroimaging, in a three-dimensional representation of what was there. Just a little more than was possible via the Hubble telescope. The major difference was that IGIE was able to reconstruct images from the input of detected gravitational waveforms from deep space targets.

While quite impressive, the hope was that with the addition of the two control pod operators, they would be able to achieve a full 360 degree overview of the targeted location in four dimensions. For the last six months, they had been working with Vera in one control pod and the others in three other drone pods, but it wasn't enough to achieve their goal of being able to manipulate a viable computer simulation of the targeted area in four dimensions.

Their newly designed purpose for IGIE was altered to detect waveforms of gravitational 'deceleration' in deep space; then gather and integrate these new waveforms within the 'theta' wave patterns of the pod operator's brain. The intent was to provide for the enhanced neuroimaging, in a four-dimensional representation of what was not there; as reconstructed from the input of detected gravitational waveforms. The team's hopes were to be the first to identify a way to quantify dark matter, or dark energy, with a 'kind of' nephelometer for dark matter.

However, Tom had decided to make a wholesale leap forward. Rather than just testing with the complete compliment of two control pod operators and four drone pod operators, using the existing proven design, Tom instructed his team to install the new interface. By skipping to the prototype run, Tom would save valuable time wasted in a trial and error phase of simulation. For Tom, speed was important as he had other more ominous goals in mind. For Tom, detecting the existence of dark matter would only be the first building block in his more nefarious plan to manipulate the universal order.

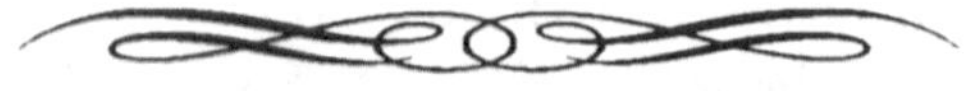

[Scene Change - Andrew's Perspective]

[Putting the pieces of the quest puzzle together]

Per the HR arrangements, we arrived early at the location indicated for our dinner with dad. As we entered the room, we were amazed to see such a large window to the outside moonscape. It was an awesome view. Dad must've been looking forward to this as well because he was already waiting when we got there.

"It's great to see both of you again," dad said with muted excitement. There was a round of hugs, and then came dad's parental tone. "What were you two thinking by stowing away on a shuttle? What if something had gone wrong? No one would even have known about you until it was too late," he said, cautioning us of the danger we were in.

"Actually something did go wrong, but it was on Earth," I admitted to dad. "The Tokoloshe showed up on the island, and mom said that we had to get off the planet."

"Oh, that's different. I didn't know. Well, I'm glad you all made it through alright," dad confessed. "Sometimes I just feel so helpless. Especially when I hear you were in danger. You could've been killed and there was nothing I could do to prevent it."

"OK, dad I get it," I acknowledged. "I love you too."

"A parent does not want to outlive their child, so try to stay safe," he recommended. "Is your mother going to be safe with the creature about on the island?"

"Turns out Kiana showed up and killed the beast, after mom managed to distract it," I explained.

"Your mother?" dad remarked with incredulity. "She never physically fought anyone. And she took on this Tokoloshe. Wow! That's big."

"Yeah, she just jumped right in to protect us," I added.

"Yes, she was great," Mairy agreed. "You should be very proud of Sandi. She saved all of us."

"I am, to be sure. So what about this Tokoloshe?" dad asked. "Last we knew it was on the mainland. How was it possible for it to follow us to the island?"

"That was actually the same reaction Sandi had," Mairy piped in. "You two are so much alike."

"OK, so did the beast say anything this time?" dad asked.

"It didn't say anything," I confessed. "It was on us before we even knew it was even there."

"Before you knew it was there, you mean," Mairy confided. "I should have known better. All this family stuff is dulling my edge."

"Oh, come now," dad said, consoling her. "You don't mean that."

"No, I guess I don't," Mairy admitted. "But I'm not about to let it happen again."

Just then, Tom walked in, saying, "Welcome to the moon station. What do you think of our home away from home here in outer space?"

"It's awesome; I've never seen anything like it," I answered quickly, hoping he had not picked up on our conversation before entering the room.

"Perhaps we can arrange a tour for you and your mother when she arrives," Tom offered. "We can show you what your father has helped us to accomplish while he has been up here."

"That would be wonderful," Mairy chimed in. "I was hoping we would be able to learn what we could, about what you and your company are doing up here."

"Yes, we understand from Dr. Beecher that the special deep space telescope is the crowning jewel of your research up here," I jumped in, thinking that Mairy had overstated her intentions.

"Indeed it is," dad said, joining in. "Their imaging technology, via IGIE, is unprecedented. With their current algorithm, they are able to demonstrate a more introspective view of just about any deep space location."

"So, better resolution than the Hubble telescope?" I had to ask.

"The resolution still leaves a little to be desired, but it provides for a full 360 degree panoramic 3D view," Tom said proudly. "Our technique provides for the 3D rendering of gravitational waves, reconstructed from the singular perspective of our deep space observatory. And if you can create a 3D model, then you can simulate its area from any angle; even from behind the targeted location."

"That is amazing!" I acknowledged. "That's like rendering a view of the body's insides via an MRI."

"Almost," dad agreed with me. "We are still looking to enhance the detail of the layered imaging.

Just then, the caterers brought in our food. It was quite the elaborate setup and much different that eating in the cafeteria.

"I hope you don't mind my ordering for you," Tom insisted. "We have a limited amount of real food up, and I do so enjoy splurging when I can. This Peking duck came up on the same transport that you two arrived on. Perhaps we can do this again when Sandi comes up."

"Oh, how convenient," I remarked. "Had we known it was with us on the way up, we might have asked you about it sooner. This looks much better than the food in the cafeteria. Hey dad, they even have Coca-Cola!"

There was a modicum of laughter expressed by all. And I wasn't at all surprised to see Mairy dig in for second helpings. The meal was capped off with a rich desert of French chocolate cheese cake, draped with caramel topping. I was feeling a little guilty about enjoying such a meal, separate of our group.

"I'm glad you all enjoyed the meal," Tom said. "Now, I'd like to make a toast. Here is to all of us. I hope all your talents will help us to change the way we view the universe forever."

We all clinked our glasses together not really knowing the true meaning of Tom's toast.

"Now if you don't mind, I will be leaving. Please feel free to stay and enjoy the view. You can have the room for as long as like."

"Thank you; and thank you for the wonderful dinner," dad said of his appreciation for the special attention.

"Yes, thank you for the dinner," I added. Mairy followed in suit, as Tom left the room.

"Are you feeling as guilty as I am for eating that wonderful dinner?" I asked of my current audience.

"Yes, I must admit it was quite a lavish indulgence," said dad, agree with me. "But I haven't had a coke in three months, and it definitely beats that cafeteria food hands down," dad remarked. "And look at that view. All those stars unfettered by our atmospheric veil. Still, it would be nice to see shooting stars up here once in awhile."

"No shooting stars to wish upon; why not?" I asked, not really thinking it through.

"For the same reason the stars look so brilliant: no atmosphere," was dad's simple answer. "Besides, there are no real shooting stars. What we see as shooting stars are just space debris or meteorites being pulled down through Earth's atmosphere."

"Well, that's a bummer," I expressed of my disappointment. "Another childhood myth busted. It's like when I first realized Santa Claus and the Easter Bunny weren't real. I believe you dispelled all of them now."

"Not sure where you two are going with this," Mairy intervened, "but we are alone now. So, perhaps we could discuss why we are up here. Steve, do you have anything to share with us?"

"Yes, but not here. Let's take a walk," dad replied in a cautious manner.

We left the meeting room and walked down toward the shops on the mezzanine. We made idle chit-chat until we reached the shops. Then dad opened up our conversation.

"Tom seemed a little too anxious for us to use the room. Moreover, one never knows who might be listening in," he explained. "This should be fine."

As we looked about, I could see we were quite alone.

"I found out that the CONS units you will be operating are meant to capture and pass gravitational waves into the mind of the pod sleepers. You can think of it like a seismmometer for measuring mini quakes in the cosmos' gravitational fabric," dad explained concisely. "The pod sleepers' brain waves are then mingle with the gravitational waves to produce data for IGIE to generate an image of the deep space target location."

"OK, that jives with what Dr. Beecher told us," I corroborated.

"Oh, you knew that already," dad guessed from my response.

"Yes; but I believe the strangest thing about our involvement in this project is that they assigned us to the master control pods. Being that we are inexperienced, I would've thought they would've used one of their more seasoned team members," I alluded as to their justification. "And their reasoning makes little sense. They say that the other pods had already been pre-fitted to the current pod operators; which is why they gave us the two special pods. But I'm not buying it."

"They also told us they wanted minds that could manipulate the dream world and work outside the normal range of consciousness," Mairy added. "Yet, I cannot imagine their decision to put us in these employee positions was solely based on our employment applications."

"Well, I may have embellished your qualifications a little on the applications," dad confessed. "I also remembered something else. I heard they needed special minds to be able to mingle and process the gravitational wave inputs for delivery to IGIE," dad explained. "It can't work without these special minds."

"Randy did say we were especially compatible for this research project," I affirmed. "But they couldn't have known that before we were actually tested. So, I'm thinking the evidence would need to be a little more convincing."

Then, it suddenly came to me. "Your books, dad," I concluded aloud. "You said they hired you after having reading your books. But did they ever say which books? Maybe it was your sci-fi story where you wrote about me; about us," I stated, referring to Mairy as the other Shadow-Forge in his novel.

"But the novel I wrote about you was marketed as science fiction," dad debated the point.

"Perhaps; but what if someone suspected or actually believed that what you wrote about me, in that science fiction novel, was actually true. I mean, why would they push for me to be part of this project at all? You're the one with the brains," I proposed.

"So you think they planned it all, like a package deal?" dad asked.

"Well, would you have requested Andrew to come along if it wasn't for the appearance of the Tokoloshe?" Mairy asked od Steve, following up on Andrew's implication.

"No, I suppose not," dad admitted.

"And none of this would have been possible without your research. Tom told us that much," she summarized of the clues they had. "In fact, they even needed to bring you up here early."

"Yes they did," dad replied.

"So what Andrew is implying is that if they believed your book to be anything other than a science fiction novel, then they may have wanted both of you all along. And if it turned out that Andrew wasn't the Shadow-Forge they thought he was, then they could just send him back to Earth," she speculated.

"I hadn't really thought of that," dad acknowledged.

Then dad turned to Mairy, asking, "But what about you; you are a Shadow-Forge as well?"

"It's not the first time my purpose has put me in harm's way," Mairy declared aloud. "So if this company is involved with the Tokoloshe, then they already know about both of us."

"Or it could be that the company is just being manipulated as well," I commented. "Perhaps we are all pawns in Discordia's plan to take control over the fate of the universe.

"Wait; if this all has to do with our quest, then let's consider how we got here," dad speculated, formalizing upon the pattern of events that had already played out. "First off, Mairy identified the Tokoloshe as a

Shadow-Forge member in league with chaos. And both times we reacted to its attack by fleeing, believing that somehow this project would provide us with some safe haven from it."

"However, if Discordia is orchestrating all of this, then we may have an even bigger problem," Andrew thought aloud. "The Tokoloshe went for me in Iowa and for you on the island," I recalled. "But I believe it actually tried to kill you. In which case, Discordia must have wanted you dead for a reason."

"It may have been that you would be easier prey if I were not around to protect you," Mairy speculated.

"Diabolical," dad said in earnest. "That must mean that you are both key to upsetting their plans."

"For my part in all of this, I just don't like being played," Mairy admitted.

"Still, we don't know anything for sure who or what we are dealing with," I reaffirmed of our speculation. "Maybe we just put the puzzle pieces together to support our own rationale."

"Did you two discover anything else?" dad asked.

"Well, Andrew had another dream," Mairy responded.

"Yes, of course, my dreams," I concurred. "There was an add-on to the earlier dream that I had on Earth. It started out like when I travelled through the universe on my first quest, but it was not quite like before where I sensed I was embodied within my own presence of being in bubble-form. It was rather that I felt more intangible. Still, I could still sense everything around me. It was as if I was part of an omnipresence that pervaded within the universe."

"Or perhaps more like a sense of astral projection to which I had discussed with you both earlier," dad commented. "Go on; what happened next?"

"Well, I was somehow aware that I was not alone. A great crack of light opened in front of me, and I was drawn into it. Whereupon passing through, I felt a rippling sensation throughout my astral form; like the tingling of an electric shock. It was followed by an abrupt loss of all sensation. After which, I was devoid of any presence or connection to the universe. And when the sensation of my 'being' was reanimated, I felt part of that sense of omnipresence again. However, this time my sense of omnipresence was as if I existed without any boundaries or containment."

"So you had made some sort of transition. Perhaps passing into another spacetime," dad surmised.

"Once there, wherever 'there' was, I felt a sense of being everywhere but without my previous connection. And yet, it was a comfortable presence of being: restful and without any distractions. It was almost as if I was a universe unto myself, outside of spacetime."

"Interesting," dad started thinking. "If you could separate the concepts of Space and Time, would you say whether it was more like you felt you were outside of Time, or outside of Space?"

"I guess I would have to say 'Space'," I decided. "I mean, I was aware of my 'Space', but in a different way. Somehow it was like I still had a sense of my Space, but without the presence of universal connections."

"It sound rather more like you achieved a sense of isolation from temporal activity," he began to think out loud. "Yes, a place of 'All Space and No Time'."

"I heard you speak of this before. You mean a black hole, don't you?" I asked, cringing at the very thought of this as a future possibility. "I must be like a black hole magnet or something," I jested about my bad luck.

"That brings to mind another clue to their objective," Mairy ventured.

"Oh, what might that be?" dad asked.

"If this company is involved and they believe that your father's novel is a real account of what happened, then they would know that Andrew had been there before and survived it," she guessed. "It may be what this is all about."

"Not if I can help it," I bellowed.

"That's the spirit!" dad acknowledged of my tenacity.

"In more ways than one," Mairy quipped. "If we are going to beat our nemesis, then I'm going to have to work with you to help you to re-discover who you are, and what it means to be a Shadow-Forge. And then I need for you to understand what powers are available to you as a Shadow-Forge."

"Powers?" I questioned, scoffing at the notion. "I never believed that I had any special abilities," I remarked.

"Your doubt is what is keeping you grounded," Mairy counseled me. "You can't develop abilities that you don't even understand. This is what I will teach you."

I looked to see Dad standing motionless, staring in through the glass of the shop in which he faced.

"I must visit this shop sometime. I see it closes early, but it also opens up earlier than the other shops," he said aloud. Then he went quiet again. I couldn't tell whether he was thinking or distracted by the figurines in the shop's window. Suddenly, he turned to us.

"You mustn't let on that you are more than you seem. I don't want you two to take any unnecessary chances," he cautioned us. "Where are you two staying?"

I filled dad in on the whereabouts of our rooms. Upon finishing, I could see the concern in his eyes.

"I never meant for my publications to put anyone in danger," dad lamented. "Good thing they are having your mother brought up on the next shuttle run. I feel better when we are working together a family unit."

"Mom's coming up on the next shuttle run?" I repeated as a question. "Why so early?"

"Guess they don't want anything to distract me from my work," dad proposed. Then looking to me directly, he said, "I need to think a little more about your dream. There is something about that crack of light and being in your own universe that is striking a chord with me. I just can't seem to put my finger on it."

We said our goodbyes for that evening and went our separate ways. As I watched dad walk away, I thought of the burden he shouldered. I walked Mairy back to her room, and I stopped just inside the opened door.

Before closing her door she said, "You can do this, you'll see. Do not turn away from our mutual destinies, lest we all suffer the consequences of our unfulfilled quest."

Our meeting left a lot for me to think about. But thinking for me just invoked more questions than answers. How does one use their Shadow-Forge powers if they are not in Shadow-Forge form? And could I wield such powers in the real world, or just in the shadow world of my etheric persistence? And how does what I do on an astral plane affect my physical host body in the real world when I am not in Shadow-Forge form?

CHAPTER

12

The Mystery Deepens

**[We are the dream-makers, the dreamers
of dreams yet to be dreamt.]**

After weeks of practice simulations with the original four members of Margaret's team, today was to be the first day of a full system test of IGIE with all six CONS units working in parallel. Just as before, they all submitted to being hooked up to the CONS units. Just as before they let themselves be put under the control of the scripted dreamscapes. However this time, Andrew and Mairy would be counted among the ranks of the pod sleepers.

It was to be a real test of the IGIE system and their designed interface into it. The expectation of this experiment was that their minds were to be used in concert to filter out gravitational wave variations in a more robust manner. The intent of this exercise was to produce detailed images of the gradient properties within targeted locations of deep space bodies. The data could then be used to render a three dimensional image of the deep space target area, both inside and out.

Still one couldn't help but to be apprehensive of someone, or something, fiddling with their brain's ability to keep them alive and sane. After all, what might be the real side effects of such a communion of man with machine? How does one really manage the comingling of waveforms within the activity of the brain?

[Andrew's Perspective]

I woke up early from a dreamless sleep. As I lay in bed, I collected my thoughts for the busy day ahead. It was wonderful connecting with dad, as we did last night, but we didn't have as much time to compare notes as I would have liked. Let's face it: I wasn't used to being without supervision for this length of time. I guess I just missed not having my parents around to steer me in one direction or other. Though, dad did say that mom would be arriving soon, so I felt a reserved sense of relief knowing that the whole family would be together. And although I felt a budding relationship with my body guard, Mairy, I did not feel ready to operate on my own. I wonder if parents ever feel that way.

As I thought about it, it was not the not necessarily the physical separation from home and family as when I traveled to Glorthocks, where I was really on my own. Rather it was that I still felt the need for their love and companionship; kind of like being homesick, I guess. Mom said it was a side effect of my acquired traumatization, like PSTD, at such a young age. She said it would probably be awhile before I was able to feel confident outside the security of my comfort zone. Although right now my comfort zone was right here in this bed; even as I knew it was time to get up.

It wasn't long before there was a knock on the door, and the activities of the day began anew. I took just enough time to change clothes, and then I was out the door. It appears the team was excited with anticipation of the day's upcoming session. I can't say I really appreciated their elated attitude toward being hooked up to a machine for hours on end. There has to be more to it.

As I exited from my room, I could hear Lindsey calling on Mairy, "Mairy, are you ready?"

Mairy's door opened, and she responded, "Yes; as is everyone else out here as well, I see."

Mairy was clearly surprise with the entourage waiting outside her door.

With the arrival of the last member into the hallway, Vera announced, "OK fellow travelers, it's time to go flying."

As Mairy walked off with Lindsey, I waited until Vera walked ahead of us. Then I got the attention of Timothy, asking, "Is it always a riddle with her? What did she mean by flying?"

"Oh, it's more than a riddle my friend. It is an experience," Timothy answered. "But I wouldn't want to spoil your surprise with my expectations. Come on, you'll love it."

"It's the ultimate feeling of freedom; virtually reality in its raw form, man. You'll see," Milo piped in.

"OK, I guess I like surprises as much as the next person," I acknowledged. Their shared secret left me with the keenness of not being in the know, and wary of what was about to come.

"But not to worry, it's a good thing," Timothy assured me.

We walked beyond the conference rooms where the group had their morning meeting yesterday. As we made our way to the research portion of the facility, we met up with Dr. Beecher, who was again waiting just inside the security entrance. Dr. Beecher singled us out from the group to wait, as the rest of the team continued their familiar route to the research lab. We followed Dr. Beecher as she continued down the hall.

"Today is going to be a full system test of IGIE with all six CONS units," Dr. Beecher started. "It is important that you two maintain control of the group at all times."

"What do you mean by maintain control?" Mairy asked.

"Oh, that's right. The units you worked with on Earth were single efficiency pods, weren't they?" she asked.

"I guess. They were definitely independent of each other," I provided as my clueless answer.

"Well, your units here are more like command modules," Dr. Beecher began to explain. "All information to and from the group will be channeled through both of you. Although you will be participating in your own lucid dreams, just as you have done previously, you will be controlling the dreamscape sequences for all of the other participants."

'Dreamscape', I thought to myself; I had seen a movie entitled 'Dreamscape' with dad. What I recalled of the movie was that the main character was able to enter other's dreams. But dad was the one who was trying to train for this, not me. I scrambled to get some semblance of what previous training they believe we had. The best I could come up with was a remembrance of my conversation with dad about being able to control my actions within my own more lucid dreams.

"Oh, you mean our ability to control our own lucid dreams," I clarified, looking wide eyed to Mairy to let her know that I was just making it up.

"Exactly," Dr. Beecher confirmed, "except that this time, your ability to control your dreamscapes will affect those of the entire group as well. You will not necessarily be in contact with them, but whatever you do in your dreams, will influence their dreamscape as well. So try to keep what you are viewing and doing in focus, and then the others will be commonly focused."

"So our attitudes and emotions will be used to set the tone of the other's dreams," Mairy asked with some concern. Perhaps she was worried about how my inexperience would get in the way of this control.

"Yes, that is a very good way of putting it," Dr. Beecher complimented her understanding of the task. "But even more, you will be keeping their more creative thoughts occupied, so they do not to interfere with their cognitive capability of the CONS units to filter and translate gravitational wave variations."

Dr. Beecher looked to us to see how much of her instructions we might have understood, and then expounded a little more.

"It is important that you keep the dream simulation alive and on task, so that the creative and social skills of the group members are kept preoccupied. Keep it simple; no high emotional states that would trigger their need for independent reasoning. Can I count on you?" she asked.

As Dr. Beecher looked to us for a response, I thought to myself that this was my last chance to opt out. But then Mairy answered for both of us.

"Yes, we have this. We can keep the simulation engaged and free from drifting. And I'm sure we can provide the group with an ample amount of distraction," Mairy stated with confidence.

I kind of wondered if her reference to an ample amount of distraction was aimed at me.

"I'm glad to hear that," said Dr. Beecher, satisfied that her instructions were understood.

As we reached the room with the rest of the group, they had already started getting hooked up into their CONS units. Dr. Beecher broke away from us to provide a 'pep talk' to the other pod operators.

I pulled Mairy over to the side, asking, "How are we going to pull this off?"

"I'm guessing that the machine is going to do most of the work," she counseled me. "So what we must do is try to stay alert and mindful enough in our own dreams to sort through whatever images she is talking about throwing at us," Mairy explained of her plan.

'And how do I do that?" I asked with apprehension.

"I'll do my best to help keep you focused, but you'll have to help. I'm thinking if anything goes wrong, they're going to blame it on the machine, anyway. After all, it is their first full system test," she stated.

"That's good thinking; that could work," I was quick to agree, as the plan didn't ask much of me. "Or at least until they can rule out whether or not any problem encountered, was really a fault of their machines. Well, I don't know about you, but I have never trained for this before."

"Trained for this? You're thinking about this all wrong. You have already lived this," Mairy stated poignantly. "You know; on your journey to Glorthocks? You explained how you were conscious of the changes happening around you. Well, you were physically unconscious for the duration of that trip."

"Yes, I see what you mean," I acknowledged. "But I wasn't really navigating; I had no real control. I was rather just a passenger. Harmony was doing all the work."

"That's fine," Mairy replied. "Leave the navigating to me this time."

The CONS technician, Randy, called over to us, "Are you two just about ready?"

"Yes," I answered for the both of us. At which time we walked over to our control pods.

Randy positioned himself between our two units, and walked us through getting ready.

"Here, you'll need to put these on," he said, handing us some baggy, white colored full body suits.

Mairy started to strip, as she had done previously in the shuttle.

"No, that's not necessary. You can just put them on right over your clothes," Randy instructed her.

I looked to see the rest of the group had already donned similar outfits, and their pods were already being prepped for the session. As I surveyed the pods designated for each group member, I could really only see each of their faces. The body suits were somewhat like the wets suits in that they only left their faces exposed. And being that they were baggy, one figure pretty much looked like any other figure.

"What no book today," I quipped, trying to conceal my nervousness?

"Nope, not today," Randy replied. "Today you'll need to be more introspective, and practice on your lucid dream participation."

The suits seemed to be lined with some kind of fluffy cotton material. And actually, despite their looks, they were quite comfortable. After we had our suits on, the Randy helped us get hooked up into our CONS units. Once we were hooked up, I felt the environment inside the suit being regulated. It was as if there was a warm dry breeze circulating around me, inside the suit.

I looked across to Mairy, saying, "Kind of comfy in here." Mairy smiled back.

"Hey Randy, can we get one of these for our own personal use?" I joked.

"They're pretty expensive," Randy pointed out. "Besides, you wouldn't want to go around looking like an 'oompa loompa' all day now, would you?"

I immediately knew that Mairy would not be able to make sense of the reference to 'oompa loompa' as the characters from the movie, 'Willy Wonka and the Chocolate Factory'.

"Guess you have a point there," I admitted. "Still you have to admit, it would be quite a fashion statement."

The technician broke out into a big smile as he continued his work.

From across the room, I could hear and see the rest of group getting themselves psyched up for the experience. They all seemed quite excited in anticipation of being put under the control of these machines. Their excitement eased my nervousness and helped me to prepare for whatever was going to come next.

"OK, amigos," Milo shouted; "it's time for a little REM exercise."

"That's about your speed," Lindsey joked.

Vera was a little more intense in her reference to the upcoming experience, saying, "Here is where we separate the girls from the boys, or should I say the adults from the children."

"Or put them together and see what you got, Bibbidi-Bobbidi-Boo," Tim quipped uneasily, seemingly using humor to ease his tension. It appeared that Tim was as excited as he was nervous. I felt I could sympathize with that feeling.

"Sweet dreams, science boy," Lindsey said to Tim, trying to get him calmed down.

"Indeed," Tim replied, continuing with his penchant for picking up song lyrics in what was being said around him. "Sweet dreams are made of these, who am I to disagree."

Once we were all situated, the technicians initialized their startup procedure. I turn to looked and see Mairy looking back at me. Like synchronized swimming, all the pod beds began sliding into place and putting us into a horizontal position, all at the same time. Similarly, I observed the lids of our units closing above each of us. However, once my lid was closed, I had no real way of seeing what was happening to anyone else.

The lid was about a foot in front of my face. I would have felt quite claustrophobic if it hadn't been for the transparency of the lid itself. All was quiet except for the electronically modulated voice of Randy. I could hear him as he talk me through the procedure on some internal intercom.

I could feel a warm liquid sensation about me, like I just peed in my pants. Then there was a weightless feeling about me as the body suit began to float in some surrounding liquid. I thought how the suit I was wearing must have been both waterproof and inflatable, because I could not feel any moisture. Rather there was only somewhat of a pleasantly cool and dry breeze, which seemed to be regulated from within the suit itself. As I lay there, I noticed how quiet it became, when the technician wasn't speaking. It was like the CONS units were systematically cancelling out our five senses. The overhead lights glaring across the transparent portion of the lid, was the last thing I remember seeing.

I awoke to a medley of tones and a collage of colored images in motion: like an aurora borealis on steroids. As if by reflex, I began analyzing my every sense, as I had done previously on my journey to Glorthocks. I did not feel the restraints of my suit, nor visualize the limitations the CONS unit that I occupied. I seemed to be floating about, as I had experienced in the shuttle cargo module on our travel to the Moon.

As I tried to get some bearing on my ability to control my surroundings, I reflexively began to think about how it was on my previous journey across the cosmos. But unlike my previous voyage through the aether of space, there was no bubble of containment. Rather I felt more free floating, as I dizzily spun end over end. Mentally I seemed to be able to propel myself from the area of my gut, while still not being able to discern any sense of a real body.

As I began to focus on my ability to control my motion, the images began to settle down as well. I then had the sudden realization that I was somehow under water. I rose up out of the water onto what appeared to be an island shore. I could see that the vegetation around the beach was more deciduous than tropical. Strange; I didn't know where I was, but it really didn't seem to matter. In trying to retrace how I may have gotten here, I finally realized that I was actually in a dream.

So this is the dreamscape, I thought to myself; nice. I would think this would be more than enough to keep the group occupied without any intervention from me or Mairy. Mairy; yes, where was Mairy? Based on what Mairy said about piloting the session, I figured she would have to be somewhere about. So I started searching for her, believing that she would be somewhere within my dreamscape. Walking through and beyond the trees of the shoreline, I could see a beach front restaurant and bar. And little farther down the road, there were hotels and traffic. This place was crowded. This seemed to be quite an elaborate dreamscape. Not something I would've considered ideal; there were just so many people. Some of the people seemed vaguely familiar, while others were just faces in the crowd. As I navigated the crowd, I found it peculiar that they were not even aware of my presence.

As I walked into one of the buildings, it took a while for my eyes to get used to the abrupt darkness. Reaching about in the darkness, I found that I was unable to feel my way through. It was like there was no furniture or walls. I wandered about trying to feel for some frame of reference. Finally, I was beginning to regain some semblance of the space I was occupying, and it wasn't a building at all.

As my interpretation of sight returned, I began to visualize an open scene of the night sky with multiple stars clustered within a gaseous cloud. I then realized that I was actually floating about in random space. Returning my attention back to the gaseous cloud, I notice a resemblance to the shape of a hand with only three fingers. As I tried to gain a perspective of the cloud shape in greater detail, it appeared to be more like a woman watching over a child holding a dog. Then the brightness began to wane again, and the stars faded into the gaseous cloud.

As I continued to watch, I felt the gaseous vapor in front of me being washed away, as if by a giant wave. It hit like the water wave that forced me into a rip current off the California coast. I couldn't tell which way was up or down, but I imagined I was back on the beach again. I surfaced from the surf, finding myself in the shadow of Mairy's visage, which appeared to be blocking a peaceful sunrise. As I reached out to her, the light of the sunrise grew brighter; blurring my vision of her.

Then suddenly, I was no longer dreaming. I knew I was back into a conscious mode again, and I could hear applause within the room. As the pod's lid was already open, I looked across to the next pod. There I could see Mairy smiling at me. I smiled back at her. I then looked about to see Dr. Beecher and the technicians, all congratulating themselves. I thought of how I could feel the fresh air against my face. As the pod beds were then repositioned automatically to a more vertical position, the technicians descended upon us. I imagined they wanted to free us from our connections to the CONS units, rather than entrust us with it.

From across the room I could hear Milo's voice, saying, "Man, what a trip that was."

"Wow," Tim joined in; "it seemed so much more intense than our previous practice sessions."

"How did the newbies fair with the experiment," Vera asked cattily.

"Well, we're still here," Mairy responded with confidence.

"But where were we?" I said aloud, still recovering from the intensity of the lucid dream.

"Venice Beach," Lindsey answered back. "They have been using that same scripted dream on and off for the last 3 months."

"At least it beats that sports game scenario they were feeding us before," Vera added.

I looked to Mairy in confusion, because that was not all I saw. Mairy signaled back to me with a hand gesture, which I interpreted to mean to be quiet about what we may have experienced in our dreams.

"In all actuality, you never left this room," Dr. Beecher responded to my query. "Your CONS units provided a scripted dream scenario in which we were able to engage your more creative or social cognitive mental processes. It's also a way of our being able to monitor your sanity while your brain waves are being used to interface with and interpret gravitational wave forms."

Maintaining sanity is a good thing, I thought to myself.

Dr. Beecher then changed her focus to the entire group, "You all perform quite well. I couldn't say anything before the session started, so as not to influence your mental perspectives, but you were all able to converge upon the same results. You see, we focus the DeepSIT telescope in an area of deep space to see if we could replicate what traditional deep space telescopes are picturing."

Dr. Beecher pulled up a picture on the monitor. "For this session the target area was the 'Pillars of Creation'. Your combined units were able to sample the gravitational wave forms emanating from that area of space, as detected via DeepSIT, while you navigated the scripted landscape of your dreams. We should be able to show you the results from today's session, tomorrow."

"Far out,'" Milo exclaimed. "Can you set my next dreamscape up to look like that? I believe I'd rather be there than return to Venice Beach again."

Andrew immediately recognized the picture, but said nothing as it appeared everyone else merely saw what was in the landscape of the scripted dream. The three pillars were what he inferred to be like a three fingered hand. He needed to confer with Mairy to understand more about what happened to him. More importantly, he wanted to know if it was expected for them to be able to exist outside of their dreamscape.

"Actually, I feel as if I have been roller skating down that boardwalk all day," Lindsey remarked. "How much longer were we out this time?" she asked Randy.

"Actually this was a short session," Randy reported. "You were out for about two hours or so, but your combined REM cycle broke a new record. The combined REM sleep was 53.4 minutes, with the longest REM synchronization being 36.7 minutes."

Andrew had never heard of REM sleep being combined and asked the technician, "What do you mean when you said combined REM?"

"Combined REM is the time when all members of the group are in REM at the same time," Randy informed me. "It's not easy to coordinate the individual REM times of each participant. Usually, REM sleep happens 90 minutes after you fall asleep. We are able to reduce that non-REM time by inducing a sensory free environment. The first period of REM typically lasts 10 minutes, with each of the later REM stages getting longer. Some of these later REM stages may last up to an hour."

"Now, the concept of REM synchronization is when we are able to orchestrate parallel feeds through the group, allowing for synchronized output of individual brain waves. We are expanding our research to include how best to merge the simulation, among each member of the group, to provide for the longest synchronization times," Randy explained.

"I agree with Lindsey," Tim spoke up. "It seemed like I spent a whole day at the beach. It was as if we were out for a much longer duration this time."

"Really; it only seems like a few minutes for me," I said without thinking.

"Same here," Mairy acknowledged, supporting my interpretation.

"That's very interesting," Dr. Beecher remarked of the disparity in our sense of the session's duration.

"OK, everyone, before any of you go to lunch, I want each of you to separately log your experiences, as we discussed earlier. As always, your choice of media to provide for this log entry is up to you. Also, please grab one of these psychological evaluation surveys before leaving. I need these surveys completed and brought back to me before our next session," she stated in a professional tone. "Excellent session all; this was our very first successful launch of data to IGIE from all six pods. And you have all performed very well."

"I'm sorry, but what do you mean about choice of media?" Mairy asked Dr. Beecher.

"Lindsey, Tim, could you orient our newest members in our evidence capture?" Dr. Beecher requested.

"Yes, of course," Lindsey replied.

"Come on you two," Tim directed us. "The equipment is already in your room."

"Oh, and one more thing," Dr. Beecher announced. "As I believe they will be crunching data well into the night on this run, you can take the rest of the afternoon off. I suggest you use it wisely to keep up with your physical training, rather than spending all your time in the gaming area of the recreational center. And yes, Milo, I am directing this at you. I will be checking your ID logs, so don't try faking it."

"Ha Ha, no gaming for you today," Vera joked with Milo as she walked out of the room. "You've been put on her watch list."

"Hey, not everyone is looking to train for the decathlon," Milo responded back.

I took Milo's response as an implication that Vera was probably more a fitness enthusiast than he was. It was also interesting to know that Dr. Beecher could and would follow up on our ID logs. I would need to keep this in mind as we moved about in the facility.

As we followed the group back towards our rooms, Lindsey and Tim explained that our 'choice of media' was a simple selection of using a word processor, dictating to a voice recognition recorder, or making our own DVD video presentation.

"It is important to get your thoughts and feelings captured while they are still fresh in your mind," Lindsey instructed us.

"Then why not just have a round table discussion right after the session?" I asked.

"Dr. Beecher is very thorough and strict about individual logs," Tim answered. "She does not want anyone's experience log to be influenced by another's description. The mind is easily subject to suggestive wording and picks up on even the slightest word choice selection. It is the psychology of social interaction that drives each culture toward a common language. Dr. Beecher wants each entry to be unique."

"Makes sense," I admitted.

"And, regardless of choice, it is a one-time capture," Lindsey cautioned us. "It is not like writing a story. So you don't really have time to think about what you are saying, or correcting mistakes on the fly."

Lindsey demonstrated the media choices to both of us from within Mairy's room. Then we all separated to retire to our own rooms.

"We'll see you at lunch," Lindsey called out as she left.

"And take your time," Tim mentored me. "It is important to log everything you remember. We're not expected back for work anymore today anyway."

I guess I was kind of old school, as I chose to use the computer's word processor. As my experience seemed brief, I had little to contribute for my first log. Instead, I wasted time trying to analyze what I had seen, and trying to keep from referring to it in my log report. From what I could remember, it started out differently from other dreams that I've had; I mean, with the tones and colors. And, although it was very visually stimulating, it was not the thrill ride I was led to believe. Perhaps my trip across the cosmos left me jaded even for these types of adventure. However, I could not tell this to Dr. Beecher. I can only imagine what Mairy might be censoring out from her own experience.

As I lay draped over the bed, there was a knock at the door; it was Mairy.

"Have you completed your log entry?" she asked as she let herself in.

"Yes, but I spent more time censoring my thoughts before writing them in," I commented. "I couldn't help comparing this experience with my previous journey across the universe."

"I know what you mean," Mairy sympathized. "It's difficult to separate new experiences from old ones."

"And it was a good thing I thought it through before writing it down," I observed. "It was like my word processor was stuck in correction mode.

Even if I tried to 'back up' or 'delete' any of my report, it wouldn't really go away. It would only provide for a strike through of the changes. It made it kind of difficult to navigate my own writing."

"It does seem that our choices of media were all meant to provide for similar documentation experiences," Mairy stated with some suspicion in her voice, as if she were 'Sherlock Holmes' himself.

"What do you mean?" I ask, as if I were playing the part of 'Dr. Watson'.

"Well, as it was explained to us, our media choices were specifically designed to do the same thing," Mairy presented her deductions like a seasoned detective. "Our first choice was ten pieces of specially marked paper, and all of which needed to be handed in whether they were blank or not. And you already described how the second choice works."

"And the third and fourth choices were either CD or DVD recordings," I added; "which had to be left on until the recording was completed. Yes, I see what you mean."

"They were all specifically designed to catch any unintentional information that we might provide," Mairy surmised. "I wonder if they know more about us than they are telling."

"You're just paranoid," I said, half believing her; or at least considering the possibility she was right in her suspicions. "I mean, it's not as if they are really targeting us with these logs. Everyone on the team has the same task and choices."

"Well, they would have to do that, or they might have tipped their hand," Mairy rationalized. "Anyway, we should be more mindful of what we do and say, lest we give ourselves away."

"Well, let's get something to eat," I suggested. "We can discuss this with dad later."

By the time we sat down for lunch with our team members, they were already finishing up their meals. As we began eating, Vera was the first to leave.

"See you at the rock climbing wall," Vera said to Milo.

"Guess I can't put it off forever," Milo agreed. "Are you ready for a little competition, Tim?"

"Sure; at least I'm not packing as much with me to this competition as you are," Tim replied, eyeing Milo's stomach. "You always eat like it's your last meal."

"Oh this," Milo rubbed his stomach, "it's all muscle."

Lindsey talked to us directly, saying, "I hate to leave you two alone, but I have an appointment with my physical trainer."

"Won't that make your husband jealous?" Mairy joked.

"Oh, that's not a problem," Lindsey replied candidly. "My physical trainer is my husband."

We stayed to finish our lunch and then went to explore the physical training center. Nothing futuristic here; the center had pretty much the same equipment I've seen at other hotels on Earth. Mairy seemed quite enthusiastic about being able to do some physical exercise. I would say she was a type 'A' personality. It appeared that the only time she settled down was either during meditation or when she was sleeping. I was never really a sports fanatic, and had done little in the way of organized sports or exercise outside of school. If fact, I had done little in the way of exercising, except for weight lifting competitions with dad. Still, it was more of a fun setting for Mairy and me to interact, instead of always being mindful of our quest.

[Scene Change – Narrator's Perspective]

[Success can be measured in many forms]

The first successful translation of deep space images were being generated through IGIE in an adjoining computer lab, which was next to the building that housed the Deep Space Interferometer Telescope. Dr. John Leighy was on his computer analyzing the data for the translated images. A bit of confusion arouse from what appeared to be a disparity in the imaging of some pictures for the same area of space.

Calling out to his associate for some clarification, Dr. Leighy asked, "Phil, didn't we set up the experiment to view the 'Pillars of Creation'?"

"Yes, that's right," Dr. Phil Berry acknowledged.

Dr. Leighy followed up, saying, "There seems to be a mix of pictures among the translated images from the six CONS units that are not part of the targeted area. What do you make of these results?" he said, pointing to his monitor.

Dr. Berry, sitting on a chair with wheels, rolled over to John's computer desk.

"I see what you mean; that is odd. It is as if there doesn't appear to be a clear synchronization of translations among the CONS units." Pausing for a moment of thought, Phil then presented a probable hypothesis to rule out. "Is it possible that, for these images, the CONS output were sent to IGIE unsynchronized?"

"I checked that already," John informed him. "There doesn't seem to be any significant timing differential for the integrated wave inputs to IGIE from the CONS. Perhaps some of the pod sleepers were not on task. After all, the gravitational wave forms are meant to be filtered via their collective brain waves to provide for this imaging," John presented as another alternative scenario.

Trying to identify the source of the translated images, Phil asked, "OK, then we need to trace it further back to see from which pods the anomalous data is coming."

John started paging through the downloaded data logs, "Let me see if I can trace it back. Yes, here it is. It appears that there were data separation integrated in with and translated through the neurological wave forms from the control pods."

Phil then speculated further, asking, "Is there a possibility that the IGIE receiver did not properly account for the split wave form outputs between the control pods and the other four CONS units?"

"You mean like a reflection or deflection of the combined gravitational wave forms?" John asked for clarification. "I don't see how that would be possible. Besides, these earlier translated images from previous control pod sessions are more consistent with imaging generated from the other four CONS units."

"You mean before the master units came on line," Phil asked.

"No, more like when Vera was running both master units in parallel," John explained. "It was only these latter wave form translations that began to differ from the norm."

"Well, maybe that is part of the problem then," Phil speculated. "There are two differing pod operators now; one each for each of the master control units."

"Perhaps that's it," John apprehensively agreed. "I hate working without a proper baseline."

"Is Margaret in," Phil asked? "Maybe she could shed some light on it."

"She's online," John acknowledged.

"Let's have her come in," Phil suggested.

Shortly after being contacted, Margaret arrives in the computer lab.

"Margaret thank you for coming," Phil greeted her politely.

Margaret questioned what they wanted her for, asking, "What do you need, Phil?"

"The generated images from the control pods seem to have morphed over time," John spoke up. "Could there be a human factor in the wave form integration and translation that we haven't accounted for?"

"Anything is possible," Margaret acknowledged. "This is the first time we've had all six pods working. However, Randy did successfully clear the two new control pod operators yesterday. He found the new operators to be 100% compatible. I guess I can have him recalibrate the neurofeedback frequencies for their neuro wave integrators."

"Actually, it was not the machine that I was questioning," John explained. "These are the newest and youngest candidates you've ever worked with. Could it be that their lack of training on this equipment could be a problem; or maybe their lack of mental discipline?"

"That's not how it works," Margaret answered defensively. "Their immaturity or temperament should have little to do with how they behave in an unconscious state. Besides, Tom personally vouched for their readiness to participate in this study. And you must admit, these first images are much more defined than anything else that IGIE was able to produce for us in the past."

"True," Phil agreed. "Still it's curious how the images were consistent with the images from the Hubble telescope at first, but then they changed over time."

"Indeed, these first set of translated images are virtually identical to the Hubble. And this is what we would expect because, as they are both bounded by the speed of light, there should be no difference in the speed of radio wave forms versus the speed of the gravitational wave forms," John pointed out.

"It is almost like the control pods targeting shifted to another area of deep space," Phil said, building upon what John described.

"OK, so let's have Randy recalibrate the neurofeedback frequencies anyway, and then we can try again tomorrow," Margaret concluded.

"Wait a minute," John paused to rethink his initial assertion. "The more I look at these two images, the more I am convinced that they are the same area of deep space."

"How can that be," Margaret asked in confusion? "You said yourself that these first images clearly show that your target area was for the 'Pillars of Creation'. So where are the three giant columns of gas protruding upwards in these succeeding images?"

"They are not pronounced, to be sure, but I believe it is the same area," John said with excitement. "Here look," John requested, manipulating the computed images, "let me overlap the pictures for you."

Dr. Leighy modified the former picture to be more transparent, but still retain its iconic view. And then he slid the more anomalous image under the modified transparency.

"Yes, just as I thought," he declared, pointing to the computer screen. "Do you see how the star patterns still line up, even without the complete gaseous columns? It is as if some data is missing in the reconstruction, so that the gaseous columns are even not being imaged anymore."

"That's just great!" Dr. Berry complained. "How is it that we are missing data? Now it appears we have a software glitch in the two new CONS. That means going through the code, line by line. We'll be here all night if you want to be ready to rerun by morning."

"Tired minds don't work well. I believe we should still reschedule the same experiment for tomorrow to see if this anomalous occurrence is reproducible," John concluded. "In the meantime, we review the software."

"But I've already told Tom that we had a successful run of IGIE," Dr. Beecher pointed out to us. "He's going to want to see the evidence."

John had a second thought, proposing, "Maybe it's just something with how master CONS units are interpreting the varying degrees of gravitational wave forms relative to the other four. We just have to delay him until we rerun the experiment over again. We'll see if the results improve tomorrow."

"Well, the last thing we want to present Tom with is a puzzle," Phil admitted. He then paused and thought for a moment, before agreeing with the others. "OK, let's see if we get differing results in tomorrow's run. Maybe it'll all work out in the end, and we won't have to change what Margaret already told him."

[Scene Change – Andrew's Perspective]

[Falling through the looking glass]

After working up a good appetite from our afternoon of physical training, we were ready to meet again with Dad at dinner to compare notes. However, this time dinner would be down in the cafeteria, where there was less privacy. As the conversation wore on through the dinner, dad had come up with an idea.

"I'm not sure my fumbling about in the dreamscape is what Dr. Beecher had in mind," I confessed.

"You two connected up once before when you were out of body, so to speak," dad stated. "Is it possible that you two would be able to do it again, during these sessions? I think you would have a better chance of success if you work together, rather than separately."

"I can try," Mairy acknowledged.

"Dad, see if you can get away tomorrow to monitor our session," I asked. "It would be good to know what images are being generated by us."

"I'll certainly follow up on it," dad stated.

As dad left, we went back to our rooms. This time, however, Mairy pulled me into her room, saying, "Let's get started on your astral training. We should practice our meditation tonight to see if we can link up."

"I haven't had any luck on my own. I don't think I can do it without Harmony," I said, doubting my abilities.

"Yes, you can," Mairy insisted. "I told you that all of the Shadow-Forge can do it. You just have to believe in yourself. Don't let the doubt, that you've carried about for years, dissuade you from believing in your abilities. That's really all that Harmony did for you, anyway. Harmony just helped you to believe in your abilities. You need to reach down inside and remember who you are."

"Alright, but I'm totally out of practice. I mean, after so many failed attempts, I just stopped," I confessed. "Hey, wait, I thought you said I was the only other Shadow-Forge member you knew."

"That is not the point here. The point is whether you have to confidence to believe in yourself. I rather think you only failed because you believed you needed Harmony. She made you feel secure from harm," Mairy guessed. "But I'm here now, so concentrate on me. Remember how it was for us together in the crystal."

"Yes, we were quite the team then, and you did save me from that Tokoloshe beast; twice," I said, remembering back. "OK, let's give it a try."

Mairy grabbed the pillows from the bed, professing, "There is no reason we should sit on the hard floor."

We both sat up facing each other with legs crossed, just against the foot of her bed; our shoulders just about touching the mattress. She briefly took my hands in hers to reassure me. As I looked into her eyes, we said nothing. This was probably the closest I had been to her since she arrived. As the overhead light lit up her eyes, it was like looking into the glowing azure blue crystal. They were decidedly azure blue with flecks of green. Between our contact and how I felt about her, I found it difficult to concentrate. I held onto the image of her eyes as I closed mine, hoping to suppress my cardinal yearnings.

It took me a little while to ignore the input from the physical senses and desires that bounded me to my fourth dimensional being in spacetime. I needed to find that sense of me that existed outside of my host body. I thought of how it felt to be in the crystal with Fairy. I remembered how it felt to project myself from within the crystal. Slowly, I began to block out my five senses in remembrance of my experience. The ambient sound was replaced by a deafening silence and my more tactile sense of touch was replaced by a buoyant feeling of weightlessness. The feeling was kind of like the sensation of being suspended in midair, upon reaching the zenith of a bounce off my trampoline, rather than actually floating.

I came to realized that I was the buoyant center of my own being. It was as if I was suspended in outer space, rather than by any lack of other gravitational influence. I became disoriented as my awareness of sight began transforming into a sense of omnidirectional cognizance about me. I tried to map out a sense of direction around me in a full 360 degrees; above and below me, to the right and left of me, as well as both forward and backward. I felt I needed something to orient me to my surroundings, as I had no real sense of containment. Where is the light, I thought; fighting off my fear of losing myself to this circumspect of unending empty darkness.

I eventually became aware of a strange melodious sound of harp-like tones echoing about me. I searched my new surroundings for its source. I began to sense the presence of another being, as if my own presence of being was being engaged. Perhaps this was a property of my aural veil I thought; the limitations of my essence that Mairy spoke about to me. This sense of presence began to embrace me in both sound and an altered sense of recognition for its frequency. It was all coming back to me now, but I needed to focus.

I quickly became very comfortable with my surroundings, as my sense of doubt faded away in anticipation of renewing this remanded experience. It was as if my unappreciated sense of smell had been remade to recognize the frequency of another aura. Slowly the emerging communication across the auras manifested itself as Mairy; or should I say Fairy. She appeared to me as she did when we were together in the crystal. Yet here and now, she appeared to have wings like an angel. And isn't that what mom called her, I recalled; my guardian angel?

"What took you so long?" Fairy jokingly asked. "I was beginning to think you weren't coming."

"I'm here, with you, I think," I replied. "Am I really here?" I asked in astonishment.

"Of course," Fairy replied encouragingly. "You just needed to believe you could."

"You make it sound so easy. This is the first time I traveled beyond the realm of my own host body since my last quest." Having thought about what I said, I quickly corrected myself, "I mean our quest. Being out her again, it feels more familiar than I remembered. And yet it feels different at the same time."

"Yes, it is quite different outside of Harmony's protective spheres," Fairy acknowledged. "Harmony was not one to lose any trainees. I always thought Harmony was rather overprotective. There is so much more a feeling of freedom outside of her control. Still, Harmony's spheres are the fastest way to travel across the universe. Even I cannot improve upon that."

"Yes, freedom," I said apprehensively. "So what should we do now?" I asked curiously.

"Do?" she asked quizzically. "This is just the 'jumping off' point. I needed to get you here, so that you could believe in your own abilities."

"Somehow, I think you had something to do with this." I stated.

"You have to stop using others as a crutch," she counseled me. "This is your accomplishment; revel in it."

"Where are we anyway?" I asked. "I can't seem to perceive anything beyond our astral selves."

"I never spend much time in here," Fairy replied, without answering my question. "It's just a means to get from one reality to another. And I don't think you want to get caught up in another alternate reality just yet."

"But what about that feeling of freedom you just spoke about?" I enquired. "Why not spend some time here?" I stated with a sense of adventure.

"Now that's an oxymoron," she chuckled with amusement. "There is no real 'here'; Time and Space is all relative. Do you see anything else; anything strange about me?"

"You mean other than you're having fairy wings," I said trying to see what I could sense about in this weird environment. I couldn't even see anything that might help me identify where we were. At least while in Harmony's spheres, I had a sense of containment, a feeling of boundaries, a seeing of lights, and the sensation of moving. "Wait, yes; I see kind of a wavy cloud of color about you."

"And do you feel anything other than our communication," she continued to quizzed me.

"No, I guess not," I admitted. "In fact, if it wasn't for your astral presence, I would have no way of knowing whether I really existed at all." Then thinking of what she said about using this 'out of body' experience to get from one reality to another, I had to ask, "So how do you know where you are going in this spirit world? I mean, how do you transfer from one reality to another."

"That is a lesson for another time," she stated playfully. "It is not good for us to be separated from our bodies for very long."

With that statement, Fairy had re-enlivened a sense of apprehension in me. She might as well hit a button for me to return home. As I had not yet mastered my fears of the unknown, my subconscious went into auto mode and I lost control again. I felt myself falling from my suspended zenith, as if in a dream; falling without ever reaching bottom. And yet it was a feeling of gravity, to be sure.

I suddenly felt my arm being grabbed, as if to save me from falling. I looked to see a hand holding onto my arm; nothing more but a hand. Slowly more came into view as I followed the hand up to Mairy's face. I began to realize that I had returned from my 'out of body' experience, and I was indeed just waking from a dream. Realizing that I was no longer dreaming, I soon returned to the conscious realm of my five senses. Still I remembered our experience together. It felt so real that I knew in my heart that we two had melded subconsciously on some astral plane of existence.

Mairy looked to me, excitedly saying, "You did it!"

"Yes, I guess I did," I said, feeling a bit groggy from just waking up. Then in realization of my accomplishment, I proclaimed with a cocky attitude, "Well, after all I am a Shadow-Forge."

"That you are," she chuckled with delight; "And a very good one at that." It was nice to hear her unique laugh. I believe I would recognize that laugh anywhere.

"How did I end up dreaming with you, anyway?" I asked. "And how is it that you had wings."

"It is a tricky portal to navigate, but you made it," Mairy mentored me. "Between the spirit world and your dream world, is an imaginary portal within the mind's eye that few will ever discover. You might say its acknowledgement is the key to the spirit world, and it is just through your own imagination. And in your imaginings, you saw me with wings. In your dreams, your imaginations are set free; for dreams are not bound by the conventions of logic and control within the conscious mind. Still, if you can't control your dreams, then you will never discover the portal."

"That's a bit eerie." I admitted to her. "I mean, what you said just reminded me of an old TV series called the 'Twilight Zone'. The narrator would say the same thing at the beginning of each episode, *'You unlock this door with the key of imagination. Beyond it is another dimension - a dimension of sound, a dimension of sight, a dimension of mind. You're moving into a land of both shadow and substance, of things and ideas. You've just crossed over into the Twilight Zone'.* Who would've thought there was actually some sense to what he was saying."

"Sounds like a man who has been to the other side of reality," Mairy acknowledged.

"Yes, I suppose so," I agreed. Then becoming distracted in wondering how I might apply this new talent of mine, I asked, "Are we going to be able to manage this while we're connected to our sleep pods?"

"Our connection was made outside of our host bodies," Mairy reminded me. "It doesn't matter where we are. You just need to be able to ignore the dreamscape, and take control of your own dream interface as you did tonight," she said with confidence. "Besides, I'll be there to help you again, as I did tonight."

"Man, I'm tired," I said, feeling the exhaustion of my experience. "I could fall asleep right here."

"Yes, exercising the mind can be more draining than exercising the body," she stated, handing me her pillow. And yet, as she said it, it didn't appear that she was affected at all. Must be her training, I thought.

I took her pillow and placed it behind me as I leaned up against the foot of the bed. Surprisingly, Mairy snuggled in a bit closer, allowing her to rest her head on my shoulder. Yes, this was a good feeling. There was something to be said for connections made inside of our host bodies as well.

"Maybe we should have some practice with more distractions; like music or TV," I thought aloud, as I snuggled in closer.

And then before I realized it, I had passed out on her head while snuggling. In my dream, I found myself wandering the woods of my childhood home; the woods where I meet Harmony. I saw Harmony breezing along the shore of the large pond that once graced the meadowlands, and ran to meet her. As I caught up to her, she levitated backwards just over the pond. The water from the pond came up to meet her. As it swirled up and around her body, she appeared to caution me to wait on shore. But I continued to follow her into the water. As I passed into the water, it slowed me down. I struggled to move faster, but my actions proved to be all in vain. As it had halted the motion of my body, I felt the weight of the water against me fade away. With my torso still above the water line, I watched in amazement as the water in the pond around me dissipated until it became a fine mist. The mist then transformed into a dense eerie fog, much like the effect of frozen gas emitted from dry ice. I then felt myself separate from my host body, as I stretched to be with Harmony.

With my physical body rooted on the ground, my spirit continued to levitate up until I came to be in front of her. As I reached around her body to hug her, I instead passed into her aural veil. As we became one, I immediately became disoriented and lost within her. It felt as if I was accelerating through the expanse of all spacetime itself. I sensed that I was transitioning into yet another dimension of existence, as I could no longer distinguish what was real and what was not. Among the several individual realities, which I could envision as somewhat like the collection of galactic clusters I had seen in the books, my perspective was now much different. Distance appeared to be a matter of size rather than a matter of motion in Time. It was as if I could embrace the entirety of universal being all at once.

As I stared in awe at the majesty of creation, I was imaging the eternity of the universe itself in just one moment of Time. It all seemed to make sense at this level of being, but it was like I didn't have enough real memory to retain it all. So instead I remained spellbound, just soaking in the experience. It was all upon this moment in Time and Space that I seemed to understand it all; it was everything all at once. It felt like the wonderful fulfillment of life itself; achieving purpose, without knowing what that purpose was. It was as if all this information, this level of being, completed me. I wonder if this is what heaven would be like; for if I had a choice, I believe I might never have wanted to pass from this feeling of grace.

I should have been satisfied to just be in the moment, and yet I wanted to explore every aspect of this singular moment. All at once before me, appeared a crack of light, contrasting the background of the event. The crack persisted like a lightning bolt frozen in Time. The fracture continued to grow, filling me with a sense of electrical shock as I bathed in its brightness. Suddenly there was a strange sensation rippling through me and throughout the aether of space around me. My view became distorted in the ever increasing illumination. The previous feeling of grace that I felt, all that I knew, was disappearing before me. I felt my 'being' absorbing all the energy of the power around me, until I became the focus of the event that was unfolding.

As the bright light was pooled within me, all became dark and I was without sensation. All at once I found myself immobile; motionless in a kind of one dimensional spacetime with nowhere to be. It was as if I was frozen in Time, or Time had stopped. Or rather it was a complete absence of Time in Space. I don't, really know. Perhaps it was a degree of Space without Time. And without Time in Space, I could not tell if even I existed anymore; for Time has always been my measure of being. I felt as if there was no longer a Present time. And, by nature of consequence, there was never to be a Future time. Instead there was only my own Past time sense of self; and that was fading fast. I was quickly losing awareness of my surroundings, as well as my sense of self. For a moment I could see Fairy coming to help, but then my vision of her slowly slipped away. Was the vision real, or just a past remembrance in the aftermath of my previous quest?

I was losing more and more control as I could actually feel my ability to think, or ideate, dissipating away. The sum of my entire life experience was somehow seemingly being erased; as if I had never existed. It was as if all my connection with universal being had been severed. And without any connection to the universe, my connection to existence itself, I had to fight to attain any real sense of purpose. And yet, even this sense of purpose was being replaced by a timeless fear of longing without knowing for what or why. For without a dimension of Time, I felt more outside of existence, than inside of it. Perhaps where there was no Present or Future, I could still remake myself from what I was in the Past. It seemed to be a nightmare from which there was no end and no return; I am because I have been, therefore I must still be.

Then in my torment, I realized that I was still thinking. While the conscripts of my surroundings were more of feelings and fear, I was still managing alternatives. Yes, of course I thought to myself, I must be dreaming; drifting in the nebulous sentience of my own subconscious. I am that I am, and naught that I can be. I could be the Present that becomes the Past; at least it was a motivation for a Future. It was enough of an impetus for me to take control of my own purpose for survival. And yet, being lost in my own dream, I needed to wake up. But I would be waking up on my terms this time, rather than being driven by fear.

But resolve is not always enough, and my nightmare had not yet finished with me. An additional distraction suddenly came upon me with the reemergence of my purpose in spacetime. It was the creature I identified as the Tokoloshe. This time however, this Tokoloshe appeared to me in the guise of an evil wizard bent on my destruction; or so that was my impression and fear. He somewhat resembled an evil version of the 'Nicodemus' character from the animated movie, 'The Secret of Nimh'. I remember how it scared me when I was a child; before I matured enough to understand the real meaning of the movie.

I felt compelled to chase him down and conquer my own fears. It was like dad said, I needed to control this dream, and not continue to let the dream control me. As I confronted my opponent, his eyes flashed and he emitted a bolt of energy from his outstreched hand. As I was struck by the bolt, I could still feel the tingling of the attack through my body. It seemed strange to me that such an attack did not do more damage. Rather It made me question the reality of my environment. Should I fear this pain or act upon it? I chose the latter. Channelling the energy running through my body, I threw a bolt of my own. The contest continued back and forth, but neither of us seemed to be gaining an advantage over the other.

All at once, I noticed the image of Fairy locked within the azure blue crystal, off in the distance. It was just like seeing her on Glorthocks all over again. Instinctively I knew she was in trouble. In that moment, I re-acquired a real selfless sense of purpose again. With a single explosive force, I managed to disorient my nemesis and take flight to save Fairy. But no matter my resolve, the faster I traveled towards her the slower I felt. My actions seemed to weigh me down. I had finally taken control of my dream in a most positive manner. And yet, it wasn't enough. Something was amiss. The thought of this simple inconsistency seemed to be the downfall of my control in the dream, and my final moment in the dream as well.

C H A P T E R

13

Encounters of the Second Kind—Uncovering Evidence

[While the Heisenberg's Uncertainty Principle speaks to the influence of the observer on the experiment, it does not address the influence of the experiment on the observer.]

It is a busy evening on the moon station, for not everyone slept as deeply as Andrew. Stephen continue to mull over the information he learned from the kids, while working to understand the interplay of the pod sleeper, the CONs, and IGIE with his theoretical concepts for dark matter.

Dr. John Leighy and Dr. Phil Berry had a puzzle to work on: If DeepSIT was able to zoom into area of deep space to capture the images of gravitational waves detected about the 'Pillars of Creation', then why were there discrepancies in the series of generated images? Dr. Margaret Beecher waded through the session logs provided by her team, trying to correlate their responses, while looking for something that might explain the discrepancies found among the series of generated images. All of them were trying to rule out any faults within their control which may have contributed to the anomaly, before presenting their results to Tom.

Tom, working separately with his team, managed to upgrade IGIE without the knowledge or consent of all involved. Based on the research Steve had already developed for dark matter detection, they had installed the prototype CONS interface. Consistent with their newly developed CONS interface, Tom's team had upgraded the software on the IGIE program for the next step in his plan to achieve a fully functional dark matter detector. The concept was to provide for a whole new perspective of the universe by incorporating the modified dark matter wave forms within the minds of the pod sleepers. Then Tom would be ready to pursue his more nefarious goal; a goal that was driven by the nature of his objective for coming to Earth.

[Andrew's Perspective]

I awoke somewhat dazed and anxious. I had a rather disturbing dream that kept resonating with me in the groggy moments just before my consciousness took hold. I could still vividly remember all the details of my dream. And to be honest, it was more the disturbing feeling that persisted, than my recollection of the details that troubled me most. While I had gone further in this recurring dream, I was haunted by the puzzle it presented. It had to mean something. What was I missing, I questioned myself? I tried to replay the dream puzzle in my conscious thoughts. Perhaps dad or Mairy could make something more of it.

Thinking of Mairy, it took a moment for me to make sense of my more conscious surroundings. I realized, oh yeah, I was still in Mairy's room. Rubbing my eyes, I looked about and did not see Mairy. I reasoned that she must've gotten up before me. But just as I was about to assume that she was gone altogether, she shows up from the bathroom to check in on me.

"Good you're awake," she said drying her hair with a towel, while wearing a robe. "Better get ready fast, or you'll miss breakfast."

As I moved to respond, I could feel the soreness of my neck where it had been contorted upon the hard surface of the floor. The moment of the dream faded with this more cognizant pain.

I asked grumpily, "Why did you let me sleep so long; and on the floor, at that?"

"Anyone who can sleep as hard as you do doesn't really need a bed," said with a smile. "Now get over to your room and get ready. The others may have already left."

"Oh, yeah; OK, just give me about 15 minutes," I said getting up off the floor.

I walked out the door of her room and noticed that the hallway was indeed deserted. As I went into my room, I thought of how my travel would've been quicker if these were connecting rooms. Now that I was in my room, I had to take a minute to consider my options. It seemed as if I been operating on autopilot and needed to put myself back into manual mode to take over my own decisions. I went to the bathroom, splashed some cold water on my face and took a quick look in the mirror. It appears that sleeping on the floor had its advantages, as I did not have worry about bed hair. Getting myself a fresh set of clothes, I was able to cover up the lack of a shower, if that's what they would call it, in my morning routine. In truth, it was little more than a sponge bath. Anyway, true to my word, I was ready in 15 minutes.

At which time, Mairy walked in without knocking, "Are you just about ready?"

"Yes, and ready to greet the sunrise," I replied, and then followed her out the door. We walked down the hall to the elevator. "Hey, Lindsey didn't wait for you this morning," I said, now that my brain was a bit more awake.

"Actually, she did," Mairy admitted. "I told her to go on without me, because I would be waiting on you." As we approached the elevator, she asked, "Did you do any more dreaming?"

"Yes, but its more than I can tell you right now," was my quick response, as I realized the conversation might be interrupted at any moment.

"But there is something I wanted to talk to you about. You know, since we started working these pod sessions up here in the research center, sometimes it is difficult to tell the difference between when I am lucid dreaming, and when I'm in the pod, or when I am out-of-body with you for that matter; especially with you being part of each experience. I can't tell were my out-of-body experiences end and where my dreams begin; it all seems so real."

"So you dreamed about me?" she asked coyly, without addressing my concerns.

"Yes," I replied with a little embarrassment. "But then I also dreamt about Harmony as well," I said, trying to divert attention from my thoughts for her.

Although I had kind of a girlfriend on Earth before all this started, but that relationship didn't seem as important as I once thought it was. I guess I wasn't really invested in my girlfriend as much as I might have thought. And, as we left without so much as a goodbye to anyone, I'm sure she feels like I skipped out on her. Anyway, now there was Mairy. And Mairy, when she was Fairy, used to get on my nerves during our last quest. However, in this reincarnation of her Shadow-Forge self, she seemed more concerned with my thoughts and feelings this time.

It was kind of a weird relationship. She started out as my protector and mentor. Then mom started out referring to her as my sister, for convenience sake. And now, it just seems strange that we would have an expectation for any different relationship. Still, it felt different; at least for me. Now, it seemed to me that we were having a more than just a brother to sister relationship. Did Mairy feel the same as I did, or is she just flirting around with me? Although I wanted to know, if I asked, and she might rejected the notion, then that might make things worse.

"Hello, Andrew; are you in there?" she jokingly inquired to get my attention. "The elevator is here."

"Oh yeah; guess I was daydreaming," I responded.

"Speaking of getting lost in one's dreams," Mairy concluded. "You need to wake up to meet today's challenge. You need to stay in control if you are going to be of any use to me."

"I guess our session last night pretty much left me 'wiped out'," I said to excuse my behavior.

"Wiped out?" she inquired.

"Oh yes; 'wiped out' is an expression that means very exhausted or tired. Perhaps I'm still not quite awake yet," I explained to her to cover up being lost in thought.

"Oh," she acknowledged my explanation. The elevators doors opened, and some of the occupants got out. As we got into the elevator alone, she requested, "Well, try to remember your dream for later then."

"No problem there," I stated confidently. "It was one really strange dream, to be sure."

As others got in the elevator before reaching the cafeteria, we remained politely silent for the rest of the trip down. In our silence, I thought more about my relationship with Mairy and about our out-of-body session last night. I actually couldn't wait to try out our new strategy for getting around the CONS machines with our new astral connection. We left the elevator, and soon joined the others in the cafeteria.

"Good morning," Tim said, being the first to greet us as we got in cafeteria line for our food selection. "We didn't really see you at all last night."

"Yes, we spent a little more family time with dad," I replied. "Did you wake up late as well?" I asked.

"No, this is my second time through the line. I am up here for my second breakfast," he answered.

"Oh, like the Hobbits from that movie 'Lord of the Rings'," I said, making small talk. I continued chatting with Tim as he was a fan of the books as well. We eventually approached the cafeteria table where the others were already assembled."

"They stayed up late after visiting with their father last night," Tim announced to the rest of the team members, as if to fill them in on any earlier gap in their conversation. "They spent last evening with their father for dinner."

"It must be nice to be able to communicate with your family on a regular basis," Vera said somewhat snidely, as if we were being given some kind of favoritism.

"From what you told us, you weren't really part of a close knit family anyway," Milo joined in, so as to deflect her somewhat negative engagement with us.

"As orphanages go, it was alright. But I had friends, and it would have been nice to be able to talk with them on a regular basis. But then that's not a problem for you, is it?" Vera fired back, looking to Milo.

"Oh really; how so," Mairy enquired, wanted to learn more of how Milo was able to communicate with his family? "I thought there was no direct contact with others on Earth."

"That's true, but then Milo's family is not really on Earth," Vera enlightened us.

"Hey, don't hold it against me that I had the foresight to broker a deal with the company to bring them on board," Milo explained. "All you do is complain."

"So why don't you meet with them for dinner, like we did with our dad?" I asked innocently.

"It's not always that easy; they work down in the lower levels," Milo answered. "And management would rather I limit my visits to the more maintenance oriented population. They even require regular debriefings upon my every visit."

"So then you don't have any problems visiting the maintenance levels," Mairy inquired, wanted to learn more about the layout of the moon station? Mairy always seemed to be working her 'spy' thing.

"Well, no more than anyone else traveling between the Israeli–Palestinian border crossings," Milo joked of the security he encounters when going to the lower levels.

Mairy looked to me as to explain Milo's reference. So I quickly jumped in, presenting Milo with a leading question that would help Mairy understand what he was insinuating. "Oh, so then the security is very controlled between the upper and lower half of this facility?" I asked for Mairy's benefit.

"Well it has to be, doesn't it?" Tim piped in. "I mean we are all dealing with some top secret research up here. This company is not about to compromise its research by allowing secrets to pass freely outside of the control of the upper level. At least not until the ten year contract is over; and maybe not even then."

"Tim, you're such a drama king," Vera pointed out. "Milo has been back and forth so many times, he doesn't feel the need to always be with them. Besides, I'll wager they don't even check his papers anymore."

"Well, they don't really have to; do they? After all, there is still a pin scanner and security backup at each location," Milo admitted.

"Oh come on, admit it; it's more or less like entering Disney World for you," Vera stated to make light of the security check. "They just want to keep track of who is coming and going. Or what you're bringing in or out with you. If there's a problem, then our manager would just clear it with security anyway. I mean, what are they really going to do to us? They need us."

"Besides, there is no real detention system up here, or I would've known about it by now," she stated with an air of prior knowledge. "They just send you up to the 13th floor for a visit with the shrink. I myself have no inclination whatsoever to visit the underground levels of this moon station."

"Do you think we could visit the lower half with you sometime?" Mairy asked of Milo straight out.

While her boldness surprised me, I remembered Mairy was never really shy about requesting what she needed or wanted to do. I was not sure why she wanted access to the underground levels of the moon station, but she was always one to think ahead.

"Yes, I wouldn't mind seeing more of how this place works myself," I commented, supporting Mairy in her request.

"Actually, I have never really seen the lower half of this station. I wouldn't mind a visit to the nether regions of this facility," Tim joked of his inclination to join in. "I'd be interested I'm rather interested in how if differs from our accommodations."

"I think that is a great idea. Maybe I can get my husband to arrange a walk through for us." Lindsey offered. "Besides, I'd like to meet Milo's family."

I looked to see Mairy rolling her eyes. My guess is she didn't want a lot of company while she did her reconnoitering and skulking about down there.

"Great, it'll be like another team work exercise," Milo joked unenthusiastically.

"Just like the company is always promoting for us to participate in," Tim acknowledged.

"Maybe it wouldn't be such a bad idea, as it would distract my parents from quizzing just me all the time for conversation," Milo agreed. "Besides, my parents like to host these types of get-togethers anyway."

"Alright then, it sounds like we are in agreement. But enough chit-chat, we do not have much time left before left before our morning meeting," Lindsey stated, keeping everyone on task.

We all finished with our breakfasts and traveled on to our meeting room. As we ended up being a little early, I excused myself saying, "I have to make a pit stop; be right back."

"Me too; I'll be right back," Mairy said, following after me. "Wait up," Mairy called to me.

When she caught up, I asked her, "So what was that all about wanting to see the underground levels?"

"I just wanted to get a layout of the area. One never knows what options they have, unless they know what their options are. I don't fancy being up here for the next ten years," Mairy explained.

"Oh, a little reconnaissance for a quick escape; good idea," I acknowledged. "But we did sign on for the full ten years."

"Did we?" Mairy asked rhetorically. "I signed on for this quest. I am not a worker drone for some industry. It's not what I do."

"Yes, of course; the quest," I acknowledged a little uneasily. I shouldn't have expected to change her nature. I had to remind myself, that she is not really part of this family; nor is she obligated to us.

"And I wasn't planning on bringing everyone on a field trip," she stated with some regret.

"Well, maybe it's a good thing. It'll introduce us to an entry into the underground levels without drawing attention to our real purpose," I said, pausing for a moment as we reached the washrooms.

Picking up on my uneasy response to her purpose, she asked, "After all, we aren't really committed to staying up here for ten years; are we?"

"I just never really thought it through," I admitted. "But now that I think about it, ten years is a really long time. It's not like a Shadow-Forge can make that kind of commitment. I mean, why would you want to stay with us for ten years?" I said with a bit of emotion, thinking of how I felt about her.

"No, I didn't mean it like that," she corrected me. "All I meant was I did not want to be up here on the moon for ten years. Are you really prepared to spend ten years of your life up here?"

"Well, it may be more difficult to get off the Moon than it was to get on," I presented my misgivings to her. "They are keen on keeping track of us up here."

"My guess is that they aren't following the same protocol with the workers below," Mairy speculated. "Perhaps we would be able to use that to our advantage."

Just then Vera came out of the women's washroom. It was a surprise as we didn't even notice when she slipped away from the team before we left.

"Planning another field trip already, are you?" Vera inquired with an air of suspicion, using one of the phrases from our conversation.

"No, just this one," Mairy replied. "You know, you're invited to come as well. That is unless you have something better to do," Mairy stated, trying to allay her suspicions. But then again, Mairy might be thinking that it would be a good tack to keep her enemies close, so as to divine what they're doing.

"Thanks, maybe I'll take you up on that. Besides, it might be fun to see something besides this upper mall environment," Vera replied.

So, with her acceptance, this venture now included the entire research group. As Vera left us and continued down the hall, I couldn't help wondering how much she might have heard.

"What do you think?" I asked abstractly. "Do you think she heard any of what we were talking about?"

"You really do worry too much," Mairy said, walking toward the women's washroom.

Without thinking, I began to follow along behind Mairy, until she paused and turned around. "This is where we separate," she said with a smile. "I really do need to use the washroom."

Looking to the sign above the door, I acknowledged clumsily, "Right. Ok then, I'll be using this men's room; which is right over here," I said, pointing to where it was. "Meet you back in the meeting room, then."

Mairy acknowledged with a smile and a nod.

When we I got back into the meeting room, I couldn't help worrying whether we gave ourselves away. I watched Vera to see if I could see a 'tell' in her body language that might indicate her intentions.

Milo couldn't help noticing my odd behavior. "She is pretty; in kind of a dark way," he said, assuming that I was staring at her. "I mean, once you get past her attitude."

"Oh, right," I answered clumsily, realizing that I must have been staring at her for him to notice. "I was just wondering what her backstory is." Actually, she was kind of pretty at that. I guess I hadn't really looked beyond my suspicions of her before.

Just then, Dr. Beecher arrived for the morning meeting. "Alright everyone, I've read all your logs. In the future, try to be more descriptive about what all of your senses pick up. And Vera, you might want to take this a little more seriously," Dr. Beecher said, paging through her tablet to find Vera's log.

"I read your argument for suggesting that we rotate everyone through the control pods, in case anything happens to the new pod operators. And while your business case was well thought out, this log was meant to provide me with an overview of your insights, health and well-being during the experiment. It was not meant as a vehicle for you to promote or discuss mission objectives," Dr. Beecher lectured her.

As Milo began to snicker, Dr. Beecher then focused on him, "And Milo, your comparison of the setup procedure to an alien abduction and examination, is not pertinent to identify whether you are experiencing any side effects from the CONS units during your session."

"You said to express how we felt," pleaded Milo. "That's how it made me feel."

"Oh, and like you would know how it feels to be abducted by aliens," Tim gaffed with Milo.

Dr. Beecher said nothing of their side discussion, but her face expressed her disapproval.

"Tim, can you dim the lights," she asked, as she turned on the room monitor. "I want to share with all of you the results we have so far from our efforts," she said, displaying a split screen of two images. "Here are two images of the 'Pillars of Creation'. The one on the left was processed from the Hubble telescope, while the one on the right was processed via IGIE. And while there is no false coloring for the raw image on the right, you can see that were able to improve on the visual perspective to provide a more 3 dimensional imaging of the individual pillars. This is one of the advantages of working with gravitational wave forms rather than either light or radio wave forms," she explained,

Switching to the next slide, she continued, "As you can see, we are now able to rotate the image in a full 360 degrees; thereby allowing us to view the far side of the target area's structure as well. However, the far side still lacks detail and definition. It is something we hope to improve as we continue to enhance IGIE."

Everyone was blown away by the incredible images they were processed via IGIE.

"That is truly amazing!" remarked Lindsey.

"I am totally blown away!" commented Milo.

"This will revolutionize how we map our galaxy, to be sure," Tim observed.

"Galaxy?" Vera questioned of Tim's scope. "This is going to totally change how everyone sees the universe."

Mairy and I sat silently studying the pictures. Could it be that we were the final ingredient needed to make this project work? Destiny is a funny thing. One might think that our destinies are just the random results of happenstance, or maybe even that our choices have some bearing on how our destinies unfold. But to think that Mairy and I might have been predestined to be here now, to make all this come together, makes one believe that perhaps fate plays a bigger role in the development of our destinies than we would like to admit.

Dr. Beecher advanced the image selections. "Now I would like to bring your attention to these two images. The one on the left is still the IGIE processed view of the 'Pillars of Creation' that we previously displayed," Dr. Beecher seemed to pause for effect.

"And the one on the right?" Lindsey questioned upon her pause.

"The one on the right is the same image without the individual columns of gaseous cloud," Dr. Beecher announced.

"Is there a reason the gas clouds are more distorted from the one on the right?" Tim questioned via of assumption.

"Well, not quite distorted," I commented out loud without thinking.

"What do you mean?" Dr. Beecher was quick to elicit any new interpretations for the disparity.

"It just seems to me that the gas clouds have just been somehow expanded to form one large cloud. See how the outside edge of the image area. The view of the individual pillars appeared to have blurred into one pillar,"

I said, pointing to the left portions of the 3 columns that made up the 'Pillars of Creation'.

"Yes, but there seems to be a bit more going on here than just a distortion of the pillars," Mairy said in support of my observation. "It is as if the gas clouds were blown off to one side," she pointed out, directing our attention to the same area of the image. "See how the gas clouds are somewhat more occluded on the lower left hand side, but more transparent on the right."

"That is a somewhat unique observation of the image," Dr. Beecher responded while taking notes.

Milo looked over to Tim, jesting in a whispered voice, "Teacher's pet."

"Anyway, the plan to today is to repeat yesterday's experiment to see if we get differing results. So if you'll all proceed back to the research lab, we can get started. And this time I want you each of you to actively interact with your individual environments. Feel free to take more creative control of the decisions in your dreams, and actually try to reshape your individual dreamscape experiences."

As everyone got up to proceed to the next room, I questioned Dr. Beecher's new instructions for the group; commenting, "Won't that make it more difficult for Mairy and I to keep them on task?"

"Not at all," Dr. Beecher assured us. "I want them to enhance their focus toward greater creativity. It should actually make your job easier, as it would further redirect their subconscious perspectives away from any logical rendition of their environment. Your jobs will remain the same."

"OK, then...," I accepted her response without further questioning, but not really grasping her explanation.

As we all reported to our assigned pods, I began to wonder whether my inept ability to stray from the dreamscape had anything to do with the way the images were distorted. I looked to Mairy, hoping to clue her in on my misgivings, but all she could do was smile back. Perhaps once we astrally join together, I could communicate with her in a more private setting.

Once again we suited up. It was becoming more of a routine now. Like astronauts filing off into the shuttle for our next mission, we took our positions within our designated pods. The techs helped us get hooked up into our individual CONS units, as they had done before. From across the room, I could hear and see the group getting themselves psyched up for the experience. They seemed quite excited in anticipation of going under control of these machines, once again.

"OK, amigos, it is time to fly again," Milo declared.

"Here is where we make history," Vera announced.

"Sure thing, see you in my dreams," Lindsey publicized of her intentions.

"Yes, indeed, Goodnight Irene, I'll see you in my dreams," Tim responded, quoting out another song lyric.

While their excitement eased my nervousness, and helped me to prepare for whatever was going to come next, I could tell Tim was still anxious about his involvement. I turn to looked and see Mairy looking back at me, I nodded back to her.

Once we were all situated, the techs initialized their startup procedure. The synchronized humming of the pod bed mechanisms matched the visual view of our pod beds sliding into their horizontal positions. Similarly, the lids of each unit closed above each of us in synchronicity. The sensation of warm liquid about me was familiar and comfortable. There was a weightless feeing within the suit as I began to sense I was floating. Perhaps the waterproof suit I was wearing was also inflatable as well.

As I lay there, it became quiet and I began to feel senseless once again. However, instead of just letting myself go under the machines influence, I focused on our connection to each other as I had practiced with Mairy the night before. I thought again of how it felt to be in the source seed with Fairy. I remembered how it felt to project myself from within the crystal.

Slowly, the environment systematically began to block out the sensation of my five senses, as I continued to feel the familiar buoyancy of my weightlessness about the center of my being. Slowly, I became disoriented from the measured release of their gaseous mixture they used to induce our sleep, but this time I understood the process. This time I was able to maintain a measure of control, even as I drifted into a more dreamlike state of insentience.

As I set up the bridge between my conscious and subconscious thoughts, my sight began transforming, again into a more omnidirectional awareness of my surroundings. I could not see, to be sure, but it was as if I could feel and hear beyond the containment of my CONS unit. Therein I waited for the familiar sounds of the melodious harp-like tones, echoing about me, which would signal to me of Mairy's arrival. Upon that ingress, I felt I actively searched my new surroundings for its source of the music.

During the duration of my search, I could no longer feel the boundaries of my containment within the research station. Rather, I had a sensation of myself slowly gyrating end over end. As I still felt a forward motion, I sought out the presence of Fairy as before in our practice.

As Fairy merged our auras once again, I sensed the emerging communication through our coupled containment. But it was not the only connection we were making; for there was still the influence of our CONS units, as well. Yet, it appeared that I had been able to bypass the scripted dreamscape.

"You made it again," Fairy said, initiating our communication. "See how your practicing has paid off," she remarked to me in congratulations.

Mentally I seemed to be propelled from the area of my gut. I still felt as if I was free floating and spinning end over end, but still I could not discern any sense of a real body.

"Do you feel as weird as I do?" I enquired, as I began to view the motion of the images about us. "This is a bit different from last night."

"Last night it was just you and me. Now we have IGIE to contend with as well," Fairy explained.

"The random pattern of lights and motion are beginning to settle down," I informed her, reporting as if we were conducting an experiment.

"That is probably the influence of the scripted dreamscape, trying to regulate your subconscious activity," Fairy explained.

Finally, I was beginning to gain some semblance of the space I was occupying. I began to imagine a scene of multiple stars clustered in clumps enveloped by a gaseous cloud. As we stayed connected, I was able to focus on more detail. As I seemingly floated, slowly rotating about in the space, my omnidirectional sentience was able to reveal the view of not one gaseous cloud, but 3 distinct gaseous columns. It was the 'Pillars of Creation', just as Dr. Beecher showed us.

"You're seeing this; right?" I asked. "How is it that we skipped right past our dreamscapes?"

"I'm not sure. This seems to be way too real to be either a dreamscape or the jumping off point for our astral state of being, as we experienced last night," Fairy confided in me.

"Could it be that they re-engineering our dreamscapes to mimic the vision?" I questioned of our observation.

"No; it's more like traveling via one of Harmony's spheres," she remarked.

"Well, the CONS units were supposed to integrate the detected wave forms with our brain waves. Perhaps we are able to see this via of the real-time wave form integration being generated," I speculated. "Maybe it's like some kind of feedback looping through our own brainwaves. Although I thought the mixing of our brainwaves and the captured gravitational waves was supposed to be more innocuous," I remarked. "You know, less intrusive."

"I don't think that this is the input for the processed image. I think we are really here," Fairy professed.

"That's impossible!" I declared, as my logical mind refused to believe the obvious. "This is thousands of light years from where we really are. These CONS units are not design for anything but detection and capture of gravitational wave formations," I stated of her revelation. "Are they?"

"Actually, this whole IGIE system is not designed to deal with us," Fairy purported of our current conditions. "Our astral states of being, or our Shadow-Forge spirits if you will, are not relegated to just this spacetime. Rather our astral presence is an outreach of our abilities to travel interdimensionally within Space and Time, wherein where ever we choose to be. Somehow, we must have projected ourselves, via our Shadow-Forge abilities, to the target area selected by DeepSIT."

Suddenly a shock wave blasted through, dispersing the iconic columns of gas. Simultaneously our auras were uncoupled, as if the propelled shock wave had knocked us apart. Fairy was quick to reconnect us.

"Did you see that?" I asked reflexively. "What was that?"

"I don't know if I saw it, but I sure felt it. Look out there" Fairy observed. "I guess we now know why the two images Dr. Beecher showed us are different. It appears the clouds were blown away by some other force."

"Yes," I agreed. "And yet I had the same feeling just as yesterday's session ended. It was like I was strongly pushed by the force of a water wave. Now, I'm guessing it was a violent gravitational wave of some sort."

There was a second shock wave, like a backwash of the first shock wave. Again we were separated, but Fairy was unable to reconnect as quickly as she had done before. Being no longer connected with Fairy, I lost my ability to maintain the focus of my surrounding space. The star scene slowly faded from view, as blackness embraced me.

And just as suddenly as I had drifted off into unconsciousness, I was brought back into a conscious mode again. I was awaking back in the lab again. However, I now felt that we might have been compromised. I panicked at the thought of how much of what happened to us could have been monitored via CONS units to the research team. And this was not something we wanted anyone to see, or even know about.

The pod lids slid open as the technicians reset our pod beds to their vertical position. I could hear Milo expressing himself in the background.

"I like the new dreamscape you're using," Milo bellowed. "These experiences get more lucid every time. I distinctly heard the waves washing up onto the shore and seagulls crying in the wind."

"Well if it was anything like mine, to me it was more real because I was actually registering a sense of touch in the coolness of the water as I flew along the shoreline," Tim revealed.

"You had a flying dream; that's fantastic. My new experience had to do more with a sensitivity for taste and smell of the saltwater ocean. Aren't we all supposed to be dreaming about the same thing all the time," Lindsey questioned Tim of their individual experiences?

"Well the experiences are all interrelated sensations of being at the beach," Tim acknowledged. "Remember they are providing us all with the same scripted dreamscape, not the same emotions."

Milo then turned his attention to Dr. Beecher, asking her, "Excuse me Dr. Beecher; perhaps you could add taste to my dreamscape for next time. I'm getting really hungry."

"OK, everyone, that's enough chit-chat," Dr. Beecher instructed us with an air of professionalism. "Now just like yesterday, before any of you go to lunch, I want each of you to separately log your experiences. And by separately, I mean no comparing of experiences prior to reporting them in whatever media record you may select. Again, grab one of the psych evaluation surveys as well, before leaving. I need these surveys completed and brought back to me before our next session." Then Dr. Beecher closed with her customary closing, "Another excellent session everyone; you have all performed quite well."

"Mairy, does it seem like she has that spiel memorized," I said joked.

"Yes, it is a little like 'déjà vu'," Mairy acknowledged with a smile.

"That includes you two, as well," she interrupted us, as if she heard us talking about her. "It's very important that you detail your experiences separately for me to determine how the experiment is affecting each of you individually."

As Dr. Beecher interrupted us before I could caution Mairy about including our shared experiences in our separate logs, I tried to surreptitiously communicate my expectation to her.

"Oh, I agree. I believe it is best if we record our 'separate' experiences separately," I said loud enough for Mairy to hear. "I think our logs should only focus on our 'separate' view of what we experienced."

"Yes, that's right," Dr. Beecher agreed, accompanying her response with a strange look.

Mairy rolled her eyes at me, and ended her gaze with a quick nod.

OK, she got my message. I was now in dad's arena, so to speak; making up stories. I needed to invent a story that was based on what I actually experienced during this experiment, but minus the part where Mairy and I both connected 'out of body'. Yep, this is going to take me the full two hours to work.

Once I completed my log and psych survey, I was ready for lunch. I knocked on Mairy's door, but she didn't answer. It wasn't surprising, as I figured she had probably left already because I took twice as long to complete my log as I did yesterday. However, it did occur to me that she might not be happy with my overt warning about the log. And maybe she was avoiding me out of anger.

As I walked toward the elevator, I looked around at some more details of the elaborate accommodations this moon station had to offer. Off in the distance, I noticed people jumping off the third floor into an air bag down below. Although it looked like fun, it appeared to be some sort of supervised training. Perhaps it had something to do with the travelling about without the weighted, semi-magnet shoes which we were all issued.

As I looked closer, I could see Mairy and the rest of the team were in line for the jump. They must have finished with lunch already. As I got closer, I could see that those jumping to the mezzanine floor below were wearing safety lines. When I finally caught up with the group, I was surprised to hear them engaged in conversation about their experiences in today's experiment. After all, I thought our experiences were meant to be private. I guess in the excitement of their new experiences, the could not contain themselves.

"I actually felt weightless; like when we were brought up on the space shuttle," Tim conveyed of his most recent session. "I couldn't really see any detail, but I imagined myself flying along the landscape of beach."

"I agree," replied Lindsey. "Even though it was the similar to our previous sessions, somehow it was different this time." Lindsey then turned her attention to Vera, commenting, "You've been awful quiet. What was your dream experience like?"

"It difficult to say," Vera started, seemingly surprised about what she saw. "But mine was actually a little different this time as well. For a moment, I think I actually saw the 'Pillars of Creation'."

"You must have been tripping," Milo expressed his concern. "How could you imagine that from the beach?"

"I hope you included that in your log," Tim recommended. "Maybe that will encourage them to provide us with some different dreamscapes."

"It could just be that I had something do with it. I mean, the ability to influence your dreamscape via the control pods," Mairy offered as rationale. "I was actually looking into the sky in my dream to see if I could visualize the target area they told us about."

"Well, Dr. Beecher did say that even a little suggestion might influence what we see," Lindsey offered as an explanation.

"Perhaps some minds are just more creative than others," Vera said, smiling cattily at Mairy's explanation. I'm sure she was still holding a grudge about our being assigned to the control pods.

"Yes, they've showed us that picture so many times now, I can see it with my eyes closed," I added, trying to distract from the whole 'Pillars of Creation' discussion. "I'm surprised it hasn't shown up in my dreams."

However, Milo was use to sparring with Vera. "So you are implying the reason some of us are seeing repeats of our dreams is only because our minds are not as creative?" Milo questioned. Looking to Tim, Milo joked, "Looks like we've just been 'dissed'."

"That's not what she said," I said in defense of Vera's rationale. "Besides, I heard dreaming is all about flushing out our feelings. Perhaps Vera just made some random attachment to the pictures."

"Maybe it has something to do with their age," speculated Lindsey quickly. "They are younger than us, and perhaps a little less disciplined in their ability to meditate and hold their thoughts."

"Or maybe, I just don't want to be bored to death in my dreams," Vera fired back. "I get tired of rehashing my emotions in these old pre-scripted dream worlds."

"Hey, Mairy hasn't really shared her dreamscape with us," Tim observed. "How was your session today, any differences from the first time?"

"Some," Mairy acknowledged. "Sometimes I have a hard time focusing on just one thought. And I don't always remember all of my dreams. But I believe that I did see the 'Pillars of Creation' as well; up high in the scripted dream sky."

"Perhaps you are onto something, Lindsey," Milo admitted to Lindsey; "about their age, I mean."

The team members were shuffling about as we continued walking through the halls, getting closest to whoever they were talking to. As the majority of the team members gravitated towards the front of the line, Mairy hung back with me.

"Did you hear how Vera also saw the 'Pillars of Creation', just as we did?" Mairy asked rhetorically in a low voice."

"Well, perhaps not just like us," I corrected her. "After all, she said it was for only a moment."

"There is something about her that is different from the others," Mairy remarked.

I immediately took a leap of logic, asking, "What; do you think she could be a Shadow-Forge, as well?"

"I don't know. Maybe she is just gifted," Mairy speculated, "but I mean to find out."

"Find out," I replied with confusion, "How?"

"If she is one of us," Mairy thought aloud, "then she could be working for Harmony or Discordia."

I was actually surprised that Mairy was quick to agree with my bizarre guess. "So we have to follow her around?" I asked. "Maybe we could just ask her."

"Ask her if she is a Shadow-Forge; really?" Mairy expressed incredulity with my suggestion.

"Well, when you say it like that, it doesn't sound like a good idea," I admitted.

"You think!" Mairy exclaimed.

"But if she is working for Harmony, then maybe it is already her quest," I deduced. "Then we could maybe pool our resources and help her."

"However unlike us, who are working independently of Harmony at the moment, she could also be working for Discordia," Mairy rebuffed, implying a negative alternative to my suggestion. "The members of chaos tend to be more supervised. If she is working for Discordia, then she must be reporting to someone. And we don't want to tip our hand until we know what she is up to."

It all seemed a bit melodramatic to me, but I haven't been at this detective stuff very long. However, even if Vera was just a gifted novice, she could still complicate things. Maybe next time she may actually see either of us. It wouldn't do to have someone snooping about on us in our astral state of being. She might even inadvertently report the nature of our activities to someone that is working with Discordia.

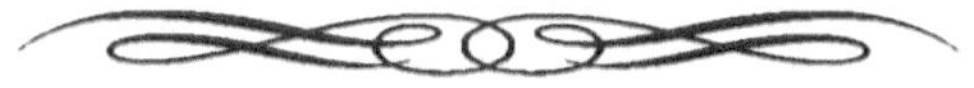

[Scene Change – Narrator's Perspective]

[Confirming the disparities of IGIE]

The second successful translation of deep space images from IGIE were being generated in an adjoining computer lab to the building that housed the Deep Space Interferometer Telescope. Dr. John Leighy was on his computer analyzing the data from the images translated via IGIE. Their prior confusion was revisited upon the team from what appeared to be the same disparity in the imaging for the same area of space. This time, both Dr. Phil Berry and Dr. Margaret Beecher were in attendance as Dr. John Leighy worked through the data from the re-simulations of the IGIE system output.

Calling out to his associates who were awaiting his analysis, John confessed, "Phil, Margaret, the succeeding images are worse than the last time we processed them. Now, I only see a unique distinction of the gaseous columns in the first few generated images."

"No, this can't be right," Phil concurred, refusing to believe this turn of events. "There must be something we are missing. I'm going back to the lab to look at the hardware equipment settings myself."

As Phil left to examine the CONS units, Margaret sat down with John to review the images. "Can you set up a time lapse phasing of the images," Margaret requested.

"You mean like a video? Sure," John agreed. "What are you looking for?"

"Just something that the pod operators noticed today," Margaret disclosed.

"You showed these to the pod sleepers," John stated in disbelief, as he set up for the time lapse. "Isn't that a bit risky?"

"Why, is it supposed to be a big secret?" Margaret replied sarcastically. "You said yourself that it could be an anomaly promoted by one of the pod sleepers."

"True; but what if it had gotten back to Tom?" John asked. "Then he would know that there is a problem that we hadn't told him about."

"Really; why would Tom go talking to the pod operators?" Margaret said with an air of condescension. "You worry too much."

"OK, here goes," John exclaimed, as he ran the images through a time lapse program simulation.

"Yes, there it is," Margaret observed. "See how some of the stars are shimmering? The time lapse should have repeated a more static imaging of those stars. What is causing them to twinkle like that?"

"I'm not sure," John agreed. "It is as if the gaseous clouds are moving along the face of the image. I'm going to reset the recycling speed for the program," he said, slowing down the time lapse view.

"And there," said Margaret as she pointed to the screen. "See on the outside edge of the image. That is not just a blur. That is gaseous matter. And it is moving," she reasoned in bewilderment.

"Yes, I see it," John confessed with astonishment. "It is as if the gas clouds are being blown off to one side."

Just then, Phil returned from his examination of the CONS units in the adjoining research lab.

"It appears I may have found our problem," Phil revealed. "The CONS for controls pods have been refitted with some new interfacing equipment. And while it does not have a part number that I can find, it does appear to be of the same quality and workmanship as the rest of the equipment."

"I'll bet it has something to do with Tom's new project with that new hire, Steve Bauer. I thought Tom agree with the board that their new project would not interfere with IGIE's primary operation," John remarked with displeasure.

"At the very least, they could have told us about the change," Margaret said in support of John position. "Now I'm not worried about approaching Tom with this problem, as it is probably his fault."

Tom suddenly arrives in the room. "And what might that problem be?" Tom asked graciously, considering he had just been blamed for something.

"The problem is that your new project is interfering with IGIE's primary operation. That's what the problem is," John said somewhat excitedly and with apprehension.

"Perhaps you could elaborate," Tom continued in his controlled demeanor.

"I discovered that the CONS have been altered without our knowledge," Phil announced, backing up John's assertion. "The controls pods have been refitted with some new interfacing equipment," he rather tersely blurted out. "Don't you think that is something that we needed to know about?"

"And how is that causing a problem?" Tom asked calmly.

"We have been trying to track down an anomaly in the images generate via IGIE for these past two days," John divulged. "Each succeeding image generated from IGIE should be representative of the same static picture, but at differing 3D perspectives. However that is not the case. In fact, the images seem to morph over time."

"And now I find that there has been this new untested equipment fitted onto the CONS units without our knowledge," Phil added. "How are we supposed to account for any new parameters that may have been introduced via this new equipment, if we have never tested the new equipment?"

"Yes, I know about the new equipment. And now you've tested it," Tom responded rather matter-of-factly. "And I can assure you that the new equipment has been thoroughly tested by my team, as well," Tom stated with an air of authority. "As for why I didn't inform you, it was because it was just supposed to separately provide for extra, enhanced imaging. So now what is this anomaly of which you are referring?"

"Here, see," John averred. "The 'Pillars of Creation' are no longer visible in the target area in this image. I mean they were there, and then they weren't."

"Can anyone start from the beginning so I can get some semblance of what the problem is," Tom asked dryly, seemingly understating the gravity of the situation.

Margaret clarified more calmly, "Yesterday, we had our first successful dry run of IGIE system with all six CONS units. We targeted the 'Pillars of Creation' because of their signature presentation of 3 unique gaseous columns. The first images of the target area matched the Hubble images, just as expected. Then the latter images morphed into a less distinguishable picture of these gaseous columns. They became less pronounced and more transparent."

"Perhaps, you are just viewing the follow on difference between these two operating protocols," Tom submitted for debate. "Rather like seeing the same area without the gaseous matter."

"Well, it is not that they are missing. Rather it is that they are differently dispersed. And now, today, there is even more to the mystery. We reran the same experiment from yersterday and now IGIE is unable to provide us with any succeeding images of the 3 gaseous columns at all, "Margaret reported, and then looked to John. "John, could you show Tom?"

As John repositioned himself at the computer and reran the time lapsed simulation he had created from the generated images. Tom studied the time lapse presentation, see much what he expected: the first images were a static presentation, while the latter images were pronouncedly different.

"What we noticed here, in the time lapse, is that there is a uniform motion of gaseous material moving from right to left," Margaret explained.

"Interesting; and you said yesterday's translated images were a problem as well?" Tom asked.

"Yes, but just in the last few images and not as detailed in its variance. Not enough to really go on," John stated, reinserting himself into the discussion. "At first, we thought it was a problem with how IGIE is interpreting the varying degrees of gravitational wave forms coming out of the CONS units," John clarified, having calm down from his earlier feelings of indignation. "But there was no change in the gravitational wave forms, or even the brain wave pattern with which it was integrated, for the succeeding images. And then Phil found your new interfacing unit."

"As to your expectation that this new unit has a role in today's anomalies, I cannot dismiss this notion. However, we only finished installing all the pieces of the new interface only last night, so it could not have interfered with the results of your first experiment yesterday."

"All the pieces?" Phil questioned. "What makes up all the pieces?"

"Well, we installed the transmitting components of the new interface on master CONS units before your first experiment, but we never activated them," Tom divulged. "Then last night we installed the receiving components of the new interface on IGIE. It was only then that we activated the new operating protocol."

"Well, we are sorry we didn't inform you earlier. But the last thing we wanted to present you with was this puzzle," Margaret explained rather apologetically.

"Not a problem at all. In fact, I applaud your initiative," Tom responded, playing into their egos. "My concern is with how these latter images changed prior to the activation of the new protocol. It may be that these problems are also in play after last night's activation."

"We can rerun some diagnostics on the software integration of the two protocols that are now sharing the program to see if we can uncover any other discrepancies," John offered.

"That's a good idea," Tom agreed. "However, I would like to bring in Steve at this point and get his opinion on all of this. The design was based on his theories, and he may have a rationale for these side effects."

[Scene Change – Andrew's Perspective]

[The group field trip to the underground portion of the Moon station.]

Having enjoyed a bit of free time, Mairy and I retired to our rooms before dinner. The intercom in my room rang. This is a first, I thought to myself. Not even my father would use the intercom for fear of internal surveillance. Yet, it was my father. He was calling to cancel out on joining Mairy and I for dinner. I called Mairy to let her know that we were on our own for tonight.

Mairy, being the type 'A' personality that she was, wasn't one to let the time go for naught. She was determined to learn more about the moon station and its inhabitants. Since she had become chummy with Lindsey, she contacted her on the off chance that her husband was free to escort them on a visit to the lower half of the moon station. As Lindsey was eager for any excuse to spend time, or even talk, with Todd, she contacted him without hesitation. Lindsey then got back to us with the good news. As it happened, Todd was scheduled to relieve the security officer at the entry gate to the lower maintenance levels in about a half hour. It was one of those serendipitous occurrences in which one would swear there is something to support an argument for predestation. Everything was falling into place for our evening expedition to the lower maintenance levels.

"Great news," Lindsey relayed to us. "Todd can't get off work right now, but he is scheduled to relieve the officer covering the entry gate in about a half hour. He says he can grant all of us limited access to the lower half mezzanine."

"Well, if he is not able to get off tonight and go with us, then perhaps you would rather wait for another time," Mairy offered.

"Actually, I could do with a bit of excitement," Lindsey admitted. "As much as I would rather spend time with Todd, my evenings without him can get pretty routine."

"Great, then we'll meet up with you in 10 minutes," Mairy arranged with Lindsey. As she opened the door to the hall, she urged me, "Grab something that you can take notes with."

Yeah, that wasn't going to happen. I never take notes. "So we are good to go then, awesome?" I asked.

"Yes, and Lindsey is coming with us. Her husband is letting us into the lower level mezzanine," Mairy explained.

"They have a mezzanine as well down there?" I asked with disbelief.

"Of course they do," Vera commented from down the hall.

We both turned around to see Vera walking behind us. Her timing was getting to be really creepy.

"It wouldn't do to have all those people down there socializing with the populace up here on a daily basis," Vera continued saying as she walked up from behind us.

We weren't sure of how much she may have overheard, so I tried to play it off. "Well, thanks," I said. "I learn something new every day about this place."

"As do I," Vera mysteriously agreed with me. "Mind if I tag along?" she asked of Mairy.

"Not at all," Mairy answered for the both of us. "I was just on my way to meet up with Lindsey."

"So why the change in plans?" Vera asked conspicuously. "I thought you two were supposed to be having dinner with your father again tonight."

"He got hung up with some last minute meeting," I answered quickly.

As we walked towards Lindsey room, she came out to the hall. And finding out that Vera had joined us, she commented to Mairy, "I didn't know you were inviting others along. This might complicate things."

Tim must've been bored as well, as he opened his door and said, "Inviting others where?"

"Were going down to the lower mezzanine," Vera informed him.

"They have a mezzanine as well down there," Tim similarly responded.

"That's what I asked," I concurred.

"Oh, come on you two. It's not the lower east side of Chicago," Vera stated like she was familiar with the Chicago area. "It's just like up here, but without natural lighting, or an outside view."

"Well, everyone paints it as such a dismal place to be," Tim justified of his query. "Wait, so you've been down there before."

"Of course, I'm not as much of a recluse as you might think," Vera said. "And since the company discourages us from us wander about, and would just not rather have us intermingling them as much, I just don't advertise it. Besides, sometimes I feel more comfortable down where no one knows me."

"There is a dark side to you," Tim remarked. "But I like it."

"OK, let's get moving before anyone else arrives," Lindsey stated apprehension.

They travel down to the mezzanine level of the upper half of the moon station. From there, they follow under the rock climber and down a corridor that was lit up with advertisement, somewhat like an airport.

At the end of the hall, Lindsey turn left and gets ahead of us. There she meets up with Todd, and gives him a quick kiss on the lips.

Lindsey greeted Todd, "Sorry for the large group. Will this be a problem?"

"Only if you're not all back in exactly four hours; that's the next time I am scheduled to relieve this station," Todd indicated. "And remember, it's only for 15 minutes at a time. Also, no one is manning that station below during the off hours. So you'll have to buzz me when you're ready to come up."

"Thanks Sweetie, you're a peach," Lindsey thanked him with an air of familiarity.

"And not bad looking for a piece of fruit, if I do say so myself," Vera commented brazenly, as she followed in behind Lindsey through the security gate.

The rest of us followed in kind, thanking Todd for the favor. We followed in behind Vera, with Tim bringing up the rear. As we all got into the elevator, I could see that this elevator panel had some new buttons that would allow us to go down. When the elevator doors opened again, we found ourselves passing through the lower half security gate and into a hallway, which was not unlike the upper half hallway to the elevator. We followed behind Lindsey and Vera to the end of the hallway, where our view opened up to the lower half mezzanine.

The difference in occupancy between the two levels was striking. The lower half was much more crowded. It was as if they tried to squeeze in all the amenities provided among the lower 5 levels of the upper half into just a few floors in the lower half. Or at least that was all I could see through the somewhat smaller openings down to the next floor. This, of course, being much more like spending time in an Earth city environment, made for an uncomfortably crowded navigating space.

"Wow, this crowd is like Christmas at the mall," I commented.

"Yes, and I 'kind of' miss not celebrating holidays," Lindsey remarked.

"I can see why most people avoid coming down here," Tim acknowledged.

"Really, you're one of those people," Vera decided. "I rather like it. It reminds me of Chicago."

"Seems like a lot to deal with, just to be nostalgic," Tim complained. "Besides, it would seem that we have more of a variety of things to do and places to go on the upper levels."

"Depends on what you're looking for," Vera remarked, as she started off in her own direction.

"Before you take off, please remember to be back in four hours," Lindsey reminded Vera. "We'll meet that the security gate."

"What I have to do, won't take 4 hours," Vera related. Then she looked to Tim, saying, "Since this your first time down here, how about I show you around." Tim obligingly followed after her, as Mairy watched them leave. It seemed to me that perhaps Mairy would rather follow after them.

"You two stick with me," Lindsey said to Mairy and I.

"How many ways are there to get in and out of here," Mairy asked.

"Todd would know; security covers the whole sphere," Lindsey revealed. "But one thing I know, the further you go down, the easier it is to get lost. Todd calls it the catacombs."

"The catacombs; sounds ominous," I indicated.

"Well, as you can see, the lower half of the sphere is not as grand looking as the upper half," Lindsey confessed. "And as the sphere narrows the further we go down, things become even more crowded. Until all that is left are the farming and maintenance sections for the entire moon station."

"Surely there is the same amount of living space?" I asked with some concern.

"True, but then there are more people down here," Lindsey explained. "Since the lower half population has been down here since the beginning, there are, well, more children."

"Children; I haven't seen many children about," Mairy stated.

"I would think it is rather late for children to be up and about right now," Lindsey indicated.

"I mean in the upper half, I haven't seen many children. Actually I don't believe I had seen any children since I've been here," Mairy indicated.

"Well, it's not the best environment for bringing up children," Lindsey explained. "Most parents choose to leave their children on Earth. In fact most women choose to return to Earth when they find out that they are pregnant. Up here on the Moon, the few children they have on the upper half are pretty much sequestered in the upper levels. It is rather like a large day care center, closer to the medical services and away from the larger populations. The company would rather not have to deal with children at all in the work environment for obvious reasons. And then there is a lot of secret research going on. In fact, the children even have their own cafeteria space up near the medical services."

"Does the lower half have their own medical services as well?" I asked.

"No, that kind of redundancy would be expensive. Extra space is not readily available. And then there would be the need for extra equipment and staff," Lindsey explained.

"So, then, there must be some way to transport patients from here back and forth. I mean, the elevator we came down on only has buttons to go between the upper and lower half mezzanines," I observed. "How do they get them to the medical center from these lower floors?"

"Yes, I would be interested in seeing that as well. I mean, I would be interested in seeing the medical services area," Mairy requested.

"I'm not really sure how they are transported, or where such an elevator might be located, from down here. Vera might know. But Todd should know, for sure," Lindsey informed us. "Besides we could always see more of that when we are up top. Actually, have either of you been scheduled for a physical yet?"

"No, not yet," I answered, wondering what additional checks would be involved in a physical where the inhabitants are constantly worried about the outside radiation levels.

It became evident to Mairy, that Todd was the one they needed to show them around the more non-touristy areas. This little trip was just a little bit of propaganda; a showy front. As Milo indicated earlier, you need to see the outlying residences to get a more complete picture of their cramp living conditions. Still, judging by the crowdedness of the lower mezzanine, it does provide a haven for those living here down under. "OK, we have four hours," Mairy said, changing the subject and redirecting the conversation. "Show us where you go when you're down in the lower mezzanine," she asked of Lindsey, hoping to learn more about the lower level.

C H A P T E R

14

Encounters of the Third Kind—Identifying Players

[Life is the illusion; it is the dream to be dreamt.]

While the pod operators were spending their time becoming familiar with the 'lower half' mezzanine, Steve was requested to meet with Tom and the IGIE research team: John, Phil, and Margaret. As Steve steps into the research lab, Tom is the first to notice him entering the room.

[Scene Change – Narrator's Perspective]

Tom greets him, "Steve, thank you for coming to meet with us at this late hour. I'm sure you must be busy."

"No, not at all," Steve said politely. "So what is it that would bring all of us into one room at the same time?"

Tom continues to introduce the group, "You know John and Phil, of course. And this is Margaret, the team lead working with the pod operators and, incidentally, your children."

452

"Is this about my children then?" Steve asked, wondering if they were under any suspicion. "Are they alright?"

"No, it is not about your children, and I'm sure they are just fine," Tom assured Steve. "And actually, they are working out quite well with the rest of the pod sleepers' team. In fact, their addition to the team has essentially helped us to get the project back on schedule. It seems that hiring you was a serendipitous selection. Who knew there was so much talent in one family," he stated rhetorically.

"Well, that is great news," Steve said, "and I thank you for such a gracious recognition. I'll be sure to let the kids know."

"Yes, it is great news," Tom agreed, and then continued. "But that is not the reason we asked you up here. Rather, the research team has uncovered an anomaly with the CONS data collected from the pod operators; which I believe you could help us with. It's a puzzle of sorts, that I think you will find very interesting."

"Oh, I always love a good puzzle," Steve acknowledged, being both intrigued by the prospect of being consulted by the scientist, but also worried whether their true purpose might have something to do with what the kids did. Had they given their selves away, he thought to himself? "What sort of anomaly are we talking about here?" Steve asked.

Turning to Margaret, Tom asked, "Margaret, could you explain to Steve what you related to me?"

Steve turned his attention to Margaret, who seemed to have anticipated Tom's request. "Yesterday, we had our first successful run of IGIE," Margaret started.

"That's wonderful," Steve congratulated her.

"Well, yes and no," Margaret continued. "Are you familiar with the work we have been doing up here?"

"I've been briefed, but I am 'sort of' removed from the work being done on the main project," Steve admitted.

"OK, then you know that the CONS units act as a filter or sorts, providing combined wave input to IGIE to help generate 3D images of deep space locations," Margaret corroborated.

"Yes, I do understand the principle behind the project's research," Steve assured her. "DeepSIT detects and collects gravitational waves which are furthered filtered and translated through the CONS units to be converted to images for our computers by IGIE."

"Yes, exactly so," she acknowledge of my simplified explanation. "So we targeted the 'Pillars of Creation' because of their signature presentation of 3 unique gaseous columns. The first images of the target area matched the Hubble images, just as we expected," she stated as she laid out a series of pictures across the top of the table. "However, after these first few images, IGIE seemed to go off track. As you can see by these latter images, it seems that either the event capture or the wave translation from the CONS, as presented to IGIE, caused a 'kind of' morphing of the optimum view for the target area. See here; the gaseous columns forming the signature pillars became less distinguishable over each succeeding image generated via IGIE."

"The way I see it, the gaseous pillars are becoming less pronounced and more transparent," John joined in, adding his own interpretation on the images.

Interjecting himself into the explanation, Phil also added to the discussion, "As a matter of protocol, we ran a diagnostics on IGIE and re-simulated the software interface on our test platform. Still, we were unable to uncover any obvious discrepancies."

"So we decided just to rerun the same experiment today," Margaret continued to pick up the presentation. "And now to add to this mystery, IGIE is not unable to provide us with any latter images having the 3 gaseous columns at all."

There seemed to be an awkward pause, from which Steve felt they were awaiting his consultation. "No gaseous columns at all," he repeated. "It could be almost anything. There could be a 'software to hardware' interface glitch, or even a problem with your CONS to IGIE network connection. Or maybe, the issue lies within DeepSIT targeting itself. Perhaps DeepSIT missed its mark."

"I reviewed the DeepSIT vectors myself," Phil piped in. "Besides, nothing has changed for DeepSIT since the first capture yesterday. We have also compared our deep space trajectory data with that of the Hubble Deep Field observations for the same location. DeepSIT is pointing in the correct area of deep space."

"How about something with the neural interface?" Steve speculated. "Perhaps not all your pod sleepers were 100% focused on the mission." Steve then paused a moment to stop his speculating, thinking he might seed some doubt on the involvement of his children in the program. "Actually, this is not even my area of expertise. Why did you think I could do to contribute to helping in resolving this mystery?"

"Well, it was something your children said," offered Margaret.

"My children?" Steve questioned. "And how are they any more qualified than I to understand this technological marvel you've built? Why should their opinions be considered, any more than mine?"

"Actually, I would be interested to hear what the children had to say. After all, you brought up the possibility that the neural interface could be pertinent to this issue," Tom interrupted; seemingly keen to know how the two new arrivals to the pod sleepers' team were involved.

"Alright then," Margaret continued, feeling the tension in the room. "Well, while Andrew noticed that the individual gas columns had been seemingly all but merged into one, John noticed the star pattern was still in place. And then I remembered that Mairy pointed out that it appeared as if the gaseous matter had been blown off to one side," she related, demonstrating the implied motion across the screen with hand gestures. "At first I discounted their observations, as you have just suggested, for their lack of expertise in astronomy. But then when I later discussed these observations with the John and Phil, I suggested that John run the images into a time lapse sequence for this last run. And, to our amazement, we began to see what Mairy had already imagined."

Margaret then looked to John, asking, "John, could you replay your prepared slideshow for Steve?"

As John projected the slideshow on the screen, Margaret continued with her explanation, "What we are seeing here, in time lapse view, is a uniform motion of gaseous material moving from right to left."

The audience in the room was captivated by the slide show John had put together and displayed upon the screen. As the time lapse images looped, over and over again, everyone could be seen studying them for some clue as to how the anomaly manifested itself. Steve was the first to provide his opinion of the generated images.

"This can't be right," he said of the time lapse presentation of the IGIE generated images. "It's rather like a science fiction movie. The time lapse you generated for these images on the nebula is reflecting an unreal time difference for the motion of the gaseous matter that makes up the three pillars. Per their distance from us, we should only be able to see a protracted visualization of minute movements. These are sweeping motions in a short period of time."

"Of course," John exclaimed, expounding upon his eureka moment, "If I hadn't been so focused on the putting the images together, I might have seen it myself."

"What are you two talking about?" Margaret queried, expressing a feeling of being left out for not being able to understand what he were seeing.

"Don't you see it?" John stated, collecting his thoughts. "It is not just a collection of sequenced images from that location, as we discussed earlier. These displayed images are actually demonstrating real-time motion," John stated with excitement. "It is as if they were taken with a stop action camera."

"Yes, I get it. Even if there was an event like a supernova, which allowed for the gas clouds to be blown aside, at that distance such movements should not be discernable," Phil contributed to their joint revelation. "Instead, the relativity of these movements at that distance should have been stretched out in image captures over the next thousands of years; not seconds."

"Exactly; so what we are seeing in this slideshow is an event that does not reflect a proper temporal displacement," Steve stated with consternation. "Rather, it is more reflective of a real-time event, as John deduced," he contributed. At this point in time, Steve was not really taking the time to think that these images might be the result of his son's and Mairy's special abilities. He was just keen on working the problem.

"Interesting," Tom remarked, intending to mediate the discussion. "And you said yesterday's translated images were generated just to match the Hubble's view of the 'Pillars of Creation'," Tom remarked, focusing on Phil. "And now it appears we are imaging an event in real-time, inconsistent with Hubble's more static view. So using the Hubble's view as a baseline, what would you make of these images?"

"As the star patterns still match," Phil started in, "I would speculate that it has to be sometime after Hubble's more static view of the nebula's past," he thought aloud. "Maybe, somehow, we are able to follow the image further down the path of light coming to us from that location;

perhaps, beyond the destination point where the light is perceived by the Hubble."

"Yes, and because we can expect that the stars were birthed within the gaseous material of the nebula," John contributed, "it must be something that would be happening in the nebula's lest recent past; or more to the point, the nebula's future with respect to the Hubble's image."

"Yes, I would agree it is the nebula's future, from the perspective of the Hubble's more static view," Steve acknowledged. "However, when I proposed that this slideshow is more reflective of a real time event, I actually meant that it had to be images of the nebula's spacetime location in the Present time; which again, from the Hubble's perspective, is also the nebula's Future time."

"Why does it have to be its spacetime location in the present?" Tom asked with confusion.

"Two reasons:" Steve started out to explain, "1; In principal, the DeepSIT is a telescope, and therefore what we see, or what the telescope can gather, is subject to the laws of wave propagation. Similar to light or radio waves from a distant star, gravitational waves can only travel at the speed of light. In short, for all intense and purposes, we should be seeing a snapshot frozen in time, similar to what Hubble now provides, rather than a series of motion capture images. And 2; Per your design, IGIE was never meant to forecast a gravitational model for the gravitational variances in these spacetime locations. Rather IGIE should only be able to interpret existing gravitational wave variances as captured by the DeepSIT."

"Perhaps, the progressive nature of the captured images has to do with the ability of the pod sleepers to imagine successive gravitational wave variances from the targeted location," offered Margaret.

"That should not possible," Phil precluded, "The pod sleepers interface with input from the CONS unit. It is the CONS units that provide the gravitational variances to the pod sleepers, and not the other way around. The pod sleepers are not part of the DeepSIT, so there is no way for them to influence how DeepSIT captures this series of existing gravitational wave variances. And the relativity of wave propagation, at that distance, precludes the ability to capture of successive sequencing of future gravitational variances that would provide a simulation for this kind of motion capture that we are seeing."

"Agreed," John acknowledged. "IGIE's ability to imaged captured gravitational waves was only meant to provide for more detailed imaging of the same area of deep space, but in 3D; thereby allowing us to enhance upon the images generated via traditional radio telescopes."

"Exactly," Steve attempted to steer the discussion, "and yet, somehow, the IGIE system is able to ignore references to radiation capture, gravitational or otherwise, that are limited by the speed of light. Somehow these multiple gravitational wave variances, as they will exist in that location's Future time relative to speed of light communication, are being generated. What's happening is either like the Hubble taking pictures of that location a thousand years apart, which we can discount, or we are actually viewing the Present time of that location in the universe."

"So, you are suggesting there is some medium of communication that is faster than the speed of light?" Phil inquired. "Even if there was, how is DeepSIT accessing it?"

"The only concept that even approaches that kind of logic is the quantum theory of nonlocality," John expressed, in considering the logic of the proposal. "Einstein termed it as 'spooky action at a distance'. And as chief engineer on this project, I can assure you there is nothing in the software that allows for any such calculations, interpretations, or translations. I don't even believe that they came up with an agreed equation for the condition of a quantum nonlocality."

"While all that may be true, somehow IGIE has managed to tap in on and detect something that ignores the rules of distance and the physics of light speed radiation. And since the current design of the system precludes faster than light speed detection, I have to ask, has the CONS units or IGIE, or even DeepSIT for that matter, been modified in anyway?" Steve inquired.

"As it happens, your team has hooked up some new interface unit on the back of the primary CONS control units, as well as on IGIE," John responded quickly.

"My team?" Steve stated with some confusion and then looked to Tom. "Tom, I thought you told me that our team was months away from completing a working prototype that would attempt to identify dark matter in deep space."

"As it happens, the team made a breakthrough based on your revolutionary theories. And I asked them to test it out," Tom admitted. It appeared Tom had chosen to keep the timing of the prototype hook up to himself. And it seemed his end goals may have been more than just for mere technological advancements.

"Then it works!" Steve expressed with excitement, knowing that he had only ever fantasized of proving his theories in his lifetime. "Still, this is a side effect that I had not accounted for," Steve remarked, trying to think on what he might not have thought of in his original working hypothesis.

"What works?" Margaret piped in, once again feeling left out.

"Our company has been sponsoring an alternative hybrid research technology that would allow us to explore the possibility of detecting and imaging dark matter, while continuing with the current project," Tom admitted. "However, our quantum researchers always hit the same stumbling block. That is, even if we were successful in our developing the concept, we didn't know what we would be looking for, or how to detect it. So we brought in Steve to see if his theories on dark matter could help us bridge our research and provide us with the understanding we needed to determine the nature of dark matter detection. And now it appears we were right about bringing him in on this project."

"I thought we agreed that your new project would not interfere with IGIEs primary operation," John stated with some annoyance.

"But don't you see? It really hasn't; if anything, it has enhanced IGIE capabilities," Steve implored, trying to keep his contributions alive. "Not only was IGIE able to identify and image incoming gravitational wave variances, but it was able to apply the same design with respect to dark matter capture. And it would appear, without regard to the temporal relativity of distance. Don't you see what this means?"

"No, I don't see. And unless you can explain it, all I see is some clever manipulation of software to produce a desired result," John said, digging in for a long drawn out argument.

Steve looked to Tom for guidance on this security matter, "We are going to need them to work with us if you want to manage the data properly."

"OK, might as well bring them in on it," Tom said, providing Steve with the permission to continue.

"Right then," Steve started. "The new interface was only expected to detect dark matter, via DeepSIT, and send it straight to IGIE. But now, it appears we are seeing the results of this newly innovative interface differently. Since we now have evidence that this new communication is being accomplished irrespective of the speed of light for the distance traversed, or even irrespective of its relativity in spacetime, I must conclude that dark energy transfer is somehow involved. So instead of just detecting dark matter, it appears that this enhancement to the primary CONS units are now able to capture variations in the interactions of dark matter with dark energy, similar to how the CONS units were successfully able to collect and use gravitational wave variations from deep space. So it would appear that now this new information is also being combined with the pod sleeper's brain waves and relayed to IGIE," Steve said, developing a working hypothesis 'on the fly'.

"You, as much, already expressed this possibility," Steve insisted, looking to John. Then addressing the larger audience, he continued, "I believe this communication via dark energy is similar to quantum nonlocality, but operating in a slightly variant manner."

Steve thought to himself that he needed to slow down, for what he was suggesting was more than just revolutionary. It had the potential to rewrite how we see the universe from the very moment of its creation. So he backed up to prepare for a viable foundation from which he could explain his new premise.

"Think of dark energy as the medium of nothingness that supersedes existence," Steve started in again. "If the foundation for our fourth dimensional universe is really based on quantum nonlocality, then the expansion of the universe as homogeneous and isotropic makes perfect sense."

Seeing that he might be losing his audience, Steve changed his tactic.

"Consider it this way," he began to explain. "There is actually no such relationship in spacetime as Past time or Future time, because Time itself is always only reflective of Present time motility. So Time is always only in the present within every part of the universe at once, regardless of its location or distance."

Steve struggled to convince his colleagues that what they were witnessing was not just a clever illusion, but a real and explainable result.

"Consequently, it is our Present time that is the mechanism by which the universe promulgates motility within existence," he provided as an intermediate conclusion. Steve then paused and looked to Tom for some validation.

"Are you suggesting that the primary CONS units are now able to add in an interpretation of dark matter via the dark energy wave variations for that area of deep space," Tom asked with renewed interest? "And by this ability to detect and communicate this dark matter, via dark energy wave variations, IGIE is now able to see into the Present time state of any deep space location?"

"Yes, exactly so," was Steve's enthusiastic acknowledgement! Finally someone got it.

However not yet convinced, John asserted, "So if the universe is continually changing, and the concept of Past time to Present time is merely an echo of these successive changes throughout the evolution of Time, then you can't ignore the temporal variations of kinetic and potential energy in an evolving universe from moment to moment," John decreed, challenging Steve's perspective of cosmology. "Subsequently, how are we able to see successive frames of real time, when the concept of Present time to Future time becomes the reflective potential of that change yet to be?"

Looking back to Steve, Tom said encouragingly, "You're doing fine. Please continue."

"You are right, of course, John. There is a consistent measure of change ongoing in the universe," Steve agreed. "But it is your understanding of the terms Past, Present, and Future which differ from my own understanding. While Time is consistent, it is not necessarily constant. Therefore, just as there is some relativity in the measure of Time in Space, there is also some relativity in the degree of Space for that dimension of Time. As a result, I have incorporated such varying degrees of Space and Time into a theoretical model of evolutionary cosmogony, which allows for these varying dimensional frames of reference by which we can measure our existence more completely."

"This should be interesting," John remarked in a skeptical tone.

"Come on, John, give him a chance," Phil chided John. "I don't know that we can rationally explain what we are seeing here. We need to entertain any rationale that might hint at some direction for resolution."

"Thank you all for your patience," Steve acknowledged of Phil's support. "I know this is a bit of a stretch beyond traditional cosmology, but is consistent with the proposals that I have presented in my book and that I believe to be true."

"It's why we brought you up here. Please continue," Tom urged Steve once again.

"Alright then; starting with the concepts of 'No Time' and 'All Time', as extreme reflections for the notion of inaccessible time, or 'stop time'. 'No Time' represents the void of Time, or time that has yet to happen, similar to what we understand for the notion of Future time. 'All Time', on the other hand, represents the fullness of time, or time that has already happened, similar to what we understand for the notion of Past time. Thus, everything between these two notions of inaccessible time is what we understand to be Present time. So it is only Present time that is defined by the notion of accessible time, or active motility, as understood of any ongoing change from its previous baseline. In fact, think of this ongoing change as the very quintessence of vibration for 'being', liken to how 'string theory' is represented."

"And if we were to string a succession of these vibrations together, no pun intended," Steve stated, adding color to his explanation, "then you would have the current animus for the nature of Present time as a succession of moment to moment units of frequency. Even the concept of a moment is, in itself, an expression of measuring change. Therefore, anything other than Present time is an illusion of the conscious mind, as it does not really factor into the nature of 'being' via the principle of causality."

While the group listened attentively, Steve paused to recollect his thoughts and then continued, "As you know, this principle was an innovation of the human perspective to be able to separate the concepts of Space and Time from spacetime, and to allow for the philosophical notions and representations of Time as Past time, Present time, and Future time. Whereupon the illusions of a Past time and a Future time merely provide a conscious articulation of continuous change in the chain of events from which to understand the breadth of evolution, or even the perception of 'being', and the extent to which evolution is accomplished."

"Consequently, ongoing evolution is the physical reality of events acting outside the conscious mind that ultimately decides all fate. Ironically, evolution can only be collected, stored, measured, and studied from within the conscious mind. Subsequently, our ultimate fate depends on how we interpret and interact with the physical reality of events acting outside our conscious mind."

He then concluded by pronouncing, "Existence, or our ability 'to be', is only ever the concept of the Present time by which there is an actuality of being in existence via continuous change."

"Yes, I take your point," John begrudgingly admits. "Our ability to exist is part and parcel of these universal changes. And what we think of as living life is merely a construct of our capability to understand how these successive changes fit together. So a real time event is just the same as Present time imaging."

"Yes, and once you have a proper foundation of the interaction of spacetime, our dimensional existence becomes more comprehensible," Steve insisted.

"But other than how you framed it in your proposal for 'All Time' and 'No Time', you are not telling us anything we don't already know," Phil disclosed.

"True, but now you see the basis for my theoretical premise: the notion of degrees by which Space and Time may interact interdependently. One of which is that a trace of radiated signals in the relativity of spacetime provides for a time capsule of information, much like the ice core samples contain information about past temperature and climate change conditions. The expectation is that, dependent on your distance to a location in space, the radiated waves present varying degrees of time for a given trace. In this way, the radiated waves are stored stream cores of interacting Past time events. And as one traverses the distance toward the event, one is able to encounter successive images of its Future time, relative to its decreasing distance to the eventual Present time event. From this perspective, Future time is reflective of a predesignated time line trace to its Present time event," Steve continued with his relative notions of Time.

Now Margaret, getting more caught up in the rationale for the philosophy of Time, noted, "But while this is the Future time of a Past time record, it is not the Future time of the Present time event."

"Exactly so," Steve acknowledged. "And yet there is another aspect of spacetime that is relevant to our discussion, which is the homogeneous and isotropic perspective of the universe. You all remember the images generated from data captured via the NASA's Wilkinson Microwave Anisotropy Probe. The WMAP gave us our first complete view of the Cosmic Microwave Background within the visible cosmos. These have been related to us as the relic radio waves from the Big Bang, which fill the universe. Our expectation of these WMAP images is that they represented a current perspective for the evolution of the universe. From the radiated signals we are able to receive by virtue of the laws of wave propagation, we had a look back in Time to a moment which we assumed was to be our moment of creation, or close enough to it."

After a short pause, he added, "However, if one were able to travel the distance from Earth to the source location of these CMBs, they would not find the beginning of the universe; nor would they be traveling to the source of these signals in either Time or Space. And this is because it was only the imagined or calculated location of the source based on the wave propagation we detected and translated in real-time."

Steve waited for some acknowledgement of understanding, but nobody was speaking up. So he took silence as an assumption that they were on the 'same page', so to speak.

"In reality what the Earth traveler would see, looking back towards Earth, would be a similar view of these CMBs where Earth should be. Accordingly, if you continued to leap-frog through the universe, you would continue to observe the same thing, over and over again; no matter where in the universe you were. This is because that while the universe only ever exists in Present time, our radiation imaging of it can only ever provide us with a perspective of any distant spacetime location based on our defined constant speed of wave propagation as it interacts with other matter," he presented as his final determination.

The silence continued to be pervasive in the room as everyone seemed to be digesting what he had purported. Steve reveled in it; letting it languish as it indicated to him that they could not refute his assertion.

"And yes, if during our journey we could successively take snapshot images along the route to this source location, as observed by Dr. Beecher, we could capture images over the evolving time of that target location. Which, or course, doesn't mean to imply that these Past time representations are substantive of any real spacetime location. Rather, they are only representative of our perspective of decreasing distance to any source location," he professed with confidence.

"OK, I get it," Phil stated impatiently. "The observable universe is larger than we can see or measure, and the distribution of matter in the universe is homogeneous and isotropic when viewed on a large enough scale; whereupon Present time is the only real representation of existence. The causality of a Past time impacting on a Future time, while ultimately probable, is an illusion of our capability to fashion our own reality."

"Right, good," Steve acknowledged.

"So are you suggesting that either the new interface on the CONS units are progressively detecting further down the path toward the target location or that the pod operators are somehow able to interpret and predict the probability of 'cause and effect' for the wave propagation that they are receiving?" Margaret had to ask.

"Neither," Steve announced with bravado, challenging everyone in the room. "As I see it, there is an underlying fourth dimensional perspective of existence via dark matter. As the new interface was altered to work with dark matter detection, and perhaps even glimpse upon dark energy wave variations, we are now able to view cosmological events beyond just the speed of wave propagation. It would appear that dark energy embraces the previous order in which the universe 'was' prior to the introduction of baryonic matter and complementary dark matter."

"Now that is an interesting concept," Phil proclaimed. "Detection of events at faster than light speed."

"Indeed; as I proposed in my book, the introduction, or creation, of baryonic matter into the universal void was an intrusion upon the non-matter imperative of nothingness which preceded it. I speculated that baryonic matter resides as the positive mass density record of this intrusion upon the original non-order of nothingness, while dark matter resides as the negative mass density record of this same intrusion. The corollary being: Where there is nothing, there is nothing to order. As a consequence, the conflagration of their complementary creations, opposing nil order, introduced the chaos that brought about a temporal ripple upon the fabric of a once empty universe; bringing about varying degrees of Space. Similarly, degrees of Time were spawned within the resultant ripple of gravitational waves. It is this gravitational partitioning upon which positive mass density is limited. Hence, this constraint imposes an equalization upon the limiting velocity for all forms of radiation: i.e., light waves, radio waves, and even microwaves."

"It is an intriguing perspective on the origin of matter; I'll give you that," John said, becoming more intrigued with his perspectives. "So tells us more about this dark matter theory of yours."

Now Steve felt more emboldened to espouse upon his theories. "So this underlying fourth dimensional foundation of universal order remains manifested as dark energy upon the intrusion of baryonic matter. That is to say, before there were these varying distinctions of positive density matter, there was only one form for universal medium without a positive or negative aspect," Steve maintained. "And yet, the intrinsic properties of this universal medium are still retained in the complimentary creation of baryonic matter and dark matter, as dark energy. The principal that dark matter exists only in Present time, rather than the gradient distinctions of baryonic matter stored in streaming cores of Past time, I believe is the concept by which nonlocality is proven. What Einstein termed as 'spooky action at a distance' is really the communicative properties of dark matter via dark energy."

"In a sense, dark matter and dark energy exist without distance because dark matter is an expression of negative matter density. In point of fact, it does not have the limiting factors which have been imposed upon positive density matter. Think of it like this: What we perceive as an inflationary universe is really the measure of dark energy attempting to restore this underlying fabric of non-order back to a degree of 'No Time and No Space'. As I see it, the universe needed to expand instantaneously in response to the intrusion and proliferation of baryonic matter; and it will continue to do so until the proliferation and effects of baryonic matter decreases," Steve explained.

"So what you are saying is that IGIE is now able to tap in on the communicative properties of dark matter, upon any targeted location anywhere in the observable universe," Tom summarized, bringing the meeting back to the focus of their issue.

"Indeed, we should be able to view Present time events taking place anywhere in the visible universe, without the limitation of speed of light transmissions," Steve proposed.

"So what you are proposing is that dark matter acts like one synergetic psychic host; and that, irrespective of distance, the whole host experiences are felt everywhere in the universe at the same time," Margaret stated, trying to make sense of it all.

"Exactly so; that is very insightfully put," Steve expressed, happy that Margaret rephrasing of it might resonate with the others. "Think of it like this: No matter what the positive density object you throw into a controlled space, it does not replace the medium within that non-space. Rather, the medium of non-space either surrounds or mixes in with the object added to that space; subsequently, resulting in an expansion of that space. And all the non-space in it still remains as an inseparable whole within this medium of dark energy. In fact, all the space can be reclaimed as one inseparable unit upon the removal of the positive density object. In contrast, any objects added to the space are distinct instantiations of positive matter, separate in of each other, and therefore they are separated by some degree of distance. Consequently, these objects must communicate through the collective of the mixed medium occupying the space."

"However, the non-space itself does not need to communicate through these objects. Rather the non-space does not really need to communicate at all, because it is not separate of itself. It is still just only one unit," Steve advocated. "Dark matter can be similarly viewed as the instantiation of dark energy at any moment in spacetime. As such, its distinction is one of less spacial density in a string of connections within the medium of dark energy. Subsequently, there is no real degree of any distance in non-space. Rather dark matter maintains a symbiotic relationship with baryonic matter, insomuch that it is complementary to it. That is to say, without baryonic matter, there is no dark matter."

"This means we can collect the data provided to us from other radio telescope at light speed and correlate that data with the data provided from IGIE via this new interface. We will be able to corroborate notions of cosmological evolution that we have yet to only theorized upon," Phil proclaimed with excitement.

"We need to have the patents established before any of this goes public," John proposed, echoing his concern about the seriousness of their discovery.

"What are you talking about? None of what we do is public now," Phil said jokingly. "You start messing with submitting patents and then other physicists start reverse engineering what we are doing. And even if we do patent it, I recommend that we do it piecemeal so that the intent is not revealed."

"Then are we in agreement to leave the interface in place for now?" Tom asked.

"I may be the only one with a neuropsychology doctorate here," Margaret began to elicit a cautionary tone, "but we haven't had a chance to study the possible effects of this new input upon the pod operators."

"Who are the pod operators?" Steve asked with concern.

"For the affected CONS units, that would be both Andrew and Mairy," Margaret answered.

Completely dismissing Steve's question, Tom breaks in to rebuff Margaret's concerns, stating, "I believe the evidence speaks for itself.

We now know that these are IGIE generated images are good since we understand the theory behind them. These images also confirm that the master CONS units were able to interface these new wave variations appropriately with the brainwaves of the pod operators to provide these images. And since you, yourself, have told me and the board that these CONS units are designed to not influence the brainwave patterns with which these new waves would integrate, then I don't see where there is a danger to the subjects."

"Excuse me, two of those subjects are members of my family," Steve interrupted."

"Yes, of course," Tom acknowledge. "I didn't mean to diminish the nature of Margaret's concern. I do just not understand the basis for her concern."

"My concern is cautionary only," Margaret reversed her cautionary tone. "I really have no evidence either way. Insomuch that the CONS units are designed not to influence the brainwave patterns, I do not see where the identification of additional monitoring would hamper the outcomes. I, too, have a lot invested in the safety of my team; not only are they irreplaceable, they are part of our family as well. I'll continue to audit the pod operator logs for any abnormalities, and keep you informed of any significant changes in their behavior."

"I guess that should be sufficient for now," Steve reluctantly agreed. Not quite convince of their optimism, Steve reluctantly agreed to continue with the new equipment in place. Although he wondered whether he was influenced by his need for recognition, he had great hope that all would go well.

Steve had no idea that the actions required to help contribute to the realization of their discovery resulted from the transcendental manifestation of the Shadow-Forge in the targeted spacetime location. Such a revelation would require him to make a more informed decision as to whether preventing the continuation of the experiment would help or hinder their chances of survival. Of that he could not know. However, he did know that he needed to talk with Andrew and Mairy before forcing his hand to pull their participation. So he would agree for now. And with his agreement, there was a unanimous consensus among the parties in attendance to transform the focus of their research to transcend the limits of known science, without knowing the ramifications of how their somewhat accidental discovery.

To be sure, somewhere between 33% to 50% of all scientific discoveries are unexpected; being either accidental or coincidental in nature. This helps explain why scientists may often frame their discoveries as more serendipitous than predictable, leaving the details to be worked out later. Such was kind of like the discovery of the neutron, which eventually led to the invention of the atomic bomb. Indeed, that night Steve joined in to become a permanent part of the corporate team; ignorant of any cause and effect that would predispose their notoriety. As the temptation to realize his dream was too noble to pass up, Steve convince himself that he was advancing the cause of science toward the ultimate truth of cosmogony.

Only Tom was aware of the true limits of their collaborative efforts; for it was he that was steering the team toward his own ends. Indeed, Tom had manipulated the situation in his favor once again. He convinced the others to join forces with his team, which thus enable him to maintain control of the project for his own nefarious designs. For him, after all these years, he had found the missing ingredient to his execute his ultimate scheme. Undeniably, he purposely neglected to point out that he believed this new capability could only be attributed to the Steve's children becoming part of the team. A realization he came to upon after reading Steve's compilation of books.

For, you see, Tom believed that Steve's tale of science fiction is what fed his more nonfictional research on dark matter, rather than the other way around. And as long as he and his family remained members of the team, no one would be the wiser. But harnessing this new ability to view deep space location in real time was not the full extent of his ambition. It was just one more step towards his ultimate scheme; a secret he shared with no one. And this unspoken, unshared, and unseen secret was keep hidden; replaced by the illusion that Tom presented to the players of his malevolent game plan.

Steve, still in the dark as to Tom's true agenda, was determined to understand how the introduction of Andrew and Mairy into this grand experiment may have enhanced its capabilities. There was really no way of telling to what extent, if any, the new interface might be either influencing their activities or vice versa. While the new interface was only meant to enhance the interpretation of captured gravitational wave variations, there may also be a chance that their scripted dreams might be more scrupulously monitored as well. For him, it had previously been all about the science for science's sake. Now with his family in the mix, he was becoming more paranoid about their other clandestine mission. He felt that he could not take a chance with his kid's safety. He felt he needed to contact and warn the kids before their next session.

[Second Star to the right and straight on until morning.]

Steve was unable to sleep after the late night spent with the intended reshaping of the research team's motivation. After a night of speculation, celebration, and reorganization, he was had a lot of input to sort through. He was finally getting the recognition he deserved, but at what cost. While he always hoped his theories would be picked up favorably within the scientific community, the source of this information had always been a secret. And there were reasons that he and his family had kept it a secret; the biggest one being the safety of all involved. He mulled over the possibilities of why the kids were even up here with him. And the answer was always the same: it was not about him and it was all about the quest.

Still, Steve couldn't see past his own accomplishments through to the nefarious aspects of what he was playing into. He had not considered that it might involve the unmasking of the Shadow-Forge guild members in his family. If nothing else, he needed to warn them about the consequences of their quest participation. He slipped out from his room, while nighttime was still being simulated on the moon station, and slid a note under the door of Andrew's room.

Unbeknownst to Steve, Andrew and Mairy spent the night, with their fellow pod operators, casing the lower levels of the spherical structure and keeping track of Vera's whereabouts. Or was it Vera that was keeping track of their whereabouts?

[Andrew's Perspective]

When Mairy and I arrived back to our rooms, I found an urgent note that dad had left for me. It didn't say much, other than to request that we all meet up together in the shops just down from the cafeteria, an hour before breakfast. So I went to inform Mairy of the change in plans. As she was already wearing a robe when she answered the door, I assumed she was eager to get some rest.

"Mairy, it seems something is up," I started in, as I brushed past her into her room. "Dad wants us to meet him in the morning, an hour before breakfast," I informed her, referring to the note in my hand.

"Does he explain why in the note?" Mairy asked, leaning in to see the note herself.

"No, just what I told you. Dad is not one to write down any details, fearing they could be intercepted," I shared with Mairy. "He pretty much doesn't trust anyone."

"So what exactly does the note say?" Mairy enquired, as she took the note from my hand.

"It just says we should meet him at the little shop that we went to after our first dinner together," I answered; "the one that opens and closes early."

"He really is playing it cautious," Mairy surmised. "He must have found out something important."

"OK, then I'll meet up with you first thing in the morning; say about fifteen minutes before we have to meet with dad," I stated of our appointment as I left for my own room.

"Sounds like a plan," Mairy replied, agreeing upon the scheduled time.

That night I had trouble falling asleep trying to second guess what dad wanted to talk to us about. And yet it was difficult to ignore the events of the day, which were wildly exciting as well. The combination of thoughts soon melded into the haze of sleep. It would seem that my mind would rather do its own sorting and storing of my conscious experiences in a more subconscious mode. That night, my dreaming was vary random, without a specific theme, and was soon forgotten upon my awakening.

The next morning, Mairy and I met at the appointed location. Dad was already biding his time by window shopping within the shop that had opened early. It was full of handcrafted knick-knacks and figurines.

"Dad, what's up?" I asked, getting his attention.

"Not here, let's walk," was dad's simple reply. As we left through the entrance of the store, dad indirectly started the conversation with an odd approach. "So, how goes the job?" he asked.

I understood from dad's leading questions that he was about to lecture me. I've been with him long enough to know when I am being set up. I tried to set up my defense by resorting to offense.

"Actually, we are a little beyond that, don't you think?" I answered, hinting about our quest. "We're not here just to work a job. We are working the quest."

"So I gather, from the deep space images they showed me last night," dad conveyed to them.

And here it comes. Anticipating the attack, I switched back into defensive posture.

"You can't blame that on us," I declared, defending our actions. And then I fired back, "Besides it was your idea for us to participate in their research up here anyway."

"And how else was I to get you up here safely, so that you and Mairy could do your investigating," dad pointed out.

Then, perhaps anticipating we were heading for another fight, dad backed off and approached the discussion differently.

"Andrew, I am not blaming anyone for anything right now. No one is being blamed for anything. So let's get that straight now before we continue. We don't have time to work through past patterns of bad communication here. Something strange is going on now with this project and it could have unpredictable ramifications. It is far too dangerous for any of us to go it alone. So are we a team?" dad asked of me.

"Yes, of course," I answered, backing down from my defensive attitude.

"So if we are not to blame, then how were the deep space images you saw generated?" Mairy asked.

"I didn't mean to say that either. Let's not use the word 'blame' at all; OK?" dad asked rhetorically. "I can't really say whether you did or didn't contribute to the situation. All I know is that those images could only have been generated in real time," dad continued; "meaning that you two were actually focused in on the target location. Which was not really a stretch for me to imagine; after all, you two have abilities unlike anyone on Earth, or on the Moon for that matter."

"Well, maybe not everyone," Mairy was quick to point out. "We found out today that Vera may have deviated from her scripted dream as well."

"Scripted dream?" dad asked with some confusion. "What do you mean?"

"As we discussed earlier, the CONS units are designed for us to synchronize with captured gravitational waves and integrate them within our own brain waves," I started to explain.

Then Mairy jumped in, explaining, "The purpose seems to be that the CONS units are first combining these incoming gravitational waveforms with our brain waveforms. And then, having already mapped out the preprogrammed patterns of our brain waves, these incoming waves trigger these patterns in accordance with their variations. Rather like conceptualizing our environment from what we see via light, we are formulating an vision of the environment being impressed upon our minds."

I then jumped back in to finish out the explanation, concluding with, "So these combined waveforms are then fed into the IGIE system to be interpreted in a more visual representation. I'm guessing this is where the IGIE system works its magic to have them translated and generated into images."

"Yes, I am familiar with the operation of how the differing combined waveforms are interpreted, translated and filtered to provide meaningful input to IGIE, resulting in these generated images," dad surmised.

"But what you don't know is that they needed to distract the brain's creative unconsciousness by using scripted dreams," Mairy informed him. "Problem is, we haven't been following the scripted dream. So we were never really being distracted."

"We have been honing our skills in preparation for any confrontation with members from the 'Legion of the Dark Guild'," I explained to excuse our actions. Yet, even as I said it, I almost didn't believe my own words. Having seen many superhero movies, it sounded almost comical to me. Not funny comical, but 'written in comic form' comical.

"Yes, well it would seem that you both have been doing a little more than that. When I said I can't say you didn't contribute to the situation, I meant that I believe that you were both actually embracing the tangible locations you were focused in on; the locations that were supposed to be detected via DeepSIT, and not by you directly," dad went on to inform them of his conjectures.

"Yeah, we kind of figured that out on our own, as well," I reluctantly admitted. "At first I thought I was just manipulating the landscape of my scripted dreams. You know, taking control of my own dreams. Like you always said I should."

"Oh, don't try and turn this back on me. By your own admission, you were not even taking part in your own dreamscape. You both were, instead, 'joyriding' outside of your dreamscape," dad retorted. "It may not have been so evident when your minds were just interfacing with gravitational waveforms, because your 'out-of-body' experiences were relatively consistent with the location of the detected gravitational wave variances. So what was expected of the CONS unit translations, for that area of deep space, is what would have been ultimately inputted to IGIE," dad pointed out.

"Wait a moment; you said 'may not have been' so evident. What has changed?" Mairy inquired.

"It's not just gravitational wave variations anymore," dad confessed. "There is another problem that we have to contend with now. The primary CONS units have been refitted with a new interface," dad injected into our conversation. "So the CONS units are no longer just translating gravitational wave form variances. Rather the two primary CONS units are now translating variations in dark energy waveforms radiating from within the dark matter of the cosmos."

"We are translating what?" I asked with surprise. "Dark Matter; how is that even possible?!"

"Funny thing is, it probably wouldn't have worked with anyone else, other than you two," dad continued to hypothesize. "I believe it has something to do with your Shadow-Forge capabilities, and your ability to transcend a fourth dimensional reference within Space and Time. It was your abilities that I was hoping to simulate to make this research work."

"So once again I was just a pawn in your pursuit and validation of dark matter detection," I fired back, feeling a bit denigrated in all of this.

"It's not like that," dad responded defensively. "I needed to understand what happened to you. I needed to understand how I could be there for you."

Unexpectedly Mairy intervened, grabbing both of our hands. "You both need this more than you know."

My mind filled with images of dad's overprotective attitude during my youth. I guess it wasn't easy raising a child with ADHD, who would impulsively put himself in harm's way. I began to see things from his point of view, which was probably Mairy's intent. We both calmed down, as dad continued with his speculation.

"It must be your special connection with the universal being that even allows you to receive and interact with these radiated waves surrounding areas of dark matter," he theorized. "I mean, the fact that your abilities are even a consideration in all of this, may have only been made possible because they chose to attach the new interface to the two primary CONS control units."

"Or maybe the two primary CONS control units we were chosen because we are the pod operators for them. Maybe this is what they intended all the time," Mairy spoke up with a sudden awareness. "I don't believe in chance or luck. I believe in fate and destiny. And I believe someone may be manipulating our destinies to achieve their own version of fate."

"What do you mean?" I asked with renewed interest, as dad just listened intently. "Someone is trying to fashion their own fate upon the future events. I thought we could only ever influence our own destiny."

"Not just their fate, but fate in general," Mairy elucidated; "the fate of everyone and everything."

"You mean like the whole universe?" I asked, utterly confounded.

"Think about it. Where fate is the purveyor of tangible interactions, destiny is the surveyor of intangible interactions," Mairy presented of her supernatural philosophy.

"Substantively, where interactions have consequences, if one seeks to influence another's destiny within the scope of their allotted fate, then they would need to understand the evolution of these coordinated destinies. Still, one can only ever influence the evolution of coordinated destinies calculated upon the windows of opportunities that each moment presents," she verbalized, as if to reason out her notions.

"So if someone wanted to influence another's destiny to serve their own ends, then they would need to understand the evolution of their intertwined destinies toward the scope of their allotted fates," dad said, building upon the concepts that Mairy presented.

"Precisely," she acknowledged.

"Wait, we have more than one allotted fate?" I asked. "You mean, like alternative futures?"

"Kind of; while the future is not set, each individual's fate is determined upon the evolution of their destiny in coordination with all other destinies," dad explained further. "Subsequently, each person's fate is predestined upon their concurrent evolutionary paths for all affected destinies."

"That's quite a leap of reasoning," I speculated. "It's problematic enough to work out the strategy of chess moves based on agreed rules. Who could possibly work out the evolution of multiple destinies?"

"The question right now is not who, but why," Mairy proclaimed. "If we try to chase down who is manipulating us, or how this is happening before we know why it is happening, we will be needlessly following meaningless clues. And we may not have that kind of time."

"I see what you mean," I began to follow her logic; "it's kind of like a chicken running around with its head chopped off."

"Really, a headless chicken?" Mairy replied with confusion. "That's disgusting. How does that have to do with anything we've been talking about?"

"No, the headless chicken running around is just an analogy," I tried correcting myself, sheepishly. "I meant to imply an analogy to the haphazard or aimless pursuit of clues without any real direction. It's just an expression."

"Oh, one of those again," Mairy responded candidly.

"OK, let's start over," said dad, interceding in our aside. "I'll think more on the 'how' of how anyone could use you two as part of this new interface for capturing and interpreting the radiated waves surrounding dark matter," dad concluded, ended their meeting. "And maybe you two can think on the 'why' of it all. I have to get going now, but you two need to be more cautious about your extracurricular activities in deep space. Hopefully once your mother arrives this week, she can talk you into being a bit more careful."

"Right," I acknowledged, "Wait, what; mom is coming up this week?" I questioned with surprise.

"Yes, so you'll probably want to clean your room," dad jested as he walked away. "Stay safe, and I'll try to see you later tonight."

I watched on as dad left for work, all the while thinking about mom's arrival sometime this week.

"We better just get into the breakfast line," Mairy advised. "We don't want to be seen going back to our rooms prior to leaving again for breakfast. I'm thinking synthetic pancakes with some synthetic syrup."

"And I believe your thinking with your stomach again," I replied, "but, then, it also make sense. I built up quite an appetite last night, wandering about in the lower levels."

Before we got to the end of the early morning smorgasbord, I could see the others arriving. That is, all except Vera. It appeared Vera had been through the breakfast line and was already seated at a table. Having been seen by her, we carried our breakfast trays to her table.

"My, my, you are an early riser," I commented to Vera as we came to sit down. "Have you been here long?"

"Not too long. As you might have noticed, I still have food on my plate," Vera replied. "But long enough to see that you did not come from the direction of the elevator."

"Yes, that would be my fault," Mairy piped in. "I convince Andrew to go in on a gift for our parents. So we came down early to check out the shops."

"Guess you didn't find what you were looking for then, as you brought nothing back with you," observed Vera.

"Well, it is still early yet," Mairy continued, "their anniversary is not for a few weeks."

"Celebrating without your mother then?" Vera inquired.

"Not at all, our mom is supposed to be coming up sometime this week," Mairy replied. I was beginning to sense a contest of wills, as Mairy monopolized the conversation with Vera.

"Whose mom will be up this week?" Lindsey asked, as she overheard upon approaching the table.

"Oh, the 'Bobbsey Twins' here say their mother is coming up this week," Vera answered. "It would seem like some families are more influential than others."

"Oh, Vera, you know that the rest of their family is already up here working," Lindsey said in our defense. "It wouldn't do to separate the family from their mother for ten years."

With that, Vera got up and left the table. I wasn't even sure if she had finished what was on her plate.

"You'll have to excuse Vera," Lindsey explained, "but I believe Vera is more homesick than she lets on."

"How long has she been up here?" Mairy asked.

"Let me think," Lindsey said, pausing. "We three have been here for about three years now. Isn't that right Tim?" she seemingly asked with some clairvoyant power of knowing Tim was approaching.

"Yes, three years, nine months, two weeks, and a day," Tim responded, as he approached from just out of our line of sight.

"OK, and then Vera came up about a year later after we did," Lindsey answered. "I remember because she was around while I was still dating."

"Yes, and she was quite the 'find' at the time," Milo piped in, arriving to join in on the conversation. "Once she came up, they changed around our training schedules to meet her needs," Milo recalled.

"Yes, Verdandi was quite the celebrity when she first came up here," Tim admitted.

"Was?" I asked, focusing in on that one word; "what happen?"

"Well, our early tests were never enough to dazzle the higher ups," Tim explained. "Even with four pods, we were only able to get some 2D resolution, similar to what Hubble is providing us now."

"Yes, and at a much higher price than the Hubble, I might add," Milo divulged.

"However, it seemed that for every advance forward, new problems cropped up. They started to become disappointed with our performance;

like we were not meeting our potential. Then they finally hit upon the solution of using six interfacing CONS units. The two new units provided innovations that allowed for marked improvements in the data presented to IGIE."

"So having six control pods was not part of the original design?" I asked, with a sense of intrigue. "I wonder why they decided to go six CONS units. When did that happen?"

"Just about two years ago now," Milo answered. "And get this; Rather than retrofit the previous four units to work as six units, they rigged it so that the two new units would act as controllers."

"Then why didn't they use them before we came up?" I asked, wanting to know more.

"Oh, they did; or they tried," continued Milo. "Each one of us had a chance at piloting the new pods, but the new interface was more difficult to link up with and it had a negative impact on our results."

"All except for Vera," Lindsey rejoined the conversation. "She seemed to take to it right away. That's when she rose to celebrity status. She helped advance the CONS to IGIE interface, keeping the project on schedule, much to the delight of the company. With Vera's help, we were back in their good graces again."

"In fact," Tim piped in, "they use Vera to fine tune the operation of the two new units. Then in an attempt to push the schedule forward, one time they even had both of the new units synced up to her in tandem."

"However, it turned out to be too much for her," Lindsey recalled with some distress. "After three weeks of tandem operations, and with the continuing disapproval of Dr. Beecher, Vera began to show signs of exaggerated stress and poor sleeping patterns. At the behest of Dr.

Beecher, they finally discontinued the tandem connection. Vera ended up being sick for some time after that.

"We all felt bad about how things worked out for her, so we just tend to ignore Vera's brash attitude and behavior. In fact, we just let Vera be Vera," Milo explained. "After that incident, no one else has been allowed to pilot those new pods. That is, not until you two showed up."

"When you two showed up and they decided to re-employ the control pods, Vera tried to get Dr. Beecher to let her back in to pilot one of the new CONS units," Tim continued. "After all, she was the best of us and she was able to handle one unit just fine. But the company did not seem to want to accept the risk again."

"And besides they had already invested a great deal of time and expense getting the four units to work with our unique brain patterns," Milo rationalized. "It was an easy decision for them to just reprogram the two new CONS units, rather than three units. But as you can see, Vera didn't take their decision very well."

"I can see where she could use the support of her family after such an ordeal," Mairy conveyed. "The brain is our ultimate safe haven. Once it is compromised, there is no telling how someone will handle stress."

"Maybe we can approach Dr. Beecher; on Vera's behalf, I mean," I suggested. "You know, have them allow her some family attendance up here."

"Yes, that would be a great idea if she wasn't already an orphan," agreed Lindsey. "But I'll talk with Dr. Beecher about it anyway. Speaking of which, we'd better get going if we want to make it on time."

"Oh, yes," Mairy acknowledged, as we all started to get up.

Mairy then did something unexpected. Mairy faked a trip and dump her empty tray on me.

"Oops, sorry," Mairy apologized. "Lindsey, we will catch up with you later," Mairy said, excusing us from following after them. We hung back and took a separate elevator up.

"You did that on purpose," I complained, knowing that Mairy was too adept for such a clumsy slip. "What was that all about, anyway? So I forgot Vera was an orphan. That was no reason to overreact."

"No it's not that. Although you did turn a lovely shade of red," Mairy joked. "It is just that we didn't have time to discuss the implications of what your father told us. I'm getting a bad feeling about this upcoming session. I believe we need to stick together during today's run. Let me take control."

"I wouldn't have it any other way. But you heard dad," I reminded her. "They might be monitoring us via our dreamscapes."

Exiting the elevator, we quickly walked towards our rooms so I could get a change of clothing.

"I don't think they can follow us," she speculated, in response to my worry. "I mean, the astral us. If they are monitoring our dreamscapes, then they would be monitoring our unconscious brain waves as they follow along within the scripted dreams that they had loaded up for each of us. The most they might see is our absence of real participation from within the dreamscape."

"It has to be more than that," I challenged her. "Yes, our physical minds are still interacting within the dreamscapes, but there is also the influence of what we are doing in our 'out-of-body' form."

"That doesn't appear to be part of our unconscious interaction within our scripted dreams," Mairy speculated. "Rather we appear to be interjecting our second sight into our own minds, intermingling with the target location's waveforms being collected and interpreted within our more physical brain waves."

"I get it. We are still connected to our physical host bodies," I reasoned.

"Right, so we just have to be careful how we focus in on each other," Mairy cautioned. "It wouldn't do for us to show up in the generated images."

"Hey, since they just started working with this new interface on our CONS units, they would probably just dismiss anything they couldn't explain as another anomaly," I continued with her line of thought.

I was easily persuaded to follow her instincts, mostly since I was not one to ignore her special sense of awareness. She seemed to have a sixth sense about things, much liked an informed hunch. I continued to put on a fresh outfit and we continued with the rest of our conversation on the way to the morning team meeting.

"Speaking of anomalies, we need to be aware of each other for any abnormalities in our auras," Mairy warned. "As we can separate from our dreamscapes and visit other deep space locations, while 'out-of-body', we need to be more cautious of our surrounding and how we interact with them. And remember what I told you, it is not good to be separated from our bodies for very long."

"OK, but you never said 'why' it's not good to be separated from our bodies for a long time," I hinted for a more direct reason.

"Well, even though it is not evident to the occasional astral traveler, there is a lot of activity within the aether of the universal being. While we use it to journey through the cosmos, or from one reality to the next, there is always the every present danger of an inadvertent diversion. For the most part, the danger is just losing our path, or our control, and being pulled into someone else's reality. But if we linger too long without some protection like Harmony's spheres, we might be detected as an unknown remnant of discarded astral energy."

"Discarded what?" I asked with some confusion.

"Discarded astral energy," Mairy repeated. "It is the form of our presence in the environment of the aether which temporally allows for our journey from one reality to another. If an astral presence is detected as separate of any reality within the aether, then it will be separated from the aether," Mairy attempted to explain without a proper reference to what I might be able to understand.

"But I am not separated. I am still connected to my host body," I stated with confusion.

"True, but your astral self is not part of that reality," Mairy replied. "An out-of-body experience is also an out of reality immersion. The aether is only the medium in which realities exist. And if you are detected as separate of any reality, a separate reality would be created for and around you."

"Do you mean to say that I could live simultaneously in two separate realities?" I asked, attempting to understand more.

"Not really," Mairy disclosed to me. "The new reality created for you is random and may not provide an easy path back to your original host reality. Although we can pass from our own reality into another, as a Shadow-Forge, we cannot truly host more than one reality at a time." Mairy concluded. "Remember, I can only return to my original source reality after my Shadow-Forge host dies."

"What do you mean by 'no easy path'?" I asked apprehensively. "Our Shadow-Forge form dies and we return back to our original bodies."

"Since you cannot truly exist in more than one hosted reality, eventually one of the hosted realities may drop from existence. We maintain our connection to our individual realities via our astral presence. And each reality maintains its connection with the universe from within the aether. And if the reality that drops from existence happens to be the one that is hosting your original body then, suffice to say, you lose that reality and all the memories that go with it. You see, the protection of your original host is paramount to your survival, or your survival as you know it. Harmony may have watched over you during your first quest, but she it is not around to help you now."

"OK, I get it; loitering in the aether is a bad thing," I summarized. "So we must always be moving to avoid detection."

Mairy smiled upon my simplification of her explanation. And rather than inundate me with more information, she did not attempt to further educate me in the way of the Shadow-Forge. Still, I was so engrossed in our conversation that I had paid little attention to our arrival at the meeting room. And after two mornings of following the same route to prepare ourselves for project, I could almost do it in my sleep.

"OK, now that everyone is here, we have a lot to go through this morning," Dr. Beecher began. "So let's get started. We have identified the anomaly in the generated images, and have accounted for it in our results. Subsequently, our last session has now been determined to be another successful run for the IGIE system. You are all performing admirably, and especially you Vera," Dr. Beecher made a point to praise her. "The detailed accounts of your last sessions provided us with the insight we needed to understand the anomaly. So thanks to Vera we are all moving forward with the program. We have realigned DeepSIT for another target, but that should not interfere with abilities to stay on task. And you'll all be glad to hear that the lab has complied with your request for new scripted dreams. Be sure to pay attention to any changes that may take place in your dreamscape sessions, however, so that you can accurately record them for our review."

Vera was beaming over the attention she was being given. But like us, I believe, she hadn't a clue as to what she did to earn such praise. Perhaps it was a psychological ploy of Dr. Beecher to elicit more data from the team members. Or perhaps there was more to Vera's abilities than even we were aware.

"So what is our new target location?" Tim inquired.

"I cannot tell you that because it may have an undue influence on how your brain translates the data to be imaged," Dr. Beecher answered. "You'll see soon enough. However, what I can do is to be sure to share the newly generated images with you and the team at our next morning meeting, tomorrow."

"Fair enough," Tim agreed.

"So what are the new scripted dreams like?" Milo inquired.

"I believe yours involves an alien abduction," Dr. Beecher joked. Everyone but Milo thought it was funny.

"Ha, Ha," Milo forced his laughter. "Well just remember that we are up here on the frontier of space now. So whom do you think the aliens will end up contacting first?"

The meeting did not take as long as I had anticipated, and soon we were all being herded down the hall as a group. I didn't have any time to discuss how the changes in our new dreamscapes might affect our ability to keep a low profile.

I turned to Mairy and, below the din of the multiple conversations, I said intently, "OK, we stay together." She looked to me and nodded.

It was never far to walk from the meeting room to the research lab. And after the routine instructions, we were prepped for our next session run in the CONS units. Just as before, we took our place in our assigned pods alongside of the other sleepers. And just as before, we let ourselves be put under the influence of the machine. As the machine moved our pods into position, I couldn't help worrying about everything we discussed with dad just a couple of hours earlier. And now this seemingly last minute change of target. I felt more like a guinea pig in an experiment, rather than a participant in research project.

I turned to look to Mairy as they prepared to go under, but her eyes were already closed. Slowly I felt the environment of the pod cutting me off from my senses and taking control of my surroundings. I hadn't prepared myself for meditation and I was suddenly found myself embracing the strange atmosphere of the scripted dream world that had been programmed for me. I found myself looking for Mairy in a large crowd of strangers; rather like being disoriented in a large theme park.

I made my way to a vantage point from which I could survey the crowd more efficiently. As I scanned the crowd, I could see, as if out of the corner of my vision, a child leaning too far over the railing that guarded the vantage point that we were on. At that point I noticed the steep drop beyond the railing to the crowd below. As the child began to fall, I kicked off from the top of the railing and seemingly floated across to prevent the child from being injured. The crowd was quite fascinated with my heroism, and I welcomed their adulation.

It was my favorite type of dreaming: the flying dream. Having felt this freedom from the gravity that normally grounded me, I wanted to explore this new experience further. After a short run, I jumped into the air and rather felt myself floating to the ground. It seemed to somewhat mimic the feeling I had without the prescribed moon shoes that we have all been provided to wear on the moon station. It was such an exhilarating feeling, and I continued to experiment to see how long I could stay afloat before touching down. I could feel a sensation within my diaphragm, that when exercised, allowed me to direct my motion. Soon I found that I could ascend at will to any distant locations.

And then it hit me. I was completely without purpose of direction. I was not thinking practically, rather I was just feeling; reacting to the rush of various mixed emotions bombarding my subconscious. I was dreaming; or more aptly put, I was reacting to the landscape of the scripted dream world that was designed for me. Knowing that I was dreaming, did not provide for an automatic escape. I needed to stop reacting to my unconscious surroundings and access my conscious mind. I tried to think of how the real world works, but I always had the influence of the scripted dream bombarding me with new input. I began to replay differing memories, but it only merged back around in my unconsciousness and became part of the dream. I had somewhat been taken control of by the scripted dream, and it was not where I wanted to be. And worse, I was not going to be allowed to wake up until the session was over.

I needed to find that sense of me that existed outside of my host body. I thought of how it felt to be in the crystal with Fairy. I remembered how it felt to project myself from within the crystal. Slowly, I began to block out the scripted sensation of my five senses; sound was replaced by a deafening silence and touch was replaced by an absence of tactile feeling. Finally, I felt no containment of being. Where is aether, I thought; fighting off my fear of losing myself to this abyss. I slowly became aware of the melodious sound of harp-like tones echoing about me. It was working; I was transitioning to my out-of-body being. As I had learned from before, I search my new surroundings for its source. I began to sense the presence of another being, as if my own presence of 'being' was being acknowledged. It was the familiar presence of Fairy. In this realm, I acknowledged Mairy's more alter ego as Fairy. As she merged our auras, I felt relieved over the emerging communication connecting between us.

"Andrew…, Andrew, your finally here," the emerging connection seemed to resonate within the echo of my being. "I'd begun to think you weren't going to make it this time."

"Yes," I said, feeling grateful for the familiar buoy of her presence in this aether of space and time. "Yes, I am here. I kind of got taken by surprise by the new dreamscape and was lost in my own subconscious for a time."

"Well, don't get too comfortable. I have another surprise for you," announced Fairy. "The target location appears to be a black hole. The tidal rift of the gravitational field almost pulled me in. It was fortunate that you had not succeeded in projecting your astrally before I got here. I just managed to escape its grip on me by backing out into the aether for a moment. But now that we are both here, I feel we can't stay here for very long without being pulled in again."

Having fully emerged, I realized the extent of our predicament. I could see the raging plasma furnace incited by the rending mass being crushed in the black hole's gravitational acceleration.

"Right, what's your plan, then?" I asked. "We can't just wander to another location. As dad suggested, our CONS units are influenced by our ability to be here at the targeted DeepSIT location, and they are expecting to translate the gravitational variances of this black hole. If we wander about, we will cause a divergence in the mixed wave variations. Or who knows what with that new dark matter interface of theirs."

"Well, we can't stay here," Fairy reiterated. "Perhaps we'll just back up a bit and move our visitation beyond the danger zone of the black hole. Not sure why they chose to image this close to a black hole anyway."

"I believe it has to do with the current theory for possible detection of dark matter," I began to articulate from what I remembered of my readings on the subject. I felt smart to be able to relate some science knowledge to her; something that she didn't already know. "The concept is that either black holes are made up of dark matter or that dark matter caused black holes to be formed during the first few seconds of our universe's existence. Dad sees the event horizon of the black hole as the boundary between primordial mass and dark matter; a place where space disintegrates and time itself stands still."

"Interesting," Fairy acknowledged. "If that is the case, then there would be no further pull from just beyond the event horizon. Let's test that theory right now. Are you ready to leave this turmoil and check out some dark matter?

"Yes; anything to avoid the rending nature of that energy ring outside the event horizon again," I agreed, with some apprehension upon previous remembrance of my first encounter with a black hole. "So let's proceed to journey into that 'never, never land' beyond the event horizon," I declared, as an analogy of the black hole's inner core.

"Curious reference," Fairy replied; "where is this 'never, never land'? Is it another of your expressions?"

"Yes," I answered, "it is a place that can only exist in one's imagination, outside of any actual reality; kind of like the aether. It's about inspiriting the nature of innocence in a character known as Peter Pan, who never grows any older. It's a favorite story of our family. Mom has quite a collection of Peter Pan memorabilia."

With that, Fairy seemed to somehow take control as she backed us out into the aether again. She then altered our destination as we both transitioned back into reality, just inside the black hole's event horizon.

It was spellbinding. The artistic depiction of it paled in the splendor of its animated grandeur. It was like we could view it even beyond just the visible frequency spectrum, which made for an even more dramatic display. The somewhat altered dimensional imaging of intermixing beacons of light frequencies, pouring in upon the event horizon, provided for a dazzling spectacle of colored lights against the boundary of outer space and dark matter. Looking around in every direction, we embraced this magnificent moment in spacetime.

And, but for that moment of resplendent reflection, I began to notice details through the vague transparency in the kaleidoscope of colored light being displayed. It appeared that this black hole was actually spinning in our presence. I could follow the articulated motion of the galactic arms as they were gently whipped about the central black hole. It was like being at the center of a giant pinwheel.

In my disbelief, I had to ask Fairy, "Are we spinning, or is the galaxy really rotating in front of us?"

"No, I don't believe it is us that are spinning," she replied. Then she expressed her own observations, "Listen to the mellifluous sound of its rotation."

"Listen," I thought to myself, a bit puzzled. I viewed this spectacle as primarily a visual display. I could see the varying density in the flow of the gaseous material on the galactic arms, as they were being pulled along, from within this rotating spacial eddy. And as of that moment, I had not considered listening.

As I focused more, I could eventually hear the harp like tones of its motion, varying with the density of the gaseous flow as it changed from one moment to the next. "Yes," I called out with excitement, "I can hear it."

As the sound seemed to fill my being, a long forgotten remembrance emerged. I thought of one of my favorite passages in Walt Whitman's poem, 'I Sing the Body Electric':

I sing the body electric,
The armies of those I love engirth me and I engirth them,

They will not let me off till I go with them, respond to them,
And discorrupt them, and charge them full with the charge of the soul.

Was it doubted that those who corrupt their own bodies conceal themselves?
And if those who defile the living are as bad as they who defile the dead?
And if the body does not do fully as much as the soul?
And if the body were not the soul, what is the soul?

Here, in deep space, I resided without body. Bathed in the energy of these musical tones and dazzling lights, I remembered how I generated similar sounds when sliding my hand through the spherical bubble surface from within which Harmony first appeared to me. I recalled hearing a symphony of varying humming tones that wavered with the motion of my arm within the sphere. I recalled enjoying the impromptu concert of sound, which emanated like the vibrations of a gently strummed harp, upon my every movement. I even remembered the odor of peppermint and roses that scented my skin upon encounters with Harmony. But there was no such scent, now.

The combination of these experiences reminded me of a 'google' search entry for 'Musica universalis' (from Latin for 'universal music'), also called 'Music of the Spheres' or 'Harmony of the Spheres'. It was an ancient philosophical concept that regards proportions in the movements of celestial bodies as an incorporation of the metaphysical principle whose mathematical relationships express qualities or "tones" of energy. It was an energy which can be manifest in numbers, visual angles, shapes and sounds, which are all connected within these patterns of proportion.

For me, I believe this representation of my being without body to be the answer to Walt Whitman's quest for the soul. As a Shadow-Forge, my being was more than mere astral energy, and more than just an out-of-body experience. Rather, I felt a true sense of soulfulness, or perhaps a fullness of soul. I was an astral presence espousing the fullness of emotion with Fairy as my soulmate.

"That was both beautiful and elegant," I could hear Fairy communicating to me. "I too, think of you as my soulmate. We have a connection that neither space nor time can separate. It is what brought me to you on Earth, and it is what is keeping you here with me now."

I was surprised and delighted at the same time, as I imagined that my thoughts were my own.

"Not in this form," Fairy answered again, as if she were listening in on my every reflection.

"It's like we are psychically and mentally connected," I said to her.

"The unadorned soul cannot harbor any secrets once they are truly connected," she explained.

"This must be what it will be like upon judgement day," I thought aloud.

"Judgement day," she said with confusion. "Yes, I recall your mother's reference to 'judgement day' as a sort of post Armageddon."

"It is also a reference to a religious philosophy for what happens to those who pass on from their host bodies when the universe comes to an end. The concept being, if the universe can be created, then it can be terminated," I started in to explain. "In this philosophy, it is a time where everyone's deeds and actions would be laid bare before the final judgement. Everyone would know everything about everyone, and there would be no way to hide secrets from this final judgement. Problem is, however, that no one can agree upon the consequences of such a judgement. Most believe there is to be a representation of a heaven and a hell, like a reward and punishment to reconcile how we have lived our lives. In general, some people want to feel vindicate for their suffering or they want retribution for those who cause the suffering."

"You said 'most'. So what do the others believe?" she inquired.

"Oh, all different things; some of the others believe that our energy is just returned to the energy of the universe," I stated flatly. "They simply believe that there is no judgement, no heaven or hell, and therefore no moral imperative to live their lives with any limitations or restrictions."

"Kind of a selfish attitude," she insisted. "They tip the balance of the universe towards chaos."

"It is rather a self-centered philosophy, I'll grant you that," I had to agree. "But not everyone abuses the absence of such limitations or restrictions. Indeed, some of them are still very giving souls, despite their agnostic disregard of any reward in the afterlife for their thoughtfulness."

"Then they will surely tip the balance of the universe towards harmony," she remarked.

"Still, in the end, isn't the universe, just the universe," I questioned of the whole balance philosophy? "I mean the universe is and then it is not; right? Maintaining the balance just prolongs it.; doesn't it?"

"The way it was conveyed to me is that there is the 'being' of the universe which permeates inside all of our realities, and there is the 'non-being' of the universe outside of all of our realities," she explained. "So it is all in how you perceive the notion of your universe. The universe is more than Time and Space; it is what 'was before' and it is what 'will be after', and all the realities within and without spacetime itself."

"That actually makes sense," I thought aloud. "If you believe the universe is just the containment of our reality in spacetime, then you would need to believe in some state from which our universe was created. However, if you try to define a state of the universe from outside of our reality, a state not bounded by the spacetime limitations of our own fourth dimensional reality, you tend to work towards breaking down things to their simplest state in a more envisaged, one dimensional reality. For such a one dimensional reality one can only imagine concepts like omnipresent, omniscient, omnipotent, or omnificent. This then leads to terms like omnipresence, omnificence, omnipotence, and omniscience; from which the term 'God' becomes the notion of an actual 'Being' outside of spacetime. Herein our own realities, abides the supreme or ultimate illusion of our restricted realities: A perfection of actual 'Being' in power, wisdom, and goodness who can be worshipped as a creator and ruler of the universe."

"But if you believe the universe is greater than our realities, then the universe is not only equivalent to the notion of 'God', but also goes beyond this imperfect illusion we created of him and for him in our realities. The concept of 'God' as the universe is not only a 'being' both inside and outside our own realities, but it is also a 'not-being' both inside and outside of spacetime. In which case, the concept of the universe should not be bounded by the spacetime, but rather by its ability to be in a state of 'being' or 'not-being'; where both are the same from the perspective of the universe." I paused for a moment longer to capture the thought more succinctly, "In point of fact, the idealism of 'being' is not the same as the identism of 'to be', or to exist. So that's what dad tried to convey to me all this time. It certainly gives me a new appreciation for his point of view."

"And then there is the notion of 'ideality', or the balance in 'being'," Fairy added, building upon my stated understanding. "For with 'identism' becomes the advent of choice, or 'free will', from which the universal being is influenced. The universal being is not representative of either positive or negative, it is both and neither. It is the evolving nature of 'being' in free will that influences the fate of all."

"Yes, I see we need to understand the mechanics of 'free will' via the chaos theory. That is to say that any random act, good or bad, has consequences," I related. "In its most absolute form, I guess we could reduce this concept of 'balance' to the ideals of omnibenevolence and omnimalevolence. So theosophically, the concept of 'God' is neither all good nor all bad, dependent on your moral ideals of what 'good' and 'bad' really is. And the notions upon which these philosophies identify with 'free will' are purported to have arisen from an understanding of our own behavior and emotions, our expectations of fairness and equality, and our imagined representations of a heaven or a hell. In fact, as I now envision 'Judgement Day', it becomes this notion of universal balance restored, by the sorting through the positive and the negative."

"There is the clarity of thought about the universe being brought about by experiencing our connection within it," Fairy contemplated of their discussion. "Don't you think?

"Yes. So while we are supporting a more positive balance, the legions of chaos are supporting a more negative balance. And what, so Harmony and Discordia just manage both factions to maintain the balance?" I asked in a complaining demeanor.

"Each faction only understands their own needs for the continuation of being within the universe, as they see it," Fairy tried to explain to me. "Maintaining a more positive balance allows for the evolutionary continuation of our realities. Maintaining a more negative balance attempts to restore the order of the universe to a more primordial, pre-evolutionary status."

"Great, we both believe we are doing the right thing," I summarized. "However, the actions of these legions of chaos are predicated upon the annihilation of the living universal being that is our current reality."

"And yet, our current reality could not exist without this force of negative balance. It is the marriage of the two that predicates the union and continuation of our existence," she revealed to me. "The essence of Time is a reflection of this marriage; where Present Time mirrors Future Time upon Past Time. Remember, Time is not constant, but it is consistent."

"That's what Harmony told me about the nature of Time: It is not constant, but it is consistent. But is that then what her reference really means?" I questioned of my own existence. "Balance is the mirror of being?"

"Yes," she responded. Then without warning, Fairy perceived another presence in the Present time of their location in spacetime. "There is another here," Fairy related to me.

"I believe I can feel it too," I responded in kind. It was as if the environment of the black hole's interior enhanced my sensitivity to everything on the outside. "Do you think it is another Shadow-Forge?"

"There in the distance, just on the other side of the plasma ring. Whoever it is, they are fading in and out of this reality, or they would've been pulled into the event horizon by now," Fairy surmised. Then, as if on an impulse, Fairy decided to check it out, "I got to find out who or what it is."

"Is that a good idea?" I asked. "I mean, that appears to be very near event horizon of the black hole."

"We could back out into the aether again," Fairy suggested to me. When I did not immediately respond, Fairy seemed to sense my reluctance. So she instead gave me another option, saying, "If you don't want to go, then just don't go any further inside or outside without me. I'll be back."

"I'm not staying here," I decided aloud. With trepidation I followed along with her, as she transitioned us back into the aether and then out again on the other side of the plasma ring. It was a weird experience to be popping in and out of this reality so quickly; like turning a light off and then on again. Yet the ordeal was quickly overshadowed by the realization of our proximity to the event horizon. Being this close to the event horizon, I couldn't deny there was still a bit of a compelling force about its nature. It felt more like a moderate current flow, rather than an inescapable suction from which we might never return. As I dwelled upon our situation, I rationalize as to the black holes weakened influence upon us: technically we have no mass, so perhaps we should not really be affected by its gravitational pull at all.

"That may be, but we are not void of energy," Fairy advised. "So there is still an attraction. I would caution you to not get ahead of me."

"I'll never get use to this astral condition," I thought aloud to Fairy. "Is there no real privacy in this astral form?"

"Not while our auras embrace each other," Fairy responded. "However, if you would rather go it alone, just let me know."

"No, I don't value my privacy that much," I answered.

"Well, we are about to become three. There is the figure just ahead," she alerted me.

As we neared the figure, it disappeared from site. I scanned the area as best as I could, looking for the unknown figure, but this was a very big area. The more we looked, the more the fear of being this close to the black hole's event horizon began to wear away at my self-confidence. And yet I couldn't help myself from peering into on the black hole from this vantage point. Even as I could see nothing, save the plasma ring outside of it, the black hole seemed to have its own metaphysical properties. It was as if the black hole were a life force unto itself, compelling me to enter.

"Don't you think we've probably spent enough time out-of-body already?" I questioned aloud to Fairy. But when there came no answer, I found her lack of response was a bit disconcerting. Knowing that when we were comingled she could always listen to my thoughts, I began to wonder if we were still connected. In my panic, I began to look around for Fairy instead of the mysterious figure which faded from sight as we approached it. Ironically, even though there was the ever present bright ring of energy just outside the event horizon, it provided no light from which to see beyond the event horizon and into the black hole. As I continued to peer into the abyss, it was strange how the dark seemed to have depth and substance. It would be easy for someone to hide in that inky blackness. Then, before I realized what I was doing, I was already closer to the event horizon than I wanted to be, and I was being pulled every closer towards it. Then, to my relief, I believed I found Fairy.

"There you are," I acknowledged. "Why didn't you answer me?"

But as I began to bring her into focus, I realized that it wasn't Fairy at all. It was instead another member of our team, Vera. And the shock of her unexpected appearance scared the bejesus out of me.

"Help me," was all I could hear Vera echo out towards me.

As I tried to focus in on her, she just seemed to fade from view again. As she disappeared, my sense of my environment went dark. I soon found myself losing control of my individual out-of-body experience. Where was Fairy? Then I imagined distinctively hearing a harp-like melody. Had Fairy taken control again?

"Andrew, Andrew," I could hear someone call out. But that someone sounded like Dr. Beecher, rather than Fairy. Slowly I began to see a light. There seemed to be a light passing back and forth in front of my eyes.

"Let me try," I could hear Mairy request. "Andrew, wake up. I need you to wake up for me."

"Wake up?" I asked. "Am I asleep?"

"Not any longer," I could hear Milo saying in the background. "You'd think you prefer your dreamscape world more than the real world."

"OK, now I know I'm awake," I announced, waking up a bit groggy. "Is the session over then?" I asked without thinking.

"For everyone except you, it would seem," Tim relayed in a similarly joking fashion.

"Man, we thought you were just going to stay in dreamland," Milo stated.

"Perhaps, we need to readjust his CONS unit a bit," I could hear Dr. Beecher speculating.

"No, I don't think that's necessary," I said, beginning to command my own consciousness again. "I was just a little overtired, I think. I didn't sleep well last night," I said, making up an excuse.

I just didn't want them readjusting anything, as there was already enough distraction going on without any further changes.

"That is not for you to decide. You still look a bit pale to me," Dr. Beecher observed aloud. "Can you two help him out of the pod," Dr. Beecher requested of Tim and Milo.

Then without warning, I momentarily blacked out. The next thing I was conscious of was Milo's voice saying, "Whoa, let's not go back to sleep now."

"What he needs is a little more rest and less sleep," Tim commented aloud.

"Can you two help him off the floor?" Dr. Beecher requested of Tim and Milo.

"I'm on the floor?" I asked with some confusion. "How did I get on the floor?"

"You know what is worse than being on floor?" Milo asked rhetorically. "Not knowing you're on the floor."

"OK, thank you guys. Lindsey and I can handle this," offered Mairy, looking to Lindsey to agree. "We can accompany him to the medical station."

"Yes, that would be an excellent idea," Lindsey agreed. "We wouldn't want you two dropping him again."

"Alright then, you two take him up to medical," Dr. Beecher agreed with Mairy and Lindsey. "But remember, you all still need to record your experiences as soon as possible," Dr. Beecher informed them. "And that especially means you as well, Andrew."

As we left the room, I could hear Dr. Beecher saying to Milo and Tim, "You two can start on your logs now."

Then she seemed to be speaking to the CONS unit technician, "Randy, can you readjust the monitoring characteristics on this unit to include modulation of brain wave patterns outside of the cognitive region."

"Won't that change the outcome of the translated output?" I heard the technician ask.

"Not if you filter it properly. Honestly, do I have to think of everything myself?" Dr. Beecher persisted.

Their voices waned with our distance from it, as Mairy and Lindsey helped me along to the elevator.

"Hang in there big guy," Mairy said, encouraging me to stay awake.

[Andrew's Perspective continued]

We continued together out of the lab and up to the medical facility. It was just a short ride to the upper floors via the elevator. I'm sure, for Mairy, this was as much of a reconnaissance mission to her as it was of an excuse to get me away from Dr. Beecher. There is no telling what I might have said in my condition. But I was not sure why she included Lindsey.

[The causality of fate is reflective of even unintended consequences.]

As we rode up the elevator, Lindsey made some small talk. "You took quite a fall out of your pod station," she said. "No thanks to Milo and Tim, who were supposed to be helping you."

"I don't remember falling," I responded.

"Then I guess you must have fainted straight away," Lindsey surmised.

Changing the subject, Mairy asked Lindsey, "I didn't see Vera after the session. Do you have any idea where she went?"

"Not really," Lindsey answered. "She was one of the first ones out the door, when the session ended. She spoke briefly with Dr. Beecher, and then left; probably to excuse herself. It would seem she missed all the excitement with your brother."

"Yes," Mairy agreed. "We'll need to tell her about what she missed."

As we exited the elevator, Lindsey guided us through to the emergency services. "I think we can take it from here," Mairy related to Lindsey. "Thank you for your help."

"OK, yes; then I must be getting back," Lindsey agreed. "Andrew, I hope you'll be feeling much better very soon. See you both in the recreation area later after lunch."

"Yes," I echoed a response to her offer, "see you in the recreation center."

I spent the next half hour signing in, filling out paperwork, and waiting in the patient receiving area to be seen. In short, it was a typical visit to the doctor's office. That is to say, it was pretty much the same here as it was on Earth. Upon completing the forms, I was ushered off to an examination room to wait again. Then, after a quick examine, they ushered me back to the patient receiving area to wait some more while they completed their paperwork. I felt like it was all a waste of my time. At least Mairy was still here. Scanning the room for privacy, I approached her about what may have happened to us in the session.

"So did you see Vera as well?" I asked; "in the aether, I mean?"

"I know what you mean," she replied. "And yes, I tried to include Vera into our aural veil, but she kept fading in and out. It seemed like she didn't have a whole lot of control, or she wasn't really there at all. I can't really say which."

"Well, she seemed real enough to me," I said, revealing my encounter. "And she seemed to be doing pretty well for a beginner. I mean, how did she even get passed her scripted dreamscape?"

"Maybe she wasn't even aware she was outside of her dreamscape," Mairy considered thoughtfully. "Maybe we inadvertently pulled her in; like via some neurological wake from our integrated brain waves."

"A neurological wake; is that even a real thing, or did you just make it up?" I asked with confusion.

"I wonder if she saw us as well," Mairy posed as a possibility.

"I believe she must have seen me," I recalled. "When I lost track of you, it was like I could hear her calling out for me to help her. 'Help me', she called out. I could've really used your help then."

"Yes, sorry about that," Mairy revealed. "I was probably the cause of it all. I believe I momentarily disconnected with you when I tried to include Vera in our group aura. I hope it didn't alarm you."

"What me? No," I replied, putting on a macho front. "I figured you must've been preoccupied. Anyway, it was quite disturbing to have our own private astral time together interrupted without any warning," I said, still remembering the shock of seeing the unexpected appearance of Vera. "And it would appear that there is more to Vera than she lets on," I added, getting back to our discussion about Vera.

"Perhaps; we can't really know more without talking to her," Mairy was quick to dismiss Vera's competence. "She could just be an innocent victim of our bumbling about. But then that could still mean, at the very least, that she has the gift."

"Yeah, I guess you could be right," I agreed. "But who knows how this new interface is messing with us or the inner workings of our CONS units anyway." Then I pursued a discussion of her previous supposition. "So what did you mean about the wake from our brain waves?" I asked more pointedly.

"Well, you remember Dr. Beecher told us that we were governing the behavior of the others via the master control pods, and that we would need to keep the group on task?" Mairy asked.

"Yes, I remember that," I acknowledged.

"And that whatever we do in our dreams would influence the dreamscape of the other team members as well?" her prodding me continued. "Perhaps our emotional responses elicited a neurological wake."

"What, like an astral distress beacon of sorts?" I replied. "I guess there is that possibility. You would know more about that stuff than I would. But in my defense, it was not something I could control while we were facing that torrent of terror."

"So her appearance may have been our own fault. We may have inadvertently put her life at risk." Then Mairy cautioned me further, "As long as we are hooked up to these pods, we need to consider the consequences of our actions on the others."

Then to our surprise, mom showed up, saying, "Andrew, are you alright?"

"Mom?" I addressed her with incredulity! "Where did you come from, and what are you doing here?"

"Well, what a nice greeting for your mother," mom responded sarcastically. "How about, it is lovely you see you again, mother. So glad you could come."

"Oh, mom, I didn't even know you were here yet," I answered apologetically, as I stood up to greet her.

Mom hugged me first, and then Mairy.

"How do you think I feel," was mom's retort. "I just got here late last night, and they told me pulled me out of orientation this morning to tell me about your episode. Imagine my alarm when they said that you had been taken to the medical facility."

We all sat down for a quick get together.

"I'm fine," I informed her. Nothing more embarrassing than an over protective parent getting involved, I thought to myself. "It was just a dizzy spell."

"Just a dizzy spell," Mairy repeated, as she joined in. "It rather goes with the job we are doing, it appears. But why are you up here so early? We heard you weren't schedule to come until the next shuttle run."

"I spoke with your father just before they hustled me on board the shuttle," mom answered. "It appears the company accelerated the schedule to bring me up here earlier after they made some great breakthrough. But your father speculates that there is more going on than he is being told."

"What do you mean?" Mairy probes further.

"I gather from what and how he said it, that they are looking to maximize their leverage over him," mom shared with us. "But that could just be your father's paranoia."

"Or that might mean they are on to us," Mairy ventured.

"I'm inclined to agree with him, as I was escorted up here personally by Kiana," mom added.

Just then a nurse walked up and introduced herself to mom, greeting her, "You must be Mrs. Bauer. I was told to expect you." After exchanging niceties, the nurse summarized my diagnosis as being under the influence of a mild flu virus, and there was really nothing to worry about.

Listening in on the diagnosis, I blurted out, "What, on the Moon? How does one get a cold on the Moon?"

The nurse obligingly provided us with an answer, explaining, "Everyone biological entity hosts a variety of bacteria and viruses. It is rather like the building blocks of life itself; a left over from our evolutionary progression to a higher life form. Some of these bacteria and viruses are good, or less harmful, and some are not. Normally bacteria and viruses are at odds with each other in the body. But it tends to be a fragile alliance that the body is able to handle it. And while viruses can actively mutate within the body, the bacteria normally keeps any mutated versions of the virus abated."

"Wow," I responded to her delivery. "I don't think I ever had it presented to me in quite that way before."

"Yes, I tend to take a more holistic approach to the human condition." The nurse continued, "As to this condition, sometimes, under stress, the body becomes vulnerable to the bacteria or viruses they host. And then, as a matter of routine, we have to make sure that these viruses are not contagious. As you can probably guess, a contagious virus, in such an enclosed proximity, could pose a significant challenge for our medical staff. For now, we recommend a couple of days off before you go back to work."

"How can you be so sure it was something I brought with me?" I asked.

"I can't, but we have a rather controlled environment from which to isolate the source of these pathogens quickly. And over the years we have found that it is actually the newcomers that tend to introduce new versions of such pathogens into this more controlled population," the nurse answered. "As you may already know, introducing new versions of bacteria and viruses into a host can cause many complications. That is why we screened out most of these pathogens on Earth before the individuals are allowed to come up to the Moon. We then rescreen individuals during their scheduled physicals. I see here that you haven't yet been scheduled for a physical up here. Well this checkup will do for now."

I guess we kind of missed the medical screening part by impulsively stowing away on board the shuttle.

"What are pathogens?" Mairy asked inquisitively.

"Pathogens, or pathogenic versions of bacteria and viruses, are those harmful bacteria and viruses that are passed between living hosts. Since the body is not prepared to handle more than what has already evolved within them, the body has little defense against any new intruders. Anyway, he's fine," the nurse concluded. The nurse then looked to mom, "He should drink more fluids and avoid any exercise for the rest of today. Oh, and have him set up a full physical with our office as soon as convenient."

It was kind of the traditional diagnosis that leaves one embarrassed for having to come to the medical center for such a menial problem: Take two aspirin and go to bed. Yet, it was better than being interrogated further by Dr. Beecher. I couldn't help feeling that she would've wanted to continue to probe me for answers until she satisfied.

"Thank goodness," mom replied. "I'm glad to hear that it is nothing to worry about. Thank you." Then as the nurse left us, mom confessed, "I'm starving; what is there to eat up here? I haven't had anything since I left Earth."

I looked to Mairy, stating, "There's something you two have in common."

Mairy gave me an accepting grin and then turned her attention to mom, saying, "It is something that I have grown accustomed to since we first met. Let me show you to the cafeteria where you can have your first real meal of synthetic pancakes in outer space."

"Synthetic food takes some getting used to," I quipped. "But I guess if you are hungry, you won't really notice."

"Oh, pay no attention to him. Having not had much food on Earth, I find the food here quite tasty," Mairy responded with a little more respect. "All he does is complain about how it doesn't quite taste the same."

"I'm sure whatever it is, I will like it," mom replied. "I haven't had a bite to eat for hours."

We reigned in our discussion of the strange and weird happenings of our recent session while in the food line, and then chose a table in the back where we could talk in private.

"Have you seen Steve yet?" Mairy asked mom.

"No, I just got in late last night," mom answered, "and then when I arrived, I was pretty tired. Then my scheduled called for this morning's orientation and then lunch with you two. Between you and me, I don't mind getting out of the orientation for a little while. How often do you get to meet with him?"

"Oh, dad," I said, jumping in on the conversation. "I don't know if it is all dad's work schedule, or the company's deference to security," I added, "but we don't see dad as much as we would like."

"And how goes the investigation?" mom inquired.

"You have some catching up to do," Mairy stated. "There have been modifications to our equipment, and we may be in danger of showing our hand before we know what their plan is."

"Or we may have already been discovered," I alluded to our encounter with Vera. "All we really know is that they have modified the equipment to work with 'dark matter'," I informed her. "And only dad knows about dark matter, so only he can predict how it might be used or abused."

"Slow down you two. I don't understand any of this. So you believe there is something going on up here?" mom asked.

"Yes, it appears that this is our path to resolving our quest," Mairy acknowledged.

"So then you believe you are close to resolving the reason that brought Mairy down to Earth?" mom pursued further.

"Mom, she didn't 'come down' to Earth," I said, correcting her. "She's not even from our dimensional reality."

"Oh, yes, I forgot," mom was quick to apologize, probably not wanting to hurt my feelings.

"It is quite beside the point, Andrew," Mairy snuffed out any distraction from the discussion. "And it not necessary for you to correct your mother in that manner all the time; especially in my presence."

"OK; sorry mom," I apologized.

"And yes, I believe there is more going on than just the strange appearance of the beast," she established. "There seems to be a great interest in the pursuit of this ability to detect dark matter. And we believe that our involvement in the project is not just a random happenstance. We think that it was by design that we were pulled into this situation. And if something going to happen, then we need to get ahead of it soon."

"You say you believe it was designed that you two where included on this project?" mom asked with curiosity. "How is that possible?"

"The Tokoloshe," I declared. "Something was driving it to push us into these decisions. And what better way to influence our decisions than to put us in danger. I mean we wouldn't even be here now, at this time, if it wasn't for that beast."

"That seems to make sense," mom agreed. "And you believe the same thing?" she asked of Mairy. "Yes," Mairy responded, and then prompted mom to continue. "Why, what are you thinking?"

"I'm thinking that if it was arranged, then they must have understood that Mairy would come to your rescue if you were threatened," mom hypothesized. "Think about it. Have seen that talking goblin since you left Earth? Someone made sure that Mairy would show up here, and that we would be willing to leave Earth with you."

"And then there is dad's mysterious job opportunity," I said, throwing my thoughts into the mix. "We would not even be here, if he wasn't recruited for this position."

"Agreed, so this dark matter experiment must be critical to the purpose of this quest," Mairy concluded.

"Hey," I thought aloud, "that's similar to my earlier quest. Remember that mad scientist who was also conducting an experiment? It later ended up threatening to tip the balance of power towards chaos."

"So what you two are doing may affect the balance of the universe?" mom asked with apprehension.

"It's what we do," I said, feeling quite proud of my involvement.

"Everything affects the balance of the universe in a small way, one way of the other," Mairy said, attempting

to calm the situation. "It is only up to us to keep the balance from bearing too far toward chaos."

"So if this is going to be a much a larger problem, with the universal balance and all," I started, "shouldn't we expect to see Harmony for some guidance?"

"Harmony only shows up when there is no one handling the problem," Mairy replied. "Be an adult already. We are handling the problem!" I could see that Mairy was getting short tempered with me always bringing up Harmony when things got tough.

"We don't even know what the problem is," I responded with exasperation. "How are we handling it?" There was a common pause, as we looked about to see what affect my outburst may have had.

Mairy finally broke the silence. "If we weren't on the right path, then Harmony would've already intervened," Mairy explained. "So since there is no Harmony, we must be doing alright."

"Unless, of course, we are horning in on someone else's quest," I ventured to speculate.

Looking past Mairy to the large screen monitor in the cafeteria, I was momentarily distracted by a breaking news story. It appeared there was a new record set for the high water tidal range. A new record of 63 feet was recorded in the Bay of Fundy on the Atlantic coast of North America. It was highest tidal range ever recorded anywhere on Earth. I then return to our conversation, not really remembering where we left off.

"Which brings to mind the sudden appearance of Vera at the site of the black hole in this morning's session," I added, just interjecting it into the conversation.

"Vera, who's Vera?" mom asked.

"She is one of the other pod operators on our team," I answered. "She was here before we came up."

"What does she have to do with any of this?" mom asked, continuing to inquire further.

"We don't know yet," I started to explain. "She showed up during our last out-of-body meeting in deep space."

"Out-of-body meeting; you mean like astral projection?" mom asked, gathering more information.

"Yes," I acknowledged. "We are astrally projected ourselves to those areas of deep space which were being targeted for detection of gravitational wave variances."

"What? Why?" mom asked, flabbergasted at the thought of what they were involved in.

"The intent of the experiment is to capture and interpret these wave variations from which they can generate these fantastic 3D perspectives. They require our minds to integrate with our own brainwave patterns in order to translate them into real images," Mairy explained in simple terms for mom.

"But for us, it was the wonder of actually being there that was the greatest thrill," I remarked.

"Yes, something like that," Mairy admitted to her complicatedness. "But I don't believe we can say the same for Vera. I don't know if Vera even realized what was happening to her. She seemed to be flickering in and out, like she was about to appear, but then didn't."

"Hey, remember you said that Vera may have just been pulled in via a neurological wake we inadvertently created," I reminded her. "Maybe there was something to how we interacted with spacetime when we astrally projected ourselves from within our dreamscapes."

At this point, it appeared mom had just given into listening in on our random recollections of what was going on; contributing where she could.

"Or maybe there was a more tangible connection that brought her with you," mom suggested, not even asking about my reference to our dreamscapes.

"What do you mean?" asked Mairy.

"There is a belief that a 'silver cord' binds the out-of-body experience to its physical host. It is said to be the path by which the soul maintains it connection with its physical body," mom recalled. "Once the connection is broken, there is no returning back to the host body and the host body dies. Perhaps these connections could somehow have been entangled or intertwined, dragging along other souls to your location."

"Kind of like an electrical short," I concluded. "Maybe that's why Vera seemed to be flickering in and out."

"Since I have little to do up here at the moment, other than cater after you two, perhaps I could research 'astral projection' on the internet," mom offered.

"That is, of course, between the paperwork and filings for a new, more family friendly residence on this moon station. I still can't get over the fact that we are on the Moon," she began to reminisce of her recent happenings. "The ride up here was more or less surreal, like the sci-fi shows your father has us watch with him, because everything was presented to us via a monitor. There were no real windows accessible to the passengers for viewing."

"Well, there is not much more to outer space, except for the clarity of view up here. We can't go outside, and we only see the landscape of the Moon through a window," I said, allowing her tell us what was going on with her. "And while we don't ever face the Earth, we do see the sun regularly every two weeks. It rises and sets just like clockwork up here, with no interference from any weather. And there is the added bonus of no natural disasters up here," I said with some resolve.

"And when it is dark, as it is now, it provides for a spectacular illusion; it is as if you could just reach out and touch the stars," Mairy said, painting a more emotional perspective of being up here.

"Perhaps it won't be as bad as I might have imagined," mom said. The tone of her voice seemed like she was already homesick for Earth. "So I guess I should get back to the orientation, or whatever it is they are doing now. I'll see you two later. We can all have dinner with your father tonight."

"Yes, we would like that," Mairy stated, speaking for the both of us.

Mairy seemed somehow comfortable speaking for us; as if she didn't imagine ever being apart from this family. We exchanged hugs with mom and then watched her walk away towards the elevator.

"We still need to complete our personal assessment logs before the afternoon meeting starts," Mairy reminded me.

"Right, back to work," I said, thinking how we might be able to stay working up here for a while. I can work with mom so that she is not so homesick, I thought to myself. Maybe they have an area up here where we could garden, or something. I mean the Moon is nothing but dirt. "Hey, it's not so bad up here," I commented to Mairy. "What do you think?"

"Here or on Earth, it is all the same to me," Mairy replied, as we made our way back to our rooms. "It just seems that up here our options for survival are rather limited to this moon station. Conceptually, it feels rather claustrophobic."

For me, it was like a homecoming. With mom now here, we were a close knit family again. Now everyone was here together on the Moon. While some say home is where the heart is, as for me, I would rather ascribed to the notion that home is where the family is. Still, I wondered what it felt like for Mairy. I wondered if she had similar feelings, and if she missed her home. I wondered if she missed her family, or if she even had a family. I hadn't really thought about her not having a family, but she never really talked about it. Then still, we were all her family now. At least I could not think of her as not part of our family.

[Narrator's Perspective]

Andrew and family were quite unaware of the unintended consequences caused by their involvement with the pod sleepers. As Mairy had stated, everything affects the balance of the universe in a small way. In this regard, on Earth, there was an influx of meteorological activity as a result of their latest session. Of this they were all unaware; everyone, save Tom. As a foreboding of Andrew's weakened condition, the Earth was having its own growing pains. There was a marked increase in the number and strength of earthquakes occurring around the world. High and low tides were beginning to supplant the norms for many centuries of stability. Volcanic activity was on the rise as well. These significant occurrences were symptomatic of a change in the relationship between the Earth and its Moon. Soon, even the timing of the 24 day would need to be recalibrated upon the consequences of their involvement.

So while these events are not seemingly contributing to a much larger problem now, much like its impact on the universal balance, they will eventually seed the potential to cause greater chaos; not only for the Earth, but for the universe at large. Indeed, the causality of fate is reflective even for the most noble of unintended consequences. It is reflective of an encapsulation for the chaos theory unto the butterfly effect: i.e., Small causes can have larger effects. The chaos that expounds upon the transitions between order and disorder can often occur in surprising ways. Because we can never really know all the initial conditions of a complex system in sufficient detail, we cannot hope to predict the ultimate fate of that complex system. Who can say whether the flapping of butterfly wings in New Mexico would not actually contribute to the power causing a hurricane in China, or whether it could even be the actual tipping point for the instigation of such a hurricane. Thus, Andrew and Mairy could not be wholly aware that what there were doing would not have far reaching unintended consequences.

CHAPTER

15

Encounters of the Fourth Kind—Loss of Control

[Living the dream is not all that it is cracked up to be.]

There is more than one kind of quest. There is the quest for wealth, power, glory, or even eternal life. There is the quest to right a wrong; providing for the adventurous journey of a hero to thwart a villain. Then there is the villain's quest, which instigated the hero's quest. Each quest has its own purpose and goal, and each ends in a clash of destinies toward one ultimate fate.

Then there is the quest for ultimate knowledge or truth. These quests are perhaps the most arduous; for how does one know when these goals have been achieved, when each success tends to move the goalpost further ahead? And if one does not realize his quest, has the journey been all for naught? While there are many successes and celebrations along the way, one tends to subvert the collateral damage which accompanies such victories. Very often the collateral damage is unimaginable, and the worth of the quest is weighs its accomplishments against its calamities.

[Scene Change – Narrator's Perspective]

Building upon the excitement of their previous accomplishments, the IGIE research team members were elated to pour over the results of the pod sleeper's last session. Andrew's medical leave was a convenient respite from which they could pause to enjoy their most recent success. The anticipation of becoming pioneers, in their respective fields of research, spurred them to carefully generate the data and complete their assigned tasks. One mistake, however, could cost them to doubt their own results. For this reason, they needed to be meticulous in the execution of their labors. They needed to prove to themselves, as well as to anyone else, that their results were pristine.

Finally completed, their expectations were rewarded, and even surpassed, by the new images that were generated and developed through IGIE. Furthermore, they were able to manipulate the images of the black hole, as planned, to provide for a larger than life, three-dimensional representation of its event horizon, along with the plasma ring just outside of it. As they did so, they were treated to IGIE's new ability to model the translated input of dark energy wave variances in real time. Indeed, they wanted to be able to see beyond the edge of the event horizon and into the black hole itself, but this was close enough for now.

"We have it!" John exclaimed with excitement. "This is the breakthrough that we had been searching for."

"I don't know how your team did it, but it is easy to see that these images are not just based on gravitational wave variances," Phil admitted to Tom. "This is beyond anything we could have imagined."

"It is as we explained to you earlier," Tom related to the team, trying to bring down their level of excitement so that they could better focus on the data at hand. "Based on Steve's theory for dark matter, we were able to craft an algorithm that would allow us to measure negative density in the degrees of absence, relative to the increase in gravitational deceleration beyond the event horizon. It is these degrees of negative density that are permitting us to generate the dark matter variances seen in these images."

"This is unprecedented," Margaret stated, looking over the 3D imaging. "We are now able to peer into and beyond the event horizon itself. It is like looking at a negative in photography in reverse, wherein the negative density areas of the developed images appear darker then the positive density areas."

Steve had remained silent in the tribute of the moment, until now. "Lady and gentlemen, we are the first to witness the universe beyond the veil of our own reality," Steve couldn't help 'preaching to the choir', for it was as he had always imagined it, but could now express it with greater self-esteem.

"Underlying our fourth dimensional perspective of existence is the medium upon which all is contained; where the void of dark energy reflects the previous order in which the universe 'was', prior to the introduction of baryonic matter. Everything we have been exploring up to now was built upon the foundation of this pre-existing medium; for it was, or should I say 'is', the progenitor for the creation of baryonic matter," he presented with the confidence gained from experimental proof."

And it is here, where positive density matter predicates an intrusion upon this medium of a non-baryonic affirmation of nothingness, that creation grounded the insistence of its establishment within negative density matter: or dark matter. As a consequence of this introduction into positive density matter, the engendering of dark energy became the natural offset to medium of gravitational energy that pervades our fourth dimensional existence. Thereby embedding both mirrored forces within the universe upon alternate evolutionary paths for our conjoined realities. And what we are now able to see here, is the collision of these two alternate paths for the consequence of our own reality," he concluded.

"Here, here," John and Phil proclaimed in tandem, as they each raised a water bottle in a toast to their success. The rest of the group obliged them by raising their water bottles in kind.

"Perhaps with time, we will even be able to discover the very engine of creation itself," Margaret related with true amazement.

"So, per your previous hypothesis, what we are seeing here is the present time existence of the black hole," John began to think aloud. "Therefore, we can expect Hubble to capture this image of matter disintegration along the event horizon in about 23 million years. And now, we also know that the Whirlpool Galaxy will still be in existence for the next 23 million years. Indeed, we actually have evidence of an ability to see into the future of our own ability to image the deep space locations."

"With this information, we will be able to more accurately plan out space travel missions to solar systems that are any number of light years away," Phil speculated.

"Sure, and now all we have to do is build a vehicle that can travel fast enough to make it feasible," Margaret spoke out contrary to the hopes and dreams of many. While not a physicist by trade, she seemed to have a good grasp of what all would be involve in practically use of this technology.

"You and your team are to be congratulated, Margaret," Tom encouraged, sensing her contributions might be overshadowed by the events of this discovery. "Without your vision, we would have still been stumbling about in a mire of technological innovations trying to do what the human brain was already designed for."

"Thank you," Margaret graciously accepted his acknowledgement of her part in this discovery.

While looking through the generated images that made up the time-lapse perspective, Steve became distracted upon viewing a few particular images. It was the images displaying the ever brightening illumination that got him thinking about his children.

"And how are our pod operators doing?" Steve inquired.

"They haven't all handed in their session logs at this time," Margaret started.

"No; I meant were there any more physical problems?" Steve interrupted to probe further.

"There were a few issues," Margaret admitted. "Your son had some trouble coming back to consciousness, and he seemed a little nauseated, so we sent him up to the medical center with his sister."

"And you didn't think I might want to know about that," Steve asked with an angry tone?

"I didn't believe it was worth troubling you, until we knew more," Margaret stated. "Besides we were able to have your wife sent up to them in your place."

"Thank you for that thoughtfulness," Steve said, calming down a bit. "But in the future I would like to be informed of any problems involving my children as well."

Steve paused a moment to consider his position and the family's ulterior motives for being here. He continued to probe further, asking more politely, "And what of the other operators; was there anything out of the ordinary?"

"For the most part, no," Margaret admitted.

"For the most part," Tom said, also expressing his concern. "What do you mean?"

"Well, Vera seemed to be a bit flustered when she woke up, and she excused herself straight away to go to the bathroom," Margaret further admitted. "And that was just before the incident with Andrew. When I later asked the others about Vera, they just related a similar impression of her behavior to me. They told me that she seemed to be a bit shaken up from the last session, but that she did not seem to want to talk about with them. I'm sure she'll explain any problems she may have had, in detail, in her session logs. She's very good about that. So as soon as I know more, I'll let you know."

"OK, all this can wait, for now," Tom announced, as he had more at stake here than even Margaret realized. "I want all the pod operators accounted for and checked out as soon as possible. Their health and well-being is of primary importance to the success of our project. They are key to this research, and I am not going to the board with a one-time success."

"Alright Tom; I'll see to it right away," Margaret agreed like she had just been scolded, and left the room.

"Thank you for your interest," Steve acknowledged of Tom seemingly sincere concern for the pod sleepers.

"Well, I'm not all business, I assure you," Tom related to me. "Still, without the pod operators, all this research comes to a screeching halt. Go on ahead; you should check on your family as well."

Then Tom directed his attention to John and Phil, saying, "You two can continue correlating this first set of data provided from IGIE. I will try and come up with some meaningful presentation for all of this. We can all meet later in the conference room and discuss it more, before presenting it to the board."

It would seem that the team's individual self-interests were enough to distract them from uncovering Tom's more ambitious and nefarious purpose. Having cleverly occupied the team with meaningful tasks, Tom was able to sift through the data at his leisure. He was seemed obsessed with what the generated images had yet to reveal. In these images Tom hoped to see a larger overview of the swirling visage of atomic plasma, just outside the event horizon boundary of the black hole of the Whirlpool Galaxy.

As he studied them more closely, he got more than he bargained for. In the latter images they had yet to review, he found what he deemed to be the signature of the Higgs Boson, or 'god particle'. A generated time lapse of the captured images demonstrating what appeared to be matter disintegrating into the swirling ring, approaching the event horizon. This is what he was looking for, and this is what he deemed that the others did not need to know. He carefully remove the revealing sequence and redirected it to his private computer; for he was not yet ready to have others stumble onto this information, especially Stephen.

Tom quickly left for his office and went through the process of developing a time lapse view of the event. It was a representation of quark–gluon plasma in the midst of an ever brightening illumination. The quark soup, he quickly conjectured, provided a medium of matter in quantum chromodynamics (QCD), which is hypothesized to exist at extremely high temperature or density, or both temperature and density. It is believed that up to a few milliseconds after the Big Bang, known as the Quark epoch, the Universe was in a quark–gluon plasma state. While discovery of the Higgs boson could validate the Standard Model of particle physics through to the mechanism of mass generation, it may also lead to another more important interaction: the 'Selfish Biocosm' hypothesis. If measurements of the Higgs boson reveal that our universe lies within a false vacuum, which is not completely stable, then the universe as we know it could effectively be destroyed by collapsing into a more stable vacuum state. This would imply that the universe's forces, particles, and structures could cease to exist as we know them.

[Scene Change – Narrator's Perspective continued]

Steve went to the Human Resource office to find the whereabouts of his family. As he passed by the windows to the exterior, he thought of how he missed the vista of blue skies and green vegetation on Earth. The stark landscape of the Moon became an everyday reminder of their isolated sanctuary. Amazing as it was to be on the Moon, he could never reach out and touch the soil of the Moon with his bare hand or be free to look out to the evening sky from its surface without a spacesuit; for there was always the ever present awareness of death by exposure to the elements. And for their location on the Moon, this would mean exposure to solar radiation, lack or pressure, lack of breathable air, and to the extreme flux in temperature; any of which would provide for a particularly painful death. It appears worrying about the family brings out the worst of possible scenarios from which things might go wrong.

Reaching the information desk, he asked about his family, "My name is Stephen Bauer, and I am looking for the members of my family: my wife Sandra, my son Andrew, and my daughter Mairy. Can you tell me where they are?"

"Do you know where they should be, or where they were last seen?" the HR administrator inquired.

"Oh yes, sorry. I understand that they were last together in the medical facility," Steve answered.

"Let me call up there," she said. She set up the call from her computer. Waiting for an answer, she started an information log.

Shortly, a nurse appeared on the computer screen, answering, "You have reached the medical center. I am Kali, the resident nurse on call."

"Yes, hello, this is the administrator. I'd like to inquire about the family members of Stephen Bauer."

"Oh, yes, they were here, but they left about an hour ago," the nurse conveyed. "Mrs. Bauer needed to get back to orientation, and the children left with her."

"Can you ask her if there were any health problems with my son, Andrew?" Steve asked.

Before the administrator could ask, the nurse offered a response, "I heard the question. Andrew is fine. It appears he had a mild case of nausea due to a viral infection. His symptomatic response is similar to motion sickness. It can be a little disorienting up here if you don't keep up with your recreational activities."

"Yes, I'm sure that is what it must have been," Steve acknowledged. "Thank you."

"Will that be all then?" the nurse asked.

I nodded to the administrator, and she replied, "Yes, thank you for your help."

"Will you be needing anything else, sir?" the administrator asked.

"Yes, do you know what room they are using for orientation today?" he asked.

"The main conference room," was her short answer. "From the schedule here, it looks like orientation is about to break for lunch in just a few minutes," she informed him.

"Thank you; you have been very helpful," he acknowledged. He then walked briskly to meet up with his wife before she left the area of the main conference room. As the main conference room was just around the corner from administration, he did not have far to go.

Upon seeing her, he called to her loudly enough to get her attention, "Sandi."

Sandi smiled and came over for a big hug and a kiss.

"Wow," he acknowledge of her enthusiastic hug. "I love you too. Any problems with the trip in?" Steve asked.

"No, it was smoother than a plane ride once the shuttle separated from the cargo airliner. I just spent my time watching the monitor and catching up on some reading," Sandi responded. "However, it was a little strange that there was no family to greet me when I arrived."

"Sorry about that," he apologized. "We just had this great breakthrough in our research on the project and Tom wanted 'all hands on deck for this one'. But Tom assured me that Kiana would be traveling up with you. Did she get you settled in alright?"

"Yes, she directed me to where orientation would be, and had my luggage brought to your room," she explained. "They seem very efficient up here."

"Indeed, it is like a grand hotel with all the 5 star treatment to go with it. Who would've thought the Moon was a vacation destination?" Steve asked.

"Yeah, some vacation; more like a secretive cultish institution, if you ask me. You can't really go anywhere outside. And where are the lakes, waterfalls, lavish forest views, and mountain vistas," Sandi lamented.

"I see it more as a theme park. And everything here is free," Steve said, trying to put it all in a better light. "You have to admit, it is quite the adventure just riding up here. Wouldn't you agree?" Steve asked.

Sandi gave an awkward glance at her surroundings. So Steve forged ahead with their conversation with blissful optimism, "Anyway, it won't be forever."

"Hey look at this," he said pulling a pen from his pocket and tossing it up into the air. As it fell in slow motion, he snatched it from the air. "We're on the Moon! This is the chance of a lifetime. Where else in the world can you have these great reflexes?" Sandi only smiled as Steve continued to support the experience.

"And you know what this means don't you?" he present in a quizzical manner. "Sex is going to be a whole new experience up here. As a matter of fact, I have been looking forward to a little time alone with you."

"I would hope so," she acknowledged, "You weren't in the room when I arrived, and it's been months since we were together."

"Another plus is that major accidents are not much of an issue up here. You'd be hard pressed to break a bone in a fall up here," he added to his positive view of being up on the Moon.

"Oh, sure, but then to offset the lack of gravity, you need to exercise twice a day," she replied.

"True, but then exercise is fun up here," he continued. "It's difficult to even raise a sweat. And speaking of accidents, I was told that you already saw the kids," he said, making a change in the conversation.

"Yes, I must admit it was a bit of a scare," she started in. "I hadn't even completed orientation before they called me out for a family emergency."

"Nothing like a good family emergency to re-orient yourself within your new surroundings," he kidded her. "No matter how old the children get, there is always something new to deal with."

"Yeah, well this one is on you," she retorted. "What have you gotten the children into anyway?

"Nothing they can't handle, I'm sure," he replied. "Besides, they are pretty much running the show up here, so to speak. So far, Andrew has had another revealing dream, and they seem to be getting closer to whatever it is that our Shadow-Forge Mairy is up here for. And since I believe all communication is monitored around here, I don't dare risk the chance of sharing anything more with you right now."

"Just remember, this is not one of your stories," Sandi said with motherly concern. "This is real life, with real consequences; and these are our children."

"Children grow up," he responded. "And you've got to let the children grow up." Steve ushered her off to a more secluded corner. "Besides, at his age, I was already in the military service with the possibility of being put in harm's way. Fortunately, it won't have to come to that with the kids. But this is who he is, and this is who were are, and this is what we need to do if that's what it takes," he paused to collect his thoughts.

"Well, this is who I am; and I worry," Sandi remarked of Steve's advice.

"And I don't mean to say that I don't worry. But I can't follow behind him all the time, like when he was little," he confessed.

"You were the worst at helicopter parenting," she agreed. "You were always hovering over him."

"And it means something to him to demonstrate his independence from me. Anyway, my point is that what we are doing up here is important.

And not that this importance is all about me, or about our research up here. Rather this is about all of our lives and maybe the all the lives of everyone on Earth," he presented, seemingly going off on a tangent.

"I don't know if any of what I am saying is making any sense at all. What I mean to say is that where the Shadow-Forge are involved, we are talking issues on a universal scale. I can't say that I know why we are all up here, but we were being hunted on Earth as it was. Perhaps we risk more than others by being here, but the others don't know and can't know about this; lest they become more of a liability than a help," he said, trying to override her concerns for the children with a higher purpose. "This is our destiny, to help our son."

Steve paused to assess Sandi's reaction and then he continued, "And you have always been there for us, no matter what life has thrown our way. So I just need you to know that we need you, and that I need you to see this through." When he could not think of anymore to say, he just pulled her close and kissed her.

As they separated, she responded, "Alright, but you know I not a soldier. And I didn't sign up for anything other than to keep our family together and safe, for better or worse."

"No problem, I'll handle the heavy lifting if it comes to that," he acknowledged. "Which it is actually easier because we are on the Moon," he joked. They looked into each other's eyes and then hugged again.

Sandi, then pulled away saying, "Oh, I told the children that we would meet them for lunch."

"OK, family time," he responded. "I missed having the whole family together."

It didn't take long for the parents to catch up with the kids. While Steve and Andrew were satisfied with the lunch menu choices, Sandi and

Mairy both chose more of a breakfast selection. It seemed that Mairy had developed quite a penchant for pancakes, even synthetic ones. As they gathered up their food, they moved to a table on the cafeteria's perimeter, far from the crowd.

"Just like old times," Andrew commented as he sat down. "I kind of miss our family meals."

Steve and Sandi smiled, as Sandi asked, "Are you feeling any better?"

"Yes, mom, I feeling fine now," Andrew noted in an obligatory manner. "I guess I'm just a little shook up about being that close to a black hole again. Fortunately, Mairy was able to pull me out of it; again."

"So that's what this was all about?" Steve asked. "How did you end up there?"

"You'd have to ask Dr. Beecher about that one," Andrew answered. "They suddenly changed up our deep space target location to a view of the area around a black hole."

"That may be partly a result of where we are at in the program," Steve remarked. Thinking through their choice to change the target location, he explained, "As I told you, they had made changes to the equipment so as to detect and image dark matter via dark energy wave variations. And since the current theory is that dark matter would most probably be revealed in a very high gravitational field, I imagine that is why they chose to target a black hole."

"So we can expect that they will continue to target more black holes then?" Andrew enquired. "I was hoping not to have to revisit that experience again."

"You don't have to do this if you don't want to," Sandi said to Andrew.

"It's OK mom; I got this," Andrew responded to her concern. "It's just that black holes are not my favorite part of the universe."

"We still have another problem we need to deal with," interrupted Mairy. "Vera has not been found yet, and we don't know what she knows, what she saw, or even if she is working in opposition to our quest."

"Working against us?" Steve echoed in a quizzical manner. "What's going on; who is Vera again?"

Ignoring dad's questions, Sandi asked of Mairy, "Where would she go?"

"Not sure," replied Mairy, "but maybe the other team members can help."

"I know Tom has directed Margaret to find and check on the well-being of all the pod operators," Steve offered. "After all, things are going especially well with the research, and he doesn't want anything to jeopardize the program, or further breakthroughs. Maybe I should check on Margaret's progress."

"Makes sense, they can't do what they are doing without the pod operators," Andrew stated in support of Steve's comment. But then Andrew thought again about what his father had just said, and asked, "Just what exactly is going 'especially well'?"

"You wouldn't believe it," Steve started in. "Based on my research, we've actually manage to filter in dark matter layering from within the black hole's event horizon. We were actually having an impromptu celebration just this morning. We are the first ever research team to be able to provide for an interactive 3D mapping of the event horizon for a black hole."

"That's wonderful, sweetheart," Sandi exclaimed with excitement. "This proves that your theories have been right all along."

"Yes," Steve continued, "but it is the mathematical proofs that will probably get the most recognition."

"Don't be so negative," Sandi consoled Steve, trying to keep Steve's confidence up. "They would've been stumbling about for decades without the foundation provided via your theories. You made this happen."

"Yes, I guess your right at that," Steve acknowledged, brightening up a bit. "And you know, with this technology, it's like we can take an x-ray of almost anywhere in the visible universe in real time. For the first time, we have the ability to capture proof of evolution, and verify theoretical predictions about the formation of planets, stars, and galaxies. The key was discerning a rationale for the discrepancies displayed in the 'Pillars of Creation' images generated by the IGIE system."

"If they liked the 'Pillars of Creation', I can't imagine what they will see of the black hole that we were in this morning," Andrew divulged."

"They are working on those even as we speak," Steve said. "I'm excited to see how they'll all turn out."

But then, as if processing his father's comments in retrospect, Andrew expressed a delayed reaction to what he had heard, "Wait, what; 'in real time'?" Andrew asked. "Just what does that mean?"

Steve continued to expound upon their team revelation, explaining, "It appears the system's ability to focus in on dark energy wave variations has a very fortunate side effect. What we are seeing is that dark energy provides for a medium of communication that is faster than the speed of light. As we deduced from the successive images generated for the 'Pillars of Creation', it is as if we are seeing the real time events as they are happening, in their own Present time frame of reference."

"As if you were actually there witnessing the event up close," Mairy asserted.

"Exactly," Steve was quick to agree.

"Then that would be us," Mairy confessed. "We discovered that in our astral state of being, we found ourselves to be truly existing at the actual location of the target location."

"Truly existing?" Steve asked, pondering the consequences. "OK, but they don't know that."

Steve's mood changed into a downward spiral of realization that his rationale may have been flawed. And even worse, that there might now be evidence of their Shadow-Forge abilities.

Steve chastised them, "You two didn't do anything crazy this time, did you? I told you two that you need to be more cautious about your extracurricular activities in deep space."

"What's the matter?" Sandi asked in confusion. "What's going on?"

"Two things primarily," Steve started to explain. "One is the fact that I may have made a mistake in my conjecture for the image discrepancies, and the other is that there may now be evidence of their Shadow-Forge abilities for everyone to see."

"Perhaps; but would they ever really believe it to be a possibility?" Sandi countered.

"You got a point there," Steve acknowledged. "I believe I can continue to stall them on working through to any such resolution on their own for this revelation; partially because I made a great logical argument to support my conjecture, and partially because it would be too fantastic for them to realize upon their own."

"Is it?" Mairy asked rhetorically. "Remember what you told us this morning? You said *Funny thing is, it probably wouldn't have worked with anyone else, other than you two. I believe it has something to do with you two being Shadow-Forge members'.*"

"That's just about word for word," Steve responded in amazement. "I'll never get over how you two are able to do that."

"So if things are going so well, because they purposely involved the use of the Shadow-Forge in their project, then it would follow that this is indeed the purpose and location of our quest," Andrew surmised.

"Perhaps we are chasing down the wrongs leads in this mystery. I mean, how might the use of this discovery impact the universal balance?" Sandi put forth the question.

"All I know is that if there is one thing I learned from talking with Mairy, it is Fate does not play favorites," Andrew stated, continuing to believe there was more to this than they had yet to uncover. "I mean, it's not like our individual destinies are really that important to the health and well-being of the overall fate of the universe."

"But perhaps the culmination of our mutual destinies, does have real import on the overall fate," Steve suggested.

Mairy sat and listened to the conversation for a long time before enter into the discussion, "I'm inclined to agree with Andrew," Mairy said. "The warning presented via the beast was - *I am here to herald the fate of all humans. The time of Ragnarok is almost upon us.* I cannot believe that was just a veiled, empty threat."

"Mom, do you remember what it is that you read about Ragnarok?" Andrew asked.

Mom recited from her recollection of what she had previously read on the subject, "Ragnarok was the apocalyptic battle to happen with the world perishing in flames; after which the world would be created anew."

"What was that last part?" Steve asked Sandi to repeat.

"…the world would perish in flames and be created anew," mom repeated, paraphrasing he response.

"Perhaps, there is more going on here than I first imagined," Steve said in an ominous tone.

"How so?" Andrew asked.

"Some time ago there was the publication of a paper that may be as important to our understanding of the Big Bang as was the detection of gravitational waves. A team from the Wuhan Institute of Physics and Mathematics in China came up with the first rigorous mathematical proof that the Big Bang could have been spontaneously generated from 'nothing'. According to Heisenberg's uncertainty principle, quantum fluctuations in the metastable false vacuum – a state seemingly absent of space, time or matter – can give rise to virtual particle pairs. What is important to note is that, as stated in this paper, the metastable false vacuum has neither matter nor spacetime. Rather it is a form of wave function referred to as 'quantum potential'. While most of us wouldn't be inclined to call this 'nothing', physicists do refer to it as such," Steve disclosed.

As Steve paused, seeming lost in thought, Andrew couldn't help filling the void, "This is just like your theory for the universal existence mechanism, in which there are degrees of space and time. They are literally 'spring boarding' off your ideas."

"My earlier books have been published for a number of years now," Steve admitted. "Still, it was just a matter of time before someone would be able to make sense of it in a mathematical proof," Steve spoke matter-of-factly. "Or come up with a similar theory of their own. In fact, it was my hope that someday someone would be able to support my theories with a mathematical proof."

"Steve," Sandi stated in her way to get me back on track.

"Anyway, getting back to this concept of 'quantum potential', it would appear that this type of a spontaneous creation event could also allow for the universe to 'overwrite' itself. Such a method would allow for the means by which the universe could continually exist by recreating its own existence outside of Space and Time. While the concept of creating such an existence from nothing is intriguing, it would be more likely that such a concept of spontaneous creation would be born from some precursor state of non-existence rather than from just this 'nothingness' itself."

"Wait," Andrew said as if hit by a conflict of reasoning, "are you saying that, like the 'Genesis Device' of 'Star Trek' four? So there is a real possibility of overwriting existence, but on a universal scale?"

"That's exactly what I am saying, I think," Steve replied. "It is just a theory."

"Well then that clinches it, Harmony has to show up now," Andrew stated, jumping to a conclusion.

"And you got all that from '…the world perishes in flame and is created anew'?" Sandi asked in confusion.

"Yes," Steve replied with stale certainty, "it's where my mind took me."

"So if this is a real possibility, then how is 'what we are doing' going to contribute to this event?" Sandi questioned aloud?

"That's what we have to figure out," Steve answered.

"So far," Sandi asked without reservation? "You're talking about the extinction of our universe, and we don't even know what right things we are doing."

"That's usually the way it goes for us, Shadow-Forge," Andrew answered. "Even when Harmony was around, she would never really tell me just what to do. She just fed us riddles about what was wrong, or indirectly left clues about how the situation should be resolved. But somehow there was always a grain of truth in what she said. It made one think that they were on the right track."

"No one can really tell us what to do, because we write our own destinies," Mairy concluded. "Having a proper direction to focus on is as good a plan as any. In fact it is better than a plan, because plans can go awry during their execution. A proper direction can be re-adapted as long as we know where we are going."

Then addressing Andrew's revisiting the notion of Harmony's involvement, Mairy countered, "As for your assumption that Harmony will appear, you can put that aside. Harmony only appears when something goes wrong. So, based on her non-appearance, I'm guessing we are doing everything right so far."

Mairy then looked to Steve, requesting, "So it is up to you to try and figure out 'how what we are doing' could end up being used to spontaneously overwrite the existence of our universe."

"I'm betting it has to be something to do with that last session today," Steve thought out loud. "There has to be another reason why our research team was directed to focus away from a stagnant nebula to the more active center of an active galaxy. That is, other than the obvious one about detecting dark matter wave variations around its black hole."

"And then there was the sudden appearance of Vera at the black hole, while we were out there," Andrew threw in his 'two cents worth' of concern.

"Perhaps targeting us towards the black hole at the center of the galaxy wasn't an accident at all," Mairy said, contributing to the clues at hand.

"OK, I need to get back to the office to see what I can find out from that last session," Steve started in like the leader of an emergency response team. "You three can track down the whereabouts of Vera."

And with that, they were off in differing directions. As they went their separate ways, Mairy had the strangest feeling that their time was short, as if they were being pressed for time. Andrew, not wanting to give up on the appearance of Harmony, continued to wonder what it would take for her to show up. Because if his father was right, then the balance of the universe would not only be upset, it would be reset.

[Scene Change – Narrator's Perspective continued]

[Unmasking our nemesis as a member of the Dark Guild]

Steve returned to the lab to sift through the reams of data they had gotten from IGIE. Phil could be seen working at his desk, just as Tom had instructed him to do. John was nowhere about, so Steve assumed that he had gone to his own office to work on the graphics simulation. As Steve labored under the low light of the computer screen, he came across sections of the data where it seemed to have been edited out.

"Phil," he shouted over to him working on the other side of the room, "Have you extracted any data; say to run a simulation on it?"

"Extracted?" he asked in a confused tone. "I wouldn't have extracted any data for my simulations; I would only have copied it."

Getting up from his seat, Phil crossed the room to Steve, asking, "Why? What's going on?"

"Data seems to be missing from IGIE's output," Steve observed.

"If that is the case, then we need to let Tom know," Phil concluded. "I don't want to be blamed for this."

"I'm not sure that is a good idea," Steve asserted.

"Why?" Phil asked. "He is the head of the company."

"Because I believe he may be the one who took them," Steve replied. "Something is not right. He doesn't include us in his decisions on the changes to the equipment, or even the intended operations of the equipment. He seems to have his own agenda when it comes to managing the DeepSIT targets and the data we collect. I mean, did you even know he change the deep space target for these black hole images?"

"No, but why do you think he should need to consult with us on any of these decisions?" Phil pressed Steve for his logic. "So maybe he did take them. But that doesn't mean his motives are especially devious."

"Perhaps," Steve feigned agreement. "Still, I don't believe he consults with anyone on these decisions. I don't believe that the 'board of directors' are even aware of his agenda; whatever it may be." Steve then proposes, "There is only one way to verify this. We need to see if the missing data is in his office. And if it is, then we need to ask him what is going on."

"You're taking a lot upon yourself," Phil cautioned Steve with his own apprehension. "Tom is the CEO and director of this project. We've made some fantastic breakthroughs this week due to his leadership. Why do you believe there is anything wrong about how he is handling the project?" Phil asked with authority.

Now Steve had backed himself into a corner. He can't explain what he and the family have speculated upon, and missing data was truly not necessarily an immediate cause for concern. "Perhaps you're right. But how are we supposed to provide for a complete time lapsed simulation of today's session if we are missing these extracted images?" Steve asked. "Do you really want to approach him with an incomplete perspective?"

"Well no," Phil admits. Phil sees that Steve is not about to drop this, so he considers a compromise. "Alright, we can go together and ask him about them," Phil insisted. "But I don't want you peddling your conspiracy theories in front of him."

Steve and Phil made their way into Tom's office. As he opened the door, we could see he wasn't in. Phil was ready to leave and return later, but Steve's curiosity got the better of him.

"What are you doing?" Phil asked, as Steve walked through the door. "He's clearly not here."

"Oh, we've been invited to his office many times," Steve persisted, excusing his actions as he walked in. "What would it hurt to look around?"

They were both awestruck to see images of this morning's session taped to the wall. It was as if Tom, himself, was looking for something. "Looks like he is running his own research operation here," Steve said, fueling his suspicions upon Phil. "And I'll bet these are the missing images from this morning's session."

"I guess you were right after all," Phil admitted. "But what is it to us? He can do what he wants."

A quick scan of the wall images revealed nothing out of the ordinary. As Phil continued to study the missing images on the wall, Steve moved on to search the furniture. Steve is rifling through images on top of Tom's desk when Tom walks in on them.

"Steve, Phil, I don't remember calling you all into my office," said Tom, as he entered the room with Kiana.

"Oh, Tom, I just came in to find you," Steve said, squelching an impetus of surprise upon his entry. "And then I ran across these generated images on your wall. This is fascinating; having recalibrated the CONS to work with my notion of dark matter detection has really improved the resolution of these generated images. I can especially see the ever increasing layering of negative density towards the interior beyond the event horizon. Indeed, the assumed density of the black hole's inner core is not the highly anticipated center of gravitational singularity everyone thought it was. Instead, I would speculate that the gravitational anomaly of the black hole is the result of concentrated negative matter density, or dark matter."

Hoping his gambit was working, Steve continued with his impromptu analysis. "See here," he said, trying to direct Tom's attention toward the generated images on his desk that supported his theory. "As pictured in the eye of this plasma storm, these images propose a central core from which there is rather the absence of spacetime; or at least the absence of positive mass density, somewhat as I predicted."

While Phil's first emotional response was to presuppose their guilt, Phil's emotional state transformed as he listened to Steve. "That is an amazing discovery," Phil noted with excited. "No real mass at the center."

"Indeed," Steve acknowledged. "Fantastically, somewhere in the transition from the concentrated plasma field, which swirls about just outside the black hole's event horizon, and the center itself, there is a separation from our known reality. That is to say, it not existence as we understand of our actuality in fourth dimensional spacetime. In which case, I would then speculate that the resulting gravitational push back, against our spacetime, is more from a dark energy focus of this concentrated dark matter."

"Yes, I can see bringing you on board with this project was just what I needed to advance my research here," Tom commented calmly. "Tell me more."

"This gravitational push back would appear to be caused instead by an inversion of spacetime, more so then the concentration of positive mass itself," Steve continued verbalizing his hypothesis, as if to try and capture it outside of his own stream of consciousness. "And I believe it is this inversion which is promoting the concentration, or synergetic increase, in gravitational acceleration for the whole of the black hole without the benefit of any more solidity in baryonic matter surrounding it."

"In fact, do you know what this means?!" Steve proclaimed excitedly. Then without waiting for an answer, Steve continued, "We can stop looking for the hypothesized graviton, because it doesn't exist. Rather, the gravitational forces governing our spacetime are the result of the interacting nature of degrees in positive and negative mass densities. In truth, as I conceived it, the more positive the mass density, the greater the offsetting negative mass density; and consequently, the greater the resultant increase in gravitational acceleration."

"Yes, of course," Tom agreed, finally being pulled into Steve's logical dissertation. "It could be that every positive mass coalescence has some immixture of negative mass central to its core."

No longer being able to contain his composure, Phil advised caution over speculation. "Slow down Steve; let's not get ahead of ourselves," he warned of everyone's emerging insights. "You're jumping off the deep end without a life preserver. We haven't even crunched the numbers on this theory of yours yet. There is a lot of personal reputation at stake here, and we need to get it right."

"But don't you feel it?" Steve challenged Phil to join in with him. "This is the new age of scientific discovery. Based on the data we have here already, we are looking at breaking down the universal code of existence. Can you imagine what this discovery alone means to concepts like wormholes?"

"Yeah," Phil acknowledged, finally let himself be swept up in the excitement. "It means that the concept of wormholes cannot be supported. And there is no traveling through this universe via a shortcut connecting two separate points in spacetime, because the black hole center does not support positive density matter at its center. In fact, the black hole center is non-existent within our perspective of reality."

Steve lauded Phil's contribution, and then built upon it, asserting, "Exactly! The black hole center is actually a negative matter density portal to a completely separate universal identity; an alternate reality to our fourth dimensional spacetime reference. Perhaps even a multidimensional frame of reference without material form or substance, bordering on the metaphysical realm of pure thought. Perhaps something more like a fifth dimensional state of being."

Surprisingly Tom just listened as the two continued to work through their suppositions based on generated images he sought to keep from them. He quickly surmised that with this additional information, they might have become more suspicious of his actions. In fact, the might even uncover his more real goal.

So Tom let his guard down, revealing, "Yes, a universal identism not unlike the foundation of your predicted 'pre-existing medium' for pre-creation. I believe you referred to it as the 'nothingness'. Let me think; how did you explain it?" he asked rhetorically. "Oh yes, the collision of two alternate realities; one being the fourth dimension and the other reflecting the previous order in which the universe 'was', prior to the introduction of baryonic matter. And it is the principal nature of this 'nothingness' that dark energy can only ever exists in the Present time, as you have conjectured by your inclusion of the co-relating concept of nonlocality. In fact, reaching the center of the black hole is like being instantly connected to everything, everywhere within the universe. Wouldn't you agree?"

"Yes," Steve endorsed as a paraphrasing of his theories. While he was taken aback upon Tom's familiarity with his concepts, he continued to further their discussion. "But not for any degree of fourth dimensional baryonic matter. Positive density matter cannot exist beyond the point of zero mass density; hence the plasma ring just outside the event horizon," Steve reminded him. "So reaching the center is not an option," Steve surmised, trying to anticipate his expectation to do exactly that.

"Perhaps; perhaps not," Tom acknowledged rather suspiciously. "You know what I find strange? It is that until you published your books, which was not really well received by your peers, we were not even aware of you and your family. Indeed it is quite ironic that out of all the scientists in your world, and with all their education and expertise, that you, a non-scientist, were the one individual able to stumble upon a plausible theory for identity and detection of dark matter. And the beauty of it all is that, even when you place the information in front of them, they were unable or unwilling to see. In point of fact, these scientists would happily tear down any contrary notion, like yours, which conflicts with their own established consensus, rather than embrace the approach of an outsider like yourself. Truly, it is amazing to see how desperately complacent the educated are to be acknowledged by their peers, even within the established scientific community, than to take a chance on an idealism with no real mathematical proof."

Steve couldn't fathom why Tom had interrupted a lively scientific discovery, to discuss this legacy. He stood there simmering in the exposures of his own shortcomings. He didn't know whether to be angry with Tom or pleased with his recognition of his understanding of his life's passion.

"Thus, this becomes your ongoing legacy," Tom unrelentingly continued; "to be shunned by the very people with whom you wish to share your new perspectives and innovative theories. And still, without their support, you persisted in exploring areas outside the accepted boundaries of the established scientific theories. In point of fact, you were the one person to question the unquestionable."

There was an eerie silence in the room, as Steve and Phil tried to anticipate Tom's rational for this sudden reversal and degradation of the scientific community.

"Perhaps you can take some measure of satisfaction in knowing that you are right," Tom professed. "You were right about everything: all of it. Indeed, your knowledge of universal cosmogony is quite inspired. But, sadly, it is a truth that no one will ever believe. I mean seriously, you can place the information directly in front of them, with all the mathematical proofs we can muster, and they will eagerly deny its veracity, and do all in their power to discredit you. And why, you might ask? Because people aren't interested in truth."

It was a confusing oration on Tom's part, which left both Steve and Phil dumfounded. Steve was the first to realize that it sounded like the confessions a villain provides just before he lets the hammer down. But even in his wariness, he realized that there was ultimately nowhere to go.

"People are interested in what's in it for them," Tom decidedly stressed. "You see people don't want to know the truth. Rather people are blissfully content with measuring their own intelligence upon previously established theories. I mean, think upon how long it took for them to accept Copernicus' or Kepler's heliocentric theory, or even concede to the logic of Darwin's theory of evolution."

"I have been tilting windmills for as long as I can remember," Steve admitted of his legacy. "For one reason or another, I could never accept the traditional conformity of my position in life. It's strange, but the more I bucked the system, the more I found that providence came in support of my naivety. It's not so much that I thought the social culture unconscionably made it difficult for me to accept my position in life. Rather I believe it was more that I was cursed with this profound insight to see life and appreciate the universe differently from everyone else. I could not be satisfied with the ignorance of social norms which seem to support incompetent attempts to recreate an isolated haven of a utopian-like universe. Still, admittedly, I cannot deny a sense of jealousy for the aimlessly affluent, who have the support of their peers."

"And when did you first gain this profound insight?" Tom asked, contesting Steve's response. "No; I believe there is more to your story, and more to your family's story, than you let on. When I said you were right, I meant you were right from the perspective of one who had experienced it all. However, being correct from the perspective of having had to work for it, via a rigorous scientific method, I did not see. Indeed, while everyone else here was willing to accept your theories as just a basis from which to publish a fictional adventure of your son's fantastical journey through spacetime, I was willing to see and accept the truth of it all. As I see it, your proposed theories did not foster you're detailing of this fictional adventure. Rather, it was this non-fictional adventure that fostered your proposed theories; or, at the very least, supported them. In all actuality, if it wasn't for the experience of your son's sacrifice, your theories might not have advanced as far as they did. There is no reason to deny it. We've studied your background quite extensively. We know that your son spent time in therapy trying to get someone, anyone other than his parents, to believe in him."

Half listening to Tom's admission of belief in their well-kept family secret, Steve began to understand that his research, even his family, had been manipulated; but to what end he could not fathom as of yet. Frantically trying to decide whether to deny it or make up a cover story 'on the fly', Steve knew he hadn't enough savvy or time to make it convincing. Ultimately Steve abandoned the notion of 'talking his way out of it' and confronted Tom's declaration.

"Putting the pieces together was not as easy as you might think," Steve confessed. "I'm guessing that's why you needed me on this project: because you couldn't do it yourself. So now explain to me why you remove these images from the research center. Why not just let this charade play out?"

Phil felt like a bystander as the two began to spar over the non-fictional nature of Steve's insights. As an established scientist himself, he decided to interject some sanity into the discussion.

"You two can't be serious," Phil remarked. "Tom, I've read his books. The concept of astrally projecting one's consciousness across the cosmos has no scientific basis whatsoever. What are we even talking about here?"

"See what I mean," Tom crowed to Steve. "It can't be real because there is no scientific basis for it."

Tom then looked to Phil, affirming, "That which has a scientific basis is only that which has been allowed to be proven. We're not just here to improve upon the observatories and the gravitational-wave detection systems currently being developed on Earth. If that were the case, then mission accomplished and more. But I want more than just 3D rendering of detection of gravitational waves and dark matter wave variances. Think about it; we cannot only see into the Present time activity of these deep space locations, we can interact with them. We could not have done that simply through the instrumented detection of dark matter at a distance. We needed to somehow observe the event in its Present time. We needed to actual be there, at its Present time location. We could not have accomplished this achievement without the possibility of working within the astral plane of existence. I knew this from the beginning."

"How do you think I even came up with the idea of approaching a meld of man and machine to reach beyond the merely perfunctory means of perceiving the heavens? I needed Margaret for her cutting edge research in neurological imaging. I needed the pod sleepers for their lucid dreaming abilities, for their metacognitive skills, and for their degree of control, including their capacity for self-awareness in the dream state. I needed John for his skill in overlaying two wave forms in tandem to refine the operation of dream scheme decoding and allow for the imaging of their combined wave forms. And I needed you for your hardware instrumentation of detection and capture for these wave forms," Tom revealed, detailing the execution of his plan.

Phil and Steve remained silent as they understood they were in the presence of a master manipulator. Steve thought to himself, this would be the one person who could orchestrate the destinies of many to predict their combined causality and produce a predetermined fate. This was the nemesis for which they had been hunting.

Tom then continued, explaining, "The final piece of the puzzle was Steve and his amazingly talented family. You see, Steve was quite right. I could not have put all the pieces together without them. If I had just Andrew and Mairy, I would have had the capability to try and harness their abilities to astrally project themselves. But what I wouldn't have had was a detailed understanding of their interaction within the universe; the how of it all, so to speak. If I had Steve alone, then I would have had this instruction manual for the universe mechanism, but without any ability to access it. So it wasn't until Steve had written his purported science fiction novel on the alleged fictional adventure of his son that everything came into place. All I needed then was for them to want to be part of our project."

"This makes no sense," Phil said, rejecting the truths which had been laid before him. "There is no evidence of any metaphysical interactions within the universe."

"There are two broad stances about the inference of metaphysics. The strong, classical view assumes that the objects studied by metaphysics exist independently of any observer, so that the subject is the most fundamental of all sciences. The weak, modern view assumes that the objects studied by metaphysics exist inside the mind of an observer, so the subject becomes a form of introspection and conceptual analysis. But is it from the mind's eye that one begins with the introspection that must be proven. Take for example the claim that electrons have charge as a scientific theory. While exploring what it means for electrons to be (or at least, to be perceived as objects), charge to be a viable property, and for both to exist in a topological entity known as spacetime is the task of metaphysics," Tom clarified.

"That which cannot be imagined, cannot be proven," Steve surmised. "Invariably, the evidence for the metaphysical is in the physical proof of the hypothesis."

"Rightly so," Tom affirmed. "And now, we can see the universe for what it really is: The 'Selfish Biocosm' of evolutionary development that is a part of the universal struggle of order against entropy for the progenesis of new life force." In professing his beliefs, Tom was emboldened to reveal more. "And the physical proof will be our ability to touch upon the very fabric of the universe. I want to set things right. And for that, I need to find creation itself."

Listening to Tom's vision of great expectations, Steve thought to distract Phil from the revelation of his family secret by joining Phil in trying to rationalize with Tom.

"There is no real creation in the Present time view of the universe," Steve stated emphatically. The Present time of creation is now Past time."

"I'm surprised to hear you say that," Tom said, claiming some disappointment in Steve's pronouncement. "As you so eloquently detailed in your dissertation on degrees of Space and Time, all Time is a valid metaphysical perspective. All Time is but the Present when view within a fifth dimensional configuration."

"Yes, of course," Steve agreed, realizing he had missed connecting a few of the puzzle pieces himself. "Still, the concept of 'Selfish Biocosm' is just another attempt at reviving the notion of 'intelligent design'. You can't possibly compare the concept of creation with that of a universe being destined to undergo a cosmic mitosis. Such a notion only promulgates the perpetuity of reproduced universes based on the preexisting condition of an ever evolving existence. Mitosis is the highly evolutionary need of the biological single cell to reproduce."

"Verily, an inherited nature of its environment; for we are all created in its image," Tom avowed.

Steve could see that Tom wasn't responding to his dissuading argument, and tried another approach, explaining, "You realize what you are proposing is not the one true, singular event from which all of creation was first realized. Even with our detection of dark matter, negative density matter is always bounded together with positive density matter via their conjoined evolution in spacetime. We'll never be able to see back all the way to the one first creation event, where neither existed."

"Maybe not, but the there is more than one way to find creation. Eventually we'll get there," Tom declared. "Oh, by the way, did you happen to know that during the last session, there was a 6% increase in the density of the Moon? And, I am assuming, it was due in no small part to your children's involvement. I'll bet that's a consequence that you had not considered. However it was, rather, an expectation of mine. You see, there is more to esoteric cosmology than just the fictional presentation of your theories," said Tom.

"To what are you alluding?" Steve demanded to know.

"I am merely alluding to you that you have much to learn," Tom pointed out. "And that your contribution to this project, along with its many side effects, shall remain …, how should I put it …, unredeemable. You will be blamed for the disastrous consequences of my research, and I will be allowed to continue my work. However this being said, you present a probabilistic liability. On the one hand I need you and your family to realize my dreams of touching upon the infinite. Let's face it; who knows how long it would take us, working within the confines of our fourth dimensional frame of reference, to achieve my goals. But then on the other hand, you are probably the only ones who could stop me. You see, like it or not, our goals are at odds. It is a real conundrum to be sure."

"What are you saying? Stop you from doing what?" Phil asked anxiously. Tom's whole espoused stream of thought totally confused Phil's view of reality. "How would you even be able to work outside the confines of our dimensional spacetime?"

"What I am saying is that you two will be confined from entering the research facility, until further notice," Tom responded, motioning to Kiana. Kiana acknowledged by contacting security on the desk intercom.

"Tom, perhaps we should've talked with you before we came to your office, but that is hardly any reason to take us off the project, or confine us," Phil stated, imploring for Tom to rethink his orders. "We can help you. You said yourself that you need us."

"Phil, I'm not just taking you off the project," Tom clarified his orders. "I am having you both arrested for corporate espionage. And yes, over time, you will help me. I just needed the appropriate leverage."

"I have a family up here," Steve stated, trying to reason with him. "They will notice if I have disappeared."

"That kind of depends on the story I give them, doesn't it," Tom replied. "Besides, no one is disappearing just yet. And you would be well advised to consider that your family is up here, and that they will stay up here as long as I deem it necessary."

"If you harm any of them, I swear …," Steve started in to say.

"You'll what?" Tom interrupted. "Besides I have no reason to harm anyone. There is nothing any of you can do to get in my way, as long as you stay apart from each other."

And just as he was about to explain the conditions of their detention, two security guards came into the room. Tom looked to the security guards, saying, "These two are guilty of corporate espionage. Please confine them to their new residences in the detention center, until we can assess the matter further."

Phil contested his position, shouting, "You can't do this! We have done nothing wrong. You are the one who stole these images from the company, not us."

"Oh, Phil, you still think this is all about the images; these images that you two were planting in my room," Tom proclaimed. Phil was dumbstruck upon Tom's lying accusations. "And Phil, I am truly sorry to learn of your involvement in all of this, perhaps we can work out something later. However, right now there are plans in motion that cannot be interrupted. And, as I am the company CEO, we will be doing this my way," Tom decreed.

[Scene Change - Narrator's Perspective continued]

The two are led by the security guards to adjoining rooms within the complex's detention area. As an added precaution, a guard is placed outside of the main entrance to the detention center. Since neither of them has access to a computer, and there are no cellphones on the Moon, they are unable to contact anyone outside their secured rooms. However, as they were the only occupants on this wing of the detention center, they could talk freely between their rooms to each other.

[The causality of fate is also reflective of intended consequences.]

Phil approached Steve about Tom's admissions, asking, "What the hell was that all about? Is he really serious about your books being based on real, non-fictional occurrences?"

Steve ignored the latter question, asking Phil about Tom, "Are you aware of any other projects that Tom is involved in; something he hasn't shared with me or other members of the team?"

Phil thinks aloud, "I'm not sure. I actually thought we were all working toward the same goal."

Steve presses Phil again, "He's seems to be alluding to some alternative use for DeepSIT and that dark matter interface he put on the master CONS units. So there is nothing you know about?"

"No," Phil answered and then continued with his own line of thought. "Did you believe him about a 6% increase in the Moon's density? How is that even possible? How does one transfer density into the Moon?"

"Transfer, of course," Steve stated aloud. "OK, there is no use keeping you in the dark. I going to need your help," Steve admitted. "What I'm going to tell you is not going to be easy for you to accept at first. However, if you put it together with what Tom just told you, it may be clearer to you."

"Enough of the mysterious introduction," Phil retorted. "What's going on?"

Steve started in, "My children are special, just as Tom said. They can astrally project themselves within the cosmos. And by doing so, they are actively visiting the Present time location of these deep spacetime events, just as Tom explained. So, it is not the equipment alone that allows us to detect dark matter. Rather it is through the children, that we are now able to image a Present time view of these distant events."

"Are you serious?" Phil challenged Steve. "How did you confirm any of this?"

"It is more than I want to get into now, but you need to trust me that it is all true," Steve requested, remembering his encounter with Harmony as she brought his son back to them.

"Let's just say that I'll keep an open mind for now," Phil agreed. "What have you got?"

"OK, consider on top of all of this, that the children are actually able to interact with these Present time events. In which case, they could be inadvertently be ferrying or channeling energy to and from these target locations in deep space," Steve began to speculate.

"What; like some kind of grounding rod?" Phil asked with a bit of incredulity. "Now you sound like Tom. Are you saying that it is not only possible to astrally project one's consciousness across the cosmos, but also to project matter back through the host body of the participant; and thereby induce greater density?"

Steve answered quickly, "Well, not positive density matter, to be sure. In their astral form, they cannot really interact with positive matter except as another form of energy. It has to be something as massless as they are; or perhaps something less than zero positive mass."

"So dark matter then," Phil deduced.

"Yes; think of it like a thought transference of energy. In this respect, then, it is their ability to transfer dark energy from dark matter, or negative density matter. So this is what Tom must have been working towards all this time. He intends to provide for a physical connection between these distant events and the pod sleepers. But to what end, I can't yet fathom. Certainly making the Moon denser would not upset the natural order of the entire universe."

"Well it certainly is not going to improve life on Earth," Phil quipped. "Alright, if I accept what you are saying about the feasibility of astral projection, then what about the ability to provide for such a connection," Phil asked, being a little more interested now in what Steve had to say.

Steve responded back quickly, "While the principal that dark matter exists only in the Present time, I believe it is the concept by which nonlocality is proven. What Einstein termed as 'spooky action at a distance' is really the communicative properties of dark matter via dark energy. If you remember from my presentation, distance is not a factor when dealing with dark matter or dark energy, as everything is everywhere all at once; like one huge spacetime fabric. And based on the new information Tom provided about the increase of the Moon's density by 6%, we now can also assume that dark matter can be transferred via dark energy through this medium."

Phil was confused by the theoretical leap Steve made, "Transferred via thought, is what you said; but how?"

Steve explained further, "Remember the analogy you made about the children acting like some kind of grounding rod? Well, in metaphysical research, there is the notion of a strong, silver-colored, elastic cord which conjoins a person's physical body with its astrally projected energy or consciousness. The concept is that this silver cord binds the out-of-body experience to its physical host. Where the physical host still resides in the fourth dimension, their astrally projected consciousness travels about in a weird alternative interdimensional frame of reference; somewhat similar to a fifth dimensional frame of reference that Tom spoke of."

"A metaphysical silver cord?" Phil questioned.

"Yes; rather likened to the connection imagined for a near-death experience, where the soul still maintains an association, or link, with its physical body. However, once this connection is broken, there is no returning back to the host body and the host body dies," Steve proclaims.

Phil creates another analogy, "So then like Ben Franklin experiment, the dark energy is grounded through their astrally projected consciousness, representative of the kite, along this silver cord down through the host body, representative of the key. And like a lightning rod, the dark energy travels beyond the host body and is grounded within the pre-existing dark matter of the Moon."

"Yes, in a sense, it would appear that is how it operates," Steve happily expresses his acknowledgement of Phil's understanding. "Therefore speculating on the ability of dark matter and dark energy to exist without having any real distance, the theory of nonlocality proposes a presupposed connection between the two locations, irrespective of their dimensional spacetime boundaries."

"So how is this a problem for the universe?" Phil questioned. "The most I can imagine as a result of this process is that enough dark matter would engender the dynamics required to create a black hole."

"Think of it like this: What we perceive as an inflationary universe is the measure of dark energy attempting to restore this underlying fabric of order," Steve explained. "So the profoundness of this activity is to change the universal order. Indeed, while the universe expands instantaneously in response to the intrusion of any fourth dimensional existence, against the force of gravity as it were. Tom has either conceived of or stumbled upon a way to localize this cause and effect. Perhaps he is even wants to interfere with it at will."

Phil concedes to Steve logic, saying, "Anyway you look at it, this sounds like a recipe for disaster. Who would've guessed IGIE, an instrument for observing the universal bodies in the cosmos, could actually be used as an instrument to influence these same universal bodies."

"Actually, it may be worse than that," Steve set the tone for the seriousness of his hypothesis. "We were discussing the concept of spontaneous creation that would be born from some previous state of nothing."

Phil, recalling what he read about the theory online, stated, "Yes, I remember the discussion. Tom wanted to find the moment of creation and touch upon the infinite."

Steve continued with his line of thinking, "If dark energy is representative of 'nothing', or at least a connection to this 'nothingness', then perhaps Tom thought of a way to engineer a biocosm-like condition within a black hole. You know, like genetic engineering, but on a more cosmic scale. Perhaps such a condition could be considered by the engendering of a singularity from within it, thereby promoting a spontaneous creation event with which to duplicate our universe in a kind of cosmic mitosis."

Phil responded, "What; like creating two universes from within a singularity, like a white hole?"

"Yes, the difference between opposing forces between a white hole within a black hole could be large enough to initiate the energy required for such an event," Steve hypothesized.

For a moment, the thoughtful silence filled the void between them as they both tried to bridge this concept of spontaneous creation from the engendering of a singularity. Then Steve continued, "I mean, is it really so difficult to imagine? In general relativity, a white hole is a hypothetical region of spacetime which cannot be entered from the outside, although matter and light can escape from it."

Phil contributed to the discussion, saying, "Yes, and it is the reverse condition of a black hole; a condition wherein gravity only allows entry from the outside, and from which matter and light cannot escape."

Steve built upon their consensus, "So in this sense, a white hole's spacetime condition is the reflection of a black hole's spacetime condition; wherein a black hole, by degree in spacetime, would be a direction toward 'No Time and All Space'. A white hole, by degree in spacetime, would be a direction toward 'All Time and No Space'," Steve deduced.

They exchanged their contributions back and forth like a tag team. Phil, drawn into the excitement of theoretical contemplations, stated, "In point of fact, the engendering of a white hole within a black hole appears in the theory of stabilized eternal black holes."

Building upon their combined conjectures, Steve began to springboard towards a probable determination.

"Yes, the stabilization of this spacetime condition is achieved via a warped equalization of past and future into the present; rather like folding Future time in on Past time, so that everything is recycled endlessly in the Present time. But where unstablized, the expanding capacity of the white hole inextricability overwhelms the gravitational effect of the black hole, exploding into a creation event that could duplicate the fabric of the universe; or at least that region of the universe, with a lesser explosion. It is difficult to say what the extent of the event would be."

"Tom said that 'All Time' is but the Present when view within a fifth dimensional configuration," Phil stated, remembering what he had heard during their discussion.

"Yes; Time is not constant, but it is consistent," Steve recalled aloud. "It is as if the essence of Time is a reflection of this consistency; where Present Time is the mirror of Future Time upon Past Time."

Phil provided a counterpoint to his conjecture, "As I understand it, a white hole is rather the continuation of a black hole and, in effect, provides for a wormhole in space."

Steve responds quickly, "Delightful reticence, I'm sure. I deem the concept of wormholes to have no real practical basis outside their mathematical proofs. They are contrived without the benefit of a reality in dark energy. The concept of wormholes ends up being the mathematical modeling of two separate locations in the same universe being bridged by some form of nonlocality through differing spacetimes. It is somewhat like in the movie 'Interstellar', or the mathematical modeling of two separate parallel universes occupying the same space in differing spacetimes, like in the movie 'Tomorrowland'."

Phil retorted, "My, you are picky as to what wild theories you agree and disagree with."

"I believe it is best to consider my postulation as being the greater probability for this event. And with Tom's control of IGIE, he could, in all probability, set up the next session for such an event as early as tomorrow." Steve paused, thinking first of the dangers posed to him and his family, and then of others. "Still, it can't work without the pod sleepers," he observed.

Phil had not been thinking about how Tom might achieve this goal, "What do you mean?"

Steve thought aloud, thinking through the clues, "I don't know why it didn't occur to me before. Andrew's and Mairy's ability to act like a lightning rod for dark matter is like the transformation from matter to energy and energy to matter; a theoretical side-effect of dark energy. If they are actually the embodiment of the dark matter transfer, then they must be able to exist within the black hole center as well. And if they should channel even a small portion of positive mass density via his astral presence into the center of this dark matter confluence, it could the method by which a biocosm might be introduced and realized."

Phil, playing 'devil's advocate', speculated on Steve's conclusion, "That is a lot of theoretical assumptions and guesswork as to Tom's intention. So, what if it doesn't go as planned?"

"If it doesn't go as planned, and there is no white hole, then there should be no danger of triggering a spontaneous creation event. However, there is still the problem of dark matter transfer through them back to the Moon. And while that may not be a problem for the reality of our existence in the universe, it would definitely wreak havoc back on Earth. However if it does go as planned, then I'm still not sure. Is it enough to introduce positive density matter into the heart of negative density matter? Perhaps I am missing something."

"I don't know how you can be sure of any of this," Phil decried of their metaphysical bantering.

"The ideal of the 'selfish bicosm' is more philosophical than a real theoretical premise. There actual prognosis for its mechanism as one of meiosis, in which a separate universe is duplicated, or birthed from within the original. And while neither of the resulting internal life forces are aware of anything other than the universe of their own contained spacetime, they are both part of a larger entity that is more cosmically-aware and sustainable," Steve put forth as his understanding of this ideal. "It is supposed to be a way around having to explain the progressive nature of an evolving universe toward its ultimate fate of demise. It's more of an 'Intelligent Design' concept to promote a foundation for the theoretical speculations about possible reasons why the universe is life-friendly. However, I see it as merely another anthropomorphization for the personification of a deified entity."

"Still, if a white whole is engendered, it could backfire on Tom. The ensuing effect could, in point of fact, be the overwriting, or resetting, of our own reality and existence within the universe," Steve professed. And the gravity of his understanding led him to only one conclusion, "Either way, we need to get the children away from this project."

Phil's concern grows ever larger, "If that is actually what he intends to do, then I see no viable alternatives for us in any of these scenarios. We really need to get him, and everyone else, off of this damned moon station. Remember, the architecture of this facility was design with the Moon's lower gravity in mind. If the Moon's gravity increases too much, the whole thing could come tumbling down around us." Then looking about and considering their situation in detention, he laments, "But first we have to get ourselves out of here. Want to try and convince the guard that Tom is about to bring about the end of the world?"

Encounters of the Fifth Kind— The Quest Revealed

[The allusion of control is our greatest vulnerability.]

Meanwhile, back in there new accommodations, Sandi and the children were waiting for Steve to return.

[Scene Change – Narrator's Perspective]

"We finally got the family back together, and Steve is working late again," Sandi sighed.

"Dad is probably just running late again," Andrew said, trying to excuse his tardiness.

"When your father gets involved in work, he forgets about everything else," Sandi complained. "It's always one more problem to solve, or one more task to complete. And then he is lost to a time warp of his own making within the nature of his own obsessive compulsive disorder."

"He's is ever so much closer to proving his theories," Andrew said, continuing to defend him. "He probably just pulled an 'all-nighter'. He's probably on his way back even as we speak."

"Then he should have called," Sandi insisted. "I don't even know if he's taken time out to eat. Perhaps we should go and find him."

"Tell you what, Sandi," Mairy jumped in. "How about I go and see what I can find out."

"I'll join you," Andrew replied.

"Now wouldn't that be nice," Mairy stated in a sarcastic tone; "You leaving your mother to worry on her own. Why don't you get involved? Interest her in some distracting entertainment. I'll be fine by myself."

As Andrew thought better of it, he agreed to stay with his mother while Mairy did what she does best: reconnaissance. "I guess you're right."

"Besides you could use some more practice in the astral world. Once you get your mother settled, try going solo," Mairy requested.

"Without you?" he questioned.

"Sure, you'll be safe enough," she replied. "Just stay in your own reality, and don't linger about in the 'jumping off' point. It would do you well to not depend on someone other than yourself. Besides, I may need you to save me one day."

He followed her to the front door, and confessed to her, "You're the one consistency in my life that I can't live without." Then he pulled her in close and gave her a passionate kiss on the lips. "Stay safe."

Mairy smiled, then admitted to him, "I was wondering when you would get up the nerve to kiss me. I'll be back soon enough, and we can have a longer discussion about this." With that, Mairy was out the door.

That evening, after helping his mother a bit to arrange their new family quarters, Andrew excused himself for bedtime. Yet it was his intention to do as Mairy requested; to practice by himself. And after having opened the portal to this astral world with Mairy, he had become more confident in his astral abilities. In fact, he began to look forward to each new session with and without the pod sleepers. Here, where his body was seemingly protected from harm, he believed his life force was free to venture anything without fear of consequence; for nothing of his previous reality can reach him here, in his astral form.

Soon he was able to embrace his out of body experience. However, as before, he was unable to transition to the 'jumping off' point without Mairy's supervision. Rather, he floated up and out of his physical form. At first he just examined the strangeness of his condition and faced his physical self relaxing in bed. He then levitated up and out of the complex to view the research center from high above. He could even see the robots moving about the outside of the facility along the wasteland of the moon's surface.

Where virtually all of spacetime begins to become his playground, Andrew dared to presume a feeling of invulnerability. With this feeling of invulnerability, he imagines that he has ultimate control over his own life, and perhaps, even of his own destiny. While his allusive fate remains intertwined within the elusive nature of the universal being, he fancies his astral energy as a controllable superpower. Within this euphoric condition, knowledge and control become the ultimate aphrodisiac. In his arrogant assumption of such control, he can't help but consider that each risk is just a calculated hazard. He journeys ever farther up and deeper into space; for after a few sessions with the pod sleepers, all this has become familiar ground. To see the stars and distant galaxies, as if he was watching the landscape from the family car on vacation, seemed quite surreal to him. Having had a few dreams like this, he even questioned the actuality of his out of body experience. Yet if this was a dream, it was the most lucid one he ever had.

Indeed, identifying with such godlike powers, with perhaps a little bit of sway from his inherent ADHD condition, Andrew had become increasingly curious about what abides beyond his self-imposed boundaries of Space and Time. And, with Fairy as his mentor, he envisioned that he would soon be able to transcend even his known reality by himself. Whereupon, with time, he dared to believe that not even his own fate would be beyond his influence. It was truly an enticing, almost seductive, temptation to know all and to be all. But all that would take time. He was not fool enough to believe he was ready now.

He was aware of the pitfalls involved. Having reasoned that to be all, he risks becoming nothing by embracing an infinity without a beginning or an end, the very thought of it was perhaps his last and greatest fear. He imagined it to be as a state so autonomous, so far removed from everything and anything he might comprehend, that his very existence could only be measured upon his emotional condition; wherein he might affect his own state of being. Still, he dared to imagine that outside the reality of his own spacetime, the answers to the enigma of his creation will become ever more clear. Would it be worth it to sacrifice all, he questioned of his own thoughts?

Enough for now; the quest is not yet done, he thought to himself. With that, Andrew returned from whence he came. Not realizing the duration and breadth of his experience, he found his way back. It was somewhat like recoiling along a line. He recalled how his mother related to him earlier about a 'silver cord' that binds the out-of-body experience to its physical host. He remembered how she said it was to be the path by which the soul maintains it connection with its physical body. For this, he was truly thankful.

[Andrew's Perspective]

Upon waking up the next morning, I tried to understand how I did not wake immediately upon returning back to my body. But Mairy did say that such experiences would be very exhausting. I got up to find mom in the kitchen. From her demeanor, I realized that dad had still not returned to our family quarters. I couldn't tell how long mom may have slept, or if she slept at all. As I could see mom was in a worrisome state, I decide to discuss whether I should go to work or wait with her. After all, the nurse did suggest I should take a few days off.

Then thinking of dad not being back, I began to wonder where Mairy was. Bringing my concern to mom, she talked me into keeping the 'status quo', so to speak, and not draw any undue attention to ourselves by pursuing either of them.

"Your father is probably just being absent-minded again," mom said. "When he gets involved in work, he forgets about everything else. I swear, sometimes I wonder if he even remembers that he has a family."

"That's a bit harsh, but I know what you mean," I said, trying to defend dad. "He may be closer to proving his theories, true enough, but he left with the intent to find out more information about our quest here. Maybe he's on to something."

"Oh, he's on to something alright," Mairy stated, as she showed up suddenly.

I wasn't even aware of their entering the room. By her side were Lindsey and Vera, who they had been looking for. I began to wonder whether I was the only one who got any sleep.

"We just came up from the lower half, and Lindsey's husband tells us that dad was arrested last night for corporate espionage. He's now being held in the detention center."

Mom went from disappointed to despondent. I could see it in her face. I needed to do something to bring her spirits back up.

"Corporate espionage?" I rhetorically questioned. "That is so unlike dad. Sounds like a trumped up charge to me. Well, we got to get him out of there," I insisted.

Vera joined in without any reservations, advising, "You can't. We are not even supposed to know about it."

Lindsey added to Vera's information, explaining, "She's right. As it is, they are only running a cover story with the research team that your father is on; there has been no general announcement of pending charges. As I understand it, they have been sequestered pending the results of the last session. They say there is going to be a big announcement about their discovery, later today."

Vera spoke up again, cautioning, "We need to go to work right now and act as if nothing is wrong."

"What is your deal in this anyway?" I asked suspiciously of Vera, not happy with her interference.

"Calm down, Andrew. We found her hold up on the lower level with Milo's family. She's confessed to everything. She has been working with Tom to keep track of us, but she really doesn't know any more," Mairy explained. "And now she is just scared."

"Or that's all she is telling us," I said, feeling the sting of betrayal. "She doesn't seem all that scared to me.

How long have you been spying on us?" I asked, interrogating Vera.

"Almost from the beginning," Vera boldly admitted. "I was approached by Tom the day after you arrived. It seems he was not fooled by your unannounced arrival to the moon station. He was the one who forged your admission into the program and assigned you two to the master CONS units."

"I thought it was dad who helped us out," I remarked.

"Anyway, one of master CONS units was supposed to be mine. When I complained about the being denied the position, he gave me this 'gig' to keep an eye on you," she revealed. "You see, he knew about my ability to control the dream simulation when I was hooked up to the control pods, and suspected that I had mastered the out-of-body experience. But my abilities pale in comparison to yours. You both seem to be able to interact with your surroundings."

Whoa, that was just a boatload of information that I did not even anticipate. I could see that Lindsey felt just as surprised as me by what she was hearing from Vera's confession.

"Is there something more about all this that I should know?" Lindsey asked Vera candidly.

As Mairy did not seem at all surprised by Vera's confession, my guess was that Vera and her shared a confidence; a shared secret to which I was not a party. I ignored Lindsey's request, and continued with my interrogation.

"So then that was you we saw yesterday, at the black hole," I deduced.

"Maybe," Vera admitted. "I mean yes, I suppose so; but I couldn't really say for sure. While I did see both of you, I couldn't real say where I was. Tom said that they were only going to align my dreamscape with yours so that I could keep track of you. But then I was unable to maintain control of my out-of-body experience as I had done in the past."

"So you did see us," I posed the leading question to her like a seasoned prosecutor. "So I am presuming that you already told Tom about our new abilities then," I asked, trying to find out how much Tom knew.

"No; and if he does know, it wasn't from me," she insisted. "That is, I haven't reported any of this to him. Somehow, he just seemed to know about you and Mairy from the start. At first, when Tom led me to believe you two were dangerous, I was apprehensive about spying on you. Then, as I got to know you better, I discovered you two weren't dangerous at all. In fact, if it wasn't for Mairy, I might have not been able to reconnect with my dream simulation at all.

I looked to Mairy, now understanding why she disappeared during the last session. "So you did end up disconnecting from me?" I questioned.

"Yes, I guess so," Mairy replied. "But only for a little while. And when I went back for you, you were gone. It was only after we were revived that I saw how it affected you. I'm really sorry, but Vera needed me more."

"No problem," I said, shrugging it off in a macho manner. "If I'm going to learn how to swim, then I had to be dropped off in the deep end sooner or later."

"So because of her sacrifice, I was instead rather conflicted as to what Tom had led me to believe. I didn't know what to believe anymore. If you weren't really dangerous, then why was Tom so eager to have you tracked? I began thinking there was something strange about the whole assignment; like I was working for the wrong side. So now I am thinking I would like to learn more about how you two do what you do."

Lindsey decided she could be patient no longer, and forcefully asked in confusion, "Why, what is it that they were doing besides all this out-of-body stuff you've been talking about?"

"Tom requested that I keep it a secret from the rest of the team," Vera replied to Lindsey, as if they had repaired their previously fractured friendship. "I'll tell you about it later."

"We appreciate your confidence in us," Mairy acknowledged of Vera's eagerness to join forces with us. "But right now, we still don't know why Tom is doing any of this."

Then, taking Mairy to the side in confidence, I suggested that the fault may not have been all their own. "Not really sure what you did to save her, but it's obvious Vera had a hand in this as well," I whispered. "So I guess you're not to blame for this whole mess."

"Well, we certainly haven't been very discrete," Mairy pointed out to me, still considering that we were largely to blame.

"You're both missing the obvious," mom said, as she finally spoke up. "Tom knows because he believes. He's read your father's books and he believes! Think about it; he wouldn't have employed your father, and us, without any advanced degree, unless he believed in him."

"That's a first," I declared in retrospect. "All this time that we were trying to keep it a secret, dad was 'spilling the beans' in his books."

"Well, there was really no reason why anyone should consider that any science fiction story would be true," mom supposed, implying to clear dad of any wrong doing. "So the question is why would Tom believe in your father's research, without any proof? It doesn't make any real sense."

"It would, if he was one of us," Mairy piped in.

I immediately pulled Mairy further away from Vera and Lindsey, politely requesting, "Could you excuse us for a moment? This is kind of a family discussion."

"One of us?" I whispered in annoyance with Mairy. "What do you mean when you say 'one of us'?"

"Not now," Mairy acknowledged dismissively, trying to brush off my question.

Being that the situation was time sensitive, Lindsey interrupted, "I'm not sure what this is all about, but we are sure to raise suspicion if we don't show up to the morning's meeting."

"Right, so then we are all in this together," Mairy implied as an agreement. "No one says anything until we find out what is really going on." Then speaking directly to Lindsey, Mairy requests, "Go on ahead, and let them know we're running a little late."

"OK," Lindsey acknowledged. "And Sandi, you can start by getting in contact with my husband, Ulrick. He should know exactly what to do for you, and how to get you to meet with Steve."

"Where will I find him," mom asked.

"He should still be working the south gate at this time of day," Lindsey answered.

"Thank you, Lindsey," mom acknowledged of her kind offer.

After Lindsey and Vera left, I asked of Mairy again, "What's going on? Are you saying that Tom is a Shadow-Forge member of the Dark Guild, working with Discordia?"

"Or just another Shadow-Forge in it for himself," Mairy corrected him. "Not everyone is working for Harmony or Discordia. Anyway, I don't really know yet. But maybe your father does," Mairy speculated. "Tom wouldn't have locked Steve up unless he was a danger to him."

"That actually makes sense, if you think about it," mom agreed. "He believes what is in your father's books, because he is just like one the characters in the story."

"Then this can't be good for us," I surmised. "If that's true, then he's has been playing us from the beginning. For all we know, he was probably working in league with that creature on Earth."

"That would be a reasonable assumption," Mairy apprised of my deduction.

"So perhaps there is more than one Shadow-Forge involved," mom speculated.

"Not anymore," Mairy emphasized. "Remember, Kiana killed that one back on Earth. Whoever it was, or from where ever it came from, it is no longer part of this reality."

"Unless, of course, it came from this reality," I replied reflexively. Everyone looked at me as if I had said something weird. "You know, like me," I said, putting it in better context.

"That is also a sensible rationale," Mairy agreed with me again. "In which case, it could resurface again; even here, on the moon."

"We need a plan," mom announced. "I don't know how your quests usually work, but we seem to be working at a disadvantage here."

"That is usually how our quests work," I disclosed to mom.

"OK; then you two continue to go to work, and I'll make some inquiries about your father. They would expect that of me by this time anyway." Then mom paused, asking, "Where is the south gate?"

After we provided mom with directions, we left her to her own devices. As we walked to the lab, I was reminded of Mairy's surprise entrance this morning, and asked, "Where have you been all night?"

"After I left you and your mother, I went over to Lindsey's room to see if she knew anything more about Vera," Mairy started. "At first

Lindsey wasn't forthcoming, but I could tell she was hiding something. She even questioned me about our activity during the last session. As the conversation seemed stilted and one-sided, I tried to persuade her, without getting into any details, that there was nothing out of the ordinary. But I could see that she was not believing what I was telling her."

"Why didn't you just use your powers to get her to tell you?" I asked. "Or is that against your code of honor, or something."

"It doesn't work like that. I can't force information out of anyone," Mairy related to me. "But I could feel that she was not telling me the truth. And I could sense that she knew something more than she was telling me. So finally, I decided to confide in her about our activity during the last session; so as to gain her trust. And not only did Lindsey know where Vera was, but she was hiding her as well."

"That makes sense," I commented. "Vera is probably closest to Lindsey, despite their problems."

"As it turns out, I learned that Vera had seen us, as she just told you, and was actually frightened by our abilities. And since Tom had told her we were dangerous, she was really conflicted as to what to do next. So she finally returned to her only real friend on the Moon. And when she caught up with Lindsey, Lindsey convinced her to hide with Milo's family, down in the lower levels."

"So now I guess Lindsey and Vera are in on our little secret?" I asked rhetorically.

"Yes; and then, of course, Lindsey and Milo discussed it so that Milo would agree to bring her down there," Mairy explained further, with a hint of guilt in her expression.

"So then Milo knows about all this as well?" I asked with surprise.

"Yes," Mairy responded. "And knowing his lack of inhibitions, I'm sure Tim probably knows by now."

"Great, they all know we're Shadow-Forge members of the Light Guild?!" I asked with alarm.

"No, not that," Mairy said, softening the blow. "They just know we can travel beyond our dream simulations. And they know, from Vera, that something strange is going on with the project. And I'm guessing it is not something that they agreed to sign up for. In fact, everyone is kind of paranoid right now. But I convince them that we were here to help. And now they want to help us."

"Well, three cheers for the cavalry!" I proclaimed sarcastically; "and just in the nick of time."

"You know, you can be really insensitive sometimes," Mairy snapped back at him, and walked on ahead of me.

"OK, OK, I'm sorry," I pleaded with her. "I promise to calm down. I guess I'm just a little on edge as well."

"Just try being a little more trusting of your own kind," Mairy advised me. "They might surprise you."

"What?" I said, pausing to reflect on a memory she had triggered.

It was a bit like what mom would say to dad. Thinking back on dad's untrusting nature, I realized I was more like dad than I would admit. In light of this reminiscence, I regretted my rude outburst. And as we were now in site of the lab entrance, I needed her to be assured of my intentions towards her before we got there.

"OK, I know you're right; I was being very rude," I said, pleading with her to not let this get between us. "I'll try to be more trusting, but I want you to know that I have always had complete trust in you."

"Alright, but just keep comments like that to yourself in the future," Mairy suggested.

"Alright, point taken," I agreed, trying to make things right with her.

"Anyway, Lindsey took me down to Milo's family home where we met up with Vera. With Lindsey's help, I was able to calm Vera down, and then found out that she had been spying on us all along. So perhaps there is a solid foundation for your untrusting nature of your own kind," Mairy stated, in an attempt to make peace with me, I suppose. "Anyway, before we came back up, we were also able to find a way from the lower level over to the shuttle bay, where we came in. There is an access door for the maintenance crew area, which as it happens, opens up directly from the lower level."

"My, you have been busy. You are one very resourceful fairy," I complimented her, hoping to offset my previous offending remarks. I saw Mairy smile. And just beyond her, I saw the door to the pods lab open.

"About time you two showed up," Dr. Beecher greeted, and then herded us into the lab. "You missed this morning's briefing, but it was short anyway. The company wanted to congratulate you both, and the team, on the excellent work you are all doing."

It looked as if they hadn't been in the lab for very long. As we went to our individual pods, I briefly thought about using the nurse's recommendation to excuse myself. Then I looked over to Mairy, in hopes of catching her eye, and realized that this was not the time to back out; regardless of any probable danger.

As we suited up for the next run, Dr. Beecher continued to talk. "We will be revisiting the same system as from yesterday's session. And Andrew, we've also tweak your CONS unit to filter data at a higher frequency, hoping to offset the difficulty of yesterday's misfortune."

"Yeah, Andrew, try not falling down on the job this time," Milo yelled from across the room. "You're slowing us all down."

"Oh, very 'pun-worthy' of you to notice," Timothy responded to Milo's comment.

"Don't you two ever take this stuff seriously?" Lindsey scolded them.

"What's to take," Milo supported of his demeanor. "We just float around and enjoy our dream simulations while our brains do all the work. It's kind of like playing computer games while your work routines are running in the background."

Then, to our surprise, Dr. Beecher made an unexpected request, "Mairy, I would like Vera to take the lead with Andrew this morning. Would you mind switching places with her?"

Mairy looked over in my direction and then back to Dr. Beecher, saying, "Yes, of course, it really doesn't matter to me. I can do what I need to do from either unit."

I took what Mairy said to mean that she would be able to hook up with me, even if we were not both hooked up to the master CONS units.

"But won't there be a problem with the calibration of the pods?" Mairy questioned. "I believe you told us the units were programmed to support a unique operator."

"Actually we had the technicians swap out your programmed boards last night," Dr. Beecher replied. "The company wanted a confirmation that we could cross train operators, should something go wrong."

"How very efficient of the company," Vera spoke up, as she walked over to replace Mairy at the control pod. "I've been wanting to get back into the driver's seat for some time now."

While this move made everyone a little uneasy, including Vera, no one was letting on.

"So, other than this switch, the mission for the rest of you in this session is still the same," Dr. Beecher continued. "Please focus on your objectives so that we can continue to get clear images."

I began to doubt the integrity of Vera resolve to help us. Although she did seem just as surprised by the change in assignments as the rest of us, my doubt seemed to resonate from all the plot twist in movies that I had watched over the years. This is the part where the main character, which I applied to myself, is double-crossed by the opposing forces in an attempt to take over control of the whole operation. It was the classic betrayal scenario.

I began to wonder how good she really was, and what were the real extent of her astral abilities, and whether Mairy had really saved her at all. Maybe that routine of being scared of our abilities was just a ruse. But then I remembered what Mairy and I had just discussed earlier about trust, and decided to let things play out. Still, even as I decided not to prejudge her, there remained a nagging doubt.

"Are you ready for this?" Vera asked me.

"Not sure what you mean by 'this'," I responded glibly for the nearby technicians. "The dream simulation interface shouldn't be any different for me no matter who is in the other master CONS unit," I said trying to play it off.

"While that should be true," the technician spoke up, "there is still a chance that the two master CONS units won't immediately sync up with the switched programs. If that is the case, you may experience some disorientation in your dream landscape simulation. Just go with it. And don't panic. We will be here to monitor the connection between you two, and we should be able to make the necessary changes."

"Oh, ok; that's good to know," I replied.

I wasn't sure what all that meant, but I thought I should brace myself for anything. I took a last look over to Mairy across the room, as my pod was being maneuvered to its operating position. As I looked through the glass of the pod lid, I gazed up to the ceiling and quickly drifted off.

I soon realized that I was right to prepare myself for anything. Everything was blurry, as if I needed glasses or something. It appeared I was dropped into a blurry dreamscape, where objects in the distance were difficult to make out and most were indistinguishable. Rather I could only envision vague shapes and colored images in motion. As tried to work through the difficulties of my handicap, I came to the realization that I was in the dream simulation. I began to attempt to take control, as I had done per previous sessions. Yet, even as the motion of the images began to settle down, it was still a bit fuzzy around the edges. My guess was that the master CONS units worked somewhat like binocular vision, and just needed to be adjusted to my new partner.

Finally, I was able to regain some semblance of the space I was occupying; and it wasn't good. It seemed I had skipped right through the dreamscape and gone directly into the deep space targeted location. It scared and disoriented me big time, as I wasn't sure who was really in control. I began to bring into view an open scene of multiple stars clustered within a swirling gaseous cloud. As the targeted location came into focus, I recognized that I was positioned near, but outside the circumference of, the plasma ring. It was similar to the Whirlpool galaxy, and yet it was not the same location as in our previous session. Or at least I had not recognized it as such. I froze in place, trying to decide what to do next. Am I here alone, I thought?

Then I began to sense the presence of another aura. It was a little different than my previous encounters with Fairy. It was as if my own presence of actuality was being engaged or intruded upon. Was it Vera, I questioned myself? Slowly the emerging communication across auras manifested itself. As I became aware of the familiar melodious sound of harp-like tones echoing about me, I realized it was Fairy's aura that had embraced me once again. She appeared to me as she did previously in other sessions, wings and all.

"My, my, your aura is a bit strange. Are you alright?" Fairy asked. "You seem to be a bit off color."

"Yeah, well a little. What took you so long? I was beginning to think I was on my own out here," I confessed, a little nervous about not knowing where Vera was.

"It took me a little longer to find you this time," she relayed to me. "Perhaps it had something to do with the new CONS set up. Or maybe being this close to the plasma ring may have caused some interference."

Vera is probably lying in wait to ambush us, I thought to myself.

"You're still thinking Vera is working in concert with Tom," Fairy picked up from me. "Somehow, I can't believe that about her."

Her statement was a gentle reminder that there was no turning off our psychic connection. I had forgotten that she could pretty much hear everything I was thinking while we were connected.

"Oh, because you had a long talk with her," I questioned, still wondering what secrets that might be sharing apart from me.

"No, because I felt it," Fairy snapped back.

"Well, I'm not sure what to think about her," I admitted. "You are the one who gained her trust. What do you think she might be doing then?" I questioned Fairy.

"Remember what you told me before the session started?" Fairy prompted me.

"Yes, that I trusted you," I replied. Something she needed to remind me of, I guess.

"There, that's much better," Fairy related to me. "Your aura is coming back to normal."

Just then I spied a twinkling brightness just outside of the event horizon; midway between the rotating ring of plasma and the swirling miasma that outlined the lower portion of the black hole.

"Wait, I believe I see something there in the direction of the black hole, just below the plasma ring. Do you think that could be her?" I asked, but Fairy gave no response. "What should we do?" I prompted again, a bit apprehensive to just move towards the rending nature of the plasma ring.

I've had only bad experiences with these monstrosities. I thought about how we might start off in a more direct line of sight, from our current position to the twinkle, while still avoiding any interaction with the effects of the plasma stream.

"You can't approach it that way," Fairy quickly cautioned me. "Remember the lessons of the crystal. You need to approach it away from its equator and more towards the bottom, where the force is weakest. I've been doing this longer than you. You stay here and I'll check it out. It may be nothing at all."

Finally, she was back in communication with me again. I wondered how I could not hear her thoughts, much the way she had already been doing with me. Anyway, I gathered from what she said that she was going to 'jump' the space between us and the twinkle without me, using the aether as she had done with me previously. As I was uneasy about Fairy's decision to detach from me, I came up with an alternative.

"Wait!" I called out to her. "Maybe there is a way we can both go. Remembering what mom said about our having a connection with our host bodies via a 'silver cord'?"

"Yes," Mairy answered. "What did you have in mind?"

"It just suddenly occurred to me that perhaps we could intertwine our 'silver cord' connections somehow," I proposed without any idea of how it might work. "Then maybe we could still maintain an aural connection, even as you make the jump to get closer the black hole's event horizon."

"Interesting idea; I'll give it a try," Fairy agreed.

Then Fairy fully embraced me as if she were going to be gone for a long time. It was quite a different experience to be embraced in our astral forms, rather them than just sharing our individual auras within her aural veil. It seemed, somehow, more sincere and bonding. It was as if we were one essence, rather than two distinct entities. She then backed up and extended our comingled auras, stretching our shared aural veil like so much silly putty. Upon her separation, we were both amazed to see a stream of ghostly light developing between us. It was as if we were tethered together by the active 'will' of our own combined consciousness.

"Whoa, that's a new one on me," she proclaimed, apparently seeing this light effect for the first time.

She momentarily grabbed and shook it, seemingly testing its strength, and then she was off. I watched as Fairy projected herself towards the bottom of the black hole's event horizon. I understood her tactic was to approach the twinkling light from the bottom up, and far away from the shredding force of the plasma ring. It was strange, but reassuring, to see the visible trail of this 'silver cord' which was extended between us. After a while, I lost sight of her in the miasma of activity beyond the plasma ring, even as the silver cord remained intact. Then, unexpectedly, Fairy communicated to check in with me. Evidently our distance from each other was not an issue for this type of astral communication, as long as our auras were comingled.

"I see her," Fairy reported. "She looks to be drifting towards the event horizon of the black hole, and she doesn't appear to have any control. If she gets beyond the event horizon, I may not be able to find her again."

"OK, I'm coming in then," I said. "I'll follow along your lighted path."

"No, not yet; something's wrong," Fairy cautioned. "Something about her is just not right."

My worst fears began to flood my reasoning, as I blurted out, "What's wrong is that we shouldn't have trusted her. She doing the same thing she did to us last time. She is pulling us into the black hole. And this time we are not together." As I waited for a quick retort from Fairy, there was instead a momentary pause.

"No, that's not it at all," Fairy informed me. "Rather, she seems to be in a trance, or something. Strange, I still perceive her but I don't sense her aura. How is maintaining her essence?"

I felt bad about my outburst and urged her on, "Well, if you have to pursue her into and beyond the event horizon, at least we are connected. You can always find your way back."

Fairy seemed preoccupied, ignoring my outburst, saying, "No matter how close I get to her, I still can't make a connection."

I suddenly thought of something that my dad and I had discussed about the interior of the black hole. "Wait, don't go any closer," I warned her. "Let me think this through. This is similar to when I came in contact with that field around the 'source seed' on Glorthocks."

"I can't stop now, or I'll surely lose her beyond the event horizon," Fairy insisted.

"When you rescued me from within the black hole during our last quest together, where did you find me exactly?" I asked.

"Just inside the event horizon; which is already where we are going now. What are you getting at?" Fairy asked of me.

"According to dad, there is no real center to the black hole. The center is just increasing degrees of negative mass density to offset the gravitational acceleration of the black hole. It's a form of dark matter, if you will; a deepening void from which there is no escape. My guess is that she is already beyond the event horizon and that she is somehow, even now, interacting with the dark matter. Have you ever been to the center of a black hole before?"

"No, not really; I never really had a reason to be in a black hole before you sent us crashing into one," she joked. "What's your point?"

"Right," I acknowledged, trying to work out the ramifications of interacting with dark matter. "So, with your not being able to sense Vera's aura, what are the possibilities then? Either Vera's aura has been cloaked by the dark matter environment, or ...," I paused in midsentence, trying to remember what it was about black holes that could skew our perspectives.

"Or what?" Fairy remarked somberly. "Or she is truly dead to us in this reality?"

But then I changed my stream of thought to deal with Fairy's anxiety, "Wait, I thought you said once you lose your aura, you are absorbed into the universal being. But you are telling me that you can still see her."

"Yes, that is odd indeed," Fairy agreed. "And she shows no signs of dissipating either. It is if she is rather frozen in spacetime."

"That's it; like how I saw you in the crystal in my dream!" I declared, as it came to me. "I believe the crystal was compacted dark matter. So this must be all about relativity. Her spacetime reference within the gravitational acceleration of the black hole, relative to our position, has her appear as if she is in a motionless trance. But rather, she really exists outside of our Time frame reference."

"Outside of our Time?" Fairy asked quizzically. "I don't understand what you are saying. How can we be in differing frames of Time?"

"Because it's not about Space, it is about the relativity of Time dilation," I informed her. "Since there is no real Space anymore, beyond the event horizon, she is just drifting towards the center of the black hole, in degrees of relative Time. You may not be familiar with the experience because you are always used to some reference point in existence, within minor variations of spacetime. That is, except when you're transitioning from one reality to the next. But even then, you are traveling faster than anything else, so it all appears normal from your perspective."

"Think of it like this: regardless of your perspective of distance to her, you are still in a Time frame reference which is much faster than where she is," I explained, trying to clarify the concept. "It's like a flying insect zipping about an elephant. The movements of the elephant appear to be exaggeratedly slow to the fly, compared with the insect's speed and reaction time. So to the insect, the elephant is moving in slow-motion. Ergo, the greater the difference in speed, the greater the perceptional variances are. From the fly's perspective, his mind is even processing information faster, consistent with his momentum."

Pausing just a moment, I formulated my hypothesis, "Perhaps you can't sense her aura because of this relative difference in degrees of Time."

"Ergo?" Fairy questioned of my word choice. "Anyway, I think I get it. Although it may seem as if she is in the same relative Space as I am, she is still in a very different relative Time from me."

"That's how I understand it," I replied. "Dad explained to me a while back, that there is no existence other than Present time, and that the universe is always evolving. It is kind of like that saying: There is no time like the Present; because Time can only exist in the Present. Anyhow, our spacetime reality cannot exist in a Past time, because the Present time source of that Past time is not a real location in spacetime anymore; it has already been changed upon its evolution into Present time."

I could recognize that I was rambling and I needed to get back on subject. "However, the difference in Time to which I am referring to is just the relativity of Present time variations; like differing frequencies running in parallel. So while we are all simultaneously existing in the same reference to Present time, we do not necessarily all exist in the same reference of Present time. It's like Harmony told me: *The Time stream is variable throughout the universe. It is not constant, but is it is consistent.*"

"Then I can still get to her, even if see doesn't sense me," Fairy construed from my explanation. "I just need to I travel faster than she is drifting, and then slow down to readjust to her reference of Time."

"Perhaps, in theory; yes," I related, thinking that I was beginning to sound like my father. "But remember, although we are all relatively in the Present, her spacetime reality is different from our own. Time passes slower relative to one's increased gravitational acceleration. It's kind of like the analogy of the 'fly and the elephant'; perception depends on how rapidly one's nervous system processes sensory information. Even as the fly is faster than the elephant, the fly can also see 250 frames per second whereas the elephant may only see about 15 frames per second."

"Can you get to the point," Fairy demanded impatiently. "Time seems to be the overriding factor here."

"Yes, OK; so we can see her, because we are moving too fast, but she cannot see us. As you continue to adjust to her relative Time, you might lose your perception of me," I said, trying to wrap it up quickly. "I'm not sure what to think about that kind of disruption to our connection in such a relative Time dilation. Let's see, dad talked about how existence is in degrees of spacetime, from 'No Space and All Time' to 'All Space and No Time'. My prediction is that the center of the black hole is absent of any mass density, or All Space, which probably accounts for its perspective of having no relevancy for Time."

I guess my time with dad was not all wasted. Actually, I wish he were here right now, I thought to myself.

"Well fortunately for us, in our current astral form, mass is not real a concern," Fairy conveyed.

"But what about what happened to me in the last black hole?" I asked, reminding her of my condition.

"That was because you did not separate from the crystal, as I did, so you disintegrated with the crystal," Fairy informed me. "It was all we could do to put you back together."

"Right, well; OK then," I continued with my previous stream of thought. "But our presence, in in our astral form, must account for something or Vera wouldn't be drifting towards the center. So the difference in relative Time still has something to do with our existence, no matter what our condition. So if the Time reference is still relative to our own existence, how shall we go about dealing with this relativity?"

"All I know is that you're wasting my time with too much indecision. I'm going in for her," Fairy declared.

"But we haven't completely assessed the risk," I pleaded with her.

"If there is a risk, then I'm in Shadow-Forge form already. If anything happens to me, then I just return to my own reality," she stated simply; "in which case you are on your own. So if something untoward happens, get out and return to your own reality. However, if nothing happens to me, then I need you to be my anchor, so that I will be able to find my way back to you. I believe we should still be able to communicate within our comingled aural connection, regardless of this Time dilation."

Before I could interject with any alternative rationale, she was moving ever faster and ever deeper into the black hole towards its center. While I wasn't sure about our ability to communicate, I could still see the lighted tether and feel our connection. I could only wait and worry whether her gamble would be worth the risk. After some time had passed, she finally communicated with me.

"I got her," Fairy proclaimed in a somewhat lethargic manner. I could almost feel her relief. "She is not in a trance at all, and I'm talking to her now. You were right about that Time reference thing. She didn't even know where she was. It's weird; from in here we can sense the motion of the universe, but nothing more. At least I think it is the motion of the universe. I can't really tell. It's like a kaleidoscope of rainbow colors in here. We must indeed be well inside the black hole's event horizon, because it's just like when we jump in here before."

While what she was saying I could make out, it was as if she was talking in slow motion. "Thank God, you're both alright!" I exclaimed, remembering to slow the cadence of my enunciation to match her lethargic rhythm. "And yes, I can hear you. I've been thinking about our current predicament. Before we went under, Dr. Beecher said they tweaked our CONS units to filter data at a higher frequency. Maybe there was a disparity in our relative Time frames even before we came into our astral forms."

"I can't see you, but I'm hoping this astral connection allows you to hear me. Right now we seem to be drifting away from the light. I think we're still being pulled in towards the center. I'm hoping, having included her in our combined aural veil, we can focus on stopping our motion towards the center."

It was like she hadn't heard anything I was saying. I began to realize that this disparity in relativity of Time was going to be more of a disruption than I might have guessed. At least I knew they were alright, and we were still connected. She was like the elephant, and I was like the fly. Hopefully, as they work their way out, the rate of our communication would begin to equalize again. All I knew was that I needed to remain as their anchor to my reality.

[Scene Change – Narrator's Perspective]

[Cause and effect – The quest is exposed]

Sandi had made her way to Steve and Phil, with the help of Lindsey's husband. They had no real plan to speak of, but they were determined to contact them anyway they could. Ulrick had led her to the detention center where they encountered one guard stationed outside the main entrance. Ulrick guessed the guard had been there a while base on the number of empty water bottles near his desk.

"I know this guy. This shouldn't be too much trouble," Ulrick stated with confidence. "You wait here."

Sandi watched as he walked right passed the lone security officer.

The security officer called out to him, "Ulrick, what are you doing down in this section?"

"I'm scheduled for guard duty over here later tonight," he replied. "I just wanted to familiarize myself with where the closest washroom is. I wouldn't want to be stuck down here not knowing where it is. See ya."

"Hey, wait; can you be a buddy, and spell me for I bit," the security officer asked. "I don't go off duty for another hour, and I don't think I can wait that long."

"Sure, no problem," Ulrick replied. "But don't take long. I have places to be."

"Thanks, you're a life saver," he said, as got up from his chair behind the desk.

Once the guard was out of sight, Sandi appeared. "How did you know that would work?" Sandi asked.

"See all the empty water bottles?" Ulrick pointed out to her. "Guard duty is boring, what else is he going to do? But we'll have to work fast before he comes back."

"Won't you get in trouble once he finds out they are not in there?" she asked.

"Probably, but that shouldn't be for a while. It's all about the illusion," he stated. With that Ulrick opened the main entrance to the detention rooms. "Now let's get your husband out of here."

As Sandi and Ulrick approached the two captives, Steve asked, "Sandi, what's going on?"

"I was going to ask you the same question," Sandi replied in kind.

"We're not sure, but it has to do with the kids," he answered.

As Ulrick opened the doors to their detention rooms, Steve came out and gave her a quick hug.

Phil thanked Ulrick for the escape, adding, "It may not just be your kids. I think he needs all the pod operators to pull this off. I believe that they are all in danger."

Ulrick hurried them along with even more purpose now, saying, "You two need to leave now. Your wife and I still have something to do to make the charade complete."

"Alright, we're going directly to research lab, just beyond where the pod operators are working," Steve informed them. "We'll meet you there."

"Sandi, you wait just down the hall," Ulrick directed her. "When you see the other security officer return, then you come back here asking to visit with Steve."

"I get it," Sandi acknowledged. "We want him to believe they are still in there, so he won't check; clever."

With that, Sandi went down the hall and hide just out of sight. They didn't have to wait too long before the other security guard returned.

"Everything come out alright for you?" Ulrick joked with him.

"Yes, thank you," he said, walking to the door of the detention room. "They give you any trouble?"

"Not at all, couldn't even tell they were in there," Ulrick said with a straight face. "Hey, someone is coming down the hall."

Sandi understood that to be her cue to approach them.

The security guard then turned his attention from the door to the woman coming down the hall, asking, "Excuse me lady, what are you doing down here?"

"I was told my husband Steve is being held down here," she answered with indignation.

"I'm not sure that's allowed right now," Ulrick intervened. "Do you have written permission?"

"Surely, just a word of comfort shouldn't be a problem," she countered.

"Please Mrs. Bauer," the first officer took charge again. "I have my orders."

"I'll tell you what, Mrs. Bauer," Ulrick approached her. "I'll take you back to where we can sort all of this out."

"Alright then," Sandi acknowledged, "but I'll be back."

"Yes, ma'am," the security guard acknowledged as he reclaimed his seat behind the desk.

As the two walked off, Sandi asked Ulrick, "Ma'am; do I look like a ma'am to you?"

"He's just being polite," Ulrick said without getting into the politics of her inquiry. "Let's find the others."

The two caught up to Steve and Phil in the research center. Steve and Phil were looking through images on the computer screen that were already being processed. Steve observes aloud, "This looks to be a different target than the Whirlpool Galaxy. Can we examine the previous images generated by IGIE?"

"I've never tried developing them in real time before," Phil admitted, "but it should be possible. But if you're just trying to identify the target location, I can check the DeepSIT navigation settings. Yes, it appears it is set to image NGC 4889, also known as Coma B, in the constellation of Coma Berenices. According to this background information, it lies at the center of the Coma Cluster. And, oddly enough, the Coma Cluster is located at exactly the center of the Coma Supercluster."

"Where have I heard about that before?" Steve questioned aloud of his memories. "Isn't that the supergiant elliptical galaxy which is hosting the supermassive black hole?"

"Yes; according to this it is one of the most massive black holes on record," Phil acknowledges. "It is measured on the order of 5,000 times more massive than the central black hole of the Milky Way."

"Can you imagine the extreme negative density of the dark matter in there?" Steve questioned.

Just then Margaret walked in on them.

"What's going on in here?" Margaret asked as she entered the center. "I thought you two were being detained for industrial espionage."

Phil responded, "And you didn't think to question that pronouncement? Think about it, Margaret, does any of it make sense to you. I've been working alongside of you for, what, four years now. You know me. It's never been about the money for me."

"Then what is this all about?" Margaret inquired further. "Because it looks like you're accessing classified data?"

"We are monitoring the session, like someone should be doing. So where is everyone?" Phil asked.

"Everyone else is in the pods lab, attending to the CONS units," she replied.

Then Ulrick spoke up in their defense.

"Come on, Margaret, don't you see that Tom made it all up so they could be detained," Ulrick attempted to explain; "to keep them, and everyone else, from seeing what he is about to do with the pod sleepers."

"Why, what do you mean?" Margaret asked protectively. "What is he planning to do with my pod team?"

Looking up from what he was doing, Steve added, "Tom is out of control. He is working on a way to connect the pod sleepers with their target environments. He not just trying to detect dark matter, he believes that he can actually channel dark energy through them here into the lab."

"That makes no sense; that's just insane; isn't it?" Margaret questioned.

"That is what we have been trying to tell you," Sandi declared. "Tom is not who he seems to be!"

"Tom just relieved me in the lab," Margaret revealed. "He came to witness this session personally. And he asked me to monitor the data directly from here. He seemed perfectly fine to me."

"Think about it, Margaret; he hasn't been interested in this aspect of the project for some years now. Why now, after all these years, does he feel the need to micromanage your pod sleepers?" Phil questioned.

Margaret gave no answer, but rather she switched the monitor over to the pods lab cameras. "They're all leaving!" Margaret observed aloud, with surprise. "It looks like Tom has dismissed all the technicians from the lab."

"In the middle of an active session?" Phil inquired. "That doesn't make sense. What is he doing now?"

As Margaret panned the camera over to the pod sleeper's CONS units, Sandi studied the activity in the lab.

"Look, he's meddling with Mairy's CONS unit!" Sandi alerted.

"Oh, my god!" Ulrick blurted out, having observing Mairy falling like a rag doll. "Did he just kill her?"

"He just removed Mairy from her CONS unit without waking her up," Margaret replied, trying to downplay the incident.

"That's not the proper protocol at all, and you know it," Phil argued. "It could have very dangerous side effects for her."

"Don't tell me that's the action of a sane man," Sandi insisted in an 'I told you so' demeanor.

"Protocol be damned!" Ulrick shouted, worried for the safety of his own wife. "Wake up Margaret. We need to get in there now!" Ulrick commanded.

"Phil, call for a medical team," Margaret ordered. "I'm going in with Ulrick."

"Now you're talking," Ulrick complied.

Ulrick and Margaret left the research center at a sprint, as they ran towards the pod labs.

"Tom is putting himself in the unit," Sandi observed, still watching the monitors.

"Is it possible to swap out a pod sleeper during a session?" Steve asked of Phil.

"I don't know. I've never seen it tried before," replied Phil, waiting for the medical station to answer.

Still working to get the generated images to show up on the monitor, Phil watched from afar. Finally succeeding in his efforts, Phil announced, "I think I got it." As the first image was being painted across the monitor, "What is that?" he questioned aloud.

"It looks like the brightest elliptical galaxy that I have ever seen," Steve responded back. "So that is NGC 4889. That is one supermassive black hole at its core," Steve reported, pausing to take it all in. "I need to see more," Steve stated with urgency, as the next image started to replace the first.

Phil finished alerting the medical team, while Steve was still pouring over the first image.

"Can we get a closer view of the black hole?" Steve asked.

"This system wasn't designed to zoom in and out on demand, much less to capture and play them back in real time," Phil explained with some frustration. "Let's see what I can do."

"They've reached the pods lab," Sandi announced, seeing Ulrick and Margaret outside the pods lab from the view of the pods lab camera facing the entrance.

Steve looked over to the monitors and could see that Ulrick and Margaret were trying to make their way in through the pod lab entrance. Margaret could be seen trying to access the pods lab with her security pin.

"I think that should work, but we will still have to wait for the next image to repaint the screen," Phil said.

Steve watched eagerly as the new imaged was being processed and painted onto the computer screen. "There, see; there seems to be a disruption in the plasma field around the event horizon," Steve noted.

"And it looks as if there is some light stretching up and over the plasma field from behind the black hole's event horizon," Phil observed aloud. "What's going on out there? That is just not possible. The gravity pull is much too strong to allow emissions at its equator. Maybe it's just an image translation problem."

"Wait a moment, let me think," Steve requested of everyone around him. "Yes, I believe I know what I was missing from our discussion before. Where there are two types of beta decay, known as beta minus and beta plus, for baryonic matter. In beta minus ($\beta-$) decay, a neutron is converted to a proton and the process creates an electron and an electron antineutrino; while in beta plus ($\beta+$) decay, a proton is converted to a neutron and the process creates a positron, or antielectron, and an electron neutrino."

Phil corroborated, "That's right; so what are you thinking?"

"What if there were a similar processes for baryonic antimatter?" Steve speculated. "I know there is no conclusive evidence for the gravitational interaction of antimatter, but the concept for their atomic mass is considered equivalent. So what if there were two types of beta decay, known as beta minus and beta plus, for baryonic antimatter. Could we possibly expect in beta minus ($\beta-$) decay, an antineutron is converted to an antiproton and the process creates an antielectron, or positron, and an antielectron anti-antineutrino; while in beta plus ($\beta+$) decay, an antiproton would convert into an antineutron, where the process would create anti-positron, or anti-antielectron and an antielectron antineutrino."

"That's a stretch to be sure," Phil remarked. "So what are you getting at?

"I'm looking for a connection between the decay of antimatter and the existence of dark matter," Steve speculated aloud. "It could be that antimatter is more stable nearer to dark matter than it is to regular matter. That being the case, then the plasma ring outside the black hole's event horizon could be the energetic interaction of matter with antimatter. However the matter-antimatter annihilation is dispersed and maintained within the gravitational pull of the black hole's center. But what if that energetic reaction were to somehow be pulled into the dark matter beyond the event horizon?" Steve hypothesized aloud of the possibility. "My guess is that it would constrict this energetic interaction into a more confined space."

"I believe I see where you are going with this," Phil concurred. "And I'm guessing that the culmination of that much matter and antimatter being forced together into dark matter could provide for enough energy to initiate a supernova from inside the black hole."

"And maybe, like how a single sperm fertilizes an ovum, it is enough energy to initiate the kind of spontaneous creation event that we were discussing," Steve asserted, thinking briefly about Andrew's previous quest in search of the source seed.

"Really, this is what you're thinking about at a time like this?" Sandi questioned tersely.

"It's just an analogous comparison," Steve attempted to correct her. "Imagine: perhaps the properties of mitosis may be inherited as a blueprint from within the universe as a property for all existence."

"Does your mind ever stop working? Our children are in danger!" Sandi observed of their dire situation.

"The solution is not always rendered upon our actions alone," Steve said in an attempt to explain.

"The medical team has shown up, and they are still not in yet," Sandi alerted. "What are we going to do?"

"This is taking too long," Steve said impatiently, "we need to be closer to what's going on. Can you feed this view to the pod lab monitors?"

"Yes, that I can do easily enough," Phil replied.

"OK, and then see if you can find John and get him down here to help you," Steve said, trying to coordinate their activities. "Sandi and I are going over to the pods lab."

Phil acknowledged with a nod, as Steve and Sandi ran out of the room towards the pods lab. Suddenly, they felt a prolonged shudder in the structure of the facility that stopped them dead in their tracks.

"What was that?" Sandi exclaimed.

"Yes, that was different," Stephen admitted, replying in a somewhat subdued manner.

A second shudder threw Sandi off balance and into Steve's arms as they fell against the wall.

"I'm guessing it is not a 'good' different," Sandi remarked with excitement.

"That would be an astute observation. I'm guessing it is a side effect of our research that I hadn't counted on happening so soon," Steve said of the event. Do to their proximity, and their situation, they shared a quick kiss. "We'd better keep moving."

As they moved with a little more caution now, they found themselves listing from side to side, at times, as they made their way towards the pods lab.

"A side effect?" Sandi repeated sarcastically. "This is what you call a side effect? What did you do now?"

"Why do you always assume that everything is my fault?" Steve queried defensively.

"Well, is it?" Sandi asked accusingly.

"Well maybe I did contribute to it. But I'm guessing whatever Tom did with the CONS unit interface is most likely the major cause. My guess is that it is causing Andrew and Mairy to act like lightning rods."

"What? Lightning on the moon is causing this?" Sandi asked with incredulity.

"No, not lightning; but rather dark matter," Steve clarified. "Somehow they are physically transferring dark matter through their astral form and down to their physical bodies, and then into the Moon. The last session caused a 6% increase in the Moon's density, or so I was told. Anyway, as the Moon's density increases, so does the probability for moonquake activity. As there was no moonquake during or since the last session, I have to wonder what the measured increase is this time."

"Moonquakes?" Sandi questioned. "How is it that you neglected to tell me about moonquakes?"

"I didn't try you keep it from you," Steve remarked defensively. "It is is just that they are very rare and not worth noting."

"Well, I'm making note of it now," Sandi retorted. "How is it even possible? It has none of the dynamics of Earth's geology."

"Yes; well, any celestial body can have quakes. Especially if one is able to mess with its gravitational pull," Steve explained. "It's like diving deep into the ocean; the deeper one goes, the greater the pressure. This increase in pressure in the ocean is due to the gradual increase in gravitational acceleration, as one approaches closer to the center of the Earth. Accordingly, the deeper one travels towards the center of any celestial body, the greater the pressure due to increased density and subsequent gravitational acceleration. As the density of the Moon increases over time, this pressure eventually needs to be released. And similar to Earth's geological response, this pressure is relieved in the form of quakes."

"Wonderful," Sandi declared acerbically.

"And there is an added problem with moonquakes," Steve revealed. "A moonquake will last much longer in duration than a regular earthquake. Or, at least that is what the recent data shows."

"Well this adventure turned out to be a pip of a vacation," she quipped sarcastically.

"Hopefully, the surface of the Moon and the structure of this facility will remain stable long enough for this moon station to survive this event," Steve stated, thinking out loud.

"Yes, hopefully; or, at least while we are still in it," Sandi joked. "Just when I begin to become comfortably with the fact that we are safe from the natural disasters on Earth, I find out there are natural disasters on the Moon as well," Sandi remarked callously.

"Actually, that's a thought," Steve pragmatically responded. "I wonder what natural disasters are happening on Earth because of the Moon's increased density."

"You mean this, up here, can affect the Earth as well?" Sandi asked.

"Oh yes," Steve was quick to explain. "Just like what we know as the tidal effects of the moon, the attraction between the Earth and its Moon can cause all kinds of havoc. But not to worry for right now. Besides, whatever happens, they'll probably just attribute to climate change anyway," Steve quipped.

While the ongoing moonquakes made them uneasy, Sandi found a bit of comfort in believing that Steve somehow knew what he was doing. Still, their primary concern was for Mairy and Andrew; who very souls remained far beyond their ability to assist. All they could do now was to try and help safeguard the bodies of the pod sleepers. Not really knowing what was going on in deep space, they rushed to assist the others trying to breach the locked pods lab.

CHAPTER

17

Encounters of the Sixth Kind— Lost in Time

[The battle for the universe begins.]

Is it possible to survive within just a singular moment in Time? And how does one even define this notion? Where Time is not a constant, regardless of its dimensional limitations or configuration, so too Space, or the lack of it, is consistent rather than constant. Therein persists the varying degrees of Space and Time within the relativity of spacetime, which allows for the fluctuating dimensional references to which we attempt to understand our existence. The concepts of 'No Time' and 'All Time' and 'No Space' and 'All Space' are combined to frame the extreme reflections for the notion of non-existence in spacetime.

'No Space' representing the lack of any actual Space, or the Space that has been choked out by the inclusion or intrusion of baryonic matter into the infinite and formless expanse of nothingness. Herein flourishes the maximum positive density of all the baryonic matter contained within the universal vibrancy of evolutionary change. Pair that with the concept of 'All Time', or the kinetic Time expended, and you have the realm of a universe in critical mass entropy that mirrors both Past time and Future time.

607

On the other hand, 'All Space', or the infinite void of unfilled Space, represents the fullness of our spacial potential with which to offset the intrusion of baryonic matter; or the maximum negative density of all the dark matter compacted. Herein subsists the Space that has achieved maximum negative density within the universal stagnation of evolutionary change. Pair that with the concept of 'No Time', or potential Time, and you have the realm of the astral plane; the fifth dimension that parallels our Present time reality.

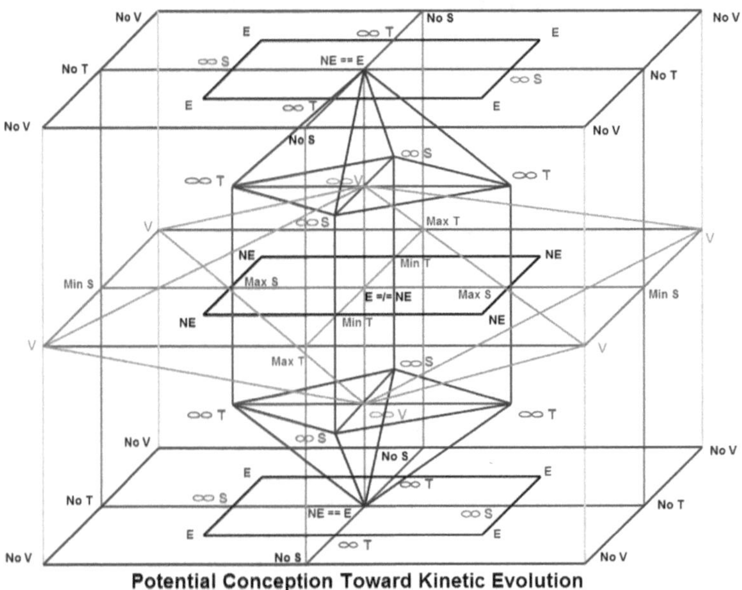

Potential Conception Toward Kinetic Evolution

Subsequently everything between these two non-existent notions of 'No Space' and 'All Space' in degrees of Time becomes the dimensional framework of our universal existence folded in on itself. In this way, existence is defined by the ongoing evolution of spacial variations and ongoing transformations in both positive and negative density. String them together in a succession of these varied density transformations, and you have the animation of our universal existence. It is an animation of being presented in a succession of evolutionary spacial changes, in both the breadth of its dimensional entanglements and the extent of its ability to contravene. Even the potential concept of these evolutionary spacial changes is, in itself, an expression of how change is achieved; ergo, it exists. It is within this imbroglio that a singular moment in Time inspires the ability 'to be' into the capability 'to do'.

[Scene Change – Andrew's Perspective]

As I remained the anchor for Mairy and Vera, so that they may return from whence Mairy traveled into the black hole, I was suddenly assaulted by a strange sensation that came rippling up into my being and throughout the aural veil within which my aura was enclosed. It felt like one of those uncontrollable shivers I would occasional get, in my more human form, which would make the hairs on my head stand up. The vibrating feeling then continued to increase, seemingly passing into and around me, causing every fiber of my sentience to cramp up in unrelenting pain. I thought experience comparable to being jolted by an unexpected surge of power; somewhat like being struck by lightning.

This assault abruptly familiarized me with the vulnerability of my astral self within this nonphysical realm of actuality, to which I was previously unaware. I had imagined that I was invincible in my astral form. And now, after this attack on my sentience, this was a very rude awakening for me. As my aura contorted about in reaction to this bizarre energy surge, I was completely disoriented. At first I thought it to be some untold side-effect of my tethered connection with Fairy into the black hole. I even entertained the notion that perhaps I had somehow snapped out of the aether and back into the landscape of my own scripted dream.

In any event, I held onto my consciousness knowing that Fairy was depending on me. I needed to stay focused on helping her. My desire was enough of an impetus for me to take back control of my astral sentience once again. And as I did so, the cramping pain of the power surge soon began to relax.

While I reclaimed my thought processes, I suddenly became cognizant of a new wariness: I was not alone. It was as if, liken to the perspective of the fictional *Spiderman* physiology, my 'Spidey' senses were tingling. It was in this moment that I realized I was actually affixed between two distinct forces; both embracing me with equal fervor. Conducting a sort of self-diagnostic of my astral connections, I perceived more than two distinct entities; both engaging in a tug of war over my astral state.

As I was still able to identify my own link up with Fairy, I was also aware that there was a second connection back to her physical body, and a third back to my own. However it made no sense to me that there would be a power surge from the direction of our physical host forms. My confusion transformed into a renewed feeling of fear when I realized the impetus of the power surge was along the second connection to Fairy's physical host. What was going on? Perhaps there was a short between the two connections leading back to our host bodies, wherein one was arcing to ground the energy of the other.

Apprehensively I astrally tracked the source of the surge, sensing my way along her connection. To my surprise, there was a new fourth connection somehow entwined with the second connection. In utter disbelief of this possibility, I deviated to follow along this new fourth connection. I soon became mindful aware of a unique presence embracing the fourth connection. While its visage was eerily familiar, it seemed to be somewhat resembling the image of an evil personification of the character 'Nicodemus', from the animated movie, *'The Secret of NIMH'*. I remembered how his appearance in the movie haunted me, and I could feel the fear taking over me in its presence. Then I realized that this was as foretold in my nightmare.

Then I had an even scarier thought. Could this was the self-same creature that had terrorized me near my home on Earth, and again on the island? If so, how has it appeared here, within this astral plane; in the one place I thought to be my safe haven from any harm? It was like the personification of the classic villain who would not die. Terror washed up over my being, as I imagined him gravitating ever closer to me. Looking to separate my connection with this beast, I realized it had been traveling up on Fairy's connection from her physical host. As Fairy had comingled her 'silver cord' with mine upon her departure, it would appear that somehow the Tokoloshe had comingled his link with her 'silver cord', which was still allied with mine.

As he continued up along the now more visible trail of Fairy's 'silver cord', I realized that there was no avoiding this confrontation. And this time Fairy would not be able to come to my rescue, because she was otherwise preoccupied in the relativity of the black hole's Time dilation. It was all happening just as it was in my dream-like vision of future events. It was like the nightmare from which there was no end and no return. As my own fear engulfed me, I recounted how this self-same creature had been twice thwarted by Fairy. Subsequently I had to believe that it was possible to fend him off again. Yet, I also remembered how that the second encounter on the island almost cost her dearly.

I backed up; astrally projecting my conjoined connection with Fairy away from this impending encounter. Traveling along our connection, beyond the plasma ring and towards the black hole's event horizon, I knew I could only get so close before I would actually enter the black hole itself. The creature gained on me as I slowed to avoid entering the event horizon. Having convinced myself this was the Tokoloshe, I braced myself for what I thought would be another vicious attack by this evil wizard-like version of him. Instead, he met with me face to face; staring me down as he seemingly looked into my soul.

"I did not come to fight with children," he stated, taunting me. "You will be safe if you do not interfere."

In reflective posture, I cowered as the creature passed over me. It was obvious from his non-engagement that it did not feel threatened by me. He even smiled sadistically upon my reaction to his presence. I was both confused and relieved that he ignored me. As I watched him continue to follow along the visible trail developed between Fairy and myself, I was newly abashed with the feeling of my own cowardice.

As the Tokoloshe continued to trail away from me, I recognized his astral connection was reacting with the energy of the plasma ring; alighting the outside of the connection between him and myself with a positive matter reaction. I reasoned that he was not at all concerned with me, because his intended target was really Fairy. And I was just his way of getting to her.

It was serendipitous that I could hear Fairy communicating to me just at this time. "Andrew, you need to focus. There is something interfering with our connection," Fairy relayed to me with some anxiousness.

I mustered up enough courage to try and communicate with Fairy through my fear, hoping she would hear me. "It's the Tokoloshe. He's here!" I seemingly yelled to her. "And he's bringing the plasma to you!"

My effort to get closer to her location must've paid off, because she was able to respond in what seemed like a more timely manner. Although still slowed down, I could make out what she was saying.

"It's not the Tokoloshe!" she affirmed. "It's just how you're seeing it through your fear. You need to concentrate and focus beyond your fear. Don't let your own demons be your downfall!"

"Easier said than done," I tried joking in the midst of absolute terror.

Yet, as Fairy had put it to me earlier, I had to fight against my own demons of fear and indecision, or they would be my downfall. Then it occurred to me; I was frightened. In fact I was terrified. So why was I still here? Why had I not just transitioned back into my mortal body, like every other time? What was keeping me here? Perhaps having a purpose other than my own survival was the key. Perhaps, simply by knowing that Fairy was in danger, I was able to override my autonomic reflex to transition back into my body. And in the clarity of that rationale, I realized something very dire about our situation.

"Wait; if you are residing in the absence of matter, and he is bringing matter to you," I said, stopping short of completing my sentence for what seemed an obvious consequence to me.

Nonetheless, it was as if Fairy could anticipate my reasoning. She completed my thought, saying, "Then it is like lighting a fuse to a bomb. It's the spontaneous creation event your father spoke of. You need to break from your connection with me, now," she ordered me. "The aural veil will contract around us, and then I can make the jump into the aether with Vera."

"I can't," I said, watching as the escaping Shadow-Forge member of the Dark Guild advanced towards Fairy. "I no longer have control of our connection."

"Well then get control," Fairy demanded. "You need to stop thinking like a human, damn it!" Fairy yelled, reprimanding me. "You do realize that you're not in your mortal form anymore; don't you? You are a Shadow-Forge member of the Light Guild. You are just as strong as he is; and maybe even stronger."

"Damn right you are! Kick his ass," I could hear Vera intervening in our conversation as if it were a party line. "Don't let him intimidate you. If you do, it is not just us that will be destroyed; it will be the entire universe."

"Yeah, no pressure," I observed. "I can do this," I asserted to myself, trying to work up the courage. "I asked anxiously. "Are we talking about that guy, Tom?"

Then Fairy tried another approach, reminding me, "Remember how it was in the crystal. You have the power to control matter. So don't let the plasma matter reach us or nothing will matter after that."

She was right of course. So I traded one fear for another, as my survival instincts took over. I put aside my fear of confrontation in the realization of my fear that all life would be extinguished should that plasma reaction spark a spontaneous creation event. It did seem, however, to be the more controllable fear of the two: on the one hand, a confrontation could bring about prolonged pain; on the other hand, we all die instantly. However right now, my life was not as important to me as that of Fairy, my mom, and my dad. As I regained my purpose and composure, I began to think more plainly.

Then it occurred to me, "Yes, of course, 'nothing matters'," I responded aloud, as I realized that I could draw upon the dark matter from which Fairy and Vera were now immersed.

If the crystal was compacted dark matter, as I had come to believe, then I must have the power to control dark matter. But first I needed a clean connection with her. Perhaps by funneling the power of the plasma energy, from my connection to the Tokoloshe, with the force of dark energy, from my connection with Fairy, I can manipulate the force of gravity. After all, to hear dad say it, dark energy is kind of like anti-gravity. All I need to do was to alternate between the positive density matter and negative density matter. It can't be that difficult. And by forcing one in concert with the other, I should be able to maneuver more quickly than the Tokoloshe within this vacuum of outer space.

I now chased after the Tokoloshe, for better or worse, whose connection was brightly emanating with the power from the plasma ring. However, I could see how the plasma energy remained active only up to him. So I needed to keep it that way. As long as he could not reach Fairy, then there was still a chance to defuse the situation.

I astrally projected myself in front of him as fast as I could, interposing myself between him and Fairy. It would be a maneuver by which I was hoping to loop our intertwined connections out in front of him, cutting him off from reaching her. Or that was my plan anyway, as I slung myself out and around him.

The Tokoloshe was taken completely by surprise with my stratagem. Though, this time he would not be ignoring me or taking me for granted.

"I should've had done with you in your mortal form," stated the Tokoloshe, in a particularly irate tone.

"Perhaps you should have," I agreed with him. "For I am not the meek boy you attempted to kill on Earth," I said, now with a little more confidence in Shadow-Forge abilities.

"True, but then me thinks I like it this way better; Shadow-Forge to Shadow-Forge, so to speak," he replied.

I knew as the Tokoloshe would attempt to overtake me yet again, that this time I would need to engage with him. This time and place, just outside the black hole's event horizon, would be my 'Alamo'. I had to keep his avenue to Fairy and the interior of the black hole cut off.

With my back to the event horizon and his back to the plasma ring, the Tokoloshe drew upon the more positive plasma rich energy in which he was shrouded. He raised his arms and projected the energy of the plasma ring at me like a giant flame thrower. The force of the projected energy pushed me further from away from him and closer to the event horizon.

I, on the other hand, with my back to the event horizon, was able to draw upon the dark matter from along my connection with Fairy. I likewise projected the force of dark energy at him in a like manner. The communion of the forces was immensely volatile, liken to the difference between extreme heat and cold. At least, I thought, the impact of the damage was confined to the area outside of the black hole.

We waged our fight for control of my conjoined connection with Fairy. Back and forth, like two wizards in a duel to the death, we assailed each other with our assaults. We vied for the use of relevant energy to fuel our weapons against the other. I had the advantage of the high ground, so to speak, and control of negative density matter; pitching spheres of dark energy from one end of our shared connection to the other. The Tokoloshe countered me by using the positive density matter of the plasma ring to match my attack. As no one was seemingly on the defensive, it became more of a contest of wills between us; and I intended to stand my ground.

"You can't win this boy. This is a stalemate from which only strategy might change the balance of power. And I have been at this much longer than you have," the Tokoloshe said, attempting to provoke me into distraction.

"I can keep this up as long as you can, old man," I ranted back at him, thinking now of him as the vision of my previous nemesis form within the crystal.

"Perhaps, but time is on my side," he implied. "In case you haven't noticed, we have been steadily drifting towards your doom and my salvation."

I hadn't noticed, but we were indeed drifting toward the event horizon of the black hole. It seems standing your ground only works when the ground is not moving. It was more like we were fighting in a river, with a current moving us toward a waterfall. As I was now deep into this battle, I called to Fairy.

"Fairy, you both need to get yourselves out of there now!" I shouted, trying to make myself clear. "I have regained control of our connection, but the plasma has now infected my end of the aural veil. And we are still drifting towards the event horizon. Make the jump!" I implored of her. "I'll break away from the connection at my end when the time is right."

Fairy responded, "I don't know how this thread thing works, but if you do break from your connection with me then you may have no escape. And I believe that in your current situation, with the plasma and dark matter as part of your being, you will be disintegrated upon entering the black hole."

"It's going to be just like when you stayed inside the crystal. You need to leave the aural veil before you touch upon the event horizon," she deduced. "Stay within your own aura and I'll find you somehow."

As the Tokoloshe pressed on with his assault, I was hard pressed to defend against his offense. I brusquely broke off with our conversation without knowing whether anything was decided. And due to the relative Time dilation between us, our communication was a little off anyway. I sent another dark energy power surge along the connection between us, as our clash continued.

"Fate is on my side, as you can see," the Tokoloshe bragged, as he warded off the power surge. "The causal circumstance has been initiated. You are just delaying the inevitable. The universe is about to become anew, and I will be its creator."

"You are fooling yourself if you believe you could survive a spontaneous creation event. Such an event will cause the entire universe to overwrite itself, with you in it. This is not a war either of us can win. You'll die with everything else," I said, trying to reason with him.

"Perhaps that will be true for you, but I serve another," the Tokoloshe proclaimed. "War always begets the renewal of life. And the behest of chaos is my quest for a better second chance. For me is the promised of a new existence in the Time that is yet to come."

"What new existence can there be for you in a universe without life?" I asked in desperation.

"Mine," he declared defiantly. "The 'Selfish Biocosm' of evolutionary balance is just another part of the universal struggle between us; between order and chaos for the progenesis of a new life force. And it will be made in my image. I am just accelerating the Time line," the Tokoloshe elucidated.

"The 'biocosm'; that's one concept I'm not familiar with," I admitted. Hard to argue with what I don't know.

"Therein lies the folly of your resistance, boy," the Tokoloshe affirmed. "Do you even know why or for what you are fighting?"

I could see there was no dissuading him with logic, as his faith and loyalty were anchored in a veiled promise from Discordia. I could see that it was probably all that was motivating him right now. As we continued on with our siege, he blocked my every attempt to force him back. It looked as if we two opposing Shadow-Forge combatants were evenly matched. My expectations for survival appeared to be slipping away from me, as we drifted ever closer to the event horizon.

Liken to a 'Venus Fly Trap', the Tokoloshe plan to use Vera as bait had lured us into this dangerous predicament only too well. It must've been what Discordia wanted from the very beginning, and we played right into her hands. I now understood that they never wanted me dead, because they needed both Fairy and I together to pull this off. They were counting on us to bridge the barrier to the void of the black hole. The barrier imposed by the event horizon, which kept out positive density matter. It was the opening through the barrier that we were providing via our aural veil. An opening wherein dark matter could be used to fuel the cataclysmic repurposing of spacetime in one inexorable and irrevocable spontaneous creation event; or whatever this 'universal biocosm' concept is all about. We were at a disadvantage from the very beginning and I still didn't even know what their endgame was.

That must've been why they had to kill the beast on the island, as the creature was really trying to kill Fairy. And had that happened, it would've spoiled their chances for us to complete our predestined destinies toward this ultimate fate. Discordia had foreseen this possibility from the beginning. She was able to play upon each of our destinies to design this one outcome. She thought of everything.

Or perhaps she had not thought of everything. Perhaps she had not thought that I might figure it out. She was playing upon the patterns of our choices. This ultimate fate can't be 'written in stone', because it hasn't happened yet; so things can be changed. I need to shake things up. I needed to do something so impulsive that it would belie any pattern from which she could manipulate this intended prognostication.

It seems that in the heat of battle, my mind works better; probably owing to my need for survival. Needing more time to think this through, I snapped our connection like a giant plasma whip.

As the whip-like snap lashed out at him, I imagined my plight from my relative spacetime reference. I suddenly remembered my dream and the vision of Fairy in the azure blue crystal. As Fairy and I had previously noticed before of Vera's condition, she was seemingly froze in time. And now both, Fairy and Vera, had the relative difference of being frozen in Time, from my perspective. As a realization of my dream, I understood my vision of Fairy in the azure blue crystal was actually a similar perspective of our existences in relatively different temporal frames of reference in spacetime. No wonder chaos was able to imprison her in the crystal for so long. She could get into the crystal, but not out. But why had she not been able to jump into the aether from her prison, as she had done with me?

Just then, I heard Fairy call out in frustration, "It's no use."

"You're both still here?" I asked with surprise. "Just make the jump."

"But that's just it; I can't make the jump," Fairy confessed. "I've tried several times. But each time I try to make the jump, we just appear to be moving deeper within the black hole."

"It must have something to do with the relative temporal instability of the Time dilation," I conjectured.

While it was easier to journey with the tide of gravitational acceleration towards the black hole's center, from a faster spacetime reference into a slower spacetime reference, it appeared building up momentum against this Time dilation, from within a slower spacetime reference to a faster one, was less of a possibility.

"Fairy, wait, this is just like the crystal. You were never meant to make it out. They needed our conjoined connection in place," I said without really providing any background. "They just needed a way in."

"Last time I was only able to escape because I was able to make the jump as the crystal began to disintegrate upon the event horizon," Fairy recalled.

"Still, there has to be more to this black hole than there was for us in the crystal," I said, formulating a plan. "Perhaps it was something like an equalization of the temporal instabilities that allowed for your escape."

"Are you saying the crystal was acting like a small black hole?" Fairy asked.

"Yes, that must be it," I agreed. "How else could this single crystal have held two planets together?"

Then a resolution to our predicament occurred to me. "If you two are both to survive this, then you need to get to the black hole's center where the Time dilation stops and equalizes," I deduced. "You need to keep jumping, so you continue to travel in the direction of least resistance, as fast as you can. Get to the center of the black hole! From there, your temporal variability should stabilize. Once stabilized, you should be able to make the jump into the aether. But it has to be from the center. That is your only way out."

"Survive this?" Fairy asked in worrisome tone. "Are you referring to the spontaneous creation event? Without our connection to this universe, there is no surviving this. Vera will be lost in the limbo of the aether. And I will transition back to my own reality, for as long as my reality may exist. And what about you and your parents, and the rest of the life forces in the universe? This can't happen! There has to be another way."

"That's what I'm working on," I replied, trying to multitask between talking and fighting. "I just need to know you're safe."

As I tried to figure a way out of this, I realized that there was more to Discordia's strategy than just my battle with the Tokoloshe. Somehow Discordia must have worked out all our destinies to purport only one probable fate. But perhaps Discordia hadn't considered that I might be able to figure out her plan. Where fate is the sum of all destinies, perhaps there is still one destiny she had not counted on deviating from her expectation: mine.

If the universe was to escape this fate, I needed to change my own destiny in some unexpected way. I needed do something completely impulsive, even if it meant shedding the protection of my own aura, as well as my individual connection to the universe. Maybe it was the hyperactive nature of my ADHD or just my indomitable spirit to resist any form of indoctrination or forced control. Maybe, ADHD was my one special ability.

There was also one other thought that I had been pursuing since Fairy arrived: Harmony's intervention. If I could create enough havoc, prior to this universal biocosm to which the Tokoloshe had referred, then maybe

Harmony would be invoked to deal with all of this. I mean, that is her reason for being; that is who she is.

Abruptly, I began to sense the Tokoloshe was recovering from my last attack.

"Fairy!" I alerted. "I believe there is another way. In fact, I believe there is only one other way. I guess there has always only been one other way. I don't know why I didn't see it before." I said, communicating my intent to Fairy.

"What are you talking about?" Fairy questioned anxiously.

"It's the way of the Shadow-Forge," I said proudly and with purpose. "This is how I saw it in my dream. This time you have to trust me."

"OK, I trust you," Fairy confirmed. "Andrew; behest of my heart and my soul will follow."

"Always," I replied to her fondly.

The creature swiftly revived his assault upon me, with a barrage of plasma snaking out from his connection to the ring. He alternated his attack strategy among a deployment of gigantic fireballs, bolts of lightning, and even an occasional yanking of the connection. As I tried to think through this dilemma, I found myself in a defensive posture from which I could only deflect his attacks. Too much thinking distracts from a good offense. It seemed that we had indeed reached a stalemate. A single mistake on my side of this contentious confrontation could be the end for all of us.

Still, as our skirmish continued, I was aware of how our combined differences in the type of matter, being used, began to test the resilience of my aural veil. It wouldn't be long before the decision would be made for me. I imagined that it was only a matter of time before our battle would ignite the catastrophic spontaneous creation event. It was difficult to sort out what to do first. I kind of knew what I had to do, but I was not quite sure how to do it. And with this maniac constantly trying to destroy me, and all of existence to boot, I needed to go on the offense again.

Recalling elements of my nightmare, I understood I needed to create a single explosive force outside of the black hole's event horizon. Hopefully it would disorient my nemesis long enough to employ this new stratagem. All the while, I was counting on the relativity of Time itself to be enough of a shield to save Fairy and Vera from the havoc that I was about to unleash.

To accomplish this, I needed to fuel the Tokoloshe's power beyond even his capacity to control. As for me, I needed to separate from the aural veil after setting up a chain reaction within it. Then somehow escape out in an attempt to transfer my astral essence into the black hole; if that was even possible. Hoping all the while that my individual aura would be enough to save me from the cataclysmic explosion I was about to impart. I knew my timing would be crucial to my surviving.

I began flooding the aural veil with dark matter, while forcing dark energy through my connection with the Tokoloshe. I figured by overwhelming the aural veil with the concentrated source of this dark energy, outside the confines of the black hole, it would react hyper-explosively with the positive density plasma stream to which the Tokoloshe was drawing his power. If I timed it just right, then the combined energies should be enough to eradicate the Tokoloshe, and maybe limit the damage to a smaller portion of the universe in one fantastic supernova. Or at least that is what I was telling myself.

As I drew the dark matter in, I dared Harmony to ignore this event.

The Tokoloshe must have been aware of what I was doing, as his aura began to inflate. Had Discordia understood my very recourse? Was there no way to avoid this seemingly predestined fate?

As the Tokoloshe grew in size, my vision of his appearance transmogrified into a titanic figure. His countenance resembled my image of the devil, horns and all. His form was alight with the plasma from which he was drawing upon to combat my next offensive.

Knowing of the impending cataclysm that was about to unfold, I separated away from our conjoined connection in the aural veil. However in doing so, I noticed the dark matter flowing back into the black hole through the aural veil remnant that was left behind. For some reason the aural veil had not contracted around my individual aura, as Fairy had predicted. So it must have been only my individual aura that was acting as a stop valve to keep the dark matter in place.

I quickly returned to the veil, which stopped the leaking. But now I had a bigger problem: I had no escape. I was the only thing that was preventing the dark matter from bleeding back into the black hole. But would my aura be enough to keep the explosion from entering into the interior of the black hole?

The Tokoloshe grew to an enormous size, dwarfing even the stars that were being drawn in and torn asunder upon the plasma ring. His presence was now aligned with the plasma ring itself, distorting the ring upon the shape of his own individual aura. Yet for all his ferocity, he was still unable to breach the event horizon without a way in; and I was still the only way in.

I needed a new tact and fast. I impulsively decided to flood my own aura, draining the aural veil of the dark matter collected. As I drew in the dark matter, I began to fashion it into a crystal of my own making. I would become the embodiment of dark matter.

Having done so, I broke away any connection to the aural veil. The aural veil quickly contracted back into the black hole, disappearing without a trace. This had basically sealed us both outside of the black hole, but with one difference: I was now filled with the quintessence of dark matter.

"I'll bet you didn't see that coming!" I shouted over to him aggressively.

"What have you done?!" the Tokoloshe wailed in contempt. "I will not be cheated of my destiny."

With that, the Tokoloshe forced all of his anger, and all of the plasma energy he could muster, through our connection and away from him. I guessed he was trying to initiate the explosion from a distance.

Instead, I projected myself into his aura before the plasma could reach me. As intended, it ignited an uncontrollable matter to anti-matter reaction that blew me out of my own aura and pushed my uncontained consciousness up against the event horizon.

As I felt my sentience touched upon the black hole's event horizon, I could see a crack of light opening up in front of me. The crack began to grow, persisting against a darker background. As the light poured in upon me like a deluge, I knew I had entered into the interior of the black hole. My omniscient perspective of the stars and distant nebulae became distorted in the ever increasing illumination that overcame my purview.

Somehow even in his demise, I could still hear the Tokoloshe ranting, "You little fool! You thought you could defeat the most powerful being in the universe! I can feel forces of chaos, even now, filling me with the phenomenal cosmic forces of the universe itself." Then the Tokoloshe expressed with ecstasy, "The 'Biocosm' begins!"

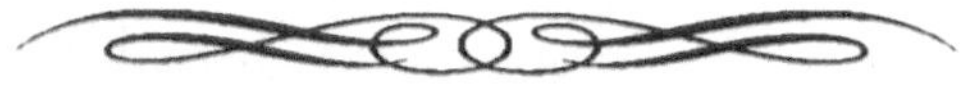

[Scene Change – Andrew's Perspective]

[Falling deeper into the rabbit hole]

If the biocosm ever did actually happen, I was oblivious to the catastrophe because it was no longer part of that reality. As I attempted to identify and learn more about this new reality, I felt an even odder gripping sensation embracing me. It was a weird absence of sensory perception, even to that of any astral senses. As I committed myself to this purpose; trying to establish some boundary of containment for my escaping astral essence, I seemingly existed outside of any Space or Time.

While I had anticipated that the chain reaction would rupture my aural containment, I could not possibly foreseen that it would end up in yet another dimension altogether. Somehow I understood this to fit a description of the fifth dimension, about which dad spoke. I was no longer just tapping into the fifth dimension as a Shadow-Forge. I was now actually in the fifth dimension. It was not just about thought transference of energy anymore. Rather it was about the transference of thought upon my previous reality. Despite the fact that I could only imagine what should have happened, it was as if I was a lucid dreamer once again. I had control over the events as they played out in front of me.

The act of diving into the heart of the beast, in my crystal form, would have most definitely provided for quite the spectacular supernova event. Though, at least it would not be spontaneous creation experience for which they had intended. I held the remembrance of how the Tokoloshe became infused within the supernova event and was diffused outside of my previous reality. And as I remembered it, so it happened. As it turned out, this fifth dimension was the ultimate way to influence fate. Liken to the tesseract, this 'spooky action' entanglement of spacetime had allowed me to manipulate the fate of the universe, as I saw it. Indeed, I was able to overwrite the ongoing events to my advantage.

And as I saw it, the volatility of the mixture proved to be too much for the Tokoloshe to handle. As a result, he was enveloped in the binding force of its core collapse. The resultant supernova implosion sent a wave of gravitational waves plowing relentlessly throughout the galaxy. And, in its wake, a new and indivisible black hole was formed, creating a binary system of merging black holes. The immediate merger of the two black holes violently shook the surrounding fabric of Space and Time, sending out a gravitational tsunami in every direction. The event was catastrophic on a cosmic scale, persisting in a blast of vibrations known as dark energy waves, rippling instantaneously through the cosmos and across the universe.

Now, within the infinity of Present spacetime, there was nowhere to go. The fifth dimension was the Present time connection to everything, with no Past time and no Future time. As I had previously severed any connection with my own reality, my familiar sense of connection and enlightenment [i.e., all that I felt, all that I knew, and all that I was] was disappearing. In my solace, I instinctively focused upon the thought of having left behind the one connection that allowed me to host my astral essence, and perhaps the only connection back to my physical form in my previous reality. In doing so, I left it all behind; for without my aural containment, I was being absorbed within the aether of spacetime itself. From every direction, I was without sensation of any kind.

It now seemed to me to be like the opposite of omnipresence; where I was no longer in touch with any part of the universal being. Separate of any known reality and excluded from it, within this eternal void, I was not so much lonely as I was alone. And yet the void was not an abyss of darkness, but rather one of light, or sorts, where there was no imagining of what could not be perceived. There were no shadows of ambiguity because there was nothing to be perceived. Nothing felt real to me forever more, as I imagine I was in the 'nowhere' that was 'now here'. I could only subsist within the solace of my own reflection upon what I used to be; or of what I used to be a part, but was no longer.

Still this introspection was not enough to maintain the sanity of my true purpose. In this blinding light, my memories were illuminated upon the hallucinogenic canvas of my own psyche. Until, within all this distraction, I felt I was truly in contact with my old friend, Harmony. I believed I could hear her thoughts being communicated to me, whispering, *"Consider who you are and where you are going. Let your hopes and dreams guide you through your darkest fears. You are more than physical form. Find the center of your life force. Only there can you realize the purpose and vehicle of your journey."*

Then, without warning, there was a renewal of sensation. It felt something like electricity, as it was sent rippling throughout my being. And all at once, I felt reconnected; once again plugged into the universe. And yet, this connection was somehow strangely foreign to me. For some odd reason, I no longer felt that I had the same feeling and understanding about my spacetime as before this unusual event. Rather I felt I was at the center of a new existence, or perhaps more like at the moment of a renewed purpose in being.

As my thoughts continue to coalesce, I felt the familiar twinge of fear from whence I once previously journeyed into another black hole some time ago; perhaps one that was even on the other side of the universe. It was there that Fairy put me back together. Yes, I needed to find her and assure myself that she was safe. I involved what was left of my astral essence in a search for Fairy. It was a long shot, but maybe the black hole still existed; the selfsame one she would've tried to transition back into the black hole to look for me. If I could just transition back into her aura, I might have a way back to my reality.

Yet, I felt my performance belying my efforts. It was like being in a like dream, where the harder you try, the more difficult it is to reach your goal. Eventually I fell motionless, drifting about in my own conscious state of doubt. It felt as though I was restrained in a two dimensional frame of spacetime, wherein my thought transference ability was being impeded within the non-containment of my new infinite abyss. I had lost my perspective of my previous reality and I had not yet found Fairy. And with no 'buoy of being', I was at an impasse to reacquire any real liaison to anything outside of my new perspective.

As my new perspective became ever more distorted, all that I felt, all that I knew, was disappearing before me. This was like in my dream, I thought, trying to infer some logic for what was happening. All at once I was without even any awareness of the black hole that I thought I was in. It was as if my essence, my 'being', was rather being enveloped within a dimensional singularity. I appeared I was either frozen in Time, or Time had stopped; or perhaps Time did not even exist for me anymore.

Still, it was not a complete absence of animation for me. Rather, it seemed as if I was no longer even in a Present time frame of reference. Instead, I understood of my existence as only in a Past sense of own self; and that was fading fast. I was quickly losing awareness of what was real about my surroundings. And as a consequence, I was losing an awareness of my own self-worth. For a moment I thought I could see Fairy coming to help me, but then the vision of her slowly slipped away. Was this all really happening, or just another remembrance of my previous thoughts and dreams?

As I was losing more and more grasp over my own sense of being, I could actually recognize my ability to think dissipating away. The sum of my entire life experience, everything that was me, was somehow being erased. Soon it would be as if I had never existed, as all my previous associations to the universe would be gone. And without this acceptance of my own self, I had to fight to attain any real sense of perseverance.

Yet, even this sense of perseverance was being replaced by a timeless fear of longing without knowing for what, or why. Eventually, I felt more outside of existence, than inside of it. In my desperation, I thought perhaps where there was no Present time or Past time, I could still remake myself in Future time. In a Future time, I could become the inspirational potential for a new life force. Yet adopting such a potential animus seemed beyond redemption within this void of nothingness. It was as if I had truly passed on, and this was to be the nightmare that would be my eternal damnation.

Abruptly I had an impression of communion, but with what I could not discern. I rationalized that if it was Fairy, she would probably have no way of knowing I was with her; for I was no longer part of her reality. I was quickly losing awareness of my own sanity, as I felt I must be dissipating into the harmony of the universal being itself. The sum of my entire life experience was slowly bleeding out away into the great void; perhaps a communion with the universe, as it were. As I was losing all sense of my own identism, I could actually once again embrace the omniscience of my greater whole, for what it was worth. Conceivably my individuality could become like so much dark matter; a container without content.

Still, I had no regrets; for no matter what happens to me, the universe would continue to support all that I loved about being me. For myself, I felt I had fulfilled my quest and achieved my true destiny. It was another grand purpose and another grand adventure, from which I was willing to sacrifice myself to save all. And whether I would ever remember being a part of another reality was no longer important. I believe I had influenced all of our fates in a most positive manner; for this is the way of the Shadow-Forge.

The last thing I remember, before losing all identity within this entanglement of my fifth dimension realm, was a familiar voice saying, "You are quite remarkable indeed, Andrew of Earth. Once again you have restored balance to the universe. Go now and live the reward of the life you have been given."

CHAPTER

18

Encounters of the Seventh & Eighth Kind—A Life for a Life

[Survival is not always an expectation of heroism, but it helps]

Indeed, who knows what fate awaits us in the promise that is our collective future when we all cooperate for the greater good of all life forces. The fate of our universe rests on the collective destinies of all life forces contained within it, regardless of their dimensional frame of reference. A life force does not stop influencing the evolution of our universal being, which is the universes ability to be, after it has passed on.

[Scene Change – Narrator's Perspective]

The scene at the entrance to the pods lab was tense, as Margaret tried rescanning her pin to unlock the door. As another tremor rippled through the structure, it did not shake their resolve. Ulrick got up to try his security access, and failed as well.

"He must've locked us all out," Ulrick shouted.

631

"It's only an electronic lock," Margaret reminded him. "Break away the sensor pad."

Ulrick made a quick search of the medical team's bag and grabbed the metal traction splints. After forcing the plate from the wall, he cut and stripped the exposed wires. Another tremor knocked them all back.

"We need to get to the safety of the lower section," one of the first responders called out.

"Not without my wife," Ulrick exclaimed.

He got up and randomly connected the wired ends until he found the right combination. As the door slide opened, they all rushed in. Ulrick immediately rushed over to his wife, while the first responders followed Margaret over to Mairy's CONS unit. As the paramedics started to work on Mairy's seemingly lifeless body, Margaret concerned herself with the operations of the CONS units.

Looking over to Ulrick, Margaret ordered, "Don't touch anything. If you don't follow the proper sequence, then you'll do more harm than good."

Margaret then began to shut down the CONS unit that Tom had taken over, as Ulrick waited for her availability. She then went over to Ulrick to repeat the shut down for Lindsey.

"She'll be alright," Margaret stated in a calming voice. "Now watch what I am doing and copy the sequence exactly as I am demonstrating. We have to get everyone out safely."

"Alright; yes, of course," Ulrick relented, as he calmed down.

Margaret then turned her attention to the master control pods. She and Ulrick then repeated this effort, in turn, for each of the pod sleepers.

Sandi and Steve arrived just as the paramedics appeared to be given up on reviving Mairy. Steve seemed to be watching on hopelessly, as Sandi rushed over to Mairy's body.

"No, it's not possible," she cried out, for Sandi knew of her secret identity and refused to believe that she could be gone. She held her body tight to her bosom as she brushed he hand tenderly across her face.

Steve came up alongside of her, trying to somehow comfort her in her grief. It all seemed so surreal to him. His dream seemed to be unraveling before his eyes. None of this was supposed to happen. He scanned the room to see Andrew's pod being raised into an upright position. He then turned his attention to Tom, who was the cause of all this havoc.

Margaret and Ulrick worked through the process of waking the pod sleepers from their hibernation. They went back and forth between the CONS units, carefully following the procedures that would safely bring them out of their unconscious states. Margaret purposely did not finish the sequence for waking up Tom. As he lay in stasis, Steve looked upon him with aversion. Curiously, as Steve watched, he noticed that Tom's skin was changing.

Steve turned to the paramedics, who were still close by, asked, "Is this normal?"

"Is what normal?" one of them questioned.

"His skin seems to be hardening," Steve observed.

"Yes, he seems to be having some reaction within the machine," he agreed. "Margaret, we need to get this one out."

Margaret came over and looked in disbelief as Tom appeared to be melding with the machine; melting into it very framework. As the pod began to shake, they all stepped back. Steve went over to pull

Sandi from Mairy's body, hoping to keep her safe from whatever was happening.

Somehow, Tom was being reformed in the image of the CONS unit. He sat up, breaking out of the pod, and sporting a robot like body. The robot looked about, as if confused by its surroundings.

"This is not right," the robot slurred. "This is not my universe created anew. What have you done?

"What is that thing?" Ulrick shouted. The robot looked to be much larger and bulkier than Tom, but managed to retain his outward visage. "How is it even possible that it is alive?"

"It is the Tokoloshe!" Sandi announced.

"What?" Steve asked, looking to her with confusion.

"Mairy told me to not be so quick to attribute the appearance of the creature from the ancient myths," Sandi started. "She said that the creature was a Shadow-Forge, and a Shadow-Forge can take any shape, or any combination of shapes, from its environment when it emerges."

"Of course," Steve surmised. "Tom and the Tokoloshe are one and the same."

With that the robot creature got up, bludgeoning the paramedic that was trying to restrain him. Then he plowed his way across the lab to Andrew's pod. Not fully in control of his new physical form, he lashed out at Andrew's CONS unit. At first he only managed to smash the supporting hardware. However upon his second blow, he knocked the pod, with Andrew still inside, right off of its stand.

Steve and Ulrick impulsively rushed in to try and stop the creature from killing Andrew. This attempt resulted in them being no more than a distraction to the robot. But it was enough of a distraction to allow for others to get involved. In the chaos, Margaret managed to revive Vera and get her out of her containment. Vera took little time to assess the situation before she sprang into action.

To everyone's surprise, Vera quickly grabbed a shaft of steel out of the debris strewn from the robot's attack. She then leaped, swinging the shaft across the face of the robot. The robot lashed out wildly, tipping her off balance and onto the floor.

Ulrick reached down to help her up, saying "Who would've thought you had all that in you. But perhaps you should let us handle it."

"Thanks, but I am not yet done with this one," Vera avowed.

The robot attacked, swiping his large arm toward Vera's midsection from behind. Anticipating the blow, she executed a perfect back flip up, over and behind his arm, with makeshift weapon in hand. Instead, Ulrick was knocked back from the blow that was intended for Vera. Ulrick slide toward Steve and Sandi.

"Is their nothing that you can think of to help her out?" Sandi asked Steve.

Vera regained her stance and jabbed the shaft into a vulnerable area of the robot's plastic body. Sparks came flying out as she pulled back on the shaft. She then flipped the shaft around and down across its robotic wrist as the creature tried to fend her off. Such moves would seem worthy of a well-trained ninja.

Steve looked to Sandi, and then to Margaret, asking, "How much voltage is running through these lines?"

"220 volts," she answered.

Helping up Ulrick, Steve asked him, "Are you thinking what I'm thinking?"

"If I'm not, then you can fill me in on it," Ulrick replied.

"I want to try and electrify one of these support rods, and jam it into the same area in the robots armor from where we saw sparks flying," Steve explained.

"Sounds like a plan," Ulrick agreed.

As Steve and Ulrick worked together to fashion an electric prod, or sorts, Vera continued her bout with the robot. Kiana then showed up out of nowhere, with pistols firing. As the robotic terror lunged at her, she leaped up and backwards, unloading a magazine atop of its head, as it slide under her. The robot continued sliding into the lab's entrance door.

As Kiana reloaded, Vera jumped on the robot's back. This time Vera jabbed her staff into the body joint where the robot's torso met his hips. For her smaller size and speed, she seemed to be equally matched against the robots larger size and sluggish responses.

As Kiana started firing again at it head, the robot jerked up off of it stomach; forcing Kiana up through the false ceiling. Vera, anticipating its movement, flipped backwards off the robot and to the floor again.

Having completed their electric prod, Ulrick jabbed at vulnerable area the knee joint. The robot reacted violently to the stimulus. Vera saw what Ulrick was doing, and jumped down toward him.

"Let me have a try at that," Vera said smartly, as he grabbed the weapon from him.

The robot righted himself and came at them again. This time Vera slide under between its legs, as Ulrick remained to be the distraction. She leaped again, jamming the rod into the small of its back. The robot reared up, tearing through the ceiling.

Another tremor knocked everyone off their feet, as the robot went crashing threw the wall into the next room where Phil was working. While his activity dislodged the electric prod, the ceiling support came tumbling in on top of the robot. Vera and Ulrick followed through the broken wall and watched as the robot ceased to function. Kiana could be seen in the background, on the other side of the robot.

"I have never seen one to be re-hosted so quickly after a manifestation," Vera commented.

[Scene Change – Andrew's Perspective]

[Reincarnation can be resolved in many ideological guises]

I awakened to see my parents, Dr. Beecher, and Vera looking in on me through the translucent cover of the pod I was stationed in. But where was Mairy? I was so used to seeing Mairy as part of the family that her absence was a stark reminder of our last encounter in the black hole. Had I not saved both Fairy and Vera? As of late, Mairy had even become more than just a sister to me. Yet, there was something in the way my mother was looking at me that led me to believe something was not right. Thinking back to the last moment I could recall anything, I even questioned how I might had survived.

"Where's Mairy?" I tried to utter, but could not even hear my own words.

Within my thoughts, I chastised myself. She was there for me when I needed her. And when she needed me most, I failed to keep her safe. Indeed, it was my worst fears come true: we had not all made it back.

"You need to calm down, Andrew," I could barely hear Dr. Beecher shouting over the sound cancelling material of the pod. "You are alright now, but you really need to calm down. We're working on trying to get your pod opened."

I could hear my father's voice saying, "I thought we lost you there for a little while. Hang in there buddy; we're here for you."

My mother's voice chimed in just after, saying, "We love you. Stay with us."

I thought to myself how I tried my best to reach Fairy, and how I tried my best to keep her safe. Yet, maybe she had made it back after all, and was only hurt. Maybe Mairy was being sequestered somewhere. As I thought about the possibility of her still being alive, I began to ease out of my self-induced panic mode and I began to start relaxing.

"That's much better," Dr. Beecher said. "We should be able to get you out of there sooner now. OK, let's start the procedure to get this pod opened."

Then I unexpectedly heard Vera speak up, and I thought I heard her say, "I don't know what I would've done without you, Elvis. You're one special individual."

Was I hearing her correctly, or had I only imagined that she was being nice to me? And had she really called me Elvis? Only Fairy used that name for me. It was something she picked up during our previous quest together. As the translucent shield was removed, I thought I saw Mairy visage flash across Vera's face for just a moment. But as I focused again, I saw it was Vera's face to be sure.

"There you go," said dad as he helped me out of the pod. I was still shaking a bit. I assumed it was a reaction to the rush of adrenaline that my body must have surely infused within me. I instinctively looked to the pod where Mairy should have been. But as I looked around, I noticed I was on the floor and the lab was completely in shambles.

"They're having the place renovated," Milo spoke up comically. "I told them they should have waited until we left. But everyone is always so much in a hurry."

Tim positioned a wheel chair in place for me to sit in, while Milo helped me into it.

"Let's move him to the medical center fast," was Dr. Beecher's directive.

As they started to move me, I spied a gurney near Mairy's pod. Oddly, the people around me appeared to be purposely blocking my view of Mairy's pod. I gently waved them aside so as to get a better look. As they relented, I saw Mairy's pod had been utterly destroyed. Overwhelmed by the thought of not seeing her again, I got up out of the wheel chair and started over to Mairy's pod. Curiously, the attendant's attention seemed to be focused on the floor next the pod.

As I staggered over towards Mairy's pod, I was approached by dad. As he attempted to stall me, he explained, "She didn't make it back."

"I want to see for myself," I replied. And then I did; next to the pod, I could see Mairy's lifeless body.

"Tom locked us out of the lab, and we couldn't get in to save her in time," dad offered up as an apology.

"It's not your fault," I confessed to him, understanding that he always took too much upon himself.

As I knelt down next to her, I bundled up her body in my arms. My mother came down in kind to hold me.

"I can't imagine our family without her," mom said, trying to console me.

I kissed Mairy's face and laid her back down. I then rose and gave my mother a hug. As I did so, dad came in to make it a group hug. I looked beyond the hug to see Lindsey, Ulrick, Milo, Tim, and Vera waiting for me to gather my feelings. I eventually went to them, as they each, in turn, provided me with their condolences. Vera seemed to be waiting separately to be the last. I couldn't really be mad at her, nor blame her for what had happened. It was not under her control, as it was not under any of our capabilities to control. I separated from the group, and approached Vera.

Vera responded in kind, meeting me half way, saying, "She was the best part of both of us."

"Thank you," I said, appreciating her concern. It seemed rather a strange sentiment, but I believe it was heartfelt nonetheless. "Thank you for being there for her when I couldn't."

Then Vera hugged me close, kind of the way Mairy would, and whispered, "You've always been there for me, Elvis. I never doubted your tenacity or courage."

There it was again; there was no mistaken it this time that she called me Elvis. Vera continued to talk.

"I've got to tell you, that was my best body ever. I believe I'll miss that most of all. But then it wasn't really all human, was it?" she posed the question to me.

I gently moved her out to arm's length and looked her in the eye. She nodded affirmatively as I felt a rush of Mairy's memories being imparted upon me. I felt overjoyed having Mairy back with me once again. Breaking from the somber moment, I pulled her back into a big hug in joyous confusion, saying, "It is you! How is any of this possible?"

"You can thank Harmony for that. It turns out, she finally did show up as you wished," Vera revealed. "And, as there was only one silver cord left between us, only one of us could return" she continued to explain.

"So Harmony gave us a choice and we made a deal with her. Vera would take my place and I would take hers."

"You can do that?" I asked in amazement. "I mean, Harmony can do that?" rephrasing my question.

"I guess so, because her I am," she acknowledged. "Now, anytime we have to transform into Shadow-Forge mode, we can always return back to be together."

"That's all I ever really wanted," I professed; "just to be with you together forever."

Then in a distance, I could hear Kiana trying to restore some order, while mom and dad waited for my return.

"It seems the moonquakes have subsided for now," Kiana declared. "Ulrick, can you check with the other officers and let me know how many people may be injured?"

"OK, I'm on it," he acknowledged, as he left with Lindsey.

"And Phil, I would appreciate if you could get me a status assessment on the safety of this facility," Kiana requested.

"How about us?" Tim asked.

"Tim, we really have to have a talk about volunteering for extra work," Milo quipped.

"Well, we will need to move these two bodies to another location," Margaret stated of Mairy and the dead paramedic. "And Andrew still needs to be checked out. Please have him taken him up to the medical."

Then in response to Dr. Beecher request, Milo volunteered, "We can help with Andrew."

"That's alright fellows," Vera replied, "but I think I got this."

The two seemed to back off, giving her much more respect than I had ever seen from them before. Vera slipped under my arm and put her other arm around my waist, walking me over to the waiting wheel chair.

I said softly to her, "It's wonderful to have you back. I can't wait to tell mom and dad."

Vera smiled and said, "Alright, but let's leave the room first. And this time I'll handle telling them by myself."

Dad took over control of the wheel chair, as mom and Vera helped me in. The rest of the pod operators allowed us to leave the room as a family unit, as I smiled back in recognition of their friendship. My first inclination was to introduce a reincarnated Fairy to mom and dad, but their somber mood had not changed since viewing the lifeless body of Mairy. So instead they walked in silence, as they accompanied us to the medical floor.

As we got a little further down the hall, I could no longer contain myself, saying, "Mom, Dad, I'd like to reintroduce you to Fairy. You previously knew her to be Mairy, but now she is Vera."

I could see Vera rolling her eyes in disbelief, similar to how Fairy used to do. "You'll never change, will you?" she said directly to me.

"Then who is the girl on the floor?" mom asked, looking half bereaved and half confused? Dad just stood silently trying to take it all in, and probably thinking I was in some form of denial.

"That was only Fairy's Shadow-Forge form," I said, trying to make mom understand. I took her hand and looked up saying, "There is nothing to be sad about now. It is just like when I died on Glorthocks, I came back to my actual physical body."

"But Fairy and Vera are two different life forces," dad said, attempting to be politically correct. "If Fairy has returned, she would not have returned back here," he rationalized, trying to make sense of my explanation.

As dad looked to Vera, Fairy acknowledged, "Normally that would have been how it all worked out, but the universe decided differently. And while Vera and I are still separate life forces, our souls are our own."

We all could see that mom could not make the leap from what all her senses told her to be the true. In her mind, Mairy, who she learned to love as a daughter, was dead. And it was a loss to be mourned. Fairy then took her hand, looked into her eyes and repeated the vow she had taken with us on Earth, "Behest of my heart and my soul will follow."

It was as if in that moment mom could see Mairy in Vera's eyes.

"Then it is true," mom acknowledge tearfully with a sense of relief.

"Great, now we can all attend my funeral, and then celebrate my rebirth all at once," she quipped.

"And what of the real Vera's soul then?" dad asked, not liking loose ends.

"In the end, it was her choice and her request of Harmony. Vera is now my kindred spirit," Fairy admitted with a sense of passion. "She will live out the rest of her life with my kin. And I can never repay her for the kindness of allowing me to live my life here, with all of you." And with that, we all hugged again.

I am not sure how Harmony managed all of this, but perhaps some secrets are best left alone. Indeed, over time, some secrets transform from the naive expressions of who we are, to become the more mature impressions, inspiring us all, to be who we can be. And after this quest, I found that I no longer yearned to have Harmony back in my life, because it appears that she never left me after all. I would only like to thank Harmony for all that she is.

Another lesson Fairy taught me this day about love: it is not just who you choose to be with, but it is who you choose to stay with, and the sacrifice both are willing to take to make it happen.

Epilogue

[The relativity of Time and the fabric of Space are not absolute]

On April 21, 2015, astronomers stumble upon eerie section of universe containing absolutely nothing. It has been so dubbed as the Eridanus Supervoid, or the 'Cold Spot'. The 'Cold Spot' refers to an empty space in the cosmic microwave background view of the visible universe. A legacy of the 13.8 billion-year-old heat environment left over from the Big Bang, our cosmos has now cooled down by the expansion of space to just 2.7 degrees above absolute zero. However, while such cosmic voids are not new and thought to have been formed in the immediate aftermath of the Big Bang, due to quantum fluctuations.

While considered a cosmic void, it appears that this mysterious void is not entirely empty. Rather, this region of the cosmos is just incredibly under-populated in terms of positive density matter. Such voids in the universe, of which the Eridanus Supervoid is the largest, are estimated to only have about 10 percent of the matter that would be expected to be found in an average region of the universe.

Still why should any cosmic voids exist at all? The cosmological principle holds the notion that the spatial distribution of matter in the universe is homogeneous and isotropic when viewed on a large enough scale. Subsequently, since the forces within the universe are expected to act uniformly throughout the universe, then the same physical laws should apply throughout. Therefore these forces should produce no observable irregularities in the large-scale structuring over the course of evolution of the matter field that was initially laid down by the Big

Bang. Consequently, the discovery of this supervoid presents a unique enigma for our scientists.

This cosmic supervoid is unique because it is the largest such structure, to date, ever identified in the universe. So say some astronomers who believe the Eridanus Supervoid is too large for this explanation of quantum fluctuations to make sense. This 'supervoid' has a radius of 1.8 billion light years; making it the largest such cosmic void detected, and also one of the largest structures known in the universe. Located 3 billion light years from Earth, its origin, and perhaps it persistence, may remain as one of the great mysteries of our ever evolving universe for a long time to come.

Wherein the presence of this huge void is difficult to explain, even in the standard cold-dark-matter model of cosmology, this anomalously cold region of the sky continues to mystify scientists. In the absence of a known cause for this effect, scientists continue to develop new and wild new explanations. Perhaps the most exciting of these explanations is that the Cold Spot may have been caused by a collision between our universe and another bubble universe; an idea fueled by the notion that we live in a 'multiverse' made up of an infinite number of parallel universes.

Nevertheless, it would appear that this cold spot is the closest embodiment to our concept of the universal medium prior to the Big Bang. And this region of spacetime would seem to have remained as such, unaffected by Time. That is, of course, unless there was some newly fabricated temporal anomaly: like an attempted overwrite of Present time within the spacetime of our own universe.

It should be noted in the post-mortem of this auspicious event, that it all happened just as Andrew had envisioned it from within his fifth dimension persistence. It should also be prefaced, within the account of this event, that the relativity of Time and the fabric of Space are not absolute. Subsequently, it is in the nature of the universe to be able to augment the establishment of these facts in providing for its own well-being. And it is from the perspective of this well-being that the circumstances surrounding the unseen secret of this cataclysmic event can truly be comprehended.

It was the appearance of Harmony, for which Andrew had hoped, at the moment of this attempted universal biocosm wherein a spontaneous creation event was contained. Although Andrew was able to influence the causal outcomes outside of the event horizon, he was not aware of the critical mass reaction that was taking place within the black hole itself. Indeed, unknowingly Andrew had created enough havoc to present an actual need to which Harmony then responded. Her actual timing expresses volumes in the healing powers of the universe to maintain its own existence.

The act of Harmony's appearance to embrace her protégés was more than a show of support. It demonstrated an actual psychic connection between them and the universe itself; for she is and ever was a part of the universe. As before, she had the capability to manipulate and operate within any dimensional spacetime environment, anywhere and anytime. This she was able to do, irrespective of the reference frame in which she was ever present; for she is simultaneously everywhere and nowhere at any moment, as an extension of the universal being. It is the necessity and nature of her sentience to be the manifestation from within the universal being that maintains the universal balance.

While she may have been brought about upon the gravity of the situation, it was her connection with Andrew which mystically brought her back into being at this exact moment and location in spacetime; through the purity of his intent and the focus of his purpose.

As before, Andrew had imagined this happenstance in his dreams. And just as he had imagined this battle between himself and his opponent, the obligation of his liable keep once again became his quest. It was a visualization in which his future self was a real participant through his connections within the universe. Yet, it was also a vision sent from his future self from within the fifth dimension; for the fifth dimension provides for the unique perspective of 'cause and effect' from anywhere to anywhere in the comingling of Time and Hyperspace. It allows for the quantum connections required of Einstein called 'spooky action at a distance'.

However, this time his quest was not part of some Present time event happening in a far off galaxy. Rather, this time, his quest was part of his ultimate fate. It was an especial fate, based on the possibilities of his own destiny and the mutual destinies of all that he held dear. It was, in fact, one of the many fated probabilities for some Future time event. Still, in all the possibilities of evolutionary animus, it was one that he himself inspired from within the fifth dimension; one that Discordia could neither predict nor control.

As such, it was Harmony that had appeared at the relevant moment of the initiated event. Coincidentally, this moment was also the serendipitous reuniting of astral participants in the relativity of 'All Space' and 'No Time': the relativity of dilated Time from within the center of the black hole. Upon her arrival into their fourth dimensional reality, Harmony once again arrived within the generation of a sphere. Though, this time her sphere was engendered within the environment of dark matter contained in the black hole.

Harmony's sphere immediately surrounded and shielded the astral forms of both Fairy and Vera, as well as the unbounded soul of Andrew. It seems Fairy and Vera never made the jump, because without Time she had no disposition to do so. It was an odd side-effect of their Time dilation, that Fairy and Vera had been literally frozen and preserved in the relative absence of Time itself. Had it not been for the arrival of Harmony, they would have been surely lost to the black hole's center forever; a slight miscalculation on Andrew's part, to be sure.

But Harmony's protective nature was not inspirited here for just her protégés. More amazingly, she produced a secondary set of nested spheres beyond the black hole's center. It contained the ever increasing negative mass density that permeated outside the black hole's center. This she did so, but not before the area between the two spheres was engulfed in a cataclysmic chain reaction. Her timing was crucial to confine and repress the provocation of a spontaneous creation triggering the 'Selfish Biocosm'.

While there was indeed a supernova, as instigated by Andrew, the intermixing of plasma matter and dark matter within the black hole was unavoidable upon the implosive, inside-out action of the event. It was a calamitous event, as Andrew had intended, that not only included the demise of the Tokoloshe, but also sparked the spontaneous creation event that Andrew was trying to avoid. It appeared that the predestined fate of the spontaneous creation event, as orchestrated by Discordia, was unavoidable.

Though, however unavoidable it was, its consequential effect had many outcomes. Had it not been for Harmony's timely arrival, ensured by Andrew's selfless act of courage to raise havoc, this spontaneous creation event would have surely initiated the 'Selfish Biocosm' from within the heart of the black hole.

As a consequence of Harmony's nested spheres, the unprecedented outcome was, without a doubt, quite miraculous. The reverberating containment of the spontaneous creation event, between the nested spheres, caused a unique rippling effect which resulted in the original black hole being turned inside-out. It had the ensuing effect of rearranging and reordering the nature of the Time within its inner most partitions. So in its place, a white hole was transmogrified into being. But only for a moment, for that is the essence and the act of creation itself. In effect, Harmony had redirected the effects of the initiated spontaneous creation event by refocusing the purpose of its intent to overwrite the entire universe upon a specific desideratum. It would seem that the most fantastic miracles are those we never really know about.

This partition allowed almost all of the Present time reality outside of her spheres to be protected from a completely new instance of temporal procreation. Liken to the nature of a wormhole, the occupants of the inner sphere were forced out through the newly manifested white hole in a single pulse. The white hole, whose inextricable entification overwhelmed the gravitational singularity, was allowed to explode into a limited creation event. It was somewhat liken to a 'Small Bang', rather than the 'Big Bang' event that is purported to have created the universe. This 'Small Bang' event minimized its reset on the fabric of the universe, in both Space and Time, forever scarring a much smaller region of the universe. And in the vacuum of this engineered collapse, a newly created black hole formed in the wake of the supernova instigated by Andrew. In this way, Harmony was able to keep the universe intact.

And what of the participants involved in this miraculous vicissitude? We already know of the choices offered to both Fairy and Vera. But what of Andrew? It would appear the universe is not yet done with our unsung hero, for Harmony was able to recreate an aural containment with which to reinsert him back into his own fourth dimensional reality. It was as if Harmony understood that no choice was more clear for him.

As a side note, it would have been difficult to imagine to what the extent such a limited spontaneous creation event would have had on spacetime itself, if not for the evidence of the Wilkinson Microwave Anisotropy Probe (WMAP) project, which was launched in 2001. For as the WMAP evidence would suggest, there is the presence of a cosmic regional cold spot that appears to have existed since the time of the Big Bang. This Cosmic Microwave Background (CMB) Cold Spot, which is more commonly referred to as the Eridanus Supervoid, was so dubbed by the cosmologists who discovered it in 2004.

And why might this side note be of any concern? It would seem that this particular phenomenon, as discovered in 2007, was hypothesized to reflect some sort of scarring in the early universe due to the interaction between two parallel universes. In fact, it could be thought of as a scarring in the fabric of spacetime itself, or even a portal to the 'never-never land' of what was before there was the reality of our existence. Furthermore, from the perspective of our ability to understand the cosmos, this portion of the universe appears to have been like this from the inception of the Big Bang.

Yet whereas these events have just recently taken place upon Harmony's arrival into the Present time, this 'Small Bang' scarring would appear to have resulted from this supreme confrontation between Harmony and Discordia. Indeed, one might further conceptualize that this region of spacetime, and the continuing fate of our universe's evolution, had been reset from this date for this portion of the universe. In point of fact, the result of the suppressed spontaneous creation event was that it only overwrote the previous spacetime for this small portion of the universe. You've got to love temporal anomalies!

It evokes the question, who will ever really know what mystery lurks in the heart of the Eridanus Supervoid? And what was there before it was overwritten? Perhaps we will never know. Subsequently, while this enigma may never have a logical explanation for scientists, the Shadow-Forge will know that they helped the cosmos to prevent a complete rewrite of the entire universe. So I put it to you, the reader: As there may be more to the degree and dimensional flexibility of spacetime than scientists have previously imagined, where in the cosmos will your imagination take you?

www.ingramcontent.com/pod-product-compliance
Lightning Source LLC
Chambersburg PA
CBHW032152180726
48284CB00001B/11